BARBAROSSA
Renaissance Corsairs

Deniz Uzunoğlu

Quintessence

BARBAROSSA
by Deniz Uzunoğlu
Copyright © 2023 Quintessence

Paperback ISBN: 978-0-9906198-7-1
eBook ISBN: 979-8-9880622-0-2

Cover art and design by Deniz Uzunoğlu
English translation from the Turkish original

Publication assistance and digital printing in the United States, Canada, the UK, Australia, the EU, and Brazil by Lightning Source®

Paperback and eBook International English language Editions distributed worldwide by Ingram

Although firmly based on historical personages and events, this novel (series) is a work of fiction. Names, characters, businesses, places, events, locales, and incidents either are the products of the author's imagination or used in a fictitious manner. Any resemblance to actual persons, living or dead, or actual events is purely coincidental.

You may forget,
     but let me tell you this,

Someone in some future time
     will think of us ...

     Sappho, *The Art of Loving Women*,
     500 BCE

To my son Derin,

The most precious gift life has ever given to me…

To Ali Murat,

Thank you for all the encouragement.

It's such a blessing to have you by my side.

To J. Erik LaPort…

Thank you for being so kind and patient with me,

and guiding me to where understanding begins.

Dear Reader,

As I've been writing this novel, which spans three continents and takes place around 600 years ago, I've made a concerted effort to remain true to the actual events that took place. As a result, I spent the most of my time focusing on an in-depth investigation of the Renaissance, which is often considered to have been the most eventful period in the history of the world. Incorporating a couple of fictional characters in the story and putting them on the same page as some of the most well-known and influential people that have ever lived turned out to be a more difficult task for me than I had anticipated. At times those close to me have occasionally commented that I was not writing a textbook for schools, but rather a novel and that it wouldn't matter if I let myself be creative a little bit, I remember myself opposing them vehemently and fighting an uphill battle to ensure that the events of the time I had been focusing on in each chapter were described as historically accurate as possible. I do not remember the precise number of books that I have read in order to stay true to my word. Yet, due to the fact that it is not easy for a person to know or recall even his great grandparents' names, and that over time, Ahmad becomes Suleiman by word of mouth; this story should certainly be considered a work of fiction.

When I first started working on the project; I had no idea that my writing would soon turn into a personal quest concerning the mystery of the Ark of the Covenant, the holiest of all the Jewish relics, which is said to have disappeared with the destruction of the Temple of Solomon. My understanding of spiritual doctrines, on the other hand, was no more advanced than that of the average cultured person. My perspective on life was more influenced by the principles of contemporary science, and I wasn't very much interested in metaphysics. Furthermore, spirituality, in my opinion, was something that a person should live within because it was society's Achilles' heel. But if I was going to write about the Ark of the Covenant, first I needed to learn more about the doctrines and the scriptures. In addition, spirituality was not something that people who lived six hundred years ago had lived solely internally. I could not write about the Ottomans without first studying Islam, the Kingdoms of Europe without looking at Christianity, and Jerusalem without first having a general, intellectual understanding of Judaism at least.

So I took Torah and began reading it. And I understood nothing. I read it once more. And again, I did not understand anything. Then I found a slightly longer version and read that as well, but I made no progress. Then I thought that maybe I should start from the beginning and started reading everything I could find pertaining to ancient wisdom. In the end, it turned out that I was truly blessed, because, along the way, I met a few very valuable guides who explained the teaching to me in detail. They kindly and patiently answered my incessant questions one by one. Days turned into nights, nights turned into days. It had gotten to the point where my loved ones were surprised to see me taking a break. When I approached my three-year-old son, he was crying out with joy, asking if I had come to play with him. And my eyes, which I had always been proud of, now had a 0.75 hyperopia...

Then, one morning at 05:46, I had a kind of understanding of what all of the prophets, philosophers, and sages of all traditions, including Sufis, Kabbalists, Hermetics, Gnostics, Zoroastrians, Shamans, Buddhists, Hindus, Taoists, Freemasons, Aristotle, Plato, Plotinus, Homer, Goethe, Shakespeare, Dante, and many more had meant. And I started crying... I realized they were all pointing to the same thing, the same single Truth... The Ark of the Covenant had been right in front of my eyes, in front of all of us, since the very beginning... All we needed were eyes to see with.

As I was putting these words down on paper, I attempted to reflect the historical events as accurately as possible while at the same time fitting the characters born of imagination into the story, much like a skilled tailor who strives to make the jacket perfectly fit for the one who is going to wear it. And I literally groped my way through the darkness. I had not the slightest idea what I was going to write in the subsequent chapter, but as soon as I completed the one I was working on, it was as if someone was waving a magic wand and whisking me away to the next. My concerns gradually faded, and in their place emerged a sense of wonder and enjoyment. Since it was no longer like writing a book with a set beginning and an end, but rather like watching a television series at the end of each episode of which I was saying, "Oh, no! This cannot be the end!"

As I wrote, I had a lot of fun. I not only laughed a lot but also cried a lot. And I wish the same for you as well. As you read the book, I wish you feel all of these different emotions with different flavors. And I sincerely hope that you find the story intriguing enough to begin your own research.

Who knows? Just as this story altered my perspective on life, it may alter yours as well.

Deniz Uzunoğlu

April 2, 2023

April 23, 1616

"An extraordinary day, when the sun extends through the clouds and blesses the lush lands of Britain..."

Cervantes, with his back turned towards the melancholic room, was standing by the window, watching the sun's orange beams slowly fade out.

"It's an unfortunate choice to die on such a beautiful day."

The words spilled from Cervantes's mouth painted a faint smile on William Shakespeare's face as he lay there in bed with fever as if he were on the verge of his life at the age of fifty-two. Cervantes swiftly turned his gaze towards the gifted playwright to further emphasize what he was about to say.

"Not a leaf is stirring. Ignore the ripples behind the ducks, the castle's reflection on the water is almost perfect. On a day like this, instead of you dying with skin as pale as common British weather, we could have been walking by the pond having a stimulating talk."

William muttered with a weak voice:

"I don't remember I was given a chance to choose, Signor..."

He was right. It was not up to man to choose a day to die, to say, "Let it be a dark and dreary one, and maybe a little rainy as well". Why would one have preferred a rainy day, anyway? Were the raindrops the teardrops of the universe? Why would one care, after he was gone, whether he would be mourned after or not? Was it really important? Was it the number of tears shed after one's death that determine the true worth of his life?

Cervantes' voice scattered his thoughts.

"Misfortune... Perhaps, we should call it misfortune..."

William looked at his wife, Anne, with whom he had shared thirty-three years of his life. He had never seen her this pale before. The look in her eyes was dull; her eyelashes were wet.

Doctor John Hall picked the dried piece of cloth on William's forehead and soaked it in water; as he gently placed it back, William muttered:

"It's raining on Anne's lands..."

Upon hearing William's mutter, Anne quickly stood up to get closer to him.

"Will?"

She stumbled. Doctor Hall grabbed her by the arm just in time to keep her from falling and helped the exhausted woman return to her seat.

"You'd better not get too close, Anne. We have no idea what caused this. If it is something contagious, it can also lay you low in a short time."

"But John, he is trying to tell us something."

"He's probably hallucinating Anne. Due to high fever."

William slowly turned his gaze towards Cervantes.

"So, you are a hallucination, Signor?"

Cervantes smiled.

"If you say I'm standing right by your side, safe and sound, yes Signor, you must be hallucinating." He sighed. "Because the 23rd of April 1616 is not my best day either..."

"Signor? Are you feeling okay? You don't look so well. Your body is swollen... and this silence..."

On that very day, ten years after Cervantes completed his famous work Don Quixote that would make his name written in history with golden letters, his house on Casa del Calle was so quiet that there was no sound except the clattering of rats running in the attic. Unlike Great Britain, the sun in Madrid was radiant as usual. As it lit Cervantes's face, who was lying in bed suffering from hydropsy[1]; his wife Catalina, eighteen years his junior, was looking for a glimmer of hope in Doctor Alonso's face.

---

[1] Diabetes Mellitus is a type of diabetes seen in old age. It causes the person to drink excessive water and an abnormal accumulation of water in the body.

"Signora, I know how sorry you are. I wish I had some good news for you, but unfortunately, I have none. None of the treatments I applied to reduce his edema turned out to be effective. There is nothing further left that I could do for him."

William was confused. He took a few steps toward the doctor.

"Nothing further left? What do you mean by saying "nothing further left"? How come you cannot figure out the cause of this swelling?"

Cervantes muttered:

"They cannot hear you, Signor. You're not even here in this room, re-member? You're in England, lying in bed with fever."

William was perplexed. Cervantes smiled.

"You are a product of my imagination. I just didn't want to die alone."

Catalina was beside herself with grief. She stood up and walked towards Doctor Alonso.

"You did your best doctor. How much do we owe you?"

Doctor Alonso looked at Catalina's pale face with compassion.

"Signora, you don't owe me anything. I know how hard you try to live through. Besides, I am an old friend of the Cervantes family. I owe a lot to deceased Signor Rodrigo."

Miguel's great-grandfather, Juan Diaz de Torreblanca, was a remarkable physician with an academic degree from the University of Salamanca. His fa-ther, Rodrigo de Cervantes, on the other hand, had no university education, possibly because he was a little deaf from a very young age and thus was un-able to follow the seminars. He had learned medicine from his grandfather and eventually had become an unlicensed healer. Back then, in Spain, at a time when nine out of ten doctors were of Jewish descent, being a surgeon neither brought high income nor required any special knowledge. Physicians, who were the only hope of especially the poor, would generally only take blood, dress open wounds, pull teeth, support fractures, and realign disloca-tions. Passing an exam and working with an experienced physician for a while was enough to become a surgeon. And the physician Doctor Alonso had worked with for a while was Miguel's father. He had learned so much from Rodrigo de Cervantes. And years later, as he was trying to treat his master's son, it had never occurred to him to charge for his services. If he could allevi-ate some of Miguel's pain, he was thinking that he would have paid his moral debt to Rodrigo de Cervantes.

He took a deep breath and placed his hand on Catalina's shoulder.
"Stay strong. He is in God's mercy now."

Catalina tried to smile and thanked Doctor Alonso. She had understood. Though she was not willing, she might have to say farewell to her Miguel sooner than she thought. Sorrow descended upon her like dark storm clouds. She was aware; their marriage had never been flawless. They had met in Esquivias, a village near Toledo famous for its vineyards and olive groves, and hastily married, but had lived apart for the majority of their lives. After her father died, all Catalina needed in her small life, taking place between home and the church in the oak-covered lush hills of Esquivias, was a man who would love and take care of her while also managing her family's estates. But blinded by love; she had failed to see the fact that Miguel's restless and nomadic spirit could never have met her needs. Though she realized soon after they got married that their souls belonged to completely different universes, Catalina had always loved Miguel.

She had her most powerful earthquake when she found out that her husband had a daughter from an extramarital affair that he had with a woman shortly before they met. Her resentment was of course not toward Isabel, who was just an innocent baby unaware of anything, but rather toward Miguel who had kept this a secret from Catalina for many years. Isabel had lost his mother at a very young age. And years later, when Catalina and Miguel's rivers of life crossed again and together they moved to Valladolid, the kingdom's new capital; Catalina had felt compassion for this motherless child and treated her as if she were her own daughter. To Catalina, the stains of the past could be washed away by the waters of time. And regardless of what had happened between them, she had to stand by her husband and not leave her beloved Miguel alone on his deathbed.

She called out to Isabel:
"Isabel, would you see Doctor Alonso to the door, please?"

With his gaze on his daughter, Cervantes spoke to William:
"Isn't she a real beauty... Just like her mother, Ana Franca... Ah! Ana Franca... How deeply I loved that Portuguese woman..."

Isabel was watching her father fighting like a knight an epic battle against the infection that had spread throughout his body when she heard him mutter. As she was about to take a step closer to hear what he was saying, she heard Catalina calling out to herself louder.

"Isabel!"

Cervantes was following with his eyes John Heminges, who was restlessly pacing up and down the room. Heminges was a man of theater, who boasted at every opportunity that all the strands of his hair had turned gray on the stages. He came to an abrupt halt; and as if he were in one of William's plays, he spoke in a deep and theatrical tone.

"I still think he would have been more comfortable if he were at home."

William turned his head towards Cervantes with difficulty.

"He turned sixty and is still in love with drama. Khidr's Felipa, your Ana Franca, John's love of drama..."

He felt blue.

"It was one of those days when he insisted that I should rearrange and publish my works... I'll never forget the expression I saw on his face when I told him I would no longer write."

Along with William Shakespeare, John Heminges had joined the company called *Lord Chamberlain's Men*. When the British Crown passed to James, following the death of Queen Elizabeth in 1603, the king had placed the actors under his protectorate and had changed the name of the company to *King's Men*. One morning in 1613, after all those years of working together, when William told John that he no longer wanted to be one of the King's Men, John had literally been baffled, and as he always did when he got angry, he had opened his arms wide and left the room grumbling.

Cervantes asked William the question he long wondered.

"Why did you quit, Signor? Why did you quit writing your plays to which you devote your life and meticulously embroidered every word?"

Suddenly the door flew open, and eight-year-old Elizabeth dashed into the room as if to answer Cervantes' question.

"Grandma! Grandma!"

With her curly hair falling to her shoulders and her lovely brown eyes, Elizabeth was a beautiful little girl. Having sensed the gloomy atmosphere prevailing lately, she had asked his father, Doctor Hall, several times why his grandfather never got out of that bed. But no one had said much to her. She knelt at her grandmother's feet.

"Why am I not allowed to see my grandpa? Do you know how many days passed since he promised to tell me the rest of the story of Barbarossa Brothers?"

Anne tried to hide her tears behind a compassionate smile she wore on her face and caressed Elizabeth's silky hair.

"Oh, honey..."

As she was struggling to figure out what to say to Elizabeth, Susanna entered the room.

"You shouldn't be here, Elizabeth. What have we talked?" She took Elizabeth by the hand and stood her up. "Your grandfather is not feeling well. Soon he will recover and tell you the rest of the story. But he needs rest right now, which is why we must leave him alone, okay?"

William vaguely smiled.

"Little Elizabeth enjoyed the breathtaking stories of the Barbarossas a lot." He paused for a moment. His face had been shadowed with gloom. "But I think I won't be able to finish it."

Cervantes had recalled his deceased granddaughter, Isabel, who was only two years old when she died. He hadn't had an opportunity to tell even a single story to his granddaughter. His heart was shattered.

As Susanna was about to take Elizabeth out, she looked at her husband, Doctor Hall. When her questions were answered by the desperate expression on her husband's face, she realized that her father would not get well soon, that he would most likely never recover. She wiped a tear that wet her cheek and, together with her daughter, left the room.

Isabel, startled by Catalina's voice, accompanied Doctor Alonso to the door. When she returned, Spain's greatest drama writer, Signor Vega, was speaking.

"Phoenix[2] of wits... After all the criticism he directed at me and my literature, I can't believe the nickname he picked for me. I can't help but wonder, Francisco, whether I'm being victimized by some sort of sarcasm that even I do not understand. He might be a poor string maker, for he was unfortunate. But I told him before, and I told him many times..."

Through his half-open eyelids, Cervantes looked at his friends, Lope de Vega, Francisco de Quevedo, and Juan Ruiz de Alarcon, who were standing by his bedside. How strange, he thought, even his last farewell fitted perfectly well to the general awkwardness of his entire life. Four men who had spent their entire lives criticizing one another had finally met in the same room. Cervantes could sense Juan's discontent with inhaling the same air as his archenemy Lope. Francisco was not fond of Juan either. He was mocking his red hair and hunchback at every opportunity without looking at his own nearsighted eyes. Lope, on the other hand, while considering himself too big for his britches, was accusing Cervantes of being uneducated, and constantly criticizing his adherence to the rules of literature. And as for Cervantes, though he wasn't the kind of man like Lope, who was carelessly splattering around his thoughts and ideas and infecting society, it couldn't be said that he also had fond memories of Lope.

Lope kept spitting poison.

"I told him! If the public pays, you will clown around if necessary. Screw the Aristotelian drama rules! Did he lend an ear? Of course, not! He said, "Pearls should not be cast before swine"[3] and walked away with pride. Stubborn as a goat! If only he could live long enough to see the truth in my words..."

Arising thoughts in Cervantes' mind transformed Lope's words into a piece of background music. Their friendship had always been full of ups and downs. Cervantes was a firm believer that a play should mirror life, that it should reflect the customs and be an undistorted representation of Truth. He had spent his entire life trying to produce works that were not only entertaining but also solemn, in which Aristotelian unity of action, place, and

---

[2] The legendary bird said to be born from its own ashes.
[3] Miguel de Cervantes Saavedra, El coloquio de los perros (The Dialogue of the Dogs), New Testament-Matthew 7

time was indispensable. According to him, literature produced with a concern for public acclaim was worthless folly; and the greatest representative of this folly was Lope himself.

Cervantes was very impressed with the young Lope when he met him in 1583, at Jerónimo Velázquez's house, and had spoken highly of him in his *La Galatea*[4]. And Lope had responded to this gesture in his pastoral romance *Arcadia* and referred to Cervantes as a "noble spirit". But Lope's accomplishments had soon turned him into an arrogant man to the point where he began equating himself with the almost holy Ancient Greek and Roman poets like Homer and Virgil and had made Cervantes feel something he had never felt before, a fit of jealousy toward Lope's ever-growing reputation. When Cervantes, enslaved by envy, began harshly criticizing some of Lope's works, his pretentious attitude had aroused Lope's enmity, who had thought of him as a man with no proper academic education. And when Lope had said, "*Of all the budding poets, there is none so bad as Cervantes, nor any so foolish as to praise his Don Quixote*"; all ties were broken; all bridges were burned.

Could Catalina be right? Could the stains of the past be truly washed away by the waters of time? Didn't the quality of the fabric, the strength of the bonds between the wefts and warps, or the type of stain have anything to say? Even if it was a stain of blood, infidelity, or slander, would it also fade over time? Or was it better to simply burn them all? The man he had been bickering with for the past ten years had somehow come to visit Cervantes on his deathbed; and his wife, Catalina, who, in fact, didn't like him at all, had courteously welcomed him. Why had he come anyway? Could it be that seeing Cervantes dying was giving Lope some sort of delight?

He snapped out of his thoughts.

"Signor Shakespeare, let me introduce you to my colleagues. Spain's greatest writers and poets..."

William smiled.

"With words pouring from their pockets, those who leave traces of thought behind..."

---

[4] Cervantes' first published work

That's exactly what Cervantes had thought of Lope at first. But his thoughts had changed over time. Did his works really lack worth? If that's the case, how come he had become so successful? Or was it jealousy Cervantes felt towards Lope's rapid rise to fame that prompted him to utter these words? After all, it was a world where some would bribe, beg, solicit, rise early, entreat, persist, without attaining the object of their suit; while another would come, and without knowing why or wherefore, would find himself invested with the place or office so many have sued for.[5] Maybe Cervantes was just jealous of Lope and if he was going to admit it to himself, it was the perfect moment.

"People, like whom I failed to have become..."

Perhaps Cervantes had never been as talented as they were. Maybe his colleagues who ignored Cervantes were right in seeing him as a mad old man, a living residue of the past century. Weren't the financial difficulties, his commercial failures that accompanied his life evidence of this? He was not an artist, but merely a craftsman; because in *Siglo de Oro*[6], prose had always been a step below poetry. After all, Cervantes had high expectations for poetry. According to him, no poet should have formed a circle in public places, reciting therein his verses; for those which were good should have been declaimed in the halls of Athens, and not in the city squares.[7] Yes, pearls should indeed not have been cast before swine. However, it was impossible not to appreciate Lope's achievements either. Lope, by chasing public applause, had made a fortune from his plays that appealed to the ignorance of the commoners. He had become so famous that no other man of literature of the era ever had such a reputation. In the years that followed, Lope's career was going to take another step forward, by Pope Urban's bestowing on him in 1627, an honorary doctorate in theology as well as the cross of the Knights of Saint John at Collegium Sapientiae[8]. Cervantes, however, would not be able to see it, for he would already have passed away from this world. Had he lived long enough to see, who knows in how many of his works he would have used it.

---

[5] Miguel de Cervantes Saavedra, Don Quixote
[6] Spanish Golden Age (1556-1659)
[7] Miguel de Cervantes Saavedra, Viaje al Parnaso
[8] Sapience College, College of Wisdom, Heidelberg

William thought that the old man was being unfair to himself.

"Yet, it appears to me that it is you, Signor Cervantes, the leading actor of the play I'm watching here. Could it be that your illness impaired your sight, or caused loss of hearing? Because if my eyes and ears are not betraying and misleading me, all these people you praise, appear to admire you."

Words flying in the air echoed off the walls of Cervantes' clouded mind. He was an autodidact; a curious, self-educated man who had learned through reading, travel; in short, through experience. But he had always been criticized by these people, because he lacked formal education. And now, he couldn't believe his ears; for praises were pouring from his colleagues' lips, softening the heavy scent of the dusty room. On the other hand, though it was true that the scent was changing, the room was still dusty. And as if his talking to his hallucinations in a run-down house where rats were roaming in the attic was not enough, Cervantes was dying.

He shifted his gaze to his bookcase. Even though he couldn't see very well from that distance, he knew exactly where his masterpiece stood. His entire life was within those two volumes on the fourth shelf of a bookcase in a dusty room of a shabby house in Madrid. It had fit in two volumes. All his experiences, all his hopes, as well as all the broken pieces of his soul that cut his hands every time he tried to grab a hold of them...

"*The Ingenious Gentleman Sir Quixote of La Mancha* received a great deal of attention from all societal classes. It hasn't even been two years since *Ballet de Don Quichotte* enchanted the Parisians. My point is, Signor Cervantes, it's not for nothing that these people admire you."

William was trying to keep Cervantes from being lost in the dreary halls of his mind. Cervantes, on the other hand, was thinking about how helpless his pure-spirited knight Don Quixote was against the power of evil; and though they made everyone burst into laughter, how sad those lines where he talked about humanity's lost virtues, actually were. Power was in the hands of the wicked now, and it was nothing but a dream for an idealist to fight against them alone.

"Knighthood has come to an end..." he muttered, "Just as I have come to an end..."

He turned his gaze to his desk on which the shuffled pages of *Los Trabajos de Persiles y Sigismunda*.[9] laid. To be able to finish this story, Cervantes had literally competed against the Angel of Death and had breasted the rope almost in his last breath. He was confident that this work would shut those up who would try to label him a mediocre author, an entertainer, after his death. Was being an intellectual more difficult, or dying an intellectual, he did not know. Perhaps because he knew he had much more to give to the world, he was swaying back and forth between getting hold of life and saying a graceful goodbye. He shut his eyes in pain.

He heard the door creak open. Whoever entered the room taking a few calm steps, the rich sound coming from his thick-heeled leather shoes indicated that he was not a member of the family of Cervantes. He didn't even want to raise his head up and look to see who his visitor was. He wasn't feeling like seeing anyone. All he wanted was to doze off at his desk. He took a quick glance at the liquor left in his glass. Though he had drunk much of it, neither his mind nor his body had relaxed. His days of fighting for what he believed in, getting wounded, and being held captive were over. But probably because he was no longer as young as he once used to be, Cervantes had recently been thinking about the past more frequently, trying to come to terms with it. He had spent five whole years in Algiers. He had been acquainted with all forms of torture, violence, slander, and cruelty, and had witnessed countless heart-shattering events. When he finished writing *Los Tratos de Argel*, he had deeply felt that his pen fell short of describing the agony he saw there; and possibly for this reason, he had decided to publish *La Galatea* as his first novel, in which he portrayed a world that was the exact opposite of the one he lived in. Cervantes had wanted a new life; he had wanted to start life over.

He remembered the taste of joy he felt when he learned that the Royal Council had approved the publication of *La Galatea* in 1584. On that day Cervantes had thought that his fortunes had changed. He was finally going

---

[9] Miguel de Cervantes Saavedra, Los trabajos de Persiles y Sigismunda (The Travails of Persiles and Sigismunda)

to be counted among the distinguished authors who had their works published. He was socially on the rise. He had married Catalina de Salazar y Palacios, the nineteen-year-old daughter of a Spanish landowner and moved from a small house in Madrid to an ostentatious one with a courtyard in Esquivias. He had thought that he finally triumphed over those who kept treating him as a *converso*.[10], even though he had in his hands the royalty-issued documents stating that he was an *Old Christian*, a *Sangre Limpia*.[11]. But his happiness had not lasted as long as he hoped for. The pastoral monotony of life in Esquivias had not satisfied Cervantes' restless soul which craved constant movement. Handling the family's financial affairs, collecting rents from the houses in Toledo was certainly not for Cervantes. *La Galatea* had not brought him much reputation either. And when the thirty-seven arrogant *hidalgo*.[12] families of Esquivias refused to regard him as one of themselves, this country life had become increasingly unbearable for him each passing day. Furthermore, after he married Catalina, the number of people Cervantes needed to look after had increased. And upon learning that Catalina's family's debts exceeded the value of their assets, he desperately had begun to look for additional jobs. Cervantes had made every effort to avoid drowning in this sea of unrest. But when he learned of his father Rodrigo's death on a cursed summer evening, he eventually had decided to pack his stuff and move to the city of commerce Sevilla.

Apparently, his fortune had not changed. He wasn't in much debt, but he was hungry. So, he took the joy he felt when he wrote, along with his pen and papers, locked them all in a drawer, and began working as a government purchasing agent requisitioning wheat and oil. It was a job that required taking people by force whatever they had and provided Cervantes with neither prestige nor a high income. On the contrary, although all he did was to follow royal orders, he would soon become the man the public despised the most and be excommunicated twice. He dealt with the councilors who sued Cervantes for money embezzlement and tried to discredit him in the eyes of the

---

[10] Jews who were forcibly converted to the Catholic faith by the Spanish Inquisition, particularly during the 14th and 15th centuries.

[11] Pure Blood

[12] Hijo de Algo (literally means "son of something"), a hereditary noble in Spain. It applies to all nobles, but especially to the lesser nobility as distinct from the magnates (ricos hombres) and commoner knights.

king and worked hard to restore his damaged reputation as he traveled back and forth between Écija and Sevilla. To get through all of this, he even had written petitions to the Council of the Indies for a post in the New World but had not been granted one. Oh, how different were the lords of the earth from the Lord of Heaven! The former, before they accept a servant, first would scrutinize his birth and parentage, examine into his qualifications, and even require knowing what clothes he has got; but for entering the service of God, the poorest was the richest, the humblest was the best born..[13] After being denied an administrative position in the Indies, Cervantes had begun working as a tax collector. However, traveling alone on perilous roads with over twenty-four kilograms of gold was not easy. And when a Sevillian banker to whom he entrusted the tax revenue in exchange for a letter of credit absconded with the money, he had found himself in the royal prison at the age of fifty. He was, as he said, better versed in misfortune than poetry. It was as if a dark cloud in the bright Spanish sky was faithfully following Cervantes and pouring all the raindrops it contained over this unfortunate man.

He took a deep sigh. Perhaps it would be better if he stopped pondering on the past and instead started a new life in Valladolid together with his wife and daughter. He had named Lope, Phoenix; but given how many times he had attempted to start life over, perhaps it was Cervantes, the true Phoenix. He was a tired, ailing, and sad Phoenix who had failed to rise from his ashes no matter how hard he tried, and who didn't want to see anyone as of now.

His visitor took a few steps toward Cervantes and came to a halt.
"Signor Cervantes?"

Cervantes reluctantly leaned upright. A neatly dressed, well-postured young English aristocrat was staring at him with an excited smile on his face.
"What can I do for you, Signor?" said Cervantes.
The young aristocrat didn't let him finish and extended his hand.
"Shakespeare! William Shakespeare!"

There wasn't even the slightest change in Cervantes' expression. After waiting for a while, William lowered his denied hand.

---

[13] Miguel de Cervantes Saavedra, Coloquio de Los Perros (1613)

"I thought you might have heard my name, Signor. Perhaps I should first introduce myself."

Cervantes reclined back in his chair.

"Don't bother, Signor Shakespeare. I didn't ask you who you are, I asked whether there was something I could do for you."

William glanced at Cervantes' desk piled with papers, books, some dirty stuff, as well as his writings. Although his liquor bottle was empty, he did not appear to be inebriated. As for the strong odor of his discontent, it was impossible not to perceive.

"You didn't respond to my letters..." said William, with a slight reproach in his voice. But after waiting for a while, he realized that he was not going to get a response to his reproach either.

Cervantes stood up and walked toward the fireplace. With an iron rod he grabbed, he began stirring the dying embers.

The Spanish winters were not as harsh as their English counterparts, but the fireplace in Cervantes' room would glow brightly throughout the winter. There were days when he would sit by the fire for hours, watching the dancing flames. He would neither speak, nor write, nor eat anything, but instead, would sit there in silence all day sipping his drink. Catalina would prepare and bring Cervantes' meals to his room. When she returned hours later to pick up the empty bowls and discovered that Cervantes hadn't even touched the food, she would stand by the door and watch her husband staring at the fire. Days like these would fill Catalina's heart with anxiety. She couldn't help but wonder about her husband's personality prior to his five-year-long captivity. Life had taken Cervantes from Madrid to Rome, dragged him from Rome to Naples, and then thrown him to Algiers. If it hadn't been for his go-getter mother, Leonor de Cortinas, who somehow managed to collect his ransom with the petitions she gave one after another, maybe the winds would not be able to bring him back home. But Catalina was feeling that her husband's years in captivity had changed him profoundly. One day, all of a sudden, he had even chosen for himself a new surname and had introduced himself as Miguel de Cervantes Saavedra from then on. Although Cervantes had claimed that he did so just to be able to silence those who unfairly continued to treat him as a *converso*, Catalina had always felt that "Cervantes"

and "Saavedra" were two different people. It was as if two different spirits had taken up residence in her Miguel's chest. On the one hand, there was this *Morisco*.[14]-hater, *Marrano*.[15]-hater "Saavedra", who was holding his head high against all the troubles, misfortunes, and traumas with a never-ending hope and great faith and respect for both the Crown and Christianity; who knew how to get up every time he stumbled; who had the courage, self-confidence, and skill to see reality as a game and had been silently living with her husband since he regained his freedom. On the other hand, under the skin of the same man, in the dreary dungeons that Catalina couldn't manage to lighten up, there was a "Cervantes" who was still living in the baños[16] of Algiers. It was as if all that he ever believed had turned into ashes and dust; and that Cervantes was shedding his yellow leaves in the fall of his life. Despite Catalina's all her efforts to show that she understood him, Cervantes would generally avoid talking about it.

"The knight errant...", Catalina had said to her husband once, as she was about to leave the room, "from so little sleeping and so much reading, your brain will finally dry up and you'll go completely out of your mind."[17]
Cervantes had replied without taking his gaze off the flames.
"I'm trying to remember..."

When enlivened flames illuminated the gloomy room and the objects concealed in the shadows became more visible, William noticed a shiny blade on the desk. He took a few steps and reached for it but clenched his fist at the last moment and gave up the idea. Cervantes did not appear to be bothered by William's presence in the room; however, William was also well aware that he was not welcomed by the Spanish author with a great deal of enthusiasm. Cervantes might consider it impolite and get annoyed if William

---

[14] Former Muslims whom the Roman Catholic church and the Spanish Crown forced to convert to Christianity or face compulsory exile after Spain outlawed the open practice of Islam in the early 16th century.
[15] In Medieval Spain, a Jew or Moor who had converted to Christianity, especially one who professed conversion in order to avoid persecution yet continued to practice Judaism in secrecy.
[16] Bathrooms that were converted into prisons.
[17] Miguel de Cervantes Saavedra, Don Quixote

played with a personal item without first obtaining his permission. Despite having read all of his works, William couldn't say that he knew him well. Hadn't he come all the way from Britain to Spain to get to know him anyway? Being kicked off this place because of some disrespectful act before he even had a chance to converse with this interesting man was the last thing William would want. As he stepped back, his attention was drawn to a sentence written on a piece of paper lying on the desk. He tried to read the handwriting:

"Don... Don Quio..."

"Don Quixote," said Cervantes and provided William with a sense of motivation to reach out and pick up the papers. After taking a quick glance and rearranging them in an order that made the most sense to him, William began reading aloud:

"Somewhere in La Mancha, in a place whose name I do not care to remember, a gentleman lived not long ago, one of those who has a lance and ancient shield on a shelf and keeps a skinny nag and a greyhound for racing."[18]

Hearing his lines spoken aloud took Cervantes to the birth of his story, back to the times he had spent in the Royal Prison of Sevilla. He recalled the glimmer of hope that shone in his heart when he learned that the king had granted him permission to publish his eighty-three-fascicle work. Juan de Amézqueta, who signed the approval as the secretary of the Council, had spoken of *Don Quixote* as a "useful and profitable work". On the other hand, what Cervantes had earned from this "useful and profitable" work was only 1500 reales, which his new publisher Francisco de Robles agreed to pay as a royalty. Cervantes had thought that the amount was much less than what he actually deserved, but he was not in a position to bargain. Francisco was the *Librero del Rey*.[19] and the preeminent bookseller in Castile. He had paid only for the Castilian rights and had not volunteered for a wider distribution covering the entirety of the Iberian Peninsula. And the amount that was paid to Cervantes per copy was 290 maravedis, which corresponded to the worth of approximately fifty-five eggs. Cervantes was, at that time, waiting for his work to be published, yet he did not say anything to William.

William kept on reading.

---

[18] Miguel de Cervantes Saavedra, Don Quixote
[19] The King's publisher

"Some claim that his family name was Quixada, or Quexada, for there is a certain amount of disagreement among the authors who write of this matter, although reliable conjecture seems to indicate that his name was Quexana."[20] He smiled. "Haven't you decided the name of your hero yet, Signor, with whom you hope to attain immortality?"

"Immortality?", said Cervantes.

He had not taken his gaze off the fire, but William was now sure that the conversation he was looking forward to, had finally begun.

"Exactly! Immortality! Don't we all have the secret desire to bring forth a hero through whom we may continue to exist in perpetuity? Immortality! The greatest passion of man!"

Cervantes stood up and walked towards William.

"To think that the affairs of this life always remain in the same state is a vain presumption; indeed, they all seem to be perpetually changing and moving in a circular course. Spring is followed by summer, summer by autumn, and autumn by winter, which is again followed by spring, and so time continues its everlasting round. But the life of man is ever racing to its end, swifter than time itself, without hope of renewal, unless in the next that is limitless and infinite."[21]

"So, death does not intimidate you?"

"If I were a man intimidated by death, I would not have enlisted in Infanteria de Marina[22], would I, Signor?

"However, you will be forgotten. Nobody will remember your name after your physical body leaves this world. Isn't it disturbing to think that all of the knowledge you obtained and experiences you had in this life would be lost forever?"

This young Englishman to whom Cervantes had not the slightest desire to engage in a conversation at first, whose letters he had not even responded to, had finally managed to get Cervantes' attention.

"You made an important point, Signor Shakespeare. As you can tell by looking at how unconcerned I am about the name of the character I presented as my hero, I don't care whether my name is remembered when I'm

---

[20] Miguel de Cervantes Saavedra, Don Quixote
[21] Miguel de Cervantes Saavedra, Don Quixote
[22] Spanish Navy

gone. But you're absolutely right when you say that the things I've learned from the experiences I had throughout my life, should be independent of my physical existence."

Cervantes walked over to his desk and got himself seated. William, on the other hand, was listening attentively and making sure not to interrupt the Spanish writer with whom he finally had a chance to converse.

Cervantes continued:

"The pen is the language of the soul, Signor. As the concepts that in it are generated, such will be its writings.[23] And a man is the sum total of the souls that touched his own. That's the reason why I'm so passionate about words. My pen is more than me, it tells the story of all others who made up the man I call "me"."

This was precisely the reason why William had traveled from the lush plains of Britain all the way down to the narrow alleys of Spain. Whose souls had reached out and touched the old Spaniard? With whose souls had Cervantes' soul been blended and it had taken this unstable form that even he himself could never have imagined? William thought that it was the right time to ask.

"So, whose souls are they, Signor, that you ink-seal on these papers?"

Cervantes' eyes were on the blade. He reached out and picked it up. Its shine lit up his face.

"I..." he said... "I am trying to remember..."

When Cervantes pushed the piled-up papers aside, William saw the Mediterranean map engraved on the wooden desk.

---

[23] Miguel de Cervantes Saavedra, Don Quixote

Lepanto, October 7, 1571

It was as if the rumbling of cannons and rifles that had been exploding for hours, the clanging of clashing swords, and the buzzing of arrows in the air had ceased for a moment. All the screams, moans, cries, and yells had come to a halt. At that precise moment, a single bullet left the barrel, hung in the air for a split second, and then pierced Ali Pasha in the chest, causing him to collapse on his knees on *Sultana*'s[24] deck. He had difficulty breathing. As the commander of the land forces, it had never occurred to him that he would meet his end on the seas.

Don Juan de Austria, Admiral of *Real*[25], possibly the greatest galley[26] in Spanish history, took a few steps toward the Kapudan Pasha[27], while a Spanish soldier drew his sword and fell on Ali Pasha, seeing him leaned on his sword trying to rise up. As he slit with his sword the Grand Admiral's throat, he hadn't even heard Don Juan's cry.

"Noooooo!"

Ali Pasha's head rolled toward the admiral's feet. Don Juan, boiling with rage, headed towards the Spaniard, and thrust his sword into his belly.

"I don't want you to live long enough to realize what a fool you are."

---

[24] The flagship of the Ottoman Navy in the Battle of Lepanto
[25] The flagship of Don John of Austria in the Battle of Lepanto
[26] Large seagoing vessel propelled primarily by oars.
[27] Grand Admiral of the Ottoman naval forces

No one dared to move. As the blood of the Spaniard dripped onto the deck from the tip of his sword, Admiral Don Juan roared at the soldiers under his command:

"God had given us the opportunity to capture the Grand Admiral of the Ottoman navy wounded! If there are any others among you as stupid as him, we can never win this battle!"

Cervantes was in one of *La Marquesa's*[28] cabins, packing his belongings. He was feeling extremely nauseous, and dizzy due to high fever and was making a concerted effort not to throw up. After placing the notes he had taken along the way in his wooden chest and closing the lid, he reached for the sword he had just put aside. But the sword was gone.

"You are sick. In your current condition, fighting is not an option. Remain inside!"

Commander Gianandrea Doria[29] was standing at the door holding Cervantes' sword. Just like his uncle Andrea Doria, he was known for maintaining his composure even during the most intense battles. Cervantes struggled to get to his feet, and walked toward him in the rocking galley, careful not to trip and fall.

"It is better that I should fight in the service of God and the king and die for them, than keep under cover."

Upon seeing the blazing look in Cervantes' eyes, Gianandrea had understood that there was no point in insisting. He took a deep breath and handed Cervantes his sword.

"May God be with you, then..."

He turned his back and joined the ongoing battle. Would Cervantes be able to see him again? Or would he be able to see Cervantes? Neither of them knew...

Ali Pasha's lifeless body was floating over the waters of Lepanto while his head on a pike was paraded around and displayed in an effort to inspire fear and demoralize the Ottoman soldiers. Uluj Ali Reis lost his zeal. As the commander of the right-wing of the crescent-shaped Ottoman formation, he had not lost a single vessel and had been successful even in capturing the

---

[28] The Christian galley Cervantes fought in the Battle of Lepanto
[29] Giovanni Andrea Doria

galleys of the Knights of Malta. He recalled the last conversation they had with Ali Pasha. The vast majority of the *sipahis*[30] and *janissaries*[31] were on the leave. The navy had just returned from the six-months-long Cyprus expedition. The ships were in need of maintenance. They were lacking enough ammunition. While in such a state, launching an attack on such a sizeable armada was a huge mistake. Both Serdar Pertev Reis and Uluj Ali Reis had explained all these to Ali Pasha and warned him, however, Ali Pasha had not listened to them. Ali Pasha was a temperamental man, but more importantly, he was a land commander with no experience in naval battles. Uluj Ali Reis had never understood why Ali Pasha was appointed as the Grand Admiral of the navy when there were so many other competent *reises*.[32] trained by Barbarossa and fought alongside him. Not heading their warnings Ali Pasha had said, *"What about the zeal of Islam, the sultan's honor? What would it matter if we are lacking five or ten men from each ship? Our Sultan ordered us to attack whenever we encountered the enemy. I'll never let them say, the sultan's soldiers have fled."*

Uluj Ali Reis commanded his *levends*.[33]:
"Retreat! We are returning to Modon!"

As he swung his sword on *La Marquesa*'s deck, Cervantes realized that his body would no longer be able to endure the fight. He had been wounded in the chest and was gasping for breath. When he paused and leaned against the rails to check his wound, he noticed the Ottoman soldiers making their way down to the lower deck.
"My notes!"

He ran down the stairs. With a single swing of his sword, he knocked down one of the soldiers, who attempted to plunder Cervantes' chest in which he had placed all his belongings. However, regarding how to deal with the other two who already had pointed their arquebuses at him, he was completely clueless. Just when he thought he was cornered, a cannonball exploded on

---

[30] Feudal cavalrymen of the Ottoman Empire whose status resembled that of the medieval European knight.

[31] Elite infantry units that formed the Ottoman Sultan's household troops and the first modern standing army in Europe

[32] Ottoman naval captains

[33] Ottoman naval soldiers

the board side of La Marquesa. It was as if both a blessing and a curse. The soldiers were dead, while Cervantes was spared. But the last thing he saw before passing out was his chest slipping through the hole that the cannon-ball had opened on the galley's hull into the murky waters of Lepanto.

"My notes!"

When he opened his eyes, he was lying on the shore. His eyes searched for his brother, Rodrigo, with whom he had fought on the same galley. The sun was setting, and Cervantes was, in fact, quite surprised to have survived the greatest naval battle he had ever seen. He was in pain. He had two severe wounds in the chest, and he had almost completely lost his left hand in a battle he would later describe as *the most memorable and lofty occasion that past centuries have beheld, or which future ages hope to see*. As he lay there alone, he looked at his right hand, wiggled his fingers, and clenched his fist. He vaguely smiled. He had remembered how he had fled to Rome to avoid having his right hand cut off, after being found guilty by the Inquisition of fighting a duel and wounding the master-builder Antonio de Sigura. It seems that his left hand was not as fortunate as his right. "I guess I still have things to write," he murmured.

Having seen Cervantes come to himself, Jose and Diego rushed up to him. "Thank God you're awake, Signor!"

Cervantes squinted his eyes to see who was speaking to him. But the sun that was shining from behind those who addressed him was making it impossible for him to recognize their faces. What he was able to see were only the silhouettes of two soldiers. When Jose kneeled, Cervantes remembered this young lad he had seen on La Marquesa's deck.

"Jose? Is that you?"

"Yes, it's me, Signor."

"Rodrigo... Have you seen Rodrigo? Is he all right?"

"Yes, Signor, don't worry, your brother is fine. He was by your side the entire time. He was the one who dressed your wounds. Since he possessed the necessary medical knowledge, Doctor Dionisio requested his assistance. And after ensuring that your condition was stable, Rodrigo went to help the doctor. What about you, Signor? How do you feel?"

As he tried to sit up, Cervantes replied:

"Like someone who survived an epic naval battle, wounded in the chest twice and lost his left hand..."

While Jose was still trying to comprehend what Cervantes had just said, Diego burst out laughing. Cervantes, on the other hand, had his gaze fixed on the reddish-blue waters of Lepanto.

"Holy Jesus, look at this..."

Both shifted their gaze to where Cervantes was looking. The smoke rising from the still-burning ships was darkening the sky, and the sea was looking like a floating cemetery with thousands of lifeless bodies on it. The shore was full of wounded. And Cervantes was in fact surprised to see that the majority of the ships that had managed to stay afloat were those belonging to the Christians.

The participants of the Holy League, eventually formed in the Strait of Messina at the call of Pope Pius V, were in such great dispute that, Cervantes initially had not believed that the Christians had the slightest chance of winning this battle. The despot king, Philippe II of Spain, had sent his best men to the Duke of Alba to quell the Dutch revolt, leaving for the navy only a bunch of inexperienced rookies. The Knights of Saint John despised the Venetians, the Venetians despised the Genoese; while the Spaniards, known for their arrogance, despised everyone who was not Spanish. It was such a hatred that, despite his yelling as "I am Christian, I am a bishop"; the Spaniards had not even hesitated to kill and rob the Albanian Bishop of Bar, Giovanni Bruni, together with his nephew, who were both enslaved by the Muslims. Though, on the one hand, they were mocked as "papagayos" because of their multicolored uniforms and red socks; on the other hand, they were unquestionably a source of great discomfort for everyone in Europe for they had control over the majority of the Italian Peninsula. As for the Venetians, their only concern was being able to trade safely in peaceful waters. To the Knights of Saint John, however, who constantly criticized the residents of La Serenissima for being only interested in their own pockets, they were the Mistress of the Ottoman Empire. But no matter what anyone would say, the marketplace set up around the Rialto Bridge was an important hub for international trade. Furthermore, they were first Venetians, then Christians; and they believed that man should first fill his stomach in this material world, and then deal with the spiritual world only if he had the time and the conditions allowed.

"What happened? Where are the Turks?" asked Cervantes.

Diego barged in.

"At the bottom of the sea, Signor. We won! We won the battle! We fought much better. We had better guns, and our soldiers were braver. After seeing their admiral's head on a pike, the Turks were demoralized. They were already out of ammunition. When they ran out of cannonballs, arrows, and bullets, they began throwing at us oranges and lemons they found on their ships. Can you imagine, they thought they could kill us with lemons. You should have seen it, it was hilarious."

Diego was a zealous young man who was in love with the blacksmith's daughter back in his village. Since the girl had grown up listening to the heroic stories of the Christian knights from her father, it was her dream to marry a knight. And Diego was adamant about becoming the knight she would marry one day. With this motivation, he had wanted to enlist in the navy as a musketeer but was only able to set foot on the deck as a seaman. Nonetheless, he was not discouraged and had thought that it was just a beginning. If he could prove useful during the battle he could be promoted to a musketeer; and if he could kill a high-ranking man, he might rise to knighthood in rank. After all, the knights, like everyone else, must have been starting from somewhere.

The ships belonging to the Christians had fared better than the ones that belonged to the Ottomans. Diego was fortunate to have been in a galley that sustained relatively little damage during the battle. He had neither been injured nor witnessed his friends' deaths. Being only a distant observer of what was, in fact, a tremendously tragic battle in which thousands of people from both sides had lost their lives had made laughing at this orange-lemon story easy for Diego.

Jose, however, had fought in the line of fire alongside Cervantes, and La Marquesa was one of the galleys that had lost the majority of its crew. Jose had witnessed such horrific events that the bitter taste of war seemed it would linger on his lips for the rest of his life.

With rage, he silenced Diego.

"Turn around and take a look at the people on the shore with their arms, their legs cut off! Turn around and take a look at the blood-red waters of Lepanto! And tell me what's so hilarious about it?"

Diego, feeling ashamed of what he had just said, lowered his head. Cervantes spoke in an effort to ease the tension.

"So, they threw us lemons and oranges huh? One cannot help but be impressed by the stubborn determination of the Turks. This must be what is called fighting to the very last drop of one's blood..."

Cervantes was aware that this victory would resound throughout Europe. In fact, he was thinking that its impact would be much greater than the victory itself. Soon, the church bells would toll in Spain, Venice, and Italy; and the streets would be filled with people inebriated with victory. They would all leave their work aside, would put signs on their doors that read "*Chiuso per la morti dei turchi*".[34], and attend the craziest celebrations. Even the British Kingdom which was, in fact, only concerned about securing its commercial advantages, but which had put forward its geographical distance from the events in the Mediterranean as an excuse when turning down the pope's call to join the Holy League, would not be late to participate in these celebrations. Dozens of poets and writers would magnify the outcome of the battle like the shadows extending in the afternoon sun; and many chansons, plays, odes, and songs overexaggerating the victory would be written about it. As for the subject matter of the artwork that the great Renaissance painters such as Bonastri, Titian, Vicentino, and Veronese would portray in no time and bequeath to eternity; it would be the great victory of Christianity that came with the assistance of God and His angels...

The Turks, who were wreaking havoc in the Mediterranean for some time, had become a nightmare for the people living on the European coastline. This fear had become so ingrained in people's hearts that it was constantly expressed in day-to-day life. When someone cried out, "*Hay Moros en la costa! Hay Moros en la costa!*", which translates to "*Maghrebis.*[35] *are on the shore!*"; everyone would be alarmed and run for their lives. It was such an intense fear that even the architectural style of the coastal cities had been drastically altered over the course of time. The windows of the houses, churches, and castles had gradually become smaller and smaller and been secured with iron bars; while many ramparts and watchtowers had been

---

[34] "We are closed due to the death of Turks."
[35] Inhabitants of the Maghreb region, the westernmost part of North Africa

built to protect the locals from the never-ending raids of the pirates. When their children misbehaved, mothers would threaten them by saying "I'll give you to the Turks!". Even according to Martin Luther, the Turks were a divine punishment that God had sent upon the so-called Christians.

Selim I had defeated the Safavids in the *Battle of Chaldiran*, the Mamluks in the Battles of *Marj Dābiq* and *Ridaniya*, and secured the eastern borders of the empire. And his heir, Suleiman the Magnificent, after succeeding to the throne, had set his eyes on Europe. During the reign of Suleiman, the Turk had become more than just a villain in a fairy tale for the Europeans; but instead, had found embodiment. The Turks were portrayed as barbarians in everything that was published, as brutal, ruthless murderers. Wild boars they were, aggressive drooling dogs, even Satan itself, who would conquer all the kingdoms one after another, would proceed from one province to the next, and if not stopped, would set the whole world on fire in the end. Despite the numerous enmities and disputes that existed between them, the European kingdoms had finally united against this evil and agreed that the Turks were *"comun y universal enemigo,"* that is, "common and universal enemy."

And the Turks had finally been defeated. One hundred and thirty-four of the two hundred and fifty Turkish ships had been captured, while fifty were sunk. Twenty thousand Turks were either killed, wounded, or taken captive. When Cervantes looked at the wreckage of the battle, he couldn't help but wonder: Was the strong one the barbarian, or the barbarian the strong? Up until that point, he had fought for what he had believed in; however, on that day he had witnessed the destruction of seventy Ottoman galleons at the hands of technologically more superior Venetian barques. The defeat Christians suffered at Preveza had finally been avenged. Was that also what had happened at Preveza? Had the sea worn in scarlet and the sky in black on that unfortunate day as well? Wasn't the number of fatalities excessive for a single day? Even if all the priests of Christendom were to remain in their cells for weeks and repent, the sin of the day was too great to be forgiven. It seems the ancient definition of valor had changed. Now it meant shooting thousands of birds with a single stone. Cervantes was slowly coming to the realization that the discovery of the New World had thrown off the economic balance of the old and the era of genuine knighthood had come to an end. He felt sad.

"La Marquesa received a lot of damage," asked Jose, "Could you be able to have kept your belongings safe? Throughout the course of the cruise, I observed, you were taking notes."

He noticed the light fading in Cervantes' eyes. Before his very eyes, Cervantes' wooden chest had slipped through the hole and disappeared in the waters of Lepanto, and he was unable to prevent it. Jose felt sorry for him.

"It's a pity..."

"It's a pity...," said William. "A lot has been written in Europe after this victory. If only you, as the one who heard the pulse of the battle from such proximity, were able to put the stories of those barbarians down on paper..."

As a matter of fact, Cervantes had; but *A Captive's Tale,* which was one of his earliest plays, had satisfied neither Cervantes nor the literary circles, and thus, had not made a significant impression. He was aware that he needed to revise his work and turn it into a more powerful theatrical play, but for some reason, he was reluctant to start. He preferred not to talk about it.

Unaware of what Cervantes was thinking, William was trying to be mindful of the words he would use to finish his sentence. He hesitated for a second, concerned about being misunderstood. Cervantes, on the other hand, did not fail to notice the hesitation of William, who was regarded as one of his time's masters of eloquence.

"I would at least have accomplished in my life, one noteworthy thing, wouldn't I, Signor Shakespeare?"

"I was going to say, perhaps it might have been a turning point for you regarding the mishaps you have experienced in your literary life, Signor Cervantes."

Cervantes sarcastically smiled.

"It's no wonder, of course, that a life lived among the British aristocrats has endowed you with diplomatic skills."

William felt relieved to have been able to avoid any tension that might arise between the two. The Spanish writer may have lost his notes, but the details of this epic battle must have been deeply engraved in his mind. After all, Cervantes was born and had grown up in these lands, where, with the fall of Granada and the completion of Reconquista, the real conflict and the ongoing battles of the world gained momentum. This was a once-in-a-life-time opportunity for William. At last, he would be able to call into question what was written in papal pamphlets as well as the traces of ink that flowed from the pens of prominent European poets. He now had the chance to find out how much of the triumphant literature of the era was based on facts and how much was a mere myth.

"Those barbarians are really…"

Cervantes interrupted. He quickly stood up from his chair and walked toward the window.

"Those barbarians, thieves, murderers, lawless, faithless assailants, those vicious arrogant and bloodsucking vampires ignorant of art, literature, and science…"

William was listening attentively.

"And on that happy day, Signor Shakespeare, when dubious fate looked on the foeman's fleet with a baleful eye, on ours with a smiling glance and fortunate, inspired with mingled dread and courage high, in thickest of the direful fight I stood, my hope still stronger than my panoply. I marked the shattered host melt like a flood, and a thousand spots upon old Neptune's breast dyed red with heathen and with Christian blood… Death, like a fury, running with foul zest, hither and thither, sending crowds in ire to lingering torture, or to speedy rest… The cries confused, the horrid din and dire, the mortal writhings of the desperate who breathed their last mid-water and mid-fire… The deep-drawn sighs, the groanings loud and great that sped from wounded breasts in many a throe, cursing their bitter and detested fate…"[36]

As Cervantes was looking out of the window he was as if staring into empty space.

"Before the turn of the century, the lands were home to not only to Christians but also to Jews and Muslims, Signor. Beginning with the period when it was ruled by the Umayyads, Andalusia had gradually become a shining sun of civilization in the eastern Islamic world. However, the fall of Granada marked the beginning of the end…"

---

[36] "Epístola a Mateo Vázquez" is the section in "Journey to Parnassus" in which Cervantes talks about what he had gone through in the Battle of Lepanto.

Cervantes had not seen those days, but his great-grandfathers, about whom he always had a sneaking suspicion that they might be conversos, had. And what Cervantes should do now, in a century scorched by the consequences of the events of the previous one, was to walk in the light of the truth that he carried in his heart, rather than in the darkness of what has been claimed. It was now time for him to figure out on his own what to think and what to believe, and then, die with dignity.

Spain, 1492

Reconquista was an eight-century-long dream. Its completion, however, had marked the beginning of an era in Granada that was more horrifying than the worst nightmare one could ever see. It was the first few hours of a dark night that was going to last for more than a century for hundreds of thousands of people. The palaces, which were the architectural wonders of the era, had been razed to the ground, and the libraries which housed thousands upon thousands of books had all been burned down. As he was about to leave the city on horseback watching Granada burning in flames, two drops of tears fell from Amir Abu Abdallah's eyes. His mother Aixa, on the other hand, was having a hard time accepting her son's despair.

"Weep like a woman for a kingdom you failed to defend as a man."

King Boabdil.[37] was crying over the civilization that was being perished. Following Cardinal Jiménez's appointment as Archbishop of Toledo, the Church of Spain had been plunged into a dramatic reformation, and over five thousand Arabic manuscripts, with the exception of those pertaining to medicine, had been burned. The lives of the people who had been living in these lands for centuries, who had the freedom to practice their faith and worship according to their traditions would, from then on, be a lot different than it was once. Because, in contrast to the Ottomans, who allowed the non-Muslims to settle in imperial lands, even if it was on the condition that they paid additional taxes; the Spanish Inquisition were not going to grant the non-Christian communities in Spain the right to live. They had to leave.

---

[37] Abu Abdallah Muhammad XII, known in Europe as Boabdil was the 22nd and last Nasrid ruler of the Emirate of Granada in Iberia

Cardinal Jiménez was holding a very firm position regarding this matter. They either had to leave or convert to Christianity.

The Muslim and Jewish communities that had been living on the Iberian Peninsula for centuries constituted the keystone of all the economic and political life in Spain. Particularly the Jews had for a long time benefited from the special privileges that were granted to them and had lived under the Crown's protectorate. Some had come to positions of power within the palace by serving the royalty as physicians and political advisers; while some had become involved in practicing usury or worked as tax collectors, taking an active role in commercial life, and gaining control of the capital. Muslims, on the other hand, who would get up earlier than everyone else, go to work, and work hard, and teach their children profession at a very young age had improved useful plants, cultivated and utilized the idle lands, and come to the fore in agriculture by keeping silk and sugar production in their hands. In such an environment, the Old Christians, who greeted the day no earlier than noon, laid down on benches for a siesta when the clocks hit two o'clock in the afternoon and who spent their days either playing cards in the streets or waiting for food at the gates of monasteries, were inevitably bound to become poorer by the day. The resentment and animosity that the *Caballeros* and *Hidalgos*.[38], who had a set of codes of honor that frowned upon working for profit, harbored toward Muslims and Jews, had led to social unrest. The opinion held by the majority of Christians was that the Muslims and the Jews would eventually completely devour Spain; and this was something that had to be prevented.

First, they were forced to resign from their positions in the palaces, universities, and churches. Antisemitism, which was gradually spreading throughout Spain, had brought with it violent attacks on neighborhoods where the Jews lived. Wealthy people were frequently subjected to false accusations and arrests. After all, it was the easiest way to seize their possessions and refill the emptied pan of the scale that measured wealth. As the flames of enmity grew, some Jews and Muslims resorted to conversion which was presented by the Inquisition as the only means to end this nightmare, and they were baptized en masse.

---

[38] Members of the lower nobility in Spain

Muslims who abandoned their traditions and converted to Christianity were called "*Moriscos*", while the Jews were referred to as "*Marranos*". However, their conversion was now leading them into yet another trap. As the New Christians, they would henceforth be constantly inspected by the *familiares*.[39] the Inquisition unleashed countrywide, and whether they really became true Christians, or they were only pretending to be one, would be under close scrutiny.

The madness of *Limpieza de sangre*.[40] would gradually spread to every part of Spain and people would begin to snitch on everyone to the Inquisition with whom they had a dispute. From that point forward, the life that awaited the New Christians on the Iberian Peninsula, was a life fraught with anxiety. Moriscos would not be permitted to use the public baths, speak or pray in Arabic. Nor would they be able to give alms or wear traditional Muslim clothes. They were not going to play musical instruments authentic to Muslim communities, burn henna or cover their faces, and were going to leave their doors open not only on Fridays but on religious holidays as well. In short, they had to completely abandon all their customs and traditions. Similar regulations also applied to the Marranos. If anyone were to disobey the orders, or get involved in any activity considered suspicious, they were either going to be placed on the *Judas Cradle*.[41] or burned alive at stakes. And in such a case, they were going to pay for their food, accommodation, and would cover the wages of the inquisitors who was going to torture them during their stay in prison. After all, nothing was free; in order to receive the service of torture, they had to pay for it.

In the end, they lost all their possessions. Mosques and synagogues were converted either into churches or barracks. Their women were forced to dress in the manner of Castilians, and their children were made to study the Bible in the churches. Those who could neither leave their homes nor abandon their beliefs, were put to sword, hanged, burned and destroyed. The ordeal of Moriscos and Marranos on the Iberian Peninsula was going to last

---

[39] Officers who apprehend the accused/suspected and convey them to prison.

[40] "Blood purity", was a system of discrimination used in early modern Spain.

[41] A common method of torture used in medieval Europe, a pyramid-shaped wooden device onto which the victim was placed.

for more than a century. Until Felipe, whom a Morisco doctor named Jerónimo Pachet would heal and save from the clutches of death at the age of eight, would grow up and expel all Moriscos from Spanish lands in 1609.

Only the Ottoman Empire had heard and responded to the prayers of the Muslims and Jews of Andalusia. While Granada was in flames, people who were pleading to get on board were being carried by boats to Kemal Reis' galleons anchored some miles away from the shore.

Piri was rowing with all of his might, his back facing the shore. As he approached Kemal Reis' galleon, the agony on the faces of those on board was beating against his heart like the salty waters of the Mediterranean beat against the hulls. Among the people holding onto each other and crying, Piri noticed an old man with a dull expression on his face sitting alone on the far edge of the boat. With a shabby robe on his back and his gaze on the shore, he was muttering. It seemed that he had no family; or perhaps, he no longer had a family. As Piri stared at his expressionless face, he recalled his uncle's words; who had once told him that Allah would not give a man a burden he could not bear and if one was still able to feel pain, one could endure it. The old man, on the other hand, as if he had felt he was being stared at, had turned his head toward Piri and begun looking him in the eye.

"And it repented the LORD that he had made man on the earth, and it grieved him at his heart."[42]

Had Piri really overheard him uttering these words? Or had he simply read the old man's lips? It was as if every word had stabbed him in the chest.

As the boat came alongside the galleon, Piri grabbed one of the rope ladders the sailors had strung up and climbed up onto the deck. Leaning against the railings, Kemal Reis was keeping a close eye on everything that was taking place on the shore. He was upset.

"Eight-hundred-year-old civilization is burning to the ground, Piri. What we are looking at right now are the last remnants of Andalusia."

Piri placed his hand on his uncle's shoulder. Perhaps it was the most effective way of showing him that he was feeling the same way. The sorrow that filled up Piri's heart would travel down his arm, and when it reached his uncle, it would meet with the anguish that was already present in his heart of hearts.

---

[42] Genesis 6:6

He muttered:

"And it repented the LORD that he had made man on the earth, and it grieved him at his heart."

"Torah!" said Kemal Reis.

Piri was confused.

"Torah, son, the Holy scripture of the Jews. The verse that you just recited is from Genesis, the first book of what is collectively referred to as the Torah, "Five Books of Moses.""

"So, he was a Jew..." Piri thought. He was deeply concerned about whether it was appropriate to take these people whom they knew nothing about on board. He shared his worries with his uncle.

"The majority of these people are not Muslims, uncle. Are you sure we are doing the right thing by carrying them to the heart of the empire?"

Without taking his gaze away from the shore, Kemal Reis replied:

"They are human, Piri. People whose homes were torched and destroyed; whose families, whose loved ones were slaughtered. Allah's people, they are. Besides, our Sultan ordered so. Come on, tell the levends to raise the anchor. We need to set sail before it gets dark."

As he was looking out of the window, it was as if Cervantes was watching Kemal Reis' galleons gliding on the waters of the Mediterranean.

"More than 150.000 Jewish and Muslim Andalusians were carried to Anatolia as well to North Africa by Kemal Reis' galleons." He suddenly turned to William. "We have spoken of them as those ignorant of science, haven't we?"

The questions in William's mind searched for themselves answers in Cervantes' eyes. Cervantes continued:

"Bayezid II's reign was a significant era in the history of the Ottoman Empire. The seeds that would later allow his son, Selim I, to bring the East to its knees and his grandson Suleiman the Magnificent, to strike fear into the hearts of the European kingdoms were sown during Bayezid's reign." He made his way over to his desk and placed his finger on the Iberian Peninsula. "If the Ottomans began this century ahead of the Europeans in terms of both economy and technology, it was due to the Sephardic Jews[43] who migrated to the Empire and made the most significant contributions. Hardworking individuals they were, who were granted permission to live in Ottoman lands with their extensive knowledge and experience. The best metal workers that history has ever seen, the most astute statesmen, and the most skillful merchants... The Andalusian immigrants who would establish for the Empire the largest network of espionage ever and would pave the way for the Turks to sweep the Mediterranean in the following century."

William took advantage of Cervantes' momentary pause and interrupted:

"If it was the completion of Reconquista which ignited the fuse and paved the way for those blasphemous barbarians to fill the Christian hearts with fear, then my heart truly wishes that what has been written about the victory of Lepanto were not simply exaggerated stories."

Cervantes responded with a sarcastic smile. Then, after searching for a while, he handed William an item he found amidst the papers on his messy desk. It was a piece of leather folded into a triangle, with a small piece of paper hidden inside, as seen through the openings between the seams. After checking it for a while, William asked:

"What is this?"

Cervantes sat back on his chair.

"An amulet Signor, something that Muslims believe brings good luck and protects them from evil."

"So, it is the power of God, packed."

"It is the power of faith, Signor Shakespeare, as another way of saying. The power they needed to shine from within when all the lights around had gone dim. The Turks whom you referred to as "heathens" believe that they fight for the sake of Allah. I would like to remind you of what Byzantine Emperor VI. Ioannis Kantakuzenos once said: It's hard to win a battle against the Muslims, for they fight either to become martyrs or veterans."

"Under the guise of religiosity, they try to justify their assaults, the purpose of which is in fact nothing but to gain economic and political power. They claim that they fight for Allah hoping that this would legitimatize their atrocity."

"Exactly Signor Shakespeare. Just like we, Christians, do..."

---

[43] Andalusian Jews settled in Avalon and Thessaloniki

William couldn't disagree. Cervantes continued:

"It is indisputable that Europe has long been going through a period of horror, and that the Christian victory in the Battle of Lepanto dealt a major blow to the Ottoman Empire. But when it comes to how barbarous, how cruel, how brutal the Turks could be, I have no doubt that the people living in Granada had thought the same about us."

William was perplexed.

"After all those years of fighting against the Turks, after losing your left hand for this cause, you are not standing up for them, are you, Signor Cervantes?"

"No, Signor, I am not. The hatred I feel towards them is no less than my admiration. To clarify, what I mean is that it was no accident that the Turks had taken control of the Mediterranean during this century. If we were to view them as nothing more than a bunch of bandits, we would be led into the murky waters of delusion. Because during that time period, the Barbarossas who were carrying on their flags the symbols of all three Abrahamic religions, who were able to speak in six different languages were much more than just a bunch of lucky pirates; they were literally the masters of the Mediterranean."

Lesbos

They were the children of the Island of Lesbos, where the peaks of Lepetymnos and Olympus dressed up with pines, oaks, firs, sycamore, and chestnut trees that stretch their heads towards the heavens, and where the olives reached forth from the slopes to the sea. The children of the Emerald Island, they were... Having been the greenest of all islands in the northeastern Mediterranean, Lesbos was the most deserving of this name out of all the others. With its housetops of red clay tiles and grayish-green olive groves that start right behind the walls, the island looked like a patchwork from afar. Its crowded port, which had not much changed since ancient times was harboring many large and small sea vessels, ranging from war galleons to *feluccas*[44] manned by the Arabs. One might encounter people of a wide variety of nationalities and religious affiliations at the port of Lesbos. Arabs in their *jellabias*[45], Greeks and Hungarians wearing multicolored shirts and straw hats, European Christians with their high-rise woolen socks, Jews wearing *kippahs*[46] from under which their curly hair hung, and of course, Turks with their impressive turbans, green striped trousers, and crossed chest straps where they placed their swords.

After being taken over by Mehmed II in 1462, the Island of Lesbos had been quickly developed into a strategically significant trade center for the Ottoman Empire. When Yakub Agha, a former cavalry from *Yanicca* who had

---

[44] A traditional wooden sailing boat used in the eastern Mediterranean.
[45] A loose-fitting traditional gown or robe worn by mostly by Arabs.
[46] A brimless cap traditionally worn by Jewish males to fulfill the customary requirement of covering the head.

participated in the island's conquest, had fallen in love with Katerina, the widow of a Greek priest, he had decided to settle on the island. He had stored his sword away in a wooden chest and begun earning his living by making pottery and engaging in trade. And the four young men, Isaac, Aruj, Khidr, and Elias, who were now laughing and joking with each other as they walked along the beach, were the offspring of this mutual love.

Katerina and Yakub Agha would occasionally step back and take a look at their children from a distance, and marvel at how quickly the years had gone by. With their skins tanned by the Lesbos sun, teeth as white as pearls, and their shiny eyes, those little boys, the day of whose births their parents recalled like yesterday, had grown up to be four young handsome men.

Isaac, the eldest of the three, had been lending a hand to his father for some time. He was sailing with Yakub Agha, transporting goods to Syria, Alexandria, and Tripoli and then, bringing back to Anatolia the goods that they purchased in those cities. But Yakub Agha was showing signs of his advanced age. He no longer possessed the youthful vitality he once had. It appeared as though snow had fallen on his hair and beard. Aruj, on the other hand, who accompanied him on his last few journeys, had impressed his father and earned his appreciation for his bravery, strength, and skills. Yakub Agha had once expressed to his wife that the time to entrust the work in the hands of Isaac and Aruj may have come. But as their mother, Katerina had not looked well upon the idea of her sons being away from home for extended periods of time, even though she had complete faith in them.

"Don't put on a sad face; don't let Aruj and Elias see you this sorrowful. Besides, the girls are with you, aren't they? Don't you love them as much as you love your sons," Yakub agha had once said.

Katerina had responded with a slight reproach in her tone:

"Of course, I love my daughters the way I love my sons, Yakub. They are all parts of my soul. My heart beats for each one of them. I'm just... I'm concerned about Khidr. You know how he is deeply attached to Aruj. Aruj has a very special place in Khidr's heart."

The brotherhood between Aruj and Khidr was indeed unique. When Aruj began accompanying his father on his excursions, Khidr had understood that he would no longer be able to spend time with his brother in the same way that they had done in the past. He had felt deeply sad yet had not shared his feelings with others. But Katerina was his mother; she could tell from the flickering light in his eyes when there was something troubling her son.

The sun was about to set. Isaac called out to Elias, the youngest of the four:

"Come on, Elias, if you want me to help you with your Spanish after dinner, let's go home before it's too late. I'm worn to my bones today, completely exhausted. If we keep hanging around here a little while longer, I'm afraid I'll nod off during dinner."

Four brothers were sitting together on the beach, bidding farewell to the day. Elias leaped to his feet.

"Don't even think about doing such a thing. I have a lot to ask. Besides, you've been putting me off for days and saying, 'not today', 'tomorrow' every time I ask you something."

Isaac had already started walking back home. As he chased after his brother, Elias turned around and called out to Aruj and Khidr:

"Hey, aren't you two coming?"

"You go," said Aruj to Elias. "We'll come soon. Oh, and by the way, tell my mother that I'm hungry like a wolf."

As Isaac and Elias walked away, Aruj and Khidr were still gazing at the sunset. Khidr began to laugh.

"I recalled the day you and I stormed the windmills. We were looking like a mess. Poor mother, she was chasing us, trying to take us back home."

"She was not only chasing us but yelling at us as well."

"Yes, but it was impossible to understand what she was saying for she was again yelling in half Turkish half Greek."

Raising four hellions alongside a grouchy husband was no easy task. Their mother had always treated them with tolerance. But there had been occasions when she was unable to hold back within her mouth the words that came on the verge of her tongue. And because she cursed in a kind of hybrid language that included both Turkish and Greek words, nobody could comprehend what she was saying at moments like this. Once, Khidr couldn't have helped and asked his mother what she had just said, but Katerina had replied, 'Just know that I'm angry, you don't need to know what I've said.' and had put him off.

Aruj's voice brought Khidr's mind back to the present moment.

"You were running down the hill, brandishing the sword that Andrea had given to you. When you suddenly stopped and yelled out, "Enemy galleeeeys!", I got absolutely petrified at first."

Both started laughing.

"But admit it, it was a good idea!"

"Yes Khidr, attacking the windmills as if they were enemy galleys, and then, getting caught by one of its blades and being thrown into the flour sacks was a brilliant idea."

"Much better than your idea of grabbing big stones from the ground and throwing them as if they were cannon balls. I still carry that scar on my forehead."

"I had thought that the amulet mother had given you would protect you."

"If it were around my neck, it certainly would. I had handed it over to Andrea earlier on that day, don't you remember?"

"Ah, yes, you are right. But I'm not the culprit of the scar on your forehead. If you hadn't been that much scared and instead had simply let our mother suture the wound, you wouldn't have a scar there today."

"I wasn't scared! I simply did not like the idea that a sharp point-edged piece of metal would go in and out of the flesh over and over again."

Aruj teased his younger brother.

"Yes, who knows that the bravest of all the warriors of Lesbos faint when he saw a needle?"

"Brother!"

"All right, all right!" said Aruj chuckling. "This will forever be our little secret, I promise!"

They sat together in silence for a while and gazed at the faint line that separated the sky from the sea. Khidr took a deep sigh.

"Since then, we haven't seen Andrea... We heard from neither him nor Signor Ceva Doria..."

"Yes, dad was telling. During the time when Lesbos was under Byzantine rule, Genoese merchants had been granted a great number of commercial privileges. But after the Ottomans took control of the island, things had changed. Though the merchants who were on good terms with the Turks continued to visit the island, dad had told that their numbers had decreased over time. Signor Doria was a good man; everyone on this island was holding him in high esteem. Who knows, maybe he had found more lucrative routes for himself."

With his eyes on the crimson sky getting darker and darker each passing minute; Khidr muttered:

"Here we had said our last goodbye..."

Andrea was the son of Genoa's prominent families, Ceva and Caracosa Doria of Oneglia. He had been sailing and trading in the Mediterranean with his father. Andrea had met Aruj and Khidr on one of their Lesbos visits, and they quickly had become friends. Ever since that time, he had sought out their company whenever he stepped foot on the island. Back then, Khidr was very young. Each time Andrea visited Lesbos, he would have brought gifts to this vivacious little boy, and Khidr would always have looked forward to seeing him. Twelve years ago, as they were about to say farewell to each other at such a sunset, Andrea had noticed the disappointment on Khidr's face. This time, he had not given Khidr what he brought to him immediately after he arrived at the island; instead, he had decided to wait until it was time to depart. During his stay, Andrea had delightedly watched Khidr become increasingly impatient, and just as they were about to say goodbye to each other, he had jumped on the boat, taken something wrapped in a cloth, and handed it to him with a playful smile on his face.

"Let's see what we've got here for you!"

Khidr's eyes glowed brightly. As he reached out and took Andrea's gift, he tried hard to conceal his excitement. When he finally unwrapped the cloth and saw what was inside, he couldn't believe his eyes. It was a short shining sword with a hilt of mother-of-pearl, decorated with precious stones from which seemed to be reflected all the shimmering lights of the Mediterranean. He was mesmerized. So speechless he was that he did not know how to properly thank him. He tried to say something to express his emotions but could only stutter.

"I... I mean... I am..."
"Didn't you like it, this time?"
Khidr gave him a big hug.
"Like it? I loved it!"

Andrea cracked a grin.
"This sword will protect you from all harm. Life out there in the open seas, far from the safety of the lands, is a life without mercy."

As a token of his gratitude, Khidr wanted to give Andrea something in return. He took off the amulet his mother had placed around his neck and handed it over to Andrea.

"And this will also shield you from all the seen and unseen dangers, believe me!"

Andrea took the triangular-shaped piece of leather that Khidr had just handed to him, and gave it a closer look, but couldn't figure out what it was or how it functioned.

"What is this?"

"An amulet! Inside, is a prayer. It'll bring you good luck. Nothing and no one will be able to harm you, as long as you have it on."

Aruj placed his hand on Andrea's shoulder.

"So far, he hasn't injured himself. Not even slightly. Given that he is such a hellion, this thing should really be working behind the scenes."

The preparations were complete, and now it was time to set sail. Signor Doria called out to his son:

"Come on, kid, it's time to say farewell to your friends."

Andrea held the amulet tight in his hand and got on the boat.

"It'll be around my neck till the day I die."

As they sail away from the shore, Aruj shouted from behind:

"Hey, Andrea! May the winds carry you to what is best for you."

"You, too!"

Khidr's gaze was on the horizon. He snapped out of his thoughts when he heard his brother speaking.

"Have you got your sword with you?"

"Of course, I have!"

Aruj grabbed two big stones from the ground.

"And I've got my cannon balls."

An arch smile appeared on their faces. Two brothers leaped to their feet and started running towards the windmills. As they hurried away from the shore, it was as if the silhouette of Dorias' boat that left the island twelve years ago was still on the horizon.

Their ship had already entered the fog. Andrea overheard his father speaking to one of the sailors.

"Perhaps, it would have been better if we spent the night on the island and set sail with the first light in the morning."

"Seasons are changing, Signor; the winds are baffling. If we hadn't set sail today, we might have had no choice but to wait till the storms passed."

Signor Doria remained silent. Sailing safely in these waters would require not only skill but also sound judgment. The sea would not mind the unripe, instead, would eliminate it in the quickest way. That's why they had to travel tonight and sail as far as they could to arrive at their destination before the storms broke out.

When Andrea heard the sound of an arrow that pierced through the dusk, he was looking at the amulet that Khidr had given to him. Startled by the whiz, he turned to his father but found him lodged with the arrow on the neck. Before Andrea's very eyes, his father collapsed onto the deck. Andrea, paralyzed with fear, stood there with eyes wide open. Amidst the misty silence, he was able to hear his own heartbeat.

One of the sailors rushed toward Signor Doria, who was lying on the ground, drenched in blood.

"Signor Doria! Signor Doria!"

He tore a piece of cloth from his soiled and salty shirt and pressed it onto the wound. But when he realized that it was impossible to remove the arrow, he desperately looked Ceva Doria in the eye and heard him uttering his last words.

"Andrea!"

It was like a silent whisper.

As the sailors drew their swords, Andrea raised his gaze and saw a pirate ship headed toward them.

At those times, the greatest threat that plagued all the trading vessels sailing in the Mediterranean was the pirates. Those who sailed under the flag of the kingdom they served would call themselves "corsairs". They would usually try to steer clear of damaging the ships or the booty they captured; and instead of killing the crew, they would often take captives so as to turn them into cash. Those who were the strongest and healthiest among the captives would be sold in slave markets for substantial sums of money, while those who were not sold, would be chained to the oars, and made to serve as galley slaves. As for the merchants who belonged to European nobility, they would be held hostage in exchange for ransom money. But those who were at that moment approaching Doria's ship were not the corsairs. Much worse, they were the sea marauders.

The marauders landed on the deck in what seemed like the blink of an eye, slaughtered the Genoese sailors, and stole all of their belongings. As he felt the tip of the sharp-edged sword resting on his neck, Andrea gulped. Were they going to sever his head from his body? Or perhaps they would stab him in the chest. Was he going to die quickly? Was it going to be painful? Had it been painful for his father? Andrea was on the verge of death, trembling with fear. As thoughts were racing through his mind, the hand that was holding the sword parted his shirt. The amulet Khidr had given to him was around his neck. He had it on. When had he put it on? He was unable to recall. Upon noticing the amulet, the bandit turned to his companions and said something. The language he spoke sounded like Arabic. Andrea hadn't understood a word of it. His mind was blurry. He closed his eyes... The voices grew distant. He gave himself over to the will of fate and surrendered.

When he opened his eyes, he was alone amidst the sea. With the amulet around his neck, and his father's lifeless body lying on the deck, Andrea was standing all by himself amidst the Mediterranean.

Spain

With the arrival of spring, the ships that were towed ashore in October had joined the waters of the Mediterranean. The port of Málaga was bustling with activity, filled with sailors dressing the wounds that storms of the previous year had inflicted on their vessels, mending torn sails, and loading onto the ships the wares that were going to be sold in the marketplaces that year.

Having been dressed like a Franciscan monk, Cristóbal Colón was rushing along. It had only been a few days since he returned from his second voyage to the New World. He was ill. Though he was in complete denial about it, he knew for quite some time that his health was deteriorating. He was also depressed and nervous. He had spent his last five years sailing the oceans. Those five years he was forced to spend with the prison escapes who had been sentenced to death but whose executions had been postponed on the condition that they would volunteer in Colón's expeditions could not be said to have been easy. When the experienced Spanish sailors of Palos who had accompanied him in his first voyage refused to join him in the next one and let Colón down; what he had been left with were a bunch of nightmares dressed in knee-length trousers and red woolen caps loitering on the deck barefoot, having an infinite vocabulary of curses and swears. It had taken Colón a long time and eventually his health to put those pains in the neck under discipline. On the other hand, he was well aware of the fact that he had failed to return from his second voyage with the results that Queen Isabel would find satisfactory. The native inhabitants of the New World had caused too much trouble. What else could he have expected from those uncivilized people who were wandering around half-naked, and wearing strange-looking feathered hats, anyway? However, on his first voyage, Colón had believed that he would somehow find a way to establish good relations with them. He was going to bring order into their lives, teach them how to speak, dress and behave properly, and convert them into faithful Christians. That's why, on his second voyage, he had taken with him the members of clergy, merchants, farmers, soldiers, horses, cattle, donkeys, sheep, goats, pigs, chickens, even cats and dogs. He had intended to establish a civilization there and declare himself as its ruler. And all he had asked for in return for all the hardship he endured for their sake, was just a fair level of obedience and, of course, some gold. Gold was not something valued by the indigenous in the same way that it was by the Europeans anyway. It was no more precious to them than any other material provided by nature. But what did they do? They rebelled! They razed the castles he built for them and murdered the Spaniards. Colón had done his best. He was a skillful administrator. And this time, on his third expedition, he was confident that he would, one by one, overcome all these problems.

As he approached the Alhambra Palace, which had been described by Moorish poets as a pearl set in emeralds for it stood out on the lush hills of Sierra Nevada overlooking Granada with its reddish color contrasting its surroundings, his mind was weary of all these thoughts. He came to a halt when he arrived at *Puerta de la Justicia*[47], which had the appearance of a giant horseshoe. His gaze was drawn to the Hand of Fatima engraved on the keystone of the outer arch of the gate. Then, to the key motif carved on the inner arch...

> *'Stop passenger! Do not enter before you remember that the five tenets of Islam are the only key to the heavens!'*

He rushed through the door with quick steps. After all, according to the legend Alhambra would be destroyed on the day that the key to heaven would unite with Fatima's Hand. What if the day was today? God forbid, Colón might find himself buried beneath the ruins before he even realized what had just taken place.

---

[47] Main entrance of Alhambra Palace, Gate of Justice, its original name is Bab al-Shari'a

He walked up the hill and turned right. After he passed by *Puerta del Vino*[48], he proceeded toward Mexuar. He had to hurry and not keep the queen waiting. As he arrived at the entrance he suddenly stopped. It appeared to him as though one of the tiles that adorned the walls had whispered to him in the ear.

'Enter and ask. Do not be afraid to seek justice for here you will find it.'

Colón muttered:
"That's what I hope so..."

As he entered Mexuar, he found himself amid a crowd he had not expected to see. A large group of people, the majority of whom appeared to be quite wealthy based on the attire they wore, had gathered in the hope that King Fernando would grant them an audience.

Mexuar was a semi-public part of the palace, where discussions regarding the administration of justice and state affairs were held. For a long time, it had served as a chamber where the Council of Ministers met, and the sultan received his subjects on certain days of the week, listened to their problems, and dispensed justice. It seemed that Fernando had kept the tradition alive and that there were a lot of people who had problems in Granada at the time.

Colón's attention was drawn to the inscription on the stucco frieze connecting the muqarnas columns.

'The Kingdom is of Allah. Strength is of Allah. The Glory is of Allah.'

"Kingdom and strength seem to be of Fernando's lately, and as for the glory, it seems that it is Jesus Christ's," he muttered and looked for himself a corner to stand out from the crowd.

The hall was lit by daylight filtering through the colored glass windows of the lanterned dome. Colón, however, was feeling low-spirited and dark as the night. If he needed to wait for all those people to get an audience with the king, how his already sick body, which could hardly stand upright, would survive the day he wondered. He was startled when he heard one of the guards calling out to him.

---

[48] Wine Gate

"Signor Colón!"

He turned toward the source of the voice.

"Signor Colón, Her Majesty is waiting for you in the Hall of Ambassadors. Please follow me."

"Thank God," murmured Colón and proceeded behind the guard.

He passed through an entrance and walked briskly through the Oratory which was originally a long balcony whose exterior wall featured twin windows. When he stepped into the courtyard decorated with flower and leaf motifs, he saw two identical doors with lintels framed with mosaics. One of them was leading to the private residential area of the palace, and the other, to the service area. He couldn't help himself but paused and gazed at the exquisite calligraphy inscriptions adorning the façade. Verses from the Qur'an had been inscribed on all the columns, arches, ceilings, and walls of Alhambra which was adorned with the unique designs of arabesque geniuses in a way that was no less elegant than the dream palaces described in the stories of One Thousand and One Nights.

"I suppose there is no palace in the world that cites Allah more than Alhambra," Colón muttered. And that talisman he frequently encountered...

'Wa lā galiba illā-llāh'

'There is no victor other than Allah'... As if a reminder for the Catholic Monarchs who had completed Reconquista and were now chasing off the remaining Muslim population on these lands...

He turned his gaze to the doors. The guard was out of sight. But through which door he had passed, Colón did not have the slightest idea.

"Signor Colón, aren't you coming?"

"Thank God," said Colón and kept following.

They walked past the Golden Room and into the *Patio de los Arrayanes*[49]. As they walked through the muqarnas-decorated archway accompanied by the sound of water flowing from the marble fountains, Colón glanced at the reflection of the Comares Tower on the surface of the thirty-four-meter-long rectangular pool. The tower was extremely strong, so much so that it had to be able to withstand even the most devastating artillery attacks. Its

---

[49] The Court of Myrtles

reflection, on the other hand, was as frail as it could fall apart with a stone thrown into the water. As if a reminder for the power holders who had forgotten the transient nature of worldly power...

Colón came to a halt at the entrance of the Hall of the Ambassadors. With its eighteen-meter-high carved muqarnas dome symbolizing the seven levels of heaven, detailed stucco decorations, and colorful mosaic tiles almost at a human height that runs along the lower walls, it was the palace's largest and most impressive hall. But, more importantly, it was the hall of reconciliation. As was reminded with an inscription carved on an arch:

'... and you will leave in peace.'

When he entered the hall, he found Queen Isabel waiting for him by one of the windows enclosed with carved wood latticework holding a bunch of papers. He took a few steps forward and bowed to the queen.

"Your Majesty..."

The queen responded to Colón by reading a sentence written on one of the papers aloud.

"As I saw that they were very friendly to us and perceived that they could be much more easily converted to our holy faith by gentle means than by force, I presented them with some red caps, and strings of beads to wear upon the neck, and many other trifles of small value, wherewith they were much delighted, and became wonderfully attached to us."[50]

With a smile on her face, Isabel turned her gaze to Colón and asked:

"These were your words, Signor Colón, weren't they?"

Colón returned the smile and bowed his head with respect. He was somewhat relieved. For the third voyage he planned, he needed the queen's help. The amount of investment required for the endeavor was too much for Colón to personally finance. The monthly salary for master sailors and maritime pilots was two thousand maravedis. The seamen had to be paid a thousand maravedis while the ship boys six hundred and sixty-six maravedis per month. The sum total of the monthly salaries that were being paid by the queen amounted to more than two hundred fifty thousand maravedis which was an amount that Colón could never afford on his own. He had prepared

---

[50] Columbus's journal entries from August to November 1492.

himself to find the queen irritated and unsatisfied as a result of the outcomes of his previous expeditions. However, the way Isabel greeted him had given Colón hope.

Isabel took a few steps towards Colón and continued:

"Now you must be wondering what is written in the other one."

Colón remained silent.

"This is a letter from one of your friends, Michele de Cuneo, who traveled with you on your second voyage, Admiral. You've known him for a long time, haven't you?"

"Yes, Your Grace. We've been friends since childhood. During the second expedition I went on, I had the good fortune to be accompanied by a long-time friend whom I could completely trust."

"Then, would you like me to read what he wrote? Or, would you rather be interested in reading it yourself, Admiral?"

"Please, proceed, Your Grace."

After taking a look at the letter and finding the section she was searching for, Isabel began to read it aloud.

"While I was in the boat I captured a very beautiful Carib woman, whom the said Lord Admiral gave to me, and with whom, having taken her into my cabin, she being naked according to their custom, I conceived desire to take pleasure. I wanted to put my desire into execution, but she did not want it and treated me with her fingernails in such a manner that I wished I had never begun. But seeing that, (to tell you to the end of it all), I took a rope and thrashed her well, for which she raised such unheard of screams that you would not have believed in your ears. Finally, we have come to an agreement in such a manner that I can tell you that she seemed to have been brought up in a school of harlots."[51]

Colón had reached the point of dying from embarrassment. His face had turned crimson red. He was required to repond and make some sort of statement but was unable to utter even a single word. He stuttered:

"My Quee.."

---

[51] Michele de Cuneo's Letter on the Second Voyage, 28 October 1495

"Is this what you meant, Signor Colón when you said you would bring order to those people's lives? You turned a blind eye to indigenous women being raped, even encouraged it, and you have expected from them obedience?"

Colón was petrified by shame.

"It's no wonder that the forts you have built have been destroyed, the people living in the lands you have conquered rebelled against you, and you have failed to establish a proper rule in the West Indies! I've been told that you had the intention of putting the natives you'd taken captive and brought to Europe on the market, and selling them as slaves so that you could convert them into gold and compensate for your losses. Tell me! Would you be able to refute any of these claims?"

When her question was answered by Colón's silence, the queen resumed her wrath.

"The lands that you have discovered thanks to the Spanish gold, belong to the Kingdom of Spain, Signor Colón, and the people who live on the Spanish lands are the subjects of the Spanish Crown. And you are not authorized to enslave even a single Spaniard, neither here in Spain, nor in the faraway lands that belong to Spain. So, you'd better act accordingly!"

Isabel, foamed with rage, was waiting for an explanation.

"Your Grace, in what has been our second expedition, we have run into a great deal of difficul..."

Upon King Fernando's sudden entrance into the hall, Colón's words were left unfinished.

"So, you have come, Signor Colón? Isabel, your yelling is echoed throughout the entire palace!"

Colón bowed low in a respectful manner and saluted the king while Isabel crumpled the letter and turned to Fernando with an artificial smile on her face.

"I was just about to ask Signor Colón his requirements from the Crown, in order for him to embark on his third expedition to the West Indies."

Colón was stupefied. After the queen's wrath that had just smacked him in the face, he had no hope left that he would ever be able to visit the New World again. Even the possibility of leaving the palace as a free man had seemed a miracle to him. What exactly was the queen talking about? After all that she had said, would the Crown be willing to fund yet another expedition?

Unaware of the conversation that had taken place between the queen and Colón a short while ago, Fernando turned to the admiral:

"Yes, Signor Colón, I also was hoping to have a conversation with you about this particular matter. As the Crown of Aragon and Castile, we are unable to say that the outcomes of your expeditions meet our expectations. I have to admit that I have started to question whether this place, which you refer to as the New World, truly does contain such a significant quantity of wealth."

"Your Majesty, due to some challenges we failed to foresee, I wasn't able to return with the results that would satisfy you. However, we gained more knowledge about both the lands and the people of those lands. I assure you, the next time you grant me an audience, you will have none of the concerns that you now have."

Isabel turned to Fernando:

"You know, Fernando, the threat posed by Turks in the east is growing rapidly. Very soon, the Mediterranean, which serves as our only connection to the trade routes, will become even more hazardous. The Turks have embraced the Muslims and Jews we expelled from Andalusia. Some were transported to the Ottoman lands by galleons, while some fled to North Africa. With the rest, we're still dealing. They will not forget the sultan's favor and will be willing to cooperate with him."

"Just like those spies of those who fled to North Africa still living on Spanish lands," remarked Fernando.

"All these point to the fact that the Mediterranean will soon become a blazing inferno. We have no choice but to take every possible step in order to foil this complex network of spies."

"I know, I assigned Juan Andre. I will give them one last chance to convert to Christianity. God damn, those heathens! There will be no single Muslim or Jew who keep living in Spain. Either they will become devout Christians, or they will be destroyed."

Fernando was not understanding Isabel. The queen's only wish was, from then on, to see her subjects living in peace, joy, and prosperity. Every one of her subjects regardless of whether they were Christians, Muslims, or Jews... Isabel had recently begun to reflect on all the drama that she and her family had gone through over the years. She was under the impression that God was punishing her family for all the people that they had killed for the sake of their political and economic ambitions. The death of her daughter while she was in the process of giving birth to her grandson Miguel, the mental breakdown of her second daughter Juana because of her husband Handsome Felipe's infidelities, having to bury her son Juan at the age of eighteen... Isabel was thinking that she was cursed by God. Otherwise, she had lived a life of piety. Why would God allow such suffering to befall a woman who had devoted her entire life to trying to bring those faithless heathens into the fold of Christianity, to uniting them all under the wings of the one and only true religion? There must have been some terrible mistake that she had made. Isabel must somehow have offended God. There could be no other explanation for the tragedy she lived through.

"They will perish, they will be destroyed! That's all you know! The same holds true for your wars! You don't stop until you completely raze a city down until you kill everyone and everything that breathes in it. Amidst the ruins, we celebrate our victories. Could you not see, what all these cost us, Fernando?"

"Isabel!"

She walked to the door and stormed out of the hall. Upon her leave, a profound silence crept in. Fernando was perturbed.

"Right after she lost her daughter, she also lost her only son, which contributed to her increasingly volatile personality and made her even more temperamental. My concern is that her sorrow will soon lay her down."

"Your Majesty, we are deeply saddened by the loss of both Prince Juan and Princess Isabel. Considering the sensitive personality of our Queen; it isn't hard to imagine how challenging it must be for her, to ward off the dark clouds that storm through her heart."

"Anyway, Signor Colón, let's get back to the topic at hand. Please let us know what it is that you require, in writing. Isabel is right. The waters of the Mediterranean will soon heat up. Before the Turks block our shipping lanes in the Mediterranean, we must find ourselves better and safer routes. Moreover, I'm sure you are aware of the fact that an alliance with the Great Khan of China will serve to strengthen our hand against the Ottomans. Portuguese also set sail. I am curious to learn what information Vasco de Gama will bring back from his eastern expedition."

"I can't say that I heard any positive remarks about Vasco de Gama," said William. "When it comes to determining how much of it is factual and how much is fiction, however, it is difficult to say."

A troubled expression spread over Cervantes' face. He had faith in his religion. He was a man who had a profound devotion to both God and Jesus Christ. An Old Christian he was, a hidalgo who had served in the *Infanteria de Marinera* for years, fought in the Battle of Lepanto, and preached encouraging sermons to the Christian captives in Algiers who were about to lose their faith just to be able to prevent them from turning away from Jesus. But throughout his life, he had been a witness to such occurrences that, he, as a good-hearted person and a good-hearted Christian, could neither comprehend, nor justify in his conscience. Events that whenever he recalled, made him feel like he was going to drown in his own sorrow...

"You are fortunate Signor Shakespeare. Sometimes ignorance can truly be bliss."

The India of the time, which lacked political unity, had been divided between the Hindus and the Muslims. Trading goods from the West Indian coastline and Asia were being transported to Europe via the Persian Gulf and the Red Sea, and the taxes collected from the spices that changed hands in centers such as Cairo and Alexandria were the most important source of income for the Mamluk sultans. European merchants, who had for a long time been concerned about the falling of Mediterranean trade routes under Turkish control, had also recently begun to feel distressed due to the increasing demands of the intermediaries and tax collectors. And it had become an absolute necessity to locate new and direct routes leading to the country of origin of all these commercial goods. A significant number of Portuguese sailors had already set sail for the western coast of Africa in the expectation of finding new ways that would lead them to the Indian Ocean. The discovery of the Cape of Good Hope by Bartolomeu Dias in the year 1487 had given them all a brand-new hope regarding the transportation of the riches of the east to the marketplaces of the west. However, this new route too, which was controlled by the Muslims, was no less dangerous for the Christian merchants than the Mediterranean.

The time had come for Manuel I to demonstrate to not only the Spanish but also to the Venetians and the Genoese, that the dominion over the eastern seas belonged to Portugal. After navigating around the Cape of Good Hope, Vasco da Gama would ensure Portuguese hegemony in the ports of Sofala, Mozambique, Mombasa, and Malindi; and from there he would set sail to Calicut. Nevertheless, things did not go as smoothly as expected, and the first question that was asked of Vasco de Gama as soon as he landed turned out to be 'What devil brought you here?'. It appeared neither the people who were living in Africa nor those on the Indian coast would renounce their faith. Just as they were not going to convert to Christianity, they would also not be willing to submit to a Portuguese King whom they had never heard of.

When the riots broke out in the region, Vasco de Gama took off his already makeshift mask of kindness that he had been wearing for a while and let his men loose on the streets of Kilwa. Settlements were ransacked; children and women were kidnapped, raped, and murdered. The arms and wrists of eight hundred women were cut off on the Swahili coast so that their jewelry could be removed more easily. And when the Talappana Namboothiri, the envoy of the Calicut King Zamorin, was sent back to the king by having his tongue and ears cut off and being stitched with two dog ears in their places instead, the political and economic relations between India and Portugal were irrevocably severed. All these political failures had driven the Portuguese admiral into a frenzy. And when he was unable to find the support he desired from the port cities, he started to attack the Muslim galleons trading in the region.

"Please, sir, take... Take all that I have. Please, have mercy, spare me for the sake of my baby."

With her newborn baby that she was holding tight in her arms, the woman was looking at the Portuguese admiral with pleading eyes. Vasco de Gama had captured a galleon that was en route from Calicut to Mecca carrying more than four hundred pilgrims. One of his men ran up to the deck.

"Admiral, it's true what they said, there's more than enough gold in this galleon to pay the ransom of all the Christian slaves in North Africa!"

The icy look that emanated from the admiral's eyes made it abundantly clear that he did not feel the slightest bit of compassion for anyone on board. He neither cared for the woman, nor for the baby, or anyone else in that galleon. It was true that, after he returned from his first expedition, the Portuguese had greeted him like a hero; but people did not know about all that had transpired. King Manuel I had cautioned him that he had to return from his second voyage with better outcomes. The fact that he still couldn't have achieved political success due to all those riots and the problems the local rulers caused, had driven him crazy. Failure was not an option for him. The flames of his vengeance quickly got out of control and spread to the galleon which contained four hundred lives within.

"Take the gold, lock everyone inside, and set the galleon on fire!"

"Happy the age, happy the time, to which the ancients gave the name of golden, not because in that fortunate age the gold so coveted in this our iron one was gained without tail, but because they lived in it knew not the words "mine" and thine..."[52]

William's face had turned white. He now had a better understanding of what Cervantes had meant. The British of the time had heard such stories about the period but had no idea whether or not they were factual. Were they truly unaware or unconcerned? Was the only thing they cared about the riches they yearned to possess? It appears that, in this century of theirs, the goods that can be sold or bought were valued more than the souls that cannot be traded. After all that he had learned, when William got out of the creaky door of this shabby house in Valladolid and returned to Britain, would he be able to resume his role as a jovial English aristocrat writing comedies?

"It was a futile attempt, of course, trying to deal with this problem in the far seas while it had not yet been completely resolved even in the heart of Granada, Signor Shakespeare."

"I was under the impression that, with the completion of Reconquista, the Jewish and Muslim issue had finally been settled in Spain."

---

[52] Miguel de Cervantes Saavedra, Don Quixote

"Isabel was a good-hearted queen. She had gotten into fierce arguments with Fernando following the fall of Granada about not forcing the remaining Jews and Muslims living on the peninsula to convert to Christianity on the condition that they agreed to submit to Christian rule. From that moment on, all that she wanted was to see her subjects living in peace and tranquility. But in reality, the war had just begun. Because the passage of time would prove Fernando right and Isabel wrong."

Spain, Andarax

She truly had no idea why she loved him so much. Maybe she did not need to know at all. She recalled the very first day that she saw him. The twinkling stars she had seen in his jet-black eyes had made Felipa smile. "Finally..." she had said... The moment she touched him, she knew, it was not their first encounter. Their souls knew one another so well that who knows how many lifetimes they had spent together. With a great deal of longing, she had wrapped her arms around his neck and whispered in his ear:

"Did it take you a long time to find me?"

He was like a joyful child illuminating his surroundings with his unruly energy. It was pointless to try to contain or control him. Restrictions were causing him distress and dimming his light. Being with him required allowing him to be free. Felipa had once approached him in silence, opened the barn door and let him out, and then she had walked away. Although she had no idea whether he would follow her, she had not even turned back and looked at him. He might run away, and Felipa might never see him again. But she had to let go of her fear and respect his freedom. No one had the right to imprison him. He was special.

Felipa had walked alone in the woods for a while. She could feel his presence. Hoping that he would hear, she had closed her eyes and called to his spirit:

"I do not want to own you; I want to live with you..."

As the winds of the valley danced among her long black hair, she had first heard his approaching footsteps, then, had felt his breath on her neck. When he leaned his head on Felipa's shoulder, she had turned around with a lovely smile on her face and caressed his black mane.

"Viento!... That should be your name."

"Once again, you're lost between the worlds Signorina."

As she was grooming Viento, Felipa was so engrossed in her thoughts that she had completely forgotten that Cergio was also in the stables.

Cergio had been working for Felipa's father for quite some time. Signor Faris, originally from the Maghreb, had bought a farm and settled in Andarax after falling in love with a Spanish woman, and devoted the rest of his life to breeding and training Andalusian horses, which are renowned for their incredible talent and stunning beauty. Since the time he first started living in Andarax, Signor Faris had liked Cergio who would accompany him all along. He had always thought of him as a member of the family, and Felipa had literally been born into Cergio's arms.

Felipa smiled.

"We were having a small talk with Viento."

"I suppose you'll go on a ride. Would you like me to assist you in saddling him up?"

"Thank you, Cergio, you take care of the others, I can handle it myself."

After she put on his bridle and took him out of the barn Felipa jumped on Viento's back.

"Are you up for a ride?"

As she galloped away, Cergio was shouting from behind her:

"Signorina, your father..."

To whom he was talking, anyway? Together with Viento, Felipa had already gotten lost out of sight.

"The nutty duo..." muttered Cergio smiling before going back to his work.

After the completion of the Reconquista, there had been an increase in the Muslim population living in this small village, located one hundred kilometers away from Granada. King Boabdil, who was sent to Andarax right after he handed over the keys of the city, had always been considered a threat by the Catholic Monarchs despite the Granada Agreement signed between the Muslims and the Christians; and therefore, had been exiled to North Africa, a year later. Neither the Muslims trusted the Christians, nor the Christians trusted the Muslims in these lands anymore. The disagreements that they had with one another would periodically escalate into riots, making it impossible for the people who lived in the area to have even one night of peaceful sleep. Following Cardinal Jiménez's appointment to the position of archbishop the number of people who were baptized against their will had reached thousands. But even this was not enough for Fernando. Many of the converts had become Christians only in appearance, and in their daily lives, they had secretly kept living in accordance with the requirements of their faith. It had come to the point where it was now time for Spain to eradicate this heresy called Islam once and for all. And as Felipa galloped in the woods of Andarax, the *familiares* of the Inquisition were advancing from one village to the next, at the orders of Cardinal Jiménez, and hunting people.

In the middle of the bustling crowd that had gathered in the town square, one of the *familiares* yelled out:

"From this day on, everyone who takes a breath in territories that belong to Spain will have faith in Holy Jesus, the one and only son of God! Not Muhammad! Islam is the religion of perversion, lies, and violence! Anyone who adheres to the teachings of Muhammad is no longer permitted to subsist on the bounties that are produced by these lands or to drink the waters that flow from these rivers."

All the books that belonged to the Muslims were being thrown into the fires. The black smoke rising from the ashes of the Islamic cultural heritage of the Iberian Peninsula was darkening the sky. When one of the *familiares* threw the Qur'an into the flames, that was the final straw, and all hell broke loose.

As Cardinal Jiménez was gazing out from the latticed windows of Alhambra he was listening to Fernando.

"Contrary to the Truth and reason! Contrary to philosophy, to logic, to astronomy, to theology! They expressly do not wish for it to be translated. They hide it from everyone, not showing it to anybody. Why? Because it is fake! Their religion, their prophet, their book—all a fabrication! A book of this perilous nature should not be taken out of private libraries and should definitely not be used for any purpose other than to be studied by the members of the clergy, who will then point out the errors contained within and show them to people, Cardinal!"

"They'll smell your fear all the way from Constantinople, Your Majesty."

It was true that Fernando was scared. But it was not the Muslim riots that would soon break out in Spain and that he would have to deal with which he found frightening, but it was Islam itself. As a matter of fact, he was afraid that this so-called religion full of strange rituals, would cause confusion in the hearts of the Christians and, after some time, it would appeal to them more than Christianity did. After all, the Garden of Eden Muhammad had promised them, which was said to be full of trees that produce delicious fruits of all kinds and where the rivers of milk, honey, and wine would continuously flow, was quite tempting to the Europeans, whose greatest fear was, at that time, starvation. And the virgins of heaven who were depicted as having smooth and pearl white skins, and jet-black eyes were almost enchanting. Moreover, if Catholic Christians were to set aside the hereafter and focused on the life they were living right now; they would find Christianity on one side of the scale, with its strict rules enforcing monogamy and a life of piety that shuns the pleasures of the world, and Islam on the other side, which shows tolerance towards people's way of life and promotes polygamy that would surely attract the Christian men. The members of the clergy had all been mobilized. What could it be more ridiculous than an afterlife that was expected to be spiritual, promising sensual pleasures? In a letter that he wrote to Mehmed II, Pope Pius had told him that, the rivers of milk, honey, and wine, intimate relationships with numerous women, angels that encourage all these; in short, a paradise where one can satisfy all his bodily desires could only be a paradise of an ox or an ass, not of a man.

"If the weeds are not removed, they would destroy the flowers in the garden, Cardinal. If we allow it to spread, the scent that they will detect from Constantinople will not be the scent of my dread; but rather, the aroma of Islam thriving in the west. And I assure you Cardinal, if we allow this to happen, they will attack us like ravenous dogs without wasting a single day."

Cardinal Jiménez replied to the king as he pointed to the Quranic verses adorning the walls of the Hall of the Ambassadors.

"I think this palace is getting on your nerves."

Fernando got enraged.

"Are you kidding me, Cardinal?"

"You don't think that I have deployed men only inside the city, do you, Your Majesty?"

He was indeed right. The cardinal, with an inexhaustible and unyielding grudge, had amassed all the soldiers of the kingdom, dispatched them to the most secluded forests, and had already embarked on a large-scale hunt for the remaining Muslims and Jews in Spain.

As soon as they got to the river, Felipa cued for a halt so that they could get some rest, and then dismounted.

"Don't you ever get tired?" she asked with a smile on her face.

Viento began rubbing his head against Felipa's shoulder to scratch his nose. It could not be said that he was enthusiastic about having to wear a bridle, but he was aware that it made the ride more comfortable for Felipa. On that very first day when Signor Faris entered the stables to meet Viento, he had struggled a lot in vain to bridle him. He hadn't even been able to convince Viento to put a saddle on him. Despite having spent much of his life training horses, he had been unable to figure out what he should do with this particular animal. Let alone allow anyone mount on him, Viento had not let anyone approach to him. Felipa had turned out to be the very first person who was able to touch him. As soon as she entered the stables, Viento had calmed down. Felipa had stared at him for a while, and then, run toward him. When Cergio witnessed the moment she wrapped her arms around his neck, he had become so stunned that he had been rendered speechless. He had dropped whatever he had in his hands and hurried over to Signor Faris. When Signor Faris came, he had found his daughter petting Viento on the mane and speaking to him in a gentle tone. Cergio had told him, 'Your daughter has a very special connection with the horses, you know that don't you Signor Faris?'; and Signor Faris had responded to him with a nod and a perplexed smile on his face.

She took the reins over Viento's head and led him down to the river so that he could drink some water. When she laid herself down on the ground, her long wavy hair spread over the tiny yellow flowers that adorned the riverbank.

"I love this valley..." Felipa muttered.

Viento was listening quietly. In fact, he was probably just grazing on the fresh clovers on the ground, but Felipa, for some reason, had felt that he was listening.

"I wish that I could spend the rest of my life in this place. But it seems it will not be possible. I overheard dad and Cergio having a conversation the other day. Dad said that these lands were no longer safe for Muslims like us and that we might soon have to leave this place."

Viento kept his quiet.

"Are you listening to me?" reproached Felipa jokingly. "Who am I talking to?"

Was he listening? It seems that Viento was just preoccupied with the clovers. Having seen this, Felipa jumped to her feet.

"Heyyy, what are you doing down there? These are fresh clovers. If Cergio discovers that I let you eat them, he will kill me! You are going to suffer from colic, and it is going to be me, who will have to take care of you till morning."

As she picked up Viento's reins, she noticed a herd of horses galloping down the valley.

"What's happening?" she muttered. "They're fleeing away from the village. We'd better go and check, Viento."

They were quite a distance away from the village, and it was starting to get dark. Felipa jumped on Viento's back and galloped towards the horses. As she got closer, she realized that those were their very own horses.

"Hey! What are you doing here? Cergio should have put you in your boxes long ago."

She got worried. And as she turned her head to look at the village, she noticed a thick plume of smoke rising into the air. Her village was engulfed in flames.

"Viento! Run Viento! Ruuuuun!"

As Viento was running at full speed Felipa was praying to be able to find her father and Cergio safe and sound. When she arrived, the stables were empty, and Cergio was lying on the ground covered in blood. Felipa got burst into tears.

"Oh my God, Cergio..."

Her father... Where was her father? She rushed home. After losing her mother at a very young age, her father had become her entire life. She couldn't lose him. Felipa couldn't lose her father too.

"Oh God, please, spare my father!"

She looked for him everywhere but to no avail. She jumped on Viento and rode him towards the town square. But what she saw when she arrived was even more terrifying than her worst nightmare. Their mosque was on fire and the people who had been locked inside were screaming as they were being burned alive. The doors had been blocked with heavy wooden boards. She pulled, pushed, kicked, punched the doors, but couldn't move them an inch. She was sobbing and wailing, pleading for help.

"Pleeeaseee! Help me, Pleeeasssee! They're dyiiing!"

There was no one around. No one, but the Christians, who merely stood there and watched. Watched until the screams of Muslims died down...

Just as Cardinal Jiménez had said, his troops had not been deployed solely in Granada. The Treaty of Granada, the Catholic Monarchs and King Boabdil signed in 1491 on behalf of the Muslims living in the Iberian Peninsula, was no longer valid. Following the Rebellion of the Alpujarras, the Inquisition had started conducting raids in each and every village, in an effort to find and kill any remaining non-Christians. They had also come to Andarax, rounded up all its Muslim inhabitants, herded them into the mosque, and set the mosque on fire. Having seen that Signor Faris was being dragged by the arm, Cergio had rushed to the stables and let all the horses out. He knew; the horses were going to follow Felipa, and when Felipa saw the horses, she was going to understand that something was wrong in the village. It was the only way for him to give her a warning. He had no time to do anything else anyway, for as soon as he had set the last horse free by giving it a hard slap on the hinds, he had been stabbed in the back and died.

As she was sobbing on her knees at the door of the burning mosque, she saw a few guards approaching. She stood up and made an effort to run towards Viento. But it was far too late. She was seized by the Spaniards.

"Viento!"

Viento was trying to escape from the guards who had caught him by the reins. Felipa cried out loud:

"Vientoooo! Rear and ruuuuunnn!

Viento reared up on his hind legs, ripped the reins out of their hands, and started running in the direction of the mountains. Perhaps it was the last time Felipa would ever see him again...

William saw in Cervantes' eyes the flames rising from the mosque, and in the silence, he relapsed into, he heard the screams of women and children being burned alive.

"Open the doors to the Spanish Inquisition!" Cervantes cried out; then, he turned to William:

"Do you recall the plays, the comedies you wrote in Britain, Signor? After hearing some of our most heartbreaking tales, I have a feeling that the themes you will cover when you return home will have a more dramatic tone."

"It's hard to deny how heart-shattering is the tragedy that those people had to go through, Signor Cervantes. Even the thought of a child whose only sin was to have been born into a Muslim family being burned alive is horrifying."

"In the same way that we look at them, so do they look at us, Signor Shakespeare. They believe our faith in Jesus Christ is what makes us blasphemers. After everything that I've been through, I can't help but wonder; what if the God we pray to is, in fact, the same God they pray to? What if the one God that we worship is also the one God that they worship? Then, how are we going to account for all of these?"

William had now a better understanding of the way Cervantes felt. When the flames of his youth fanned the torch of his faith, Cervantes had found himself serving in the *Third Spanish Regiment*, much like a knight of Saint John fighting with a sword in his hand and his love of Christ in his heart. But years later, when he reflected on everything that he had been through, he was unable to decide. Who was right? Or would it really matter, being right or wrong, after the chandelier of the heaven was brought crashing to the ground? William's procession of thoughts was disrupted by Cervantes's words.

"I've always had a sneaking suspicion that the Catholic Monarchs' primary motivation was purely economic and political. But when it comes to the Knights of Saint John, I was absolutely sure that they were the genuine defenders of the Christian faith."

The purpose of the Order of the Knights of Saint John[53], founded in the Holy land by the merchants of Amalfi in the late eleventh century was to provide assistance to the needy and sick Christian pilgrims who somehow had managed to make their way to Jerusalem. Because the prospective pilgrims, some of whom had set out on this costly and perilous road to fulfill the penance given by a priest, and others hoping to be forgiven for the sins they had committed so far, would usually have arrived in Jerusalem, if at all, exhausted and afflicted with a variety of diseases. And Gerard Thom, with that in mind, had founded a hospice to provide these people with the care and treatment they needed.

When Jerusalem fell into the hands of Christians, this small hospice had begun to amass great wealth through land donations, and after some time, it had been converted into an infirmary. By 1113, the hospital had not only become a wealthy and powerful organization within the borders of the city; the Order had expanded its sphere of influence by setting up inns and nursery homes on the way to Jerusalem. It was no longer enough to simply treat the pilgrims. It was also necessary to protect the donated lands and property, as well as to ensure that the pilgrims could come here without being robbed, hurt, or killed. Since the priests who spent their days studying the sacred mysteries and preaching sermons could not be expected to be responsible for security as well; under Raymond du Puy, the successor of Gerard Thom, the Order became increasingly militarized; and with the authority that they received from the pope, they eventually put their arms and armors on and declared themselves as the Defenders of the Faith in the Holy land. The knights were well aware that Christian dominance in Jerusalem was hanging by a thin cotton thread. Though there were some among the members of the Order who were opposed to taking up arms, over time they were silenced; and the notion that they could not greet the ruthless hordes of heathens with bouquets of flowers in their hands, gained more adherents. They had formed a fraternity in the lands far away from Europe where their families and people with whom they shared the same faith lived; they had given this brotherhood a divine purpose and sworn to protect everything that they both materially and spiritually possessed.

---

[53] Knights Hospitaller

By the time the calendar showed the year 1160 when Raymond du Puy passed away, the Order had already ensured its position with the wealth and the privileges it possessed. They had begun to conduct themselves in the region as independent princes and made significant progress toward becoming an international organization independent of the local authorities thanks to their possessions in Europe as well as the powers and freedom of action the pope had granted them. But the day eventually came, and that thin cotton thread broke with the Battle of Hattin in 1187 when Saladin encircled the army of crusaders and destroyed them, putting an end to the existence of both the Knights of Saint John and the Knights Templar in Jerusalem.

After they were driven out of Jerusalem, they relocated to Acre, their last stronghold in the Levant; and when they were also forced to leave Acre, they settled in Cyprus. But the political climate in Cyprus was tumultuous and when they found themselves being drawn towards the political whirlpools, this time they set their sight on the Island of Rhodes. For the Templars, however, the end was near. The Order's growing influence in Europe had long been a source of concern for King Phillipe IV of France, who owed them a significant debt. He eventually persuaded Pope Clement V, and the Templars were formally disbanded in 1312, while their possessions were transferred to the Knights of Saint John. The Templars had been erased from traceable history; the Knights of Saint John, on the other hand, who were now much stronger than before, had settled in Rhodes.

The conquest of Rhodes by the Knights of Saint John had heralded that the ongoing conflict between Muslims and Christians in the Levant would soon spread into the Mediterranean. The knights were resolute in their mission to sabotage the trade and undermine all the activities carried out by Muslim merchants. They had settled on the island with the intention of being a sword that would cut through the shipping lanes. And in line with their purpose, the first thing they did after establishing their base was to fortify the walls of the Castle of Rhodes. As for the second, to seize control of the Dodecanese Islands.

One by one, the islands of Kos, Kalymnos, Leros, Tilos, Nisyros, and Symi surrendered to the knights. With their rich soil allowed for a wide variety of fruits, vegetables, and spices to be grown, surrounding waters teeming with redfish, octopuses, shrimps, and lobsters, and their convenient harbors that provided a safe shelter to the wintering ships, the islands of these waters were like the stars that God sprinkled across the clear night sky.

The canal between Nisyros and Tilos was serving as the main artery of trade both in the Aegean and the Mediterranean. The watch posts the knights had built on the islands were reporting every vessel that approached these waters. The fires burning at the peaks of the mountains that stretched their heads up above the misty sea were filling people's hearts with fear like the sound arising from the war horns. The Knights of Saint John, with their strongholds and naval power bolstered by the support they received from the European Kingdoms, and their surcoats emblazoned with a white cross, would, in that century, be the worst nightmare of the Muslims trading in the Mediterranean.

Cervantes knocked over with his finger a small hand-carved wooden galleon standing on the Mediterranean map engraved on his desk.

"But the time had come for the Defenders of Faith. What they lost in these waters would herald the end of a two-century-long Christian rule in the eastern Mediterranean."

Mediterranean

"There is a galleon on the starboard!"

Piri, like all the other children born in Gallipoli, had spent the majority of his life on the seas. He had begun his career as a yeoman on Kemal Reis' galleon at a very young age, sailed throughout the western Aegean as well as the Mediterranean, and fought alongside his uncle in numerous battles. In the end, when his long years of experience was recognized by Sultan Bayezid II, he had been promoted to the rank of warship commander in the Ottoman Navy, serving in the expeditions of Lepanto and Modon. Still, Piri would prefer setting sail with Kemal Reis during the quieter seasons of the Mediterranean, when arrows did not fly through the air and cannons did not fire off. He would look forward to the times when he and his uncle get together on the poop deck of the Goke and work on the maps he had drawn.

Goke was one of the two grandiose galleons that had been built in the *Tersâne-i Âmire*[54] by a shipmaster working for Sultan Mehmed who had learned the secrets of the Venetian's first steerable galleons. This massive galleon, which was seventy-arshins long, thirty-arshins wide, and had a pole with a four-arshins diameter made up of several parts, had on its upper deck forty-four oars, each of which could only be pulled by at least nine men. It also had a spacious crow's nest which could easily carry the weight of forty armed men at once.

---

[54] Ottoman Imperial Arsenal, the main base and naval shipyard of the Ottoman Empire located on the Golden Horn.

Upon hearing the voices coming from the upper deck, Kemal and Piri Reis rushed upstairs.

Piri shielded his eyes from the sun with his hand.
"It is one of our Sultan's galleons... Seems like it's drifting, uncle. As I always say, no wind is no good for the galleons."
Kemal Reis looked at the galleon for a while without saying a word and became concerned when he observed that there was no activity taking place on its deck.
"It does not seem that they are drifting solely due to the calm weather, Piri. It's dead silent on the deck. Perhaps we should go and take a look."
Piri called out to the levends:
"To starboaaaard!"

When they boarded the silent galleon there seemed to be no one around. Kemal Reis gave his men the signal to get on board. A few minutes later, one of the levends called out to Kemal Reis.
"Everyone is dead here!"

As soon as they stepped foot onto the deck, they noticed that there were dead bodies all over the place. Piri was trying to understand what had happened to these people.

"Uncle, do you think they were attacked?"
"I don't think that's the case, Piri. There is neither evidence of a struggle nor any sign of blood here."

When Kemal Reis moved closer to have a better look, he became even more convinced that these sailors did not perish as a result of an enemy attack. The bruises, boils, and lesions on their faces, the cause of which were unknown to them, had quickly brought the souls of these sailors before the presence of God. Could it be the Black Death? What could possibly have befallen these men? They needed to talk to someone who was still alive. They needed to find a single heart that was still beating to learn from him what had transpired. At that moment, Piri heard a weak voice of a groaning sailor.
"Stay away... Get out of this place..."

Piri ran towards the man as soon as he heard him. Kemal Reis called out to Piri:

"Piri, do not touch anything. Their flesh appears to have been rotten. It may be something infectious."

Upon hearing his uncle's warning, Piri came to a halt before he got too close.

"What happened here?"

"We... we saw an enemy galley... we attacked. It belonged to the knights."

"Did the knights do this to you?"

"No, we seized the galley. Among the spoils there was..."

"Reis, there is an ark here!"

Levends had entered in and carried to the upper deck a gold-plated ark that they found in the ship's hold. Having seen the ark, decorated with two golden angel statues, the dying man screamed in horror:

"Away! Go away!"

No one had understood what was happening. Those were his last words; it was the last breath he took...

"Go away..."

Silence took over. Everyone was wondering what their Reis was going to tell. What were they going to do now? Were they going to take it or leave it? What about the galleon? Kemal Reis took a deep breath and gave his orders:

"Carry the ark to Goke! Set fire to the galleon!"

Piri ran toward his uncle and grabbed his arm as he was just about to return to Goke.

"Uncle, are you sure?"

"This galleon belongs to our Sultan, Piri. We must inform him and deliver this ark to him. He'd know what to do with it. I can't let such a valuable treasure go down the waters without first getting his permission."

As the ark was being transported to Goke Kemal Reis called out to his levends:

"No one is allowed to open it! No one is allowed to approach it! We're going to Constantinople!

Cervantes had become excited. He had gotten out of his chair and started walking around the room. Then, as he stared at the crimson-colored woods crackling in the fireplace, he once again, had become lost in thought.

William's voice summoned him from his voyage across the Mediterranean.

"What was it in that ark?"

Cervantes smiled.

"You are impatient, Signor Shakespeare... You are quite impatient. Whereas we are in Lesbos yet."

Lesbos

"Are you sure you got everything."
"Yes, I got!"
"The olives?"
"Yes!"
"Soaps?"
"All are here."
"Grapes, acorns?"
"Brother, I told you I took all the sacks."
"Sails? Swords? Arrows? Are the arquebuses loaded as well?"

The preparations were almost complete, and they were about to set sail. Elias put everything in his hands aside and rose against his older brother who was standing on the shore, issuing to him commands.

"I tell you; I will never sail with you again."
Aruj was in a good mood. He picked up a stone from the ground and threw it at Elias.

"Look at that! Haven't you just said that you got everything? What are these small-caliber cannonballs doing on the beach, then? What kind of a sailor are you? What kind of a levend are you?"

"A levend? Brother, all we're going to do is sell some soaps, but you make it sound like we're going to wage war against the knights."

"You have a poor imagination. We are just having some fun. Aside from that, who knows, perhaps one day we will set sail to fight against them, too."

"Hah! As if it was something to look forward to!"
Aruj turned to Khidr who had come to the shore to send them off.

"I swear! The next time I'll go sailing with you!"

Khidr was enjoying his brother's upbeat demeanor and hearty laughter. On the other hand, the few weeks he'd have to spend on the island without Aruj felt like an eternity.

"I don't understand why we can't set sail together. You know, I get bored without you around."

Aruj smiled and placed his hand on Khidr's shoulder. As he began to talk with a gentle, but resolute tone of an older brother trying to convince his younger, Khidr had understood that he was going to remain on the island regardless of how fervently he pleaded.

"You have to stay on the island, Khidr, you know that. Dad is not well. And Isaac has not yet made his way back. We cannot leave our mother alone. In addition, we need a valiant and brave warrior to stay behind to defend our home against any possible attack."

Elias burst out into laughter upon hearing what Aruj had just said. Khidr went on:

"Why wouldn't Elias stay behind? He's not fond of sailing anyway."

"Because he lacks the strength and bravery necessary to defend our home against the enemy hordes! The only thing he does well is to laugh like that."

"I'm going to be a theologian, not a warrior. Brother, please let me stay!"

Aruj turned to Elias with a joking fury in his tone.

"You! If you don't want to remove olive seeds along the way, get back to your work!"

After that, maintaining the same demeanor, he turned to Khidr:

"And you! Run quickly and get what my mother has brought."

Khidr was so focused on his siblings' leaving that he had failed to notice their mother chasing after them with two bowls of cookies in her hands.

"You forgot! It took me all night to prepare these for you. You are supposed to be adults, yet I'm still chasing after you so that you can have a bite to eat."

Khidr immediately dashed off to Katerina to take the bowls and then brought them to Elias so that he could load them into the boat.

Aruj hugged his mother, took both of her hands in his, and then kissed them.

"Thank you, mom."

He then turned his gaze towards Elias and shouted so that he can hear as well.

"It's all because of your younger son. We were going to starve in the middle of the sea. And yet shamelessly, he still claims that he took everything."

"Oh, come on, brother! Wouldn't it be better if you reminded me about the food instead of asking about the arquebuses?"

Katarina was baffled. She became concerned.

"Arquebuses? Son, are you going to war?"

Khidr laughed.

"No mom, my brother is just teasing Elias."

"Come on, we have to leave before it's late!"

After saying goodbye to both his mother and brother, Aruj jumped on the boat. As the boat sailed away, Khidr felt as if a part of his soul was leaving him.

Aruj called out to Khidr:

"It's like walking on the seas!"

Khidr shouted back with sparkling eyes.

"Walking on the seas!"

They were walking on the seas. As the waves of the Aegean were gently rocking their boat like a cradle, this was the exact sensation that Aruj was having. Ever since he was a child, he had loved being on the seas. He recalled the jealousy he felt when Isaac began to accompany his father in his journeys. "Be patient, son. Your time will also come" his father had once told him. And the time had finally arrived. After spending some time at the seas with his father, Aruj was now able to successfully navigate the waters on his own. He had gained enough experience, and he now knew these waters like the back of his hand. From the treacherous reefs that lay hidden beneath the surface to the safest routes to take, from the most dangerous flags to the best harbors to take shelter, and the winds that whisper impending storms... He had learned them all. Aruj was in love with the sea. He was in love with these waters as if it was his beloved...

He closed his eyes, took in a long, deep breath, and inhaled her intoxicating fragrance...

"Am I in love with you, or with your setting me so free?" he said to himself. And then he smiled. "I'm both in love with you, and the way you liberate me. I'm in love with the freedom that I feel to my bones when I'm with you..."

While he was lost in thought in the blue waters of the Aegean, their boat had already arrived at the pirate reefs a few miles away from their village. But once they got past the reefs, what they came across nailed them both to their places. They were about to come face to face with the Mediterranean's most feared flag.

Elias had turned pale with fear.

"The knights!"

Aruj rose to his feet. He was concerned, but he shouldn't have acted as such in order not to frighten Elias further.

"Don't worry. They're not going to do us any harm."

Even he himself had not believed what he just had said, for the galley was coming straight towards them at full speed. As if it had only one goal, as if the knights had traveled all this way just to seize their tiny boat...

"No, they'll pass us by. Why would they even bother attacking us, anyway?"

Had he said it aloud? Or had he just uttered those words to himself? Aruj couldn't recall ever hearing his own voice. After a while, however, neither what he said nor what he thought would matter. Because four of the six knights were going to leap from the spur of "Our Lady of Conception", the most famous galley of the Knights of Saint John hunting in the Mediterranean, onto the deck of their small boat, and pin Aruj down.

They were interrogating him, but Aruj had no idea what they were talking about. He was worried about his younger brother. As he struggled to free himself from the rope they wrapped around his neck, he called out Elias:

"Eliaaasssss! Eliaaaaaaaasss!"

The last thing Aruj saw before losing consciousness due to a blow to the head was Elias' head being severed by the knights.

"Eliaaaasssss!"

"The Knights of Saint John... Why would the Knights of Saint John attack a small sailing boat, anyway?" said William.

"Perhaps they were searching for the Ark, Signor Shakespeare. Perhaps they were just looking for the Ark that they had recently lost, throughout the Mediterranean."

The Ottoman-Venetian warfare was in full swing, and the Mediterranean was witnessing the never-ending victories of Kemal and Piri reises, who were lavishly funded by the Empire. The Ottomans' strategic victory in Sapienza over the Venetian navy under the command of Antonio Grimani had opened a new chapter for the Turks in the Mediterranean. All the Venetian ports in Greece had one by one fallen into the hands of the Turks. As for the greatest blow to the Italians, however, it had been their loss of Modon and Coron, both of which were literally their eyes in Ionia. Kemal Reis who later turned his route towards Pianosa, Sardinia, and the Balearic Islands, had organized an attack on Majorca and enslaved over a thousand Christians. Concerning the booty acquired during these expeditions, it was quite satisfactory for both the levends and Sultan Bayezid II.

Piri was fighting alongside his uncle and swinging his sword, participating in all these battles, while at the same time, meticulously embroidering the Mediterranean onto his maps. But the surprise that awaited him in one of the seven Spanish galleons they had captured off the coast of Valencia that evening, would be the thing that had excited Piri the most up until that day.

As the chests containing gold and silver found in the seized galleons were being carried to Goke, Piri overheard one of the levends laughing. When he got close enough to understand what was going on, he was surprised to see the strange-looking feathered headdresses that came out of the boxes.

He kneeled and took one in his hands.
"Allah Allah, what is this?"
Then, he laughed and put the headdress on one of the levends.
"While we were preoccupied with Ionia, it appears that Castilian fashion had changed drastically."

Levends started laughing.

Kemal Reis took one of the headdresses and approached the captives.

"Is there anyone among you, who can tell me what this is? In exchange, perhaps I may give him some food before being chained to the oars."

"Perhaps I can talk, if you give me my freedom instead of your rotten food," one of the sailors replied arrogantly.

Piri became enraged, he grabbed the hilt of his sword.

"You, impudent!"

But when Kemal Reis raised his hand, he stopped. With his hands clasped behind his back, Kemal Reis took a few steps toward the sailor.

"Depending on how valuable I will find the information you provide, I may reconsider my decision."

The expression on his face indicated that he had a great deal of hesitancy. His gaze was drawn to the remaining Christian slaves, who were throwing at him daggers with their eyes. As a matter of fact, it was no longer relevant to him what anyone else was going to think from that moment on. If this was the path that would save him from slavery, he was going to walk it.

"They are from lands beyond the dark seas."

"You simpleton! You really believe that they will let you go?"

Piri gave the interloper a slap to the face.

Kemal Reis was confused.

"The lands beyond the dark seas?"

"Some of us here, including myself, sailed with Cristóbal Colón."

When Piri heard the name 'Colón', he took the headdress that one of the levends had just put on his head and took a few steps towards the sailor.

"Did you bring these from the New World?"

"Yes, these are the hats the indigenous were wearing. We had no luck with gold or spices, but Admiral Colón mapped out the entire coastline."

Piri's eyes glowed.

"So, where are those maps now?"

"Where Colón is."

Piri and Kemal Reis caught each other's eye. As if he had read what Piri had in mind, Kemal Reis spoke to the captives:

"Whoever takes us to Admiral Colón will be given his freedom!"

The sailor cried out in protest.

"You've said we'd be released if we answered your question."

Kemal reis roared.

"I said I might reconsider!"

After a brief pause, Kemal Reis repeated:

"Whoever takes us to Admiral Colón will be given his freedom!"

"It is impossible, Signor."

They all turned back to see who was speaking in the back row.

"Admiral Colón is imprisoned."

"Imprisoned? But why?" said Piri.

"Probably because he was obsessed with gold," replied another.

Piri had not understood.

"I was one of the sailors who went on his second voyage with him. After seeing him cut off the hands and arms of natives who were unable to find and bring him the gold he wanted, I swore to myself that I would never ever set sail with Colón again."

"If I had known, I wouldn't have sailed either, brother."

"If you had asked, I would have told you, Ramon!"

Piri was confused.

"You two, are brothers?"

"Brothers at odds!" said the elder one, "Brothers at odds with one another, for the past three years..."

"Brother!"

Piri squinted his eyes and checked them from head to toe. Their stature and features were indeed strikingly similar.

"So, you were there, Ramon, along with him on his third expedition?"

"Yes, Signor."

"And, you know where they keep Colón?"

"Francisco de Bobadilla, the judge who was appointed with orders to investigate the complaints about the Colón's policies in the New World, brought the admiral back to Spain from his third expedition in chains. I don't know where he is right now. The last time I've seen him, he and his brothers were imprisoned in La Gorda."

"La Gorda?"

"One of his caravels."

Piri had no intention of giving up. He had to see those maps.

"And where is La Gorda?"

"In Cádiz, Signor. In the harbor."

Kemal Reis commanded his levends with a resolute tone:

"To Gibraltar!"

It was as if seeing with his eyes was not enough and he wanted to feel the coastline with his calloused fingertips; Cervantes started to trace with his fingers the outline of the Mediterranean map carved on his desk. He began his journey on the embroidered shores of the Aegean Sea and moved on to Peloponnesia. He, then, turned around the Italian boot and continued to Valencia. When he arrived at the Pillars of Hercules[55], he paused for a moment, and then, passed through them at once.

"Cartography was on par with literature to Piri. It was like poetry, or like a well-written play. If words are the doors of our souls with broken locks for authors like us; if the syllables are the candles that illuminate our darkness within; every line, every point, every location that was drawn on a map, was as if granting Piri his liberation. A well-drawn chart would mean new worlds to him... New lives, new adventures that awaited him..."

They hoisted the Spanish flag that they took from the galleon they captured on the main mast and anchored off the coast of Cádiz. Then, Kemal and Piri reises took Ramon and Gómez with them as well as two levends who were dressed like the Spaniards and they all got on a small boat that would take them to La Gorda. They were gliding on the dark waters of the Mediterranean in silence. Piri, lying on his belly at the front side of the boat, was guiding the levends so that they would not crash on the sharp reefs lurking beneath the waters. They had only one goal: to find Colón. Gómez was going to wait in the boat while Ramon got on La Gorda. If Gómez were to cause trouble, Ramon was going to get hurt; if Ramon gave them a headache, it was going to be Gómez who was going to pay the price. If everything would go well and the mission was completed, both would be released as promised.

---

[55] The phrase that was used in antiquity to the promontories that flank the entrance to the Strait of Gibraltar.

Because they had waited until late at night, there was little activity in the port. But they needed to be quick and cautious until they reached La Gorda. Ramon had said that he knew where they anchored the caravel. When they came abreast, Ramon was going to climb up; and as soon as he found out where they kept the admiral, he was going to return to the boat. "The rest is easy," Piri had said. Although he had no idea what awaited them next.

They approached the caravel quietly. Ramon grabbed hold of a rope and made his way up to the deck.

"Who is there? Who is there?"
"It's me, Juan, Ramon!"
"Ramon?"
Juan was surprised to see his friend back in La Gorda after three weeks.
"Where have you been all this time?"
"Off the coast of Valencia."
"Valencia?"
"I was on a cargo ship bound for Ibiza."
"So, what brought you back?"
"The pirates!"

The dialogue that was taking place between Juan and Ramon caught Piri's attention. A single blunder Ramon would make could have exposed them. Gómez became concerned. What nonsense was his little brother babbling about? After all, it wasn't Ramon who was waiting on the boat feeling the tip of Kemal Reis' dagger resting on his back.

"Pirates?"
"They are helping Muslims who fled Spain and made their way to Africa. I heard they'd been seen near Ibiza harassing merchant ships. So I fled... just in case."
Piri was relieved. When Kemal Reis loosened his grip on the dagger Gómez let out a sigh.
"Well, what are you going to do now?"
"I'll speak with the captain."
"Signor Colón?"

DENİZ UZUNOĞLU

"What's the use of talking to Signor Colón. He is no longer the captain. I'm looking for Signor Andrea Martín de la Gorda."

"Right. He is no longer the captain. After they dropped anchor, they locked him up in La Villa. I've heard that they were planning to transport him to Sevilla tomorrow."

"So he is still in Cádiz, then?"

"I've heard so."

"La Villa..." murmured Piri. But where was La Villa, anyway?

"And where is Signor Andrea Martín."

"I don't know. Ask those at the port if you'd like."

"All right, I'll do that."

Silence prevailed for a while. Ramon had managed to get an answer to his question. He now needed put an end to the conversation and get back to the boat as quickly as he could.

"I'll go then."

"Are you making your way ashore?"

"Yes."

"Hold on a second, let me gather my stuff, and we'll go together."

Juan rushed inside the caravel while Ramon's knees knocked together. What was he going to do now? He was not alone in the boat. He hurried towards the railing and looked down. Piri was waiting for him holding his sword while the rest had already hidden themselves out.

"Let Juan come down first!" whispered Piri. Ramon confirmed with a nod.

Juan got his stuff and came back as quickly as he left. Ramon, on the other hand, stepped aside to encourage Juan to be the first to go down.

"After you..."

But fate had laid an ambush. Unaware of what was about to befall him, Juan jumped on the boat. And as soon as he jumped, he was knocked unconscious with a blow to the neck.

Piri called out to Juan:

"Hurry up! We need to get ashore before he wakes up."

- 86 -

"La Villa...," said Cervantes. "La Villa was a fortress with strong walls and battlements perched atop the highest point of El Monturrio. But they were indeed very fortunate, because, it had been serving as a warehouse for a while, rather than an arsenal."

Juan was still unconscious when they got ashore; Ramon, on the other hand, was concerned.

"The slope on the south is steep, but it is our only option. We cannot sneak into the castle from the city side. They must have imprisoned the admiral within the keep. I'm not sure how many guards are stationed inside, but I do know that the guards' tower is located in the keep. Do you see that circular bastion situated right next to the main gate?"

"Yes," said Piri.

"That's where you are going to enter the castle. The main gate is guarded by the battlements located on top. But it is likely that there are no guards stationed there at this hour of the night. I'll distract those who keep watch at the entrance. Once inside, proceed through the gate on your right facing the court, and climb the stairs. The passageway that you'll come across will lead you to the inner castle. Then, it's all up to you."

"All right," said Piri.

"What if you don't return?" Ramon asked. "Will the levends set my brother free?"

Ramon's question was answered by Kemal Reis.

"If we don't make it back, it means we're dead, Ramon. And if one of us dies, one of you dies too. Therefore, just doing your best may not be enough, you'd better pray as well."

Ramon quickly made a sign of a cross on his chest.

"If I were you, Ramon, I'd pray to our God," said Kemal Reis and began walking towards the rocky slope.

Ramon was worried. Piri offered Ramon some solace by placing his hand on his shoulder.

"We'll be back, Ramon. Don't worry."

After they climbed up the slope, Ramon left them. He was going to pretend as if he was one of the town dwellers who had drunk too much and got inebriated. He was going to approach the guards while staggering around;

and as if it was the *Arco de los Blanco*, the gate that leads to the town; he was going to try to pass through the main gate of the castle. If Ramon was lucky, he would be able to trick at least one guard and convince him to leave his place to lead him to the right gate. If he was very lucky, he might convince them both.

"But Ramon had no luck, at all," said Cervantes. "No matter what he did, the guards neither let him in nor did they budge from their positions in the slightest. He did not want to yell out loud either, because he did not want to make an unnecessary fuss which would draw the attention of the rest of the soldiers stationed inside the castle to the main entrance."

After hiding behind the bushes for a while, and watching Ramon's fruitless efforts, Kemal Reis couldn't wait any longer and decided to enter the scene.
"Come on, Piri."

They bided their time and took advantage of the struggle between Ramon and the guards before charging straight through the main gate. In the darkness, the guards couldn't see what was approaching them. It had only taken a minute or two, and two lifeless bodies were now smeared in blood lying on the ground.

They took the bodies aside and hid them behind a bush, Piri turned to Ramon:
"Ramon! At least, show us the way."
They went through the gate and raced up the winding stairs of the bastion, then, they quietly walked through the dark vaulted corridor and reached the inner castle.

Colón was sitting in a cell on the cold wet floor, with his back propped up against the stone walls. His heads were in-between his hands, and he was swaying back and forth while muttering to himself. After unlocking the door with the assistance of a curved pointed-tip piece of metal, Piri entered the cell and took a few steps toward the admiral.
"Signor Colón..."

God knows how long he had been held in this place. His hair and his beard had grown long, and he was in a terrible shape. The shackles on his hands and feet had been chained to an iron ring on the wall. He didn't seem to have been tortured; however, it was clear that he was sick.

He raised his head and looked up and was taken aback to see two men standing before him. They had been dressed like Spaniards but did in no way appear to be of Spanish descent.

"Who are you?".
Just as Piri was about to start speaking, Kemal Reis intervened.
"People who can get you out of this place."
Colón laughed in a sarcastic manner.
"And in exchange for what?"
"Your cooperation."

The admiral had not the slightest idea what Kemal Reis was talking about. When he saw Ramon entering in, he was surprised.
"Ramon?"

"Signor Colón, Piri, and Kemal reises would like to see your maps."
Colón got in a stew.
"Did you just say, Kemal and Piri reises?"
Kemal Reis lost his calm. He smacked Ramon on the back of his neck.
"You goof!"

Piri tried to put the admiral at ease.
"Signor Colón, we are not here to do you any harm. We came here to help. All we ask in return is that you allow us to take a look at some of your charts."
It had worked. Colón was somewhat calmer now.
"Who sent you here? Sultan Bayezid? If this is the case, and if he is after the gold, you should go and tell him that the amount of gold I found in the New World does not even come close to matching what he already has."
Kemal Reis spoke:
"We are not interested in your gold. We've already told you, all we want is to see your maps! If you cooperate with us, we can get you out of here. Well, if you don't; you'll end up in the dungeons of Sevilla no later than to-morrow."

Colón bit his lips. After all, the dungeons of Sevilla were notorious. The racks designed to fracture the bones; the Heretic's Fork placed on the victim's neck to pierce his flesh with the slightest move as he stood there with hands tied behind his back, the head crushers.... The Inquisition had creative ways to purify the sinners' souls... And if he were to give it a thought, Colón knew that he would long be dead, if all the sins he had committed so far were to be cleansed.

"If he had provided the Christian Monarchs, who had not hesitated to have murdered tens of thousands of innocent people for the sake of Reconquista, with some valid reasons to justify his actions toward the indigenous people of the New World, they would have released Colón the very next day. But what if his true identity was revealed? What if the Queen of Spain would find out that he was, in fact, a Portuguese spy sent to Spain at the orders of King Juan II of Portugal... Then, without a doubt, he would end up in Judas' Cradle."

"How so?" said William with astonishment.

But Cervantes did not reply. Now, it was his turn to give him a sarcastic smile.

His uncle's blaze had made Piri anxious. At that moment, the last thing he wanted to do was make Colón feel insecure. If the admiral called out to the guards, none of them would be able to leave the castle.

"I am a cartographer, too, Signor Colón. I know of the significance that your charts hold for you."

"You know nothing, Piri Reis." said Colón. "You don't even know why I traveled there in the first place..."

"For gold!" Ramon chipped in, but as soon as he noticed the anger on Kemal Reis' face, he shut his mouth up.

Colón laughed with sarcasm.

"Gold...," said Colón. "You do not have the faintest idea about what the real gold is, Ramon."

His expression was clouded. He recalled the letters he had written to Queen Isabel. She had not responded to any of them, but had met all of Francisco Roldán's demands, who was the real leader of the riots, and unleashed Bobadilla on himself. Bobadilla had confiscated all of Colón's property and had sent him back to Spain in chains to stand trial. He remembered the words he had said to Captain Andrea Martín de la Gorda when he offered to remove his shackles once he got on board. In a manner befitting a knight, Colón had said, "These chains have been put on me by the royal authority, and I shall wear them until the sovereigns themselves should order them removed". But it had been more than three weeks since he arrived in Cádiz, and he was still in prison. He felt depressed. Colón had set sail hoping to find the Garden of Eden, but it appears that the only thing he found was hell. He couldn't help but glance over at his wooden chest sitting in the far corner of the cell. "Gold..." he muttered.

Ramon had not missed this fleeting glance. He went to the wooden chest and opened its lid. Even though it was not gold that he found, it was, at that time, something that was much more valuable to him, it was his freedom.

"Here! For me, this is real gold!"

Colón had sprung to his feet, but the chains had prevented him from stopping Ramon.

"Stay away from that chest!", he cried out.

Piri took a few steps toward the chest to take a closer look at what was inside. It had piqued his interest as to what might be in that chest that had made Ramon excited and the admiral disturbed, at the same time.

"Here, Signor, Admiral Colón's charts!" said Ramon, "Take it and we'll leave."

But Piri maintained his silence and stared at the chest for a while. Inside was a cylindrical leather case that most likely contained some of the admiral's personal belongings as well as the maps Ramon had spoken of. He reached out and took the case; he, then, handed it over to Colón.

Ramon was baffled.

"Signor! What exactly are you up to?"

"I did not come here with the intention of stealing a mapmaker's charts," replied Piri.

This time it was Colón who was baffled.

Kemal Reis, who had been silently watching the ongoing conversation for a while, eventually turned to Colón, and asked:

"Are you coming with us, Signor Colón? Or are you planning a trip to Sevilla?"

Colón took a deep breath and showed them the shackles on his wrists. Piri took out the curved metal pin from his pocket and freed him from his chains. All that they had to do now was to leave this place in the same stealthy way they had entered.

Upon hearing the guards approaching, Kemal Reis turned to Piri:
"We have to go!"

Colón had been set free, but he was too sick and exhausted to walk without assistance. Piri handed over the maps to Kemal Reis and went to give the admiral a helping hand. Colón recalled his brothers who were also imprisoned in a cell next to his.

"My brothers! We must save them, too."

Kemal Reis had no intention of putting themselves in such a risky situation.

"May Allah save them, Admiral. We simply have no time for them."

For some reason unknown to them, the guards in the castle had begun mobilizing. They were rushing down the stairs as their commander was barking orders. One among them, who had donned his armor and grabbed his sword ran outside in no time flat, fortunately not noticing Kemal and Piri reises who were hiding in the nooks and crannies.

Taking advantage of a split-second silence Piri asked:
"What's happening?"

A voice that was coming from the main entrance made the answer clear.

"Commander! The guards stationed at the gates are dead! On the shore! They're on the shore!"

Ramon got excited.
"Gómez!"
"Levends!"
"Juan!"

"Juan woke up!" said William.

"He had not only woken up, Signor Shakespeare, but as soon as he woke up, Juan had taken advantage of a split-second time when the levends were distracted and had begun running towards the rocky slopes while at the same time shouting out loud for help. When the guards heard of his shouts, they had rushed to the shore; and a sword-to-sword fight with the levends had commenced."

They got out of the castle as quickly as they could. Kemal Reis was knocking every Spaniard standing in their way. Piri, on the other hand, was trying to advance while he was assisting Colón with one arm and swinging his sword with the other. As for Ramon, he was shouting at the top of his lungs calling out to Gómez as he was trying to escape, jumping from rock to rock.

"Brotheeerrr! Brotheeerrr!"

Gómez, with his hands bound, was running with all his might to be able to get away from that place. Just when his eyes locked with those of his younger brother, one of the arrows raining down from the ramparts pierced through his chest.

"Brotheeerrr!"

A moment later, one of the levends fell to ground...
Kemal Reis cried out in pain:
"Mehmeeeeed!"
And then, the other...
"Yunuusssss!"
He was late...

Uncle and nephew fought standing back-to-back. The flames of their vengeance took the form of a lightning bolt and struck the dead of night. As Ramon was swinging the sword that he had picked up from the ground, he was at the same time crying out loud as "I am a Spaniard, a Christian I am!". But no one was hearing him, no one believed in him.

After finishing off the last Spaniard he fought, Kemal Reis pushed the boat into the water. But the guards were running down the slopes and charging at them like hordes of spiders. They had to leave this place as quickly as they could.

He called out to Piri:

"Piiiiiriiii! To the booooat!"

Piri caught Ramon by the arm and dragged him to the boat.

"Come on, Ramon! They're going to kill you here!"

They had just gotten on board and started rowing when one of the guards grabbed Colón by the jacket and yanked him into the waters at once. Kemal Reis caught Piri by the arm and prevented him from jumping after the admiral.

"You have to solve the mystery of the maps on your own, Piri!"

Kemal Reis was right. The Spaniards had already dragged Colón ashore. Under the heavy rain of arrows coming from the ramparts there was nothing more they could have done for the admiral. They had to leave.

The Spanish author's eyes sparkled with the lights reflected from the blade he was holding. It was as if Piri's soul had inhabited Cervantes' body. It was as if his hands were Piri's hands, his sword was Piri's sword; his heart was as if beating with Piri's...

William couldn't hold back.

"It is as if Piri is looking from behind your eyes. Your fingers clutch the hilt as if they were his fingers. You... Hadn't you fought against them for years? Hadn't you stood up against those bloodthirsty barbarians, against those marauding homeless pirates?"

"Marauding homeless pirates, huh?" said Cervantes in a cynical manner. Whether they carried a cross, the crescent of Islam, or the Star of David on their flags, Signor Shakespeare, one thing is certain: no one in that century had the heart of a true knight like those Turks of the Mediterranean."

William couldn't say a thing. Anything he would say would have hung in the air like the morning mist hanging over the seas.

As soon as they got on board, the levends who remained behind and waited for their reises' return had understood from the devastated expression on Kemal Reis' face. Nothing they had planned had gone as they hoped and only three of the six people who left the ship had been able to return safe and sound. However, neither Kemal Reis nor Piri or Ramon was willing to utter a word. When no one could muster the courage to ask the questions lingering in minds, all remained unanswered.

After washing his hands and changing his clothes, Kemal Reis made his way to the upper deck and pointed with his head at the Spanish flag hoisted on the main mast.

"Lower that damn flag and get ready to set sail!"
"Right away Reis!"

The day was about to be reborn. Kemal Reis was looking forward to sailing away from these cursed waters as quickly as possible. Ramon had seated in a far corner. He was taken aback when a sack of gold fell into his lap. When he raised his gaze, he saw Piri standing in front of him.

"Go Ramon..." said Piri. "Go home... I'm sorry about your brother..."
Ramon took a deep sigh and stood up.
"I lost a brother... you lost two..."
Then, he got on the small boat waiting for him and sailed away in the twi-light.

"They were unable to save Colón," said Cervantes, "But his maps were now in Piri's hands."
William got excited.

Piri worked on the charts without a rest, and as they approached Kilitba-hir, he dashed up to the deck.
"Uncle! I think I know what is in that ark?"
Kemal Reis was confused.
"You mean the gold-plated ark we found in the drifting galleon?"
"Yes, uncle!"
"And?"
"The Stones of Death!"

Cervantes put the shiny blade on the table and with a mischievous smile on his face, leaned back.

"In fact, Piri had one more thing in mind, but for a little while longer, he preferred to keep silent on this subject."

William got curious.

"What? What did he have in mind?"

Cervantes did not reply and, just like Piri; he also preferred to keep silent on the subject for a little while longer.

Italy, Imola

Italy was not like Spain. If there indeed was a country in that century that could be called Italy. Because of the never-ending internal strife among the Italian city-states, their ever-conflicting economic and political interests, hatred for one another, and the bloody hands of Pope Alexander, who had been running Saint Peter's as if it were a corporation; Italy had become defenseless not only against the threats that might come from outside but also against those that might arise from within the country. It was in fact this political disunity that had paved the way for the Ottomans, who were less experienced than the Italians in maritime affairs, to show up in these waters so easily and ravage the ports in Ionia. This situation, however, did not seem to bother the Borgia Pope at all, who was supposed to be an enemy of the Turks. While his son, Cesare, was conquering Italy from within, the fact that the city-states were at the same time dealing with the threat posed by the Ottomans appeared to have been serving the Borgian interests well. The only thing in Alexander Sixtus' mind at the time was to wear the boot of Italy on his own holy feet, and turn the papacy into an institution that would be passed down from father to son. First, he was going to become king, then declare himself the caliph. As for the rest of the world that dared to threaten the power God had given him, he would deal with them later.

Cesare had served his father in his political intrigues as a cardinal within the walls of Vatican for years. And as soon as he was given his sword back and an army under his command, he had attacked the Italian city-states like a starving lion released from his cage. But when he finally realized that he was lonelier than he thought in this fight, he had decided to take refuge in Niccolo Machiavelli's wisdom.

"Do you know who is the most glorious leader who has ever lived? A visionary who had sown the seeds of a new religion as well as a new state at the right time, in the right place, and in the right way. A man of God, a statesman, a philosopher, a warrior. A prince!"

Machiavelli's calm voice was like a glass of water poured over the flames of vengeance burning within Cesare's heart. Being stabbed in the back by his so-called fellow men with whom he fought alongside at the Siege of Forli a few years ago, and in whom he placed so much trust, was not a kind of betrayal that Cesare Borgia, the Duke of Romagna of the time, could easily forgive. He had given his father a promise of an empire. And as he was dealing with the difficult task of bringing the ruling families of the Italian city-states onto their knees; the loss of the Castle of San Leo, the revolt of Urbino, and the hostility towards the Borgias spreading like a plague in the heart of Sicily had enclosed him within the borders of Romagna.

"Who, Signor Machiavelli?"
"Moses!"

Cesare smiled with sarcasm. He knew Machiavelli. He was a Florentine diplomat, an intellectual, a philosopher, a strategist... Yes, he was all of these... But a religious man? He certainly was not!

"If you had faith in Jesus as much as you had in Moses, we may have seen Florence fighting alongside the Vatican!"
"Oh, the Vatican! The Saint Peter's, the holiest of all the churches of God! Defender of the Truth, Preserver of Order and Faith." Machiavelli paused for a moment and without moving his eyes away from the duke, he continued: "The most precious toy of the Borgias! A nest of conspiracy, intrigue, bribery, and assassination!"
"While expecting to see Florence by our side, are we going to find it standing against us, Signor Machiavelli? Especially while we host the weakened Medicis in Rome."

Upon hearing Cesare's words, Machiavelli smiled. Even if he was trapped in Romagna with only a handful of men at his disposal, a Borgia was always a Borgia. Their insane courage flowing through their veins, endless ambitions, and an unquenchable thirst for power and wealth, must have been hereditary.

"Have you ever heard of the story of Mizaru, Kikazaru, and Iwazaru, My Lord? If you haven't, allow me to tell you. Once upon a time there would live a wise and good-hearted monkey king on a mountainside, and on the other side of the mountain, the devil. The monkeys would believe that if anyone among them saw the devil or heard his voice, that one would be cursed forever and turned to stone, and the monkey kingdom would fall into an irreversible collapse. The monkeys, so scared that the prophecy would come true, would not even turn their gaze up and look towards the hills adorned with colorful and fragrant flowers so that they would not accidentally encounter the devil. One day the king's three advisers, Mizaru, Kikazaru, and Iwazaru, decided to set on a quest to collect some of these beautiful and rarely-found flowers for their king. As they looked about, they heard a voice coming from behind the bushes and got curious. And when they parted the bushes, they came face to face with the devil screaming out with a dreadful voice. Mizaru covered his eyes with his hands so he wouldn't see him. But Kikazaru who had unfortunately seen him covered his ears to at least, avoid hearing his voice. But petrified Iwazaru had both seen and heard him. In order not to talk mention it to anyone he immediately covered his mouth. Since then, these three monkeys, who had been waiting for the day the prophecy would be fulfilled and their hearts would turn to stone, kept this a secret until the end of their lives so that the devil would not harm their kingdom. The first one, with hands upon his eyes, the second, on his ears, and the third one, on his mouth..."

Cesare had failed to grasp what Machiavelli wanted to point out.
"What exactly is your point, Signor Machiavelli?"
Machiavelli smiled.
"My point is that the diplomatic demeanor of Florence will not be any different from what you have witnessed so far. Florence will neither see, nor hear or speak, as she always did."

Cesare took a sip of his wine.
"So, Moses, huh?"
"The prophets who take up arms triumph, while those who are unarmed, would perish under the ruins, My Lord. Just like Savonarola!"
"Savonarola was not a prophet. He was just a heretic who claimed that God had spoken to him and led Florence into animosity towards Rome."

"Because he had no weapons, My Lord! What makes your father, who sits in the Vatican and claims that he is God's voice on earth, different from Savonarola, is the resources he has. I do not advise you to be more ruthless, you are vicious enough already. I'm just stating the facts. It's time for you to stop believing in the idea that the author of the play the Borgia family was staging in the Vatican is God. If you want to unite people under the flag of a single empire, the religion you'll impose on them would do it on your behalf. Trying to bring people with conflicting sets of beliefs under single a political umbrella is nothing but a futile endeavor. No matter how flawless the system you would establish, it would collapse in a short time. However, never forget, religion is a human invention and is valuable to the extent that it contributes to the social order. And if it is the security that is at stake, it should be waived. As for the code of ethics, given your father's admirable indifference on this matter, here's what I wouldn't hesitate to tell you: If there is a God, you can be certain that, there will be other concerns with which He will be preoccupied during a battle. A true prince should never be religious; those who should be pious, are his subjects. Moses, Romulus, Cyrus the Great, Theseus... The glorious swords who had written the rules of diplomacy!"

With the last words that spilled from Machiavelli's mouth everyone in the inn had stopped speaking and silence had taken over. Machiavelli, possessed by excitement, had unintentionally raised his voice.

He remained silent for a while and waited for the people inside the inn to mind their own business. Then, he continued in a calmer way.

"The ends justify the means, My Lord. Now is the time to replace the so-called fear of God of the Italian aristocrats with a genuine fear of a true prince! Wondering why I prefer Moses over Jesus? Then, find the Ark of the Covenant."

"The Ark of the Covenant... Could the ark Kemal and Piri reises found in the Mediterranean be the Ark of the Covenant, the holiest of all the Jewish relics?" William was excited. "But I thought that the Ark had disappeared with the destruction of the Temple of Solomon."

William felt drawn deeper into the conversation they were having with Cervantes. Although the story of this Spanish author appeared to have sprouted in geography where some of history's bloodiest maritime conflicts occurred, it seemed to have been rooted in much earlier times. "I am trying to remember", Cervantes had said. William was slowly coming to a better understanding of what he had actually meant. He was not only trying to re-member but also trying to understand. Three teachings, three prophets, three holy books... Though it is life, faith, righteousness, justice, compassion, and love that they all honor, why were the streets smelling so much death?

"Do you know the reason why the cardinals would dress in reds, Signor Shakespeare?"

"For it is the color of their blood they say that they would not hesitate to shed for the sake of Jesus Christ."

"But it has always been the blood of women, children, shepherds, farm-ers, artisans, commoners having been shed... You think goodness some-times requires a bit of evil, don't you Signor Shakespeare?"

After his final words, Cervantes had again become lost in thoughts as he watched the dancing flames. Although William was more than impatient to hear the rest of the story, he kept his silence and waited so that he would not abruptly unlink him from his thoughts and emotions.

"The Ark of the Covenant..." muttered Cesare. "A secular statesman like you... Haven't you just said that the first thing that I should do to unite the Italian city-states under my rule is to stay away from God?"

Machiavelli smiled.

"The narrative of the Ark of the Covenant is an intriguing one, My Lord; it is claimed to have played a critical role in the history of the Israelites, who fled Egypt and headed out for the promised land. For the Jews, the Ark rep-resents the power, the glory of God. Being in possession of the Ark is an indication that God's will is on their side. Armies that carry the Ark of the Covenant win the battles they fight; nations, live in peace and abundance. Have you ever pondered why? Have you ever wondered what could be in-side the Ark?"

"The sacred relics?" said Cesare in a sarcastic tone. "Imitations of which are produced almost everywhere. You'd be surprised to learn how good the Jews are at creating their replicas, Signor."

"Stones, My Lord! The Stones of Death!"

The sarcastic smirk on Cesare's face left its place for a more serious expression. Confident that Cesare would be listening to him more attentively, Machiavelli continued his words:

"I believe you realize better that I'm more interested in the physical power of the Ark, rather than its spiritual influence over people. Whatever is inside that Ark, My Lord, makes its owner come out triumphant in battles; helps him establish kingdoms. And I don't think it is logical to bring an explanation to this matter with the irrational idea that the Ark has in it the power of God. If one would consider the fact that the Babylonians, Romans, Persians, and Muslims have all been searching for this Ark since antiquity; it would not be irrelevant to guess that these Stones of Death are as poisonous as cantarella[56] to anyone who would approach without knowing how to make use of them. What you need to do first is to find the Ark. When it comes to dealing with what's inside, you are going to need someone who doesn't put much stock in religious matters. As soon as you figure out how to operate the Ark, you'll be no different from Messiah, My Lord. Just like Moses! "

"I thought that we were going to talk science."

Machiavelli was startled by the voice coming from behind. Cesare, pleased to see that the visitor he had been expecting finally arrived, stood up.

"Let me introduce you, Signor Machiavelli. My adviser on military matters, Signor..."

A witty smile covered Machiavelli's face. Was there anyone at that time who had not heard about Leonardo?

"Leonardo... Leonardo da Vinci..."

---

[56] A poison allegedly used by the Borgias during the papacy of Pope Alexander VI

"Leonardo da Vinci," said William. "The most famous painter, architect, and engineer of the era..."

"The genius of the era..." added Cervantes.

William could not disagree. All of Leonardo's designs, all his projects were truly the work of a genius. But the problem was that; all were incomplete. What would the golden pages of history have to say about Leonardo in the years to come, William wondered.

Cervantes leaned back in his chair.

"Leonardo had not found what he had been looking for in Milan, just as he had not found it in Florence where he had grown up. He had worked for Ludovico Sforza, or better known as Il Moro, for seventeen years during which Milan was ruled by the Sforzas. When Ludovico had lost it all, however, after the French occupied the city, Leonardo had lost his patron. When the war knocked on the door, art was silenced. But during the years Leonardo spent in Milan, which was a city always prepared for a fight because it was located in northern Italy and open to continuous French attacks, Leonardo had given a lot of thought to matters concerning strategic military engineering. This was the reason why Cesare Borgia had believed that he could benefit from Leonardo and had chosen him to serve as his military adviser."

"All you need to do now, Signor Borgia, is to find the Ark. The question of who is going to take care of the rest seems to have been sorted out."

Even though she did not speak about it much, Katerina had been anxiously waiting for Aruj and Elias to return from their trips. Once, she had attempted to say a few words to Yakub Agha to express her frustration regarding the length of time it had taken for her sons to return, but her old, grouchy, and recently ill husband had silenced her by saying, "Woman! The sea is as the sea does! Perhaps the winds had shifted, and they had taken precautions and avoided setting sail. Why do you constantly assume the worst possible outcome?". In order not to ponder too much and to worry less, Katerina had to keep herself occupied. Besides, in this way, the seconds that disguised themselves as hours in the absence of her sons might speed up, and time might flow faster.

First, she had decided to keep herself busy with knitting and had taken out of the closet all the leftover yarns she previously stored just in case. She had spent the next three weeks purling and knitting and had produced two cardigans, four scarves, and two berets, but neither her sons had returned, nor had she received any news from them. She then had given herself to baking buns and cookies; but this time, she had gotten herself into trouble with Yakub Agha who was not allowed to eat a single cookie for he had long been suffering from diabetes. When he had become inebriated from the aroma of freshly baked cookies his wife was handing out to neighbors, Yakub Agha had turned into a much grumpier man and had eventually started yelling at poor Katerina.

It had been weeks, but nothing had helped to lessen her worries. She eventually let go of everything, sat on the sofa by the window, and began waiting for her sons. The light in her eyes had become dim, the color of her words had turned pale. Katerina had become quieter and quieter each passing day.

It was one of those days when her heart was with her sons and her gaze outside when Pierro arrived with a letter from Aleko in his hands. Could it be possible that he had brought Katerina some words from Aruj and Elias? Or more importantly, were the words written in that letter the words Katerina's pale heart was hoping to hear? Khidr... Khidr would know... Where was Khidr, anyway?

"Khidrrrr!.. Khidrrrrrr!.."

Khidr, who had spent that entire afternoon on the shore repairing his small boat, leaped to his feet when he heard his name reverberating throughout the island. Pierro, in his haste to reach Khidr as soon as he can, had run all the way down the hill, and by the time he arrived, he was completely out of breath.

"Khid... Khidr..."
"Hey, slow down!"
"Aleko... It's from Aleko, Your mother... letter..."
"I don't understand what you are saying, take a breath. What's going on, what does my mother say?"
"I say, from Aleko, a letter came from Aleko. Your mother wants you to read it to her."

Khidr, like the rest of Yakub Agha's sons, was well educated. He had learned to speak at a young age Spanish, French, Italian, and Greek which were at those times the languages spoken by the maritime nations. Aleko was a Greek with whom Aruj had met on the Island of Kalymnos during one of his journeys. He would bring news to Lesbos about the goings on elsewhere in the Mediterranean. The news, which was usually not good... Khidr got worried. It had been a long time since Aruj and Elias had gone, and there was still no sign of them. As a matter of fact, what Khidr had been doing for the past few days was spending time on the shore under the pretense of repairing his boat until the orange sun would bid him farewell, waiting for his brother. He put the scraper aside and wiped his hands on his pants.

"A letter? Okay, I'm coming."

When he creaked open the door, he found his mother standing there waiting for him with Aleko's letter in her hands. With a look on her face overshadowed by anxiety, Katerina gave the letter to Khidr.

"Here, read it, son. You know, Aleko hardly ever writes good news. And, you know, it's been a long time since your brothers have left..."

"Don't assume the worst-case scenario mom, let's read it first."

He reached out, took the letter from Katerina's trembling hands, and started to read. Like a piece of food that grew in size inside one's mouth and eventually choke him up, Khidr felt that his soul was suffocated by Aleko's words. His face turned pale, he felt tightness in his chest, and a lump formed in his throat. He clenched his fist and crumpled up the letter. Katerina had understood, the news that Aleko wrote about was no good. She had felt it days ago. She had felt it the day she ran out of yarn, the day when was left with no choice but to knit the rest of the cardigan with a different color.

"Son? What does Aleko say?"

"The news is not good, mom. Come, have a seat."

Khidr took her by the arm and helped her sit on the sofa.

"Elias, mom. Aleko says that Elias was killed, that the Knights of Saint John has taken his life..."

Katerina's eyes welled up with tears. Her lips were trembling, and she could barely speak.

"Aruj?"

"He was taken captive."

Katerina was devastated. She was at a loss for what to do or say. She started sobbing. Khidr knelt beside his mother and took her delicate, her snow-white hands in his own. His eyes were bloodshot from grief and rage.

"I'll save my brother, mom. I will find him and bring him to you. Don't you ever worry."

He got to his feet, dashed through the open door and ran towards the shore. The flames of vengeance were scorching his heart. However, he also knew he had to devise a plan and rescue Aruj from the hands of the knights. The indescribable agony he felt within his heart brought him to his knees.

"I swear... I swear on the blood of our forefathers and of all the martyrs, Elias. Nobody will be safe in the Mediterranean until your revenge is taken!"

Cervantes turned to William and looked him in the eye.

"And he was going to keep his word..."

"Get up! We're leaving for Petrium[57]."

Grikko was a Greek merchant trading in the Mediterranean. He had been traveling back and forth between Constantinople and the Island of Rhodes which was, at that time, ruled by the Knights of Saint John. The big earthen jars that he was carrying on his ship would usually contain wax, wine, and corn; and the chests would be full of precious stones as well as a variety of trading goods. On each of his journeys, he would stop by Lesbos to buy soap, olives and grapes, stay on the island for a few days to rest, and after loading his ship with everything he bought from the island, he would sail to Rhodes. As for his favorite place to rest where he spent much of his time during his stay, it was Yossi's inn.

Startled by the clanking sound of the gold sac that Khidr had thrown onto the table, Grikko sat himself up and rubbed his eyes. As was his custom, he was drunk.

"Petrium? I just got here. Even the Janissaries would come, no one can make me leave this place any sooner than three days."
"I said get up! We're leaving. I don't have three days."

Khidr was breathing fire. It was obvious that he was in a hurry. Grikko had never seen him like this before. He shifted his focus to the sac tossed onto the table.
"What's this?"

---

[57] Bodrum, Turkey. The city was named 'Petrium' after the city was dedicated to Saint Peter, together with the castle called Saint Peter's Castle.

"Eighteen thousand akches."

"Woah!"

He reached for the sac, loosened its knot, and peeked inside. It was not stuffed with akches, but rather with gold. His eyes popped out of his head.

"These are not akches, these are Venetian ducats!"

"It's worth eighteen thousand akches."

Grikko took one ducat from the sac, examined it, turned it over, bit it, spit on it, and rubbed it with his fingers. There was no doubt that it was gold.

"Why are you giving me such a large sum of money?"

"To ransom my brother!"

"Aruj? What happened to Aruj?"

"A letter came from Aleko. He says that the Knights of Saint John had killed Elias and taken Aruj captive. There are people you know on the island. I want you to set sail to Rhodes and ransom Aruj."

Grikko scratched his beard and asked the first question that came into his mind.

"How are we going to find him? What if it turns out that he is not in Rhodes? What if it turns out that they've already sold him at the market? What if they've made out of him a galley slave, shaved his hair, chained him to oars and whipped him? What if they've already killed him?"

Khidr slammed his fist on the table in full blast!

"I said get up! We're leaving!"

Rhodes

Aruj had been chained to the oars at first, but he was subsequently incarcerated in a dark cell when his inciting remarks eventually drove the knights mad. When he was brought up to the upper deck after the galley had dropped anchor at Mandraki, the ancient city's port, his eyes, which had become accustomed to darkness for weeks, nearly burned due to sudden exposure to bright sunlight. As soon as he came ashore with the rest of the slaves who were chained to one another, and saw the majestic walls rising before him, he realized that he was in Rhodes.

The walls had been built in such close proximity to the sea that they must have been absolutely sure that no one could attack the castle from this side. His attention was drawn to the inscription at the entrance:

Pro Aris et Focis, Cruce, Ense et Aratro

"For hearth and home, with cross, sword and plow..."

There was no doubt that the knights had built their kingdoms with these. After the island came under the knights' rule in 1308, these skillful stonemasons, who were the masters of Gothic architecture, had rebuilt the city walls that dated back to the Byzantine era. The knights had built a network of narrow roads resembling a spider web, designed mobile bridge systems, and constructed castles, walls, bastions, ditches, and silos integrated with the rocky surface. As Aruj gazed in admiration at the Virgin Mary, Saint John, and Saint Peter reliefs adorning the Marine Gate, the primary entrance that connected the port and the city, the clanking sound of the shackles on the captives' feet was filling out the harbor.

Under the scent of the pines, he began to walk towards the city, located on the northern side of the island covered with pink hibiscus, peonies, and other wild Aegean herbs.

"And here it is! The Island of Helios[58]! The island that the gods had hauled up out of the depths of the waters!"

It was the voice of that young man who had been chained to the oars next to Aruj. He looked like he was in his early twenties. They had made eye contact several times while they were on the galley but had no chance to converse.

Aruj squinted his eyes.
"The gods?"
"Yes, the gods! The legend says that there was no such island at this location. Then, when Zeus emerged triumphant from the war he fought against the Titans, he made the decision to draw lots to divide the world among the gods. However, since Helios, the Sun God, was not present when the lots were drawn and therefore did not receive his portion of the land, he requested that an island be pulled up from the depths of the seas just for himself."
"So, the gods drew lots among themselves?"
"The legend says they did; to ensure that there was no injustice."
"And they dipped into the waters and pulled this bit of land out from the depths?"
"They may also have pulled it up with a fishing rod, or a hook they attached to a rope as the fishermen do, who knows. In fact, there's also a rumor that they formed the island from the foams of waves. After all, they were gods!"
Aruj, who had been enjoying the conversation since the very beginning, erupted into fits of laughter at the very last words the young man said. When a knight slapped him on the back of the neck, however, he stumbled.
"The days you spent behind the bars seem to have taught you nothing!"

They kept walking in silence for a while. But the young man couldn't help himself and soon began to talk.

---

[58] Sun God in Ancient Greek tradition

"There was once a massive statue of Helios here. A bronze monument forty arshin high that they had constructed to commemorate their victory against King Demetrius of Macedonia! Do you know what was inscribed on it?"

"What?"

"To you, O Sun, the people of Dorian Rhodes set up this bronze statue reaching to Olympus, when they had pacified the waves of war and crowned their city with the spoils taken from the enemy. Not only over the seas but also on land did they kindle the lovely torch of freedom and independence. For to the descendants of Herakles[59] belongs dominion over sea and land."

The young man kept speaking in a confident tone:

"This is why, Rhodes is invincible! And since the knights also knew this fact, they turned Mehmed II's offer. Mehmed II had asked them two thousand ducats per year. Two thousand! Do you know how much akches it makes? Eighty thousand akches!"

Aruj smiled.

"What's your name?"

"Dragut!"

"Could it be that Rhodes is invincible because it is surrounded by these mighty walls, which the knights constantly restore, Dragut?"

"I've never seen a wall mighty enough to withstand against Mehmed II's navy of one hundred and seventy warships carrying a hundred thousand soldiers. Can you imagine? These walls withstood three thousand five hundred cannon balls fired, as well as the great earthquake that shook the island like a cradle and killed thirty thousand people in the following year. The gods must surely have a finger in the pie!"

Aruj, impressed by this apparently well-equipped young man, was enjoying himself as he listened to Dragut.

"Wow, it appears you are also knowledgeable about military matters."

Dragut, with a shiny look on his face, replied confidently:

"I am skilled at archery, and I am a competent sailor as well. I'm getting artillery and castle siege training in the Ottoman Navy."

"In the Ottoman navy?"

---

[59] A divine hero in Greek mythology, the son of Zeus and Alcmene. Hercules in Roman mythology.

Aruj was taken aback.

"What are you doing here then, shackled by the feet and looking like a mess?"

Dragut grinned.

"I came here to find that finger of the gods I mentioned. I will find and take it to Sultan Bayezid."

"So, the fingers of gods, huh? I was thinking that they believed in one God in Muhammad's religion."

Cervantes stood up and walked toward his bookshelf. For a while of searching among the shelved books, he took one out and handed it to William. As soon as William took the book and saw what it was, it was as if a glass of ice-cold water was poured over his face.

"But Signor Cervantes, this is Qur'an! Wasn't it banned in Europe? Haven't you said that all except a few copies preserved in the Vatican were burned?"

"Yes, Signor, they were all burned. Fearing that Islam could become more appealing to the people over time, Christian Monarchs seized and destroyed all its translations. A few copies are retained in the Vatican to be studied when needed, alongside that copy which in your hands right now."

"So, Signor, did you... did you convert to Islam?"

Cervantes laughed at William's bewilderment and quickly drew a cross on his chest.

"Hah! No, Signor. I'm an Old Christian. I'm a soldier of Christ. I needed to know against what I would be fighting. And a writer, I am. And as you would also appreciate; if you want to be a good writer, you must first be a good reader."

As William was turning its pages one by one and checking out the scripture, Cervantes continued:

"Islam worships to one God, Signor. Muslims say, "Allah" is One. But their scripture, the Qur'an, does not deny the religions and the prophets who preceded Muhammad. In the Qur'an it reads: *"Say, O believers; we have believed in Allah and what has been revealed to us and what has been revealed to Abraham and Ishmael and Isaac and Jacob and their descendants and what was given to Moses and Jesus and what was given to the prophets from their Lord. We make no distinction between any of them. And to Allah we all submit."* [60] While all preceding scripture heralds the coming of a messiah, the Qur'an claims that it is the final book and Muhammad is the last prophet. For this reason, the Turks allow the people who live in the lands they conquered to keep fulfilling the requirements of their own faith and worship as they please."

"As long as they continue to pay their taxes."

"As long as they bow to their rule, Signor."

William's gaze was drawn to the Qur'an in his palms.

"An empire of horror!"

"Are we the Christians not scared? Doesn't the idea of being subjected to God's wrath in retaliation for all the crimes we've committed so far, and the possibility of our souls being consumed by the eternal fires of hell frighten us? Isn't it what compels us confess? In order to be forgiven, in order to feel cleansed..."

William added his own justifications to those already stated by Cervantes.

"To let someone else know the wrongs we've done consciously, in order not to be crushed under the burden of being the only witness to the sins we've committed thus far."

Upon hearing the words that spilled from William's mouth, Cervantes paused. He had never considered the concept of confession in this light before. He smiled and slightly nodded to confirm.

"Yes, Signor. You're right. While we're stronger than the strongest when it comes to defend ourselves against everyone else, how desperate, how naked we are while trying to justify our ourselves to our souls."

Silence reigned in the room for a while. Cervantes took a deep breath and continued:

"What was I telling?"

"Dragut! You were telling about Dragut!"

Glad that Cervantes returned to the story, William reclined back in his chair.

"Ah yes, Dragut!" said Cervantes. "Who would eventually become probably the greatest pirate warrior of all time... and about whom a French admiral would one day say, *"A living chart of the Mediterranean, skillful enough on land to be compared to the finest generals of the time. No one was more*

---

[60] Qur'an, Al-Baqarah 136

worthy than he to bear the name of 'King'". I was telling you about Dragut... The uncrowned King of the Mediterranean..."

He took a deep breath and then continued:

"Dragut was born in Petrium to a Muslim household. He was a gifted young boy, intelligent and well-trained. He was an avid reader who enjoyed learning about Greek mythology, Ancient Egypt, the Babylonians, Persians, and the Romans. He was tremendously interested in history and would strive to learn every detail. His military skills in addition to all the knowledge he acquired so far was going to allow him to take an active role in state administration in the following years. In short, Signor Shakespeare, it would not be wrong to claim that his capacity to think strategically ranked him, in that century, the second most important figure after Khidr."

"What about Aruj?"

"Ah, Aruj was a first-class warrior. But he was just a warrior, Signor. He was audacious and fearless, not a man of thorough thinking. He would like to act quickly on whatever came to his mind. He was never diplomatic. He would speak what he says, do what he does. Stubborn as a goat, he was, hated being challenged and would ask no one for their opinion on things, except Khidr. He was not uneducated; it was just his nature. Perhaps because he did not take life so seriously, he was not intimidated by anything. Aruj could burst into laughter even in the most trying situations. He was able to laugh to death five minutes after exploding with wrath."

"No wonder the knights had locked him in a cell then."

"Yes, Signor. And on that day when they arrived in Rhodes, while being led to the city center; neither being pushed around, nor the shackles that caused his ankles to bleed, or the calamities that might befall him must have been bothering him that he was able to chuckle at the stories Dragut was telling."

"What do these symbols represent?"

Aruj had noticed that the insignia sewn on the knee-length robes of some of the knights differed from the rest.

"The Order of the Knights is comprised of volunteered warriors who come to Rhodes from all around Europe. The knights of each country are identifiable by the distinctive emblems that are sewn on their clothes. The northern part of the city, for instance, is under the control of the Grand Master.

Whereas the western and the southern parts are ruled by the French, Spanish, Germans, and Italians. Not only do they reside in different regions, but the foods they eat and the languages they speak also vary."

"It makes no difference to me what language they speak. I can speak in all anyway."

At first, Dragut was surprised, and then he broke into a grin. But as he saw the blood leaking from Aruj's ankle, his expression turned sour.

"They're bleeding."

"What's bleeding?"

"Your feet."

Aruj looked at his feet.

"They're more itching."

"Why don't you scratch, then?"

"I can't. My shackles are not only linked to yours but to those of that stinky Arab standing next to me. So, in order for me to kneel down and scratch my feet, both of you will need to kneel down with me. See the slaves who are chained to your shackles? They need to kneel as well."

Dragut began to laugh.

"So, you think you don't stink!"

"At least, I don't smell like shit."

"Yeah, you're right. You smell more like puke and chicken dung."

When Aruj started laughing as well, one of the knights drew his sword and whacked both of them on the face with the hilt, almost breaking their chins.

"Shut your mouths up!"

They were in the slave market. The buyers were mostly merchants from Venice and Genoa. Prices would vary from year to year depending on the abundance of slaves as well as the prevalence of epidemics. Physical features had a direct effect on the price of a slave. While the strong, sturdy, tall, and healthy ones would be sold at higher prices, those who were weak were not worth much. If those who were sold were lucky, they would serve their new owners in their homes. If not, they would be chained to oars. Everyone always needed slaves for their galleys. Because the slaves, who were chained to the oars stripped naked with shaved heads and a piece of bread soaked in wine stuffed in their mouths, who were forced to eat, drink, defecate, urinate and sleep in the same place and regularly whipped, would not live for a long time. The captives that were being sold on the market were first brought before the knights, who would choose the best among them. The remainder would be sold to the buyers who offered the highest price.

After the knight who had beaten them up walked away, Aruj whispered so that none other than Dragut would hear what he was about to say.

"Could it be because I smell like chicken poop that they did not choose me?"

"I don't believe it to be the case; the scent of puke is more dominant."

As a matter of fact, the reason why Aruj had not been selected was the same reason why he had been locked behind the bars in the galley. His refusal to keep his mouth shut, his talks that provoked the rest of the slaves, and his sarcastic attitude and laughter as he was being whipped, had driven the knights mad. Let alone having him on board, they would have preferred never seeing him again. All they wanted was to get rid of Aruj as quickly as they possibly could.

Khidr, on the other hand, had arrived in Petrium and handed over eighteen thousand akches to Grikko before sending him on his way to Rhodes to ransom Aruj. But the primary reason why Grikko was doing quite well during all those years as he sailed back and forth between Rhodes and Asia Minor carrying goods, was not because he was trading good quality products. What provided him a smooth entry into the port was his good relations with the knights. The knights, who were more interested in the news that he brought from Constantinople than the goods he sold, would not even check his boat as Grikko entered or left the port. And this time, he had brought Philippe Villiers de L'Isle Adam, the Admiral of the flagship of the Knights of Saint John, news that he thought the admiral was going to find interesting.

After handing over the gold sac to the admiral, Grikko did not hesitate to provide the admiral with some information about Aruj and his family as well.

"Eighteen thousand! Khidr says it's all his money. Aruj's family has a long history of successful trade in the Mediterranean. You have recently killed one of their four boys and enslaved the other. If you keep him for a period of six months, or perhaps a year, who knows how much Khidr will offer."

"Let's go and visit the market."

"Red... He has a red beard. He is also quite study. He can serve you well until you agree on a higher price."

Content with the information he was provided with, the admiral returned the sac to Grikko and then left the room, making his way to the marketplace where the sales had just started. When he arrived, a Venetian merchant was negotiating for Aruj.

"No way I would pay more than six hundred!"

"I'd like at least a thousand!"

"Look at him, he's a wreck. He doesn't seem to have been adequately fed in weeks. God only knows how long it would take him to regain his strength, assuming he won't fall sick."

"He will not get sick! He's a Turk, tough as a boar."

"Seven hundred at max."

"I can't sell a man that sturdy to seven hundred. Let's shake on nine hundred!"

"Look at his feet, they're bleeding."

"He speaks several languages and is also well-educated."

"Seven hundred and fifty!"

"Eight hundred final!"

The Venetian was just about to agree when he suddenly felt the tip of Admiral Philippe Villiers' sword on his back. He took a few steps back and walked away from Aruj. The sword was now resting on Aruj's neck.

"What's your name?"

"Aruj"

"Aruj... Red bearded Aruj... Barbarossa..."

Without taking his gaze off from Aruj, the admiral spoke to the Venetian:

"You must have forgotten that the knights have priority when it comes to choosing among slaves, Signor..."

"Benito."

"Signor Benito."

Thinking there was a misunderstanding, one of the guards interrupted and showed the admiral the slaves who had been already selected to serve on the knights' galleys.

"Sir, the knights have already made their choice. There they are! The ones who stand here in front of you are those for sale. He pointed at Aruj. "Believe me, you wouldn't want this man on board. For causing so much trouble, he was imprisoned in the galley for weeks. Besides, as I already stated, the slaves who would be serving you on your ships are there. There's no room left in the galleys, anyway."

With a sudden move, the admiral yanked the guard's dagger from his waist and flung it at one of the slaves reserved to serve the knights, stabbing him in the heart. The man, covered in blood, fell to the ground.

"Now, there is room for one!"

Cervantes reclined back in his chair.

"Aruj spent the entire winter with the rest of the slaves, working in the restoration of the castle walls and serving the knights in their daily lives. Grikko, on the other hand, had been tasked with informing the admiral about the conversations that were to take place between Khidr and Aruj without raising any suspicions."

"So, Aruj discovered that Khidr came to Petrium with eighteen thousand akches to ransom him."

"Oh yes, of course, he discovered, Signor Shakespeare, the admiral was a smart man. He was aware that Aruj would cause him too much trouble while trying to escape from their hands."

"But they could have simply locked him up."

"Without a doubt. But then, they would not have made use of this sturdy young man, right? His family might not be able to recover the ransom the admiral demanded for him in a short time; and Aruj might have remained in a cell, consuming their food, until he got rotten and was of no use to them. Motivating him by making him believe that one day he might earn back his freedom or at least the money he needed to be ransomed was the wisest way to keep this defiant young man under control."

"Yes, it seems that the admiral was indeed very smart."

"Aruj had learned that Khidr had placed all of the money he had saved up to that point in a sac and given it to Grikko."

"Go and give this sac back to Khidr."

"You have got to be out of your mind!"

"I say give it back! And also, take this letter to him."

Aruj extended a piece of paper to Grikko. Grikko's eyes, however, were still fixed on the sac that was sitting on the table.

"He sent you this money so that you pay the ransom and return home. I really don't get why you refuse it."

"This is all his money Grikko. The money he worked so painstakingly to earn. This calamity befell on me, I cannot buy my freedom with my brother's savings."

"So, what are you going to do?"

"I'll work. I'll work and earn the money I need on my own, and then I'll pay my own ransom."

"Hah! Who has ever seen that the knights accepted the ransom a slave paid for himself? You can only see it in your dreams. If it were not the knights who enslaved you but an ordinary Venetian merchant, you might have had a chance. Then, you could have said, "-How much did you pay for me? - This much. - Ok, take what you have paid, and give me my freedom." But the knights...."

"They are not going to sell me to me. They'll sell me to Centurione."

"To Nicolás Centurione? You mean the former knight, who was taken captive by Kemal Reis and then released?"

"Yes, he is a man of influence liked by everyone. He also knows what it means to be enslaved. His being a former Knight is an advantage. He participated in many battles on behalf of the Order. It's unlikely that the admiral will say no to him. I just need more time. First, I must earn Centurione's favor and convince him that I will provide him with excellent service if he ever decides to buy me. After that, I'll start giving him problems and ensure that he thinks it would be in his best interest to get rid of me as soon as possible. Who knows, maybe at that time, I may have the opportunity to buy my freedom at a reduced price. Go and let Khidr know all this. Tell him to take all his savings and sail back to Lesbos. Tell him to wait until he hears from me."

William was listening attentively.

"Grikko went...," said Cervantes. "But not to Khidr; rather, he went to the admiral and told him about all of Aruj's plans. The admiral was pleased to have been informed about everything that was spoken. He had guaranteed to get the best possible efficiency that he ever could get from a slave. Concerning Centurione, he was going to deal with him later. Now, he had to turn his attention to something far more important, something that was giving him a great deal of concern. To finding the Ark which, Phillipe's five-generation ancestor Jean de Villiers who was once the twenty-second Grand Master of the Knights of Saint John, had protected at the cost of his life when Acre fell into the hands of Mamluks in 1291... The Ark, which Phillipe's men had shamefully lost in the Mediterranean just recently."

Cathedral of Córdoba, Spain

Even though it was converted into a mosque in the Middle Ages, the Córdoba Mosque, which had originally been built as a Catholic church by the Visigoths, in the city of Córdoba, the former capital of the Umayyad Dynasty of Andalusia, was one of the most stunning monumental works of Moorish architecture. Each of its one thousand two hundred ninety-three pillars that stood ten meters in height had been constructed out of the world's most exquisite marbles. It was as if the cedars of Lebanon, the pearls, emeralds, and ivories that had been brought from various parts of the Orient had come alive in the mosque's interior ornaments. With its ten thousand silver candle holders illuminating the interior, its minbar secured with golden nails, the engravings adorning both the walls and the ceiling, its extraordinarily elegant mosaics, azulejos[61], red and white painted arches, and the splendor of the pillar heads, the mosque would give the chills to anyone who entered.

When the city had fallen into the hands of the Christians in 1236, and King Fernando III of Castile had entered the mosque for the first time, he had said, 'This place must surely be the house of God'. But since Córdoba was cleared of Muslims, the mosque was also required to be converted into a cathedral. When the king gave the orders to make the necessary alterations, he most likely had not considered the amount of damage that would be inflicted on this architectural masterpiece. Nevertheless, exactly 268 years after the Castilians set foot in Córdoba, none among the people, gathered in this place, this time, to bid farewell to the queen who won the hearts of all

---

[61] A form of Portuguese and Spanish painted tin-glazed ceramic tilework

by conquering Granada, completing the Reconquista, and putting the entire Iberian Peninsula under Christian control, was able to hide their admiration for the beauty of this former mosque.

King Fernando, however, was on that day, furious.
"Felipe? Felipe the Handsome?"

During her reign, Isabel was known for her tender heart and for her prioritizing the peace and welfare of her subjects above all else. She had desired to see the whole of Spain under Christian rule but had not shared the same views with Cardinal Jiménez and Fernando on the use of bloody methods to convert the inhabitants of Granada to Christianity; at least not after she realized her dream and completed Reconquista. She had not found it just to ruthlessly murder the people who long had known these lands as their home. Killing innocent people was an unforgivable sin in God's sight. Hadn't they been punished by God for the errors they made while trying to differentiate between the innocent ones and the sinners? As they took the lives of Muslims and Jews, God had taken from them their only heir to the crown. He had left only Juana alive; but not without taking away her ability to reason.

Isabel had always regarded the weakening of her daughter Juana's mental abilities as God's punishment to remind them of their previous sins. For Fernando, on the other hand, the true punishment of God were the conversos. He feared that those pests, some of whom they banished from the lands of Spain, would soon begin to undermine the Spanish interests on the African coast. And what they needed to do now, without wasting more time, was to suppress those Andalusian exiles before they became stronger on the opposite shores, and if necessary, chase them to the deserts of Africa and destroy them all. But just as he was about to put the plans that he diligently made with Cardinal Jiménez into action, he had learned that the crown would not be handed to him. The true heir to the Crown was their grandson Carlos V who was only four years old at that time. And since his mother Juana la Loca[62] could not possibly inherit the throne, his father Felipe had been proclaimed King until Carlos was of proper age.

Fernando was enraged. The cardinal tried to calm him down.

---

[62] Juana the Mad, Juana of Castile

"Your Majesty, you should know that your concerns are unfounded. Allow Felipe to succeed to the throne. You can be sure that his reign will not last long. Now, with your permission, let us go and say our dear queen farewell on her final journey, leaving state affairs for tomorrow."

Cardinal was right. This was neither the right place nor the right time to discuss the issue at hand. The Spanish Prince of Machiavelli who had always been skilled at abusing his followers' trust in God and pushing them to war, should now bury his queen.

"Very well, Cardinal, but don't forget that I'd like to talk to you about this topic in greater depth."

Jiménez gestured toward the door and extended an invitation to Fernando to attend the funeral. Then, striding through the kings and queens that had come from all over Europe he approached Isabel's lifeless body and turned to face the crowd.

"Spain has lost a queen she cannot sufficiently mourn. We have known the superiority of her intellect, the goodness of her heart, the purity of her conscience, the sincerity of her piety, her justice toward all the world, her desire to give abundance and tranquility to her people. Her errors were those of her education and her century; her virtues were those of a great queen and a great woman. The most important thing that she taught to the nobles was that they were born to serve and not to oppress. She made them remember the oldest of all the Castilian rules that a cavalier of noble blood should treat his subjects with love and gentleness. She believed that freedom could only be the fruit of a wise government. She showed the world the importance of being committed to justice and morality and with her commitment she succeeded in advancing the civilization up to the highest level."

His eyes fixed on Isabel's coffin, Fernando seemed to be listening to Cardinal Jiménez. But the expression on his face was indicating that the noise in his mind repressed the cardinal's voice.

"The passion for wealth and power, Signor Shakespeare, is like a fire that must be fed continuously." Cervantes stood up and walked towards the fireplace, which was about to die out, while it was lighting up the dim room with its warmth and light a moment ago. "If I were to get lost in this glowing ember and not feed the fire with more wood, I would begin to shiver soon."

William was trying to understand where Cervantes was trying to get to.

"The kingdoms are also ruled likewise," continued Cervantes. "If your subjects are living in peace, security, and prosperity, then, they won't need you. If they don't need you, they won't feed you. Because now, you are the only one who is burdening them, both materially and spiritually. They can cultivate their own crops and raise their own children. If they don't have an adversary who will attempt to seize what they have, they don't need your protection."

"Then, the wisest attitude to maintain the power you've already obtained is to maintain the continuity of the conditions that gave you that power."

"Exactly, Signor Shakespeare, and that is to create a permanent enemy against whom you would fight to protect your subjects."

"Wars are what keep armies alive."

"Fernando had managed to get everything he wanted by keeping the nobility on a knife's edge for years. Soldiers, weapons, wealth... everything. The last thing that he would have wanted was for the years following the fall of Granada to be years of peace and abundance for people as Isabel had dreamt of."

"And I guess Felipe the Handsome was more attracted to women than to wars. It's easy to see why Fernando was bothered about Felipe's inheriting the throne."

"Fortunately, two years later, Jiménez's prophecy came out true and Felipe the Handsome died of typhoid fever shortly after becoming ill. And Juana lost the last bits of her sanity, with Felipe's death. Unable to accept his husband's shedding his body with which she was madly in love, Juana would grab a torch, go visit the chapel where Felipe's body was kept, and would force the guards to open his coffin. The woman who kept embracing every night not only love but also death, had turned into a ghost soaring over the palace halls. When Felipe was eventually buried, Juana, who clearly could not be entrusted with a kingdom, was confined in the Royal Convent of Santa Clara in Tordesillas and the golden crown of Castile had once more been placed on Fernando's head. But it had taken longer than he had expected, and the adversaries Fernando would have to deal with on the African coast were no longer merely the Andalusian exiles."

Mediterranean

With their figureheads at the bow and ornaments adorning their sterns, the galleys of this century were like statues gliding on water. Their enchanting beauty seen from afar was covering the wailing of the slaves that one would hear as one got nearby. It was better to die, in this century, than to be put to oars. The galley slaves, strip naked, chained in groups of six to oars, were required to row nonstop to the beat of the guard's whistle for ten, twelve, or sometimes even twenty hours so as to avoid having their backs lashed to pieces. To keep them from passing out, a piece of bread dipped in wine would be placed in their mouths. Those who completely lost their physical strength, on the other hand, would be thrown overboard and immediately replaced with fresh ones. In this century, these galley slaves who had to live under such deplorable conditions might easily change the outcome of a war, especially if they were to rebel as the fight went on.

"The season had arrived, and the hulls had been cleaned and greased before the galleys were once more launched into the sea. Aruj's plans, however, had not gone the way he had hoped."

William flashed a grin.

"I guess he was unable to convince Centurione."

"Oh no, Signor. That winter, Aruj had managed to establish good relations with Centurione. It can even be said that they had become friends. If Centurione was able to buy Aruj from the knights; he would have gladly granted him his freedom in return for a short period of his services. However, neither the admiral nor the Grand Master had agreed to sell Aruj, for they thought releasing a man so skilled in maritime affairs could cause them trouble in the future."

"Aruj must have lost all hope. From then on, he must have become less willing to serve the knights."

"Less willing?" Cervantes was amused. "From that day on, Signor Shakespeare, Aruj had become a real pain in the neck for the knights; and consequently, he had been put in the worst possible place of servitude for a slave and chained to the oars."

"The greatest mistake the knights could have ever made... After all, escaping from a galley must be a lot easier for Aruj, than escaping from Rhodes."

"Given that he opposed the Grand Master regarding Aruj's serving on board, it can be assumed that the admiral must have held the same opinion. But the Grand Master was reluctant to continue feeding a slave whose ransom seemed unlikely to be paid soon, without making him work. Yes, a sailor like Aruj should not have been set free, but if the ransom would not be paid, perhaps it would be better if he died. And if he was going to die, he would die much faster on board."

"So, what did Aruj do?"

"While chained to the oars, Aruj observed the way the knights behaved during an expedition, but he also did his best to drive them all mad."

The soldier approached the commander in desperation.

"If we keep whipping him, he's going to die. It's almost as though he is mocking us. We can neither put him on oars. He is throwing us off our rhythm, which in turn slows us down. He has all the attention of the remainder of the slaves. No one is paying heed to our word anymore."

The commander was enraged. Had it been someone else, he had already minced him into pieces and fed him to the fish; but regarding this Turk, the admiral had orders. And the amount demanded for ransom did not seem that it would ever be paid... They heard a burst of laughter.

"Here, Commander, it's him again."

"I guess I have to deal with this bastard myself."

He pushed the soldier aside and headed toward Aruj.

He had been severely tortured. Blood dripping from the wounds on his back was flowing down his legs onto the deck causing his feet to slip. Aruj, on the other hand, was singing and dancing as though he was not feeling any pain at all.

Having seen the commander approaching, the remainder of the slaves became silent; as for Aruj, he did not care.

"You should learn this dance, Commander; you should not only learn it, but also teach it to all of the soldiers under your command."

"To be enslaved in a galley that takes a hundred captives ransomed by Prince Korkud to their homes... The scent of your homeland must be reaching to your nose, Barbarossa."

"Oh, I wish it was as you say it is, Commander, for the odor of your filthy galley suppresses the fragrance of my beautiful Asia Minor."

The commander took a few steps and approached Aruj; he then gripped his chin and looked him in the eye.

"It is in fact enough that you're breathing, you know that don't you? I mean, how about we cripple those legs, for example, or chop off that long tongue of yours..."

With all his arrogance, Aruj defied the commander.

"I will not care, whether you'll still be breathing or not, you know that don't you, Commander? I mean, when my brother and I will once again get back together; I'm going to engrave the map of the Mediterranean onto your back, whether you are still alive or already dead."

"When you and your brother get back together, huh? You mean your stupid brother who believed that he could save you with the eighteen thousand akches he handed to Grikko? Do you think that the admiral was unaware of what's been going on? It seems that you are ignorant about how well our ears hear."

Aruj spat the blood accumulated in his mouth onto the commander's face. As he wiped the blood off his face with the back of his palm, the commander was trying to keep calm.

"You and your brother will get back together soon Turk, don't worry. Very soon, I promise, I will chain him right beside you. Even a hundred thousand akches is no longer sufficient to save you."

He turned around and called out to the supervising soldier:

"Give the Turk twenty whips for lunch today! I'll be back later for dessert!"

Cervantes threw a piece of wood into the fire.

"But on that day, when the knights' galley was caught in a storm off the coast of Antalya, God would be on Aruj's side..."

Southern Aegean was perhaps the only region in the Mediterranean blessed by regular winds. The galleys that had been beached for maintenance during wintertime and rested in safe harbors, would return to the seas by the arrival of spring. The etesian winds that blew from the north during the summer months, filling the sails, would start right after the sunrise and reach its maximum speed in the evenings, making the galleys to fly above the waters and giving the oarsmen a chance to take a break. And their slowing down just before sunset was an indication that the people on board would have a calm night ahead. That night, however, off the coast of the Island of Meis, the ferocious westerly winds appeared to have no intention of dying down anytime soon. The storm was at its height. Everyone on board was running up and down the deck as the galley swayed like a cradle in the midst of the sea, while Aruj, who had been tied to the mast, was watching all that was happening around him.

"Brail up the sailssss!"

"Commander, we would drift!"

"Otherwise, we'll sink, you idiot. The masts cannot carry this load!"

To ensure that the order was heard by all the sailors on board, the helmsman shouted at the top of his lungs:

"Braaaaailllll upppp!"

Those who were running around, slipping and falling on the deck, those who were throwing up, who were trying to bail out the water with the buckets they grabbed, those who were praying and making a sign of cross on their chests, who were forcing the Muslim slaves pray to Allah, who tied themselves with ropes in order not to fall overboard... It looked like everyone had forgotten about Aruj.

A strong wind finally broke the mast off and Aruj fell overboard. His hands were tied. He was trying hard to swim. As the saline waters of the Mediterranean were scorching his wounded back, he was struggling to keep his head above water, ignoring the pain. When he finally reached the rocks on the shore and with a last-ditched effort climbed up, he burst into a hysterical chuckle.

"The commander will be furious in the morning."

He was exhausted. He had no idea where he was, but he neither had any strength left to stand up. He closed his eyes and passed out.

At the break of dawn, he came to himself with the warm breath of Ali Reis' horse he felt on his face. A few men at the service of Prince Korkud, who was at that time the governor of the province of Antalya, had seen Aruj lying on the beach and had come by to check whether he was dead. As soon as he saw the horsemen circling him, Aruj realized that he was on Turkish soil.

"Thank Allah!"

"For what you are thankful I did not get it, son."

"I hope you'll never have to, sir. If the storm from yesterday hadn't turned the knights' galley upside down, I would still be getting whipped."

A bitter expression appeared on Ali Reis' face. He turned his elderly gaze toward the sea.

"The knights... So, the snake is nested in our bosom now."

"The storm tore apart their mast and tossed me overboard. I don't know what happened to them. I hope they've got what they deserved."

"What's your name, son?"

Aruj was trying to stand up and get himself together.

"I'm Aruj. I am from Lesbos. I'm one of Yakub Agha's sons."

When Ali Reis gestured with his head, one of his men approached Aruj and extended him his hand.

"Jump!"

Following a moment of doubt, Aruj caught his hand and jumped on the back of the horse. Then, together they galloped away.

Though their galleys had been severely damaged, the knights had survived the storm. But now they had no idea how they would survive the commander's rage storming through the deck who eventually learned that Aruj had fled.

"Whose head should I cut off now?" the commander bellowed out.

He was furious. He caught one of the slaves by the arm and stabbed him in the stomach.

"This one would not have mattered!"

He flung the lifeless body into the sea. Then, he slaughtered another.

"Neither this one!"

When the second slave was fed to the fish as well, the commander pointed his sword at the remainder of the slaves.

"None of them would have mattered, except him! Now tell me, whose head I should separate from his body."

As Aruj was cleaning himself up and changing his clothes at Ali Reis' modest home, the long-prevailing silence between them finally broke.

"I know your mother and your father. They are good people. I've heard Elias had passed away, is that right?"

Aruj paused for a moment and then clenched his teeth so firmly that his rage pulsated in his temples.

"He was murdered. Elias was murdered, Ali Reis. The knights severed his head. We were carrying goods; we had just set sail from Lesbos."

"They attack every vessel which comes on their way. The winds of serenity had long departed these waters, son. There's hardly a single day on the seas that passes by quietly. Last month, they've butchered twenty of my finest men."

Aruj took a few brisk steps towards Ali Reis.

"Ali Reis, do you know how many Muslims are being held captive on the island? All are being tortured, all are being whipped to death. We can't just sit here and wait. We must fight against these murderers. Help me! Help me take Elias' revenge."

"Against whom you are fighting, son? What do you have in your hands that would make it possible for you to stand against the knights? You need ships, you need weapons, companions... Where will you find all these?"

"I'll build it myself! I'll build my own ships if necessary. I'd taken an oath, don't you understand? I no longer can lay my head on the pillow in peace even for a single night until Elias is avenged. Until my brothers of faith are saved from persecution, my soul cannot be at ease."

Having seen Aruj's determination, Ali Reis placed his hand on his shoulder.

"Come to Alexandria with me! The Sultan of Egypt requested that I build him ships. Let's go and talk to him. He had a long-standing enmity toward the knights."

Aruj, feeling thankful, held Ali Reis' hand on his own shoulder.

"What about Khidr?" asked William. "What did he do when he heard no news from Aruj?"

"He stayed in Petrium for months and waited to hear from his brother. But when no news came out either from Grikko or from Aruj, he returned to Lesbos and started building himself a bigger boat. No matter what he was going to rescue his brother, either with money or with sword."

"Didn't he ever consider the possibility that he might be dead?"

"No, never. Khidr had always believed that Aruj was alive. Perhaps it was due to his faith in Allah, or perhaps because he had too much faith in his brother, he had not even considered the possibility of Aruj's being dead."

"After all that had happened, all he had left was faith, huh?"

"Faith is something interesting, Signor Shakespeare. It is like the tangible form of hope. It is the proof of the unseen. When one has faith, one would not only hope for God's help but, he would be sure of it."

"What about Grikko?"

"No one saw Grikko again. Neither on the island nor in Asia Minor."

When Khidr entered the house with a letter in his hands, he was almost out of breath. He had run as quickly as he could from the beach to his house and was drenched in sweat.

"Mom! Dad! Aruj! Aruj is alive! I've got a letter from him. He mentions that he will be traveling to Alexandria with Ali Reis!"

Tears of joy welled up in Katerina's eyes.

"Yakub Agha! Did you hear that, Yakub Agha? Our son, our beloved son is alive!". She opened her arms wide and raised her hands up in the air thanking God. "Thank you, my Allah! Thank you you've spared my son! You've spared my Aruj!"

The good news they all had been waiting for had finally arrived. Although it was true that there had been times when Yakub Agha had lost all hope, Katerina knew that this day would eventually come. God would protect his son; Katerina had faith in Him. And indeed, God had protected him.

"When will he come? Does he say anything?" asked Yakub Agha.
"Soon," he says, father. It's possible that he's already in Alexandria."

Payas, Alexandretta

Ever since the Ptolemaic era, the bay of Payas in Alexandretta had been an important commercial port used to transport the timber sourced from Adana to Alexandria. When Qansuh II al-Ghawri, the Sultan of the Mamluks, decided to deploy a fleet of forty galiots[63] to India; he had commissioned Ali Reis to go to Payas and purchase from there timbers suitable for shipbuilding. Ali Reis, however, when he asked Aruj for his assistance in loading the timbers on board, had some other ideas floating around in the back of his mind.

"From these will be built forty galiots, at least that's I've heard. I think you can build more. Forty galiots, we can present to the sultan; regarding the rest we keep silent."

Aruj smiled.

"There's more than enough timber here to build a small armada. Even just loading them onto the ship will take at least a week."

They heard a sailor crying out:

"Knights are on the horizoooooooonnnn!"

Everyone was alarmed. Though they would usually intimidate the locals with a few gunshots and sail away, the knights who had recently begun to penetrate deeper into the shallow waters of Asia Minor were a great source of discomfort for the people living in the region. And this time, it seemed as though the galleys were heading straight toward the port.

---

[63] A small galley boat propelled by sail or oars that has 16-24 seats, two masts and 2-10 small caliber cannons. It has a capacity of 50-150 people.

Ali Reis took a deep breath. He was demoralized.

"They must have heard of the timbers."

With his gaze fixed on the galleys, Aruj mumbled under his breath:

"They must have heard of me."

Aruj was looking forward to engaging in combat, but Ali Reis convinced him to give up the idea.

"Those are heavily armed war galleys, Aruj. They'll smash us as if we are insects. We must drive the ships ashore stem-on and run inland."

Ali Reis was right. They had no other choice but to abandon their ships, and the timbers, and make their escape. Aruj was fuming with rage. The fact that he had to run away when all he wanted to do was draw his sword and sever each of their heads off one by one, was hard on him. They mounted on their horses and rode towards the inland of Payas. As for the soldiers who let Aruj slip through their fingers and returned to Rhodes with nothing but the timbers they seized, they were going to be severely punished for their incompetence.

Ali Reis, upon learning that Prince Korkud, who had just recently been appointed as the governor of Manisa, would soon be leaving Antalya, thought that they might ask him for help; and at the inn where they stopped by to take some rest, he told Aruj what he had in mind.

"Let's ride to Antalya, Aruj. Let's go and talk to Prince Korkud. The brazen behavior of the knights has been bothering him for a very long time. It's possible that he'll lend us a hand."

Ali Reis was an unusual man. Even though he wouldn't talk much, it seemed as though he had seen a lot while trading in these waters. He had long been sailing back and forth between Alexandretta and Egypt and had cultivated good relations with Qansuh II al-Ghawri. Although he gave off the impression of being a man with a short fuse; in spirit, he was calm. He had always been kind to his men and attentive to their requirements, which was why they regarded him so highly and showed him such respect. The knights were certainly their greatest enemies; and Ali Reis, having years of experience, would usually predict where the threat would come from and prefer to plan his routes accordingly so as to avoid engaging with the knights in a sword-to-sword battle. Was it because he was scared, or because he was no longer as young as he used to be, Aruj couldn't help but wonder. As a matter of fact, it was because of neither.

"Let's ride, Ali Reis," Aruj said in despair.

Ali Reis smiled slightly.

"But first, you should eat something. Get some sleep and rest. If you lose your strength, you will not have the energy even to lift your arm when it is time for you to make your sword speak."

Ali Reis was right. The only thing that Aruj was nourishing was the flames of vengeance within. He was neither eating nor sleeping properly.

"Now, it's time to cultivate patience, son. Listen to what Shams Tabrizi says: '*Whatever happens in your life, no matter how troubling things might seem, do not enter the neighborhood of despair. Even when all doors remain closed, God will open up a new path only for you. Be thankful! It is easy to be grateful when all is well. A Sufi is thankful not only for what he has been given but also for all that he has been denied.*'[64] This path which is unseen to you now will first take us to Prince Korkud. Have a good sleep tonight, son, we have a long way to go tomorrow.

Cervantes reclined back.

"It was true that that a long way to go, but it was an open path. Prince Korkud had long known and liked Ali Reis. When he heard the story of Aruj, he called him to his presence; immediately wrote a letter to the qadi[65] of Smyrna[66], and ordered two small galiots with twenty-two seats to be built for Aruj."

"Two small galiots? But how could Aruj possibly challenge the fleet of the knights with two small galiots, Signor Cervantes?"

"Scorpions are small too, Signor Shakespeare, but how lethal the poison they have within. With these two small galiots, Aruj would soon be as lethal as a scorpion in the Mediterranean. He equipped the galleys, gathered around him levends, paid homage to Prince Korkud, and received his blessings. Then, he set sail to where he had been longing for."

---

[64] Shams Tabrizi

[65] A Muslim judge who renders decisions according to Islamic law in civil as well as criminal matters

[66] İzmir

William had grasped what Cervantes meant by the smirk that had settled on the corner of his lips.

"To Lesbos!"

Aruj's unwillingness to part ways with Ali Reis was written all over his face. He placed his hand on the old man's shoulder.

"Join me! Perhaps it's time... perhaps it's time to quit trade, huh?"

"I can't, son. It's been a long time since I locked my sword in a chest. The times are changing. It seems more blood will blend into the waters of the Mediterranean than ever before. But if such brave hearts like you have sprouted in these lands, then it means, the empire would stand long."

"It would be great to have by my side someone like you, someone in whose mind I can put my trust..."

"Set my mind aside, and put your trust in your own heart, son!"

He took a small leather-bound notebook out of his belt and handed it to Aruj.

"If the stars happen to go dim and the darkness falls on you; if the moon were to descend into the waters and you lose your way, open and read it, son, so that you turn your gaze inwards; so that you leave aside the moon and the stars and find the sun within..."

"What is this?"

"Something for you to read every once in a while, son."

It was time to set sail. After expressing gratitude to Ali Reis, Aruj turned to his men:

"You sail to Djerba. I'll stop by Lesbos. I'll meet you in Djerba in three weeks."

Naples, Italy

"Every man is for himself... Whereas you could have become a real prince."

"I've had so many chances to kill him..."

Machiavelli was not surprised to see Cesare, whom he had not encountered since their last meeting in Imola, confined in the dungeons of Naples. In the years following Rodrigo Borgia's death, Borgias' arch-enemy Della Rovere's ascension to Papacy as Pope Julius II had heralded the downfall of Cesare.

"Although I have warned you about not putting your faith even in God, I really struggle to comprehend how you could put your trust in that hypocrite Della Rovere, who spent his life trying to erase the name of Borgia from the pages of history."

In a fit of rage, Cesare leaped to his feet and grasped with his hands the icy iron bars of the dungeon. He was exhaling flames like a bull that had been cornered and fatally stabbed in the back.

"It's not over yet!"

Machiavelli did not lose his composure.

"It's over, My Lord. Borgias are over in Italy. In order to ensure that no traces of the Borgias were left on these lands, Della Rovere even had the graves of your ancestors been dug up and uncovered their bones. The sacks that will accompany you in your journey to Spain, are stuffed with the bones of members of your family."

"So, I'm being taken to Spain," murmured Cesare.

"I've heard that King Fernando has reserved a special place for you in the dungeons of the Castle of Chinchilla."

"Naples... Spain's never-healing headache... I am sure that I will find a way to come to terms with the king."

"The curtain of the play that France and Spain had been performing in Naples for a while will never close. But speaking from my own perspective, I do not believe that Fernando would agree to anything that you would offer to him. In this regard, he has Gonzalo Fernández de Córdoba at his command. But if you... perhaps if you..."

It was finally time for Cesare to embark on his journey to Spain. Having seen the guards who came to take Cesare to the galleon Machiavelli stopped speaking. While being taken out of the cell and dragged to the stairs, Cesare had to learn what Machiavelli had in mind.

He cried out:

"Perhaps what? Perhaps what?"

Machiavelli knew that Fernando was a King who had achieved great accomplishments while hiding behind the guise of Christianity; but he was also well aware that he was, in fact, a ruthless monarch. Even though he knew for a fact that it was the last time that he would ever see Cesare, he still went on and said it.

"Perhaps you can tell him about the Ark!"

Cervantes stood up, grabbed the jug of milk that was sitting on his bookcase, and poured part of the milk into a bowl. He, then, placed the bowl on the table.

"As Machiavelli had predicted, Cesare's mentioning about the Ark to Fernando would not be any use to him. But this rumor would excite the cardinal; and with an insatiable thirst for power, Jiménez would ferociously sack the North African coastline in the days ahead, to get his hands on this relic before anybody else."

"For whom is that milk?"

"For Mia and Mancha, of course."

"Mia and Mancha?"

"Yes, it's their lunchtime. They'll be here soon."

Just when he concluded his sentence, two kittens, having smelled the aroma of the milk, came out from under the couch, meowing, and ran next to Cervantes' feet.

"Oh, come here little sweethearts."

Cervantes kneeled down, scooped up the kittens, and placed them on the table to drink milk. He could now continue the story while William was smiling in bewilderment. But of course, if only he could recall what he was talking about.

"What was I telling?"

"Cesare..."

"Oh yes, Cesare... Cesare's relocation to Spain had been entrusted to competent hands. To make sure that he was thrown into the dungeons of Spain, Pope Julius II had commissioned Andrea Doria, the Genoese commander who had recently become a blazing star catching everyone's attention. Andrea's stories of naval success as a condottiere were spreading throughout the Italian city-states by word of mouth, and the elegance of his magnificent galleon which he had built in Genoa's best shipyard was fascinating everyone who saw it. But a cell was a cell. Even if it was a golden one, being imprisoned was a nightmare for Cesare. He had recalled the day he put Caterina Sforza, Countess of Forli, in chains, locked her in a golden cage, took her to his father, and had her kneel down. It seemed as if history was repeating itself. But, this time, it was Cesare who had been confined."

Andrea approached Gonzalo Fernández, who was looking out over the sea while leaning against the railings of the galleon that was sailing toward Spain.

"There was no need for you to accompany me. I, myself, could have ensured that he was delivered to King Fernando. As the Viceroy of Naples, you must have more significant matters that you have to deal with."

"I sail with you, not because I do not trust you, Signor Doria. The power struggle in Naples taking place between France and Spain has turned into guerrilla wars. I must report to the king on this matter. And also..."

Andrea did not fail to notice his hesitation.

"Also?"

"It is imperative that I discuss my ideas with him regarding his objectives in North Africa. The surface that Spain is trying to dance on is much more slippery than he believes it to be. It seems that the overly ambitious nature of our King would soon drag us all into greater conflicts."

Gonzalo Fernández was a commander renowned for his commitment to putting the adversary to the sword to its last man, even in situations in which the opposing army had conceded defeat and hoisted the white flag of retreat. He appreciated the king's intense desire to strike at the root of the Andalusians who had fled to North Africa, but he was also worried about the ongoing unrest in the Mediterranean. It was possible that there might be even more perilous threats that likely to await the Spaniards on the Barbary Coast. The campaigns that would be organized might keep them preoccupied for a longer period of time than they expected, which would in turn place an additional financial burden on Spain and cause an unnecessary loss of manpower. Even if all these risks were to set aside, it was an indisputable fact that France had been seeking for the slightest opportunity to catch Spain weakened in order to attack. In such a case, King Louis, would waste no time and invade not only Milan but also Naples. The commander had felt that he was obligated to confer with the king, inform him of the potential threats that they might be required to face, and warn him.

"So, it seems that your queen's passing away was a great misfortune for Spain," remarked Andrea.

"It is, Signor Doria. In my humble opinion, King Fernando's actions will soon stir up the hornet's nest."

Andrea was not interested in carrying on this conversation they were having on the political affairs of Spain. He neither had a king nor a queen that he had to give account. Unbound by a yoke of a ruler, he was a mercenary serving whoever paid him the most. If it was Genoa today, then it was Genoa. Tomorrow it might be France, and then, maybe one day, it would be Spain...

"You are right, Signor. As one of the senior commanders of the Spanish military forces, I'm certain that the king would place a high value on your counsel. Now, if you would excuse me, I'd like to retreat into my cabin and relax for a while. Enjoy the rest of the journey. In case you need anything, my men will be at your disposal."

Pleased with Andrea's hospitality, Gonzalo Fernández bowed his head and thanked him.

"Please, enjoy your rest. I'll see you at the port of Málaga."

The bowl was almost emptied. For the sake of that last drop of milk, the kittens had dragged it all the way to the edge of the desk, causing it to roll over and fall at William's feet. Cervantes opened his hands wide.

"They do this all the time!"

William smiled, bent down, picked up the fallen bowl, and placed it back on the desk. As the kittens licked their paws and cleaned their cheeks, he turned his gaze towards Cervantes and watched the old man caressing the kittens with a compassionate smile on his face. He enjoyed the scene. A man who would not hesitate to stab his sword in his enemy's chest, during a battle, could give milk to his cats at home and play with them without caring whether they were Muslims or Christians. "How strange", William thought and laughed at his own thoughts. Even the idea of a cat being Muslim, or Christian had seemed absurd to William. But if religion didn't apply to cats, why did it apply to man?

A serious expression covered Cervantes' face. It was clear that, in his mind, the story was continuing its course at a top speed. William placed his thoughts inside one of his mental drawers which housed matters that he later would reflect on and directed his attention back to Cervantes.

"As Andrea was taking Cesare to Spain, Aruj had already arrived in Lesbos together with the three Venetian galleons he had captured off the coast of the Island of Euboea…"

Euboea, Aegean Sea

After spending some time in the waters of the northeastern Mediterranean, they eventually had set their route toward Lesbos. But the weather had turned bad, and the reversed winds had whispered in their ears that they had a grumpy visitor that they would have to welcome by night. Storm was coming.

The levends, drenched by the waters rising from above the galiot's ram and washing the deck, had started to complain.

"Reis, storm is at hand, we have to take shelter in Euboea!"

However, when they entered the bay, they saw three Venetian galleons that had already dropped anchor. The galleons warned the approaching galiot with three shots of cannon fire.

Mehmed turned to Aruj:

"I suppose they courteously tell us that we should go and find ourselves another shelter."

"By cannon fire? That's an unusual take on how to exhibit courtesy, Mehmed."

Upon seeing that the galleons were in a more advantageous position than they were, Aruj contemplated for a while. Should he have gone his way and risked the storm, or should have summoned up the courage?

"You will not make us wrestle with the storm tonight, will you, Reis? Let's seize these galleons. We can move them aside to make some room for ourselves, and then, drop anchor."

Aruj looked into Mehmed's bright eyes and noticed the arch smile that smeared across his face.

"They don't call you Mad Mehmed for nothing, do they, Mehmed?"

Mehmed grinned like a Cheshire cat.

"I take it as a compliment, Reis!"

They had nothing but their hooks, daggers, and swords at their disposal in order to throw themselves on board as they got abreast. The Venetians not only outnumbered them, but it was also evident that they were significantly better equipped. But a little bit of madness would save the day in these waters. One had to be a little mad like Mehmed.

Aruj called out to his levends:

"Slack the port, haul the starboard braces."

The levends started executing the orders. They would stay out of the firing range, approach the galleons from the port side, sail downwind and maneuver to block their route of escape. And as soon as deployed themselves in the desired position, they were going to rain down on the adversary the arrows they had dipped in tar and set on fire.

"Reeeeaaaady to Taaaack!"

Aruj's plan worked out perfectly. The galleons that were stuck in the bay had their sails pierced, their decks destroyed, and their masts set ablaze. When the Christians mobilized to put out the fires, Aruj threw himself on board alongside his men.

Mehmed was standing on the deck, trying to catch his breath. He placed his sword on his belt and spoke to the Christian captives:

"Now, I'm going to untie a few of you. Lend a hand in moving these galleys a little bit to the side. There's enough room for all of us here."

Aruj, upon hearing Mehmed's words as he wiped the sweat off of his forehead with his blood-covered hands, couldn't help but let out a hearty laugh.

"You are madder than said, Mehmed!"

Lesbos

It had been years since he had seen his family. Aruj had entrusted his lateen sails to the Aegean winds and fixed his gaze on the Emerald Island appearing on the horizon. The greenest of all the islands in the Aegean... He thought how much he missed the aroma of the olive oil, the scent of the freshly baked bread rising from the stone ovens, and the taste of the Aegean's most delicious sardines. Then, he recalled his mother, her cotton-like hands... How halfhearted she was when she came to bid them farewell. The loss of her youngest son, Aruj's being taken captive must have crushed her to the sharp reefs of indescribable grief. Khidr... How was Khidr doing lately, Aruj wondered. He thought back to the times they had spent sitting on the rocks facing the sea and imagining that they waged war against the enemy. Then, a shroud of darkness descended on his heart, and a desire for vengeance burned brightly in his eyes. He had recalled the day when the knights decapitated Elias.

Since then, he had been waking up in the dead of the night from his nightmares, drenched in sweat. He thought of the slaves chained to the oars and being whipped to death, those who were thrown overboard and fed to the fish for they no longer had the strength to row, those who were drowning in these waters while Aruj and his family were trading pottery... Aruj now had a much better understanding of the reason why his father had always been reluctant to tell them about the times he served the Ottoman Empire as a janissary. All had to be avenged, he thought. From then on, every cross that he would come across in these waters would be an enemy of Aruj. He closed his eyes and searched within his heart for a bit of mercy that was left but was unable to find.

With his gaze set on his home, where he knew he wouldn't be staying for long, he muttered from Sappho[67]:

'You may forget but let me tell you this,
Someone in some future time will think of us.'

The salvo fire levends launched to greet the islanders caught him off guard. He was so engrossed in his thoughts that he had forgotten that he had ordered his levends to fire the cannons. His levends appeared to be men he could rely on. Prince Korkud had given at Aruj's command his best men. Aruj was grateful. But the real surprise was, in fact, awaiting him on the Island of Djerba, located off the coast of Tunisia. Prince Korkud had told him to get his brothers from Lesbos and sail there. Aruj would certainly follow his orders, but when he inquired out of curiosity as to why, Prince had simply smiled and said, "You just go!".

Osman quickly grabbed up the heavy anchor and flung it at once into the waters of Lesbos. Then, he turned to Aruj:
"Reis, we've arrived. Your boat is ready. The men are waiting to take you ashore."

Osman was a sturdy young sailor. Since he was never patient and acted without always thinking first, his friends would usually call him "Bodos", which means "half-cocked". Aruj had understood better why he was nicknamed as such when they decided to attack the three Venetian galleons they encountered on the way to Lesbos. Bodos was always in hurry. While the levends thought thoroughly, calculated the risks, and planned their attacks accordingly, Bodos would generally have already snatched his mace and plunged into the fight headlong. He was neither a tactician nor a strategist. He was a quick man, who did not give much thought to anything.

Aruj reproached Osman:
"Well, you're early again! You should've waited till we got closer! What are we going to do with your impetuousness?"

Osman laughed. Once again, he had failed to hold himself back. Waiting was surely not in his vocabulary.

---

[67] A famous Ancient Greek lyric poet from Lesbos.

The islanders who had raced to the shore after hearing the salvo fire were shocked to discover three Venetian galleons following the wave steps of a small galiot. Some of them had kept their calm, while others, recalling the assault they suffered a few years ago, had taken the bags they kept ready and fled to the mountains. When they realized that it was Aruj, Yakub Agha's son, returning to the island, they were going to come back to the village complaining, but would be labeled as being cowardly hens and mocked by those who had managed to keep their calm.

Khidr was thrilled when he saw the approaching galiot and raced home. He had taken with him Katerina and Yakub Agha, and together they had rushed towards the shore. Khidr had sensed; it was Aruj, his beloved brother, approaching the island.

As soon as he saw his family awaiting him on the shore, Aruj waited no more and jumped into the waters. His heart filled with longing he rushed ashore and gave his family a big hug.

"Mother!"

Katerina couldn't believe her eyes. Her prayers had been answered.

"Oh, My Allah! Look at this young man! My once little boy had become a sturdy young sailor!"

The days he spent at the seas had changed Aruj profoundly. With his hardened bones, muscular arms, and his sharp-edged face chiseled like a statue he had been transformed into a genuine sailor. He squinted his fiery brown eyes and looked at his mother with a smile revealing his snow-white teeth. Isaac was likewise surprised by how much Aruj had changed since they had last seen each other.

"Hey! I liked your beard!"

Aruj hugged his brother and then rubbed his beard.

"They'll remember this beard forever brother, rest assured brother!"

He reached into his belt and pulled out a sword wrapped in a piece of green velvet, embroidered with jewels on its hilt, and handed it to Isaac. Isaac couldn't hide his admiration as he gazed upon it.

"Where did you find this?"

"I took it from a man whose hands were blood-stained. Since I also took his arms, he would no longer need it."

The expression on Isaac's face grew serious. His brother had returned, but it was clear that he was not going to stay long. He seemed to have had plans. Isaac did not say a word.

Aruj did some looking around. His eyes were searching for Khidr.
"Well, where is Khidr?"
"Right behind you brother! As always!"

Aruj knew this voice. Aruj had long missed hearing this voice. As soon as he turned around, Khidr gave him a hug so tight that he was almost going to break Aruj's bones.
"Thank Allah, none of my enemies are as strong as you are. If that weren't the case, how desperate my situation would be."

Just like Aruj, Khidr had also changed. He now was a twenty-eight-year-old young man. In the absence of his brother, he had taken care of his family and built a boat for himself.

Aruj looked at him from head to toe, then, gave him a pat on the cheek.
"Hey! Such a handsome sailor you've become!"
"Yes, but the girls on the island are still asking about you. No one is interested in me!"
"Fools, they are! Moreover, they should know that I have only one beloved."

As he said his last words, Aruj had turned his face towards the sea, towards his one and only beloved. Khidr had understood; his brother had returned but it was clear that he was not going to stay long. He did not say a word.

Málaga, Spain

Andrea's galleon approaching the port had caught everyone's attention. Its hulk had been constructed out of some of Europe's finest oaks, while the masts on which the sails were let out were made up of some of Europe's most durable pines. Hundreds of shipwrights, carpenters, and blacksmiths had put laborious effort for this galleon which was built in Genoa's best shipyard.

Back then, galleons would mostly be built for commercial purposes, and their construction would cost their owners a significant amount of money. The Genoese, however, were literally obliged to build for themselves merchant ships, because the barren hinterland of Genoa and the surrounding Alpines were not allowing them to engage in any other activity other than maritime trade. Genoa was a republic of the merchants that was run like a company rather than ruled like a state. And the most critical thing for these wealthy aristocrats of feudal origin who regarded themselves to be importers of eastern riches to Europe was the alliances they had established over the course of years. For them, alliance meant peace, and peace meant free trade. And to be able to freely engage in any commercial activity, they had founded a number of commercial colonies and vehemently supported the maritime power of the Kingdom of Spain throughout the Mediterranean. However, the waters of the Mediterranean had started to become more turbulent following the years of the Reconquista's completion. The expansionist policies of the Christian princes were no longer the only threat. Pirates were lurking in almost every bay of the Mediterranean. Piracy meant war, and wars would bring commerce to a standstill.

After losing his father, Andrea had pledged to offer no respite to pirates hunting in these waters, and had this magnificent galleon been built solely for this purpose. He would serve as an admiral for the kingdom that paid him the most and drown the pirates in the Mediterranean at any cost.

When they arrived at the port, the royal guards were waiting for Cesare Borgia to be delivered to them. As Cesare was led to the upper deck after being taken out of the cell he had been imprisoned, Andrea and Gonzalo Fernández walked over to the guards.

The head of the guards greeted them both.

"Welcome to Spain! I'll inform His Majesty that the prisoner was successfully brought to Spain. My men will take him to the dungeons where he will be imprisoned for the rest of his life."

Cesare's head had been wrapped in a sack. Andrea's men got him off the galleon and handed him over to the guards. Gonzalo Fernández mounted on one of the horses and turned to Andrea:

"Signor Doria, thank you for the journey. I shall leave, now. I'll see to it that this Borgia is placed behind the iron bars, and then I'll pay a visit to the king. Take good care of yourself, and may the winds be with you, always."

It was the best of all wishes for a galleon captain. After all, the galleons would rely on the friendly winds to advance and therefore were always at a disadvantage compared to the galleys, which could readily maneuver even during the calm summer months, thanks to their oars.

Andrea thanked the commander by slightly bowing his head and watched Gonzalo Fernández gallop away.

The head of the guards turned to Andrea:

"I hope you enjoyed your journey."

"Both the seas and the winds were quite friendly, Signor."

"I'm glad to hear that. And how long are you planning to stay in Spain?"

"A couple of days."

"His Majesty has requested that I let you know that he would like to see you in the palace."

Apparently, there were several issues over which Fernando wanted to talk to Andrea. Andrea was aware that people all around the Mediterranean had begun invoking his name thanks to the recent uprisings he suppressed in Italian seas. His growing reputation in these water as a capable and reliable captain had to be the reason why they had entrusted with him such an important prisoner like Cesare.

"It is an honor," said Andrea.

Then, he jumped on the back of a horse and together with the guards that accompanied him, he rode to the palace.

Lesbos

"But you have just got here!"

Isaac looked at his younger brother Khidr, hoping that he would support him in his argument. But Khidr remained silent.

As soon as he saw Aruj, Khidr had understood that he was not going to stay in Lesbos for long and would be sailing soon. Khidr had known it all along, as a matter of fact, Khidr had been looking forward to it. The anguish he felt about Elias' death had been nested deep in his heart, as well. As he was building a boat for himself during all those months he had not heard from Aruj, during which he did not even know whether his brother was still alive, Khidr had waited for this day to arrive. Aruj would come, and when he came, he would say Khidr, "Come!", "Come with me, we have vengeance to take,". Isaac, too, was inconsolable when he learned about Elias's death, but Khidr was different, he could not easily accept. Even if years would pass, he would not forget. Yet, he could wait. He knew that everything had its time. He would not rush into things like Aruj, but he also would not consider the misfortunes that befell them as Allah's will like Isaac did. An agony of such sort could not just be regarded as fate. And it was worth the wait! Aruj had come and said to him "Come!". While his heart was more than ready to answer his call, how could Khidr refuse Aruj's offer and say "No!" to his brother?

Isaac, upon coming to the realization that he would not be able to secure Khidr's backing, turned to Aruj:

"What about our mother? What are we going to say to her?"

Aruj looked Isaac in the eye and spoke firmly:

"Times are changing, brother. After everything that I've been through, after all that I've seen so far, I cannot pretend as if nothing has happened. For you, perhaps, Elias died once; but for me, he keeps dying over and over again at each night I surrender myself to sleep. And there's more! We can no longer trade in these waters with the same ease and security that we once did. There are currently more than three thousand Turks who are enslaved and who were waiting for the day they would be flogged to death. And this is just the situation in Rhodes. During the summer months, they are chained to the oars, and during the winter, they are forced to dig ditches, clean the ducts, cut wood, carry stones, and reinforce the walls. The Mediterranean is no longer the same Mediterranean we are familiar with. Your life depends on how mightily you fight in these waters!"

"I am in!"

Khidr had not hesitated. His brother was right, but even if he was not, it would not have made a difference. Khidr had no intention of staying behind this time; he had no intention of letting his brother go alone. Both turned their gaze to Isaac. Isaac was struggling to find the right words. He was the eldest of them all. He also had to think about their mother. Yakub Agha was no longer as young as he once used to be. Even though he was willing to embark on this journey, he was also aware that he could not stay away from this emerald island for an extended period of time.

He let out a long sigh.

"I'll sail with you to Djerba. I want to make sure that you know what you're doing. Then, I'll return... then, we'll see..."

From the bottle of wine that Yossi had opened to celebrate Aruj's return, only a few sips were left in their cups. After Isaac had finished speaking, they toasted to their reunion, to their brotherhood.

"Djerba... Why Djerba?"

There were other islands in the Mediterranean recently seized by the Ottomans. Kemal Reis, who was in command of the Ottoman naval forces at the time, had been storming through Ionian waters. Even the unfortunate incident occurred in Cephalonia had not slowed them down. William was wondering as to why Prince Korkud had sent them to Djerba while there were so many other alternatives available.

As he petted Mancha, fallen asleep once the milk was done, purring on his lap, Cervantes replied:

"They had to be neither too close to nor too far away from the European shores. Besides, Aruj would need men. In order to succeed in his path, he would require brave crew members such as sailors, helmsmen, scouts, cooks, carpenters, caulkers, gunners, and archers. Prince Korkud was aware of it. And at that time, the Island of Djerba, located off the coast of Tunisia, was a haven for pirates. Among them, there were renegades, debt-ridden merchants, and slaves who had had enough of being whipped. The majority of them were men who had been hurt in some way; who did not follow any norms and who were not accountable to any laws. They had no families, no children, not even a country, and thus, had nothing to lose..."

"A bunch of thieves!"

"There were a great number of skilled and experienced seafarers among them, Signor Shakespeare; men who regarded their ships as their homes, men who committed their lives to the sea. They were experts on all there was to know about the Mediterranean. They knew these waters like the back of their hands. The only problem was that they were in total disarray and that they never trusted anyone but themselves. But they also had an insatiable thirst for adventure. And Prince Korkud had well foreseen how they may have contributed to the Ottoman navy, in case they were gathered under the command of a courageous man like Aruj."

"How could he be so certain that these men would accept to be subject to someone who was less experienced at the seas than they were?"

"You are right, Aruj would need help. But the help he needed was already on its way. Kemal Reis and Piri were on their way to Djerba!"

Málaga, Spain

Andrea maintained his silence as he entered the door the accompanying guards had opened and proceeded to the hall where King Fernando and Cardinal Jiménez awaited him. Along the way to the palace, he had refrained from engaging in any sort of conversation, provided only cursory responses to the questions posed to him, and made it clear with his demeanor that he wanted to appear in front of the king as soon as possible. He had no idea why the king wished to see him in person, but he had speculated that King Fernando was probably going to play a more active role in the affairs of the Mediterranean after his queen's death. Though it was true that the guerrilla fights were still going on, at least for the time being, Spain seemed to have been successful in expelling France from Naples. Fernando must have had other plans.

"Welcome, Signor Doria!"
Andrea bowed down and greeted the king."
"Your Majesty..."
"I hope you enjoyed your journey to Spain. Yet, if your galleon is as exceptional as Gonzalo Fernández reported, I see no reason for it to be otherwise."
"Compared to your magnificent war galleons serving in the royal navy, my ship can only be considered an ordinary trade vessel, Your Majesty."
As a member of the Italian nobility, Andrea knew very well how to talk to a King. Fernando smiled. Fernando's passion for wealth and power was no secret to anyone. He was always pitching for more. And Cardinal Jiménez, the Inquisition's sharp sword, was there solely for this purpose; to ensure that the days Fernando ruled the Mediterranean would come soon.

The cardinal addressed Andrea:

"Who knows Signor Doria, perhaps one day, those war galleons will be given under the command of an experienced captain like you."

Andrea had the sensation that the cardinal had been quietly observing all the steps he so far had taken in the Mediterranean. It was probably his idea to bring Andrea before the king's presence. Even his assignment regarding Cesare Borgia's transfer to Spain may have been nothing more than a pretext.

"It would be a privilege for me, Your Eminence, to have the opportunity to serve His Majesty at some point in the future."

Fernando turned to Andrea:

"The cardinal is right, Signor Doria. Your endeavors for the Genoese navy are worthy of praise. I have to acknowledge that the cries of the French were heard all the way from Spain. Your strategic intelligence appears to outshine your navigational expertise."

Andrea bowed his head to show his gratitude.

"Knowing the enemy, Your Majesty... Knowing the enemy is just as crucial as being familiar with the battlefield."

"Signor Doria, the Mediterranean is starting to warm up. The commerce that takes place on these seas is the backbone upon which the European economy is based. The long-standing partnership that Genoa and Spain have maintained in the Mediterranean is more crucial than it has ever been. As you are also aware, the fact that Spain has once again taken control in Naples is a tremendous acquisition in terms of securing the investments that Genoa has in both Naples and Sicily. We shall most surely proceed with providing special commercial privileges to Genoese merchants operating in Spanish territory. In return, we count on your continued support for Spain's naval forces so that peace may be maintained in these waters. Whoever rules the Mediterranean rules entire Europe. I have no doubt whatsoever that the Turks will quickly come to the same realization and will not squander time in taking appropriate action. The Ottoman Empire is like a dragon on the verge of waking up. Although its head has not yet reached us, when its breath begins to scorch Europe, we will need the waters of the Mediterranean to put the fires out."

"What is it exactly that you require of me, Your Majesty?"

Fernando took a few steps toward Andrea.

"The corsairs, Signor Doria, the Turkish Corsairs. Very soon, we will be compelled to encounter them. I want you to maintain a vigilant watch on them at all times. I am interested in knowing each and every step they take."

Silence prevailed for a while. Andrea shifted his gaze to the cardinal. Whatever the king was thinking, it was clear that, behind it, was the cardinal's mind.

"Those people whom you expelled from their homes are not only quite familiar with the lands, but they also have an impeccable command of the Spanish language. When they dress like the Spanish, it is almost impossible to distinguish them from the Christians. And they are now burning with vengeance on the African coasts. They will cooperate with the Maghrebis as well as the Turks and arrive on our shores in small boats. They'll raid the coastal towns where the centralized government is ineffective, hampering trade causing trouble for all Christians. I am quite concerned, Your Majesty. If you had allowed them to stay, it would have been much easier for you to maintain control over them."

Lightning bolts flashed in Fernando's eyes.

"We don't want to control them, Signor Doria, we want to exterminate them! Those we expelled from the Spain are not warriors; nor are they knowledgeable on military matters. They are artists, scientists, authors, craftsmen... But as you have just stated, they are going to ignore their inadequacy, and in the hope of reclaiming their homes, they are going to approach the corsairs for help. Meanwhile, we will make sure that they are unsuccessful in their endeavor. If we want to carry out unrestricted operations in the Mediterranean, our presence along the coast of North Africa needs to be bolstered. We will establish garrisons and bribe the local rulers to assure their allegiance. If it becomes necessary, we will launch campaigns and send our naval forces to attack their port cities, but we will under no circumstances let them to band together under a flag and interfere with trade in the Mediterranean. Mers El Kébir is in our grasp, next is Oran. Rest assured that you will not be alone in those waters. It won't be long before you may see the Spanish flag waving along the African coast!"

Andrea had understood Fernando. The king was asking for him to maintain his acute sense of smell and gather the necessary information that would soon deliver the Mediterranean into his royal hands. He visualized himself as the Grand Admiral of the Spanish Armada. "Why not?" he thought; and smiled.

"Rest assured, Your Majesty, I'll even lead their carrier pigeons astray and make sure that they fly to Spain first."

The king seemed to have been satisfied with Andrea's reply. The meeting could be considered over.

"Yes, Signor Doria. I wanted to take this opportunity to personally thank you for your assistance in delivering Cesare Borgia for us. But I have one more request from you."

"I'm listening to you, Your Majesty."

"I have a present I would like you take to Sheikh Yahya, the governor of the island of Djerba. A horse trainer, one of the best. I am counting on you to see to it that my present gets to him unharmed."

Cardinal Jiménez added as if to highlight the relevance of the king's request to what they had been discussing for a while.

"You know, Djerba is a pirate's nest."

Andrea made a mental note of the cardinal's remark and turned to the king:

"Rest assured, Your Majesty, your present will be delivered."

He,then, bowed down with respect and asked for the king's permission to leave.

As he made his way to the door, Cardinal Jiménez accompanied him.

"Before you leave, Signor Doria, there's one more thing I want to ask you."
"Please, go ahead."

"The prisoner you have delivered us, Borgia, Cesare Borgia. I heard that he had uttered a few words in the vain hope of being released. I heard that he uttered a few words. A few words which I found inappropriate to share with the king before making sure that he speaks the truth..."

"What can I do to be of service to you, Your Eminence?

"He referred to an Ark that was rumored to contain some stones of death. A holy ark that ensures victory in battles. An Ark that is said to have been lost in the Mediterranean... If..."

The cardinal took a little pause.
"If?"
"If this ark is truly what I think it is..."

While Andrea waited for the cardinal to finish his sentence, Jiménez hesitated whether to convey his thoughts as they were.

"Yes, Cardinal?"
The cardinal took a deep breath.
"If this ark is what I think it is, it is imperative that we find it, Signor Doria."

The cardinal thought that there was no need for Andrea to learn more about the matter for the time being. Andrea, on the other hand, had no knowledge of such an ark, but even the rumor of it had piqued his interest.

"May the winds be favorable, Commander!"

Lesbos

All the preparations were complete. The levends had rested and regained their vigor, the ships were caulked and greased, the necessary repair work had been carried out and the sails were mended. A few weeks in Lesbos was certainly not enough to satisfy Aruj's longing for his mother, but the time was ripe to set sail. Katerina had come to the shore to bid farewell to her sons and send them off to an unknown future. With her delicate fingers, she gently caressed their faces.

"May Allah bless you, always. May God watch over every one of you and keep you safe."

Her voice had come from such depths that Khidr found it heart-shattering. Even though Katerina had full confidence in each of her sons, yet still, she was their mother.

Aruj cupped her teeny hands in his own calloused palms and softly looked her in the eye.

"We'll return, mom. We'll bring you good news. You just keep us in your prayers."

"You are always in my prayers, son, you know that don't you?"

"I do mom, of course, I do."

Isaac brushed aside a stray hair resting on Katerina's face.

"Don't let your heart be shadowed by grief. We'll all be fine. Don't you ever worry. Besides, I'll find my way back home sooner than Aruj, I promise."

"It would be good, son. You know... your father is not well. And the three of you now leaving together at once..."

They said their farewell. Katerina, who had long been secretly praying to Jesus Christ in addition to performing her Muslim practices, drew a sign of the cross on her sons' chests. Khidr smiled and gave her mother a warm embrace.

"We are Muslims, mom, I think you forgot."

"God is one, son, I think it is you who forgot."

The moment Aruj stepped onto the deck he felt the fresh breeze caressing his heart. He knew; nothing other than being on the seas would evoke in him the same feeling. Nothing was blessing his soul more than the seas did. It was his one and only beloved. It was a love that was beyond hope, a love that could never be explained by reason alone, and that was precisely why it was so beautiful. Aruj had been born into the seas, and as he was traveling south in the arms of his beloved, this time, he also had his brothers with him. From under his mustache which appeared even more crimson due to the orange beams of the setting sun, Aruj smiled. And when Khidr approached him and put his arm around his shoulder, he felt even more wonderful. Khidr looked his brother in the eye. The joy of being together had also lit up Khidr's face.

"Finally... we're finally walking on the seas together, huh?"

Aruj responded with a smile. They had set sail for a new life, and the Mediterranean had already blessed them with a calm and warm weather on the first day of their journey.

As the day faded to night, they dropped anchor near the rocks off the coast of one of the islands in the Aegean. Under the awning covering the poop deck, they were having their meals and chatting with one another. The levends were all in a cheerful mood, with the exception of Cemal, who was sitting quietly in a corner, gazing at the moon glade, smoking tobacco.

Aruj called out to Cemal:

"How are we going to put a smile on your face? I'd rather not have a miserable dude on board."

"He fell in love, Reis!"

It was Sinan speaking. He would enjoy teasing Cemal. As a matter of fact, Cemal was not the only one he loved teasing, Sinan would make fun of everyone whenever he got the slightest opportunity. When he chose a victim for himself and began mocking him, it meant that the unfortunate man would have to put up with him for weeks. Until such time as Sinan would either forget about the incident or come up with an even more amusing topic for himself to make fun of.

Aruj let out a hearty chuckle.

"What? He fell in love again? Wasn't it just last month that you had fallen in love?"

Cemal was a sentimental man. On each island they stopped by, in every tavern they visited, he would find himself a beautiful woman to whom he would generously offer his heart. A pair of dark smoldering eyes would tear his soul apart from the seas, enslaving him on lands; and he immediately would begin fantasizing about putting his sword aside in favor of a more settled life with wife, and children.

"Oh, Reis! I was hoping that at least you wouldn't make fun of me!"

"I'm not making fun of you, Cemal. I'm just trying to understand."

"Understand what, Reis. It's not me to decide whether to fall in love or with whom I fall in love."

Sinan chipped in.

"How quickly you took back your heart from Agnes of Chios and gave it to Aisha of Lesbos. Besides, we were together all thorough the time."

"I know of a Gulbahar from Smyrna. I thought she was the very last one." said Aruj.

Following Aruj's remark, the laughter of levends echoed off the rocky shore. Mehmed turned to Aruj:

"Reis, we'd better leave him on of the islands on our way and let him marry the first woman he sees."

"The first woman I see? I'd rather marry the first woman I fall for!"

"The first woman you see or the first woman you fall for, what difference does it make? You're constantly falling for the first woman you see, anyway."

Aruj fiercely opposed.

"I'll never let that happen! Don't waste your breath! How will I ever find an archer as skilled as him? He had already pinned down at least five men when we attacked the Venetian galleons before you even had your swords drawn."

Aruj was right. Cemal would shoot the flying eagle in the eye. This young man, leaned against the railing daydreaming about the plump red lips and jasmine-scented hair of Aisha he met a few days ago in Yossi's inn, would change in an instant upon hearing the battle cries, and would hunt down a third of the enemy, even before the ships got abreast.

Mehmed tried to justify himself.

"We were so dumbfounded when we saw Osman fighting the Venetians with the anchor that he had picked up that we couldn't find our swords in our belts. And Reis, you also know that; it was not a scene that one can witness every day!"

Mehmed was also right. When Osman couldn't find his mace on the day they attacked the galleons; he had grabbed the anchor, thrown himself onto the enemy deck, and attacked the Venetians. Osman had smashed the chins and noses of at least twenty men in three rounds while spinning around and swinging the anchor with all his strength and sent them all like pebbles to the azure waters of the Aegean.

Khidr was stupefied.
"With the anchor? Oh, my Allah!"
"He is Bodos! He always goes half-cocked! As soon as he smells the scent of the enemy, he never thinks twice; he grabs his mace, and runs to the deck breathless. Now watch!"
Aruj gestured with his hand for the levends to keep silent. And when silence prevailed on the deck, he exclaimed:
"Ambuuussshhhh!"

Osman, who had already called it a day and retired to the foredeck cabin, grabbed his mace, and dashed as soon as he heard his reis' cry. While on the one hand he was trying to pull himself together, he was also spinning around himself like a wooden peg top tossed by a capable hand.
"Make waaay!"

They burst out laughing. Aruj was making a valiant effort to be able speak:
"Thank Allah that we've never been attacked by the enemy so far while you pee, or else, it would have been really unpleasant for all of us."

It was getting late. Except for the levends who were going to take over the night watch, they should all go to sleep. "Good night"s and "Sleep tight"s were exchanged and the levends retired to get some rest. With the dawning of the new day, they were going to set sail to Djerba.

Aruj walked towards Isaac and placed his hand on his brother's shoulder.
"If only you knew how happy I am that you agreed to join us."
"I know, Aruj, I am happy as well. But you know..."
"I know. You must soon return to home, to your wife. You must take care of our mother, and deal with the work you've left unfinished. You were okay in Lesbos. Being a carpenter, a potter like our father, and carrying goods to Syria and Alexandria, is all that you expect from life."
"I am not like you, Aruj. I want a peaceful life."
"Don't you see brother? A different future awaits us all. With your experience in carpentry, we're going to build the best galiots anyone has ever seen. Our enemies in the Mediterranean will tremble with fear when they see the flag of Barbarossa!"
"Barbarossa?"
"Yes, Barbarossa... The Admiral of the Knights had addressed me like this... Barbarossa... Red Beard..."
Isaac grinned.
"Now I see why you let nobody touch your beard."

The look in Aruj's eyes had become chilly and the lines on his face, more defined. The man who was laughing a few minutes ago had gone leaving his place to someone filled with vengeance.
"This beard will be the Christians' worst nightmare, I promise you, brother!"

He had recalled the days he spent in captivity. It was not only Aruj's physical features that had changed. Isaac was aware of it. The storms surging through his heart could topple even the greatest armadas. And that was exactly what he was planning. He was going to reflect the storms within, onto the waters of the Mediterranean.

Isaac placed his hand upon his brother's shoulder.
"I'll be with you, always, just like the winds!

When his storms calmed down and the sun began to shine through his eyes, Aruj's face lit up with joy.

"Look! Tomorrow is going to be a beautiful day!"

They gazed upon the stars sparkling like diamonds sprinkled on black velvet.

"Let's get some sleep!"

Mediterranean

Andrea was gliding through the Mediterranean headed toward Djerba. His gaze on the horizon, he was pondering on the conversation they had with King Fernando and Cardinal Jiménez. The cardinal was right about his assessment; Island of Djerba, located in the Gulf of Gabes off the coast of Tunisia, was indeed a pirate's nest which lacked proper administration since the death of Abu Osman, the Hafsid Sultan of Tunisia. Due to the freedom that it provided, it had become a favorite stop for the pirates. Because the governors who came to power after Abu Osman had been turning a blind eye to all the illegalities as long as they got their share of the booty.

Djerba was a small island embellished with white-washed houses with red clay roofs and surrounded by azure waters. Its main settlement was Humt Suk. It was an island with a semi-tropical climate where the fragrance of the date palms, olive trees, and eucalyptuses blended with each other; a place where camels, cloth dyers, and potters lay over the poppies grown in the shades of the fig trees and enjoyed the idleness whipped up by the hot Mediterranean sun.

The waters that surrounded Djerba were very shallow, and the island was well-known for its tides. It was necessary for the sailors approaching the island to take the soundings and cast the leadline overboard as soon as they spotted the date palms of the island and drop anchor at a distance of at least five miles off the coast. Only the galiots, which were the smallest of all the vessels, were able to enter the harbor provided that the captain was familiar with the route.

As a matter of fact, Djerba was nothing more than a heap of sand where the sailors spent their share of the booty to rip up the clothes of prostitutes who awaited them in the taverns; where they drank all night and woke up the following morning without even remembering with whom they spent the night; and where they mended, equipped, or sold their ships at noon which was the only time of day when they were somewhat sober. And the men who inhabited this place were the men who lived one day at a time. If they could fill their tummies during the day, find a woman in the evenings to spread her legs, if they had enough money in their pockets to get drunk; they would stay in Djerba. They would get the most recent news from the spies, sell their share of the booty in the marketplace; and when they ran short of cash, they would once again, hoist their sails. However, it was true that Djerba was the heart of the Barbary Coast. It was the place where all going ons in North Africa was talked about. Therefore, it was certainly no coincidence that King Fernando had decided to send a gift to Sheik Yahya, the so-called governor of Djerba.

With the clamor coming from the lower deck, the thoughts that had been occupying Andrea's mind were flushed away. When he headed toward the stair to learn what was going on, he saw one of his sailors come up with a desperate look on his face.

"Commander... one of the chains has been broken. The slave is hurling at us whatever he finds around."

Andrea shoved the sailor aside and proceeded downstairs.

On the lower deck, it appeared that all hell was broken loose. When a nail securing the iron rings to which the captive was chained became dislodged and fell loose, he had started hurling whatever he found in the vicinity at the sailors responsible for keeping an eye on him. And since the sailors knew how sensitive Andrea was about delivering the king's present to the sheikh unharmed, none of them had dared to approach and take measures to protect themselves from all those utensils raining down.

Andrea roared:
"Stop it, right away!"

A porcelain plate that sailed right past his head and slammed into the wall behind him before he could even finish his sentence was certainly not the kind of response Andrea was expecting. He tried to keep his calm. He could vaguely see two black eyes peering at him from beneath the sack that was covering the captive's head. The captive was gasping for air. Andrea took advantage of a momentary pause and approached.

"If you don't want to travel under worse conditions for the rest of your journey, you'd better stop acting like this!"

His threat did not seem to have been effective. Another response came, this time in the form of a copper jug aimed straight at Andrea.

Andrea ordered his men:

"Seize him!"

Two of his sailors seized the captive by the arms. The captive, on the other hand, had not given in and was struggling to break free from their grasp. When the sack slipped and the captive's long, dark hair tumbled across her shoulders, everyone rendered speechless.

"A woman..."

With a swift shake, the woman broke herself free from the clutches of Andrea's men. As she stared from behind her long, wavy hair that had fallen on her face, the flames of rage bursting out from her dark eyes seemed that they could set the entire galleon ablaze at once.

Andrea spoke to his men:

"Leave us alone!"

When the sailors left the cabin, Andrea took a few steps toward the woman.

"So, a woman... a woman who trains horses..."

He was trying hard to cover up his bewilderment. It was the first time he had ever met a woman horse trainer. The woman, on the other hand, was as though challenging Andrea with her posture by standing tall and staring him in the eye.

"What's your name?"

She was just about getting ready to take the frying pan sitting on the counter and smash him on the head when Andrea got her by the wrists and trapped her against the wall.

"Hooo, hoo... It looks like you are the mare that needs some training here! Now tell me, will it be possible for us to communicate with words?"

She was gasping for breath. Her chest was still heaving due to her struggle to free herself from the grip of the sailors.

"Felipa... My name is Felipa..." she said.

"So, Felipa, I'll let go of you now. And in return, you'll stop hurling pots and pans at me. If you have a important problem, maybe I can help."

"An important problem? What important problem do you think I might have, Commander?"

Having seen that Felipa had quit fighting and started talking to him, Andrea let go of her wrists.

"You're taking me as a slave to a place I don't know, to serve someone I've never met. Does this problem of mine, which is literally a matter of life and death to me, sound important to you as well?"

"I'm taking you to the sheikh as a gift. Likely, you will spend the rest of your life training his horses in Djerba. There are thousands, who would prefer such a life over a life of freedom in which they struggled with poverty and diseases."

Felipa shouted with rage.

"I am not a slave!"

After a short period of silence, Andrea took a deep breath.

"So, you are not a slave, huh? Who then is, the one who was shackled with chains, boarded on a galleon, and being taken to her new owner with a sack covering her head?"

Felipa's eyes welled up with tears. Andrea reached up and touched her stained cheek. If only she had been able to cry, not only her cheeks but also her heart may have been cleansed; but Felipa was a strong woman, Andrea had understood, those tears were not going to fall from those dark eyes. Her despair had caused her to become somewhat calmer.

"Who are you? Where are you from?"

"From Andarax"

"You are not Spanish..."

"I am a Moor."

"All right..."

"The Inquisition arrived in our village, seized every Muslim living in Andarax, locked them inside the mosque, burned them alive. I was in the valley with my horse. I had gone for a ride. As soon as I saw the thick smoke coming from the village, I rushed back. They had sealed the entrance with massive wooden boards..."

Andrea could hear the screams of those who had been burned alive from the look in Felipa's damp eyes.

"The soldiers caught me. I couldn't open the doors They all died..."

Andrea had understood. In an endeavor to purge the Spanish lands of all the non-Christians, the Inquisition had swept through the country, marched from one village to the next, and left behind streets that smelled death. He wanted to console Felipa.

"Hadn't you been in the valley at the time they arrived, you would have died as well, you know that don't you? They were going to shut you in that mosque and burn you alive along with the others."

Lightning bolts flashed in Felipa's eyes.

"I'd rather be burned there together with my family and die free than spend the rest of my life as a slave!"

At those times, it was unusual to run into a woman who was so enamored with her freedom. For someone of this nature, being enslaved was even more dreadful than death itself.

"Be careful what you wish for, Signorina!"

Andrea turned back; as he walked toward the door, Felipa spoke in a calmer tone.

"I'll find a way and escape, you know that don't you, Commander?"

"Never from my galleon; whenever you like, from the hands of the sheikh."

As he was just about to leave the cabin, he stopped.

"You don't have to stay here. If you'd like, you can come up to the upper deck. I'll send my men down to set free you from the chains. If you don't hit them on the head with the pottery you grab, I'd appreciate it."

Mediterranean

As they sat under the awning, Aruj was explaining his brothers about his long-planned goals.

"We need to convince as many men as possible to join us in Djerba. Since we sail toward their nest, I want the most capable ones."

Isaac was concerned.

"But how are we going to convince them, Aruj? We cannot say "Come with us, swing your swords, and claim your share of the booty. They'll want to see the gold with their own eyes and weigh the sacs with their own hands first. They are pirates. They are not like us; they're not brothers to us."

"If that's the case, then we'd hand over the sacs."

Isaac took a deep breath and leaned back.

"Which sacs, Aruj? We are sailing towards Djerba in a galiot with three Venetian galleons in tow. We don't even know what awaits us there. Unless there's a secret place you stored the gold; I personally don't have enough to share with all those men."

"Summer is not over yet, brother!"

Aruj had raised his voice. He was aware that it was not going to be easy, but he did not want to start off feeling discouraged right from day one either. Khidr put an end to the icy hush that had descended upon the brothers.

"We cast anchor and come ashore first, then see what we can do. There must be a reason why Prince Korkud insisted that we should go to Djerba. We can sell the galleons there; in these waters, they're useless to us, anyway. What we need is vessels propelled with oars, galiots that will allow us to maneuver effortlessly."

Khidr had caught Aruj's lowered morale halfway down the road and restored it.

"There will be another galiot waiting for us on the island. With the money we'll receive in exchange for the galleons, we can equip the galiots, and set sail for one last hunt before the winter. If we succeed, then, we can use half of the loot to turn Djerba into a secure base for ourselves, and regarding the rest, we can share it with those who would be interested in joining our cause."

Having heard the clamor of levends, Aruj stopped speaking. And when they all rushed to see what was going on, they noticed the approaching galleons.

Bodos had already picked up his mace, while Sinan nocked his arrow. Mad Mehmed was standing with his hand on his forehead shading his eyes from bright sunlight as he was trying to figure out by looking at their flags to which kingdom the galleons belonged.

He turned to Aruj:
"It seems that they belong to Papacy, Reis!"
"Look at the waterline! Their hulls are submerged. They must be carrying a substantial load."
Aruj smiled. Isaac's question had literally been answered.
"You were asking me about the sacs, weren't you brother?"

Yahya rushed down from the main mast and informed Aruj:
"Three-masted galleons... Each has at least fifty cannons."

Yahya would enjoy spending time on masts and keeping watch. He usually would be the first one to notify and warn the crew, whenever a galleon appears on the horizon. With eyes no less sharp than an eagle, Yahya could identify in an instant, the kingdom that the ship belonged to, as well as the number of cannons and oars that were on board and give report. Aruj had once told him in a sarcastic way that it would have been nice if he also could tell them the number of men on board so that he could divide his levends into groups accordingly. But when Yahya had replied by saying, "There seem to be three hundred and fifty men on board, but the weather is a bit misty, Reis, I may be mistaken"; Aruj was left speechless.

"Fifty cannons on each, huh!", muttered Aruj.

He was thinking. He needed the booty. But because they had not yet arrived at Djerba, there were not enough men on board to fight and seize three galleons with a total of fifty cannons. Khidr studied the expression on his brother's face, trying to read what he had in mind. It was not a prey that could be easily ensnared but Aruj had to be quick to decide. The levends were getting restless. The slightest hesitation they would see on Aruj's face could deter them all at once.

"What are we going to do, brother? Are we going to fight or flee?"
Aruj's eyes met with Mad Mehmed's. It was as if Mehmed was telling him with his eyes that one needs to be a bit mad in these waters, one needs to be a bit like Mad Mehmed.
"We decide more easily if we run out of options," replied Aruj, and then, ordered his levends:
"Pull half of the oars on board and tie them with ropes!"
The levends began looking at each other. None had understood the reason why Aruj had given such command.
Having seen that they hesitated, Aruj roared:
"Do as I say and pull the oars on board!"

Having heard Aruj's roar, levends got themselves together at once. They pulled the oars on board and secured them with ropes as they were commanded. Everyone was waiting for their reis' next command. Aruj did not make them wait long.
"Toss the oars overboard!"

After the oars were tossed overboard, Aruj turned to Khidr.
"Fleeing is no longer an option."
Khidr flashed a grin and drew his sword.
"So, we'll fight, brother!"

Abandoned like orphans, floundering helplessly in the midst of the sea, the square-rigged galleons were desperately praying for a breath of wind. Even though galleons were the perfect vessels for withstanding the raging ocean waves and carrying loads of cargo at once in their lockers; the fact that they could not maneuver easily in the shallow waters of the Mediterranean would always put them in a more disadvantageous position. The only aspect in which galleons had an advantage in the Mediterranean was in their high firepower. With their cannons stationed just above the waterline in the portholes below deck, they could easily open fire from above against the galleys and galiots, which had relatively lower decks; and if they deployed well, they could sink the enemy ship in a short time. However, chasing a galiot in these waters was like chasing a centipede; because the oars that these low-deck vessels had on either side were giving them a tremendous advantage whenever they needed to maneuver.

Aruj now had the chance to approach the galleons with the remaining oars and easily maneuver without getting within the firing range of the cannons that were stationed on both the port and the starboard sides of the vessel. And the levends did exactly as they were commanded and rowed toward the papal galleons headlong.

When the Christians started running around to avoid being targeted by the arrows that Cemal and his men raining on them, a commotion broke on the upper deck. But arrows were simply an appetizer because Bodos Osman, who had already grabbed his mace, was getting ready to serve the Italians the main dish. It was imperative that he be the first person to throw himself aboard; he could not let anyone else take his turn. Otherwise, the levends would have to endure his sullen face for who knows how many days.

When they got abreast with one of the galleons, the nets, ropes, and hooks were thrown. The levends set the oars aside as they drew their swords. This was perhaps the most valuable lesson Aruj had learned during the years of his captivity: to select his oarsmen from among the levends. The entire crew needed to be comprised of fighters for the absence of slaves ensured that there would be no revolts. And "no revolts" would mean that it was the swiftness of their feet, the superiority of their wits, the strength in their arms, the sharpness of their swords, and the bravery in their hearts that was going to determine the outcome of the fight. As Aruj stood confidently on the deck looking at the Christians whom his men took captive and tied after they had taken control of all three papal galleons; he once more felt assured that none of his levends lacked any of these traits. He was now in possession of six galleons in addition to his own two galiots, as well as enough funds to transform Djerba into a naval base for themselves and persuade any sailor to join him in his campaigns.

Djerba

As Andrea dropped anchor off the coast of Djerba, the last beams of the setting sun were giving way to the rising moon. The night was falling down, and the kingdom of darkness was ready to reign. Andrea was feeling depressed. Though he knew not why; the fact that he would soon be required to hand Felipa over to her new owner was troubling him. This woman with dark eyes who stormed through his entire galleon had kept Andrea's mind preoccupied all along the way. "What if I say, she escaped?" he thought. They were in the midst of the sea; how could it be possible for her to have escaped? "What if I say, she died?", Andrea said to himself. It was not convincing either; for nobody would believe that one of the most reputable admirals in Europe had failed to deliver a captive unharmed. There was simply no way for him to avoid handing over Felipa. Then, he recalled her shining dark eyes. His lands were struck by lightning bolts, his seas heaved by violent storms.

When turned his gaze to the island, he noticed a group of men waiting on the shore mounted on white horses. They must have been the sheikh's guards waiting for Felipa's arrival. It seems Sheikh Yahya was pretty excited and looking forward to getting his present. Andrea felt even more depressed.

Felipa was brought to the upper deck with her wrists tied and her head covered with a sack. The men were ready. Felipa was ready. Even the words Andrea had planned to say to bid her a farewell were ready... If only he was able to speak...

Meanwhile, the thoughts, which were racing through Felipa's mind as she was gazing at the fluttering sea, were as if drifting along by the currents of the Mediterranean.

When they landed ashore, sheikh's men greeted them.
"Welcome to Djerba, Signor Doria. I hope that the journey was a smooth one."

Andrea turned his gaze to Felipa. This young woman, who hurled at them whatever it was in the galleon that she managed to get a hold of, must have been exhausted from her own wrath for she was looking calm. Andrea would surely have preferred to wrestle with the raging waters of the Mediterranean rather than a duel with Felipa. The journey was certainly not a smooth one. Neither on the deck nor in Andrea's heart...

"It was pretty smooth, thank you for your concern. The season provided us with all the convenience we needed."
"It was not the weather that concerned me, Signor. As you also are aware, sailing in the Mediterranean is not as safe as it once used to be. Pirates, who have recently increased in number, are also taking advantage of favorable weather as such."
Andrea smiled with arrogance.
"During all those years I set sail in these waters, you don't suppose I've been fishing for octopus, do you Signor? I have enough nautical and military experience to deal with any pirate ship that I may encounter."
"I'm glad to see that my concerns were unfounded and that you have arrived at Djerba without any incident. So, we can set out and deliver King's present to our sheikh. Also, Sheikh Yahya wanted me to inform you that he would consider it a privilege if you could join him for dinner."

The hues had gone red as the day desperately tried to cling on to the last beams of the sun, and the silvery moon had begun to rise on the horizon so that the streets would not be plunged into complete darkness all at once. Around this time of the day, all of the sailors in Djerba, except for those who were going to stand watch, would flock to the inns to enjoy their drinks and blow off some steam. They would chat about the most recent events that was taking place in the Mediterranean until it was late at night, and then, their tipsy gaze would begin to drift toward the plump-breasted women. Andrea was not going to stay in Djerba for long. He was mercenary hunting down pirates, and he had no intention of becoming prey in this den. He had planned to set sail as soon as he got the information he was looking for without revealing his identity much. And he was very much aware that sheikh's residence was not the best place where he could smell the air.

"I'm quite tired. If you'll excuse me, I need to get some rest tonight. But I'd like to pay him a visit in the morning if it also suits your sheikh."

"Of course, Signor Doria. I'll relay your request. If there's nothing else I can do for you tonight, I ask for a leave. As you would also guess, Sheikh Yahya is looking forward to seeing the king's present."

Andrea looked at Felipa who had already mounted on a white horse. "I hope she'll forgive me one day," he thought to himself.

"Nothing special, thank you."

As they galloped away Andrea began walking toward the inns where he intended to spend the night. The night had descended, and the narrow streets of Djerba were illuminated by the flickering lights emanating from the lanterns that were hanging on doorsteps. Coughs rising from the wheezing chests of the boozed were echoing through the streets as if they were cursing at their solitary stars glowing alone in the darkness of the night. A usurer, who seemed to have had the pouch he tucked in his belt stolen, was chasing a ten-year-old who was running away laughing, and threatening to shatter his bones as soon as he caught him. But Andrea was neither aware of anyone nor what was going on around him. His mind was too preoccupied to notice even the lascivious looks that the women of Djerba were throwing at him from behind their dark eyelashes as they strolled around extending out their tanned legs while holding their skirts up to their thighs. He had to dust himself off and get out of this melancholic mood as soon as possible. What he now had to do was to find an inn where the events on the Barbary Coast were being discussed, to sit in a quiet corner, have a drink, and give an ear to the conversations going around.

When he heard the humming of people conversing with one another inside one of the inns, he paused. He took a few steps and peeked through the filthy window. It seemed to be crowded inside. He walked down the weathered stone stairs, pushed the wooden door open, and quietly entered the inn.

Mehmed was laughing at what Cemal was saying, while Khidr, Aruj, and Isaac were following them without any haste. As for Sinan and Yahya, they had stayed on the ships along with a few other levends, in order to keep watch.

Upon hearing Cemal's hearty laughter, Khidr turned to his brother:
"He seems to have got his joyful mood back. I suppose he's through with the love of Aisha of Lesbos."
"Don't be surprised if he finds himself another one inside the inn who has a slim waist and full lips."
"Have you ever been in love, brother?"
Aruj laughed.
"You mean, while I was chained to the oars? Or, being flogged in the dungeons?"
Isaac jumped in.
"So, you say, you didn't have the time?"
"In other words."

Love was an emotion that none of them had experienced it in its fullest sense so far. Given his handsome looks with its snow-white teeth, strong stature, quick with and cheerful character, there was no woman who would not have felt herself drawn to Aruj; yet after all that he'd been through in the recent years, Aruj had taken an oath. The only thing that his mind was occupied with would, from that day on, be his ships. He had one and only true passion, and that was the sea. He did not believe that he could ever find in any woman the depth, the serenity and that heartly bond he had found in the waters of the Mediterranean. The sea was his, yet at the same time it was not; Aruj was bound to the seas, yet at the same time he was free.

For Isaac, it was enough if he simply liked a woman, shared his life with someone whose company he would find enjoyable. He desired a settled life in which he could raise his children, just like the life of his father. At least that was his intention before Aruj came to Lesbos and dragged him into this adventure. Isaac wanted to be a father. Was whether or not he was truly in love with his woman that important?

Khidr was different from both of his brothers. He could not spend the rest of his life engaging in carpentry. Just like Aruj, he was also after a life that would take place on the seas. However, he did not have that strong passion for the seas in the same way that Aruj had. They were bonded in a different way, the sea was his friend, his companion. But he also needed a woman on whose bosom he could rest his weary soul, who would enchant him with the fragrance of her skin and brighten his days with her words. A woman who would tenderly caress his crimson-brown beard with her delicate hands and heal his wounds with a gentle touch of her lips. Khidr had to be engrossed in the love he felt for his woman. He had to be in love with her beauty, her depth, her compassionate heart, her generous spirit, and profound wisdom. He was not like Isaac. Simply "liking" a woman had never been enough for Khidr.

"Do you believe in coincidences, Signor Shakespeare?"

"If we have faith in God, then, we also should have faith that there's something called fate, shouldn't we, Signor? Is what you're asking me in a hushed tone whether or not I have faith?"

"It is clear from the fact that you preferred to reply with a query, that there are times during which you question your own faith. Are you buying time, or you also have doubts about the existence of God, Signor?"

William relaxed his posture and leaned back in his chair. He was certainly not trying to buy time, but it could neither be said that he had a flawless argument that supported and proved to himself the existence of God.

"I do have faith in God, Signor Cervantes. It's impossible for me to dismiss the fact that there are occasions when I can feel God's presence. It is impossible for everything that has ever taken place in to be the consequence of random occurrences. We cannot possibly be making our journey along the path of life merely by colliding with one another in a chaotic system." He paused. It was as though he was searching for a glimmer of light in Cervantes' eyes that would back his intuition. He inquired with a sense of doubt. "We cannot, can we?"

Cervantes bent down and lift Mia up who was sound asleep snuggled up at his feet. With a belly full of milk, the kitten curled up and settled on Cervantes' lap, purring.

"I believe in miracles, Signor Shakespeare. When I found Mia and Mancha they were almost on their last breath. Had they been abandoned or whether anything dreadful had happened to their mother, I do not know; but they were making a valiant effort to hold onto life. Their faces were completely covered with mud and dust, and it was clear that they hadn't eaten anything for days. It was a dark and silent night, and I heard Mia calling out to me with a weak voice."

All of a sudden, a rumble was heard. The three-story house where Cervantes lived was in a residential neighborhood of shelter houses that overlooked the south branch of the Esgueva River, which had been built near Puerto Del Campo[68] to meet the demand that was created as a result of the surge in population that occurred after the capital was moved to Valladolid. An intolerable odor was being produced as a result of the combination of wastes of the slaughterhouse that were being thrown into the river combined with the garbage from the neighborhood. But the beggars, children, and prostitutes who were competing with one another to collect the usable stuff among the trash would usually not care much about this heavy stench. And this was also the case with Signor Esteban, who would spend his days off sitting in the butchers' clubhouse located on the ground level of the building.

Signor Esteban had one of the prostitutes in his sights and had been watching her for quite a while. He was thinking that he was not giving out his intentions much, but people around him were aware of the thoughts that had been going through his head. And Signora Esteban, who now had reached the point where she could no longer ignore the rumors being whispered in her ears, had finally raced to the clubhouse, and broken her long wooden broomstick on her husband's back.

While William ran towards the window, Cervantes did not even move.

"It was one of those rare nights, as a matter of fact, when the streets were quiet."

After Signora Esteban dragged her husband home and things settled down, Mia's purrs became audible once again bringing serenity to the souls of the two men who happened to come together in that room on that very day whether by coincidence or by fate.

---

[68] Campo Gate

"At that precise moment..." said Cervantes, "As I was just walking purposelessly in the dark quiet of the night, this little kitten called out to me with a faint "mia". She was on the verge of taking her very last breath. Do you think it's possible that it was just a coincidence?"

"Isn't it possible?"

"It isn't", Cervantes should have to say. It was what William would like to hear from him in response. Life couldn't be made up of coincidences. He thought about the works he produced. Could it be possible that he had become a playwright by chance, that he was writing plays simply because life had led him in that direction? It was impossible! He had been born a playwright! Man would soon or later fulfill the purpose for which he was born. There ought to be a point to living. There had to have been a purpose behind his existence. After all, he was not the one who had chosen to have been born into this world. Or was he? He was unable to recall. William was even unable to recall his infancy.

Cervantes read all that William had in mind from the expression on his face, from the lights flickering in his eyes. He smiled.

"No, it cannot be a coincidence," he said; "in the same way that Khidr's encounter with Felipa that night was not a coincidence."

They all came to a halt when all of a sudden, they heard a scream that rang through the streets. Felipa had found a way to escape the clutches of sheikh's men and was now fleeing like a scared cat. She was being chased by three men and already out of breath, so it was only a matter of time before she fell into their hands. When she came across the Barbarossas and noticed the way they dressed, Felipa thought that they might be Muslims. She cried out for help.

"For the sake of Allah, save me from these men!"

Khidr caught the gasping woman by the shoulders. Aruj and his levends stood in the way.

"Hey heyyy! Take it easy! Three men against a woman, eh? I'm astounded by your bravery!"

The guards were breathing fire. They drew their swords.

"Stand aside, barbarian! Or I'll cut your tongue off!"

It took only a couple of minutes. Aruj, known for losing his cool when threatened, drew his sword without giving the guards another chance to speak. Upon seeing three lifeless bodies lying on the ground drenched in blood, Felipa froze in Khidr's arms.

Mehmed moved closer to Aruj, sliding his sword into his belt.

"When you went insane, we've knocked them all down in haste. But wouldn't it be better if we spared one and asked what they wanted from this woman?"

Khidr slowly moved Felipa away from his arms and looked at her face. Felipa, on the other hand, still gasping, was now aware that she was the one expected to answer their questions.

"I don't know where to start."

Holding his sword dripping blood from its tip, Aruj took a few steps toward Felipa.

"How about starting with your name?"

"Felipa... My name is Felipa."

"Well, Felipa, who are you? Where are you from? And what did these men want from you?"

"I am a Moor. In fact, my mother is Spanish, my father is Moor. They were... they were, at least."

She was still shaking. Khidr took his waterskin out of his belt and offered it to Felipa.

"Here! Drink some water! It'll help you to calm down."

Felipa took a deep breath. She had no idea who those men were that she encountered as she was trying to escape from the sheikh's men. It was possible that she had pulled them into a situation where they shouldn't have been involved in the first place unwittingly. She turned his gaze towards the dead bodies lying on the ground. It hadn't taken a few minutes for those three souls to leave their bodies. Felipa had not seen the moment of their death though. Khidr had pulled her into his large chest and hugged her so tightly that it was as if he had wanted to prevent her from witnessing such a scene. It was as if he had cared for her. Perhaps she might trust him. She desperately wanted to trust him. But she couldn't.

"I... I don't know... I have no idea why they were after me."

No one seemed to be satisfied with her answer.

"I really don't know. They suddenly emerged from out of nowhere and began chasing me. I had to run away. One can trust no one on this island."

She had not even come close to convincing them. Some eyes were not very good at backing up the lies that spilled from the mouths. Khidr had realized; it was clear that Felipa was hesitant to place her trust in these men whom she had just met. She was right, if honesty was what they expected from her, then, they were the ones who needed to put in the effort first. He briefly introduced himself and his brothers.

"I'm Khidr. These are my brothers, Aruj, and Isaac. Mehmed and Cemal are our comrades. We are the children of the Ottoman. We will not hurt you. We all saw that those men were not interested in talking at all. Now, tell us, who are you? No matter who you are, we are going to let you go, anyway."

"I hope you don't..."

Her heart had spilled from her lips in an instant. She was alone in a place she knew not. She had nowhere to go. This island was a pirate nest. Besides, Khidr... It was as if Khidr had cared for her...

"I was living in Andarax, Spain. Christians killed my entire family. My father, Cergio... all are dead. They took me captive. The King of Spain sent me to the governor of this island as a gift. I... I..." Her voice was trembling. "I have nowhere to go..."

Had she said it aloud? The stern expression on Aruj's face had softened. He tucked his sword into his belt and rubbed his face with his hands.

"Damn Christians!" he said. "They persecute people not only on the seas, but the lands as well."

Khidr's eyes were fixed on Aruj. He knew exactly well what he wanted to do, but he needed his brother's approval. Aruj, on the other hand, read his little brother like an open book, for the expression on Khidr's face was giving away everything he had in mind. He took a deep breath and looked Khidr in the eye.

"Take her to the ship. We'll talk later."

Mehmed and Cemal became concerned. The presence of a woman on board would have brought about ill fortune. But Khidr acted quickly.

"As you command, brother!"

He caught Felipa by the arm and led her to the ship.

"The presence of a woman on board would bring about ill fortune..."

William was pondering on what Cervantes had just said. He turned his gaze to the Spanish writer.

"Why?"

"Why what?"

"You said, the presence of a woman on board would bring about ill fortune. Why? I'm curious as to why you hold such a perspective, Signor Cervantes."

"Woman, Signor Shakespeare, woman is the very essence of life. Woman gives life but she also takes lives. To the one who knows, woman is the breath of life; to the ignorant, however, she is the nafs[69]. The legend says that there once lived the Sirens around the Sirenus islands, who are said to have been half women and half birds. These pixies of Achelous[70], who lined up like bronze statues glittering beneath the silvery moonlight, were so beautiful, so charming that there was not a single man in the whole world who would not fall desperately in love with these women. When the sailors wandering around the sharp reefs that surrounded the island heard the enchanting voices of these fairies, they would fall under the spell of their beautiful songs, steer their boats in that direction and eventually crash on the rocks. And their vessels would split in half like a walnut shell. All those mighty seamen would be dragged into the dark waters, ultimately becoming bait for those sea women."

"Why wouldn't they have stayed away even though they knew the legend?"

"For they couldn't, Signor Shakespeare. As soon as those enchanting tones reached their ears, they would forget all the vows they previously took. According to the legend, only Jason and the Argonauts, and Odysseus were able to escape death. Jason, with the help of Orpheus; and Odysseus thanks to Circe the Enchantress."

William was attentive to every word.

---

[69] Shams Tabrizi
[70] Shape-shifting Greek river god who was the personification of the Achelous River, one of the longest rivers in Greece.

"When Greek sailors who set sail for their hometown after the Trojan War began to fall one by one into the sirens' traps, Odysseus was haunted by fear. After looking for days for a means to be able to get back to his wife and son without falling under the spell of the sirens he had decided to consult Circe for guidance. "There is a way," Circe had said, "No man who has ever heard the songs of the Sirens and lived to tell the tale, but you can! Tell your crew to plug their ears with wax, and tie you to the main mast." Odysseus had done as Circe had instructed and ordered his crew to secure him to the main mast with the strongest ropes. But the song he heard as they approached the rocks had swept him off his feet. No matter what might happen to him, Odysseus had wanted to see with his own eyes those creatures with such beautiful voices. Even the certain death that awaited him in the end, had not frightened him, and he had started shouting from the mast he was tied to, calling out to his men, saying: "Untie me! Untie me! Untie me and steer the ship towards the reefs!". But since the wax with which they plugged their ears had rendered them all deaf, none of his men had heard Odysseus; and they had continued their way unaware of what was going on. The Sirens, upon seeing that the sailors were not paying attention to them, had begun singing even louder, and Odysseus had begun burning with even a greater desire which, in the end, rendered him unconscious. When he finally come to himself, even though the threat was no longer present and Odysseus was able to make it through the ordeal, the songs of the Sirens had always remained in his ears."

"The past is rife with such legends, of which we can never be quite certain of their veracity."

"If we were able to prove their veracity, we would have called these stories 'history', not 'legends', Signor Shakespeare."

"Could it be possible that the true reason for associating women on board with ill fortune is the fact that the presence of even a single woman on board is enough to cause conflict among the crew members who were all males? Could that be the reason why all these stories have been made up, Signor Cervantes?"

Cervantes smiled.

"Among those brave and strong-willed warriors who grab his weapon and hurl himself into the bloodiest battles, do you know anyone who would not surrender to the beauty of an elegant woman, Signor Shakespeare?"

"As a matter of fact, Signor Cervantes, you are the only warrior I've ever known so far who had participated in battles of such nature."

William had Cervantes cornered. But he was no longer afraid whether he would offend him. They had been talking with each other for hours. Maybe they still could not be considered close friends, but they certainly had developed a friendship of some sort. Cervantes was so taken away by the fascination of the story he himself was telling that he no longer considered this young Englishman a stranger in his house. Still, he paused for a moment for he had been taken aback by the response William gave to his question.

"I see that you're challenging me to a duel with your wordplay, Signor Shakespeare. If what you're wondering is whether I would be able to keep my composure in a situation like that, let me tell you frankly, I could have proudly forgotten even where I had put my sword in the presence of a woman as glamorous as Felipa. Just like Khidr, who had forgotten where they had left their boat that night."

When it was dark, it was as if all the streets of Djerba were alike. They were finally able to make it to the shore; and Khidr was now frantically trying to recall on which side of the sand they had left their boats before Felipa would realize that he forgot and start laughing at him.

He felt relieved when he finally saw Yahya.
"Yahya!"
Yahya had his given instructions to those who was going to stay onboard, come ashore after completing all his chores, and headed toward the inns.
"Reis!"
"There's someone I'd like you to take to the ship, Yahya. But you must do it quietly! You should not let anyone hear about it!"

Yahya was surprised. It was somewhat strange that Khidr had requested such a thing from him. Since Felipa had her head covered under her hood, he had not yet noticed in the darkness that the person who was standing right next to Khidr was a woman.

"As you say, Reis! But why do you want to keep it a secret?"

When Khidr turned his gaze towards Felipa, she slowly took off her hood. Having seen her long dark hair tumbling across her shoulders, Yahya's knees knocked together.

"Bismillahirrahmanirrahim... But Reis, woman on board..."
"Hush Yahya, do as I say!"
"But what would Aruj Reis say?"
"I said hush, Yahya! That was his instruction. You do as I say and take her to somewhere she would feel comfortable."
"All right, Reis! Don't worry. Even the waters will not hear about her."
Khidr turned to Felipa:
"Go with him. I'll drop by when I get back. Sleep, get some rest."

Felipa did not reply. After putting on her hood, she climbed aboard the boat with Yahya's help. As they moved away from the shore, Felipa did not take her gaze away from Khidr, not even for a moment.

Khidr, on the other hand, waited till the boat disappeared in the darkness and then set out toward the inns. First, he started humming a tune, and then, he noticed that his steps had become a little weird. What exactly was going on with him? No way! He stopped, cleared his throat, took a deep breath, and shrugged himself off. After that, he began walking more like a levend.

When he reached the street where the inns were, he looked around. Just as he was trying to figure out where his brothers might be, Aruj's earth-shaking laughter served as a compass. He entered the inn and saw two men whom he had never seen before, sitting next to his brothers. He approached them with curiosity. Kemal and Piri reises who had been sent to Djerba on Prince Korkud's orders to meet with Aruj, were recounting how they had obtained the maps from Cristóbal Colón.

Aruj took a sip of his drink and turned to Piri.
"Don't tell me you failed to save Colón, Piri Reis."
Kemal Reis intervened:
"I don't know how many guards we've knocked down with Piri; they were crawling down the cliff like spiders."
Piri took out the maps and laid them in front of Aruj.
"Here, Colón's maps!"

They all looked at the maps. Aruj squinted his eyes and started reading them like a book. After he studied them for a while, he noticed a peculiar symbol on one of the maps. He turned to Piri and asked:

"What does this symbol mean?"

Piri smiled.

"I have no idea, but that's Jerusalem."

"I thought that these maps depicted the New World."

"The vast majority of them, do indeed."

Piri took one of them and handed it to Aruj.

"This one, for instance. Have a look at it. It depicts the coastal line of the New World."

Aruj gave the map a serious examination. He was surprised.

"Isn't that Star of David? What could be the reason for it to have been drawn on a map that depicted the New World?"

"If you had seen it over Jerusalem, it wouldn't come as much of a surprise to you, would it?" replied Piri, and continued his words while pointing at the symbol Aruj had asked about. "And if you had seen this one on the lands of the New World..."

"Yes" said Aruj. "After all, these are not the symbols we are used to seeing in these waters."

Aruj's attention was drawn to a handwriting beneath the Star of David. He leaned forward to give it a closer look.

$$\text{אֲרֹן הַבְּרִית}$$

It hadn't evoked anything in Aruj. Piri took a small mirror out of his pocket and positioned it so that it was vertically aligned with the writing.

"Perhaps you can read better now."

$$\text{אֲרֹון הַבְּרִית}$$

"It looks like Hebrew," said Aruj.

Piri looked him in the eye.

"Ărōn habbrīṭ."

Nobody had understood a thing. Kemal Reis translated.

"The Ark of the Covenant!"

The words spilled from Kemal Reis's lips passed tangent by the weary ears of the sailors sprawled around exhausted in every corner of the dim inn and blended with the last sip of Andrea's drink. When Andrea was just about to turn his head into that direction, he gave up the idea at the last moment. He had crept in the inn like a shadow and given ear to what was being talked about for hours in silence. The island was the heart of the Barbary Coast, which meant that most of its inhabitants were Muslims. If the Genoese commander were to be cautious about not revealing his identity much, it would surely have been in his best interest.

"Taboot-e-Sakina?[71]" asked Khidr. He was surprised. "I'd heard that it disappeared with the destruction of the Temple of Solomon."

A stern expression appeared on Aruj's face.

Kemal and Piri reises looked at each other. They were on the fence regarding whether they should let the Barbarossas know about the ark that they had found in the Mediterranean. Their irresolution did not go unnoticed by Mehmed.

"Gentlemen, Prince Korkud sent you here, right?"

Piri replied:

"Yes, he did."

"To meet with Aruj."

"Yes."

"Then why don't you just spill the beans of out your mouth?"

"I guess, Sultan Bayezid and Prince Korkud are not on good terms," said Cemal.

Kemal Reis intervened.

"We hold the deepest regard for Prince Korkud, and we have complete confidence in him. But you must keep in mind, gentlemen, that we are the Imperial Navy."

Silence prevailed for a while. Aruj took a deep breath.

"And we are from the Island of Lesbos, Kemal Reis. We are Yakub Agha's sons, a former janissary in the service of Sultan Mehmed."

"We've been informed about your family."

"So, you know that we are also the children of Ottoman," said Isaac.

---

[71] Qur'an refers to The Ark of the Covenant as Taboot-e-Sakina.

"We also know that you have a Greek mother who continues to worship like the Christians," said Kemal Reis.

Cemal laughed with sarcasm.

"So what? The fact that his father had fallen in love with a Christian woman would not make them spies!"

Aruj got angry.

"What does my mother's religious practices have to do with the matter at hand, Kemal Reis. Allah is one! I suppose you forgot. We are the enemies of neither Prophet Jesus nor Prophet Moses. We stand against those hypocrites, those who dare to persecute people as they utter the names of the prophets of Allah."

Kemal Reis smiled.

"Those were the words I was hoping to hear from you, son. Now I understand better why Prince Korkud wanted me to see you. We wouldn't have traveled all the way down to Djerba to meet you if we did not have trust in you. But this secret that we're about to disclose to you is an imperial secret. First, we have to be sure that you are going to swing your swords on the behalf of the Empire, no matter what the situation may be."

Aruj had calmed down.

"They cut off my little brother's head. And when I was chained to the oars, being whipped almost to death, I knew that my brother was the lucky one."

"It's a miracle that you're still alive," said Piri.

"We had set sail with Elias. We were carrying goods. At first, we had thought that they would pass us by. Why would the knights attack a small trading boat stocked with olives, soap, and pottery, anyway? But they didn't pass us by. Later on, I found out that they had been searching throughout the Mediterranean for an ark that they recently lost, and that they had been ordered to seize all the vessels they came across until it was found."

"An ark? What ark, brother?"

Khidr was perplexed. Aruj had never mentioned such an ark up until that moment. He had said that they could no longer trade safely in these waters due to the threats posed by the knights. He also had said that they should be able to stand up and fight against them if they had to. But an ark... It was the first time Khidr was hearing from his brother something about an ark.

Aruj left Khidr's question unanswered. With eyes fixed on Kemal Reis he continued his words:

"This means we, too, are the soldiers of the Ottoman Empire. Just like you and Piri. I've sworn to avenge my brother, to avenge the days I've been held captive and chained to oars, the days I've been locked in the dungeons. Prince Korkud lent me a helping hand for he saw my fury." He placed a hand on Mehmed's shoulder. "He gave me his best men, equipped two galiots and sent us here to meet with you so that we cooperate, so that we fight side by side. Now, is it fair to keep secrets from us? Tell me, have you found the Ark?"

No one uttered a word. Khidr and Isaac had realized that Aruj's intentions far exceeded hunting in the Mediterranean during the summer months, capturing a few Christian merchant ships, and amassing plunder to survive the winter. Aruj was planning to make Christians pay a much heavier price for Elias' life. Not only was he going to take revenge of Elias, but also of all the Muslims who were imprisoned or chained to oars; and he was literally going to be a thorn in the flesh for the Christian kingdoms by hampering all their activities in the Mediterranean.

Kemal Reis gave the young sailor a once-over with eyes that glistened like two diamonds on his wrinkled face. He was not only full of vengeance but courageous and determined as well. While maintaining a slight smile adorning the corner of his lips, he said to himself, "Prince Korkud must also have seen these."

"We took it to the sultan, son," said Kemal Reis. "We found the Ark in a galleon and took it to our Sultan. We don't know what's inside. We didn't open it. We found it in one of our Sultan's galleons drifting in the Mediterranean. We learned that they had seized it during the battle they fought against the knights, but that after they brought it on board one at a time, they began to die. When we arrived, there was just one remaining sailor on board who was still alive. He begged us to throw the Ark into the water. We couldn't have done that. When he also died, we set the galleon on fire, transported the Ark to Goke and took it to Sultan Bayezid, son."

Kemal Reis had recounted the story in such a low tone that was impossible for Andrea to pick up the few words he heard from where he was seated and convert them into intelligible sentences. He stood up and searched for a spot where he could more easily overhear what was being discussed. But just as he was passing by, upon tripping on Khidr's foot which he suddenly extended into the narrow corridor, Andrea faltered, lost his balance, and tumbled down. Having heard the rumble, every head in the inn had turned in that direction. Andrea's deliberate silence that lasted for hours was rendered meaningless by the hush that descended upon the inn. He had attracted everyone's attention which was something he had tried hard to avoid. His rage got out of control. Just when he grabbed the jug on the round copper tray and poured the wine onto Khidr's face; he felt the sharp tip of Aruj's sword on his neck.

They gazed into one another's eyes and saw their own childhoods reflected in the other's face. They saw the Orthodox Basilica, the Ancient Greek and Persian ruins on which they perched, and joked around with each other, the little houses with red tiled roofs, the reflection of the pines on the waters, the coves nestled within the rocks on the shores of Lesbos, and the final sunset when they said their last goodbyes... Andrea knew this face, Andrea knew this swift young man with sparkling eyes.

The daring look on Aruj's face had been replaced by one of perplexity. Then, it swiftly morphed into one of excitement and joy. Khidr, on the other hand, was chuckling as wine was dripping down from his face.

"Khidr? Aruj? What are you doing here?"

Khidr got a handkerchief out of his pocket and wiped his face off; and then he stood up and gave his good old pal a big hug. They all started laughing.

Aruj, filled with curiosity, couldn't help but ask:
"Where have you been for all this time? Why didn't you ever show up in Lesbos?"
Andrea got seated.
"Do you remember the day when we said our last goodbye?"
"Of course," said Aruj.
Andrea's expression had turned serious.
"That was the day I said goodbye to my father, too."
Khidr's sunny expression was clouded by perplexity and concern.
"Your father? What happened to him?"
"Shortly after we cast off from Lesbos and set sail, we were attacked by the Arab pirates. They killed everyone on board, plundered all that was in the ship, and left me there alone."

Khidr felt deeply sorry.

"So, Signor Ceva is dead?"

For a while, none of them spoke. Then, Aruj turned to Andrea and asked:

"And you? How did you survive?"

Andrea took his hand to his chest and revealed the amulet that Khidr had given to him that day.

"When they saw this on my neck, they did not harm me."

No one could find a word to say. They were all heartbroken.

"It appears the storms of the Mediterranean had blown through you before it swept through us," Aruj said, taking a sip of his drink.

Andrea was not sure what Aruj meant.

"Yakub Agha?"

"Elias," said Khidr.

Andrea was taken aback. When they had last seen one other, Elias was a little boy.

"Tell me what happened?"

The cold look settled in Aruj's eyes was showing that his thoughts had already traveled to that dreaded day.

"My father's health was getting worse. We had been sailing together for a long time. I thought it might be better for him if he stayed on the island this time. I could have taken Elias with me. Just when we reached the reefs, we saw one of the galleys of the knights approaching. At first, we tried to stay calm. There were only a few jars of oil, some olives, and some soap in our boat, nothing that could be interesting for the knights. But it turned out that, at the time, they were interested in every single vessel sailing in the Mediterranean."

Khidr had clenched his teeth. His features had become sharper and more defined. Kemal Reis, on the other hand, was staring Aruj dead in the eye, to prevent him from disclosing anything to Andrea regarding the Ark.

Aruj went on:

"They severed Elias' head from his body and took me captive. During the time that I was chained to the oars and confined in dungeons, I amassed enough hatred toward the Christians. And now it is time to bring it into daylight."

Andrea felt troubled. He recalled his father lying on the deck with an arrow on his neck. He recalled the oath he had taken as he stood there in the midst of the sea all alone in tears. He could feel the cool breeze of his desire for vengeance blowing through his heart. Then, his mind set sail to the little village Bonova, where together they dreamed about the future... He looked at the veins of rage that had puffed up on Khidr's temples, at Isaac's clenched teeth, and at Aruj's bloodshot eyes...

"So, you'll become pirates?"

Under Aruj's fiery mustache settled an allusive smile, but his eyes had not joined his lips this time.

"We shall be the masters of the Mediterranean, Andrea. From now on, we will be the ones to rule in these waters."

"What is it, Signor Cervantes, that which determines the course of history? Is it Plutarch's brave, strong-willed, determined individuals who, with their invisible staffs in their hands, divert rivers away from their beds? Or is it destiny that had brought these two childhood friends to sword-to-sword in the Mediterranean?"

As he lifted his gaze from the Mediterranean map, Cervantes replied:

"We live our lives under the illusion that it is us, who are in command, that we have ideals, principles. However, whether you call it coincidence or fate, we are all driven along the path of life by occurrences that are not of our own free choosing."

Cervantes was right. Andrea's father's murder by an Arab arrow, Elias' death by a sword stroke, all those years Aruj had spent in captivity... None of these were in their childhood dreams. And years later, they, once again, had stumbled into one other on a tiny island in the Mediterranean. With their hearts hardened by life's nasty surprises and agonizing grief that had slowly crept into them like a sneaky snake...

Having seen the defiant look in Aruj's eyes, Andrea again put on his insincere mask that he had long grown accustomed to wearing.

"I do trade, I follow my father's footsteps..."

He didn't tell. With his eyes fixed on the maps lying in front of Piri, Andrea didn't tell Aruj that he was a mercenary serving the kingdom that paid him the most, hunting down pirates in the Mediterranean.

"We haven't introduced you," said Isaac. He had noticed that Andrea's attention was drawn to the maps. "Piri and Kemal Reis. Our new companions. Piri is a talented cartographer."

Andrea gestured with his head.

"Are those your maps?"

Piri was reluctant about trusting this sly-looking man they just had met. He decided to throw a little bait to see how he would react.

"These are Cristóbal Colón's maps."

"Cristóbal Colón, huh? I'd heard that he was imprisoned after having been returned from his third expedition."

"You had heard it right, Signor." said Kemal Reis. "Don't you also think that you have big ears for a simple merchant?"

Andrea cracked a grin.

"What's so unusual about the news related to the fate of a Genoese admiral should reach the ears of a Genoese merchant quickly? Besides, the Mediterranean is not that vast, is it Kemal Reis? Even just a few hours on this tiny island is enough to learn about what's recently been occurring in these waters."

Kemal Reis was a wise old wolf. Just like Piri's deciphering the charts, he was more than capable when it came to figuring out the true intentions of everyone he encountered in these waters thanks to his advanced age and vast experience. And in fact, although Andrea was pretending as if he did not, he knew very well who Kemal Reis was. But he was also aware of the fact that he might have found himself in serious trouble if someone were to mention the surname 'Doria'. So, it would surely be better for him if he bid farewell to his old friends, before his mask was ripped off from his face.

"I have to leave now, I'm glad to see you all."
Khidr smiled.

"We're glad to see you too, Andrea. May the winds be fair to you, may these waters bring us together again."

"Yes... May it be as you say..."

He couldn't complete his sentence. If Andrea could be sure that they would never run into each other again, he would certainly be more pleased. If only the Mediterranean had not been as small as he had just asserted, and these waters had not pitted them against each other. He took his hand to his neck and grabbed a hold of his amulet. He saluted all with a nod of his head and walked out of the inn.

Although he was paying attention to every single detail of the story, William's integrity of thought was still intact, and the young Englishman was relentlessly searching for the divine power behind everything that had taken place.

"So, it seems, both coincidence and fate play a large part, but one's will and determination as well, Signor Cervantes."

"That day, Signor Shakespeare, when Andrea and the Barbarossas stumbled upon each other may truly be coincidental. But the plan that would eventually pit these two childhood friends against one other in a swordfight in the Mediterranean was unquestionably a divine one. God had sown the seeds in both of them; Felipa had settled in both of their hearts. And Andrea's seed would begin to germinate the moment he realized he lost Felipa."

It had become late. The Barbarossas knew that the day that lay ahead of them would be an exciting one packed with action. Kemal Reis had said that the levends who would come to Djerba to meet with them at the orders of Prince Korkud were the mightiest warriors in the Mediterranean. Some were on their way to join forces with the Barbarossas, while some were going to offer their fellowship. Aruj was so impatient that he was not even sure whether he was going to be granted a restful night's sleep that night. Nonetheless, they had to return to their ships now.

After they all left the inn, Kemal Reis turned to Aruj:

"Son, go now and get some rest so that your worn-out bodies would rejuvenate. Better the evil of the day than the good of the night. Tomorrow, early in the morning, we'll be waiting for you in Goke."

"We'll be there, Kemal Reis. Wish you a good night."

"Oh, and just so you know, nobody will learn out about the Ark. Keeping this a secret will be the first thing you do to earn the Empire's trust. The Ark is in safe hands now, you just watch over the Mediterranean."

"What Ark, Kemal Reis?"

Kemal Reis smiled. No one uttered a word. They all had understood that they should not talk about this matter even with each other and forget whatever they had learned that night.

Most of the lanterns that illuminated the dark, narrow streets of Djerba were already put down. The island had pulled over herself her quilt of clouds and was now getting ready to sleep. Under the flickering lights of a few lamps still burning, they set out to their ships. This time it was Mehmed and Cemal who were lagging behind the Barbarossas, following them from a distance. The night was in fact not over for any of them. They were all thinking about what they were going to do with that dark-eyed woman who awaited them onboard, but none among them had the courage to speak to Aruj about it.

Khidr was following his brother's steps; from time to time giving him a glance, searching for Felipa in his contemplative eyes. But the expression on his brother's face was not revealing anything that he had in mind. Nonetheless, they had almost arrived at the shore. They had to talk.

"Brother..."

Aruj came to a halt and waited for Mehmed and Cemal to draw closer so they, too, could hear; then, he spoke in a resolute tone:

"No one will hear about her. No one will learn that there is a woman on board."

His orders were as sharp as their swords. There was no further discussion to be had. If anyone would dare to utter a word, it was clear that Aruj would choke him up with the word he uttered. If their reis said so, then, it would be so. Together, they got on the boat.

Mehmed whispered to Cemal:

"Nobody will hear about the Ark; nobody will hear about the woman. Then, what exactly did we see, and what exactly did we hear tonight?"

"Husshh! Shut your mouth up! Reis will hear."

"No, he won't. Nobody hears anything tonight."

When they got on board Khidr's eyes searched for Yahya.

"Reis."

"What did you do Yahya?"

"I did as you said, Reis. Even the waters didn't hear. I thought no one would enter the captain's cabin so I decided to take her there. But I was unable to check on her later, to see if she needed anything. I was worried that the levends would be suspicious if I went in and out of the cabin frequently."

"You'd thought well Yahya. You just keep quiet; I'll go and check her now."

When Khidr entered the cabin with quiet steps, he found Felipa sleeping on the mattress. Her wavy black hair was scattered on the velvet cushion and her one arm was hanging feebly from the mattress. She was holding a small leather-bound notebook in her other hand, which she had it pressed against her chest so tightly that it was as if she had wished to place it inside her heart. What was the last thing Felipa had read, Khidr wondered. Whose words had sent her into the healing arms of deep sleep? In the streets of what kind of a dream was her soul currently wandering? Khidr slowly reached out and took the notebook and read the handwriting on the open page:

'And it is you, my love; the first thing I think of every morning I wake up and the last thing I see in my mind's eye each and every night...'

"O, she doth teach the torches to burn bright! It seems she hangs upon the cheek of night Like a rich jewel in an Ethiop's ear; beauty too rich for use, for earth too dear!"[72]

"Whereas she gets richer when used, Signor Shakespeare, for the woman blossoms with her beloved's touch."

---

[72] William Shakespeare, Romeo and Juliet

"But how could the fire fall so quickly to the heart? While his ears have not yet drunk a hundred word of that tongue's uttering. How could it fall so quickly and turn into an ember at first sight?"

"Do you think that there must be a reason to love? Then, you must be looking at the beloved with the eyes of the flesh instead of your heart's eye."

"I think I'd relish a duel between you and me, Signor Cervantes."

"With pen or sword, Signor Shakespeare?"

"With pen, of course. I suppose you too wouldn't want a plain English playwright like myself to perish at the hands of an experienced soldier like you, would you?"

Sorrow descended upon Cervantes.

"In truth, Signor, I wish I never had to part a soul from the body it resides in, not even one in my entire lifetime."

William was at a loss for words. But it was clear that what he just said had caused Cervantes feel sad. He had to give him a lift.

"None of what had transpired, Signor, was your fault, you know that don't you? It's more the fault of the terrible times we live in."

"War justifies ferocity, doesn't it?"

Cervantes gazed off into space for a while, then, he raised his eyebrows and took a deep breath to resume the story where he left off.

"Anyway... What was I saying? I suppose I was talking about love... Love, which man falls into without knowing when or why..."

That night, Khidr did not enjoy a single drop of sleep. He lay awake on the deck and gazed upon the sparkling stars scattered across the night sky. All through the night, that one sentence kept echoing within his heart... The one that begins with, "And it is you, my love..."

As the golden fingers of the sun touched the waters with the dawning of the day, Khidr stood up. Aruj, who was already awake, was washing the sleep off his face with clean water from one of the barrels. Khidr slowly walked toward Aruj.

"I had thought that Djerba could offer us a shelter. An island in the midst the Mediterranean that is close to trade routes... An island which lacks a ruler as well as rules."

Khidr was listening. After wiping off his face with a piece of cloth Aruj continued:

"But it also lacks water. There is no water on this island!"

He was right. Drought was Djerba's most serious challenge. This was a bone-dry island; it was the parched lips of the Mediterranean. Rains would only visit the island for a few months each year, and that was from November to January.

"Aside from that, there is no stone... and no timber... Djerba cannot provide us with the timber suitable for shipbuilding. We have to dig ditches, construct palisades, and reinforce the walls. Otherwise, this pile of sand cannot withstand any assault."

"What do you have in mind?"

"I haven't fully made up my mind yet, but I'm thinking of establishing some sort of common ground with Mulay Muhammad, the Sultan of Tunisia."

Khidr was surprised. Kemal Reis had said that Tunisia was an oasis in the heart of the desert with its magnificent gardens, aqueducts, majestic pillars, and countless taverns, baths, and shops. However, he also had emphasized Sultan Mulay Abu Abdullah Muhammad's unquenchable passion for power and wealth. Since the day he had ascended the throne, his sole objective had been to become the *Amir al-Mu'minin*[73] and the Defender of Mecca. But since he did not possess the financial strength to hold such a rank, he had made deals with the Venetian and Genoese merchants and granted Christians plenty of privileges to provide his dynasty with an additional income. And while acting in this manner, the sultan had shown no regard for the potential consequences that this would have for his precious Tunisia.

"La Goulette[74] may provide us with all that we need so that we can equip the ships and set sail."

"But Piri had said that La Goulette had nothing but a series of low fortifications constructed on the sand. Besides I've heard that it had shallow waters."

---

[73] An Arabic title designating the supreme leader of an Islamic community, which is usually translated as "Commander of the Faithful" or "Prince of the Believers".

[74] A port in Tunisia, also known as La Goulette

"Then, we would raise the walls higher and reinforce them if necessary. And the fact that its waters are shallow works in our favor. We can easily enter in and out of the port with our shallow drafted galiots. And if Christians ever make an attempt to pursue us, the prevailing northern winds will take care of their galleons."

"If you'll recall from yesterday, they mentioned that the issues of water and timber were problematic in La Goulette as well."

"Cherchell seems to be the only location on the Barbary Coast where there's no shortage of timber, water, or food, anyway. But for us, it is too far west. Khidr, we must be prepared to overcome difficulties. Before we set sail from Lesbos, I don't remember telling you that it would be an easy task."

"But brother..."

"We cannot stay in Djerba, Khidr. This place, with its fragrant eucalyptus trees, white sandy shores, and inns filled with women, may seem like paradise for the levends; but for us, it is just a pile of sand and rubble."

"I couldn't care less about the women or the inns, brother. I will, without a doubt, accompany you wherever you choose to steer the ship, but..."

"But what?"

"Where are going to find the gold that would quench Mulay Muhammad's thirst? With the booty we were able to seize on our way to Djerba, we can only appease the hunger of those who are willing to join us. And also, there is this..."

"There is what?"

"Felipa... What are we going to do with Felipa?"

The last words that had spilled from Khidr's mouth were more of a whisper compared to the earlier ones. There was no way that Felipa could remain on board. They were, without a doubt, going to leave her off somewhere. Khidr had the idea running through his head that it would be nice if this "somewhere" would be "somewhere" where he could at the very least pay Felipa a visit every once in a while.

Aruj began to laugh. The spicy lights emanating from his eyes illuminated the day, more than the morning sun did at the time. And yes, Khidr's fears were soon going to be realized. First, Aruj was going to grin like a Cheshire cat; then he was going to burst into laughter so loud that, at this early hour in the morning, it was going to make both the levends and Felipa leap from their beds.

"Brother... Brother, please don't!"

It was too late. No later than half a minute or so after Aruj's laughter was heard reverberated off the shore, sleepy Osman appeared on the deck with his mace in his hands.

"Maaaakeee wayyy! Ambush or what? I think I've heard a rumbling."

"There are times when you feel that the decisions you make are backed up by the Divine. The times when you don't have to strive hard to manifest your dreams... The circumstances quickly change in your favor turning what seemed to you at first impossible into something possible. The saints bring and place it in your palms what has always been yours. You either notice or miss..."

William was listening to Cervantes attentively. Cervantes' eyes, on the other hand, were once again fixed on his carved map. He placed his finger on Tunisia; then he turned his gaze towards William.

"Tunisia, Signor Shakespeare. Aruj's decision on setting sail to Tunisia was the right one."

In the years that followed the death of Queen Isabel, Cardinal Jiménez had begun to serve as the king's ruthless arm reaching to the coasts of North Africa; and Pedro Navarro, Count of Olivetto, was the sharp sword that the cardinal was holding. The Spanish had gained control of the strategically important naval base of Mers El Kébir. And then, as their next step, they had their sights set on Oran, another precious port located in the north of Algiers. These two ports were of critical importance for keeping the pulse of the Mediterranean and ensuring the safety of the trade routes that the Christian merchant ships navigated through. However, the Sultan of Tunisia, Mulay Muhammad, was aware that Cardinal Jiménez would never be satisfied with the influence he had succeeded in establishing in the region. He knew that the bells would soon toll for La Goulette.

Aruj knew this sparkling smile from somewhere; and not from very long ago, from only a few years back. The lines on his face had become a little bit more defined and therefore more noticeable, and his beard had grown a little longer and that's all. It was almost as if Dragut had emerged from childhood and become more of a man.

"Dragut? You are here in Djerba? It appears that you had found a way to escape from the island."

They gave each other a warm hug.

"Escape? If my memory serves me well, I had already told you at the beginning that I purposefully had let the knights take me captive. My plan of leaving the island as soon as I was done with them was ready from day one. And you? How did you manage to get away?"

"My account is somewhat lengthy. A little bit depressing, somewhat difficult, but by the will of Allah I am here now."

"You'll tell me, and I'll listen."

"Sure, I'll tell you sometime."

Kemal Reis was delighted to see that Aruj and Dragut already knew each other. Khidr, on the other hand, realized that he still had a lot to learn from his brother about what he had been through.

Aruj rested one arm on Khidr's shoulder, and the other on Isaac's.

"These two men are my brothers, Dragut. We are of the same essence!"

"So, they are fellows, comrades, brothers!"

Aruj flashed a dazzling smile, revealing his pearly white teeth.

Dragut gestured with his hand.

"Come! Let me introduce you to your new fellows, comrades, your new brothers!"

Together they went up to Goke's forecastle deck. Khidr could not believe his eyes. Sailors, who were obviously the children of the Ottoman Empire as their red berets, multi-color vests they had worn on their white shirts, baggy trousers, and recently sharpened swords on their belts indicated, were waiting to meet with the Barbarossas. As Dragut introduced them one at a time, the levends advanced a step forward.

"Koca Dayi...Kara Kadi... Kara Hodja, also known as Caracossa... Gazi Mustafa... Sancaktar... Ali Ahmed... Aydin Reis, whom the Italians called Cachidiablo..."

"The one who beats the Devil," said Aruj with a grin on his face. "I can't say I haven't heard this name."

"Salih Reis... Shaban Reis... Muhyiddin Reis, who is Piri's cousin..."

Piri smiled.

"Guzelce Mehmed... Sholok Mehmed... Mad Cafer... You will, in due time, understand the reason why he is referred to that way."

Aruj looked over to Mad Mehmed, who had been his comrade since they left Smyrna.

"Mehmed, it seems you now have a competitor."

"You know what they say, Reis, better to have two mad levends on board than just one."

Dragut continued:

"Sadik... Seydi Ali... Kurdoglu, with whom I am acquainted from Rhodes. The knights took from him two of his brothers, and his third brother is still being held captive."

Aruj looked Kurdoglu straight in the eye. He had understood very well why Dragut had shared this information with him. He recalled his little brother Elias, he felt his heart begin to pound in his temples, and a shadow of hatred descended upon his soul.

"So, it seems our animosity towards the knights would be the foundation upon which our fellowship would be built."

Kurdoglu was a quiet man. He would neither talk nor smile much. He placed his hand on the hilt of his sword and slightly lowered his head to salute Aruj.

Andrea gazed at Sheikh Yahya's big white house while he waited for the guards to let him through the garden gate. The sheikh must have been living a life of a prisoner on an island like this where there were all kinds of illegalities wandering in its narrow, stinky, and steamy streets, he thought, he must probably have been unable to take even a single step out of the house alone. He was not the lawgiver on the island, for there were no laws on the island. The sole law that applied in Djerba was perpetuating lawlessness, and it was the sheikh's responsibility to ensure that this single law was enforced while he kept reporting to Spain what was happening along the Barbary Coast.

The pirates, who had to follow strict rules while they were out at the sea, would like to enjoy complete freedom as soon as they set foot on the island. In exchange for granting them freedom of action, the sheikh had ensured that they would not touch him. This was the only rule, the only law in Djerba. On an island that established its own order in accordance with its own dynamics, the sheikh was not concerned if one bandit slit the throat of another. Why would he, anyway? After all, all were murderers. If one would go, another would come from North Africa bringing with him the latest news.

After a while, the guards arrived and opened the massive gates, allowing Andrea to enter.

"Welcome, Signor Doria, Sheikh Yahya awaits you in the front yard."

Andrea followed the guard as he showed him the way with calm steps. As they passed the stables, he paused. His gaze wandered around, looking for Felipa. He was curious as to how she was doing. He was startled by the guard's calling.

"This way, Signor."

They walked through the marble courtyard and reached the yard where Sheikh Yahya was waiting for Andrea.

"Welcome to my house, Signor Doria. We were just talking about you with Signor Navarro. I suppose you know him."

"Thank you, governor... Signor..."

After he greeted them both, Andrea continued:

"Of course, I know Signor Navarro, the Count of Oliveto, the Grand Captain Gonzalo Fernández de Córdoba's eyes in Ionia. I'd heard that you had successfully breached the walls of the Castle of Saint George in Cephalonia by your skillfully laid mines and driven the Ottomans out of their stronghold. Is there anyone who hasn't heard of Signor Pedro Navarro?"

Pedro Navarro was not able to figure out from Andrea's words if he was praising him or harboring jealousy toward him. He smiled and preferred to keep his doubts to himself.

"I was only doing my job, Signor Doria, nothing to brag about. Someone needed to put a halt to Kemal Reis and his hounds' reckless advance in Ionia. Having been commissioned for this assignment by Pope Alexander Sixtus was an honor."

"Alexander Sixtus..." said Andrea and smiled with sarcasm. "Aka Rodrigo Borgia, whose bones I recently handed over to the King of Spain along with his son in chains... I cannot say we were on good terms with him during his Papacy."

Pedro Navarro was convinced beyond a shadow of a doubt that Andrea was jealous of him.

"Could it be because you served in the Neapolitan Army of Alfonso of Aragon during those years, whom Rodrigo Borgia was not fond of much? What do you think, Signor Doria?"

Andrea smiled.

"Why does it seem so strange to you, Signor Navarro, after all, we are cut from the same cloth. We are mercenaries; we serve those who pay us the most. Had Rodrigo Borgia invested the gold he preferred to spend for his own luxury for the papal army, today, we might have been talking about the military power of a unified Italy rather than the Turkish threat in Ionia."

"You're mistaken, Signor Doria, we are not cut from the same cloth. You may enter in the service of whoever pays you the most, but I serve only to King Fernando, only to the Kingdom of Spain."

"I see that you are a man of principles. To what does King Fernando owes this over patriotism of yours?"

"If we are discussing the Turkish threat in Ionia today, it is not the Holy Roman Church that is to blame; rather, it is the Eastern Church, which took a stance against Rome and severed its ties with Saint Peter's with the Great Schism, paving the way for the tragedy of Constantinople's takeover by the Ottomans. The conquest of Constantinople is God's response, God's punishment to the Orthodox. The Great Schism is the first and foremost issue Christianity must resolve. Today, what Christianity needs is far beyond the unification of Italy; the whole of Europe needs to be united under a single flag. And if there's someone who can make this dream a reality and put Jesus' spilled blood back into the Holy Grail, it is King Fernando."

After Pedro Navarro finished his tirade that he recited as if by heart, Andrea couldn't help but applauded his admirable ideals.

"You are a true Spaniard, Signor Navarro. With such brave-hearted patriots like you at his disposal, I have no doubt that Fernando will soon recapture not only Constantinople but even Jerusalem."

Was he really jealous, or was he making fun of him? This time Andrea had cut the conversation short. After what he had just said, Pedro Navarro was confident that they would have a contentious discussion with Andrea. But just as he was getting ready to counterattack Andrea's possible opposition, he had been silenced.

Sheikh Yahya seized the opportunity presented by the brief lull.

"It is abundantly clear that you gentlemen have a great deal to discuss. Let's keep this conversation going as we eat our breakfast together."

They walked over to the table prepared by servants in long hooded robes sewn of a light cotton fabric called burnus. To ease the tension in the air, Sheikh Yahya put on a fake smile.

"Yes! It's such an honor for me to be able to host two of the greatest commanders of the Mediterranean at my humble house. Signor Navarro, Signor Doria, again, welcome!"

Aruj informed Kemal Reis about his intentions to pay a visit to the Sultan of Tunisia and got encouraged by his supportive attitude.

"What do you think I should offer to him?"

"One-fifth, one-fifth of the booty, Aruj. He will accept."

"Are you sure?"

"I am! After Queen Isabel's death, Cardinal Jiménez became increasingly ambitious in his role. Mers El Kébir was only a stopover on the way to Oran. Although he is being friendly to the Spaniards and is maintaining relations with a soft demeanor, Mulay Muhammad is aware that the doors of his white Tunisia are soon going to be knocked on."

"Then, the destination is La Goulette."

"Your decision is right. I have no doubt that you will flourish there, son. Be warned, though, that if a man is skilled in playing the ally, you should be aware that the smiley face he displays to you is also a disguise. Consider it a piece of sound advice that you should bear in mind."

"I trust in no one save my brothers, Kemal Reis; don't be concerned."

"That's exactly what I thought, and when I saw that you only had a few siblings, I introduced you to the others".

They laughed. Kemal Reis continued:

"Look Aruj, even though the men you got to know here today are not your blood brothers, nonetheless consider them your heart brothers. They never waver in their allegiances, and their statements carry the weight of an oath. I have complete trust in all of them. They will be your comrades while you navigate in these treacherous waters; at times they will be on your galiots sailing under your command, and at other times, they will join forces with you in their own galiots and with levends sailing under their command. When you see their flag on the horizon, rest assured, you will never fall flat on your face."

"Thank you, Kemal Reis. From now on, all are brothers to me. I will always appreciate the helping hand the Ottoman has extended. Upon your return, please convey our gratitude and regards to Prince Korkud. May Allah bestows upon him victory and prosperity both in this life and in the life to come."

"I will, son. Today is the day to set sail for Tunisia. There is no point in lingering on this island any longer and wasting time. May you be guided by Allah's grace and wisdom."

They hugged each other and bid farewell. Aruj's concerns had begun to fade away as they made their way back to their ships. His eyes had once more started to gleam, and his demeanor had become a little more softened.

Khidr could not let this opportunity pass him by, so he turned to his brother and asked:

"Brother, so what about Feli..."

"I said we're going to Tunisia, Khidr. Why are you worrying? We're going to Tunisia and Felipa is also coming with us."

Khidr was still in search of proper words, but Aruj had already given his reply. First, he got confused, then he became surprized and cracked a grin.

"We are going to Tunisia... Felipa... Felipa is also going to Tunisia..."

His face lit up and his eyes gleamed. Khidr had regained his mood. He raised his hand high and gave Aruj a firm pat on the back.

"You are the king of brothers!"

When Aruj lost his balance and stumbled with the blow, he turned and yelled at Khidr.

"Heeey, you'd better keep that lion in the cage! I was almost going to spit my lungs out!"

"So, what encouraged you to set sail from the Italian waters all the way down to the Barbary Coast, Signor Navarro?"

Bored with the small talk, Andrea had finally asked Pedro Navarro the question he was wondering the most. Without waiting to swallow the last bite he was still chewing in his mouth Pedro Navarro replied:

"Cardinal Jiménez of course, Signor Doria. And as the admiral of the fleet, my first gift to King Fernando was Mers El Kébir."

Andrea couldn't hide his bewilderment.

"So, you've risen to the rank of admiral in the Royal Navy."

"True, Signor. Following the death of the queen, His Majesty and His Eminence Cardinal Jiménez decided to put their plans for North Africa into action. And with the approval of Gonzalo Fernández de Córdoba, the Spanish fleet was given under my command."

"If I recall correctly, you had said that the first and foremost issue Christianity had to address was the division of the Church. Are you not concerned about the possibility that Fernando's aspirations on the Barbary Coast would distract him and prevent Spain from accomplishing this lofty goal?"

"Once we take Oran after Mers El Kébir, the kingdom will have two strategic bases on the North African coast, both of which are of immense value. During a crusade to Constantinople and subsequently, to the Holy land, we need to make sure that we are not stabbed in the back in the Mediterranean."

It was now Pedro Navarro's turn to ask questions.

"What about you, Signor Doria? What brought you here?"

Sheikh Yahya intervened.

"Signor Doria has come to deliver the priceless present that was sent to me by your generous King. But it is rather unfortunate, of course, that the woman he successfully brought from Spain all the way down to Djerba and entrusted to my men, was kidnapped by the pirates before it even reached me."

Andrea was utterly shocked. After hearing Sheik's last words, a sip of water lost its way and got stuck in his throat, and to be able to clear the way and breathe again Andrea started coughing. The veins on his forehead swelled up and his face started to turn crimson.

The sheikh got worried:

"Signor Doria, are you okay?"

Andrea was having trouble breathing. Had he heard right? Had Felipa been kidnapped? He made an effort to speak in between the coughs.

"Didn't you receive your gift?"

"Never mind the gift, Signor Doria. You're not even capable of breathing."

"I'm... I'm fine. It's just a drop of water that lost its way down and that's all."

Andrea was slowly coming to himself. Yet this time, his face was turning from crimson to white. But since he was already a pale-faced man, neither Sheikh Yahya nor Pedro Navarro noticed how he was troubled by the news.

"So, she was kidnapped by the pirates..."

"From what I've been told, after she escape from my men, she fell into the hands of a bunch of men who were wearing baggy trousers. I've heard that they had berets on their heads and multicolored vests that they had worn on their white shirts."

Pedro Navarro jumped in.

"Given the way that they were dressed, they might be Turkish corsairs."

"I have no idea, Admiral. What I've been told is that the one with the red beard had pulled his sword and slaughtered all my men in a matter of minutes. And we presume that they're ensuring our safety here. God damn guards, they're even incapable of looking out for themselves."

Turkish corsairs... Turkish corsairs with baggy trousers, swords, and red beards... Andrea had his fists clenched so tight that he could feel his nails digging into his flesh.

"I'm sorry to hear that. At the special request of King Fernando, I had brought her here..."

Sheikh Yahya cut Andrea off before he finished.

"Signor Doria, please. You have nothing to do with this incident, it's my feckless guards to blame. I dispatched men after her to search the island thoroughly. Rest assured; they will soon find that woman. And when that bitch is brought in here, she will be punished so severely for her attempt that she will not even dare to make the same mistake again."

Andrea felt his heartbeat quicken. It was as if the sheikh's words were ringing within his head. At that moment, he could have stabbed him in the throat without the slightest hesitation with any sharp object he would grab; but finding Felipa before the guards, was more important.

"I hope... I hope you find her quickly. I have to leave now, as I plan to set sail this afternoon."

Andrea and Pedro Navarro looked each other in the eye. The sheikh had somewhat been relieved upon hearing about Andrea's desire to leave, for he was feeling quite nervous due to the tension between the two commanders.

Andrea stood up and bid farewell to both.
"Sheikh Yahya... Admiral..."
Pedro Navarro said Andrea a sarcastic goodbye.
"Looking forward to seeing you again, Signor Doria. In another place, another time, but hopefully on the same sides..."

Andrea had no time to retaliate. He turned around and began walking briskly. All those men who were supposed to accompany him to the door were left behind. They all stood there and looked at Andrea as he quickly got out of sight.

As soon as Khidr stepped aboard, he raced to the captain's cabin. Felipa leaped to her feet as she saw him enter headlong. She had dropped the notepad on the floor, but she neither could speak nor kneel down to pick it up. She could just stand still.

"I was... I was just... reading..."

"Damn me!" said Khidr to himself. He had grown so impatient to tell Felipa that they were also going to take her to Tunisia with them that he had literally barged in the cabin. Felipa must have thought of Khidr as someone lacking manners now. "Bravo!" he murmured to himself. He needed to do something to make amend for his discourteousness and he needed to do it quickly, but what could he do? After taking a few steps toward Felipa, Khidr knelt, picked up the notebook from the ground, and then replaced it in the hands of the young woman. He helped her to get seated, turned around, and left the cabin. As Felipa sitting on the edge of the wooden stool with the notebook in her hands, she was trying to understand what was going on. She heard three knocks on the door. Khidr cracked the door open about halfway and slowly entered. He was glad he didn't make Felipa jump out of fright this time.

"I apologize for being so impolite."

Felipa greeted Khidr with a smile that appeared to be one of bewilderment.

"I was just reading..."

"You've been reading since last night."

"Last night?... but you... how... How do you know?"

"After we got back aboard, I wondered how you've been doing, so I dropped by to check on you. I saw you sleeping on the mattress with this notebook in your hands and didn't want to wake you up."

Felipa smiled.

"So, it was you who covered me with a blanket."

"Oh, My Allah, it seems that I woke you up from your sleep."

"Oh, no! You didn't! It was already morning when I noticed."

"The nights are usually breezy on the seas. You've already had a rough day. I wanted to keep you warm."

"A rough day, huh?" It was as if mist descended on her sparkling eyes. "If only you knew how long I've been going through these rough days. Sometimes it feels morning will never arrive."

"The darkest hour of the night, they say, is just before the dawn."

Felipa took a deep breath. She was in despair.

"I miss them a lot... I miss my father, my home, Cergio... and Viento... I suppose I'll never be able to see him again."

Felipa's eyes welled up with tears.

"How many years had passed?"

"Three, five... what difference does it make? It feels like eons to me..."

"I'm sorry about your father and about Cergio, but a new day has dawned Felipa. Today is the day you got your freedom back. You can set up a new home for yourself and start a new life. And I'm sure Viento is also..."

Was he sure? How could he possibly be sure? Khidr didn't even know who Viento was. Was he, her brother? Her friend? Her husband? Felipa read all these questions from the strange look in Khidr's eyes.

"He was my horse... Viento was my horse. With his long silky mane, shiny fur, deep black eyes, and a spirit that can never be contained, Viento was my best friend."

The flames of Andarax passed by her eyes. She thought back to the last time she saw him, the time when she saw him galloping away...

"They had me in their grasp... I cried out to Viento for him to run away... and he did..." Felipa wiped that single drop of tear that fell from her eyes leaving her lashes an orphan. "Anyway..." she said. "None of these should make you upset. One has to learn to live with one's scars. Besides, maybe they will heal in time. I mean... I guess... I hope..." She paused for a moment and then gathered her composure. "I... I suppose it's time for me to leave. I don't want to burden you."

"We're going to Tunisia!"

Khidr had said it in an instant. It was obvious that Felipa had spent the previous night, which was probably the only night in a long time that she had felt safe, drowned in these thoughts. She had reflected on her past and tried to foresee her future, settled accounts with her demons and sought refuge in her prayers before she eventually surrendered her worn body into the healing arms of sleep.

"So, you're going to Tunisia?"

"We're going to Tunisia!" This time Khidr had put more stress on his words.

"We're all going... We're going together. You're coming too."

Khidr seemed he had no intention to let her speak. Even if he would, what was she going to say, anyway? She could not stay here in Djerba, the Sheik's men would find her on this small island in less than an hour. She neither could return to Spain. Spain had become a graveyard for the Muslims. Khidr was her one and only chance. In a weak tone, she said "Okay."

"Good!" said Khidr with a grin on his face. "So, now I'd better go to the upper deck and lend my brothers a hand. Soon, we'll set sail for La Goulette."

He turned around and walked towards the door. Just when he was about to leave, he turned to Felipa.

"Did Yahya bring you something to eat this morning?"

Felipa was so perplexed that it took her a moment to understand what she was being asked.

"Yahya... something to eat... Oh, yes. I ate."

"Perfect! I'll drop by later."

He was gone. Felipa, on the other hand, was still sitting on the edge of the stool and staring at the door. She muttered to herself:

"Tunisia... but where is Tunisia?"

"Come on! Run you sluggard!"

After had left the sheikh's house was now galloping at full speed towards the port. Red-bearded Turkish corsairs... They could be none other than Aruj and Khidr. He knew that they were planning to set sail this morning, but to where the winds would take them, he was clueless. Oh, such a fool he was! Why hadn't he asked them the previous night when he had the chance? He had gone so far as to wish that he would never see them again. What if he would get exactly what he wished for? How would Andrea ever find Felipa again? Oh, such a fool he was. He was galloping at full speed on the trails of Djerba leaving a cloud of dust behind. He had to catch them, no matter what he had to catch them!

Mooring lines were loosened, and the anchors were weighed. The levends treaded on the ratlines tied between the shrouds that had already been coated with tar to avoid a slip. They got on the yards and let the sails drop down. And as the oars began to move in and up the waters like the wings of a monarch butterfly, two galiots followed by galleons full of sailors set sail for Tunisia.

Aruj was singing and joking around. The weather was warm, the sea was calm and everyone on board was in a cheerful mood. Khidr had leaned on the railings and was enjoying the sunlight. Isaac approached him and wrapped his arm around his shoulder.

With eyes on the horizon, Khidr muttered:
"La Goulette..."
"What do you think?"
"Good days are ahead of us."
"Sometimes it really surprises me seeing how you two are exactly alike."
Khidr smiled.
"My beard is a bit more brownish."
"Oh, come on Khidr! You know what I mean."
"Even on such a beautiful day, you're still concerned."
"Cautious... cautious let's say."

They began to laugh. It was true, Isaac was always cautious. It was his character. He had never been one for adventure and was well aware that he had not set sail toward a life he imagined for himself. However, his brothers needed him.

For a while, they kept silent. Both were gazing at the white silhouette of Tunisia reminiscent of an oasis with its flower-filled gardens. Khidr wanted to cheer his elder brother up.

"It wouldn't be long before the leaves said their final goodbyes to the branches. There is a good chance that we will set sail once or twice more. After then, the weather would no longer cooperate. We return to Tunisia with the booty and please the sultan. Then, La Goulette is ours."

"Perhaps I'll go to Lesbos, before the winter settles, to see mom, to see if there's anything she needs. Then I'll return."

"We're going to build ships this winter, you know."

"I know."

La Goulette which connected the Lake of Tunisia to the sea was an ideal location for them to spend the winter. Even though it was not a port that was as equipped as it once was, and it no longer had the deep waters that could host the great armadas as the last and greatest historian of antiquity Procopius, had once said; Barbarossas could build here their ships, repair the thick walls dated back to the Roman times, and turn La Goulette into a perfect naval base for themselves. Moreover, Khidr was glad that the port was situated in close proximity to Tunisia which overlooked Carthage, the largest city of the Hellenistic period. It was not only a prosperous place but also a secure one. Every nightfall, the guards would lock the city gates of this white city that was surrounded by battlements, and they would patrol the city throughout the entire night. This place could turn out to be a safe home for Felipa. Yes, Felipa could truly love Tunisia. While Khidr was immersed in these thoughts and Isaac was almost lost in his dreams of Lesbos, Aruj's blossoming voice brought both back into the present moment.

"And there it is! La Goulette. Those walls that you see are the walls of our new home."

They were gone. There was no trace of the galiots, nor the galleons or the levends. The sun was high up in the sky beaming out rays that cast shorter shadows. Andrea placed his hand on his forehead to shade his eyes from the bright sunlight and scanned the horizon. Felipa was gone. Who knows where she had been taken to? He ripped off his cap, squeezed it in his hands, and slammed it to the ground with rage.

"Damn!"

Cervantes got up from his chair, walked towards his library, and began searching for something through the dusty books sitting on the dusty shelves.

"It should be somewhere around here. Hah! Here it is!". He picked up a rolled-up piece of parchment from amid the volumes and returned to his desk. After blowing off the dust, he rolled it open with care.

"Here! Mulay Muhammad's white court!"

With its carved column heads, meticulously shaped thujas, magnificent arches, and fountains among the pines, medlar, and mango trees, it was a drawing of Mulay Muhammad's stunning palace in Casbah which was obviously a work of a very talented artist.

William took the drawing in his hands.

"Gosh! It's so beautiful! Is this masterpiece a work of yours, Signor Cervantes?"

Cervantes smiled and showed William his right hand.

"No, Signor Shakespeare. Look at this hand. Since its companion had abandoned us, this hand shouldered all the responsibilities of my miserable life. Look how worn, how rough it eventually became. How on earth I can possibly produce such a breathtaking piece of art with this poor hand of mine?"

William shifted his gaze from Cervantes' weary right hand to the city of Tunisia that he was holding in his hands.

"Then, whose work is this?"

"The work of a woman with tiny hands and delicate fingers... A woman who had fallen in love with Tunisia the moment she saw it."

William looked Cervantes in the eye.

"Felipa's..."

Tunisia

"Come! This way, Signorina."

Upon hearing the word "Signorina", Felipa smiled. Cergio was most likely the last person to call her in that manner. Mounted on a bay horse, she was following a stranger called Yahya without knowing where she was being taken to; still, she had been captivated by the beauty of this white city blooming flowers all around.

"So, this is where they call Tunisia..."
"Medina, Signorina. Do you like it?"
"Like it?"

She had been expelled from her home. Her family had been murdered and she had been enslaved by Christians. Just when she was finally granted her freedom back, did she have the luxury of liking or despising any place that might give her a second chance to start over?

Medina was located approximately a hundred miles of north of Kairouan, which had been built as a military post by the Arab general Uqba Ibn Nāfi of the Umayyads right in the middle of the steppe and had become over time one of the most magnificent works of the Western Islamic art. Its location on the fertile plains of North Africa, at the intersection of the caravan routes, had soon made Medina the heart of Tunisia. After declaring their independence in 1229, the Hafsids, the rulers of the Almohad Ifriqiya, had moved the center of administration to the Casbah that was leaning against the western wall of the city. They had thoroughly renovated the fort and strengthened its defenses, built two palaces inside the fort, in one of which they would dwell, in the other, they would discuss state affairs and had begun ruling the city from Casbah. Except for the northeastern façade featured with porticoes, it was as if the walls were swathing the entire city. The city itself had been laid out like a sprawling maze of narrow streets and alleyways revolving around the Al-Zaytuna Mosque which was surrounded by numerous covered souks. The intersection of the crossing streets connecting Bab Souika[75] in the north and Bab el Jazira[76] in the south with the two main arteries leading to Bab el Bahr was dividing the city into four main suburbs. Exquisitely decorated Bab el Bahr was the city's largest gate leading to the port. Its double-wing gates made up of date wood would be closed in the evenings and the guards stationed in front of the gate would keep watch throughout the night.

Felipa had been mesmerized by the charm of the narrow streets leading to courtyards covered with mosaic tiles in-between the low-rise dwellings. As she passed beneath the horseshoe arches, she gazed at the houses with blue framed windows from which colorful flowers were hanging, as well as at the small shops selling silk and velvet fabrics, and the carpets finely woven by the Tunisian women. As for the flags sewn with a black horse motif hanging in the streets of this enchanting white city; it was impossible for Felipa not to notice.

"This place is very beautiful, Yahya... and these flags..."
"It is the Hafsid flag, Signorina. Members of the Hafsid Dynasty are known by their love of horses, dogs, and parrots."
"It reminded me of Viento..."
"Viento?"
"My horse, Yahya Reis, my horse..."

Felipa had noticed the warm and friendly expression on people's faces as she followed Yahya into the narrow shadowy alleys. Tunisians of the time were not arrogant like those of the Algerians. They seemed be people with soft temperaments and gentle hearts.

Yahya smiled.
"I think you'll feel comfortable in here."

---

[75] The northern gate of Medina
[76] The southern gate of Medina

"Where are we going?"

"To Mother Firuze's house."

They came to a halt in front of a house with blue-framed windows, resembling the rest of the houses in the Medina. Yahya jumped off his horse, approached Felipa, and offered her his hand.

"We're here, Signorina. Allow me to help yo..."

As Felipa dismounted all at once without any assistance, his hand was left hanging in midair.

He took a few steps climbing up to the threshold and knocked on the door. After a short while, the wooden door creaked open and two azure eyes brightened by the daylight flowing into the foyer gleamed in the darkness.

"Yahya? My son?"

"It's me, Mother Firuze.

They hugged each other in the doorway.

"You've wanted a daughter ever since I knew you. See? Allah heard your prayers."

Mother Firuze did not utter a word. She reached out for Felipa with her wrinkly hands, caught her by the shoulder and pulled her inside. Pleased with this warm welcome, Yahya quietly followed them in and shut the door on the face of the narrow street.

The northwestern eyes of the Casbah were looking at the hills lined with bastions and battlements that had been built to defend the city; while its southwest was facing the Sebkha Séjoumi which was a natural salt lake frequently visited by migratory birds. A narrow lane surrounded by high walls was connecting the fortress to the gardens of Ras Tabia.

As soon as they arrived at the mansion Mulay Muhammad used to for the purposes of collecting taxes from his subjects and inspecting his troops, Khidr could help himself and muttered:

"The glamorous Maghreb..."

He was dazzled by the abundance and luxury that surrounded them. The column heads inscribed with verses from the Qur'an, countless halls illuminated by the flickering lights of lanterns, rose-scented gardens nested within each other, the stunning mosaic tiles...

"This place is a true oasis in the midst of the desert."

Aruj smiled.

"I'm pleased to hear that you liked your new home."

Aruj had made his plans. He had reserved for the sultan the most exquisite silk fabrics, the most precious jewels, and the brightest swords with diamond adorned hilts from the booty they seized from the Venetian galleons. He had placed them in the chests and had them all brought to the palace on his men's shoulders. He had rehearsed the speech he intended to make, sorted out the promises he was going to give, was now ready to appear before the sultan.

When the guards drew the curtains opening to the throne room asunder, the Barbarossas suddenly found themselves in front of Mulay Muhammad. Their placed their hands on their broad chests and bowed low to salute the sultan.

Mulay Muhammad leaned back in his throne and after keeping his silent for a while he welcomed the Barbarossas with a sarcastic tone.

"Aruj Reis... Khidr Reis... Isaac Reis..."

They were taken aback. It was apparent that their names had paid a previous visit to the sultan before they did so themselves. Mulay Muhammad continued:

"I suppose you did not think that my ears would not hear what's being said about you while the winds whispering your escape from the Knights of Saint John were still blowing in the Mediterranean, did you Aruj Reis?"

Aruj replied cautiously.

"I hope the words those winds had whispered in your ears, are words of praise, My Sultan."

"Oh yes, yes, don't be concerned. What's generally spoken of you is your vast knowledge of maritime affairs, your valiance, bravery, persistence along with many other..."

The sultan's caustic and demeaning tone was extremely irritating. The expression on Aruj's face who was already a hot-tempered man by nature had now become even sharper.

"You seem to imply that these are easily acquired virtues."

Sultan rose to his feet.

"Of course not, but as you would also know, what makes the world go round is not one's virtues, but wealth, Aruj Reis."

Isaac gritted his teeth and cast a sidelong glance at Aruj. He was right to have had concerns. During all those years that he sailed alongside his father, Isaac had met all kinds of people. The moneylenders who keep an account of every single ducat; the drapers who run out of the mosque screaming during Friday prayer thinking that they had their money stolen when, in reality, it had only slipped into a hole in their pocket; the bakers who count each and every sesame seed they put on each loaf of bread... When it comes to money it would make no difference whether one was a baker or a sultan; everyone would behave the same way regardless of their social status. They would all look at, at the end of the day, the akches, ducats or florins they had whether they held it in their palms or kept it in their chests.

The sultan raised his hands and showed them the splendor of the hall they were in.

"As you would also appreciate, valiance and persistence alone are not enough to live a life as magnificent as this one. It requires not only trading skills and administrative acumen, but also well-established relationships and a level of diplomacy for these oases to come into existence. Or else, this white city before your very eyes would have been nothing but a mirage in the dunes of Maghreb." He took a few steps and walked towards Aruj. And then; he confronted him by staring him directly in the eye. "I said, as you would appreciate, but I hope, you would, Aruj Reis."

Khidr took advantage of a brief silence and chipped in:

"Of course, My Sultan. But what is more important is the fact that a statesman like you, who has extensive experience in matters of administration, foreign affairs, and diplomacy, require support and protection when wielding authority. We are sailors. We spend our summers on waters, our winters on land, but always close to our ships. We know how to build, how to mend; and how to fight with all our might when the seas allow. What distinguishes us, the Barbarossas, from the rest, is the strength of our hearts to which we resort in case our arms have no more. And now, we'd want to put our swords at your service."

Aruj relaxed his grip on Khidr's arm. His younger brother appeared to have succeeded in swaying the sultan's opinion in their favor.

Mulay Muhammad clasped his hands behind and addressed Khidr:

"So, you want to swing your swords for me, huh?"

His arrogance had somewhat dissipated, and his initial sardonic tone of voice had changed.

Khidr continued his words:

"Mediterranean, My Sultan… Mediterranean is no longer as safe as it once used to be. Let us restore the walls of La Goulette, assure the safety of your merchant ships and chase the thieves away from your door. All that we need in return is to be sheltered throughout the winter and to rest our summer-worn galiots at the port."

Mulay Muhammad was aware that the Mediterranean had begun to heat up following the fall of Granada. Even while the Hafsids enjoyed cordial relations with the kingdoms of Europe, he had no idea how his dynasty would tolerate if the demands of the Christians grew more stringent over time. He was content with the prosperous life he was living. The primary objective of his diplomatic efforts, as well as the driving force behind his conciliatory demeanor, had always been to protect what he already possessed. He had not been equipped for battle from birth. What he wanted was to spend the rest of his life to pursuing intellectual endeavors in various arts and sciences. He had libraries filled with manuscripts, and scribes who were transcribing the works of ancient historians and writers. His greatest fulfillment was engaging in scholarly discourse with the various intellectuals he hosted at his palace. He would find delight in attending games and arranging banquets and relish the company of his horses, dogs, and parrots. He was certainly a man of wits, for he needed to be witty to possess all these things. And as he was looking at these three men standing before him; he had already seen how well the Barbarossas might serve him in severing the Spanish hands in case Spain would dare to touch his Tunisia in the future.

"One-fifth… I want one-fifth of the booty."
"One-fifth of the booty is yours, My Sultan…"

Aruj had not hesitated. Providing protections for his ships, reinforcing the walls of La Goulette might be well-thought promises to convince the sultan, but Aruj knew that Mulay Muhammad would not be content with these alone. There was no doubt that the sultan would request a share of the booty they would seize and seeing that he eventually did, had not surprised him.

The sultan flashed a grin. He signaled to his guards by clapping his hands.

"Then I bid you a warm welcome to Tunisia!"

The guards entered the room, carrying with them an aigrette bedecked with diamonds and three delicately woven caftans laid out on cushions of green velvet.

"Accept these as a gesture of my appreciation for your presence in Tunisia" said Mulay Muhammad and then he draped the caftans over their shoulders.

After taking the presents and expressing their gratitude, the Barbarossas could now request Sultan's permission to return to their ships.

"Thank you, My Sultan. Provided that the weather cooperates with our plans and the Mediterranean continues to bless us with gentle breezes and placid waters, we hope to set sail once more before the onset of winter. If we have your permission, we would like to return to our ships to make the necessary arrangements for the upcoming expedition."

"You have my permission to leave, valiant levends. But I'd love to have you over here for dinner tonight. In celebration of your coming to Tunisia, I will host a banquet in the palace in your honor. Tonight, I'd like you to fill your tummies with delectable foods as my lovely dancers replenish your souls."

In two minutes flat, they had become "valiant levends". The guards who entered with a clap of a hand, had obviously been ordered to stand ready behind the closed doors, with presents in one hand and swords in the other. In the event of a disagreement between the sultan and the Barbarossas, it was obvious that what was going to be left behind would be the presents. Fortunately, both sides had come to terms with one another, and this time, it had been the swords that remained behind.

As they were being led out the door, Khidr was thinking about neither the food nor the dancers. It was Felipa his mind was preoccupied with. He was curious as to Yahya's whereabouts. He had said "Leave it to me, Reis. I know to whom I am going to entrust her" and had left. Obviously, it was not Yahya's first visit to this white city, for he seemed to have people around whom he knew and trusted. But still, Khidr was worried. He was thinking that he needed to return to the ships as soon as he could to see whether Yahya had returned. It was at that precise moment, he stumbled with Aruj's pat him on the back. Khidr was almost going to give the Moorish carpet on the floor a kiss when his long caftan wrapped around his feet.

He turned to his brother with reproach:

"But you do this all the time!"

Aruj was smiling and looking away, whistling as if he was not the one who had just hit him on the back.

"Every time my mind sets sail, I either get a slap on the neck or a firm pat on the back."

"You left me with no other choice; I saw that you were getting too far away from the shore, and I wanted to bring you back."

"I have a thousand things in mind, brother."

"Come on, you have only one thing in mind, we all know what it is." Aruj suddenly stopped. "I mean, who she is..."

"Brother!"

Mother Firuze was one of the expats who had moved to Tunisia many years ago and started living in a tiny house with his crimpled grandson Yusuf. Yahya had raced to her help just as she was about to taste death at the hands of the Spaniards, saving her from suffering the same fate as her slain husband. Despite being seriously wounded in the chest by a Spanish sword, Yahya had managed to get Yusuf out of the blazing house and carry the old woman and her grandson to the boats. After the galleons set sail to North Africa, Yahya had laid with fever for days. And the ship's doctor was not unable to bring the fever down despite his best efforts. When Mother Firuze saw this, she had offered her help. She had prepared a mash with some dried tipton's weed, fresh melissa leaves, and a handful of nettle seeds she had taken out of her pocket and applied to the wound for the next two weeks. Yahya could only barely recall all of this. When he opened his eyes, he had found himself in Tunisia, lying on a low sofa inside this tiny house.

Every time Yahya traveled to Tunisia, he would pay a visit to Mother Firuze, but would never go empty-handed. He had supported Yusuf in opening a small shop in the souk, and had always set aside for them, a part of his earned income. He had become a son for Mother Firuze; as for Mother Firuze... she was no less than a mother to him.

Felipa had settled in Mother Firuze's house, and the ships had docked in La Goulette. Barbarossas, on the other hand, had decided to visit the baths of Medina to wash rid of the salty smell of seaweed that their days at the seas had left on them before attending to the banquet.

Aruj pulled a substantial of akches from his pocket, placed it in the palms of the burly Ethiopian at the entrance, and together with his brothers he entered the pine resin, rosemary, and myrtle-scented bath.

Medina was famous for its baths. With its pools of clean water reminiscent of the Antoine baths of the Carthaginian times and its elaborately decorated walls and vaulted ceilings; the baths, like in many other parts of the Maghreb, were serving the people who always complained about the water shortage in Tunisia as places not only for cleaning but also for meeting up and socializing.

Khidr yawned with a loincloth wrapped around his waist and a copper pitcher in his hand:
"Ah, this is so good."
Isaac was also feeling relaxed.
"This heat will relieve the pain in my bones."
Aruj poured some hot water down his head and turned to his brothers:
"What the hell is wrong with you? One of you talk like a grandpa; while the other sound like an old woman suffering from arthritis."

Khidr hadn't even heard what Aruj just said. His attention had been drawn to a Latin inscription on one of the pillars.

IMP. CAESAR
DIVI NERVAE NEPOS
DIVI TRAIANA PARTHICI F.
TRAIANVS HADRIANVS
AVG. PONT. MAX. TRIB.
POT. VII. COS. III.
VIAM A CARTHAGINE
THEVESTEN STRAVIT
PER LEG. III. AVG.
P. METILIO SECVNDO
LEG. AVG. PR. PR.[77]

---

[77] Shaw, T. (2022, October 9). Travels, or observations relating to several parts of Barbary and the Levant Volume Copy 1,2 1738.

A rotund voice echoed in the bath.

"Inscriptions from the times of the Ancient Romans..."

They all turned their gaze in the direction of the voice. A tall and slender man with dark skin, dark eyes, dark hair, and protruding cheekbones was sitting in the bath's darkest corner, watching them.

"I guess, you're new here..."

"Dating back to Julius Caesar's reign?"

William had always found the era of the Ancient Romans intriguing.

"Mostly from the reign of Emperor Hadrian, Signor Shakespeare. From Egypt to the Atlantic, from the northern shores of North Africa to the vast Saharan deserts; these lands are teeming with stones and marble that recount the stories of generosity and valor of all the communities that have ever lived in this region since antiquity. In these lands, the history of man has been engraved onto stones."

"Then, there must be thousands of papyri dating back to ancient times in Tunisia. Holy Jesus, I would have gladly given up everything just to have a glimpse of them."

"Not quite, Signor. After the defeat of the famous general Hannibal, the shores of the Maghreb, which had previously been ruled by the Phoenicians and then by the Carthaginians, had fallen into the hands of the Romans." Cervantes' fingers had started to trace the Mediterranean map. "After losing dominion over Sicily, Hannibal had crossed the Iberian Peninsula, the Pyrenees, and the Alps, stepped onto Italian soil with his elephants and a massive army. However, even though he had defeated the Romans in a number of significant battles; he had been unable to prevent the Romans from quickly regaining their strength and launching another assault on Carthage."

"I'd heard that Hannibal had committed suicide by drinking the poison he carried in his ring," said William. Cervantes went on:

"After the Third Punic War, which resulted in the complete destruction of Carthage and the enslavement of its population, all the ancient records had been moved to the Great Library of Alexandria founded during the reign of Ptolemy II, the Hellenistic King of Egypt. Back then, Alexandria was a center for science and learning. According to what Strabo had said, it was Aristotle himself, the teacher of Alexander the Great, who had gathered books and taught the Hellenistic kings of Egypt how to set up a library. But in the year 48 AD, during Julius Caesar's conquest of Alexandria, the library was severely damaged by the flames that spread from the boats. And after Christianity was declared the official religion of the Roman Empire, all the ancient manuscripts were destroyed by the order of Emperor Theodosius I, which resulted in the tumbling down of one of the most important bridges that connected the old and new worlds."

"All the records? Were all the records destroyed?"

"The majority of them. Except for those translated and copied by the Arabs and those the Helens transported to Anatolia over time, all were destroyed. And those scribes who had been working for Mulay Muhammad for quite a while, were, at that time, busy with copying whatever had remained of these priceless manuscripts."

After leaving the bath, Barbarossas wore over their tanned myrtle-scented skins pearl white shirts. They put on their backs the caftans Mulay Muhammad had given them as a gift, and went to the palace. As they waited for the sultan in the courtyard they were welcomed in, it was as if the light beaming through one of the arches leading to the courtyard was calling Aruj to itself.

He took a few steps and partially opened the veil. What he saw had taken him by surprise. He turned and called out to his brothers:

"Khidr…. Psssst… Come on over and take a look!"

"Brother, stop! Don't barge in!"

Aruj hadn't even waited for Aruj Khidr to finish his sentence and entered the room. Khidr went after Aruj, dragging Isaac along with him, grumbling.

"You can't just walk in anywhere you…"

He was unable to complete his words. All of them had become awestruck upon what they saw. His gaze fixed on the shelves, Khidr mumbled:

"This place must be twice the size of the Great Library of Alexandria!"

"Ha ha! I wish it were, Khidr Reis, I wish it were as you say."

It was Mulay Muhammad speaking. They all bowed low and greeted the sultan. Mulay Muhammad invited them to stroll along the aisles.

"Come, please, take a closer look!"

Barbarossas were astounded by the magnificence of Sultan's library which seemed to house countless books and manuscripts. It was as though all those authors, historians, and poets of antiquity had come out of the books they hid themselves in and were walking among the shelves alongside the brothers.

"As if I can hear them whispering," muttered Khidr.
Aruj leaned towards Khidr and whispered in his ears.
"Who knows what they're saying."
"Hushh!"

As they approached the shelves that held the most ancient of all the pre-served papyri, the sultan began talking.

"These are from the Roman times. It's a misfortune that they are the old-est texts we have in our hands. I would have given anything to have been able to find the records of the Carthaginians."

"The Carthaginians...The forefathers of seafaring and trade," muttered Isaac.

"Carthage is said to have been founded by Dido, the Queen of Tyre, who had fled from her ruthless and autocratic brother Pygmalion. When she first set foot on the coasts of North Africa, Dido had requested from the natives a piece of land not larger than an ox-hide would cover. And when her wish was granted, she had cut a single ox-hide into thin threads, attached them at their ends, laid the long strip forming a circle, and acquired an area large enough to found her a kingdom. So had the Kingdom of Carthage been founded on these lands; and thanks to its location right across Sicily, the people of Tyre had been able to continue engaging in trade. The people who live here today, believe that the spirit of Dido is still roaming the Carthagin-ian hills even today. Just like the spirit of Hannibal they say."

"Commander Hannibal... Rome's implacable enemy... I'd heard his story."

"The Mediterranean, gentlemen... The Mediterranean that you claim heated up with the fall of Granada... Her waters never cooled down through-out history. She is a lover, for the sake whom all societies that ever lived in this region eventually perished as they tried to possess her. With her deep blue brilliance, she is a dazzling beauty from afar... A dazzling beauty that can drown you in an instant, even in her most shallow bays..."

"And just when you least expect..."

They all seemed to have recalled this tall and slender man with dark skin, dark eyes, dark hair, and protruding cheekbones who suddenly appeared before them as they walked through the shelves. Had they met before? Or had they simply had the impression that they had met before? If it was just an impression how come, they all had gotten the same impression at the same time?

"Oh, Huseyn, so you are here, too?"
"I was looking for you, My Sultan."
Mulay Muhammad turned to the Barbarossas.
"I'd like to introduce you to Huseyn. He is my adviser, my right hand, the person in whose judgment I have the utmost confidence."

Huseyn greeted the Barbarossas with a slight bow of his head. His eyes, however, had not moved in tandem with the motion of his head. None among the three brothers had liked Huseyn. His moves were slow and the expression on his face suggested that he was an expert at hiding his true colors. They were all under the impression that there was something sinister about him, yet there was also the possibility of this impression being un-founded. But it if was really unfounded, how come they all had gotten the same impression at the same time?

"We met before, My Sultan...", said Isaac, "If our encounter counts as such. In the bath..."
"Of course!" Khidr thought to himself. Khidr's mind must have been blurred due to the heat, or else, how could he have forgotten this irritating man?

Huseyn turned his gaze away from the Barbarossas to Mulay Muhammad.
"I wanted to inform you that the food is served."
The sultan clasped his hands in front of his chest.
"Wonderful! Then we can all go and enjoy!"

The banquet Mulay Muhammad hosted in honor of the Barbarossas was so magnificent that the levends, who had nothing to eat but salted meat and rusks while at sea, could only dream of such a feast. The round copper trays adorned with prayers of abundance were full of various kinds of vegetables cooked with harissa, olive oil and vinegar, camel meat that had been marinated underground for weeks in earthenware pots, couscous pilaf, and a selection of various kinds of seafood. The tunes rising from the instruments of saz players were dancing on the curved bodies of the beautiful belly dancers, enchanting everyone in the room except Khidr, whose mind was at that time captive to Felipa.

As she sat on the edge of the mattress, Felipa was gazing at an exquisite needlework of a bird pattern on the wall. It had vivid colors and a crown of feathers on top its head. She had no idea what kind of bird it was, but she had never seen one this elegant before. She was so engrossed in its beauty that she didn't notice Mother Firuze enter the room.

"Anqa al-Mughrib[78]," said Mother Firuze.
"She's very beautiful..." Felipa muttered.
Mother Firuze handed Felipa a white night gown.
"Here, my girl. You can put this on."
Then, she sat next to Felipa and caressed her long hair scattered across her shoulders.
"Rest well tonight. Tomorrow, Yusuf will take you to the shop. There you can choose fabrics to your liking and bring them to me so that I'll tailor new clothes for you."
Felipa was grateful. She wanted to say something to express her feelings but struggled to find the proper words.
"I... Mother Firuze... But you go into all this trouble for me."
"Oh, you are most welcome, my dear girl. Yahya entrusted you to me. This house is your home now. Stay as long as you like."
Felipa took Mother Firuze's hands into her own and kissed them.
"How am I going to repay you for all these?"
Mother Firuze's face was lit up with a heartfelt smile. The light gleaming from her sapphire eyes warmed Felipa's heart.
"You keep me company. Since Yusuf has to stay at the shop during the day, I was feeling lonely here. Being alone is not always pleasant, my dear. One wants to feel the breath of another. I'm so glad that I have a daughter now. Get some sleep tonight. Let your body, mind, and soul rest a little."

---

[78] A legendary bird referred to as Phoenix in Greek mythology, Simurgh in Persian mythology.

Felipa reached out and took the gown from Mother Firuze's delicate hands. After putting it on, she slid under the bed cover. Mother Firuze gave her a goodnight kiss on the forehead. Then, she stood up and grabbed the lantern hanging on the wall. As she was ready to leave the room she turned around and stared into Felipa's dark eyes.

"Good night, sweetheart. May Allah bless you with a restful night."

As soon as the door was closed, darkness descended on the room. For a while, Felipa listened to the sound of silence whispering into her ears, but she eventually succumbed to the enticement of sleep and her weary eyelids softly closed.

Aruj was working on a somewhat detailed map of Mediterranean laid before him, trying to plan a route for the expedition he intended to launch in a few days. He spoke without taking his eyes away:

"Couldn't sleep?"

"I couldn't."

"You're thinking too much."

"And you?"

Aruj took up the hourglass on the table and flipped it over.

"We have a lot to do... and only three days."

"Three days? But we've just got here!"

"I know."

He placed his finger on the map and spoke firmly:

"We will hit the Italian coasts!"

Khidr was perplexed.

"We have a lot to do this winter, Khidr. We must fortify the walls, repair the ships, and build new ones. To accomplish all these, we need more men, which would necessitate more money. Come, take a look."

Khidr approached and turned his attention to the Mediterranean map resting beneath Aruj's calloused fingers. Aruj started to explain to his little brother the plans he had been working for.

"The prevailing northern winds of the Mediterranean hurl ships sailing in the south toward the coasts of Africa, which results in European trade being confined to the north. In the Ligurian sea; Genoa, and the waters between the islands of Elba, Corsica, and Hyeres. The Balearic Islands and the coasts of Spain, the southwest waters of Sardinia, the islands of Lipari and the northern part of the strait of Messina; and lastly, the Strait of Otranto and the western coast of Peloponnese... These are the routes that merchant ships in the western Mediterranean take."

"We need to scout out good spots to lay an ambush."

"East of Sicily and the Ionian Sea, the Tyrrhenian Sea to the north up to the Gulf of Naples, southwestern part of Sardinia; in Liguria the waters between Elba, Corsica, and Genoa; and of course, the Balearic Islands. These are perfect locations to hide. The Venetians do not have a naval base on the Italian coasts. Corfu is too far south and the bases on the Dalmatian coast are too small. The galleys don't patrol for there's no suitable harbor to take shelter. We need to make use of this opportunity."

"Where shall we begin?"

"The merchant ships sailing to Rome usually follow the route between Elba and Piombino. This is going to be our primary area of focus. Also, I don't trust Mulay Muhammad. His only concern is keeping the status quo and preserve his luxurious life. He can easily cooperate with the Spaniards just as he did with the Genoese. If, on the other hand, we can be the ones to bring him this wealth, then, we can consolidate our position in La Goulette."

Aruj was right. It was true that they had the sultan's permission to anchor at the port, but if they wanted to spend this winter more comfortable, both the sultan and the Tunisians needed to see with their own eyes what the Barbarossas were capable of. And the best way to demonstrate this, was to set out for a final hunt in the Mediterranean before the onset of winter.

Khidr took a deep breath.

"We need more galiots, as well as more men. We can't go hunting with the galleons."

"There are galiots with paired oars at the port. Tomorrow, I'll talk to their owners. Meanwhile, together with Isaac take a few levends with you and go to the sailors' district to see whether there are any experienced sailors around eager to join us."

"All right, brother..."

Aruj turned his gaze back to the map. Khidr, on the other hand, after staring at his brother for a little while longer, turned around and walked toward the door. Just as he was about to leave the cabin, he heard his brother's voice.

"It is because of Felipa, isn't it?"

Khidr gazed over his shoulder at Aruj without turning his back.

"What is because of Felipa?"

"Your lack of sleep..."

"Whereas sleep is a drop of honey. If there's nothing bothering one's mind, neither the ghosts would disturb him, nor his dreams."

"However, sleep, like the Venetian ducat, has two faces," added Cervantes. "Being able to fall asleep is one's ability to calm his mind, for it is not always sorrow or concern that causes sleep to depart. Sometimes one's own dreams about future reach to such heights that even the excitement one feels from having such dreams would reverberate through the halls of the mind, leaving one sleepless. Other times, as you mentioned, sleep flees because it fears his ghosts... When the mind cannot cope with the suffering of the soul, sleep leaves one alone. Fortunately, it was their dreams rather than their ghosts that kept both Aruj and Khidr awake, at least for the time being, Signor Shakespeare... At least for the time being..."

Within three days, they had completed all the necessary preparations. They had traded several of the galleons for smaller galiots anchored at the port and found experienced sailors who were ready to join the crew. They had stored enough clean water, olive oil, salted meat, fish, cheese, cereals, tallow, and rusks to get them through the journey; and they had carried spare boats, gunters, topgallant masts, sails, and leadlines on board. And after stocking a sufficient amount of bitumen, tar, and lint that they might need to repair the ship's hull in case that it got damaged during a fight; the Barbarossas had set sail toward the coasts of Italy, where no one had come across Muslim corsairs for years. However, when the winds of the first week gave way to a hot, misty, and still air, the sails had become idle and the levends had no choice but to advance using the oars.

It had been three weeks since they had set sail from La Goulette, and the fact that they still hadn't spotted a chase carrying a big cargo was bothering them. But, as they cruised through the waters to the north of Sicily, hundreds of miles away from Tunisia, where the coasts of Piombino reached out to the sea as if to touch the Island of Elba, Aruj was scanning the horizon with no intention of returning to La Goulette empty handed.

Yahya's shouting from one of the poles aroused his attention.
"Galleoooon on the starboaaarddd! Galleeeooooonnssss... There are two of them!"

With the pennant of Saint Peter's embroidered on their flags, rails ornamented with gilded bronze lanterns, and the cardinal's coat of arms, these two galleons, apparently belonging to the Papacy, were sailing from Genoa to Civitavecchia. The Barbarossas had not yet any idea about their cargo; but judging by the guards with spears in their hands and daggers in their belts, by the noble women with their hair tinseled with ribbons and jewels, loitering on the deck in their silk blouses and the crinolines that they had worn under their embroidered belts; they seemed to be laden with treasure.

Yahya dashed down the mast and reported to Aruj.
"They seem to be four leagues apart from each other, Reis. The first one is three-masted, at least sixty-arshin-long and equipped with eighty cannons."
"What about the second?"
"It's difficult for me to say anything about the second one from this distance."
"I wonder how many men they've got..." muttered Khidr, while keeping his gaze fixed on the galleons.
"I've counted as many helmets as I can. They outnumber us by at least two to one."
Nobody uttered a word. Everyone was curiously waiting to hear what Aruj had to say. Aruj, as soon as he noticed the concerned expression settled on their faces, tightened his grip on the hilt of his sword.
"So, what are you waiting for? Are we going to watch them pass by?"

Aruj's galliot had the weather gage, and thanks to its being lightweight, they also had the advantage of speed. However, it was impossible to get within shooting range of a galleon that had forty cannons on each side and get abreast without being struck by the cannon fire. As the levends rowed closer to the galleons, Aruj had to devise a plan.

Cemal, who had not been around for some time, ran to Aruj with a piece of cloth in his hands, panting.

"Reis, let's bring down our flag and raise this up instead."

When Aruj looked at what Cemal was holding, he saw that it was the white flag of Genoa with a red cross sewn on it.

"What is this, Cemal? Where did you get this?"

"Reis... when we were in Tunisia... at one of these little shops... I met a girl, a girl called Hanna..."

Cemal seemed to have found himself a new girl to enamor with. Aruj was taken aback.

"We stayed in Tunisia for only a few days, Cemal. It's really beyond my comprehension how you manage find those girls in such a short period time."

Sinan showed up behind Cemal, put his arm on his shoulder and began to recount what had happened.

"While we were running around like crazy trying to get the supplies and load them onto the ship, Cemal walked inside one of those shops, Reis, and hasn't come out for I don't know how long. I was the one who carried all the grain sacks on my back. Hours later, we saw him making his way towards the ships with this piece of cloth he was holding his hands. He appears to have tried to buy something to attract the girl's attention, but with the money he had, he could only afford this rag."

Sinan had begun to mock Cemal once more, and Cemal had been steamed up naturally.

"Never mind where I found it, Reis. Let's hoist this flag up on the mast!"

Aruj first looked at the flag in his hands, and then he turned his gaze toward the papal galleons. It was a very clever idea. They could raise this flag up, disguise themselves and approach the galleons as if they were Genoese merchants. He grinned and gently patted Cemal a few times on the cheek.

"Good job, Cemal! Finally, one of your love affairs will benefit us."

He ordered his levends to run the Genoese flag up. Cemal on the other hand was complaining to himself.

"There is no problem with falling in love; but to have an affair, I need more time, Reis."

Sinan grabbed the flag; but before he began to run, he couldn't help himself and whispered in Cemal's ears.

"For hours, I waited for you outside the shop for hours, Cemal."

"Oh, Come on! You're overstating."

Sinan had already gone.

After positioning his miniature wooden ships in the narrow canal of Piombino Cervantes turned to William:

"It really was a clever idea. The Christians, who hadn't encountered a pirate threat in the region in a long time, had mistaken the Barbarossas for Genoese merchants. None of the guards, who'd been leaning on their spears and watching around with sleepy eyes, had suspected a thing. And as the clergy in their crimson cloaks and the rosy-cheeked women in their gold embroidered gowns loitered on the deck, the galleons continued their ways."

The fog had started to descend. Piri approached Khidr and kept his focus on the second galleon, which was about to disappear into the mist.

"If we're lucky, we'll be able to get away as soon as we take the first galleon in tow."

"You're nervous."

"They outnumber us."

"They haven't noticed us."

"They haven't noticed us, yet."

They were getting closer. Aruj instructed his levends to keep a low profile. With berets on their heads, shalwars on their legs, and swords on their waists they needed to stay away from the Christians' sight for at least a little while longer to avoid drawing the guards' attention.

"Don't worry Piri! Just wait until we get abreast."

"We must take advantage of the distance between the two galleons, as well as the fog. We must seize the first galleon before the second galleon rushes to her help. Or else, we'll get caught in the crossfire."

As he approached, Dragut overheard Piri's remarks. He placed his hand on Piri's shoulder and tried to give him some relief.

"Don't worry Piri! Just wait until we get abreast."

Khidr started laughing and left without saying a word.

Dragut was puzzled.

"What is so funny about what I said?"

Commander Vittorio was working in his cabin. He had his usual gloomy expression on his austere face that had been lost in the shadows cast by the light filtering through the window behind him. He was startled by the sudden opening of the door. After bursting into the captain's cabin, breathless, the guard quickly bowed his head as if to express regret for the disturbance he had caused and then started speaking.

"Commander! There are galiots on the port side."

"What's their flag?"

"Genoa."

"Then what's the problem?"

"Because to this day, I haven't seen a single Genoese wearing a shalwar."

Commander Vittorio sprung to his feet, quickly snatched his sword and hurried to the upper deck. He squinted his eyes and peered at the approaching galiots. Without a shadow of a doubt, they did not belong to the Republic of Genoa.

"Damn!"

They were very close. He began to give his men orders.

"To arrrmmmsss! Everyoneeee!"

The silver whistle was blown. As soon as the war drums began to beat, everyone was alarmed. Khidr was watching the rush of the cardinals, the scattering of the noble women around screaming, and the guards grabbing their weapons and getting ready to fight at Commander Vittorio's orders.

"They noticed."

His hand tightly grabbing the hilt of his sword, Aruj muttered:

"It's too late."

After pushing Aruj's galiot and positioning it alongside the papal galleon, Cervantes turned his gaze to William.

"It was indeed too late. Before the heavy galleon could even attempt to make a maneuver, the Barbarossas had already gotten abreast. The ropes, the nets, the hooks that were going to allow them to get on board had already been thrown. Had the gunners considered closing the port lids, they would have been able to make use of their relatively higher decks; but as Aruj had said, it was already too late. The levends had begun to surge into the galleon. Aruj grabbed a rope and hurled himself onto the enemy deck."

A sword-to-sword fight broke out. Swords, daggers, spears, staffs... Both sides were swinging whatever they could get their hands on. The flying arrows were whistling in the air just before they pierced through someone's head, some other's eye, throat, or chest. And the howling of the galley slaves rattling their shackles were blending into the wailings of the nobility.

Yahya and Sinan were swinging their swords back-to-back, watching each other's back as they knocked down every Italian that came their way.

Sinan yelled angrily at Yahya.

"You've said, 'two to one'! You've said, they outnumber us two to one!"

"Should I have said, 'ten to one' and scared the hell out of all the men? Reis was going to launch the assault anyhow!"

He was right. Aruj was adamant about not returning to Tunisia empty-handed. The fight had evolved into a bloodbath on the deck. Every time he turned around himself swinging his mace, Osman was tossing the Italians overboard. Deli Mehmed, on the other hand, was keeping his position next to the railings, waiting for those who managed to climb back onto the deck so as to be able to send them all back into the waters of the Mediterranean.

Seydi Ali was complaining as well as battling with all his might.

"For the sake of keeping quiet we didn't pray to Allah. And now look what we have to deal with!"

Piri yelled at Seydi Ali.

"Who told you not to pray! Do you have to fire the cannons and beat the war drums for Allah to hear your prayers?"

"Allah Allah, maybe Allah is too busy to hear our whispers, how do you know?"

Commander Vittorio had been severely wounded by Aruj's dagger stabbed in his throat. He pressed his hand against his wound in an attempt to stop bleeding, but blood was running between his fingers in streams, and his soul was slowly departing his body. The light in his eyes faded quickly, and the commander collapsed on the deck, falling right at Aruj's feet. The clanging of swords, the firing of arms had ceased. Aruj, covered in sweat and blood, knew the fight was over. The Italians had lost their leader. They laid their weapons down, raised their hands, and surrendered. The galleon had been captured by the Barbarossas.

Mancha leaped upon the desk and knocked over the papal galleon with a pat. Cervantes embraced him in his arms.

"Yes, Mancha, that's exactly how it happened."

William smiled. Then, he got curious. He had an idea about why Cervantes had called the other one Mia, but he was clueless as to why he had named this little one Mancha.

"Why Mancha?"

"You mean his name?"

"Yes, you most likely gave the name "Mia" to the other one because she cried out to you with a "mia" on that particular night. But I'm curious as to why you choose Mancha as a name for this little one."

Cervantes showed William the kitten's face.

"In Spanish, 'la Mancha' means 'a spot, a speck', Signor. Look! Do you see the little speck on the left side of his nose?"

William let out a chuckle. He had fed his curiosity about little Mancha. When his mind flew back to the story, he found for himself new things to wonder.

"The Barbarossas captured the first galleon. What about the second one? The firing of arms, the clanging of swords.... Have they not heard the screams or notices the bustle going on?"

"Sure, they heard; but blinded by the fog, they were unable to see what was going on clearly. And Aruj couldn't have asked for a better opportunity than that!"

"Yes, Barbarossas could have made use of the fog and easily escaped before the second galleon came to its consort's help."

"Escape? Do you believe that Aruj was planning to escape after such a victory, Signor Shakespeare? No, Aruj had other plans."

Everyone was waiting for Aruj's next commands. Aruj, on the other hand, was aware that they were running out of time.

"Throw the dead overboard! Gather the injured together, tie their hands and strip them off their clothes."

The levends, expecting to take the first galleon in tow and sail away as quickly as possible, were taken aback. But Cemal had understood. In the same way, that they had raised the flag of Genoa and misled the Italians when they attacked the first galleon, they were now going to dress like Italians, take their own galiot in tow, and head in the direction of the second one.

Aruj's orders were falling like rain.

"Aydin! Release the Muslims among the slaves and give each one a sword. Let the rest remain chained."

"As you wish, Reis!"

"Keep the soldiers and guards out of sight. If someone makes an attempt to yell, cut off his head!"

"As you command, Reis!"

After the levends tied the Italians, stuffed a piece of cloth in each one's mouth, and ensured that they would keep silent, some concealed his sword under a cardinal's robe he wore, while some placed it inside a guard's jacket he had grabbed and put on his back. As for the noble ladies who had been loitering on the deck a few hours earlier, they were all escorted to the captain's cabin so that they would not be harmed. After all, they all belonged to the Sultan of Tunisia now.

It was now time for them to take their stand.

"Sinan! Take Khidr's galiot. Hold your position and be ready to attack from the opposite direction!"

"At your command, Reis!"

"Cemal! Mehmed! Take command of my galiot, now! Archers, get ready. Gunners, fill the gunpowder and wait for my signal!"

Within a short time, everyone had settled into their positions. The galiots were lined up one after the other as if they had been taken in tow by the papal galleon. As the flag of Saint Peter's continued to flutter, what the Italians in the second galleon had understood from what they saw was that it was their companion who had come out from the battle victorious. And it was this misinterpretation that was going to prevent them from noticing the dark clouds that would soon descend upon them, as well as the arrows, cannon balls, and bullets that would shower down from those clouds beforehand.

The levends swarmed into the galleon with cries of "Allah! Allah!". Those who resisted were put to sword, those who begged for mercy were taken captive. The fate of the battle was as if had been written on stone. It didn't take long; the shackles around the wrists of the Muslim slaves were put on the Christians, and the Italians were confined in the ship's hold.

The Barbarossas were amazed by the sheer volume of the booty that they had captured.

"These galleons are like floating mansions!"

The cabinets embellished with mirrors were full of invaluable wares. Plates made of porcelain, bowls of silver, golden stoups, necklaces, and rings adorned with precious stones, chests stuffed with silk, taffeta, and velvets...

"We no longer have to worry about the winter," said Aruj with a triumphant smile on his face. Even yet, he had not even seen the barrels filled with cereals, tobacco, and all sorts of spices that were waiting for them in the ship's hold.

Khidr called out to his men:

"Call the clerk, have him fetch his scales, and come down here. We need to keep inventory."

Yahya came in. He was more baffled than anyone else on board.

"Reis, you should see this!"

They got out of the hold and followed Yahya. They were at a loss for words upon seeing all those beautiful horses, special hunting hounds, colorful parrots, and many other exotic animals that were being taken as a gift to the pope. Aruj approached one of the horses and ran his fingers through his mane. Then, he turned to Khidr with a smile on his face:

"I guess we're going to need Felipa!"

William's eyes twinkled.

"Love always finds a way."

"Yes, Signor. Those horses that they found in the papal galleons were an excellent opportunity for Khidr. He was now impatient to go back to Tunisia and see Felipa."

They hoisted the sails up and steered their ships south. But along the way, as they traveled by the Gulf of Salerno and the Calabrian coasts, they thought it would be nice to whisper the name of Barbarossa. The barque they seized on their way back would be greatly appreciated by the Tunisians who had long been suffering from shortage of wheat. And the galley called "Cavalleria" they captured off the coast of the Island of Lipari would infuriate King Fernando. As for the idea of releasing some of the captives as they passed by the Italian shores, it was Khidr's. Those who had been flung to the Christian lands in a state of desolation would cry out the name of Barbarossas, and the winds of these mighty corsairs who had just recently begun hunting in the Mediterranean would stir up storms over European realms.

Toledo, Spain

"Cavalleria! On her way to Naples!"

When Fernando entered the cardinal's bare-walled cell in Toledo, Jiménez was on his knees, praying with his hands clasped before Jesus. When this man, who considered even the arduous life of an ordinary monk to be too luxurious for a man of God, and by his own free choosing, wore a cilice, slept on bare ground, and enthusiastically devoted himself to suffering and preaching, was proposed by Mendoza, the Archbishop of Toledo, as a confessor to Queen Isabel, he had accepted the position only on the condition that no one would ever interfere with his rigorously ascetic way of life. Even when Isabel began to seek his counsel on state affairs in addition to religious matters, Jiménez had preferred to kneel next to a prayer stool rather than sit in the velvet armchairs of the palace. He was a man of iron will, an unyielding man who never hesitated when it came to paying the price that his faith necessitated.

Despite he had heard the king, Jiménez ignored him.
"Are you listening to me, Cardinal?"
He replied without making the slightest movement.
"No, Your Majesty, because now, I'm listening to God."

His face obscured by the hood of the cowl he had put on his shaved head was slightly lit by the light pouring through the small, latticed window of the high-walled cell. As for the expression on his corpse-like face; it was unmistakable: He was not going to lend ear to the king until God finished speaking.

Fernando was trying to maintain his calm as he stood in the midst of the low-rise stands loaded with leather-bound hefty volumes and prayer books, waiting for the cardinal to finish his prayers. Couldn't he have chosen another time to converse with God while they had such an important topic to discuss?

Jiménez remained silent for a little while longer, and then rose to his feet. With his long robe on his back and sandals tied to his ankles, he took a few steps toward the king.

"Cavalleria!" shouted Fernando.

"I've heard," said Jiménez. "I'm praying for their souls."

"Do you have any idea, how many nobles were on board, Cardinal? I don't believe that your prayers alone will be enough to save them at this point. This will cost us a fortune!"

"I'm not praying for them to be saved, Your Majesty."

The cardinal had heard the name "Barbarossa" storming through the Italian coasts from Andrea Doria who had visited him a few days ago. But Fernando was yet unaware of his plans. In sharp contrast to the king's bubbling rage, Jiménez spoke calmly:

"We are leaving for Oran!"

Cervantes reclined in his chair.

"As a man gets older, Signor Shakespeare his physical features begin to reflect what he carries within his heart. It is the beauty of their heart that shines through the faces of those who age well. And the darkness nested in one's eyes shows that his soul is lost in the Kingdom of Hades."

"It is as if an iceberg is locked within his rib cage."

"An iceberg? You're being polite, Signor. What the cardinal had kept within his rib cage was pain, agony, and death. And the death that had been confined in this cage back when he was just a regular Franciscan friar, was now unleashed; and with an immense authority in his hands..."

William muttered from the Bible:

"Therefore, as God's chosen people, holy and dearly loved, clothe your-selves with compassion, kindness, humility, gentleness, and patience. Bear with each other and forgive one another if any of you has a grievance against someone. Forgive as the Lord forgave you..."[79]

Cervantes smiled with sarcasm.

"Compassion, kindness, humility, gentleness, and patience... On the contrary, according to Cardinal Jiménez, the only means to save a soul was by hurling the body into the wood fires."

"How contrived appears faith in such a conscience... Like someone attempting to fit into a place he knows that he does not belong to; like an unwelcomed guest to whom is shown that his presence disturbs the rest..."

Cervantes rose and threw a piece of wood into the dying fire. As he was watching the dancing sparks he confessed.

"I fought so many years... So many that in the end, I forgot what I'd been fighting for... Or perhaps what I believed I was fighting for had undergone a change so profound that I no longer recognize it."

"What about Fernando?" asked William.

"King Fernando was a monarch, Signor. He had men who would both commit evil and do good on his behalf. Men who would smear blood on their palms for him... If he needed to slay more people, he would recruit more priests and make them pray more in the churches. And what was the pope for, anyway? Couldn't Fernando buy off God's forgiveness with the gold he offered the Vatican? Wasn't that the pope's vocation? Selling indulgences..."

William couldn't agree more. Cervantes went on to say:

"When the Barbarossas anchored in La Goulette with the loot, their saga circulating on the Italian shores had reached the cardinal's ears; and Jiménez had summoned Pedro Navarro and ordered him to make the necessary preparations for an expedition to Oran. But it was neither Cavalleria, captured on its way to Naples, nor the nobles who were taken captive by the pirates, the cardinal was concerned with. What he was after was something else. Among the news Andrea Doria had brought from Djerba was an Ark that was said to have been found by Kemal and Piri reises. And if this Ark was the lost Ark of the Covenant as Cesare Borgia had mentioned, it had to be recovered before the Turks unraveled its mystery."

"So, Jiménez knew how to make use of the Ark."

---

[79] Colossians 3:12-13

"No, he didn't, Signor Shakespeare. Since 587 BC, when the Babylonians demolished the Temple of Solomon and the Ark vanished into thin air, no one knew how to harness the power of the Ark. The cardinal's knowledge about the Ark was no more than what was written in the holy texts. According to the Old Testament, only the High Priest of the Israelites was permitted to enter the place where the Ark was kept. And only on the Day of Atonement... The fate that awaited those who did not know the rules, who did not adhere to the rules, was a dreadful fate. When the Israelites were defeated in the Battle of Aphek and the Ark was captured by the Palestinians, the people living in Ashdod, Gath, and Ekron had begun to suffer from diseases. If what was written in Septuagint is true, rats had begun to swarm in the streets of Palestine. Without the shadow of a doubt, it was the work of Yahweh!"

"How ironic it is that as a cardinal he is challenging the power of God," said William.

"Yahweh was the god of the Israelites, Signor Shakespeare, not Cardinal Jiménez's. In the same way that Yahweh had destroyed Dagon, the god of the Palestinians, the cardinal would bring Yahweh to his knees with the help of Jesus. However, Jesus' help alone might not be enough. So, he took his pen and wrote a letter to Leonardo."

"The All is mind, Leonardo. The universe is mental."

Leonardo did not reply. He was digging into the ground and tossing the tiny pebbles he found into the shimmering waters of the stream that was flowing by them. Francesco kept on:

"If you truly know what you want, the first thing you need to do is create it in your mind."

"He will never accept me! I will spend the rest of my life in Vinci as his illegitimate son and die here!"

"If that's what you're thinking, then yes, that's most likely what you will experience in this life."

Leonardo sprang to his feet. His white socks were stained with mud, and one of his overall straps had come off his shoulder. He looked to his uncle Francesco, his eyes puffy and his lashes wet.

"But that's not what I want, uncle! I don't want to spend the rest of my life planting olive trees, doing the yardwork, plowing the fields, and taking care of the animals like you do. I want to go to Florence with him!"

He was about to turn fourteen. As a child born from an extramarital affair, Leonardo had not been sent to school and thus had no formal education.

"Don't you remember how much fun we had back in those times when we spent our days watching those lizards, fireflies, and hundreds of other little creatures that haunt the vineyard? Or the day we planted this acacia tree? Do you no longer enjoy spending time with me as you used to, Leonardo?"

A blue smile spread across Leonardo's face. Since the day that his father took him from his mother's arms and brought him to this farmhouse in Vinci, it had been his uncle who spent time with him, raised him, and took care of him. Leonardo had learned so much from his uncle Francesco. As they rested under the shade of the acacia tree that they once planted together, he thought back to the thrill he had felt the day when they entrusted that tiny seed to the earth. "Every farmer who has a good seed in his hands, first has to choose a fertile field," his uncle had said to him, "and only after he plows the land, manures it well, and weeds it of all tares, he should sow his seed." All that needed to be done after that, was to let nature perform its art. The rains would decompose the seed and raise a new life and the sun would bring it to maturity with its warmth. All Leonardo needed to do was be patient.

"I don't want to be away from you but... but..." His gaze was on the glittering dance that rays of the sun performed on the waters. He wiped his runny nose with the sleeve of his shirt. "Just like this acacia, I've grown up. I want to learn. I want to have a proper education, uncle."

Francesco smiled.

"Then, focus on that. Instead of focusing on the things you don't want, think about the things you desire, Leonardo. Remember, the universe is mental; it's a thought materialized."

"It's a thought materialized..."

William smiled.

"Othello, Hamlet, Iago, Romeo, Juliet... None of them existed before I first thought about them. They all came into existence with a thought. Like life born from a woman's womb, all the characters of my plays first came alive within my mind."

"Each of them has its own soul and its own version of reality, but each carries a fragment of your soul and reality too. You are the one who breathed life into them. It is you who animated them. Like the Venus of Cleomenes, David of Michelangelo, Sistine Madonna of Raphael..."

"The spirit of my Creator is within me... but I am not Him."

The expression on William's face turned serious.

"I... Could it be possible that I am nothing but thought, Signor Cervantes? A thought God conceived in His mind..."

Salai's voice snapped him out of his thoughts.

"Leonardoooooooooo!"

"What, little devil, what?"

"Don't you hear what I say? There is a letter for you from Cardinal Jiménez. He says, Il Valentino[80] is dead."

Following their encounter in Imola, Leonardo had worked for Cesare Borgia for about a year and designed for him defense lines, towers, bastions, and trenches. Cesare's cruelty, however, had taken on a more personal meaning for Leonardo when he suspected Leonardo's friend Vitelozzo Vitelli of treason and murdered him. Leonardo was thinking that man was far more savage than animals. While even animals would not take a life without a reason, man could kill just for the sake of killing. Leonardo had felt nothing when he learned about the death of Cesare Borgia, the man who had become the inspiration for Machiavelli's book "The Prince"; the man who, according to Leonardo, surpassed all the other demons of the bad times they were in when it came to perfidy. But the death of someone else, which he had just learned through another letter, had shattered Leonardo's heart to pieces.

"Did it trouble you? I thought you'd be happy."

"My uncle has passed away, Salai. Pack your things up, we're going to Florence."

"Are we going to stay long, or we'll simply take a look inside and leave?"

"In the letter that informed Leonardo of his uncle's death, it was mentioned that Francesco had left a chest full of his belongings to Leonardo before he passed away. Francesco had wished for Leonardo to have all his notebooks as well as his drawings. But as Leonardo traveled to Florence to claim his uncle's inheritance, his mind was preoccupied with what Cardinal Jiménez had written in his letter."

---

[80] Cesare Borgia

As it traveled along the bumpy roads, the jolt of the carriage had made him nauseous. For the last few years, it was as if he had been shuttling between Florence, Venice, Pisa, and Milan with Salai. In Milan, *The Virgin of the Rocks*; in Florence, *The Battle of Anghiari* were both left unfinished. And Leonardo had no longer any desire to complete any of them. Despite his years of hard work and achievements, he was troubled to see that he still was struggling to make a living. The Council of Florence was accusing him of taking their money and not doing the job, without ever considering how Leonardo could survive with the amount they had paid to him. Michelangelo, on the other hand, had received 3000 ducats for his cartoon-like work. Leonardo had even solicited funds from his friends and submitted 150 florins to the Council, but the Council had not accepted it either. So, it was certainly not a matter of money, but of stinginess. If only Leonardo had been commissioned for the construction of the six hundred-braccia-long bridge which he had designed for Sultan Bayezid to connect Pera to Constantinople; then, he could have journeyed to Ottoman lands and gotten away from all this nonsense.

"Anyway..." he grumbled to himself.

He took Cardinal Jiménez's letter out of his pocket and gave it another look. The cardinal was writing about an Ark that was rumored to have been lost in the Mediterranean. Judging from what Cesare Borgia revealed to the cardinal in the hopes of gaining his freedom back, there was the possibility of this Ark being the holy Ark of the Covenant. And if the cardinal was right in his suspicions, the Stones of Death housed within the Ark should not have fallen into the wrong hands. After a secret meeting they held, Spain had promised the pope to find and bring him this Ark. However, the cardinal was concerned; because if the mystery of the Ark could not be solved before it reached Rome, it may have been disastrous for all of Europe. Leonardo gave some thought to the things he recalled from the Old Testament. People who were expelled from heaven, towers that had been built to challenge God's power, bushes that were burned but not consumed, plagues that had ravaged Egypt, waters splitting in half, staffs turning into snakes, arks that kill everyone... Leonardo had been fascinated by Moses' imagination when he first read the Torah. Even if it would be assumed for a moment that all the events recounted in the Old Testament actually occurred at some point in the past, how could it be possible for Moses to have written about his own death? There were so many things in the Torah that made no sense to Leonardo that he was unable to understand why people took it so seriously. "Moses..." he muttered to himself... He was placed in a basket and abandoned in a river to avoid being slain, and luckily it happened to be the Pharaoh's sister who eventually found him. If Leonardo had one-tenth the chance that Moses had, he wouldn't be in so much trouble at this age.

He grumbled again: "Anyway..."

"How about thinking of something that would make you happy every once in a while?"

Leonardo had not understood.

"Anyway... anyway... You're continuously repeating this word, Leonardo."

Leonardo raised his finger up in the air.

"Master! You'll call me master, not Leonardo!"

He turned his attention within and resumed thinking. He was planning to take what Francisco had left for him and return to Milan. Seigneur de Chaumont, Charles d'Amboise, seemed like a compliant man. He had sent one of Leonardo's works to King Louis of France, who was getting ready for a new expedition to Milan. If Louis would happen to appreciate the work and if he happens to take over Milan, he might be Leonardo's new patron. He sighed deeply and grumbled to himself:

"Anyway..."

Cervantes leaned back.

"However, a few manuscripts his uncle had left for Leonardo would cause him to spend the entire winter at the Santa Maria Nouva Hospital examining the lifeless body of a man who died shortly after turning one hundred."

Florence, Italy

"As above, so below; as below, so above."
"How so?"

They were lying on the grass one sunny afternoon, inspecting a dead lizard. Francesco took a small knife from his back pocket and cut the lizard from neck to belly.

"See, Leonardo? This is the heart. Its function is to pump blood to the rest of the body. The blood leaves the heart via the veins that are attached to it, travels through the rest of the body, and nourishes the lizard's organs with the nutrients it contains."
"These veins are just like rivers."
"Yes, Leonardo, you are right. And you know what, rivers are also like veins. They nourish the world on which we dwell."
"So, is the world a big lizard, uncle?"
Leonardo's question made Francesco laugh. How vast a six-year-old's imagination could indeed be, he thought to himself.
"Of course not. But they have a lot in common, Leonardo. See the lizards' organs? Although they are all interconnected, and each of them serves a unique purpose..."
Leonardo was paying close attention to what his uncle had to say. After closing the lizard by putting its two halves together, Francesco shifted his gaze to Leonardo.
"... they are all parts of the same whole; just as the seas, rivers, mountains, and all living beings which are all parts of the same whole that we call 'The World'. And would you like me to give you a little secret?"

He moved closer and whispered in Leonardo's ear:

"This world has a soul, and every being that lives on it have a secret bond with that soul. Just like the divine bond that exists between our bodies and souls... And you, little one, one day you will embark on a journey to find that hidden bond."

"But, uncle, if this bond is hidden, how am I going to find it?"

"By looking within when you want to understand something which is outside, and by observing outside when you want to discover something within. You will ask the world to be able to understand the lizard and ask the lizard to be able to discover something about the world."

Leonardo fell silent. He was feeling blue. Francesco wondered.

"What happened, Leonardo?"

"I suppose the lizard can no longer answer me."

He was exhausted. The day was about to dawn. For days, he had been working on the lifeless body of a man he didn't even know about. He was creating sketches of every muscle, bone, and organ in his body as he studied them. Although he did not say much about it, his uncle's death had been hard on Leonardo. He couldn't figure out why human intelligence was unable to avert death so far. In those holy books, they valued a lot, it was written that people lived for seven, or even eight hundred years. When it came to believing, everyone would believe, but no one was asking why he himself could not see past sixty. Leonardo was asking. He was questioning why his uncle had to leave, where he had gone. He was wondering about '*That*' which kept man conscious and alive.

If Francesco was right, the only way he could understand what was going on outside was to first figure out what was going on inside. Just like the nature he adored; the human body was something exceptional. He picked up one of his uncle's notes.

'Consider how the human being is crafted in the womb, examine the skill of the craftwork carefully, and learn who it is that crafts this beautiful, godlike image of mankind. Who traced the line round the eyes? Who pierced the holes for nostrils and ears? Who opened up the mouth? Who stretched out the sinews and tied them down? Who made the channels for the veins? Who hardened the bones? Who drew skin over the flesh?

How many labors within the compass of a single work... All of them exquisite things, all finely measured, yet all different.[81] How can creation be thought of as separate from its creator? How can the creator be envisioned separate from its creation? Is it possible to find something in the cosmos that he is not?'

"A perfectly designed instrument in which everything was connected," he thought. He was thinking that coarse men of bad habits and little power of reason do not deserve so fine an instrument, so great a variety of mechanism[82]. But could this exquisite work of engineering that has a soul and a mind be the creation of a mindless and soulless machine? If his uncle was right, could the essence of the cosmos have been residing in man?

"Ch'i, Prana, Vis Viva..."[83] muttered Leonardo.

The bond had been severed. This old man, who must have experienced numerous moments of joy, sadness, disappointment, excitement, and who knows what else during his lifetime, was now lying before the very eyes of Leonardo like a piece of lifeless meat. Had all the experiences he had acquired over the course of a century disappeared into thin air? Where was the "energeia" that made this old man someone's husband, some other's grandfather, or a friend, up until very recently? Was death really the end? Or was it a dissolution, a separation of the subtle from the gross? When this soulless body was buried, it was going to decompose like an acacia seed. But what was going to become of the divine essence that was contained within? Was it going to bloom into a new life? There was nothing in the universe that totally vanished. It was only the form that was changing.

He glanced over his uncle's notes. His gaze landed on a pearl of wisdom Francesco had left for Leonardo:

'Life Leonardo, life does not begin with birth, it begins with awareness... And death is not the end, it is just a remembering...'

---

[81] Hermetica
[82] From Leonardo da Vinci's notes
[83] Life energy

Leonardo observed the veins that emerged from the old man's heart and extended across his entire body like a spider web. The heart, with its pyramidal shape, was at the center of this distribution system.

"The heart..." he muttered... "The seat of the soul..."

Then, he turned his attention toward the old man's vacant eyes. The eyes, the gateway via which Plato's 'Logos' can access Aristotle's 'Reality', were linked to the brain.

For a long time, Leonardo had held the belief that a man's soul resided in his eyes. After all, among the five sense organs, the eyes were the most reliable ones. Yet they still would err from time to time. Sometimes they would perceive the objects as being smaller than they were in fact, and sometimes they would see them as being larger. They even had trouble distinguishing between the colors from time to time, especially if there was not enough light in the environment. Perhaps two eyes were not enough to perceive reality as it was. After all, even though the mechanism was laid in front of Leonardo's very eyes, he still had not been able to find the answers he'd been looking for. It would be nice if man had an additional eye located in between his eyebrows as the ancients once had described. He paused for a moment. Maybe man did, indeed, have an additional eye, couldn't it be? He dissected the old man's skull and removed the brain. At that same moment, he heard Salai's footsteps coming down the stairs to see Leonardo.

"Salai, could you pass me that little knife?"

When Salai saw the brain Leonardo was holding, he covered his mouth with his hands to prevent himself from vomiting the undigested parts of the pork stew he had eaten for dinner and raced upstairs faster than he came down.

"And he is calling himself my assistant..." muttered Leonardo.

He reached for his knife himself and carefully sliced the brain in half. Something about the size of a peanut behind the tissues that connect the eyes to the brain caught his attention. It was looking like a tiny pinecone seed located right in the middle of the brain. He recalled how much his uncle loved the pinecones, and the conversations they had together while they wandered through the forest collecting the cones that had fallen down the trees. All those beautiful moments they had shared with each other had faded into eternity, leaving behind only memories of his uncle. And a few journals replete with notes, sketches, symbols, and riddles for Leonardo... He shifted his focus to one of the notebooks lying open on the table. A strange eye his uncle had drawn in the margin of a page seemed to be watching Leonardo. Leonardo knew this symbol, but from where, he couldn't recall. When he pulled the notebook to himself, he saw a text scribbled underneath.

The All-Seeing Eye... The eye of Horus.
Do not forget, Moses was from Egypt.

"Moses..." muttered Leonardo, "The Ark of the Covenant..." He was trying to think straight. He took one half of the brain, washed it in a pail of water with care, and dried it off with his apron. He then grabbed a soft-tipped brush and carefully painted the cross-section. After that, he pressed it on a clean sheet of paper and lifted it. There it was! The All-Seeing Eye, The Eye of Horus his uncle had depicted in his notebook was right in the middle of the brain! He now needed some of the books he had entrusted to his friend Giovanni when he had decided to set out for Milan years ago.

He took off his apron, got his books under his arms, put his hat on, and headed towards the stairs. As he climbed up, he bumped into Salai who had again decided to come down and see Leonardo once he washed his face and gathered himself.

"Where are you going?"
Leonardo quickly passed by Salai.
"Eyes don't see everything, Salai!"
"Well, isn't it natural? You're aged, Leonardo."

When Salai went down the stairs and saw the old man's body parts scattered around in a jumble, he shouted after Leonardo:

"It would be good if you had packed him up!"

He heard Leonardo's voice from a distance.

"Bury him for me!"

After Gemistos Plethon, considered one of the most renowned philosophers of the late Byzantine era, re-introduced Western Europe to Plato's teachings; the most ardent supporter of the Platonic Academy of Florence founded by Marsilio Ficino, had been Cosimo de Medici. Marsilio, who was brought up by the Medicis and had become in Florence one of the most influential philosophers of his time; had begun translating all of Plato's works, Plotinus' Enneads, and various other books and manuscripts that contained the secrets of collective ancient wisdom, making Florence one of the pioneering cities where the humanist movement blossomed in Europe. The Public Library which was founded by Cosimo de Medici in San Marco and cost him nearly all his wealth had begun to host more and more books each day with the support of his grandson Lorenzo the Magnificent; and alongside the Academy, the library had become a place where Leonardo spent most of his time to quench his insatiable thirst for knowledge during his days of youth he lived in Florence.

Giovanni di Benci, the eldest son of the Sanna family who had long served the Medicis' as their right hand and who were among the most wealthy and intellectual aristocrats of Florence, was also one of those inspired by this humanist movement that quickly spread across Florence. Aside from their shared interest in Latin-translated manuscripts, Leonardo and Giovanni's common love for horses had turned this acquaintance into a close friendship soon after they met. Leonardo had too much trust in Giovanni, so much so that when he set out for Milan, he had left some of his most valuable books and personal belongings in Giovanni's care. And now, after all those years, it was nice to see that their friendship had endured the tides of time.

Giovanni welcomed Leonardo at his new house.

"The house by the Santa Croce Basilica was more appealing."

He hugged his longtime friend tightly.

"For we were young back then."

"O Time, thou that consumest all things! O envious age, thou destroyest all things and devourest all things with the hard teeth of the years, little by little, in slow death!" [84]

Giovanni cracked a grin.

"Metamorphoses by Ovid!... Are you still seeking, Leonardo?"

"I've been seeking for as long as I can remember, Giovanni."

"On the other hand, if you could simply be content with accepting what's being said as true and did not chase the Truth, your life would have been a lot easier."

"You know me, I've never been a true follower of Plato."

Giovanni let out a hearty laughter.

"Yes, observation is essential to you."

Leonardo grimaced.

"The world is rife with false images, Giovanni. Eyes deceive, it is the light that determines everything."

"And Aristotle, too, does no longer quench your thirst, right?"

"If something is neither hot nor cold... nor wet or dry... how can we perceive it with our senses?"

The expression on Giovanni's face turned serious.

"What are you seeking Leonardo?"

Leonardo did not reply. His gaze was drawn to the ostrich eggs on Giovanni's wood-engraved table.

"Leonardo?"

"Do you mind if I take those ostrich eggs?"

Giovanni turned his gaze to the table.

"No, I mean yes, of course, you can take them."

Leonardo took a few steps toward the table, picked up the eggs, and carefully tucked them into his bag. He then turned to face Giovanni.

"Well, before I left for Milan, I had handed you a few of my books as well as some personal stuff."

---

[84] Ovid, Metamorphoses (From Leonardo da Vinci's notebooks)

"Yes."

"I need one of those books now."

Giovanni turned around and gestured for Leonardo to follow him.

"Follow me. They're in my study room."

As he followed his old friend's footsteps along the dim corridor lit by the light flowing through the drapes, Leonardo's mind was wandering somewhere else.

"De Vita Libri Tres..." he muttered.

"Marsilio's books?", asked Giovanni. "Unfortunately, I do not have a copy. I'm not sure if you can find it in the library either." He kept speaking as he walked. "After Piero the Unfortunate was banished from Florence, the entire collection of the Medicis was left at San Marco Monastery to rot. Are you looking for those?"

"No... No", said Leonardo.

He was thinking. He needed to read. He had thought that he might find what he was looking for in Marsilio's translations. The closure of the library was unfortunate.

When they arrived at the study room, Giovanni opened the lid of a wooden chest, took out a large box, and handed it to Leonardo.

"Here they are! Everything you entrusted to me."

Leonardo wiped off the dust covering the box and slowly opened it. He smiled.

"Here it is! Il Pimandro di Mercurio Trimegisto![85]"

William was excited.

"Corpus Hermeticum!"

Cervantes flashed a grin.

"Moses was from Egypt, which meant the secret of the Ark might well be hidden in Egypt. Since what Moses had said did not make sense to Leonardo, maybe he should have looked at what Hermes had once said."

---

[85] Italian translation of Corpus Hermeticum translated by Tommaso Benci

William smiled.

"It seems that Leonardo was ten times luckier than Moses."

Cervantes concluded William's sentence with his own words.

"Especially considering the fact that the Italian translation of Corpus Hermeticum had recently been completed."

Giovanni was staring at Leonardo.

"What?"

Giovanni did not say a word.

"Didn't Marsilio start with Aristotle as well?" He tucked the book into his bag, raised his finger, and looked Giovanni in the eye, standing there staring straight at him. "Besides, there are some points I disagree with Aristotle. The language of the universe is mathematics, and it reveals its secrets only to those who speak its language."

He turned around and started walking.

Giovanni muttered behind his old friend.

"What are you seeking, Leonardo?"

"What was he seeking?" asked William curiously.

Cervantes leaned back.

"The works of Marsilio and his contemporaries had challenged the hundreds of years long authority of the teachings of Aristotle, Ptolemy, and Galen who had sought to understand nature by way of utilizing empirical observation. For the Renaissance man, it was no longer sufficient to simply understand nature; he also needed to learn how to control it. Leonardo, who had always constructed his ideas based on empirical evidence rather than musing on Plato's idealistic abstractions, had now returned to the point that he had been rejecting from the very beginning. The universe had its own rules operating behind the scenes that kept it ticking like a clock and that man could not perceive with his five senses."

As he walked along the same dim corridor and made his way to the front door, Leonardo paused for a moment. He had realized that Giovanni wasn't following him.

"Will you not see your old friend to the door?" he said, as he turned around.

"Wait a second, there's one more thing I want to give you."

He took a little key he had secreted between the pages of one of the shelved books and unlocked his desk drawer. He pulled a bound book and a stack of papers from the drawer. He heard Leonardo speaking at the entrance.

"I need to get going; I don't have much time."

"I'll be there in a second."

He strolled down the corridor, and when he arrived at the door, he handed the book and the papers to Leonardo.

"Here, take these."

"What are these?"

"These are the things you should stay away from, Leonardo."

"If that's the case, then why are you handing these to me?"

"Because I know you. This thread you've started to pull will directly lead you to Him. When you get there, I want my words to ring in your ears... Words that I've just said to forewarn you in advance; so that you let go of that thread...."

After taking a look at what Giovanni had just handed him, Leonardo laughed.

"Zohar[86]... The Book of Splendor... and Pico della Mirandola's Nine Hundred Theses, huh? You don't think that I'll become a Jew while I couldn't even have become the kind of Christian the church would like, do you?"

"If you were the kind of Christian the Church would like, you wouldn't have come to me and asked for Corpus Hermeticum in the first place."

Giovanni was not smiling like Leonardo. His face, which had been gleaming like the sun when he had welcomed his old friend had become clouded as he was about to bid him farewell.

---

[86] Foundational work in the literature of Jewish teachings known as Kabbalah.

"This Nine Hundred Theses he had concluded, Leonardo, sent Pico to death at the age of thirty-one."

"You also think that he was poisoned?"

Giovanni did not reply. But Leonardo could tell what he was thinking by his expression.

"Don't worry. It has been a long time since I was thirty-one."

He thanked Giovanni with a nod. Then, he turned around, walked out of the door, and disappeared out of sight in the crowded street.

"Bereshit bara Elohim![87]" muttered William.

"These are the words that those who feed on what this land has to offer must refrain from muttering, Signor; especially during these centuries when the Jews are being forced to renounce their faith, persecuted and exiled."

"How ironic it is that while the Catholics chase the Jews from the west, and Sunni Muslims clash with the Shiites in the east, the Gnostics, Kabbalists, and Sufis have been affirming the same idea of unity for centuries."

"Maybe the closer one gets to the source, Signor Shakespeare, the more clearly one can hear. What do you think?"

"For there is nothing hidden which will not be revealed, nor has anything been kept secret but that it should come to light. If anyone has ears to hear, let him hear."[88]

Cervantes smiled.

"The Ark's journey had begun in the Desert of Sinai and continued all the way to Jerusalem."

"And with the demolition of the Temple, the Ark had dissipated like smoke into thin air."

"Perchance not, Signor Shakespeare."

William became intrigued. Cervantes started telling:

"The ongoing ecclesiastical differences and theological disputes between the Hellenistic East and the Latin West had reached their climax in 1054 and brought the two pillars of Christianity, the churches of Rome and Constanti-

---

[87] Torah, Genesis 1:1
[88] Mark, 4:22-23

nople into confrontation with one another. And given that the pope's ultimate goal was to place the entire Christian world under his own authority,
this split between Eastern Orthodox Christians and Roman Catholics referred to as the Great Schism, was not something that he was pleased with.
However, when the Seljuk Turks who had entered Anatolia after defeating
the Byzantines in the Battle of Malazgirt, also captured Nicaea and Antioch
from the hands of the Christians, Emperor Alexios I Komnenos had no alternative but to approach the pope for help. The fact that the emperor required
the pope's help had strengthened the Western Church's hand. When Pope
Urban II called for a crusade at the Council of Clermont, his primary goal was
to demonstrate the Eastern Church who was in charge. As for his second
crucial goal, it was to take Jerusalem back."

"Considering that Christ's army were able to successfully make it to the
Holy land, it seems that both the pope and the Emperor got what they
wanted. The Western Church appears to have proved its power to the East,
and the emperor must have felt some measure of relief when the Turkish
threat at his doorstep was repelled."

"Had the pope restored the lands he had captured to their previous
owner, what you just said would have been right. The pope, on the other
hand, had no intention of handing over either Nicaea, Antioch, or Jerusalem
to the Byzantines. According to him, Jesus had entrusted the treasures of
Jerusalem to the Catholics of the West, not to the Orthodox of the East."

"I'm sure Emperor Alexios had thought otherwise."

"Ever since the year 300, all manuscripts containing the secrets of collective ancient wisdom had been housed in the libraries of Constantinople, Signor Shakespeare. Therefore, Alexios was thinking that he knew better than
the pope about the treasures of Jerusalem. On the other hand, he had no
intention of personally joining the crusaders that had just come from all
across Europe like swarms of locusts and camped outside the walls of Constantinople. Alexios could not possibly leave his empire which was already
under threat from all sides. It was necessary for him to devise a strategy to
entice the four French nobles who were the commanders of the troops to
swear allegiance to him. In the end, he decided to host the commanders at
the Blachernae Palace.[89]"

---

[89] An imperial Byzantine residence in the suburb of Blachernae, located in the northwestern section of Constantinople.

"The French must have been surprised to see that Alexios had no such intention, despite their expectation that he would head the campaign."

"They were both surprised and disappointed, Signor. However, when Alexios offered to send General Taticius to the campaign with two thousand light cavalries under his command as a sign of his goodwill, he had managed to obtain a swear of allegiance from three of the four French nobles; especially from Godfrey de Boullion. Raymond IV, Count of Toulouse, on the other hand, had promised the emperor only his friendship."

"The emperor appears to have had no choice but to have settled for it. After all, the crusader army that had camped just outside the walls of Constantinople had to have made him apprehensive."

"He was undoubtedly nervous, and thus had felt relieved when the armies began their march against Nicaea. Nonetheless, Raymond was the most significant figure out of these four French nobles. Because among his men was one secretly commissioned by Hugh de Payens, Count of Champagne, who would soon become the first Grand Master of the Knights Templar."

"So, the leaders of the campaign were all French."

"Not by chance, Signor. Thanks to the religious tolerance the Count had showed towards the Jewish families who had migrated from southern Europe, the city of Troyes had quickly become the center of education in France within a relatively short period of time. In the city considered a paradise for scholars and intellectuals, the sacred texts were being studied comprehensively. The Jewish rabbis and the Cistercian monks were collaborating and comparing the old texts with more recent ones. When the synagogue founded in the city by Rashi, who was a man of Jewish descent born in Troyes, had gained popularity; so too Rashi had become someone who was looked upon in meetings hosted by the Count. The Count was enjoying himself immensely listening to the Talmudic stories Rashi told, and his interest in the sacred scriptures was growing even more stronger with each passing day. Rashi was mentioning a number of manuscripts that had been carefully concealed; and claiming that if he had the chance to visit Jerusalem, he could find them as if he had put them there himself. The Count needed to go to Jerusalem. There was a lot to be discovered in that holy city. At the time, however, family matters and some issues related to his lands were keeping him from joining the crusaders who were about to embark on their campaign. Eventually, he decided to send his cousin, Hugues de Payens, in his place. When the crusaders triumphed and Hugues returned to France with certain manuscripts in his hold, the Count understood that those narratives Rashi had been talking about were more than mere legends, because Hugues had discovered the texts exactly where Rashi had specified. And these texts Hugues had brought with him were none other than the texts of the *Zohar* which would soon be translated in Europe and captivate the attention of many. The texts, a copy of which Giovanni would subsequently give to Leonardo."

William got excited. He sat up straight in his chair.

"The sacred relics! Oh, my goodness, did Rashi know where the sacred relics were?"

"Rashi was just saying that he could read the texts. Everything was already written in the scripture. Nothing was hidden from those who had eyes to see. What mattered was which eye one used to seek the Truth. According to the wisdom of Kabbalah, the Torah, like a flower bud, was wrapped with multiple meanings. While the beauty of the bud that one would appreciate while reading the Torah for the first time presented a moral compass, the essence revealed as the bud blossomed was the path to the Tree of Life that would eventually lead him to the Truth. The ten gates that would allow one to recognize what is unutterable... Every word that was written in Torah had an essence. But in order for one to be able to comprehend and reveal its essence, he himself had to blossom like a bud first; he had to shake off from himself all the dust and the dirt."

"Rashi must have been surprised when he saw the manuscripts. After all, you mentioned that they discovered them right in the spot where he believed they would be."

"Knowing and believing are two different concepts, Signor. A person would not believe in what he already knows, but knows it. Believing or denying is a choice we make in matters about which we are uncertain."

"Such as believing in God... It's like making a choice between believing and denying, for we do not know for certain whether God exists."

The room fell silent for a while. Neither Cervantes made a remark, nor William waited for one.

"It was the Count of Champagne who was surprised, Signor," said Cervantes. "Because he had approached all those stories as if they were fairy tales. Finally, he couldn't help but travel to Jerusalem to see for himself. And when he returned to France in 1108, the first thing he did was to search for Rashi. Rashi, however, had passed away some time after the Count had set out on his journey. This horrible news left the Count in utter grief. He was at such a point that he could not give up. So he went straight to Stephen Harding, one of the founders of the Cistercian Order who was at that time busy comparing the translations of the Old and the New Testaments that had been used since ancient times with their originals and correcting the errors contained within. With the help of Jewish scholars in the area, they began to shed light on the problematic parts of the texts. After years of hard work, the Count had finally made up his mind on his second expedition. The treasures of Jerusalem had to be unearthed. With the king's approval, an Order should be established, and the Temple Mount, as Rashi had pointed out, had to be investigated thoroughly."

"After the Knights Hospitaller, a second order in Jerusalem... So, this is how the Order of the Knights Templar was founded, huh? Poor Fellow Soldiers of Jesus Christ and of the Temple of Solomon..."

"Not Jesus Christ's, Signor Shakespeare; only Christ's... Poor Fellow Soldiers of Christ and of the Temple of Solomon. Of course, I shall not dare to teach a literary master like you how significant each word can be at times; but I couldn't help myself."

William smiled.

"I'm here to learn from you, Signor. To replace rumors with what you know."

Cervantes was relieved that he had not offended William. He kept on telling the story.

"Hugues de Payens, along with eight other knights, founded the Order of Knights Templar in great secrecy. Their so-called task was to protect the relics in Jerusalem and ensure the safety of the Christian pilgrims. However, for some reason, the Templars did not become embroiled in any of the regional conflicts that took place between the Saracens and the Christians."

"This must have been the reason why the Knight Hospitaller got increasingly militarized; the Templars' not leaving their Temple."

"The Templars were quite busy, Signor. Excavating the Temple Mount and transporting all they discovered to Europe was taking all their time. They had no time left to protect the Christian pilgrims."

"I can't help but wonder what they discovered."

"A great deal of things... Gold, silver, ancient manuscripts, alembics used in alchemical experiments, even double pelicans... The Templars retrieved a great deal of priceless artifacts that dated back to antiquity. But the most precious of them all was an Ark which the Knights of Saint John would eventually lose in the Mediterranean after all those years of guarding it. An ark, the whereabouts of which in the sixteenth century were only going to be known to Barbarossas..."

Tunisia

When the Tunisians saw that the Barbarossas, who had left La Goulette with their galiots a few weeks ago, now returning with two papal galleons and a giant barque in tow, they rushed to the port to greet them. People had climbed up the city's walls and minarets to get a better view and see for themselves the enormity of the loot these 'valiant levends' had brought to their city. Khidr was excited. This triumph was undoubtedly going to help them gain a good reputation among the locals. The port was already swarming with people. Aruj should have been there to see it. Where was Aruj, anyway? Khidr hadn't seen him since they had captured the wheat-laden barque.

He snatched Yahya's arm.
"Where is Aruj?"
"I haven't seen him, Reis."
As Aydin approached from behind, he replied to Khidr:
"He is in the galleon. In the captain's cabin."
"Didn't he come out the whole time?"
"No, he didn't. The two men standing at his door told me that he wanted to get some rest. I was hoping to talk to him, but they didn't let me in."
"Perhaps I should go and check. Get closer to the galleon. I'll jump on board."
"As you command, Reis."

When they were close enough, Khidr grabbed a rope and threw himself on board. He went down the stairs and made his way toward the ship's stern. There appeared to be no one around. He slowly opened the door and found

Aruj standing there half-naked. He was injured. The linen he used to patch his wound was stained with blood. He had just taken it off to wash it when he spotted Khidr staring at him. He became enraged.

"I had ordered them not to allow anyone in!"

Khidr was petrified.

"Brother! You're... you're wounded!"

Aruj did not respond. He soaked the blood-stained linen in a barrel of clean water a few times and squeezed it.

"Why didn't you say anything?"

"Nothing serious."

"What do you mean, nothing serious? It's pretty serious, don't you see? Besides, how could you keep secrets from your brother?"

In response to Khidr's rebuke, Aruj raised his tone.

"I said, nothing serious!"

Khidr kept silent. He stood at the door with his eyes fixed on Aruj.

Aruj was aware that he had failed to hold back his wrath and that he yelled at his brother when there was in fact no reason to do so. He sought to make amends.

"I mean it, Khidr. It's not serious. I didn't want levends to find out."

"I want you to see a doctor in Tunisia. This wound absolutely must be sutured."

"Okay... let's just get there first."

"I'm serious!"

"I said OKAY! Don't push me any further! Get out now or the men will become suspicious."

Khidr stood there for a while and waited for his brother to thoroughly clean the wound and re-bandage it with a fresh piece of cloth. When Aruj noticed that Khidr was still standing there staring at him as he put his white shirt on, he became enraged once more.

"Who am I talking to? Come on, shove off!"

Khidr turned around. As he was just about to leave the cabin, he heard Aruj.

"No one is going to hear about this! Do you understand?"

Khidr went to the upper deck. He was upset.

"I suppose it was his first serious wound."

"Yes, Signor Shakespeare. Contrary to what he said, his wound was indeed quite serious. Perhaps because he didn't want to demoralize his men, or because he couldn't accept the fact that he, too, was of flesh and bones; he had wanted to keep this a secret. But Khidr would fail to keep his mouth shut."

Yahya had been concerned and had discreetly followed Khidr. He immediately understood something was amiss as soon as he saw the expression on Khidr's face.

"What's wrong, Reis?"

"Nothing... nothing is wrong, Yahya."

"But your eyes tell otherwise."

"I said, nothing, Yahya."

"Okay, if there's nothing wrong then I can go and see Aruj. There was something that I needed to talk to him about anyhow."

Yahya quickly passed by Khidr to make his way to the captain's cabin, but Khidr caught him by the arm.

"You are as stubborn as a goat!"

They stared at each other in silence for a while. Yahya was more than determined to find out what had happened to Aruj. Khidr took a deep breath.

"Aruj was wounded."

"Wounded?"

"Yes, he seems to have been stabbed in the belly."

"How so? Is it something serious? Why didn't he tell us anything? Why did he..."

"Hushhh Yahya! He doesn't want anyone to hear it. He seemed to have taken care of himself."

"How, though? Did he suture the wound by himself?"

"Yes, with a few temporary stitches; but he is still bleeding. He must be handled as soon as we set foot on land."

"We can take him to Mother Firuze. She'd know what to do."

"The woman you'd taken Felipa to?"

"Yes."

"Okay."

"Okay."

"Okay, but quietly, okay?"

"Okay."

"Okay."

They entered La Goulette with salvo fire and were welcomed by cheers, whistles, and whoops of delight. That day, which was evocative of the processions that took place in Ancient Rome, would be remembered by Tunisians for a very long time. The well-dressed gentry walking with their hands tied were being followed by the wavy-haired women who had been mounted on horses with jewel-encrusted bridles and embroidered leather saddles. Two of these women in particular had captivated everyone's attention with their noble stance as well as the lavishness of the way they dressed. These two maidens having been mounted on white armored horses and being taken to Mulay Muhammad, were the daughters of the Spanish governor of Naples. And there was no doubt that the sultan was going to receive a hefty amount of ransom from the governor in exchange for the release of his daughters.

Following the Barbarossas who were riding towards the Casbah with falcons perched on their fists, were the levends and the captives, carrying chests of booty on their shoulders. The port was so crowded that if someone were to toss a needle into the air, it would take a considerable amount of time to make its way to the ground. The Tunisians were competing with one another to get a closer look at those who had managed to capture such a great booty, while on the other hand struggling with each other to collect the items that were falling off the chests being carried to the Casbah.

Felipa had been stuck in the crowd. Her eyes were looking for Khidr. When she finally saw him, she tried to find a way to get through the mob and reach him. She got on her knees, slid from under someone's arm and between the legs of another, and eventually caught Khidr's horse by the reins.

"So, you're back!"

By Felipa's sudden appearance next to him, Khidr was taken aback.

"Heyy..."

"Heyy..."

"You... Here?"

He flashed her a broad smile that showed off his sparkling white teeth.

"Did you come for a welcome?"

"Yes, I was concerned. You've been gone for a long time."

When Aruj slightly lost his balance on the horse, Felipa noticed the blood oozing down Aruj's white shirt.

"Your brother... What happened to your brother?

"Hushh! He is okay. Don't worry. Go now, I'll come by later."

"But Khidr, he doesn't look..."

She had been stuck. She was trying hard to catch up with Khidr but was being dragged further away by the crowd. She had to follow them. She had to, but how? She covered her hair with the silk shawl around her neck, found herself a horse, and jumped on its back.

A chunk of the loot had been taken to the town square so that it could be distributed among the people of Tunisia. Other precious items selected for the sultan, such as satin fabrics, red velvets, mirrors with gilded frames, jewel-inlaid daggers, and engraved armors, were being transported to the palace on the backs of donkeys, horses, and slaves. As for Felipa, she was among the women who had been captured and were being taken to the sultan's harem. They would soon pass through the flower gardens and arrive at the palace. Felipa was going to understand the mistake she had done when one of the guards forced her to dismount, but by that time, it would already be too late.

"Stand in line! You'll be appearing before the sultan soon!"

She wanted to speak but was prevented. The guards mistook her for one of the woman captives that the Barbarossas had brought the sultan as a gift. Wasn't it natural for them to think this way? Hadn't Felipa gotten on a horse and ridden to the palace together with those women? Ah, such a fool she was! Her eyes were searching for Khidr, but Khidr was not there. Neither Khidr, Aruj nor Yahya was around.

"Are we there yet, Yahya?"

"Almost."

Despite all Aruj's protests, Khidr had decided to take him to Mother Firuze upon seeing that his condition was deteriorating. He had asked Yahya to lead them out of the procession and they were now following him through the narrow streets of Tunisia racing to get Aruj to Mother Firuze's house as fast as possible.

As he struggled to sit upright on his horse, Aruj weakly mumbled:

"You must go to the palace!"

"I will, brother, I will. After I entrust you in safe hands."

When they arrived, Yahya jumped from his horse and rushed toward Aruj.

"We've arrived, Reis! Just hang on!"

He helped Aruj to dismount and carried him to the door. After a few knocks, the door creaked open slowly. When she noticed Aruj's blood-stained shirt, Mother Firuze immediately invited them in.

"Yahya, my son, on the couch... lay him on the couch. I'll go get some hot water and return."

As she rushed to the kitchen Yahya and Khidr laid Aruj on the couch.

Khidr was concerned.

"Sweat is beading up on his forehead."

"Do not worry, Reis, Mother Firuze will know what to do."

Aruj reached out and snatched Khidr's arm.

"You must go to the palace!"

"I'm not going anywhere!"

"I'm your brother! You'll do as I say!"

A little while later, Mother Firuze came back bringing with her a bowl of hot water and some pungent herbs. She sat down on the couch next to Aruj and put her hand on Khidr's cheek in an effort to provide him with some relief.

"Do not worry, son. I will take care of him. He'll be fine by tomorrow. You just leave."

Yahya accompanied Khidr to the door. It was evident that he was unwilling to leave his brother. Yahya wanted to comfort him.

"Keep your heart at ease, Reis. Aruj Reis is right; you must go to the palace and present the sultan his share of the booty. I'll stay by his side. You'll see, tomorrow he is going to feel much better."

"How do you speak with such certainty, Yahya?"

Yahya parted his shirt. On his muscular chest was a scar from what appeared to be a serious injury in the past. Khidr did not say a word. Yahya took the lead and opened the door.

"Do you remember the way?"

"I do."

"Good. Go, then. The sultan must be waiting for you."

Khidr sprang onto his horse and took off running.

"Look how Allah rewards the brave!"

Chests brimming with Venetian ducats, Spanish maravedis, Portuguese golden coins, Flemish florins, opulent silks, silver-inlaid boxes... Mulay Muhammad had never seen a booty of this magnitude before. While marveling at the treasure that had been laid out before him, he was unable to disguise his joy and astonishment and kept reiterating how fortunate the Tunisians were to have such valiant levends at their service as the Barbarossas.

"You are no longer merely guests in Tunisia! From now on, this place is your permanent home!"

Isaac expressed his respect by bowing his head.

"We are grateful, My Sultan."

"Oh, no, no! On the contrary, it is we, Tunisians, the ones who are grateful. Especially concerning the wheat you've brought. Do you know how long Tunisians have been pining for wheat?"

The sultan continued to speak as if he truly cared about the Tunisians.

"The streets will be filled with the aroma of freshly baked bread... and sugar... and tobacco... olive oil and carobs... I'm at a loss for words to express my gratitude."

"I'm sure you'll figure something out, My Sultan."

Isaac was trying to gain time in the absence of his brothers but, at the same time, he couldn't help but wonder how Aruj was doing. Huseyn, on the other hand, who was standing right by the throne in his long caftan and his insidious gaze fixated on Isaac, was getting on Isaac's nerves more and more.

The sultan turned to Huseyn:

"Huseyn, Isaac Reis is right! We must find a means to express our appreciation. I say, we reserve one of my residences overlooking Carthage for the accommodation of these valiant levends."

Huseyn did not seem to like the idea.

"But, My Sultan, is it appropriate to allocate the residences where we welcome our Spanish visitors to these people you've only recently met?"

"Then what should we do? Are we going to let them stay at the port? Is this how we are going to show our hospitality towards these brave hearts who have just laid a fortune at our feet?"

Isaac was hesitant to accept the offer.

"My Sultan, please do not bother yourselves. We can..."

Mulay Muhammad did not allow him to finish.

"No way! It will be just as I say! Did you hear me Huseyn?"

Huseyn had no other choice.

"I did, My Sultan! It will be done according to your instructions. Please give me a few days so that I may select the most suitable residence for these levends to spend the winter and make the necessary arrangements according to their needs."

"Superb! Also, I'd want to throw a banquet in their honor this evening."

As Mulay Muhammad clapped his hands, the servants began to gather in front of the sultan and wait for his orders.

"You've heard me! The tables will be flowing milk and honey. And the dancers... I'd like to see them perform throughout the evening. And... and the saz players..."

"As you command, My Sultan."

Taking advantage of a momentary silence, Isaac intervened:

"My Sultan, please excuse us for tonight. We've come a long way. Furthermore, Aruj Reis..."

At that very moment, Khidr walked into the court and bowed before the sultan.

"Forgive me for I am late, My Sultan. There was a minor mishap on the ships that required some attention. My brother had to stay at the port."

"There's nothing to apologize for, Khidr Reis. I was just telling your brother Isaac that I would be delighted to host you at the court this evening."

"It would be an honor for us to have a place at your table, but if you'll excuse us, we'd best stay at our ships tonight. You know, we've come a long way and we need some rest. We would be revitalized by tomorrow and be looking forward to having a taste of not only your food but also your talks."

"All right, Khidr Reis. As you wish, then. You have my permission to leave."

After Khidr and Isaac had left the court, it was now time for Mulay Muhammad to select the women who would join his harem. Felipa was trying to maintain a low profile among the other women who were standing in front of the sultan in their Medici-style dresses of brocade taffeta, which revealed all their physical beauty with a tight belt at the waist, and a low breast line. But when the sultan looked Felipa in the eye after scanning all those women from head to toe; Felipa realized that God did not even hear let alone responded to her prayers.

"This one! I especially want this one!"

As she was dragged away, she tried to explain that she was not one of the captives, but no one was listening to her. And the sultan had already shifted his attention to the remainder of the captives with whom he was planning to enrich his harem.

Khidr and Isaac had mounted their horses, heading toward Mother Firuze's home. When they arrived, Aruj was sleeping on the couch. His wound had been cleaned, sutured, and bandaged.

"Yahya, how is my brother doing?"
"He's fine, Reis. Mother did what needs to be done."
"He is no more sweating."
"Yes, Reis. You'll see, tomorrow he is going to be much better."

When Mother Firuze walked into the room and noticed them standing near Aruj, talking quietly to one another, she summoned them all with a hand gesture. They followed her into a tiny kitchen that was stocked to the brim with glass jars containing a wide variety of herbs, and roots, such as rosemary, commonly referred to as "bird tongue", senna leaves, juniper berries, licorice, belladonna, cinnamon, mandragora, sweet myrrh, nettle's leaves, zedoary, ginger, turmeric, myrtle leaves, and hundreds of other plants that one would ever think about. As he stood there and looked at the jars, Khidr was unable to conceal his astonishment.

Upon noticing the puzzled expression on his face, Mother Firuze smiled.
"Nature, son... Nature provides us with everything we need. We just need to figure out what to use where, when to use it, and how much we should use."
Isaac was speechless.
"But how do you find all of these herbs in Tunisia?"
Mother Firuze turned to face Yahya with gratitude in her eyes.
"Thanks to my son, Yahya. He is the one who finds these herbs as he travels back and forth and brings them to me."
"I am not the one who should be thanked, Mother. Who would benefit from all of this if it weren't for your knowledge and skills?"

Mother Firuze took the boiling water off the stove and poured it over the dried leaves she had previously put in a copper bowl.

"Give it a little time to brew, then it will heal you all." After that, she addressed Khidr directly. "It will especially help you with regard to your anxiety."

"We can't thank you enough," replied Khidr.

"There's no need to thank me, son. Your brother's wound was not that serious." Her sapphire eyes met Yahya's. "I've seen a lot more serious ones, ones that not only torment bodies but also hearts..."

When Khidr turned his attention within his own heart, he recalled Felipa. The last time he had seen her, she was in the crowd. He had hoped to find her here, but for some reason, Felipa was not around.

"Well... it's not just my brother. That girl that Yahya had brought you."

"Are you talking about Felipa?"

A warm, heartfelt smile spread across her face.

"For her, I should be the one to thank you. She became a daughter to me."

"Is she around here?"

"She left early in the morning. She must have gone to see Yusuf. She spends one day with me, and then goes to my grandson's small shop the next day to lend him help."

"I was hoping to see her while I'm here."

"If you have time to wait for a while, they will come shortly. They'll definitely make it to dinner."

Isaac took hold of Khidr's arm.

"We need to get back to the ships. The men are waiting for us."

"But, what about Aruj?"

"Aruj is in safe hands. We must give the men their share of the booty. They've been out at the seas for weeks. They'd want to spend the night on dry land."

Isaac had a valid point. Levends had already begun to grow impatient. And because they had no idea what Aruj had been going through, the only thing on their minds at the time was to spend whatever money they had in their pockets at one of the inns in the sailors' district.

Yahya confirmed Isaac's words:

"Reis is right. Levends have been dreaming about this day for weeks."

Khidr was not only concerned about Aruj. Even though he did not say a word about it, another reason why he was unwilling to leave the place was Felipa. "Anyway," he said to himself, she would find her way home eventually. Felipa would most likely be there to greet Khidr when he returned to visit his brother the next morning. Hadn't Mother Firuze said that she visited Yusuf every other day? Since she was absent today, that means she was going to be at home tomorrow.

"Provided that she can find a way out of the sultan's harem."
Cervantes smiled.
"And that, Signor, that surely was not going to be easy for Felipa."
"Was the harem so well-protected?"
"Having said so, I did not mean that she would be restricted from leaving the palace. However, it was no longer possible for Felipa and Khidr to be together as two free individuals."
"So, just because there was a misunderstanding, are you telling me that Felipa had to spend the rest of her life enslaved to the sultan's bed?"
"In order for you to comprehend the answer I'll provide to your question; you first need to come to a better understanding of the notion of Harem in eastern cultures."

William had heard some rumors about the Ottoman Harem. If it was as depicted in the works of European painters, Harem was a place where hundreds of naked women were being kept among whom the sultan would choose for himself one and satisfy his manhood anytime he pleased. An abhorrent place where the women enslaved in battles were sexually abused.

"So, allow me to clarify, Signor Shakespeare. *Harem* means "that which is protected", "that which is sacred and inviolable" in Arabic. In Islamic tradition, "sélamlique", the living quarter reserved for men where the administrative affairs are held, and "harem", the domestic space reserved for the women and family members, are separated from each other. Women taken captive in battles are included in the harem as odalisques[90], which means

---

[90] A chambermaid or a female attendant in the Ottoman seraglio, particularly the court ladies in the household of the Ottoman sultan.

they become a member of the family. If there are any women among these slaves who belong to European nobility, they are placed in the harem for a period and treated as guests. And when are ransomed, they are returned to their families. If a woman is not of noble lineage, she is, from that moment on, considered the sultan's harem."

"So, again, as in every other area of life, it is wealth, the primary factor that contributes to inequality and establishes one's level of good fortune. If, as a woman, you belong to a wealthy family, you do not have to bear the odor of a man you do not desire. Otherwise, it is really upsetting even to visualize the horrible life awaiting those women."

"You obviously seem to have strong preconceptions about the harem, that you have formed based on what you've already been told. Neither the harem nor the life that awaits those women in the harem is as horrible as you assume, Signor. If that were the case, they wouldn't be vying against each other to be the sultan's favorite, would they?"

William was surprised.

"They vie against each other?"

"The women who bore a son to the sultan are regarded as the sultan's wives. They even have the opportunity to become the sultana when their princes reach adulthood. Concerning the sultana, she is the most powerful person in the empire; and not only in matters pertaining to harem but, in fact, in administrative matters as well."

"What about the other women, those who are unable to provide the sultan with a male heir?"

"Harem is governed by a number of strict laws, Signor Shakespeare. It is not a place where the sultan may simply enter whenever he pleases and sleeps with whoever he desires. Odalisques are war captives; and in the Ottoman culture, it is essential to treat the women who were taken captive in battlefields well."

"What exactly do you mean by well?"

"First, they are taught decent manners and the principles of Islam. After they become Muslims, they are subjected to practical training in a number of disciplines. In addition to learning how to write, read, and speak properly, they are given an education that adheres to the Islamic moral code and theological knowledge. They pursue their interests in music, tailoring, and needlework through a variety of classes tailored to their skills. And when the time comes, they are wed to high-ranking statesmen, which would allow them to spend the rest of their lives in mansions with servants running around doing their bidding. Returning to Tunisia, Mulay Muhammad's harem was, of course, not comparable to the Ottoman harem. Nonetheless, the circumstances that awaited Felipa were not that dire. After all, given the fact that the sultan had been suffering from sexual impotence for some time, the only thing he could have asked Felipa to do for him could have been to serve him in an area she was gifted."

A peculiar kind of despair descended on Cervantes' expression.

"But that was not going to change the fact that Felipa was now the sultan's harem. Khidr could not even look at her let alone touch her."

William's face also lost its bloom along with Cervantes'.

"Alas that Love, so gentle in his view, should be so tyrannous and rough in proof!"[91]

"But passion lends them power, time means, to meet tempering extremities with extreme sweet..."[92]

William's eyes gleamed.

"So, you've read my letters!"

Cervantes arched a grin.

"Romeo and Juliet... Of course, I read them."

Although each bowl of water poured from her head was wiping off the tears streaming down her cheeks, her eyes were welling up with new tears until Kalfa refilled the bowl.

"Oh, please don't cry any longer. There's no reason for you to be upset. This place is not as terrible as you think."

Felipa turned to Kalfa with reproach.

"I am not a slave! I am not one of those women taken captive in battle!"

"Oh, sweetheart, you've already said it so many times."

"Then, why don't you let me go? Why are you trying to force it into the sultan's bed?"

---

[91] William Shakespeare, Romeo and Juliet
[92] William Shakespeare, Romeo and Juliet

She was in deep despair; her voice was trembling. Kalfa, on the other hand, upon hearing Felipa's last words, couldn't help herself and started chuckling.

"The sultan's bed, huh? Oh, dear..."

She was unable to stop her laughter. Felipa was confused.

"Why are you laughing? What's so funny about it?"

After wrapping Felipa's wet wavy hair in a loincloth and rubbing her elegant shoulders with fragrant oils, she replied:

"I don't suppose there's much you can do in the sultan's bed. You can at most replace his linen and fluff his pillows, but that's about it."

Felipa was puzzled.

"What do you mean?"

Kalfa sat next to Felipa. After pulling aside a strand of hair that had fallen on her face, she reached out and gently took hold of her delicate hands.

"The sultan is not as sexually potent as he once used to be, my dear. He wants you in his harem because seeing such a beauty like you around each morning will bring him delight. That's only the reason he wants to have you. And this is true for not only you but for all the other women in his harem."

Felipa was surprised. After all, the sultan was the power holder in the country, yet it seemed that he was recently unable to enjoy this power in bed. Kalfa carried on with a cheerful expression on her face.

"Therefore, you'll most likely be assigned a job in the palace that matches your skills. If you know how to write, you will most likely spend your days copying manuscripts; otherwise, you will paint, play music, or make needlework. You will eat nice food and wear nice clothes and the sultan is not going to touch you, not even once."

"Needlework?" said Felipa. She'd never done needlework before, not even once in her life.

"Tell me, is there something you are skilled at? Something you were taught when you were little."

"Well... there is... I..."

"You?"

"I... I train horses..."

Kalfa was surprised.

"You train horses? I had never met a woman horse trainer before."

"I grew up in a farmhouse in Spain. My father was a horse trainer."

"Really? And how about your mother?"

"I have no memories of my mother. She had died when I was too little."
Kalfa felt sorry for Felipa.

"Oh, I'm sorry sweetie; sometimes we lose our loved ones far too soon."
Felipa remained silent.

"You're one of those who escaped from the Inquisition, right?"

"Yes..."

"And your father? Where is your father now?"
Felipa's voice trembled.

"He is with my mother..."

Maybe it would be better if Kalfa stopped inquiring. It was obvious that this young woman had gone through hard times. Every question would seize her by the heart and would force her travel back and forth between the present moment and her unchangeable past, remind her of her family she would not be able to see again and eventually tire her out. She took a deep breath and smiled at Felipa.

"Listen! Maybe I can help you!"

Felipa's was staring at the copper pitcher sitting on the floor. Upon hearing what Kalfa had just said, her face lit up, and she lifted her hopeful gaze.

"I can't get you out of here. After all, the sultan has taken you into his harem. However... From what I heard, that among the treasures those men had brought to the sultan, were some horses of great value."

Felipa got excited.

"Horses?"

"Yes, horses. The sultan is very fond of his horses. One of his favorite things to do is to go hunting with his hounds, horses on a weekly basis. If you want, I can talk to the sultan and tell him that you can take care of the newly arrived ones. What do you say?"

Felipa smiled in between her tears.

"Good! I'm glad that I was finally able to put a smile on your face. After you've dried off, the girls will show you where you'll be staying for the night. Rest well until tomorrow."

"Well... when are you going to talk to him?"

"Soon, dear."

Kalfa stood up.

"Before he gives his permission, he will most likely want to see you ride. That wouldn't be a problem for you, right?"

"No... no, of course not..."

That night, Khidr did not get a wink of sleep. He rose with the first rays of sunlight, mounted his horse, and headed for Mother Firuze's home. When Mother Firuze opened the door with drowsy eyes, she was surprised to see Khidr standing at her door at such an early hour in the morning.

"Son? Didn't you get any sleep?"

"I couldn't, Mother. I was worried about my brother."

"Come, come in..."

When Khidr entered the room, Aruj had already awoken and was perched on the edge of the sofa. He was relieved.

"Oh, thank Allah! How do you feel brother?"

"As if I was stabbed in a battle, taken to a house I've never been to before, and healed by a woman with magical hands who watched over me the entire night."

They chuckled. His brother was okay. Given that he had managed to construct such a lengthy statement with only one breath, Aruj must have been fine.

"So, Mother remained with you all night, huh?" He turned around to face her. "I don't know what to say, Mother. Thank you very much!"

"It was not me, son. My old, depleted body apparently had given up, and I'd fallen asleep as a result. It was Yusuf who spent the night by your brother's side after he took me to my bed. When I woke up, Aruj was already up."

"Since I was feeling much better, I told Yusuf to go to bed and get some rest. Anyway, not too long after Yusuf left, Mother came by, and then, you arrived."

"Yusuf..." muttered Khidr. He had recalled Felipa. Yesterday Mother Firuze had said that they would make it to the dinner. Khidr wondered whether she was around. Perhaps it would have been better if he asked.

"So, Yusuf stayed by my brother, huh? May Allah bless him. Well, Felipa... Is Felipa around, Mother?"

"I don't know, she must have come home together with Yusuf last night. Like I said, I had fallen asleep."

She leaned on the hands she had placed on her knees to assist herself as she slowly rose to her feet.

"Wait here, I go check on her and let her know that you are here so that she may come and see you."

She walked out of the room with slow steps, but after a short while she returned with a worried expression on her face.

"Son, Felipa is not in her room. I asked Yusuf, too."

Khidr was standing stock-still.

"He said he hasn't seen her since yesterday morning..."

"While Aruj was recuperating at Mother Firuze's house, Khidr searched for Felipa in all of Tunisia's alleyways. Since they had just recently settled in this white city, there was only a handful of locals whom Khidr could have asked about Felipa. And they all said the same thing, none of them had seen her."

"What about the levends? Had nobody among the levends seen her, either? Hadn't anyone noticed as she rode towards the palace?"

"Nobody knew anything about her, Signor, don't you remember? How hard they had tried to keep Felipa's presence on board secret."

"Love is like a dream in the white city... Like a mirage amid the desert that vanishes as you get closer..."

"Pull yourself together. We'll be in the sultan's presence soon."

"I'm fine."

"We'll find her don't worry. After all, the ground could not have split open and pulled her in."

"I said I'm fine!"

"Khidr, I know you care for that woman. However, today we should be heading to the palace feeling jubilant and proud, just as any victorious warrior would do." He placed his hand on his belly. His wound was still causing him pain. "And we've been putting off the sultan's invitation for days. Therefore, pull yourself together, and don't let anyone know that you're floundering in such a state of weakness."

"Brother! Enough! I am not floundering in weakness. Yes, it's true, I'm worried about her because we've brought her here. And neither she nor we are familiar with this place. Just because we're not in Christian territory doesn't mean that she is safe here!"

"She is a free woman, Khidr! She is a young, beautiful, and free woman!"

"What do you mean brother?"

"Isn't it possible that she'd started seeing someone?"

Khidr couldn't keep his tone calm.

"No, it is not!"

Aruj kept silent. It was the first time that he had seen his younger brother oppose him with such fury.

"You don't know her, not even a little bit. You don't even know whether she thinks of you as much as you think of her."

"I don't need to know. I feel it."

"Do you know what I'm feeling, Khidr? I'm feeling that this woman will storm through your seas."

He turned around and walked out of the room.

With their embroidered caftans on their back, Barbarossas entered the hall in silence. The splendor of the banquet that awaited them, was proof of how feverishly the palace servants worked all day. The sinis set amid the red velvet cushions were full of venison that had obviously been cooked for that particular night, piping hot loaves of bread, delicious deserts prepared with almond and dates, all kinds of fruits and vegetables as well as wine. Regarding the interior it was considerably more crowded than they had expected. It appeared that the sultan had not only wanted to get to know them better; but he had also invited the city notables to introduce them to the Barbarossas. And of course, Huseyn, as the chief adviser, had also taken his seat right next to the sultan so that he could keep a careful eye on the brothers throughout the evening.

The clocks were ticking, yet it seemed like the night would never end for Khidr. As the sultan continued to speak about the history of the Hafsid Dynasty, the importance of Tunisia's strategic location, relations with the European monarchs, and the future of the Mediterranean; he also kept reiterating in between his two sentences that how fortunate they were to have the privilege to host these 'valiant levends' in Tunisia.

"Especially the beauty of the women you brought. Those Spaniards in reds."

Aruj took a sip of his wine and spoke.

"You mean the daughters of the Spanish governor of Naples?"

"You do not intend to include them into your harem, do you, My Sultan?"

It was Huseyn speaking. Throughout the course of the night, he had barely uttered a few words. He fixed his gaze on Aruj and continued:

"Unless you want to utterly severe the relations between Tunisia and Spain, of course..."

Aruj turned to the sultan:

"They are war captives. You are free to do whatever you want with them, including keeping them to yourself; alternatively, you can return them to their family in exchange for a ransom. We brought them to you for we knew that they have value. The rest is your own business."

The expression on Mulay Muhammad's face turned sour. He was clearly not willing to give up on any of those women. On the other hand, he was cognizant of the fact that he should not disregard Huseyn's words.

"So, how about the brunette? The one with deep dark eyes and the long wavy hair. Is she also a daughter of the governor?"

Huseyn had quickly deduced which woman the sultan was referring to. Nonetheless, he inquired.

"Which one, My Sultan? The horse trainer?"

"Yes, the horse trainer. Did you speak with Kalfa and learn who she was?"

"I did, My Sultan. She is a Moor. She is one of the Muslims who were able to escape the Inquisition. She is a loner who had lost her entire family in Spain and somehow come to Tunisia. You can keep her for as long as you want; she has no one who cares about her."

Khidr's face became flushed with blood. His heart had begun to pound on his temples. Aruj, on the other hand, was concerned of his brother's possible sudden reaction and that he might lash at the sultan with a foul remark that would come out of his mouth. His eyes met with Isaac's.

Isaac turned to the sultan:

"Are you planning to hold a Muslim woman in servitude, My Sultan? Isn't it contrary to our religious tenets?"

"Isn't the wine you're drinking also contrary to our religious tenets, Isaac Reis? But in Tunisia, you can drink as much wine as you like. Tunisia is a land of freedom. Religion doesn't disturb the Tunisians. A person prays to Allah whenever his heart desires. If he has to, he fasts; If he has money, he drinks wine, and if he drinks too much, he gets drunk. Gentlemen, I suppose you are confusing Tunisia with Constantinople."

Isaac had no answer to give. This place was Maghreb. One should not have hoped to find the empire's order here. He shifted his gaze to Aruj. Aruj's heart was still in his mouth. As for Huseyn, he had noticed the sensitivity they displayed toward this woman. He decided to inquire further.

"May I inquire as to why you are so interested with this woman, Aruj Reis?"

Aruj could not let Huseyn learn that they knew Felipa. Since the first day they had met, this man was getting on his nerves.

"We are not. I suppose my brother wanted to have an idea about how things work in Tunisia."

Isaac approved Aruj.

"Yes, of course. Why should we care?"

The sultan intervened as he reached for one of the dates on the table.

"As a matter of fact, Huseyn, it's good that she is here. You know, among the treasure are some exceptionally valuable Spanish horses. And she is a horse trainer..."

"Are you going to put the care of those priceless horses in the hands of a woman, My Sultan?"

"Why not?"

Khidr could not have passed up this opportunity. The only way he could tell whether the woman in question was indeed Felipa, was to see her himself. He jumped in:

"My Sultan, if you would allow me to see as she rides..."

Aruj cleared his throat so loudly that it was obvious he was eager to change the subject. Khidr, however, simply ignored him.

"If she is really a skilled rider, why not give her a chance as you say?"

The sultan liked the idea.

"Huseyn, what do you think? I think that is an excellent idea. Khidr Reis can tell us whether this woman is qualified for the job."

Huseyn was not pleased that the sultan was giving so much credit to those men about whom they knew nothing about their identities or intentions. He had a sneaky suspicion, though, that one of them had some kind of relationship with the woman in question. If he was right in his doubts, he could validate it in this manner.

"Yes, My Sultan. I also think that it's a very good idea."

Aruj was somewhat relieved. At least for tonight, things would not get more complicated.

Khidr asked with a phony smile on his face:

"Good. Then, tomorrow. Your stables... May I ask the location of the stables that you have allocated for the newly arrived horses, My Sultan?"

"At the port, Khidr Reis, in La Goulette."

"Ay me, for aught that I could ever read, could ever hear by tale or history, the course of true love never did run smooth."[93]

Cervantes smiled.

"There is no greater folly in the world than for a man to despair, Signor.[94] For there is nothing in life that is not transient, and each dawning day brings with it fresh wonders and fated encounters. Just like the one that awaited Felipa in the stables she visited that morning."

"Hoooo hoooo! Easy boy! Easy!"

Two men had caught the reins of a black stallion with a long mane almost brushing the ground, were trying to calm him down. When one of them stepped on some dung and slipped, the horse got out of control; and after smashing the other man against the wall with a head throw, he got himself freed. He was bucking, rearing, banging himself against the walls, looking for a way out of the stables. Felipa took a couple of steps and got closer.

"Miss! You better not come too close!"

It was Mustafa's voice, the stableman who had retreated into a corner after escaping from being crushed under the horse's hooves at the last moment. But Felipa just ignored his warning. Kalfa, on the other hand, was concerned.

"Felipa!"

Felipa had not even heard her. Her gaze was fixed on the stallion, which glistened like ebony velvet under the light streaming through the windows.

"Felipa, it appears that this horse has been overfed. I have doubts about whether it's a smart idea to continue with this training thing."

---

[93] William Shakespeare, A Midsummer Night's Dream
[94] Miguel de Cervantes Saavedra

The stables were dim. Felipa walked over to the horse taking slow and steady steps. She could hear him breathing. She could even hear his heartbeat.

"Oh, my Allah!" said Felipa.

Could it be possible that it was really him? She walked closer and closer and stared him in the eye. It was indeed him! She wrapped her arms around his neck. She knew this scent... She knew this texture of skin... With a delightful smile on her face, she turned to face Kalfa.

"He is Viento!"

"I want you to promise me!"

They were walking toward the stables nervous as well as excited. Khidr was about to find out if the woman the sultan was referring to was Felipa. Nevertheless, he was unsure as to which of the two possibilities was giving him the greater cause for concern.

"Do you hear me? I said I want you to give me your word!"
"What word do you want, brother?"
"If it turns out that she is Felipa, you won't say a word."
Khidr came to a sudden halt and spun around to face Aruj.
"If it turns out that she is Felipa, she's coming with me!"
"She's coming nowhere Khidr, do you understand?"

Aruj's voice had blasted out so loud that all the other voices around had evaporated in the air as if terrified by his fury. Aruj took a deep breath. Khidr, on the other hand, turned around and kept walking with the same determination.

"Look, Khidr! If she is indeed Felipa, it's so fortunate that nothing had happened to her. If she's indeed Felipa, then it is truly a stroke of good luck that she eventually found herself a safe place to live. If she is indeed Felipa..."
The woman, mounted on a black stallion, riding, and letting out hearty laughs as her hair was blowing in the breeze was indeed Felipa.
Khidr muttered:
"Is it because of the sun that her hair is so shiny?"

"Or is the sun shining in the sky so as to be able to touch her radiant hair?" said Cervantes.

"Loves messengers should be thoughts, which fly ten times faster than sun beams and drive the shadows back over the dark and scowling hills. That's how fast swift-winged doves carry the goddess of love in her chariot, and why Cupid has wings that propel him as quickly as the wind."[95]

Mustafa was trying hard to hide his astonishment as Felipa brought Viento back to the stables.

"Miss, never in my life I've seen anyone who rides like you. Especially a horse like this one!"

Felipa smiled as she stroked Viento's mane.

"I'd be glad if you would allow me to take care of this horse from now on."

"Mustafa. My name is Mustafa. And yes, of course, Miss. In any case, I do not believe that anyone besides you can even approach this horse. Take me, for example; even if they were to put me in chains, force me to oars, whip me to death, I'd never ever mount on that animal. This creature would not be content with simply knocking me down, rather, it would also trample me with its hooves."

Felipa let out a chuckle; and as Mustafa walked out of the stables, she turned and whispered to Kalfa.

"Thank you..."

Kalfa replied in a hushed tone as she pointed at the sky.

"Do not thank me, thank Allah!"

Mustafa returned to the stables in less than a minute or so.

"Miss, there are two men outside, waiting for you. They claim to have come on behalf of the sultan to see whether you are qualified to train these horses."

Felipa was taken aback.

"Okay, Mustafa, I'll be there in a second."

As she was leaving the stables with Kalfa, Felipa's joy had been clouded.

---

[95] William Shakespeare, Romeo ve Juliet

"Two men, huh? Who are these two men? What are they going to tell the sultan?"

"Calm down, Felipa. There's nothing for you to be concerned. How could they possibly have anything unpleasant to say about you if they've seen you on Viento's back?"

Felipa paused and took a deep breath.

"I don't want to lose him again."

"I know, and you're not going to lose him."

Upon seeing that it was Khidr and Aruj who had been waiting for her to come out of the stables, Felipa's eyes twinkled with delight.

"Yes! You are right Kalfa! I'm not going to lose him!"

Kalfa hadn't understood a thing. Weren't these two men with tanned skins, sharp features and red beards waiting for them outside, the levends who had just recently returned to Tunisia with a treasure everyone had been talking about? It was obvious that Felipa knew them; and there was also no doubt that they likewise knew Felipa. Felipa was as glad to see them as she was glad to have Viento back.

"You look very happy..."

Khidr was relieved to see Felipa safe and sound.

"That black stallion you were riding... It reminded me of your horse, Viento, that you had mentioned..."

"He is Viento, Khidr!"

Khidr was surprised.

"How so?"

"He is Viento! It is inconceivable that I could ever mistake him for any other horse. Isn't it true that the galleon you seized belonged to Spain?"

"Yes, it is," said Khidr. "It was laden with treasure being taken to the pope."

"Well, that explains everything. It seems that Viento was captured and included in the group of horses chosen to be delivered to the pope. The king is absolutely right! He could never have found a horse in entire Spain as magnificent as Viento!"

"Wow!"

"Wow, indeed. He is Viento, Khidr, can you believe it? After all this time... you... you..."

"Me... me what?"

"You returned my horse to me. And now that I have the sultan's approval, I will be able to spend as much time as I want with him. I... I don't know how to thank you."

She was beaming with joy to the point that one might have mistaken her for the sun. Khidr admired her petite face, the stars twinkling in her dark eyes, and gazed at her long hair that reminded him of Mediterranean waves. Felipa was undeniably a beautiful woman; but Khidr could swear that he had never seen her look so breathtaking before.

"By always being as happy as now."

Felipa was confused.

"You may thank me by always being as happy as now," said Khidr. "For seeing you sparkle like the sun will be what pleases me the most."

Felipa smiled. He wanted to wrap her arms around his neck and give him a hug; but she took a step back after hearing Kalfa's warning by clearing her throat.

"Felipa, we have to leave now," said Kalfa. "I'm confident these gentlemen will persuade the sultan that you are more than capable of caring for this horse."

Theirs was a quiet farewell. Not a word spilled from their lips. They just stood there in silence and looked at each other, and who knows what they said to one another with their eyes...

Khidr and Aruj stared after the carriage for a while that was soon going to disappear in the dust clouds rising from the hooves of the white horses galloping away; then, Aruj turned to Khidr and asked:

"Why didn't you say anything?"

"Didn't you see the jasmines blooming in her smile and the butterflies taking off from her hair, brother?"

"He must have really loved her..."

"He indeed did," said Cervantes. "And that day, not only Aruj but Khidr as well had realized it much better."

"Letting someone go when all that you want is to be with them..."

"Separating Felipa from her Viento she had been missing for so many years just when they were recently reunited, would be plucking the jasmines from her smile, chasing the butterflies in her hair. How would Khidr ever have done that while he was thinking how wonderful her tiara of butterflies looked on her head?"

"That dreadful hunger tormenting the body while the soul is fully fed..."

Cervantes took out a little leather-bound notebook from his pocket. After he searched for a while he turned to William, pleased to have found the page he was looking for.

"Knowledge is three things, says Shams... The chanting tongue, the grateful heart, the patient body."

"He didn't ask..."

They were returning to the palace. Felipa was looking out of the window as the carriage lurched down the dusty road.

"He didn't ask what?"

"I had assumed that he may have wondered about me. I mean when he couldn't find me..."

"I don't understand what you're trying to say. Who did you think might have wondered about you?

"Khidr..."

William was feeling upset.

"Did the entire universe conspire to bring them together, so that in the end they would break apart?"

"If the winds are going to put out the fires, why does God ignite them in the first place, isn't it, Signor Shakespeare?"

Cervantes continued to read from the notebook in his hands.

"Love wants a heart that burns like hell, one that would even ravage hell, so that if two hundred seas are to open up before that heart, it should burn them all at once. Its single wave should run rings around all the known seas. It should crumple the skies like a handkerchief in its hands and hang it on the firmament like an infinite, imperishable shining candle; so that it battles like a lion, has the heart of a crocodile, and that it would not leave anyone else on the face of the earth other than itself."[96]

---

[96] Shams Tabrizi

William was as if he was gazing off into empty space.

"Khidr needed this love...", he muttered.

"Yes, Signor Shakespeare. Khidr needed this love... So that when the Kingdom of Spain turned Oran into hell, he could withstand the flames... So that he would not leave anyone else in the Mediterranean other than himself..."

Oran, Algiers

"That's enough!"

Oran, with its twelve thousand inhabitants, had been razed to the ground. Cardinal Jiménez, who had spent most of the fortune he saved in Toledo for this cause, had unleashed upon the African coasts perhaps the greatest military force that the kingdom had ever amassed. While there were only thirty casualties among the twenty thousand Christian soldiers, one-quarter of the Muslim population had been slaughtered.

After witnessing the heartbreaking scene of a child attempting to suckle milk from her mother's breast as she lay on ground drenched in blood, Pedro Navarro hurled his blood-soaked sword at the feet of the cardinal.
He was gasping.

"This is no war! This... this is a massacre!"
The cardinal turned his merciless gaze to the rebelling commander.
"What were you expecting, Commander?"
"These people... they're not fighting... not even resisting, don't you see? Why are we keep killing them though they've already surrendered?"
"Because I didn't come all the way down to North Africa to make them surrender."

Cardinal Jiménez was as if he was not breathing in the life of this world. He was feeling proud to have successfully completed a task given to him by God. It was as though his soul had shed his body, ascended to the heavens, and was now waiting for Christ to bless him for his services.

"We... we embarked on this expedition to consolidate Spanish control over the region. Just like we did in Melilla, and in Mers El Kébir... To build a watch post, a garrison... We arrived here to prevent the locals from assisting the pirates."

The cardinal took a couple of steps toward Pedro Navarro with an arrogant smile spread across his face.

"Ah, I see, so that's why you came here, Commander."

No further explanation was needed. Jiménez had clearly made his point. Pedro Navarro, on the other hand, had no intention of further contributing to this massacre in any way.

"You... you are out of your mind, Your Eminence!"

Cervantes placed his finger on the North African shores and went on:

"At first, the Maghreb had appeared to be a land of possibilities for the Muslims who were expelled from Spain. However, although they had invested a great deal of effort in an attempt to settle there and plant the seeds of a new life, the Atlas Mountains and the lands of Northern Sahara were infertile. Algiers, Oran, Mostaganem were minor alluvial deltas. And when the exiled Muslims were unable to establish in the region the same glorious life they had enjoyed in Andalusia, particularly due to the never-ending tribal warfare, they had been doomed to a semi-nomadic life. The policy of 'letting the sleeping dogs lie' followed by the rulers of Tunisia, Bejaia and Tlemcen, was giving the Christian monarchs the ability to call the shots in the region according to their own preferences. And for Algiers, which is located smack dab in the center of this raging storm, peace and prosperity did not appear to be on the horizon any time soon."

He reclined in his chair.

"They neither could return to Spain, nor they were pleased to stay in the Maghreb. The hatred they harbored in their hearts for the Christians who had driven them out of their homes surged within them like a volcano that was about to erupt. Their thirst for vengeance grew so strong that they eventually set sail, pillaged the Valencian shores, disrupted commerce, and enslaved the inhabitants of the coastal areas."

"They knew the Spanish lands. They must have established an impeccable network of espionage with the help of the Moriscos who remained in the area."

"The Moriscos were like a cunning snake growing inside the womb of Spain. They had no qualms about collaborating with the pirates and making them stronger with each passing day."

"A valid reason for the Catholic Monarchs to become a lightning bolt and strike the ports on the African shores."

Silence fell on the room. Both writers sat there for a while in one of the rooms of a shabby house in Valladolid, with their gaze on the flames dancing in fireplace and their minds wandering in the dreary alleyways of the century before theirs.

"And who is to blame for all of this, Signor Cervantes? Who started this chase, who started this fight in the first place?" He sat up straight in his chair. "I mean, if the Christians hadn't driven these people away from their homes..."

"Then there would have been no reason for the Moriscos to ally themselves with the pirates on the Barbary Coast."

"Exactly!"

"Or if the Nasrids had not taken the Iberian Peninsula from the hands of the Visigoths... Or the Visigoths from the Romans, the Romans from the Carthaginians, the Carthaginians from the Greeks, the Greeks from the Phoenicians..." He paused... He took a deep breath. "Christianity in the west is fighting against Islam in the east. Have you ever given any thought to what would have transpired if there was not another faith to fight against, Signor Shakespeare?"

William remained silent.

"Christianity would have been divided into sects, and people following different sects of the same faith would have fought against each other. What if the reality underlying all of the conflicts that are taking place in the world right now, all of these wars that we assume are a battle between good and evil, is, in fact, the fight of 'what one person believes versus the belief of another'?"

"Then, what's the truth about the religions?"

"Religions... Systems integrated with socio-cultural history which had been founded by people who were not enlightened as their prophets... Conditioned institutions that further condition people...Whereas all the prophets had just sought to remind us of something we already knew but had long forgotten, that we are all parts of a single, undivided whole..." Cervantes took a deep breath. "There was only one Truth, one religion emanated from the enlightened ones, and that was to refrain from doing to another what you consider unjust. But man did everything else except for this, for the sake of being faithful ."

William had realized how pointless was to look past history from the perspective of "if"s. Cervantes was right. The Protestant movement, which was ignited in 1517 with Martin Luther nailing his *Ninety-five Theses* to the gates of the Wittenberg Castle Church, had literally divided Europe into two and led to hundreds of deaths until the Holy Roman Emperor Carlos V officially recognized the Protestants in 1532.It seems humanity was quite adept at finding reasons to battle with one another. And the true motivation behind all of those wars that were fought whether in the name of Jesus, Muhammad, or God in general, had in fact always been something quite different.

Bizerte, Tunisia

"Melilla, Mers El Kébir, Oran..."

Kurdoglu's calm but also concerned deep blue gaze was anchored at the galiots resting in the port of Bizerte, which had once hosted not only the fleets of the Carthaginians and the Romans but also, the Byzantine ships due to its strategic location in northernmost Africa. The port which would soon awaken into a fresh fuss with the dawning of the day with all the caulkers, foremen, cooks, gunners, helmsmen, bosuns, ship boys, and carpenters who would be swarming around, was yet sleeping under the starry quilt of the night. There was no sound, except for the shrill cries of a few seagulls that had completely lost the track of time.

With its surrounding forested mountains and sheltered harbor connecting the Mediterranean to the inland lake, Bizerte was one of North Africa's most important capes. Protruded like a nose that has an acute sense of smell, it had been serving as a naval base for Kurdoglu for a while, providing him the opportunity to learn about everything that had been happening in the Mediterranean before anyone else. However, the recent news the winds had just whispered into his ears was troubling; so much that it had prompted him to pen a letter to Aruj, give it to one of his most reliable men, and make it delivered to La Goulette. Aruj, on the other hand, having read Kurdoglu's letter brimming with words of anxiety, had decided that he had to have a face-to-face conversation with this blue-eyed man with whom he met in Djerba a few years ago. He neither had wasted time nor notified anyone and had ridden his horse towards Bizerte in the dead of night.

"I rode as quickly as I could."

"What about Khidr?"

"He is in La Goulette. He doesn't know I'm here."

It was a quiet night. The full moon, gleaming as if a lantern suspended in the sky, was filtering through the window, lighting up the room.

Aruj looked at the maps that were laid out on the table.

"The siege has been lifted... Is it true?"

"True. On the sultan's command, Kemal Reis and I transported thirty-seven galleons of janissaries to the island; nonetheless..."

"The walls are too strong..."

"It's not just that. There are other clouds circling over the Empire. The army is divided. Following Shah Ismail's ascension to power in Persia, the sultan deployed a frontier force of one hundred fifteen thousand soldiers in Anatolia to fight against the Qizilbashs[97]. Kemal Reis was tasked with sailing to the southern seas. And..."

"And *Kıyamet-i Sugra*[98]..."

"It took forty-five days for the aftershocks to cease. The raging sea breached through the walls of Constantinople and Galata. Mosques, masjids, houses, water arches... all were destroyed. Thousands of people died under the rubble. And most importantly, the shipyard in Iznik..."

The expression on Kurdoglu's face troubled Aruj.

"How bad?"

"It became useless..."

Aruj was at a loss for words. From what he had heard from Kemal Reis; Kurdoglu had long been living and breathing with the Island of Rhodes. The knights, who had drowned his fiancée in the waters of the Mediterranean and taken the lives of two of his brothers, were his archenemy. He had been attacking every galley without hesitation and plundering the coves of Rhodes at every opportunity. However, the castle... The castle was strong. Kurdoglu was fully aware that his forces alone were not enough to besiege

---

[97] Shia militant groups that flourished in Iranian Azerbaijan, Anatolia, the Armenian Highlands, the Caucasus, and Kurdistan from the late 15th century onwards, and contributed to the foundation of the Safavid dynasty of Iran.

[98] The 1509 Constantinople earthquake known as the Minor Judgment Day, occurred in the Sea of Marmara on 10 September 1509

the castle. What he was counting on was the imperial power. Kurdoglu was sure, that day would come and the sultan would command his troops to launch an attack on Rhodes. Even if Kurdoglu was already dead, he was going to rise from his grave and join the battle that day. But it seems there was still time for the sultan to issue the command.

He walked up to the table and, after looking through the maps, chose one with the coast of North Africa embroidered on it like needlepoint and set it in front of Aruj.

"Melilla, Mers El Kébir, Oran... They're coming Aruj. They're coming to Djerba to surround Tunisia from all sides."

Aruj kept silent. Kurdoglu, on the other hand, had his eyes fixed on him.

"Italy, France, and Venice are currently keeping Fernando preoccupied. The cardinal, however, had the mosques transformed into churches in Oran and appointed an inquisitor to oversee the religious affairs of the congregations. He had gallows and scaffolds installed in public squares, and established monasteries to persuade people to convert to Christianity."

"Right under our nose..."

"They are not intimidated in the least by the hunts that we conducted in the Mediterranean. On the contrary, it stirs up the cardinal's already-burning hatred. And the sultan has such a full schedule."

"Sultan Bayezid's administration always relied on diplomacy. Yet, Allah created the Turks to fight! Prince Korkud... Prince Korkud is aware of this; that's why he gave us a helping hand. When he rises to power..."

Kurdoglu intervened.

"Prince Korkud will not rise to power, Aruj. It will be Prince Selim who will inherit the throne. The only Ottoman prince who did not have his share of his father's merciful nature. And given that the truce with the Venetians is still in effect, Prince Selim will almost certainly march towards East, to crush the Safavids who have been bothering him for quite a while."

"This indicates we'll be alone in these waters for a little while longer."

Kurdoglu walked over to the window and gazed outside.

"These waters are entrusted to us for a little while longer, and..."

The sound of a knock on the wooden door echoed throughout the room. Kurdoglu turned to face Aruj before completing his words.

"I thought we might need some help."

Aruj shifted his curious looks to the door. Whoever it was that showed up in the middle of the night had certainly done so at Kurdoglu's invitation. Who could it be, Aruj wondered.

"Reis, Daughter of Granada has arrived."

"Daughter of Granada?" William was intrigued. "So, the helping hand extending to the most formidable pirates of the Mediterranean of the time is of a woman?"

"Daughter of Granada, Fatima, or the daughter of the Amir of Chefchaouen, a descendant of Muhammad... She was the wife of blind Ali Al-Mandari who had migrated to Tetouan in northern Morocco a year before the Christians seized power in Granada and become a true nightmare for both the Spanish and the Portuguese in the Mediterranean since then."

"The eyes of the Blind Man..." said William.

Cervantes let out a chuckle.

"A fitting description, Signor Shakespeare..."

"I'm taking it as a compliment."

"On the contrary, I think your assessment is perfect. Because the city of Tetouan, which was already in ruins after the Castilians razed it to the ground and enslaved its population, had become one of the most important naval bases for pirates after being reconstructed by Ali Al Mandari, especially due to its proximity to the Strait of Gibraltar. The expeditions known as *Jihad Fil-Bahr*[99] that his fleet of pirates embarked on every summer, had been disrupting trade, inflicting heavy losses on the Christians. They literally had made the Christians enslaved during the hunts rebuild the city. And the one who was arranging it all, keeping accounts down to the last detail, taking the pulse of the Mediterranean, and leading their fleet was, in fact, Fatima. So, your analogy to the vengeful Daughter of Granada as the eyes of the Blind Man is indeed pretty accurate, Signor."

---

[99] Holy Sea Battles

When she lowered the hood of her silver-embroidered dark green cloak, Fatima's long brown hair spilled over her shoulders. As she stood there looking at Kurdoglu, the lantern light bouncing off her elegant crown dazzled Aruj's eyes. Whoever this woman, who started making her way toward Kurdoglu with a slight smile on her face was, it was certain they had known each other for quite some time. They might even have a deeper relationship that could hardly be described as merely a friendship, Aruj thought.

Kurdoglu, enchanted by her beauty, was unable to take his eyes off Fatima as she took one step at a time with a serene grace.

"Daughter of Granada...", muttered Kurdoglu and lamented, "Such a toil your beauty is to my eyes..."

Aruj stood there silently watching. He was now almost certain that these two had a history that went beyond what could be considered a simple friendship.

Kurdoglu took Fatima's delicate hand and raised it to his lips.

"Long time passed... Yet, it does not appear to have paid you a visit."

Fatima smiled. She reached out for Kurdoglu's hair, touched his forehead, his eyelids with her fingertips, and caressed his cheeks.

"It seems to have paid you a brief one. Your blue glance appears to have deepened and darkened. Tell me, was it the seas that wore you out to this extent?"

"Your yearning..."

Shadows slid across Fatima's emerald eyes. She parted her lips, wanting to say something.

"If only you hadn't left..."

"If only I hadn't left and had endured the agony of seeing you alongside Ali Al-Mandari."

Fatima took a deep breath.

"I'm not resentful of you. I've never been. But don't be resentful of me, either. You know I'm bound to... In the same way that you're bound to Rhodes."

"Only because of your Christian hatred... Only because of your oath of vengeance..."

Fatima couldn't help but raised her tone. Her voice was trembling.

"What makes my oath less firm than yours? And... and... Ali is dying Kurdoglu! He is leaving under my command a huge fleet of pirates, a kingdom to rule, and dying."

Silence fell over the shoulders of the room. Fatima took a deep breath.

"Come... come to Tetouan, come to my kingdom."

Words became clogged in Kurdoglu's throat.

"I can't..."

Fatima remained silent.

"The Mediterranean, Fatima, Mediterranean needs me more than ever."

"I do, too."

"You do not understand!"

Fatima sighed deeply. It was clear that this discussion would lead them nowhere. She changed the subject.

"The Spaniards are conquering all of the ports on the Barbary Coast one by one, like stringing beads on a rosary; thousands of Muslims were slain, and tens of thousands of them were taken as prisoners."

"I know."

"I came here to tell you more. Pedro Navarro left Oran with fourteen thousand men at his command and sailed to Bejaia. The ruler of Bejaia, Abderrahmane, took his brother Al-Abbas and fled south into the mountains."

"How about Salim al-Tumi? Didn't he come for assistance?"

Fatima gave him a sarcastic smile.

"Come for assistance? The difficult circumstances the Hafsid rulers of Algiers had found themselves in, as well as Abdelaziz's loss of his two sons during the Spanish assault, may have even suited Salim al-Tumi. After all, he is nothing more than a local ruler."

"So, he took no action in response to his neighbor's defeat?"

"He did. He announced that he would submit to the Spaniards on behalf of himself, the chieftains of Mitica, and the leaders of the coastline line."

"He surrendered Algiers to the Spaniards without even so much as a single swing of a sword, huh?"

"Fernando had Salim al-Tumi take an oath of obedience, acknowledge the Spanish presence in Algiers, and agree to pay an annual tribute. He also ordered him to release the Christian captives, and had the ports blocked not just to the pirates, but also all ships hostile to Spain."

"But how could he keep it under control?"

"Machín de Rentería is about to complete the construction of *Peñón de Argel* he'd been building on the islet off the coast of Algiers. If he wants, he can even unleash cannon fire and attack the city from there, do you understand? In short, Algiers is now under Spanish control."

"They will come to Tunisia. The Ottoman Empire is waging its own wars. There's no one else here to stand against the Spaniards other than us."

As he was finishing up his remarks, Kurdoglu had turned his eyes to Aruj.

"Barbarossa and I..."

Fatima turned to face Aruj, hiding under the dark cloak of the room listening to their conversation in complete silence.

"The Red Beard... So, it is you..."

Aruj bowed his head and saluted Fatima.

"The cries of your raids on the coasts of Italy are heard all the way from Morocco. According to what I've heard, Christians have been scaring their children by yelling, 'Red Beard is coming!'"

"They haven't seen anything yet," replied Aruj.

"Another pirate king full of vengeance, huh? It's nice to meet you, Aruj Reis."

"The pleasure is mine, My Queen."

"Not yet Aruj Reis... Not yet."

The night was advancing, the hours were flying out the window.

"We need your support, Fatima," said Kurdoglu. "Cannons, guns, men, provisions.... They are going to attack Djerba."

"How do you know?"

"I always know, you know."

"I know. I've never seen a nose that has such a strong sense of smell as yours."

"What do you say?"

Fatima fastened her emerald eyes on Kurdoglu's.

"Whatever it is that you need..."

Kurdoglu took a deep breath as if to say, "it is you...".

Fatima smiled, took a few steps toward Kurdoglu, and left a gentle kiss on his lips.

"I have a dying husband whom I will have to bury soon, and a kingdom to rule afterward. Also keep in mind that, we are fighting the same war. You against the Spaniards, me against the Portuguese. However, I will do everything in my power to back you up."

She turned around, walked out the door, and vanished into the darkness of the night as gracefully as she had entered the room.

La Goulette, Tunisia

"It's good to see you smiling."
Felipa was in a good mood as she rode Viento along the Séjoumi lake.
"Thanks to you, Kalfa."
"Oh, come on Felipa. We both know thanks to whom."
Felipa started chuckling.
"Yes, but it wouldn't have been possible if it weren't for you; let alone seeing him, I probably wouldn't have been able to step outside the palace."
"Hah ha, you? Don't make me laugh, Felipa; you would climb the walls and still find a way out."
"I don't know if I'd be able to do it, but I definitely would have tried."
"I know... The first time I saw the two of you together, I had understood." She paused and looked at Felipa for a moment. Then, she pursed her lips and let out a kiss sound before pulling her earlobe. But when she couldn't find anything wooden to knock on, she knocked three times on her own head. "Allah forbid, who knows what would have happened to you?"

After leaping off Viento, Felipa pulled his bridle off his curved neck and wrapped the reins over her wrists. Together they made their way to the lakeshore.

"But how did you find out?"
"From the dazzling light that surrounded both of you..."
Felipa let out a chuckle.
"You've got to be kidding!"
Yet, Kalfa was not.

"It was not difficult to see, Felipa. Your face was gleaming with joy, the sound of your heartbeat was so loud that it could be heard from Bizerte, and I'm not even going to mention your trembling voice and flushed cheeks."

"You can't be serious! I thought I was playing it cool."

"Cool? Honey, you were hot as the desert sand."

"Oh, please!"

Their honey-sweet conversation gave way to a brief silence. Felipa was watching the waterfowls taking a bath in the lake. When one of them, after repeatedly dipping its head in the water, cleaning itself, and preening to align each feather, finally fluttered its wings and took flight, Felipa's sky got clouded.

"I once used to be as free as they are."

"However, back then you did not have Khidr with you."

Felipa quickly turned to face Kalfa.

"But what will become of us, Kalfa? I mean, yes, I can see him thanks to you, but..."

"You have to be patient Felipa. The brothers earned the favor of both the sultan and the Tunisians thanks to the booty they captured. With each passing day, their influence in Tunisia will grow, making them more indispensable to the sultan. You will wait, Felipa."

"I'll wait for what?"

"For fresh captives to arrive."

"Fresh captives?"

"Yes, as the Barbarossas introduce new women captives for the sultan's harem, Mulay Muhammad's interest in you will wane."

"But there are already so many women in the harem."

Kalfa smiled.

"Yet, none of them can compare to how beautiful you are."

"Then, I don't want to be beautiful."

She had frowned.

"Yes, that's it. Do exactly that and you're not even pretty."

Kalfa's remark had once again cheered up Felipa.

"But you always make fun of me!"

They heard the hoof beats of a galloping horse approaching. Felipa got excited.

"It's him! He's coming"
She tidied herself up and turned to Kalfa.
"How do I look?"
Kalfa replied with a hearty smile on her face.
"As always, sweetie... Like a precious pearl."

"And in the wood where often you and I, upon faint primrose beds were wont to lie, emptying our bosoms of their counsel sweet, there my Lysander and myself shall meet..."[100]

"Yes, Signor Shakespeare, theirs was a midsummer night's dream. But their souls, drawn to one another by a summer breeze, would drown in the autumn rains that never cease. And the clouds were already forming in the Tunisian sky."

"It is as though the sun has never risen in their skies, and their hearts remained hazy at all times."

"You are mistaken, Signor Shakespeare. Every drop of time they spent together either became the sunlight that keep them warm, or the moonlight that brighten their hearts. From their lips, dripped honey as they talked. They yearned for the hours they were in each other's company and saw it as a treasured gift from God. And although in secrecy, their eyes always caught one another's, enjoying that heartfelt, that intimate bond. Because hope, Signor Shakespeare, hope is always born at the same time as love[101]."

Khidr jumped off his horse and walked over to Felipa.

"Hey..."
"Hey..."
He turned to face Kalfa:
"How are you, Kalfa?"
"Thank you, Khidr."

---

[100] William Shakespeare, A Midsummer Night's Dream
[101] Miguel de Cervantes Saavedra, Don Quixote

The expression on his face was troubled. Felipa got concerned.

"How about you?"

Khidr remained silent.

"Something seems to have happened..."

"My brother..."

"Your brother? Oh, my Allah, did something bad happen to Aruj?"

"No, no... Aruj is fine."

He took Felipa's hands, raised them to his lips, and kissed. What he was about to say, he had to say all at once; or else Felipa's heart was going to fail.

"It appears that Aruj had traveled to Bizerte without telling anyone."

"To Kurdoglu?"

"Yes, upon receiving Kurdoglu's letter, Aruj had jumped on his horse and rode to Bizerte in the middle of the night so that they had a talk."

"And? What's the deal with all that worry that's pouring down your face?"

"News is not good, Felipa. The Spaniards had attacked the majority of the ports on the African coasts. After Mers El Kébir, Oran, Bejaia, and Algiers also had fallen into Christian hands. Thousands of people are said to have died, and thousands more were enslaved."

Felipa shut her eyes in pain.

"Oh, my Allah, would this war never come to an end?"

"The war has just begun, Felipa. Those ports must be reclaimed, or else, none of us can survive here. But first..."

"First?"

"Djerba. We've learned that they're preparing to attack on Djerba."

Kalfa covered his mouth with her hands, hoping to contain the dread that was ready to spill forth within.

"So close to Tunisia!"

Khidr turned to Kalfa.

"If they succeed in taking Djerba, they will have everything at their disposal to launch an assault on Tunisia from every side."

"What about the sultan? Did you talk to him? What does he say?"

Felipa tuned her attentive gaze toward Khidr. But Khidr did not reply.

"You strengthened La Goulette's fortifications. You are more than capable of repelling the attack and defending the white city. You can make them deeply regret attacking Tunisia in the first place."

"Felipa, Mulay Muhammad does not want us to defend Tunisia."

Felipa was puzzled.

"What do you mean, he doesn't want you to defend Tunisia? Does he want the Spanish to take the city and massacre us all?"

"He is looking forward to securing an agreement with them. In the same way that the ruler of Algiers, Salim al-Tumi, did. The sultan thinks that we are to blame for all that has happened. He believes that granting us permission to settle in La Goulette was a tremendous mistake."

Kalfa stepped in.

"Huseyn has to be the brains behind this. He must have planted these foolish beliefs in Sultan's mind."

"I don't know who is the brains behind this, Kalfa, but I have to say, there's some truth in it. It was us who carried the war to the European coasts. And now the Christians want to pull the battle line back to the shores of North Africa. They are planning to establish garrisons at the ports that they have taken control of and secure their shipping lanes in the Mediterranean."

Felipa got angry.

"Do your ears hear the words spilling from your mouth, Khidr? How could you say that you are the ones who carried the fight to European shores? Aren't they the ones who drove Muslims out of the lands they had called home for centuries? Aren't they the ones who took away from us all our possessions, our families?"

When Khidr was unable to give her an answer, Felipa resumed her reproach.

"Moreover, while he was looking at the wealth that you set at his feet, gazing from head to toe at all those women you had brought for his harem; Mulay Muhammad was licking his lips. And now he thinks it's all a mistake?"

"Felipa, the Spaniards killed two of his four grandchildren. The other two were only allowed to live on the condition that they retreat into the mountains. The Hafsids were forced to give up the most important port that they had possessed in eastern Algeria."

Kalfa sought to calm Felipa down.

"Felipa, I'm sure Aruj and Khidr had something in their minds."

Khidr took a deep breath.

"We have, Kalfa, of course, we have. However, the way things are currently set up will keep us apart for a while. The sultan wants us to leave Tunisia. In this way, he thinks that he will prove to the Spaniards that he's no longer cooperating with us. We're leaving La Goulette. We are going back to Djerba."

"I'm coming too!"

The look of sheer panic spread across Kalfa's face.

"Felipa!"

"What? Of course, I will go with him, Kalfa!"

"You must be out of your mind!"

Felipa was just about to respond back to Kalfa when Khidr caught her by the arm and prevented her from doing so.

"You should stay here in Tunisia. This place is safe for now. My mind shouldn't be preoccupied with you. The fight has only just begun. We will not let them take Djerba. After that, we will reclaim the ports they seized on the African coasts, one by one. When the waters calm down, I'll come back for you."

Felipa silently waited for Khidr to finish his words. When he sealed his speech with a dot, she raised her head and looked him in the eye.

"I said I'm coming too!"

She jumped on Viento and leaving both Kalfa and Khidr by the lake, she galloped away

Kalfa was in despair.

"Ah, my beautiful, my obstinate Felipa..."

Khidr turned to Kalfa:

"Would you be able to hold her back?"

"I have no idea, what about you?"

Genoa, Italy

"There is no trace of her..."

Andrea's despair was fanning his rage. With the back of his hand, he slammed the crystal wine glass sitting on the table and smashed it into smithereens.

"Damn! Where could she possibly be?"

"Anywhere, Signor Doria. In a North African town, at the service of a European aristocrat, or in the Ottoman harem."

"No, she cannot! She must be with Khidr."

"How can you be so certain? He may have dropped her somewhere and never seen her again. He may have even enslaved her and sold her in the marketplace; isn't that a possibility?"

"No, it isn't!"

Pedro Navarro took a deep breath.

"Signor Doria, this woman, Felipa; why does she hold such significance to you?"

Andrea clenched his fists. The fury he felt erupted in his eyes like the flames in the fireplace.

"This, Signor Navarro, is none of your concern!"

He shifted his attention to the Mediterranean map spread out on the table. After quietly examining the African coastline for a while, he eventually turned to Pedro Navarro.

"She must be in Tunisia. There's no question about it!"

"Signor, we can't just walk into Tunisia. Kurdoglu is keeping an eye on Bizerte. Concerning La Goulette, the port is not quite as defenseless as it once was. Over the last three to four years, they made the thousands of Christians they enslaved work on rebuilding the fortifications."

"Have you seized all those North African ports for fun? Why don't you consider enlisting the assistance of the forces that you left behind in those towns?"

"What Fernando left on those shores is nothing more than a few minor garrisons, Signor Doria. A substantial sum of money was spent. Almost a fortune. But when tension with the pope started to build up, the kingdom was compelled to withdraw its troops. The king has no standing armies. Every military campaign Fernando undertakes requires him to reach out to aristocrats whom he is not very fond of. Only Cardinal Jiménez is currently interested in the issues pertaining to North Africa, but his resources are not sufficient for us to advance further into the Maghreb. Those who remained on those shores are a financial burden on the kingdom's shoulders. I hope that you now have a better understanding of the significance of the cardinal's request from you."

"The only thing I get from what you've just said, Signor Navarro, is that you don't want the Ark quite enough. Am I incorrect in assuming that if it was as essential to you as you say it is, you would be making more of an effort to obtain it?"

Pedro Navarro took a deep breath.

"Our relationship with the cardinal is not as it used to be, Signor Doria. The primary reason behind the massacre that took place in Oran was the cardinal's stubborn refusal to pay attention to the warnings of competent commanders and his ambition to exert his own authority over the troops. And I have to say that things got even worse when one of the cardinal's men died as a result of a quarrel he got into with one of my sailors. It is not Tunisia, but rather Tripoli that the kingdom plans to launch an assault. At the moment, Mulay Muhammad is an indispensable pawn in the game Fernando is playing in North Africa. Furthermore, we cannot take the risk of strengthening the hands of the tribes that are already showing a propensity to unite under a call for jihad by also giving them the opportunity to get the backing of the dynasty."

Pedro Navarro paused for a moment. He wasn't sure if he would be able to successfully carry out what he was about to propose to Andrea. There was a chance, though, that his strategy would help to settle Andrea's storms.

"On our way back, we may launch an attack on Djerba."

"You'd be late."

"It won't be long before we gain control of Tripoli. A castle built on flat terrain right by the sea. As soon as we take control of the port, our ships will spit fire. You will see that the siege will be over in a very short amount of time."

"Oh, come on, Signor Navarro, you're as familiar with those seas as I am. When you are done with Tripoli, it will be the end of the summer, and we both know that you are going to steer your route to Spain to be able to get away from those waters as fast as possible."

"Signor Doria, I'm afraid I don't have any alternative offer for you at this time."

Andrea had no choice but to accept. If Spain would manage to succeed in capturing Djerba, the relations between Fernando and Mulay Muhammad would deteriorate. Moreover, if it turned out that the Ark was neither in Tripoli nor in Djerba, Cardinal Jiménez would be left with no choice but to attack La Goulette. All that Andrea needed to do was wait a little longer. For just a little while longer, he needed to practice patience.

He took the crystal carafe and poured the final drops of the exquisite wine into the other glass that had survived his recent rage. He made a toast to Pedro Navarro before raising it to his lips.

"To your taking Djerba before your fleet is capsized during that season."

Pedro Navarro remained silent. He now had to leave. He slightly bowed his head to bid Andrea farewell before turning around to make his way to the door. Andrea, on the other hand, after sending the final sip of wine he'd been twirling in his mouth down his throat, couldn't help but ask the commander as he was about to leave the room.

"When the cardinal took possession of that Ark rumored to contain the Stones of Death; does he have something in mind that would allow him to avoid the death spilling from the Ark from splashing on himself?"

Pedro Navarro turned to Andrea.

"If you're wondering how the kingdom would use the power of the Ark, I'd say there's no need for you to be concerned, Signor Doria. Because one of the greatest minds that Europe had ever seen has been working on this matter for quite some time."

"One of the greatest minds that Europe had ever seen, huh... May I inquire as to who this individual is?"

"Leonardo, Signor Doria, Leonardo da Vinci."

Pavia, Italy

The University of Pavia, which was established in 825 as a school of law, by King Lothair I, son of the Holy Roman Emperor Louis the Pious, was one of the oldest institutions of higher education in Europe. When Charles IV decreed in 1361 that the school, hitherto devoted to ecclesiastical and civil law, should also teach philosophy, medicine, and liberal arts, and open its doors to everyone with a hunger for knowledge; the city had developed into a center of learning in northern Italy. With its interconnected courtyards, this edifice, which Ludovico Sforza donated to the university at the end of the 15th century, was reminiscent of a labyrinth. Leonardo had lately been visiting this place rather frequently. Together with Marcantonio della Torre, a brilliant, young, and energetic anatomy professor whom he befriended, they were conducting studies on the human body and drawing sketches. There were questions that haunted Leonardo, questions to which he had been seeking answers. Marcantonio was referring to the human body as "the most exquisite instrument designed by the Grand Master". Leonardo, on the other hand, had no idea who this Grand Master was, yet he admired the job that he had done in the same manner as his friend did.

With his back turned to the naked body of a man who apparently had passed away before he could reach his sixties, Leonardo was trying to form a mold by pouring the melted wax into the heart he was holding in his hands. He was so caught up in what he was doing that he hadn't even heard Marcantonio's entering in.

"How are you doing today, Leonardo?"

Leonardo leapt in fright. He almost dropped the heart he was holding.

"Well done, Marco!"

Marcantonio let out a laugh.

"What? You thought that the man was resurrected?" He took off his coat and put it up on the hanger at the entrance. "You're early today, I hope everything is okay."

"Something got stuck in my mind last night, and when I couldn't get it unstuck, I couldn't sleep."

Marc Antonio moved closer to the lifeless body that was lying on the table.

"And in order to remove what got stuck in your mind you decided to remove the old man's heart, huh?"

After setting the heart aside so that the wax could harden, Leonardo retrieved his sketchbook and walked over to Marcantonio.

"Look, if the heart is a muscle, and like every other muscle, it is animated by the signals coming from the nerves attached to the brain; then Plato was right, the brain is the seat of the soul! Because it is the action of the brain that is manifested in the heart. But if the heart beats on its own, then Plato is wrong, the soul is in the heart."

"Plato had divided the soul into three parts, though," said Marcantonio.

After leaving his notebook aside Leonardo reached for his scalpel.

"According to Descartes, on the other hand..."

He took the brain out of the man's skull, sliced it in half, removed the chunk the size of a pinecone that he had discovered while working in the Santa Maria Nuova Hospital, and then showed it to Marcantonio.

"This is the seat of the soul!"

"You mean, Glandula Pinealis[102]? But Galen had said that it serves the same purpose as all the other glands in the body, which is to act as a support for the blood vessels."

Leonardo let out a sigh.

"I know..."

He was unable to come up with a conclusion. Marcantonio wanted to help.

---

[102] The pineal gland, a small endocrine gland in the brain of most vertebrates.

"I think we should examine the spinal cord that connects this whole system. It can give us the answers we seek. Think about it, the frogs can continue to live for some time without a head or a heart, but they die the moment their spinal column is ruptured."

"You could be right, Marco... You could very well be right."

Cervantes leaned back.

"Leonardo was resolved to unravel the mysteries of the human body, which all philosophers have compared to a tree that has its roots in the sky. In the same way as Felipa, who was quite firm in her determination to sail to Djerba with Khidr."

Tunisia

The night had etched its way deep into the guards' bones, whispering silent tales into their ears as they stood watch. After putting her cloak on and hiding her wavy hair beneath its cloak, Felipa cautiously opened the door and took a peek around. She had already made up her mind about which route she was going to take, and which lanterns she was going to put off along the way. She had spent the previous week strolling along the corridors in her white nightgown to become familiar with the path that would lead her to the most secluded corner of the gardens. Even though there had been instances she was spotted by the guards; she had managed to get away by telling them that she had trouble sleeping and had quietly returned to her room.

Tonight, though, since there was no turning back for Felipa, not a single soul should hear about her. As soon as the new day broke, Khidr would set sail for Djerba, and Felipa was aware that she did not have much time. If she managed to escape from the palace, she had a long way to walk before reaching the port. She could not possibly leave on horseback since it was impossible for anyone to sneak a horse out of the palace without being noticed. She also had no one who could help her, for she had kept her plans to herself. Khidr had been objecting since the very beginning. She had tried to persuade Yahya, but he also was not keen on her sailing to Djerba with them. Regarding Kalfa, Felipa could not let her know. She did not want her to be involved in this risky adventure. She would undoubtedly find a way to help Felipa, but if the sultan were to figure this out, Kalfa may have gotten into trouble.

With all these thoughts wandering in her head, Felipa tiptoed through the halls. She disguised herself behind the pillars, hid among the velvet drapes, and eventually managed to get to the garden. The night was pitch dark. Even the moon had retreated behind the thick blanket of clouds depriving the roses of its silky rays as if it were part of a larger plot to assist her. She was very close... If Huseyn hadn't been waiting for Felipa in the garden with two of his guards at his side, Felipa was really close to getting out of the palace.

"Did you decide to go down to the garden this time, young lady, because you couldn't sleep?"

"Well, yes... I... I've been having trouble sleeping lately. I thought getting some fresh air might help."

"So, you've been having trouble sleeping, huh? Maybe you should see a doctor; after all, you've been suffering from insomnia for quite some time."

Felipa was frozen in place. Huseyn could not possibly be here at this hour of the night merely by chance. He had to have been waiting for her. But how could that be possible? Felipa had told no one about her plans.

"Oh, I'm.., I'm fine. Really, there is nothing to be concerned about. In any case, I was going to return to my room in a few minutes. I'd already started feeling a bit chilly."

Felipa had no intention of returning; she was simply looking for a way to get around Huseyn. Huseyn, on the other hand, was well aware of her plans.

"Let my guards accompany you to your room, then."

When the guards took a step towards her, Felipa retreated to keep them at bay.

"Oh, no... There's no need for that, really. I can go by myself..."

They did not stand back and caught her by the arms. Felipa was yelling at them to let go of her while at the same time struggling to release herself from their hold. Huseyn took a few steps and approached Felipa.

"If you think that I am unaware of your aspirations, you're erroneous, young lady. So, you were hoping to flee the palace and slip into the arms of your lover, huh? Let alone going to the port, you're not even allowed to set foot outside the garden again."

He ordered his men:

"Take her to her chamber! Keep an eye on her, she won't be leaving her room anytime soon!"

Felipa was yelling and calling out to Kalfa. Kalfa, however, could not possibly help her, for she was at that time pacing up and down in the room where she was confined by Huseyn's men.

"But how did Huseyn find out about Felipa's plans?"

"Ever since the day they had first arrived at La Goulette, Huseyn had disliked the Barbarossas. Believing that their presence in Tunisia would eventually cause them trouble, he had never, not even for a moment, taken his sneaky eyes off the brothers. He had spies at the port informing Huseyn of every step they took. And, of course, he was quick to notice Khidr and Felipa's frequent encounters. He had long been waiting for a single mistake the brothers would make. It might have been an arrogant act, or perhaps a defeat that they would have suffered. However, things had not gone as he had anticipated. The Barbarossas had returned from all their hunts with invaluable treasure and had put one-fifth of the booty at Mulay Muhammad's feet, as they had promised. Fortunately, the Spaniards had begun to seize the ports along the African coasts, giving Huseyn the opportunity to plant the seeds of fear in the sultan's heart. And Huseyn had convinced Mulay Muhammad that Tunisia's safety would be in jeopardy so long as he maintained his alliance with the Barbarossas."

By the time the next morning arrived, and the waters had begun turning blue with dawn, almost all the preparations were complete. Khidr had leaned against the railings, gazing out at the white city in the distance. He was startled by Yahya's voice.

"Everything is set up, Reis. We now can raise the anchor and set sail."
"Spare boats?"
"In their proper place."
"Provisions?"
"We've got enough to get us a long way."

"Gunpowder?"

"Glazed. We can hurl nine-ounce cannonballs a mile afar."

"Good."

"Aruj said that Kurdoglu's ships returning from Alexandria would join us as well."

"I hope they bring good quality timber and men to work on strengthening the defenses. Anyway, let's get to Djerba first and we'll think about the rest later."

"You are right, Reis, we will surely figure out a way."

Khidr placed his hand on Yahya's shoulder.

"Yahya."

"Yes, Reis."

"I'll go ashore and then come back. You make sure that nothing falls short. I will not be late."

He turned around and began to walk.

"To bid farewell, Reis?"

Khidr stood still. He replied without turning his back.

"To bid farewell, Yahya."

"He knew neither what had transpired the night before, nor that Felipa was locked in her chamber. The last time they saw each other, Khidr had been a little harsh on Felipa and had felt bad about it afterward."

"Absence from those we love is self from self - a deadly banishment."[103]

"Khidr was feeling exactly the same at that moment," said Cervantes. "But he didn't have much of a choice. Khidr could not possibly drag Felipa into such a perilous adventure. She needed to stay in Tunisia and they both had to be patient for a little while longer. Khidr and his brothers would defend Djerba; and then, they would search for a better and safer harbor for themselves somewhere along the coast of Africa. After they settled, it would be easy for him to go and get Felipa out of Tunisia. Who could have possibly stood up to him? Huseyn? The sultan?"

William laughed.

---

[103] William Shakespeare, The Two Gentlemen of Verona

"Stand up to those who land on Christian lands and kidnap the dukes' daughters while they sleep in their lace gowns?"

"As he made his way to the stables, his mind was preoccupied with all these thoughts. He was going to apologize to Felipa and ask her to be a little bit more patient. After that, he was going to place a kiss on the corner of her lovely lips and say goodbye. But when he couldn't find her at the stables, all that he couldn't say became a huge stone that sat on his chest."

"Mustafa?"

"Yes Khidr Reis."

"Felipa... Is Felipa around?"

"She's not here, Reis. She hasn't arrived yet."

"Allah Allah..."

"It's still quite early. She may be still sleeping."

"She knew that we would be sailing early in the morning."

Mustafa did not have a clue. He raised his hands up in the air.

"I don't know, Reis. Since yesterday afternoon, I've seen neither Felipa nor Kalfa."

Khidr didn't know what to say.

"All right, Mustafa. Thanks, anyway. It's time for us to set sail. If Felipa comes..."

He paused for a moment. What could he possibly ask Mustafa to say to Felipa? Could he ask him to tell her that, though he knew it was only tempo-rary, being away from her was wreaking havoc on his heart? Or that, how much he would have preferred to take her with him...... or that, how much he loved her...

Mustafa deduced everything from the expression on Khidr's face; then, he took them all at once and replied to him with a single sentence.

"I'll tell her, Reis, I'll tell her that you came to bid farewell."

"Thank you, Mustafa..."

Upon noticing Viento running freely inside the fenced field, Khidr slowly walked toward him. And Viento, as he spotted Khidr, came running. Khidr caressed his mane and patted him on the neck. Then, he leaned up close and whispered.

"Would you, as well, tell her, Viento? Would you tell Felipa that I love her? That I love her and will be back for her..."

The mooring lines were loosened, and the sails were hoisted. As the ships sailed away from La Goulette, Felipa was watching through her tears. She hadn't even been able to bid farewell to the man she loved.

"Oh, please stop crying Felipa, you ruined yourself."

"How shall I not cry, Kalfa? Khidr is gone and I am now trapped in a room with two men keeping guard outside to ensure that I won't escape. I'll not even be able to see my Viento again."

"Oh Felipa, if only you paid heed to my words. You are the one who brought this on yourself with your obstinacy. Why on earth would you ever attempt to escape in the middle of the night? I really don't get it. And without even letting me know!"

"I couldn't have let you know. I couldn't have made you a part of this. Who knows what he would have done to you."

"Who? Huseyn? Huseyn can do nothing to me. Don't pay attention to his hissing. Do not assume that he has any power over me from the fact that he stationed guards at my door and compelled me to spend the night inside. Come on, sweetie, wipe away your tears. Allow Khidr to leave; he will return, you'll see. And concerning Viento, don't worry, I will speak with the sultan about him."

Her damp gaze riveted on the ships vanishing into the mist; she placed her head on Kalfa's shoulder.

That winter was not easy for either of them. Even though Kalfa had convinced the sultan to allow Felipa to meet with Viento again, the young woman was neither eating properly nor speaking. She was spending her days tending to the horses with Mustafa. She was dealing with their training, cleaning, and grooming them in the mornings; while in the afternoons, she was galloping away from the city with Viento, arriving at the lakeside where she once used to meet up with Khidr. There was no trace of her former joy. Her face was usually looking pale and tired. Kalfa was observing, with each passing day, Felipa was becoming more like a shadow. She had attempted to talk to her several times but had felt that whatever she said was lost in the ether; for her words had not even passed Felipa's pensive gaze allowing them to reach her ears. Finally, she had decided to pay Mother Firuze a visit and tell her about Felipa's condition. Mother Firuze had become concerned; because she knew that a cut in the heart may be so deep that it could not be compared to any other wound in the body. She had gone to her kitchen brimming with medicinal herbs, and after giving some thought to it, she had taken a few of those leaves, roots, and barks, wrapped them in a piece of cloth and gave them over to Kalfa. And Kalfa had started carrying pots of tea she brewed by boiling these herbs to Felipa's room every night.

Khidr could not be said to have been well, either. All day, he was working on digging trenches, shoring up the defenses, mending the sails, fixing the boats, and assisting the shipwrights in building new galiots with the high-quality timber Kurdoglu's men brought from Alexandria. Isaac had gone to Lesbos for a brief length of time and had sent them a letter informing his brothers about Yakub Agha's passing away. Aruj, on the other hand, was continuously making plans. He was getting excited as soon as he saw on the horizon Kurdoglu's red flag, on which was embroidered a motif of a dark blue wolf head. They were sitting together until the wee hours of the morning, discussing the measures that they would take against the impending Spanish onslaught. Then, Kurdoglu was once again hoisting his sails and sailing toward Rhodes, the island that had been his greatest lover as well as his bloodiest nemesis.

The men working on the ships during the daytime were spending the nights with the women they met in the inns, and most of them were returning to their ships the next day hungover. Aruj was concerned that if the lethargic nature of Djerba were to overtake the levends, then they would all become lazy in the end, and their drive for fighting that had been keeping them alive would melt away in the scorching sands of the island. However, the Barbarossas had no choice but to remain in Djerba at the time; which was why they had worked for months to turn the island into a secure shelter.

When November arrived and the Spanish flags emerged over the horizon, it became clear that nothing they had done was in vain. Kurdoglu was correct in his predictions. The Spaniards were getting ready to attack Djerba.

Cervantes picked up the model ships that he had positioned off the coast of Piombino, added to them a few more of those, and then placed the entire fleet in the southern waters of Djerba.

"However, just as Andrea had predicted, the time they wasted in Tripoli would cost the Spaniards dearly."

He began whistling as he drew circles around the island. His hand accelerated and eventually knocked down all the ships.

William had a sardonic grin on his face.

"You've said it was November, correct?"

"Yes, Signor, I did say November."

"I suppose we made it."

Khidr was smiling. They had been able to successfully ward off the Spanish assault. And Aruj's one and only love, the sea, had helped them a lot this time. The storm had swallowed up four Spanish galleons and plunged them to the depths of the seas, taking the lives of a huge number of Spanish sailors alongside. The waters surrounding Djerba had become a graveyard for the Spaniards.

Once he had secured his sword to his belt, Aruj responded to Khidr:

"We made it, brother... We made it!"

"The news of their victory over the Spaniards traveled fast to Tunisia," said Cervantes.

"Huseyn must have been disappointed."

"Indeed, Signor. Mulay Muhammad, on the other hand, was now brooding over how to mend the bridges he had burned and smooth out the relations with the Barbarossas. It was true that the raids the brothers carried out on the European shores had drawn the Spaniards to African coasts. But Mulay Muhammad was fully aware that if he could not reach an agreement with the Christians, there was no one else to defend his white city but the Barbarossas. The solution he was desperately looking for came from someone unexpected."

"As daring as it sounds, I'd like to suggest a solution, My Sultan."

Kalfa had been serving Mulay Muhammad for many years responsible for keeping the harem in order. She would never interfere in anything other than matters directly related to his private chambers, but she would ensure that the harem ran smoothly at all times. Thanks to her intelligence and discipline, the women in the harem would receive appropriate training and be inspired to improve themselves in the areas in which they were gifted. "Women should never be left idle", Kalfa would always say; and would add, "It's always preferable to keep their hands busy, rather than their tongues." Mulay Muhammad had always liked and appreciated Kalfa and had complete trust in her competence pertaining to matters of her expertise. Seeing her hesitating this time, had astonished the sultan.

"What is it that you want to say, Kalfa?"

There were standing amidst the garden of roses. As the sultan curiously waited to hear what she had to say, Kalfa was trying to choose the right words.

"My Sultan, I... you know... until now..." She took a breath. "You know that I have never spoken to you about anything other than matters pertaining to your harem until now. But I learned that something is troubling you in your relations with those Turkish corsairs. And in case you'd like to hear, I have a suggestion."
"You have a suggestion?"
Mulay Muhammad was baffled.
"Yes, My Sultan. If I'm not overstepping my bounds, perhaps I can help you in this matter."

The sultan got even more curious. What kind of suggestion could Kalfa possibly have had for the sultan about the Turkish corsairs? He squinted his eyes and stared at her for a while; then, he decided to grant her an audience.

"What is it, then?"
"I know that you want to mend fences with the Barbarossas. I am also aware that you are feeling a little uncertain about what to say to them, for you were at odds with each other just before they left La Goulette last winter. Perhaps... Perhaps, as a symbol of your goodwill, you might send them something insignificant to you but very important to one of the brothers."

The sultan repeated Kalfa's words.

"Something insignificant to me but important to one of the brothers?"

"I mean, someone."

"Someone?"

"Yes, My Sultan. Someone from your harem."

"Someone from my harem?"

Mulay Muhammad was befuddled. Kalfa, on the other hand, had decided not to juggle the beans in her mouth any longer, and spill them out all at once.

"Felipa, My Sultan, that long-haired woman in charge of your horses you keep at La Goulette. For a long time, I'm aware that the younger of the Barbarossas has feelings for her. However, since she is part of your harem, he never spoke a word about it, nor he did ever touch a strand of her hair. If your desire is to see the brothers at La Goulette once more, perhaps you may send Felipa to Khidr as a present to please him."

"Felipa? Does Khidr have feelings for Felipa?"

"In all honesty, he has, My Sultan. I beg your pardon if I've crossed the line in any way, but I've seen that you've been giving a lot of thought to this matter as of late."

The sultan was indeed surprised. It was the first time Kalfa had asked him such a thing. He reflected on her idea for a while as he rubbed his beard. Why not, he reasoned. If the Turk did indeed have feelings for Felipa, in this way, he might well be able to win over the Barbarossas again.

"What about the horses, Kalfa? She'd been doing an excellent job with the horses."

"Felipa loves horses, My Sultan. She'll certainly continue taking care of them. There's absolutely no need for you to be concerned about it."

"All right, Kalfa. Then, go get the woman ready. Get on a boat and take her to Djerba."

"As you command, My Sultan."

After leaving the sultan in the garden alone with his roses, Kalfa rushed to Felipa's room trying not to reveal her joy much. She found Felipa sitting by the window as usual with her gaze on the horizon. She took a few steps, reached out, and grabbed her hands, then, rose her to her feet. She began twirling her around in circles.

"Kalfa, stop! What are you doing?"

Kalfa was giggling and singing songs.

"Kalfa, please, I'm already tired."

After a few rounds, Felipa managed to get away from Kalfa's hold and flung herself onto the couch. Kalfa sat down next to her. She looked at her with twinkling eyes.

"You are not tired! You cannot be tired! You shouldn't be tired! So long you've been waiting for this day to come! Get up! Get up quickly!"

Felipa had not the slightest idea what was going on. She just sat there, perplexed, staring at Kalfa. But Kalfa took her hands and stood her back up.

"I said, get up! We're going!"

"We're going? Where are we going?"

"To Djerba, of course!"

"To Djerba?"

"Yes, to Djerba! to Khidr. The sultan was looking for a way to win back the brothers' hearts and I told him that Khidr's heart belonged only to you and no one else."

Stars shone brightly in Felipa's eyes, her face began to glow, her voice trembled.

"Kalfaaaaa?"

"Yes, sweetheart. The sultan is sending you to Khidr as a gift!"

Felipa was at a loss for words.

"Oh, my Allah! Oh, my Allah!"

She wrapped her arms around Kalfa's neck and gave her a big hug. Then, she brought her to her feet and began twirling her around in circles.

Kalfa was screaming.

"Oh Felipa, stop! Slow down! Oh, my Allah! We're going to fall!"

"O Mistress mine where are you roaming? O stay and hear, your true love's coming, that can sing both high and low. Trip no further pretty sweeting. Journeys end in lovers' meeting, every wise man's son doth know. What is love, 'tis not hereafter, Present mirth, hath present laughter: What's to come, is still unsure. In delay there lies no plenty, then come kiss me sweet and twenty: Youth's a stuff will not endure."[104]

William was feeling so joyful that if it were up to him, Felipa should have sailed to Djerba, pressed her thirsty lips to Khidr's, three apples should have fallen from the heavens, and so the play should have ended. He had leaped on his feet with excitement, spread his arms wide, and after completing his sonnet bowed before Cervantes to salute him. He now was waiting for the veil to come down. And yes, the hazy veil of sorrow had already come down on Cervantes's eyes who knew the rest of the story.

---

[104] William Shakespeare, The Sonnet "O Mistress Mine"

Djerba

The boat had docked at the wooden pier. As soon as she landed onshore and removed her hoodie, it was as if spring had arrived on the island with the fragrance of her hair blowing in the wind.

Khidr muttered without taking his eyes off her:
"Oh, my Allah... She is Felipa!"

He couldn't believe what he was seeing. At first, he thought that she had escaped from the court. But how could that be possible? Even if she had found a way, there was no way that she could have traveled all the way down to Djerba. Could it be possible that she had struck a bargain with the pirates? Or had she secretly gotten in touch with Yahya and convinced him to arrange a boat to bring her here? Or was it Aruj? No, it was impossible. Aruj would never do something like that. Besides, Aruj was only interested in his plans concerning the ports along the African coasts. He had devoted his days to nothing but repairing the ships and getting the crew ready for the upcoming campaigns that he intended to embark on in the spring. His brother hadn't even allowed himself the opportunity to ride the wave of victory they had over the Spaniards. While the levends were drinking wine, singing songs, becoming engrossed in their daydreams, and getting drunk with the spicy aroma of the Moorish women they encountered in the inns, he had continued to work, day and night. He also seemed to have been a little nervous as of late. Even though he was, for the time being, keeping his restlessness to himself; it was quite likely that he would storm at someone in the near future. No, there was no way that Aruj could be the one who had brought Felipa here. It must have been Yahya.

But... But wait a minute... Was that Kalfa, walking next to Felipa? But how so? Had Kalfa as well made her escape?

"Aha! He will certainly think that I am the one who is responsible for all of this. And so, it is crystal clear to whom my brother would soon storm at."

"Storm at? I'm going to shatter your bones into zillion pieces."
He was startled. He hadn't noticed Aruj approaching from behind.
"Brother, I have nothing to do with what's going on.; believe me, I'm telling you the truth."
"If you do not immediately go and welcome her, I will crush your bones, Khidr, and I'm pretty serious about it."
"Brother, I say I know nothing about this matter, why don't you believe me?"
"She turned into a tree, man; she grew roots as she waited for you."
"Brother, I am just as baffled as you are. How could you possibly think that I'd ever attempt such a thing without getting your opinion first?"
"Keep her await a little while longer and watch what happens. I swear, I'll chain you to the oars!"
"Brother..."
"Oh, damn your brother, Khidr! Go and greet her you fool!"

He paused for a moment to reflect on the words his brother had been telling him for the past two minutes. His jaw dropped open. Aruj, on the other hand, was staring at him with a wide grin adorning his face.

"Brother? You? So, you knew this? I mean, Felipa...
Aruj folded his arms on his chest and scowled at Khidr.
"I'll not only chain you to the oars but whip you, as well, Khidr. When five to ten lashes pierce the skin of your back, then you will understand what awaits those who disobey their reis' orders."
"But brother..."
"Oh, come on, man! Run!"
"As you command brother!"

William was enjoying the story; a gleaming smile had lit up his face.

"I see, Signor Shakespeare, that hearing about Khidr's moonstricken, foolish state of heart has given you a lot of delight."

"Yes, Signor, it truly brings a smile to my face, as I consider the love of this sort to be so pure that I believe it is ideally suited to the most vulnerable part of the heart."

"That part of the heart which you refer to as most vulnerable, Signor Shakespeare, is in fact, the strongest part. It is where the mightiest of all storms occurs. It is the part that withstands the heaviest cannon fire of love... The strongest of all the fortresses in the world guarded by no one..."

"But how can a fortress withstand if it is not guarded, Signor?"

"By opening its doors and yielding, Signor, by surrendering to love."

It was true that Aruj knew about Felipa's coming, but he was also aware that it was not a case of abduction from the seraglio, but rather a part of Mulay Muhammad's plan to win over their hearts. The sultan was convinced that he should heed Kalfa's advice about sending Felipa as a gift to Khidr and penned a letter to Aruj to let him know about his decision. Aruj, after reading the letter that arrived Djerba shortly before Felipa, had preferred to keep this a secret from his brother to surprise him. And, in fact, he had been successful in doing so, since Khidr had been caught off guard by all that had transpired.

Khidr's joy was indescribable, but unfortunately, it was eclipsed by some unexpected news from Constantinople. A raging storm had swallowed up Kemal Reis' galleon. And Kemal Reis, the greatest admiral of the Ottoman naval forces, the worst nightmare of European Kingdoms, was no more...

Khidr was at a loss for words. With his hand on the railings and a foot planted on the first step of the staircase, he stood still. What could he possibly say to Piri? The man who would grab his sword boldly and reveal his chest to the adversary, who would not be daunted by anyone save Allah, had been carried by the seas, washed along by the storms. What might Khidr possibly say and bring some solace to Piri? Piri had lost his best friend, his comrade, his second father, his greatest master... Perhaps it would be best if he said nothing at all. Perhaps it would have been enough if Khidr made Piri feel that he was there to share his pain. He steeled himself and then made his way to the upper floor.

"How are you?"
Piri was packing up his stuff.
"He went... and left us alone in this world..."

For a while, silence prevailed.

"You're packing."
"Yes, Khidr... I am."
"Where are you going?"
"To Gallipoli."
"On the orders of the sultan?"
"No."
"Why, then?"

With his notebooks in one hand, and his charts in the other, Piri turned to face Khidr. For a moment, the two comrades looked at each other in silence. Then, Piri spoke:
"I'm leaving, Khidr... I'm going home..."
"But Piri, our fight has only just begun. We have a vengeance to take, there are times ahead of us when we will swing our swords back-to-back."
Piri took a deep breath.
"Of course, there are... but..."
"But what?"
"I'll be gone for a while, Khidr. I must first fight my own war."
"Your own war?"
"Yes, my own war. The war I must wage against my own rage, my pain, my frustrations... First, I must defeat my own demons and convert them to Muslims. Only then, I can draw my sword and point it at the enemy. If I pull it with a rage that scorches my heart, it will miss its mark and injure the people I care about."

Khidr could not reply. Piri was right. When out in the waters, one should have nothing in mind but the waves. The seas would never spare those and would devour the scattered minds.

"Besides, I have some responsibilities to fulfill. My uncle's untimely death reminded me that I need to wrap up some loose ends and complete the projects that I'd long been putting off for I was too caught up by the excitement of the campaigns and battle cries. Because it is a mystery to all of us how many breaths we have left as we fight in these waters."

"Are you afraid of death, Piri?"

"What I'm afraid of is not death, Khidr, but rather, a death that would come before I finished my charts and presented all my years of hard work to our Sultan. I don't think I can embrace such a death."

Khidr had understood better the reasons behind Piri's leaving. He was going to be away only for short while. He would soon return, and together with his comrades, they were going to put the finishing blow to the enemy. And as he returned, this time, he would be bringing with him his very own maps...

Piri had his eyes fixed on the horizon, on that thin line that separated the earth from the sky. Prior to Christopher Colón, the world was believed to be flat like a tray. It had a visible end, and if someone were to get there by accident, he would fall into the void and vanish. That's what the vast majority of the people were thinking. But not everyone!

He took the manuscripts and unwrapped them. As he ran his fingers across the pages, he muttered:
"Zohar... The Book of Splendor..."

It had been kept hidden from the eyes for centuries. Within the caverns, cellars, and forests; in earthen jars; under the stones, bushes, beneath the ground... And after millennia, the Splendor had decided to reappear in daylight. It had begun to shine in Spain around the 11th century, and along with its cousin Sufism, and contributed to Andalusia's rise as the light of civilization in the west. Until the Catholic Monarchs came and turned this light off... Who knows how many copies were set ablaze in wood fires... Who knows how many of them had survived, like the one Piri was holding in his palms... He slowly flipped the pages and opened the chapter he had been reading over and over.

> *'The world is as round as a ball. When the sun comes out in the east, it goes in a circle until it reaches below the earth, and then it becomes evening. At that time, it gradually descends by circles of certain steps, descending and circling the whole earth and the whole world. When the sun comes down and is covered by it, it grows dark upon us and lights up to those who are dwelling below us, those who are on the other side of the earth, below our feet...'*

Someone knew... 1300 years ago, someone knew that the world was round like a ball. And because Colón also knew this, he had mounted his sailing horse and ridden straight into the raging waves of the ocean without hesitation. He had not been intimidated by the possibility of reaching the horizon and falling into the void. Or else, how on earth, could someone have risked his life by relying solely on intuition to guide him through the unknown waters? Piri was curious as to how Colón got a hold of these manuscripts. Who could have possibly given him the Zohar, which holds who knows how many more secrets in it? Piri needed solitude. He needed to go somewhere where he could work in silence. He needed to go to Kilitbahir.

He rewrapped the manuscripts in cloth and secured them in his chest, where he also kept Colón's charts, as well as the Qur'an and Torah that he inherited from his uncle. Just like anybody who had ever gotten their hands on the Zohar had done throughout history, he intended to hide the Splendor, protecting the Splendor from the blind.

He got on his feet and called out to his levends:
"To Gallipoli!"

"Why?" said William.
"Why what?" asked Cervantes.
"Colón was a staunch Christian. He could not possibly have given the Turks his priceless maps in the sole expectation that they would free him from prison."
Cervantes grinned.
"Cristóbal Colón... Aka Salvador Fernandes Zarco."
William had not understood.
"If you think that Cristóbal Colón was an ordinary sailor born to a poor Genoese family of fabric dyers, who had spent his days of youth watching the boats in the harbor and studying the charts, and then somehow managed to draw the attention of the Spanish Monarchs, you are mistaken, Signor Shakespeare. Colón couldn't even speak Italian. He had never written anything in Italian. But his Spanish and Portuguese were like his mother tongue."
William was confused. Cervantes kept on:

"He was Salvador Fernandes Zarco, the illegitimate son of Isabel Gonsalves Zarco who was of Jewish descent, and the Duke of Beja, Don Fernando, brother of King Juan II of Portugal."

William was so dumbfounded that he was almost going to fall off his chair.

"Then Colón was a member of the Portuguese royal family, he was of royal blood!"

"Exactly, Signor. Cristobal Colón was a spy who had learned his navigational skills at the nautical school of Prince Henry the Navigator. He was not the first to set foot in the New World. He was not even the first admiral in his family. Although Spain was ignorant of it, Portugal had arrived at those shores quite some time ago. Colón had been sent on a secret mission by King John II of Portugal to keep the Catholic Monarchs away from the southern part of the New World, which held vast quantities of gold, silver, raw materials, jewels of inestimable value, and metals. Think about it for a moment, even though it was Isabel who financed his voyages, the admiral's first stop after returning from his first voyage had been Lisbon, and the first King he went to see to report was King John II of Portugal. It was Colón who had advised the king to raise objection to the Treaty of Tordesillas before it was ratified in 1494. This was a true act of espionage. The purpose of the treaty was to settle the conflict between Spain and Portugal over uncharted territories. However, King Juan II had insisted that Portugal should be given a larger portion than what had been previously agreed upon and that the demarcation line should be moved 180 leagues to the west which eventually provided the Portuguese dominion over the lands the existence of which had been a closely guarded secret, known only to Portugal's great navigators."

"Holy Jesus!" said William.

However, that still did not clarify why Colón had consented so quickly to the offer Piri and Kemal reises made to him; because even if he was Portuguese, he must have been a staunch Christian.

"I cannot say that I am not startled by what you have just said, yet that still does not answer my question."

"The Templar Cross was emblazoned on the sails of the caravels that Colón used to sail to the New World, Signor Shakespeare. The triangular kabbalistic cipher that he had been using as his signature was the same triangular symbol that is used by Jewish money lenders and bankers."

After spending some time sifting through the jumble of papers spread out on his table, Cervantes picked one and handed it to William.

"Take a look at this, Signor Shakespeare, look at those letters."

"*x, t, p, o*. It is '*Salvador*' which means 'Christ', 'the Savior', the very person the Templars paid homage to. Also, '*ferens*' stands for 'Son of Fernando'. He took a small mirror out of his pocket and placed it vertically right next to the cipher. "And lastly, look at that last 's' letter at the very end. See how it turns to 'z' when you look at it with a mirror. It is the 'z' of 'Zarco'."

William turned his gaze to Cervantes.

"So, he was not a Christian?"

Cervantes smiled and revealed to William another of the mystery about Colón's cipher.

"The word 'Columbus' means 'dove' in Latin, so 'Xtpofer Columbus' is..."

William completed Cervantes' words.

"The Dove of Christ..."

"He was a Christian as well as a Jew. He wouldn't be able to embark on a voyage of this sort unless he was a Templar himself operating in the name of King Portugal, Signor. And you know, the Templars were the bankers. He had set sail to the New World on August 6th, the very same day, the Catholic Monarchs had given the Jews of Andalusia the choice of converting to Christianity, leaving the Spanish territory, or enduring the consequences. So, he had to get out of that prison before Queen Isabel discovered who he truly was. He had utilized such ciphers in all his papers and charts that deciphering them was nearly impossible for anyone who didn't know what Colón was after. And he could have easily bought his freedom by giving Piri a few maps of the New World's coasts."

"But the Templars..."

William was confused. How on earth was it ever possible for Colón to have any kind of connection to the Templars? Wasn't the Order of the Knights Templar disbanded some two hundred years ago?

Cervantes read William's confusion from the expression on his face.

"The Templars, which Pope Clement V disbanded in 1312 by tying their 23rd and final Grand Master Jacques de Molay to a stake and setting him ablaze, have, in reality, never been completely eradicated, Signor Shakespeare. They changed their names, disguised themselves in other outfits, and continued their operations in secrecy in a variety of countries. In Portugal, they had renowned members such as Magellan and Vasco de Gama. And as for Don Fernando, Duke of Beja, who was Colón's real father, he was the Grand Master of the Order of Christ, the Portuguese branch of the Knights Templar."

William let out a laugh.

"It seems Colón had given Piri the questions, not the answers."

"However, things had not gone as planned. When the guards dragged Colón into the waters at the last moment, he had been obliged to stay in Cádiz while his charts set sail with Piri. And although it was true that he had carefully ciphered them all, Piri was just as competent a cartographer as he was."

Soon after Piri set sail for Gallipoli, a few of Amir Abu Bakr's men had come to Djerba to meet with Aruj. The news they brought from the Barbary Coast presented an excellent opportunity for Aruj, who had grown tired of being stuck on this small island, to hoist his sails and set sail.

After the Almohad Caliphate lost its last stronghold in Marrakesh in 1296 and disappeared from the historical scene, the three influential dynasties of North Africa had declared their independence. While the Marinids governed Morocco and its surroundings, the Zayyanids were in control of Tlemcen and the Hafsids ruled in Tunisia. The Algerian province, on the other hand, had been divided into two between the Zayyanids and the Hafsids. As if the tension created by these dynasties, which were constantly at odds with one another, was not enough, wars between tribes did not seem to end anytime soon. Emerging emirates were promptly gaining control of the weaker ones, and this constantly shifting balance of power was posing an increasingly serious threat to dynasties.

Constantine was under the control of one of Mulay Muhammad's sons Abu Bakr, and Bejaia was governed by his other son, Abdelaziz. When Abdelaziz, long fed up with having been constantly harassed by his brother, lost his patience in 1508 and marched on Constantine; Abu Bakr had fled south to the Belezma Mountains. As for Abdelaziz, after leaving Bejaia in the hands of his son Abderrahmane, he had settled in Constantine.

DENİZ UZUNOĞLU

Cervantes reclined back in his chair.

"But when the calendars showed the year 1510, the bells had begun to toll for Abdelaziz. During the Spanish siege of Bejaia, Abdelaziz had lost two of his sons. His other sons, Abderrahmane and El Abbas, on the other hand, were spared, but only in exchange for surrendering the city to the Spanish. Abu Bakr was furious; his brother had failed to protect Bejaia. A city with such significant strategic importance should not have been handed over to the Spaniards at any cost. He gathered his men and set out to Bejaia."

"What else did he expect from a man who had lost both of his sons as they defend the city, other than his surrendering it to the Spanish?"

"Bejaia was Abu Bakr's fondest desire; if he failed to take it from his brother's hands, he was going to take it from the Spaniards. But when Abdelaziz stood against him, the two brothers clashed, which resulted in Abdelaziz's capture and death."

"What about Abderrahmane and El Abbas?"

"They retreated to Biban Mountains in Lesser Kabylia[105]; then, they looked for a means to come to terms with the Spanish. Abu Bakr had to do everything in his power to reclaim the city before his nephew become a puppet for Spain and settled in Bejaia. He retreated to Constantine and started formulating a strategy."

"He must have sought assistance from his father, Mulay Muhammad."

"He surely did, but the sultan did not respond as he had anticipated. Because of his insatiable thirst for power, Abu Bakr had slain his brother and weakened their dynasty. Moreover, the rightful heirs to the throne were Abderrahmane and El Abbas. Therefore, Mulay Muhammad gathered his forces and dispatched them to eastern Algeria to rein back on Abu Bakr."

"Abu Bakr was left alone."

"Abu Bakr's plan was to rally all the tribes around him and proclaim himself as the leader of a jihad against the Spaniards. However, he was aware that none of his ambitions would ever become more than a fantasy unless he could get the support of the dynasty. The forces that Pedro Navarro left in Bejaia were superior compared to those of Abu Bakr. Abu Bakr needed help."

---

[105] Kabylia, "Land of Kabyles"(Land of the Tribes) is a cultural, natural, and historical region in northern Algeria, the homeland of the Kabyle people.

"The Barbarossas!" said William, grinning.

Cervantes was glad to see that William had a good grasp of the intricate dynamics at play in North African politics. He smiled and confirmed William with a nod.

"After all, their names had been circulating all throughout the Maghreb. If Abu Bakr were to convince these mighty warriors to join his cause as partners, he would not only be able to unite the tribes and place them under his own command but also exact revenge on his father by freeing them from his father's patronage. He sent envoys to Aruj Reis."

"Everybody is talking about you, and not just the Moors, but the Christians as well."

Three men, sitting on velvet cushions strewn on Moorish carpets, had come to Aruj on Abu Bakr's behalf, to notify him of the recent events that had taken place and seek his assistance.

"What does Abu Bakr want from me?"

"He wants your help to stand against the Spaniards, Aruj Reis. They assault the city whenever they feel like it. They do not allow the ships to enter the harbor. All Christian captives were released. Abderrahmane, on the other hand, is hiding in the Biban Mountains, hoping to make an accord with the Spaniards."

Aruj was silently listening to what the men had to say. As a matter of fact, none of what they said really mattered to Aruj, for he had already set his mind to sail to North Africa. All he needed to do was to make a decision about his first destination.

"If you accept, Amir Abu Bakr will render his forces at your disposal. Once he gets rid of those Spaniards; then, the ports are yours to use as you see fit."

They had set their eyes on Aruj, wondering if he would respond in the way they had hoped for. As they waited for an answer, Aruj got on his feet. He was as if saying there was nothing more to talk about and silently asking for them to leave. They stood up and made their way to the door. Just as they were about to leave, Aruj announced his decision.

"Tell your Amir that we're coming to besiege Bejaia. We will teach those arrogant Spaniards a lesson that even their three generations of grandchildren will not forget."

"The preparations, however, took longer than expected, and by the time they set sail for Bejaia, it was already the month of August."

"Almost the end of summer..."

"They were having a shortage of gunpowder and food. And the help that they had been hoping to get from Mulay Muhammad had for some reason not come."

"There is no way we can get there before ten days!"

As the men loaded the provisions aboard, Aruj was rolling up the rope in his hands, not even looking at Khidr, who was expecting him to respond in some way.

"No help came from Tunisia, either," Khidr added.

Aruj was frustrated. He slung the rope over his shoulder and started walking toward the boats.

"I doubt the sultan is overjoyed that we're sailing to Bejaia, brother."

"Neither do I," said Aruj. "Neither do I think he's pleased that we're sailing to Bejaia at Abu Bakr's request."

"Isn't Abu Bakr a Hafsid as well?"

"How do you know Abu Bakr does not aspire also to the Tunisian throne?"

"Then, why are we going, brother? Why are we launching this campaign if it is only going to fulfill Abu Bakr's avarice? Wasn't that your idea?"

Aruj came to an abrupt halt and turned to face Khidr.

"We lingered in La Goulette far too long. I no longer intend to spare a fifth of the booty for the sultan. We need to find ourselves a base where we're not accountable to anyone and are not required to share even a duka of our earnings. Abu Bakr is taking advantage of us, and we are exploiting his troops. So, as you can see, Khidr, we are not launching this campaign to nourish Abu Bakr's avarice, we're launching it for ourselves."

"We worked hard to make Djerba secure."

"This island sucks! It is far from the shipping lanes where real trade takes place. Every time we set sail, we have to get ashore numerous times to restock our food and water supplies. We cannot go to the east, either. If Sultan Selim acknowledges us as being Prince Korkud's men, that'll get us into trouble with the capital. Our fortune lies in the western Mediterranean."

After leaving the rope on his shoulders to the boat, Aruj kept on listing his justifications.

"Bejaia is the most convenient port between Gibraltar and Bizerte. It is also capable of sheltering large armadas both in the summer and winter."

Khidr took a deep breath. He knew that his brother was right, but his intuition was telling him that the time was not right to launch an attack on a place like Bejaia. In the approaching season, the North African waters were notorious for their sudden and unexpected storms, hurling the ships against the reefs. Nevertheless, Khidr would once again stand by his brother in his decision, as he always did.

"Then, may Allah help us, brother. I hope you know what you're doing."

Cervantes positioned his miniature ships in front of Bejaia.

"They set out with twelve galiots. It did not take them too long to arrive at the small port near the bay, where they dropped anchor. Known as the Little Mecca, this city of 8,000 households nestled among pine trees and olive groves was so close to both Spain and the Balearic Islands that, if it were to fall into the hands of the Barbarossas it would undoubtedly cause Spain a lot of trouble. Fortunately, this time, Aruj's hastiness was going to coil around his feet."

They pounded the castle with heavy cannon fire for weeks. They were running low on food and gunpowder. The levends had lost all zeal, and the Moors who had joined forces to assist the Barbarossas by encircling the castle from behind were of little help to Aruj.

Khidr was concerned.

"The levends are getting restless. Perhaps, we should retreat brother."

Aruj was pacing up and down the deck, trying to find a way to alter the tide of events in their favor.

"Retreat, huh? We've sailed all the way down here, squandered tons of gunpowder, and just as we're poised to finish what we've started, you say, 'Perhaps we should retreat, brother'. Let's retreat and watch how our names spread across the Maghreb. Everyone will talk about how we messed up."

"Brother, the storm is coming. All our ships will capsize. Please, heed what I say for once. Winter is on its way. We can regain our strength in winter and set sail first thing in the spring. At that time if you like, we'll raze the entire castle to the ground."

Aruj did not even hear Khidr. After a while of pacing up and down, he suddenly stopped.

"We're getting ashore!"

Khidr was shocked.

"You must be out of your mind! We don't even know how many soldiers are deployed within the castle. We have no idea how well-equipped they are."

"The Moors will come to our aid."

"The Moors? Which Moors, brother? Most of them already fled from the battlefield. Rains have begun. These are not warriors, but farmers who must return to their fields and tend their crops if they don't want to starve during the winter. How many of the tribes had responded to Abu Bakr's call, anyway?"

Khidr was talking in vain. Aruj had long made up his mind.

"Take control of the ships! I'll be ashore with two hundred men tomorrow."

"No one is deafer than the one who does not want to hear, Signor."

"He could accept being defeated. Even that cold-skinned death might make its way into Aruj's vocabulary at some point. But giving up... Giving up was something Aruj did not know its meaning."

"But it's not giving up that Khidr had proposed, just to put off his dreams until next spring."

"On the path to wisdom, Signor, the most formidable enemy of man is impatience."

Cervantes reached out for the leather-bound notebook on the table. After spending some time browsing through its pages, he started reading:

"Patience is not sitting and waiting, it is foreseeing. It is looking at the thorn and seeing the rose, looking at the night and seeing the day. Lovers are patient and know that even the moon needs time to become full."[106]

He closed the notebook and turned to William.

"On that day, Signor Shakespeare, Aruj's defeat at the hands of his impatience would cost him dearly."

Aruj and his men landed near the mouth of the Soummam creek, a few miles from the city, and headed toward the castle at full speed. He had left everything to chance. He had neither an accurate assessment of the number of soldiers in the castle nor any idea about the firepower the Spaniards possessed. Despite being outnumbered, their armament was filled with carbines, crossbows, and various other weapons. Aruj, on the other hand, had only bows, spears, wooden shields, and short-range cannons at his disposal. As for Khidr, he had disobeyed Aruj's orders and after leaving the ships under Sinan's command, gone ashore with his brother.

Seeing the enemy approaching the castle, the commander of the castle launched an artillery fire over the walls. The levends were falling like autumn leaves, and Aruj's fury grew more and more as he watched them fall one by one. Sinan had opened cannon fire, was pounding the walls. He was desperately trying to open a breach for the levends before they were all destroyed by the poured boiling oil and boulders falling from the battlements.

The breach had finally been opened, but Aruj, who had been gravely injured by a small-caliber cannonball shot to his left arm, had collapsed on the ground. The battle was over for Khidr. After that point, even if the Spaniards would have wrapped the castle in silk and presented it to the Barbarossas as a gift, it was worthless to him. They were retreating.

---

[106] Shams Tabrizi

As he ran to his brother he was calling out to his men:

"Heeeeellpp!... Aruj fell!... Bodoooooosss!... Mehmeeeeed! Saliiiiiihh! Heeeellppp!... Retreaaaatt!"

They carried their reis to the ships and sailed away from Bejaia. His arm propped up with a board, Aruj was lying with a high fever. Khidr, on the other hand, was trying to put out the flames scorching his heart.

"Reis..."

"Come Yahya."

"I wondered how he was doing."

"Not so good. They had his arm tightly secured. The bleeding slowed but did not stop."

"We must find a means to stop the bleeding."

"It may not be enough, Yahya."

"Let's go to Tunisia and take him to Mother Firuze. She'll know what needs to be done."

Khidr rubbed his anxious face.

"Huseyn would unleash his man on us."

"We may send the rest of the ships to Djerba, then, lower our flag and enter the port quietly. After that, I go and bring Mother onto the ship."

They neither had much time nor any other options. Yahya was right; Mother Firuze was the only person Khidr could entrust Aruj to.

"Okay, Yahya. Let's do as you say..."

"The levends sneaked into the port on the orders of their Reis. They neither hoisted their flag nor fired their cannons to salute the Tunisians. They glided across the waters like an ordinary trade boat and dropped anchor."

"How long could they hide in a city where everyone knew who they were?"

"Not for too long, Signor, certainly not for too long. Depending on Aruj's condition, Khidr would be required to pay a visit to the sultan and get his permission for them to stay in La Goulette for a while. However, at the moment, Aruj was his top priority. His wound needed to be treated as soon as possible. Yahya left the port late at night and made his way to Mother

Firuze's house; then, he brought her to the ship. Khidr was worried. After he waited for her to check the wound, he had deduced from the expression on her face that what she was about to say concerning his brother's arm was not good."

Mother Firuze turned to Yahya:

"Yahya, my son, bring me a bowl of hot water. I first need to clean the wound with myrtle leaves, dry laurel, and salt."

"Right away, Mother."

When Yahya left, Mother Firuze turned her gaze to Khidr.

"I'll do whatever I can, but if this wound would not get healed and the inflammation would not reduce..." Her words were as if twisting in her throat. "Nothing good will come from this arm, son."

Cervantes' eyes were on his crippled hand.

"A gun shut in between two breaths and a part of you that had accompanied you all along is no longer there...", said William.

"Have you ever thought, Signor Shakespeare, how miraculous it is, in fact, that we are able to live so long?"

He reached for his blade and scratched his crippled arm. Having seen the blood seeping from his skin, William got excited.

"Signor Cervantes! What are you doing? Your arm..."

"There's nothing to be worried about, Signor Shakespeare, it's just a minor scrape. It'll quickly make you better understand what I mean and then dry out."

"That wasn't necessary!"

"It was, Signor. For you to understand, for me to recall just how fragile our bodies in fact are..."

He took a drop of blood in between his two fingers.

"Our skin... our most valuable armor which adapts itself to us from the day we are born until the very last moment of our lives... How incredibly light it is..." He turned his attention to the blade in his hand. "How vulnerable, in the face of such sharp things... Or our bones... how fragile our skeleton actually is in the face of any heavy load or blow that it might receive... Yet we rely on it as we walk, run or jump, can you believe it?"

William was listening intently.

"Our eyes... our portals to life; even an inverted eyelash may well them up with tears... Or our organs, which may fail to function due to the simplest poison we may be exposed to... We may even die from anything as simple as an insect sting." He raised his head and looked William in the eye. "How is it possible, Signor Shakespeare, that we live for such a long period of time?"

William gained insight when he observed how rapidly the blood coagulated and how quickly Cervantes' wound dried out.

"I suppose it is because we heal... Because our bodies find a way to heal itself somehow..."

"What about our souls, Signor? Do you think that our souls also healed in the same manner? Was Aruj's soul going to heal itself as well?"

La Goulette, Tunisia

The treatment was not working. Despite Mother Firuze's best efforts and daily dressings of the wound with mixtures she prepared using various medicinal herbs, Aruj's arm had turned purplish-black, and his flesh was flaking off piece by piece. There was nothing left to be done. The arm had developed gangrene, and it was most likely going to be amputated. Khidr was utterly devastated by the news. Why hadn't his brother listened to him, anyway? How many times Khidr had warned him...

He took a deep breath, washed his face with the clean water inside the barrels, put on his white shirt and embroidered vest, and slung his sword over his waist. He was going to visit the sultan, and just as he had predicted, he would not be well received.

"You've sneaked into La Goulette, Khidr Reis, you seem to have forgotten that I have eyes and ears everywhere."

"We had no intention of hiding from you, My Sultan. We simply didn't want everyone to learn about the misfortune that befell on my brother."

"You utilize my ports to support my enemy; then, you screw up with your siege and come to seek refuge in me. Why didn't you go to Constantine, to Abu Bakr, huh?"

"Isn't your son, Abu Bakr, a Hafsid as well? What ulterior motive could there be in our attempt to reclaim the territories your dynasty lost?"

Mulay Muhammad was enraged. He leaped on his feet and roared:

"How dare you advise me on state affairs! My grandsons, Abderrahmane and El Abbas are Bejaia's rightful heirs, not that traitor, not that brother-slayer Abu Bakr. Abderrahmane will succeed to the throne as soon as he reaches an agreement with the Spaniards. In the meantime, Khidr Reis, you'd better mind your own business and refrain from sticking your nose into matters that are non of your concern!"

Khidr was trying to keep calm. The last thing he would want right now was to enrage the sultan and be expelled from La Goulette. He took a deep breath and waited for Mulay Muhammad to regain his composure. When he did and sat back to his throne, he spoke:

"My Sultan, my brother's condition is unstable. If the Christians learn about it and show up at your door like bloodthirsty sharks, we can neither defend La Goulette nor Bizerte unless my brother recovers quickly. As you may be aware, following the unexpected death of Kemal Reis, Sultan Selim summoned Kurdoglu to Constantinople. So, it's in Tunisia's best interests for Aruj to get back on his feet as quickly as possible. Because, for the time being, there is no one other than us, who can rush to your aid in these waters in case you require it."

"So, there is no one other than you who would come to our aid, huh? Woe to us, then, woe to us!"

Upon hearing Huseyn's snakelike hiss as he entered the throne room with an evil smile on his face; Khidr had lost the last bits of his already low mood.

Huseyn kept on hissing:

"What you do not understand is this, Khidr Reis, the only issue that puts Tunisia in trouble with the Christians is your presence in La Goulette. Imagine it this way: If the Christians are the bloodthirsty sharks, as you just described, you are the very putrid blood that they're after."

Khidr ignored Huseyn and turned to the sultan.

"I've come to ask you for permission to stay in La Goulette for a little longer. My brother's arm may need to be removed. We need the most skilled surgeon in Tunisia. And after that, we need to allow Aruj some time to rest and recover. We'll be gone in two seasons. In the meantime, if your men were to keep their mouths shut, nobody would find out that we are here, in Tunisia."

As he said his last words, Khidr had turned his gaze to Huseyn. He didn't have the least trust in him, and he had valid reasons for it. As for the sultan's decision, Mulay Muhammad granted them permission to remain in La Goulette for a little while longer on the condition that they pay for their accommodation, preferably in Spanish maravedis, Venetian ducats, or Italian florins for the duration of their stay. Khidr had no choice, but to accept.

After leaving the court he returned to the ship and gathered his levends around. He had made his plan.

"Yahya!"

"Yes, Reis."

"We'll settle in the residence reserved for us. I want you to carry Aruj there safely. Mother Firuze, too. I'd like her to stay with us for a little while longer."

"Salih!"

"I'm listening Reis!"

"Bring me the best surgeons of this white city! If any of them finds a means to save Aruj's arm, I will reward him greatly. If he is a prisoner, I will free him; if not, I will put him on one side of the scale and fill the other side with gold."

"As you command, Reis."

"And you, Sinan, find me the most skilled blacksmith of Tunisia. He'll forge Aruj a silver arm... In case, he has to let go of the one Allah gave him...."

"Right away, Reis!"

"Aydin, go to Djerba and bring Felipa here."

"As you say, Reis."

"Osman, Mehmed, and Cemal, you are to set sail with Aydin and take command of the ships that we sent to Djerba on our way back from Bejaia. I want you to bring them here. Do not depart on the same day and be sure that your leave is a quiet one. Do not raise the flag as you enter La Goulette, nor drop anchor side by side."

"Don't worry, Reis."

"I want ten to twelve ships to be brought here; the remainder should stay in Djerba. Place them under the command of the levends, and then put those levends under the supervision of those other... No one will lay idle this winter."

Sinan looked at Khidr.

"What's your plan?"

"We will spend the winter quiet. None other than Allah will know that we're in Tunisia. We'll complete our preparations till the spring."

"So, you intend to set sail in the spring? Do you think Aruj would get better by that time?"

"I hope, he will. In case he won't have the strength, we'll go without him. You didn't suppose, Mulay Muhammad would let us stay here for free, did you?"

Nobody uttered a word. They all had realized how unpleasant Khidr's meeting with the sultan had been.

Khidr looked each one of them right in the eye and said his last words.

"We'll go after Genoese ships!"

"They found the best surgeons in Tunisia." Cervantes' eyes were fixed on his crippled hand. "They were obviously, not poor as a church mouse like me. Khidr wanted every one of them to examine his brother's arm. He promised a fortune to anyone who would save the arm from being cut off. In the end, however, they all came to the same conclusion: If Khidr wanted his brother to live, that arm had to be gone."

When he entered the room, he saw Mother Firuze standing by the fire, boiling some herbs she had brought from home.

"Mandragora leaves... mandragora leaves and poppy. If you make him smell this, he'll become asleep. Also, apply this flaxseed and dill mash. It will alleviate his pain."

Mother Firuze handed all that she prepared to Khidr. She was sad.
"Sorry son... I couldn't help..."
"You did your best, Mother. Beyond that, it is Allah's will."

After wiping her hands on her faded gown, she snatched Khidr's arm and pushed him toward the door.

"Go now, son. May Allah give strength to you all. May Allah heal him quickly."

Khidr had chosen Kose Ismail Effendi[107] to amputate his brother's arm. Ismail Effendi, renowned for his pointy teeth and pale skin, was by far Tunisia's most accomplished surgeon. As soon as he arrived, he had taken out of his bag his pincers, scalpels, tongs, and the other tools that he thought he might need; and after sterilizing them all with fire, he had carefully placed them on the table. He was now standing there with a bone saw he held tight in his hand and an apron made of ox hide wrapped around his waist, waiting for Khidr to bring the herbs Mother Firuze had prepared. Aruj had been tied and secured to his spot. Yahya was right by his side, as usual; while Sinan was lost in thought as he watched the embers that would be used to cauterize the wound after the arm is removed.

Khidr dipped a clean piece of cloth into the bowl and placed it on his brother's nostrils. But it had not sent Aruj immediately into the alley of dreams. When he saw Ismail Effendi approaching, he grabbed his arm.

"He hasn't fallen asleep yet!"

Then, he realized that he was holding a chunk of wood in his hands. As soon as Khidr saw the bite marks on it, he understood, he was not going to be able to stay by his brother till the end.

As Ismail Effendi inserted the wood between Aruj's teeth, he grumbled:

"His mind will get a little fuzzy and that's all, Khidr Reis. If you think that you'll brother will sleep like a baby while I cut this bone, you're mistaken. Now, pull that piece of rag away from his nose, too much of mandragora is poison."

Cervantes paused for a moment. His gaze was still on his crippled hand.

"It's really difficult to find the appropriate words that would describe the pain Aruj had to suffer, Signor Shakespeare; yet it is quite likely that his soul had resounded with the cries of others who had their teeth marks left on that piece of wood."

---

[107] A title of respect or courtesy, particularly given to a man of high education or social standing in an eastern Mediterranean country

William felt his mouth getting dry. Cervantes added:

"Especially when it is time for the wound that had its nerves plucked before it was stitched, to be cauterized with a blazing rod of iron..."

Just as he had anticipated, Khidr was unable to keep the word he gave about staying by his brother until the very end. He rushed down the ratty stairs of the residence and ran to the beach. His agony, despair, and sorrow, all blended together and manifested as a resentful cry that echoed through the narrow streets of the white city.

Shortly after Aruj's arm had been treated, Khidr started putting his plans into action. Felipa was brought to Tunisia by Aydin. In accordance with Khidr's instructions, the galleys entered the harbor covertly over the course of a month and dropped anchor. A work as feverish as it was secret got underway. Sails were mended, the hulls were scrubbed; and gradually, all the additional equipment as well as the provisions that they would require were supplied. And all done without arousing the curiosity of a single Tunisian. But Huseyn had already whispered everything that had been going on at La Goulette to the Christian ears. They were apprised of every move that the Barbarossas had made thanks to the letters Huseyn had written to the cardinal.

Genoa, Italy

    'Aruj was severely wounded during the siege. He lost his left arm. They forged him a silver arm instead. His men are usually spending time by their ships, tending to any necessary repairs and preparing to set sail in the spring. The pirate, however, does not make very frequent appearances at the port. He spends most of his time in his house. I've been told that he is reciting verses from the Qur'an. I can only assume that he is having a difficult time accepting the fact that he was defeated, and that's why he must be seeking refuge in God for solace. I do not believe that he is mentally stable at this point. I've heard that he's been occasionally going to the shore and spending lengthy hours walking on the sand as he stares at the horizon and lets out hysterical laughs talking to himself but mostly yelling. Several of my men have told me that they had even witnessed him sobbing on a few occasions. They say he has dropped a lot of weight, and his face was as white as chalk. He's been spending most of his time alone, rarely seeing his brother. I've heard they've been arguing every time Khidr goes to visit him. The younger, even penned a letter to their elder brother Isaac and sent it to Lesbos asking him to come to Tunisia. I was able to read the letter before it was dispatched, so I learned some of what I've just relayed to you directly from Khidr. To conclude, Your Eminence, it appears that it is not just Aruj's arm that has been severely wounded in Bejaia, but more, his soul.'

    After reading a portion of the letter Huseyn had sent to the cardinal, Pedro Navarro turned to Andrea with a cynical smile adorning his face.

"It appears that the Red Beard has reached a state that he may be toppled with a blow of breath. Do you also agree that it is time to give that beard a shave?"

Andrea was not smiling. As a man of moderation and circumspection, he had donned his usual icy and apathetic expression.

William got curious.

"What may be Pedro Navarro's motivation in bringing Huseyn's letter to the cardinal to Andrea?"

"After the setback that they had endured at Djerba, Fernando had once more been forced to direct most of his attention to France and Italy. He had formed a Holy League with the Republic of Venice and the Vatican in order to recover some of the possessions of the pontificate that had been occupied by the French. Particularly because he was an expert in explosives, the king had not wanted to give up on Pedro Navarro solely because of the friction that had been going on for a while between him and the cardinal and had appointed him Head of the Spanish Infantry Troops. As for matters pertaining to the administration of the Barbary Coast, they had been entirely left in the bony hands of Cardinal Jiménez. The cardinal, on the other hand, who had spent the majority of his fortune on the Oran campaign, had not got a single maravedi left to finance a new expedition that would be carried out along the African coast.

"Hah! The cardinal is trying to persuade Andrea this time, to launch an assault at La Goulette."

"Exactly, but he also was aware that Andrea had to convince the Senate before he could embark on such an endeavor. And Huseyn's letter had arrived at that precise moment. Aruj was in an unstable situation health wise; and Khidr had been going through troubled times. And based on what was written in the continuation of the letter, Khidr would shortly embark on a hunt for Genoese."

Andrea rubbed his chin as he walked up and down the study.

"Genoa appears to have restored its autonomy, at least for the time being. On the other hand, if they find themselves threatened in any way, I have no doubt that they will embrace French rule. Before that happens... If I can convince the Senate to launch an attack on La Goulette..."

"In the letter it says, Khidr will set sail in the spring. This time to pillage Genoese ships... "

"The sultan must have requested booty."

"Most probably. Here, Signor Doria, a valid reason for you to present the Senate. Before they strike Genoa, Genoa should strike them! And especially when they are so weak in terms of strength..."

William flashed a cynical smile.

"It seems Pedro Navarro had not delivered Andrea the news of an impending Spanish attack on La Goulette, but he had provided him with a reason by which he could convince the Senate to carry out this campaign himself."

"The expeditions he led along the African coast had drained Jiménez's personal wealth. All he had left was his cunning wit and persuasion skills, which he would not shy away from employing."

"Did he have any intention of keeping his word about surrendering the Ark to the pope when he eventually got his hands on it?"

"Come on, Signor Shakespeare, he was a cardinal. Popes would die on a regular basis and be succeeded by new ones. How would the future Pope know about the promises that had been made to the previous one?"

"Then, the only thing he needed to figure out was how to utilize the power of the Ark."

"Exactly, and one of the greatest minds of Europe would probably bring him this knowledge very soon."

Milan, Italy

It had turned out just like Salai had predicted and Leonardo had returned to Milan not long after he traveled to Florence following the death of his uncle. As he stood by the window in his house right across Santa Maria delle Grazie and watched the pouring rain, he thought of Ludovico Sforza, who had given him this place as a recompense for his unpaid wages. After being left to decay for ten years in the dungeons of Loches in Touraine, Il Moro[108] had died on French domains. And now the French were ruling over his domains. When King Louise XII consented to pay his wage of 114 livres and hired him, Leonardo had decided to stay in Milan. Until the pope allied himself with the Swiss to drive the French out of the city once and for all...

He recalled the day when the Swiss Soldiers of the Holy League opened fire on Desio, less than ten miles from the city walls. He had made a note in his notebook and wrote, '*On the sixteenth day of December, at the fifteenth-hour[109] fires were set.*' When tension began to escalate in the city, the members of the household had decided to move to Villa Melzi, twenty miles outside the city. Even though the French had triumphed against the Holy League's forces at the Battle of Ravenna, their victory was marred by the death of their elegant young chevalier Gaston de Foix. It was now clear that the French would not be able to maintain their hold over Milan for long. For the time being, Leonardo was occasionally visiting his house, however, he was aware that if the Sforzas were to retake control of the city's administration, he would have no choice but to leave Milan permanently. He was upset... upset and exhausted from being dragged around...

---

[108] Ludovico Sforza
[109] 10:30 AM

This vineyard was dear to Leonardo. He was enjoying its garden, the peace and tranquility it offered, as well as its vines from which he produced delectable wines. The one and only thing that he did not like about this place was that it kept reminding him of his failure in *The Last Supper* fresco he painted on the north wall of the monastery's refectory right across the street. When Il Moro intended to renovate a part of the monastery so that it would one day serve as a mausoleum for the Sforza family, he probably had thought that he had chosen the top talents in all of Italy for the task. As Donato Bramante crowned the sixteen-sided drum with a majestic cupola, he had blended the classical Gothic architecture of Lombardy with the innovative Renaissance style; Leonardo, on the other hand, had spent a considerable amount of time painting the last supper Jesus had with his apostles. Bramante had done an impeccable job. Yet, the new painting technique that Leonardo developed to obtain more vibrant colors, had proved to be a complete disappointment. Even before the fresco was complete the paint had started to flake off and Leonardo had been obliged to repaint the areas that had deteriorated. If only he had listened to Geroastro[110] and instead of mixing oil and tempera[111], had employed the traditional *buon fresco*[112] technique of painting on fresh plaster. Because it was clear; his work would not be inherited for eternity, it would not be able to withstand the passage of time. How time was transmuting everything. The universe was constantly renewing itself and shedding its skin, much like a serpent, an Ouroboros[113] devouring its own tail. As Michelangelo's star was rising, Leonardo was aging; while David was being reborn from marble, the fresco of Jesus was falling apart. Was he pondering more about death as he got older or what?

---

[110] Tomasso di Giovanni Masini, Italian metallurgist, and alchemist, a friend and collaborator of Leonardo da Vinci generally known by the imposing alias of 'Zoroastro'. He probably joined Leonardo's workshop in Florence as a teenager in the late 1470s and is later mentioned as 'Geroastro' as part of Leonardo's entourage in Milan.

[111] Tempera, also known as egg tempera, is a permanent, fast-drying painting medium consisting of colored pigments mixed with a water-soluble binder medium, usually glutinous material such as egg yolk.

[112] 'Buon', or "true," fresco is the most durable method of painting murals since the pigments are completely fused with a damp plaster ground to become an integral part of the wall surface.

[113] Ouroboros, the emblematic serpent of ancient Egypt and Greece represented with its tail in its mouth, continually devouring itself and being reborn from itself.

"The Last Supper...." he muttered. Which of Leonardo's suppers was going to be his last one? Was he going to sleep one night and not be able to get up the next morning? Or would God tell him that it was time on one sunny afternoon? He had no clue. But Jesus knew. How could he possibly know? How was he able to continue to drink his wine, and eat his bread despite the fact that he knew?

Lately, Leonardo had realized that just as he thought that he was learning to live, he had, in fact, been learning how to die. His eyes were as not sharp as they once were, and arthritis in his hands had become increasingly annoying. But there were some loose ends that Leonardo had to tie up. Because just as a well-spent day would have brought a happy sleep, a life well-spent would have brought a happy death. It should have been conclusions, the legacy one had to leave behind, rather than the sought-after but unattained wisdom. But his quest after the Ark of the Covenant had impregnated Leonardo's mind with fresh inquiries at this age, rather than explanations. It appears that there was still time for Leonardo to arrive at the conclusions the cardinal expected to hear.

As if to say "Salute!" to Jesus, he raised a toast toward Santa Maria Delle Grazie. Then, he sent off the sip he twirled in his mouth down from his elderly throat.

He was snapped out of his thoughts by a knock on the door.
It was Donato Bramante.

"I'm feeling like a rat out of water."
Leonardo laughed as Bramante took his drenched clothes off.
"I suppose you were going to say, 'a fish out of water'."
"Where do you find fish in the streets of Milan? But rats... Rats are everywhere. It is only a matter of time before a new plague strikes. I hope that the Black Death will do to the occupying French what the Swiss were unable to."

Bramante despised the French. After all, every time war broke out on Italian lands, the artist's bread and wine were first to be taken away. And, according to him, the French had no intention of taking their damn feet off Milan. On the other hand, when the plague arrived, it would not only strike the French. Leonardo had just recently lost Marcantonio to the plague. That bright, lively, young anatomist with whom he had worked together for a year at the University of Pavia, had bid farewell to life on the banks of Lake Garda at the age of twenty-nine, due to the plague that had ravaged Verona that year. Whereas, they had dreamed about publishing a comprehensive work on human anatomy, in which they were going to document all their findings and conclusions they reached in all those dissections together they had carried out. During their study, Leonardo had drawn at least seven hundred and fifty sketches. He now knew the human body like the back of his hand. But just like a bird taking off from that hand, all their dreams had flown away by Marcantonio's death.

After wiping off rain-baptized face with a handkerchief, Bramante turned to Leonardo:

"You didn't say anything. I suppose you were getting along well with the French."

"It was Louis, paying my wage."

"So, it seems you've lost your patron again," said Bramante with a bit of innuendo and reproach.

"As you also know very well, Donnino; in order for the genius to deliver what is expected of him, he requires nourishment as well as an environment that offers him a chance to succeed."

Leonardo was right. Bramante took in the aroma of burning wood wafting from the fireplace, filling the hall.

"If I love winter, just for the sake of this aroma." He looked around. "Where's everyone?"

"They're at Villa Melzi."

"Gerolamo's[114] house? That foursquare villa perched on a bluff by the Adda River?"

"Yes, war makes it impossible to live in the city. I come here occasionally. To take care of my vines..."

"You mean, to get away from all the fuss?"

Leonardo laughed.

"Is that little devil still with you?" asked Bramante.

"Are you referring to Salai? Yes, he is."

As he poured himself a glass of wine, Bramante continued talking:

---

[114] Gerolamo Melzi; Father of Francesco Melzi, one of Leonardo's pupils as well as the literary executor of all his papers.

"That little brat is the main source of all your current financial troubles. If you'd been able to save even a fraction of what he had stolen from you up to this point, you wouldn't be searching for a patron at this age."

"He is a talented boy, and he's loyal. Also, honest in a way. At least he doesn't deny what he did when he got caught."

"You seem to have an interesting understanding of honesty, Leonardo. Well, it's your business. How long are you planning to stay here?"

Leonardo walked over to the fireplace and invited Bramante to the comfiness of the velvet armchairs.

"I don't know. It depends on whether the French would be able to hold the city or not. In case the Sforzas were to re-seize power, I don't think Massimiliano[115] would be eager to be my new patron."

Bramante let out a hearty laugh.

"Hah! Weep Heraclitus, weep! Furrow your brows, and curl down your lips! Weren't you the one who had said you cannot bathe in the same river twice?"

This time it was Leonardo laughing. His long-time friend was alluding to the artwork he had painted shortly after they became acquainted. Inspired by Leonardo's notes he had taken for his *Trattato della Pittura*[116] which he intended to publish one day, Bramante had portrayed grief and joy. Leonardo as weeping Heraclitus, and himself as laughing Democritus...

Leonardo was quick to respond.

"Laugh, Democritus, laugh! To you, not even death is worthy of being taken seriously, let alone grief!"

Bramante took a big sip of his wine.

"Don't you get bored living in the countryside?"

"There's a strange kind of tranquility that I'm not used to its taste. Away from the hustle and bustle of the city, away from all its hostilities and the sticky obligations... And then, there's Francesco..."

"Gerolamo's son?"

"Yes, we spend a lot of time together by the river, studying its currents and tossing pebbles into the water. He reminds me of my youth, the hours I

---

[115] Massimiliano Sforza, Ludovico Sforza's son

[116] A Treatise on Painting, a collection of Leonardo da Vinci's writings entered in his notebooks under the general heading "On Painting".

spent with my uncle in nature, observing, experimenting, and sketching. Francesco enjoys painting, too. He just recently told me that he wants to be my pupil."

"Well, give that little devil a kick in the ass and make Francesco your assistant instead. I've known the Melzis for a long time; they're of noble blood. Is the boy talented?"

"Yes, quite a lot."

"Look Leonardo, I'm aware that you have a habit of not paying heed to your friends' advice, but this time, take my word for it."

Leonardo hurled him a grin.

"Am I not paying heed? Tell me whose words I haven't paid heed?"

"Tomasso, for example."

"Geroastro?"

"Yes, that crazy magician, that keeper of strange reptiles, had warned you numerous times as you worked on *The Last Supper*; so that the paint would not flake off and that it wouldn't be the last supper you worked on. He is an alchemist, a metalworker, a color grinder; working with metals and substances is his profession. But what did you do? You took your own way."

"I like Geroastro."

"He has some strange opinions."

"Like what?"

"Like dressing in nothing but linen."

"He wouldn't like to cloth himself with the skin of a dead animal and would say that linen may well cover his body. What's so strange about it?"

"As strange as your refusal to eat meat."

"Yes, there are things we have in common. But alchemy is not one of them."

"You've never been a fan of alchemists, anyway."

"Nature, Donnino, provides us with such things that one can create a variety of useful materials by their combinations. But the only concern of alchemists is to turn lead into gold."

"Well, that's gold, the most useful material."

"The natural desire of good men is knowledge, Donnino, for just as the soul is worthier than the body, so much are the soul's riches worthier than those of the body."

He took a sip from his wine. His gaze was on the flames dancing in the fireplace.

Bramante remained silent for a while and waited for Leonardo's mind to return to the room.

"Do you see those flames Donnino? What do you think is the cause of those flames?"

Bramante gave the first logical answer that sprang to his mind.

"Burning of wood?"

"And what do you think is the cause of the burning of wood?"

"Flames?"

"The universe is like a serpent devouring its own tail..." Leonardo muttered and turned his gaze to Bramante. "Every effect has its cause, and every cause has its effect. Yet every effect is also a cause, and every cause is also an effect. Because in order for something to be a 'cause', there must be an 'effect' that it has to produce; and that 'effect' that the 'cause' has to produce is nothing other than the cause of the 'cause', Donnino. A vicious circle encircling the entire universe... An Ouroboros..."

Bramante let out a laugh.

"Hah, you've picked the wrong person to enjoy a discourse on such topics, Leonardo. I'm a simple architect. I understand from mathematics, not from philosophy!"

Leonardo sprung to his feet.

"If there was no connection between mathematics and philosophy, we would not be learning from Pythagoras today. You are one of the few people whose analytical mind I trust the most. Hold on a second, there's something I want to show you."

He rushed out of the room and continued talking on his way to the study. As Leonardo walked away, it had become increasingly difficult for Bramante to hear what he was saying.

He yelled from his seat:

"I don't understand what you're saying."

"Wait! You will!"

A few minutes later, Leonardo returned to the room.

"I want you to have a look at this."

"What is this?"

"The Temple of Solomon!"

Bramante was surprised. Leonardo continued to explain:

"I drew it exactly in line with the dimensions that are specified in the Torah."

"Where do you intend to build this?"

"Of course, I have no intention to build it, Donnino. I'm simply interested in hearing your thoughts on this architectural plan."

Bramante took the drawings from Leonardo's hand and checked.

"Well, it's a massive structure. Yet it is not complex. In fact, it is quite plain compared to the more sophisticated structures of today. What is this place for?"

He was pointing to the inner sanctuary of the temple known as the Holy of Holies.

"It is where the Israelites had placed the Ark of the Covenant," said Leonardo, and added, "Literally, God's throne room."

Bramante laughed.

"Well, in comparison to the throne rooms of today's European Kingdoms, the God of the Jews appears to have been pretty humble, huh? That is, of course, provided that the entire structure was not made of gold."

"Don't trivialize and listen to me, Donnino." He placed his finger on the drawing. '*Hekhal*, 'the Sanctuary', 'The Palace of the Lord', was twenty cubits wide by forty cubits long, making it a double cube based on its 2:1 proportion. And given that the section you've just asked me about, the Holy of Holies, was itself a cube with twenty cubits on each side; this floor plan yielding the square root of five, divides the Temple into 1/3 and 2/3rds."

Bramante was listening intently, trying to figure out what Leonardo was trying to get to.

"Now, if we take the place where the diagonals intersect as the center point of our compass, which is in fact precisely at the center of the veil that separates these two parts according to this double cube floor plan; and draw a circle that touches every corner of the double cube; a line drawn from this adjoining side to the top of the circle gives us...."

Bramante jumped in.

"1.6... The Golden Ratio!"

Leonardo was grinning.

"Also, look at the porch at the entrance that they referred to as 'Ulam'. It is twelve cubits by twenty cubits, which when divided by each other it makes..."

"1.6..." muttered Bramante.

"Precisely! Vitruvius[117] had talked about three main attributes that every architect should focus on in his *De Architectura*: *Firmitas, Utilitas, and Venustas*[118]. He had argued that it was the human body that should serve as a foundation for the classical architecture, especially in the construction of temples, for the designs of nature are based on the universal laws of symmetry and the golden ratio inherent in the human body."

After taking a quick look at the papers in his hands, Leonardo extended one to Bramante on which was a sketch of a nude man drawn in two superimposed positions with his arms and legs apart, one fitting in a square and the other in a circle. As Bramante reached for the sketch, he asked:

"What is this?"

"Vitruvian Man! According to Vitruvius, an ideal human body fits perfectly inside both a circle and a square. It is based on patterns of five, which is also the basis for the Golden Ratio, and hence all proportions in the human body perfectly reflect the Golden Ratio. Look at the proportions of the face, arms, and legs. Look at the entire body. The human body is the living book of nature! And Donnino, you know what? I believe that the Temple of Solomon, with all its details, mirrors the human body."

Bramante's smile slowly dissolved.

Leonardo let out a laugh.

"What happened Democritus? Looks like we finally found something worthy of your attention."

After slurping down his last sip of wine, Bramante asked:

"What was in that Ark, Leonardo?"

Leonardo gathered his drawings together and reclined in his seat.

"The two tablets on which were written the Ten Commandments, Aaron's rod and a cup of Manna."

"Manna?"

"Something they ate. It is written that Moses instructed them to place it in the Ark so that it may be preserved for future generations."

"Like a donut? But it'd spoil in the Ark!"

---

[117] Roman architect and engineer during the 1st century BC, known for his multi-volume work entitled De Architectura
[118] Strength, Utility, Beauty

"I have no clue, Donnino. It appears that it was be more like a kind of yeast, something they mixed with flour to make bread."

"But what makes it so unique? I mean, if it is the throne room of God, why put a yeast there in the first place?"

"Manna is something that six thousand men, or two and a half to three million people if you include their wives and children, are said to have eaten for forty years while they wandered in the Desert of Sinai before being allowed to enter the Promised Land. Do you know how many people are currently living in Rome?"

"Eighty thousand? A hundred thousand?"

"These lands are so fertile that, it would be ingratitude not to appreciate the generosity that nature has shown the Italians. Despite this, everyone is starving! On the other hand, it is said that those three million people managed to survive for forty years in that desolate place by eating Manna only."

Bramante was confused.

"What's your point Leonardo?"

"Have you ever considered the possibility that all those stories told in the Torah may simply be the sequin dress of some other knowledge meant to be conveyed?"

"I must admit that I haven't given much thought to the Torah. But I know someone who studied it extensively. A young man in his twenties who wrote a book on the subject. You may want to talk to him. He may be of help. I've heard that he was just getting ready to give a presentation at the University of Pavia. You may even have heard his name before. Heinrich Cornelius Agrippa!"

William smiled.

"Walking occult encyclopedia of Renaissance..."

"Agrippa was born to a family of middle nobility who had been in the service of the House of Habsburg for generations. His fascination with magic and the mysteries of the occult had begun when he was a child. Albertus Magnus' *Speculum* was perhaps one of the first study texts he had read. To him, magic was the most effective, the most sacred means to transform a soul. And when it comes to God's magic, it was certainly Kabbalah. He had already compiled all his writings related to occult when he was still in his early twenties."

"How young to be knowledgeable enough to write a book on such a broad subject as the mysteries of occult..."

"He was one of those who was born before his time. When his lectures had received universal acceptance, he had been conferred a doctorate in theology by academics at the age of twenty-three. People from all over Europe were attending his conferences and looking forward to having a discourse with him about occult mysteries. He was eloquent, bold, and intelligent. But perhaps he was still too young, or because it was his very nature; his heart had the nativity of a little child. Because he had such a deep appreciation for the Truth, he had assumed that everyone would love it. Because he was a man of honor, he had expected honor from everyone. While his tireless mind was exploring the limits of the universe, he had thought that those people whose ignorance he had brought to the daylight would be grateful to him."

"Whereas ignorance is the curse of God while knowledge is the wing wherewith, we fly to heaven."[119]

"Man is blind in the darkness of ignorance, Signor Shakespeare. He never accepts ignorance as an attribute. Those who admit that they are ignorant are those who are not as ignorant as those who deny."

"And Leonardo was not ignorant."

"Leonardo was determined to unravel the mystery of the Ark by any means necessary, therefore he was making use of all the resources at his disposal. In the same way as Andrea Doria who was, at that time, trying to persuade the Senate to launch an attack on La Goulette for the same hidden reason..."

---

[119] William Shakespeare, Henry VI

Genoa, Italy

"Someone needs to put an end to the activities of these damn pirates!"

The Senate was in turmoil. Its members were having a heated debate about how to deal with the Barbarossas. The financial losses they had incurred because of the expeditions Khidr had been leading in the Mediterranean were unfathomable. Members of Genoa's most powerful families had finally banded together in an attempt to find a permanent solution to this problem.

"With their oars heaving like hawk wings, they're able to progress even against contrary winds."

"They spot their prey from miles away and then adjust their positions accordingly. And we are always late noticing them. It's as though they struck a bargain with the devil to keep their ships hidden from the Christian eyes."

"We were relieved when the demon Kemal had died, but now this red-bearded scourge has descended upon us. And not just one, there are two of them."

"They're pillaging our coasts, kidnapping our women and daughters."

"Soon, there won't be anywhere on the Italian shore that's safe."

"They took six of our barques laden with valuable goods. Our loss is incalculable."

"I've heard that they'd also seized a French barque."

"To hell with the French."

They were all talking at the same time. Before one of them was done with what he had to say, another frustrated aristocrat was beginning to voice his complaints.

When all the voices blended together and became a buzzing hum, Andrea realized it was time to step in.

"Gentlemen!"

All eyes turned to Andrea and silence started its reign in the room.

"You're repeating yourselves. Since there's none among you who does not know what the Barbarossas are capable of, it would serve us much better if we discussed the countermeasures we will take against them than chit-chatting about what had transpired."

Andrea was right; they all acknowledged him by nodding their heads.

Commander Doria is right!"

"We have to do something about it!"

"Yes, we absolutely ought to take action in response to this!"

"But what are we going to do?"

"There must be some course of action we can take!"

"We must teach these pirates a lesson!"

"We must make them pay for their actions!"

The room was once again humming.

"Gentlemen!"

And then, there was the recurring silence...

"The elder of the Barbarossas had lost his one arm, before they acquire their full vigor back, we must attack to their nest!"

"We don't even know where they've set up their nests. Where are we going to launch our assault?"

"You don't know where they are hiding, Signor Fregoso! I know!"

Nobody said a word. As they sat there in their lace-collared silk shirts and velvet jackets, unsure of what the next step should be, Andrea went about looking into the eyes of the representatives of Genoese nobility

"I want twelve war galleons! Crammed to the brim with soldiers, cannons, arquebuses, and provisions... "

Signor Lomellini couldn't help himself.

"Those devils have recently taken possession of one of my ships that was on its way to my trading post in Tabarca. As if it was not enough; they also seized the flagship of the fleet we dispatched after them to reclaim what they usurped. And now you're asking from us war galleons? For what purpose, Signor Doria? So that the Barbarossas would take them as well?"

Andrea reached for his crystal glass. After taking a sip from his wine and placing the glass back on the table, he replied to Signor Lomellini:

"To attack La Goulette!"

Gallipoli

After settling in the Castle of Kilitbahir, which had been built by Mehmed the Conqueror to prevent the papal navy from providing aid to the Byzantines during the siege of Constantinople; Piri had begun working on his colorful maps he had meticulously drawn on gazelle skin to turn them into a book that he could present to the sultan. Kilitbahir meant, "The Key of The Sea", and Piri knew that it was him who had the possession of this key. Lately, he had been devoting all his time comparing the notes he had taken while he was on the seas with the writings and drawings he had found from among the spoils of the ships. He had been trying to create a good blend by combining his own observations with the experiences of people of different languages and nationalities. The book that he intended to present to the sultan needed to be absolutely flawless and contain as much information as possible in order for it to serve as a guide for every levend that would sail under the Ottoman flag. On the other hand, there were a few maps that Piri had never let to leave his sight. He had even been tucking them under his pillow during nights. Few maps, that every time he got his hands on them, he had been abandoning the idea and diverting his attention to something else. Those few maps were none other than the maps they had acquired from Colón.

Once again Piri had picked them up. When had he picked them up? Wasn't he working on the Corsican coasts the last time? What had intrigued him and prompted his mind to take a trip from west to east?

He ran his fingers over the area marked with the strange symbol.

"Jerusalem…" he muttered, "The city that had suffered countless assaults, that had been occupied for who knows how many times, and built over and over again after being razed to the ground. The cradle of all three Abrahamic religions… The city where King Solomon constructed his temple, where Jesus was crucified, and where Prophet Muhammad had ascended to the heavens…"

He unfolded the maps and placed them in front of him. The pyramids resembling those of the Egyptians had been drawn on the New World; the symbols which Piri would not be astonished if he were to find them in the New World, on the other hand, had for some reason been shown on Jerusalem. The Ark of the Covenant had been depicted in Egypt while its name was recorded on the maps that showed the newly discovered lands. As for the connection between the Star of David and the New World, Piri was completely in the dark with regard to it. In addition, the maps were filled with Hebrew letters, yet no matter where he had positioned the mirror, Piri was not able to decipher even a single word except the Ark of the Covenant. The letters appeared to be randomly dispersed across the map. Although it was evident that Colón had meant to either disclose or conceal some information, Piri was not even able to figure out even what the admiral had intended yet.

So that he could have a better look, he drew one of the maps closer to himself, on which was drawn something that looked like a labyrinth. Where might this location be, he wondered. Was it underground or above ground? Was it in the New World or in Jerusalem?

He was startled by a knock on the door. Who might have possibly come at this time of the night?

After quickly hiding the maps, he called out:
"Come in!"

The wooden door creaked open. When Piri saw Muhyiddin standing at the door staring at him, he was both surprised and pleased.

"Muhyiddin? What are you doing here?"
Muhyiddin walked in smiling.
"Is it possible that I missed my cousin?"

They hadn't seen each other in quite some time. Muhyiddin would write to Piri every now and then to let him know what was going on in the Maghrib. He was undoubtedly the most reliable source from which Piri obtained the most recent news. They hugged each other tightly.

"Of course, it's possible. However, I can't deny that seeing you here at this hour of the night startled me greatly."

Muhyiddin remained silent. Piri's curiosity was piqued as soon as he spotted his concerned countenance.

"Muhyiddin? Is there something wrong? Did you get into a quarrel with your comrades, or what?"

"Oh, no, Piri. Of course, I did not. But..."

"But, what?"

Muhyiddin was struggling to find the right words. Hearing what he had to say was going to make Piri very upset. Piri, on the other hand, had become extremely concerned.

"Oh, come on Muhyiddin, spill the beans out!"

Muhyiddin took a deep breath.

"I brought you news from Khidr and Baba Aruj, news that are not quite good."

"What do you mean by that? The last time you were planning to go on an expedition. You had said that you were getting ready to set sail to Bejaia. Or did one of them suffer a misfortune? Is it Khidr?"

"No, not Khidr, but Baba Aruj. Baba Aruj lost an arm in front of the walls of Bejaia."

Piri made his way to his chair and slowly sat down. He was extremely upset.

"And I was wondering why I hadn't heard from you in a while."

"I couldn't write you. I thought it would be better if I came in person and told you what happened. When the support we'd been expecting from Tunisia did not arrive, we were unable to set sail before August. Khidr Reis warned his brother numerous times, but you know Baba Aruj... When he sets his mind on something..."

"He goes for it..."

"The castle proved to be far stronger than we had anticipated. We pounded it with intense cannon fire for days. Although we inflicted damage, we were unable to open a breach in the walls. When the weather began to turn bad, Khidr Reis told his brother that we should return to Djerba. In vain, he tried to persuade Baba Aruj by suggesting that we lay siege to the castle the following spring."

"Aruj would never return... He is stubborn as a goat!"

"He went ashore together with his five hundred men. The Spaniards showered upon us arrows and musket balls. We had a lot of casualties. Baba Aruj became further enraged as he saw the soldiers fell. Sinan Reis was pounding the castle with cannon fire. Just as a small breach had been opened, just as we had headed in that direction to pour inside the castle, Baba Aruj was hit."

Piri was devastated at the news. He knew very well of Aruj's demeanor when he set his sights on a goal. But how could a man with this much experience had acted so recklessly?

"Where are they, now?"

"In Tunisia. Khidr Reis took him to Tunisia. They tried everything to save his arm, but they couldn't. They eventually cut off the arm and replaced it with a silver one."

"In Tunisia? But how did Mulay Muhammad..."

"Khidr Reis talked to him and promised him booty in the spring. They worked hard all winter and finished their preparations in utmost secrecy."

"Why in secrecy?"

"When they were in such a vulnerable state, they did not want anyone to discover where they were hiding. Baba Aruj rested throughout the winter. He didn't even come to the port to spent time with his levends. The levends also spent the winter in silence. Then we all set sail. They headed to the coasts of Italy, while I headed here."

Muhyiddin seemed to have meant what he said when he said that the news he had brought was not good. Piri rubbed his face.

"So how is Aruj, now?"

"His arm is getting better. But his soul..."

A dreary silence crept on the room. Piri was so upset that he didn't know what to say or do.

"They need help, Piri... We need help..."

"So, it's time..." mumbled Piri, "It's time to see Sultan Selim."

"He had one thing in his mind; and it was that Ark that they had found in the Mediterranean."

"The Ark that bestows victory on its possessor...", added William.

"Piri was thinking that if he could solve the mystery of the Ark, he would be able to alter the outcome of the battles. And he had an inner sense that those few maps he had acquired from Colón were somehow related to the Ark. Perhaps it was time... Perhaps the time to let Sultan Selim know about the Ark had indeed arrived."

"The experiences that we've gone through, though we had no idea as to why at the time we go through them, reveal their meaning to us when the time is ripe. As the fog lifts, the paths leading to the castles of which we could only see their silhouettes so far, begin to unfold right in front of our eyes. However, the fog lifts only when it is time, and there is no way for man to foresee when that time will be."

"That's why it's crucial to be on the road even if you're unable to see what is ahead of you, and never ever take your gaze off the road even if you have no idea where it leads you to."

The room had immersed in silence and both of their eyes were gazing into distance. Who could say which of their paths had become more visible to them? And who could say which ones were still in the darkness.

"And then?" asked William, being the first to break the silence, and brought Cervantes' mind to the throne city, Constantinople.

"Sultan Selim...", said Cervantes, "Sultan Bayezid's son..."

And he began relating the story.

"The succession to the Ottoman throne had once more been eventful. Prince Selim, who had a considerably harsher temperament in comparison to his two other brothers, Prince Korkud and Ahmed, had ousted his father and ascended to the throne. But before he could turn his attention to the east, which had been giving him trouble for quite a while, he had to ensure the stability of his reign."

"You mean he had to slaughter his brothers."

"If Selim had marched east ignoring the threat posed by Ahmed, who refused to recognize his brother's rise to power and was ready to do whatever it would take to reclaim the throne he saw as his birthright; this might have resulted in Selim's overthrown, Signor Shakespeare."

"So, you think that the practice of fratricide in the Ottoman Empire is acceptable."

Cervantes replied with a sarcastic smile.

"Time is a teacher who adheres to the curriculum so strictly that it never teaches anything in advance. It kneads man in its hands like a dough for years; and just when he thinks that he is no longer a novice and has learned everything there is to know about life; it reveals to him the first truth. It topples down his well-constructed towers of judgment and makes him realize that what he has learned thus far is no worthier than a useless scrap of junk. Those days of judging whether something was acceptable or not, are long gone for me, Signor Shakespeare. I'm no longer that young. I'm just telling you what happened. The greatest battles ever fought in the Ottoman Empire were those fought for the throne. Being the sultan means having the one and only say in all matters regardless of whether it is related to education or art, state administration or military affairs. The sultanate is the unification of all power in the hands of a single individual, even the destiny to occur in between the two lips of the sultan. When the princes reach a certain age, each is being given the administration of a specific province for them to gain experience and develop administrative skills. To determine which one of them possesses that innate power to rule; to understand which one of them was born to become the sultan. Because in the Ottoman Empire, what is important is the survival of the state, not the emotional bond between the sultan and his children."

"The survival of the state is important for the European Kingdoms as well, but they do not murder their brothers for this purpose."

"I'm not so certain as to what would have happened in the event that the Archduke of Austria Fernando had challenged his brother Carlos V; however, the roads built to serve the expansionist policies of the power holders in Europe are typically paved with the stones of marriage. That's why the children of those lords, dukes, kings, all are betroth to each other. To expand the territories under their rule and provide additional military support in case of a war. On the other hand, history is littered with examples of rulers who had not hesitated to wage war against their relatives in cases where they had conflicting interests. In short, although it may seem so, power in Europe has never been concentrated in the hands of a single person as it is in the Ottoman Empire."

"What about the people's support?"

"The fact that Prince Korkud and Ahmed were living in relatively safer provinces while Selim was fighting at the border had cemented Selim's position as the rightful heir to the throne in the eyes of both the people and the troops. The Janissaries had not recognized Ahmad's rule as sultan and had continued to support Selim until Sultan Bayezid agreed to hand over the throne to him. And once this period of turmoil was over, the first thing that Selim had felt compelled to do was to get rid of his brothers once and for all. After Ahmed and Korkud were strangled, Selim could now turn his attention to the east."

"And before the sultan embarked on his expedition, it was imperative that Piri should visit him and show Sultan Selim the maps he had acquired from Colón."

Cervantes flashed a grin.

"Sultan Selim was about to learn about the maps. Leonardo, on the other hand, was on the verge of unraveling the mystery of the Ark."

Pavia, Italy

As he walked through the marble colonnaded barrel-vaulted corridors of the University of Pavia, Leonardo was rubbing his aching wrists, trying to gather his thoughts on what he should say to Agrippa. He had started swimming in dangerous waters, he could feel it. The church had prohibited all topics within Agrippa's area of expertise. The occult, Ancient Greek philosophy, Kabbalah, Hermeticism... All were poison, according to the church; all were a form of Black Plague. All the ancient manuscripts, all books pertaining to these subjects were being thrown into the fires set up in town squares; the Jewish people, who were still held responsible for the crucifixion of Jesus after fifteen centuries, were being forced to convert to Christianity. The time was not right; it was certainly not the right time to seeks answers to the questions bothering Leonardo's mind.

He decided to use Agrippa's voice echoing in the corridors as a compass and headed for the stairs. Leaning against the stone railings for support, he climbed upstairs and found there Agrippa answering the questions posed by a middle-aged man who, judging by his attire, appeared quite wealthy.

"Make of a man and woman a circle; then a quadrangle; out of the this a triangle; make again a circle, and you will have *the Stone of the Wise*. If that's not clear enough, go learn geometry first!"
His voice had an angry hue. He had not yet noticed Leonardo approaching. He raised his hand as if to say "Enough!", turned around and started walking away from the man's incessant questions.

"Harmony of the opposites... the dual nature of man...Yin and Yang..."
Agrippa came to a halt.

Leonardo continued:

"Four elements washed with fire and transformed into body, soul, and spirit... Its body belonging to the earth, its soul to man, spirit to God..."

Agrippa turned around to see who was speaking. He squinted his eyes and stood there for a while under the golden hair of the sun filtering through the columns spreading across the corridor and stared at Leonardo.

"Do I know you?"

"You've probably heard of my name. If I am my name then you know me, but only to the extent that you know my name."

Leonardo took a few steps toward Agrippa to take refuge in a shadow and made himself more visible.

"Leonardo, Leonardo da Vinci."

Agrippa's face was lit up. After taking a couple of steps toward Leonardo, he reached out to shake his hand.

"So, it is you, the Master! It's a pleasure to finally meet you."

Agrippa's hand was suspended in midair. Leonardo, who had been suffering from arthritis for quite some time, was unable to reach out and shake his hand.

"It's my pleasure... I hope you'll pardon me."

"What's the matter with your hands?"

"It's just the ravages of old age."

"I'm sorry to hear that, Master Leonardo. Heinrich, please call me Heinrich."

"If it's possible, Signor Heinrich, I'd like to have a chat with you."

"Yes, of course, but I must apologize in advance because I will not have nearly as much time as I would like. I must get ready for the presentation I'm about give about Plato's *Symposium*. There are a few key issues that need to be addressed in Marsilio Ficino's translations."

They started walking with a slow pace.

"I loved Marsilio."

"Did you know him in person?"

"It was the Medicis who made us both. Though I've never been as passionate a Platonist as he was."

"I see, Master. Would you mind if I asked you what you'd like to talk to me about?"

Leonardo looked around. He seemed that he wanted to make sure that what he had to say would not be picked up by other ears.

"About the Torah!"

Agrippa came to a halt. He lifted his gaze from the stone floor to meet with Leonardo's. It was as if he was hoping to receive an honest answer to the question he was about to ask, free from conditioned fear.

"Do you have faith, Master Leonardo?"

"To the wise, there's no religion Signor Heinrich."

"I haven't asked you whether you have faith in religion."

"I don't believe in fairy tales. But I do believe in goodness."

Agrippa smiled.

"Let's find ourselves a quiet place to talk, then."

They started walking. Agrippa was surprised to see that Leonardo had no trouble navigating the corridors of the university which was resembling a labyrinth with its intertwined courtyards.

"Something tells me you're familiar with this place."

"We studied human anatomy with Marcantonio della Torre for about a year here. He was a dear friend."

"Where is your dear friend now?"

"In the Kingdom of Heaven... If such a kingdom exists, of course..."

"I'm sorry to hear that. When a person dies, his essence is said to be separated from his body, with each returning to where it belongs. Body to the earth, essence to the skies. Do you know that in Ancient Egypt, they used the term 'set' rather than 'died' to refer to a person who had passed on from this world?"

Leonardo laughed.

"Like the sun?"

"Yes, like the sun. Like the sun that has to set to be able to rise again."

Leonardo rubbed his aching fingers.

"I suppose I'm also living the afternoon of my life."

"Who knows, except you, Master, whether your mission in this world is complete?"

"God? If he exists, or course..."

Agrippa smiled.

"Even your firm conviction that God does not exist, not prevents you from seeking Him."

"You can't blame me for having doubts."

"Blame? I can only applaud you for having doubts. Because doubt is the first step on the path to knowledge. Knowledge is not enlightenment, but enlightenment begins with knowledge."

"The Truth is the truth; belief has no effect on reality. If science must prove the existence of something to confirm its existence, it must prove its non-existence to claim that it does not exist. Otherwise, we would have been going in circles and not making a progress even one step forward."

"How far a mind can go in its search for God is depends on its fearlessness. To the ignorant and indifferent, God may be a white-bearded tyrant sitting on his golden throne in the heavens, issuing orders and threatening to cast those who disobey his rules into the fiery pits of hell, whereas to a scientist, God may be a topic of research. On the other hand, the opinion of a philosopher who has just lifted the veil of Ultimate Reality will also differ from that of an initiate who has been conversing with God face to face."

"Whereas to me, God is nothing more than a sociocultural concept the Church imposed on people under the guise of maintaining order. A product of imagination which I cannot perceive with any of my five senses..."

Agrippa smiled.

"Do you hear those bird calls, Master Leonardo?"

As they flew from one courtyard to the next, the birds were singing their songs in harmony, almost as if they were paying homage to the sunlight that was breaking through the clouds.

"Listen, please close your eyes and listen to it."

Leonardo closed his eyes and washed his ears with bird calls.

Agrippa continued:

"If it were your ears that were closed, would you be able to hear this symphony?"

Leonardo slowly opened his eyes.

"You can only perceive God with your five senses, to the extent that your eyes can hear the music. Or to the extent that you can taste the flavor of a delicious wine with your fingertips... Or appreciate the splendor of a sunset in Ponto Coperno with your ears... Your five senses, Master Leonardo, are only there to provide you with information about the external world. Maybe what you're looking for is not out there, isn't it possible?"

Leonardo laughed.

"I can assure you, Signor Heinrich, that what I'm looking for is not inside either. I have studied the human body for such a long time that I know about all its muscles, fibers, nerves, veins... Let alone finding God inside, I haven't been able to discover even the location of the soul yet."

"What a futile attempt to search for the soul within the body it had shed. What is the body, Master Leonardo? What is it, besides being tool utilized by the soul to experience the corporeal world? A tool that had been borrowed from and thus had to be returned to the earth... The soul, on the other hand, can neither be seen with the eyes, heard with the ears, nor felt with the fingers. The body is the tomb of the soul, while the soul is the Temple of God."

Leonardo muttered as he rubbed his aching fingers:

"Know ye not that ye are the temple of God, and that the Spirit of God dwelleth in you? If any man defile the temple of God, him shall God destroy; for the temple of God is holy, which temple ye are."[120]

They went down the stone stairs and stepped in the courtyard.

"There is nothing in God that does not have a representation in man. Man is the image of God; and if one wants to know God, one must first know himself. Do you know yourself, Master Leonardo? Do you know who you are? Or do you know yourself only to the extent that I know you, to the extent that you know your name?"

"The Temple of Solomon..." muttered Leonardo, "The Kingdom of Heaven and the Temple of Solomon..."

Agrippa came to a halt and looked at Leonardo's bright eyes shining from under his hat.

"What do you want to know, Master Leonardo?"

Leonardo answered with all honesty.

"The Truth..."

William stood up and started walking in the room.

"Like Enoch, who wanted to know everything, Leonardo was seeking answers to the questions that plagued his mind."

---

[120] Corinthians 3:16-17

"And beyond that abyss I saw a place which had no firmament of the heaven above, and no firmly founded earth beneath it; there was no water upon it, and no birds... I saw there seven stars like great burning mountains, and to me the angel said: 'This place is the end of heaven and earth'... And I, Enoch, alone saw the vision, the ends of all things: and no man shall see as I have seen."[121]

After a moment of reflection on Cervantes' final words, William turned his gaze to the Spanish author.

"Enoch did not die. Enoch walked with God; and he was not, for God took him.[122]*"*

Cervantes smiled.

"Enoch was the first man in history to climb the thirty-two steps of wisdom, Signor Shakespeare. He had transcended his mortality. He was now Archangel Metatron, whom God placed on a throne next to the *Throne of Glory*. His flesh had turned to flame, his sinews to blazing fire, his bones to juniper coals, his eyeballs to fiery torches, his eyelashes to flashes of lightning, his hair to hot flames, all his limbs to wings of burning fire... Enoch was now the Face of God, the Divine Essence of Adam, *Adam Kadmon*, the Primordial Man. However, his love for humanity kept him from completely merging with God. He desired to be the scribe of God and remain in the world to help people until everyone in the world had climbed the same ladder of wisdom that he had climbed and realized the Truth."

"The scribe of God..." muttered William. "Thoth, the patron of scribes and the god of wisdom in Ancient Egypt..."

The names that flashed through his mind had begun to make sense one by one.

"Hermes Trismegistus had also written down all everything he knew for future generations to read." He got excited. "The Egyptians referred to him as Thoth, the Greeks as Hermes, the Romans as Mercurius!"

Cervantes was pleased to see that William was coming to some sort of understanding.

"The Scandinavians as Odin, Hindus as Mahavishnu, Buddhists as Buddha, Christians as Christ, Muslims as Khidr...That divine bond between Man and God was none other than Metatron, the guardian of the Universe..."

---

[121] The Book of Enoch
[122] Genesis 5:24

"He was the one who had helped Osiris[123] in his transformation into Horus[124], as well as Jesus in his resurrection as Christ. It was thanks to him, Siddharta had become Buddha after fasting for forty days under that bodhi tree."

"He was the one who was with Jesus during those forty days he spent in the wilderness; who was alongside Moses during his forty-day retreat in Mount Sinai as he inscribed the Ten Commandments; and who fed the Israelites for forty years as they wandered in the desert."

William muttered:

"And when Muhammad received his first revelation at the age of forty..."

He squinted his eyes. He had wondered.

"Why forty?"

"*For forty days the flood kept coming on the earth. As the waters rose higher, they lifted the ark high above the earth*[125]" He took a deep breath and continued. "Forty, Signor Shakespeare, is the numerical value of the letter 'Mem' (מ) in the Hebrew alphabet. It has the shape of a closed box, similar to Noah's Ark. If a person can isolate himself from the rest of the world for forty days by avoiding its allures, deceptions, and other diversions, focusing solely on the Divine; only then does his soul falls into the waters inside the Divine Mother's womb. He is now an embryo, an embryo under the Creator's care until it is mature enough to leave the ship through that single window of reality."

William found this explanation somewhat poetic.

"I never thought of Noah's ark from that perspective."

"It's because we read the holy texts which were actually intended to tell us about the Divine, to teach us what is spiritual, with our eyes, Signor Shakespeare, not with our hearts; because we translate the Hebrew word 'tevah' simply as 'ship' when it actually means 'an ark that preserves the Divine', 'a word that preserves the meaning'."

---

[123] God of fertility, agriculture, the afterlife, the dead, resurrection, life, and vegetation in Ancient Egyptian religion
[124] The falcon-headed god in Egyptian religion, Son of Osiris and Isis
[125] Genesis 7:17

"Bereshit bara Elohim." said Agrippa. "Since you want to know the Truth, let's start from the Beginning."

Leonardo muttered the first verses of the Book of Genesis:

"In the beginning God created the heavens and the earth. The earth was formless and empty, darkness was over the surface of the deep, and the Spirit of God was hovering over the waters. And God said, "Let there be light," and there was light. God saw that the light was good, and he separated the light from the darkness. God called the light "day," and the darkness he called "night." And there was evening, and there was morning—the first day."[126]

"However, in order for a day to be referred to as 'the first day,' there must be a 'second day' that follows it, isn't that right, Master Leonardo?"

"Yes, but the second day had not arrived yet."

"Which means, there was also no such day that could be referred to as 'the first day'."

Leonardo was confused. He scratched his beard with aching fingers. Agrippa tried to clarify his point.

"In order to create something, one has to first form a thought about it. To be able to form a thought about something, one has to have an understanding, which is the child of wisdom. But even before understanding and wisdom there's something that precedes them both, and that is, will! Desires and wishes are not things that are tangible. Therefore, they are not part of the physical universe, but rather parts of the mental universe. Mental universe is infinite, and eternity is not contained within time and space. Rather it is time and space that reside in eternity, which means 'time' does not exist in the mental universe. But thought does. Because whatever was thought, it had come into existence in the mental world. Whereas 'time' is relative. To be able to define time, one needs an 'end' as well as a 'beginning'. And for the beginning to be 'the beginning' there must be nothing that comes before it. And this nothing, is the very 'no-thing' that we call God!"

Leonardo let out a laugh.

"It's no surprise the pope excommunicated you!"

"Do not worry, Master Leonardo. When the pope understands that 'nothing' is 'everything', he will revoke my excommunication."

---

[126] Genesis 1-5

Leonardo was in fact more worried for himself than he was for Agrippa, because everything this young intellectual had said thus far sounded reasonable to Leonardo.

"Let's rephrase the creation using different words. In the beginning, there was an eternal, unbounded, formless 'no-thingness' that no human mind can comprehend. This 'no-thingness' was the very essence of creation; it's absolute potential. It was the possibility of 'Relative Non-Existence' to manifest as 'Existence'. It was the dark light of God that pervades eternity. It was dark because it was extremely bright to be visible."

"An eternal existence beyond space and time..." muttered Leonardo.

"And the 'will to manifest' within this infinite potential created a vacuum in itself, in same manner we make room in our minds when we want to think about something. Like the waves retreat before they rush to the shore, God took a deep breath and inhaled his light."

"And opened up a space in Its mind for the universe It willed to create."

"A beam of light then followed from that Divine Essence into space, becoming the beginning of everything. It was the beginning because there was nothing before it. 'Bereshit' was the first of the Ten Commandments, or better be said, the Ten Utterances."

"The 'no-thing' before the beginning became 'everything' with the beginning. Leonardo turned his gaze to Agrippa. "God became manifested as everything that ever existed. It placed Itself within the limits of understanding through Its wisdom."

Agrippa smiled.

"You're beginning to understand, Master Leonardo. Ehyeh asher Ehyeh, Will - Wisdom - Understanding, Keter - Hochma - Binah, Father - Son - The Holy Spirit, Brahma - Vishnu - Shiva, Ahmad - Muhammad - Mustafa... Existence - Consciousness - Bliss... Nothing, all things, and everything in between... The eternal, absolute, tranquil state of being. Just like God said to Moses on Mount Sinai, I AM, that I AM."

"Nothingness is the source of all things, but it is also the end of all things. Like a serpent devouring its own tail, everything begins where it ends and ends where it begins... An endless cycle of creation... a single perpetual motion..."

"*I am Alpha and Omega, the first and last, the beginning and the end.*"[127]

---

[127] Revelation 22:13

"Everything had already been created, before being brought into material existence."

Leonardo was unsure whether he had understood Agrippa correctly, thus he had his eyes fixed on the young scholar.

"Exactly, Master Leonardo. To put it in another way, everything that existed in the past, exists today, and will exist in the future already existed in the beginning. Therefore, it is written; 'one day'; rather than 'first day' in the Torah."

"A state of being independent of space and time. The perfect state of existence of all things in the universe!"

"And, in fact, it is the only state of existence; because there's nothing except the beginning, nothing before and after the beginning. The beginning has neither past nor future. All the other days, or better be said, all the other parallels of creation are in this day, in this very moment with all their brilliance —on God's birthday!"

Leonardo muttered from the Bible:

"What has been will be again, what has been done will be done again, there is nothing new under the sun."[128]

"So, everything is a part of God's grand plan. There are no coincidences, no such thing as acting with free will. All the world is a stage, and all the men and women merely players... They have their exits and entrances; and one man in his time plays many parts[129]..."

"Everything is a part of God's perfectly laid out grand plan, Signor Shakespeare; so is man's acting with free will when the time comes."

William felt unsettled. He thought about all that he had been through in life, all the decisions he made, the paths he chose, the conclusions he arrived at. How many of them were his own, how many were predetermined by fate, he wondered.

"Who am I to act with my own free will..." he muttered.

---

[128] Ecclesiastes 1:9
[129] William Shakespeare, As You Like It

"In all seriousness, who are you, Signor Shakespeare?"

William shifted his inquisitive gaze to Cervantes.

"The reality has three levels, Signor: absolute, empirical, and personal. While the absolute is unchanging; the empirical and personal realities constantly change with each new piece of data we acquire and the way we perceive and interpret it. Consider a scientist who is seeking the truth about something; as he gathers more information through his observations and experiments, his opinion about the reality of that particular subject will inevitably change. Likewise, your personal reality is constantly changing depending on how you perceive and interpret your environment, am I correct? Only the Absolute Reality which is not dependent on time, space, or conditions, is real. Now tell me, Signor Shakespeare, who are you really?"

"I... I am not this body. My body belongs to me, but I am not just a body. I have feelings, I have a mind. On the other hand, my heart is like a sea churning in a storm; it is constantly heaving up with joys, sorrows, concerns, hopes, and dreams; which means, nor can I be merely my feelings..." He looked at Cervantes. "Then, all that remains is my intellect."

"Do your thoughts and ideas never change, Signor? Are they unaffected by time, space, or conditions?"

William was unable to provide an answer. Perhaps it would be best if he asked.

"Who am I, Signor Cervantes?"

"There's something inside that is aware of all those waving emotions, all those opinions that are constantly shifting. Something that is aware of this piece of cloth you wear and refer to as 'body'. Something called 'You', that is conscious of everything."

William muttered from the Torah:

"I AM, that I AM..."

"You are this Consciousness, Signor Shakespeare, you are this Consciousness that is aware of everything happening inside and outside of you! Eternal and unchanging... Just like God! For God created man in his own image."

They were walking slowly through the partially shaded courtyard, accompanied by the chirping of birds.

"Everything came into existence as a result of a will that emerged in God; a will to bestow. God desired to give, but there was no one to receive. It had to give a form to its eternal, unbounded light, by limiting Itself."

"I recall you saying that the light was not visible."

"It was, indeed; for light to be seen, it needs to be surrounded by darkness. Thus, he inhaled his light and created darkness. Within the darkness, a single spark shone... God's essence, God's wife Shekhinah..."

Leonardo was surprised.

"I didn't know that God had a wife."

"That unknowable, incomprehensible eternal source of everything was both everything and nothing, remember? It was 'One' and 'Whole' that had neither a beginning, nor an end, that was neither male nor female, but both male and female at the same time. So, in order to create the side that would receive what It had to offer, It had to polarize itself as a He and a She. And Shekhinah emerging from this Essence surrendered herself and flowed into that vast void to bring the universe into existence, to be the side who would receive Her consort's blessings."

Leonardo smiled.

"And God said, 'Let there be light!'"

"Ten tiny little orbs shone in the darkness and Shekhinah embodied the Spirit, becoming the Soul of Adam Kadmon, the Perfect Man, as the Universal Consciousness."

"The foundation of the universe..." muttered William. "The Divine womb pregnant with the universe."

"The white page on which the sparks of our minds take shape and become letters, yet is noticed by no one who read what's written on it..."

"The woman who molds the man and shields him from his own blaze. Shekhinah, Mother of the universe, patiently awaiting the birth of her child."

William muttered with a slight smile tucked in the corner of his mouth.

"Who could be trusted more to look after the children than their mother?"

"And how could the mother abandon her children alone in this cruel world?"

"Shekhinah became the soul of the Perfect Man, and the Perfect Man became the soul of Adam Ha-Rishon... and Adam Ha-Rishon[130], of all of humanity... Orbs within orbs within orbs..."

"Universes within universes..." muttered Leonardo.

"Your body, Master Leonardo, your body that wears out over time is just an illusory garment. Everything you see in this vast universe, everything that you hold in your hands is nothing but God's light. Because, in reality, God created only one thing by inhaling Its light: The grail into which It would place Its Essence."

"Holy Grail!" exclaimed Leonardo. His eyes were gleaming. "It is not within the universe; it is the universe itself!"

"The Glory of God... Just like the soul that enlivens this body of bone and flesh; just like the moon that receives and reflects the sunlight; just like mother nature..."

"The feminine face of God..."

"Or as the alchemists put it, the Salt of the Earth."

Things were getting off the rails. Leonardo scratched his beard.

"Shekhinah was God's covenant with man."

"The covenant that the Spirit made with the corporeal, that the infinite, the unbounded and the transcendent made with the finite, that Brahman[131] made with A-braham..."

Leonardo locked his gaze on Agrippa.

"If that's the case, Ark of the Covenant is a metaphor, a symbol!"

He was perplexed. He rubbed his face with his aching hands.

"What about the Exodus? The Israelites' flight from Egypt? Did none of the events written in the Torah occur in history?"

"The body seen with the eyes is the garment that envelops the soul, Master Leonardo; it is not the soul itself. And when one sees a lovely garment, one does not notice the soul that wears it. However, just as clothing serves as a covering for the body, the body serves as a covering for the soul, and the soul is a covering for the Spirit. That is exactly how the Torah is. It has a body made of narratives you call fairy tales; but also has a soul and Spirit

---

[130] The first man, Adam

[131] In Hinduism, the unchanging, infinite, immanent, and transcendent reality, the Divine Ground of all matter, energy, time, space, being, and everything beyond in this Universe.

within. Because just like wine that requires a glass to sit in, it requires a body to hold its soul and Spirit."

"Do you mean that the Torah is a text that can be understood only by those who know its language? A code that only the Jews, God's chosen people, can decipher..."

"What I mean, Master Leonardo is that the Torah already contains the key to its own cipher. Shekhinah of the Israelites, Inanna of the Sumerians, Asherah of the Akkadians, Astarte of the Canaanites, Shakti[132] of Hindus, Isis of Ancient Egyptians, Mother Mary of the Christians, or Mother Fatima of the Muslims... She has so many names that you can refer to Her in any way you want. That Sacred Tree of Life is not inside God's chosen people, but inside those who have chosen God. She is the word of God, the very essence of the word Jesus tried to spread..."

Leonardo shut his eyes.

"That is why they crucified him..."

"Woe to you, teachers of the law and Pharisees, you hypocrites! You shut the kingdom of heaven in men's faces. You yourselves do not enter, nor will you let those enter who are trying to."[133]

Leonardo had understood.

"Jesus had deciphered the Torah, and the Sanhedrin[134], whose members were the wealthy power holders, were of course, not eager to share the secret."

"Jesus had put an end to all the bloody rituals, offerings, and donations made to the temple, and eliminated the intermediaries. He was trying to make people understand that the *Word* was with everyone; and for man to know God or for God to hear a man's cries, there was no need for any animal to be slaughtered or for a priest to mediate. All that man had to do to return home was climb Jacob's ladder."

---

[132] The primordial cosmic energy, female in aspect, and represents the dynamic forces that are thought to move through the universe. She is thought of as creative, sustaining, as well as destructive, and is sometimes referred to as auspicious source energy.

[133] Matthew 23:13

[134] Jewish judicial and administrative body in the ancient land of Israel, composed of local elites, including members of the high-priestly family, scribes, religious experts, and lay elders.

Leonardo muttered from the Torah:

'You are to make for Me an altar of earth, and sacrifice on it your burnt offerings and peace offerings, your sheep and goats and cattle. In every place where I cause My name to be remembered, I will come to you and bless you. Now if you make an altar of stones for Me, you must not build it with stones shaped by tools; for if you use a chisel on it, you will defile it.[135]* "* He turned his gaze to Agrippa. "An altar of stones not shaped by tools... an altar made of earth... From earth, God had created Adam's body. Man himself was the Temple. He wanted us to sacrifice the animal within..."

Agrippa smiled.

"See, Master? Everything is already clearly stated in the text."

"Yet the Church continues to sell God's forgiveness and rob people through indulgences."

"In Rome, you see more ritual and less religion, Master. In rural parts of Britain, on the other hand, there is less ritual and more religion. Whereas to the indigenous, there's neither ritual nor religion; only the principles of nature. Jesus was not a Christian; Christianity spread as the teachings of Jesus. But those who considered themselves to be God's Chosen People and preferred to keep the secret to themselves knew that, after Jesus died, no one would understand what he really meant."

"A new religion was not going to pose any threat, on the contrary, it was going to move the capital from Jerusalem to Rome, shifting the focus away from the Secret." Leonardo paused. "They had to kill him before he could spread the word... and they did!"

"But at that last supper, Jesus had disclosed everything to his apostles."

"Peter brought the word to Rome and was crucified upside down by Emperor Nero. Likewise, Andrew ended up on the cross. James and Paul were beheaded. Matthew was stoned and burned at the stake, and Thomas was speared to death in India. You say that the word had spread. Italy is a battlefield. The Vatican is simultaneously attempting to ally itself both with the French and the Spanish. The Inquisition is tossing into the fires whose attire it disapproves of. In the east, the Turk is biding his time. And instead of mist, it is the smoke from the cannon fire that is settling on the waters of the Mediterranean. Doesn't it also appear to you, Signor Heinrich, that the Shekhinah — the soul of God — has long since left this world? Perhaps the

---

[135] Exodus 20:24-25

- 411 -

Torah is not as encrypted as you claimed, and it says precisely what it says. And perhaps, just as it is written, God had decided to abandon the world after the destruction of the Temple of Solomon and the disappearance of the Ark."

A compassionate smile spread across Agrippa's face.

"Why are you in so much despair, Master Leonardo?"

Leonardo sighed; after a brief moment, he replied:

"I suppose it's because I'm getting old." He rubbed his aching hands. "My hands are no longer capable of achieving the perfection of art while realizing what I envision. I am getting old, and despite all my good intentions and endeavors, my soul is unsatisfied. I realize that I can only study reality superficially; and the fact that the universe is too complicated for my mind to fully comprehend gives me pain."

"It's such a pity that the body has only feet while the soul has wings, isn't it, Master Leonardo? He smiled. "Hell... the state of a person who is ignorant of the Truth, who has been trapped in his individual perspective, seeing only what is the relative... The Kingdom of Hades, which scorches the souls... You are right in the middle of it."

Leonardo was feeling depressed.

"You have said that you wanted to know the Truth, right? Then, please allow me to share it with you, at least to the extent that I am allowed to know. Because the universe is not as complicated as you think."

Leonardo lifted his gaze from the ground, shifting his attention to Agrippa.

"The universe was created through Thirty-two Ways of Wisdom; ten utterances, and twenty-two letters each of which has a numerical value. Because letters expressing quality and numbers expressing quantity are enough to transform the incorporeal into the corporeal. One, represents the point. Two points connect to make a line. Three points give you a surface, and four points the four elements. Their sum equals to ten; the number of the fingers on the hands, no more no less, which includes all numbers and therefore all probabilities. The Temple of Solomon, which you said was destroyed, is the representation of Adam Kadmon's body in our corporeal world. There is nothing in the universe that does not have a representation within man. Man is the microcosm. You've told me that you've studied the human body for such a long time that you know it like the palm of your hand, right?"

"To the extent that I am allowed to know..."

"In the dissections, you've performed, you must certainly have encountered the Thirty-two Ways of Wisdom, am I mistaken?"

Leonardo remained silent for a while and tried to gather his thoughts and recall the subtle details of the human body that he and Marcantonio had discovered together. Then, he muttered:

"Thirty-two... Thirty-one pairs of spinal nerves, one on each side of the vertebral column... And one more, emerging from above the first vertebrae, branching into twelve pairs inside the skull..."

"Golgotha... Just outside Jerusalem's walls, the Skull Hill where Jesus was crucified and the twelve pairs of cranial nerves within the human head... Like the twelve Ancient Greek gods dwelling in Mount Olympus, like the twelve sons of Jacob, twelve tribes of the Israelites, twelve apostles of Jesus, twelve imams of Muslims... What a strange coincidence... In addition, Moses, depicted with two horns protruding from his head, had lived in the Age of Aries, which is the sign, representing 'I AM' consciousness. Jesus, on the other hand, had lived in the Age of Pisces, representing the subconscious. And do you know what Muhammad is said to have replied when he was asked on what the world rests, Master Leonardo? He had said that it rested on a fish and an ox which is another horned animal that represents consciousness."

"The zodiac with its twelve signs..." muttered Leonardo, "The zodiac starts with Aries and ends with Pisces... And its end marks its beginning..."

"Thirty-two. Three and two. Lamed and Bet. 'Lev' in Hebrew. Meaning 'heart'!" Agrippa raised his hands up and turned his gaze toward the sky. *"Blessed are the pure in heart, for they will see God![136]"*

Leonardo was muttering as he rubbed his aching wrists.

"The action of the brain manifests in the heart. If the brain ceases to function, the heart stops. And vice versa..."

"Do you understand better now why God, that Divine Mind, will never abandon us, Master Leonardo? Do you understand why Jesus said he was the Son of God; or that you are the Son of God?"

---

[136] Matthew 5:8

William was holding his breath as he listened to Cervantes. He would even silence his beating heart if he could so that he wouldn't be distracted.

Cervantes summed up all of Agrippa's words.

"God willed to bestow because It was kind and loving. It envisioned a dream and manifested it. And by using the three most powerful forces, Will, Thought, and Speech, It created man in Its own image."

"And bestowed all these three powers on man," said William. "The three forces of creation!"

In Pavia, in the City of Hundred Towers, the ancient home of the Lombard Kings, science and religion were staring at each other down in the middle of a university courtyard surrounded by colonnades. It was as if black was trying to comprehend the white, while white was trying to understand the black; hot was trying to unite with the cold, fire with the earth. Leonardo recalled his uncle Francesco's words. *Everything is dual; everything has poles; everything has its pair of opposites; like and unlike are the same; opposites are identical in nature, but different in degree; extremes meet; all truths are but half-truths; all paradoxes may be reconciled[137]* according to the seven laws of the universe...

"Religion and science..." Leonardo muttered. "How could religion and science be possibly reconciled?"

"G-enerātiō O-perātiō D-issolūtiō[138]" said Agrippa in Latin; then, he smiled at Leonardo. "The only thing that bothers you is that we refer to It as God, isn't it Master Leonardo? As a scientist, as soon as you hear the word God, you immediately put on your glasses of prejudice."

Leonardo remained silent. Agrippa placed his hand on Leonardo's shoulder, with a smile as vibrant as the sun.

"The Universe is a single living Universal Consciousness. All the seeming separations are merely illusions. We call this Cosmic Consciousness as God. The Ancients had referred to It as 'The Soul of The Universe'. You can call it 'Tree' if that makes you feel better."

---

[137] Hermetic Principle of Polarity, The Kybalion
[138] G-O-D, Latin root of God.

"Signor Agrippa!"

They both turned their heads toward the voice coming from upstairs. One of the students was calling out for Agrippa.

"Signor Agrippa, the time has come for your presentation."

Agrippa turned to Leonardo.

"I hope I have helped the light that already exists in your mind to shine a little brighter. I shall leave now."

He reached into his pocket, took something wrapped in a handkerchief, and handed it to Leonardo.

"Here, take this."

As he reached for it, Leonardo asked:

"What is this?"

"For your aching hands. It will help!"

After paying his respects to Leonardo, Agrippa turned around and walked away with youthful steps.

William's curiosity was piqued.

"What was it in that handkerchief?"

Cervantes flashed a grin.

"Something that would make Leonardo rush to the Vatican, Signor Shakespeare."

He leaned back.

"Leonardo was thinking that he was only a heartbeat away from unraveling the secret of the Ark. Just like Andrea, who was at the time, gazing at La Goulette, thinking that he was on the verge of seizing the Ark itself."

La Goulette, Tunisia

After returning from expedition, Khidr had not found Aruj in a good state. While he was out at seas, Aruj had made a few visits to the port to check around. On one of these days as he wandered around in the sailors' quarters, when a Tunisian made fun of his lameness, he had become enraged, broken the man's chin with his silver arm, and then returned home. After that day, Aruj had not taken a step outside. At times when the pain became intolerable for him, he had called Mother Firuze and asked her to give some opium. He was spending his days mostly sleeping. And during the times that he was awake, he was a source of rage for everyone around him. There was not a single day in which he did not yell at his men for petty reasons, not even a single day when he did not violently slam the door of his room...

"He must have been blaming himself. He must have felt ashamed of himself for having been succumbed to his own greed. That must have been the source of his rage at times when he was awake; and those long hours of sleep must have been serving him as a way of escape."

"All I know is that while I'm asleep, I'm never afraid, and I have no hopes, no struggles, no glories; and bless the man who invented sleep, a cloak over all human thought, food that drives away hunger, water that banishes thirst, fire that heats up cold, chill that moderates passion, and, finally, universal currency with which all things can be bought, weight and balance that brings the shepherd and the king, the fool and the wise, to the same level."[139]

---

[139] Miguel de Cervantes Saavedra, Don Quixote

Cervantes paused, turned his gaze toward William and added:

"There's only one bad thing about sleep, as far as I've ever heard, Signor Shakespeare, and that is that it resembles death, since there's very little difference between a sleeping man and a corpse."[140]

Cervantes was right. Aruj was thinking that if would have been better if he was dead, and this was devastating Khidr.

Time had flown by, and it was already midnight. Khidr was working on the records of their last hunt. The treasure they had captured was worthwhile. On their way back to Tunisia, Khidr had dispatched some of the loot to Djerba. And when they landed ashore, he had penned a letter to Piri, thinking that it would have been a good idea if they set aside some of the loot for Sultan Selim who had just recently ascended to the throne, as a token of their loyalty. Sultan Korkud's strangling had become a source of concern for all the levends sailing in the Mediterranean under his auspices. After all, having the Empire's support was essential. In addition to making plans for his upcoming expeditions, Khidr was feeling obligated to fulfill the requirements of diplomacy. He, unlike Aruj, would pay attention to such details. As for the remainder of the booty, it would be presented to Mulay Muhammad as promised.

He had been working for hours, taking notes, doing calculations, and trying to determine their next move. He was feeling tired. At least for tonight, he should not have been working any longer. He heard the door creak open. When he lifted his eyes to see who was coming in, he saw Felipa standing at the door in her snow-white gown, staring at him. He was surprised.

"Heyy..."
Felipa smiled. Her dark wavy hair had fallen over her elegant shoulders.
"Heyy..."
"Are you still awake?"
"I couldn't sleep..."
"Why?"
"Because of your longing."

---

[140] Miguel de Cervantes Saavedra, Don Quixote

Khidr had been out at the seas for weeks. Besides that, ever since Aruj lost his arm, almost all the responsibility had been resting on Khidr's shoulders. Felipa hadn't seen him properly since the days they were in Djerba, and she had missed her beloved greatly. She took a few steps toward the man she was deeply in love with and caressed his reddish-brown beard and cheeks with her delicate hands. She moved closer and placed gentle kisses on his brows, eyelids, and ears; then, rested her face on his neck and deeply inhaled his sweet scent. Khidr ran his fingers through her swan neck and shoulders; his thirsty lips wandered around the hollows of her collarbones. When the straps of her featherlike gown fell off her shoulders Felipa trembled under her lover's hands sliding down her back. Her eyes were burning, her body was trembling; love had taken captive her entire being. Khidr kissed the two drops of tears that streamed down her cheeks.

"Why are you crying?"
Felipa smiled behind her wet lashes.
"Your love did fit in nowhere but my heart. Yet it no longer fits there either and drips from my eyes."[141]

That night, the waves of the Mediterranean were in Felipa's hair and its salt was on her silky skin. The breeze that accompanied the moonlight streaming through the window passed through the tulle curtains and extinguished the light from the candle on the table. Khidr's breath became Felipa's as Felipa became a breath for Khidr.

William muttered:
"Set me as a seal upon thine heart, as a seal upon thine arm: for love is strong as death; jealousy is cruel as the grave: the coals thereof are coals of fire, which hath a most vehement flame..."[142]

---

[141] Rumi
[142] Song of Solomon 8:6

"The enemy fleet! "The enemy fleet is closing in!"

The following day, when one of the levends stationed at the bastion over-looking the port saw the approaching Genoese fleet, he had begun shouting at the top of his lungs. As his warning spread like wildfire among the other sailors working on their ships, a commotion broke out at the port.

Kurdoglu rushed to Khidr, who was with Aruj at the time, and found him standing by the window watching the approaching fleet with concern when he entered the room. Aruj, on the other hand, was in his bed, battling his hallucinations. Although his wound had healed, he was still suffering from severe aches in his bones. It was one of those days again, he was lying in bed, dizzy from the effects of the opium the doctors had given him to relieve his pain. Kurdoglu tried to remain calm.

"We've got twelve ships. But the levends lack morale."
Khidr turned his gaze toward Aruj who was tossing and turning in bed drenched in sweat.
"It is what we all lack..."

He was indeed right. Khidr had foreseen this coming. Aruj's reckless cour-age would one day get them into trouble. Kurdoglu made his way toward the window and fixed his eyes on the approaching armada.

"It seems Aruj's news had crossed the waters in no time."
"They have men everywhere. They walk among us like shadows in the streets of Tunisia, as if they are one of us."
"What's your plan?
"We cannot fight. I must protect Aruj. Sink half the ships. Divert their at-tention with the other half and buy me some time."
He took a deep breath and turned his gaze to Aruj.
"I have to take him someplace behind the walls, someplace safe..."
Kurdoglu placed his hand on Khidr's shoulder.
"I'll do my best. Be quick, they're close."

He turned around and made his way to the door. Just as he was about to leave the room, he turned to face Khidr.
"All this is taking place so that the revenge we'll take tastes even sweeter."
Khidr vaguely smiled to show he appreciated his friend's efforts to boost his morale.

Everyone who saw the approaching fleet had swarmed to the shore. Felipa had rushed to the port, worried, was looking everywhere searching for Khidr. She caught Kurdoglu by the arm.

"What's happening? Where is Khidr? What the heck are these galleons?" She was in a panic. Kurdoglu pulled her aside.
"They obviously heard of Aruj."

They were startled by the blaring of the battle horns blasting on the walls of La Goulette. The enemy was drawing closer. They were coming to raze La Goulette down.

Kurdoglu turned to Felipa.
"He is going to take Aruj to a safe place behind the city walls. I'll buy them some time. Go, find Khidr! Retreat behind the walls!"

After leaving Felipa Kurdoglu began to rain down orders.
"Sink half the ships! On boaaaaard! Everyone!!!"

As the levends hurried to carry out his orders, Kurdoglu muttered under his breath without taking his dark blue gaze away from the approaching armada.
"I hope you enjoy the welcome ceremony..."

Felipa rushed to the residence. But what about her horses? What would happen to her horses? The stables were very close to the port. The port would be turned into hell as soon as the Christians opened cannon fire. If the fires were to spread, Felipa might have lost them all. She could not let this happen. She turned back and started to run towards the stables.

Andrea was standing on the forecastle, watching the hustle and bustle going on at the port. Just as he had intended, he was going to strike them when they were least expecting it. But seeing the ships at the port being sunk had bothered him. It seemed Khidr was trying to avoid them from being captured by the Genoese. Kurdoglu had left the port with six galiots, he was approaching the enemy fleet from the starboard side in an effort to divert their attention. Andrea, on the other hand, had no time to waste with Kurdoglu.

He ordered his men:
"Full speed ahead!"

He was not after a bunch of galiots; rather, his job was with the walls of La Goulette; his job was with Khidr. And he had this gut feeling that was telling him that Khidr was not on any of those galiots. As soon as Andrea razed La Goulette down, Khidr would undoubtedly emerge from the rubble.

The bombardment began. The people on the shore were running away in terror, screaming, trying to take shelter in order not to be crushed under the rocks falling from the collapsing walls. The cannons installed on the fort were spewing fire at the Genoese in a vain effort to prevent the enemy from approaching. It didn't take long, and La Goulette was completely engulfed in flames.

Khidr was galloping at full speed leaving a cloud of dust in his wake, taking Aruj to the white city. As soon as he arrived at the gates, he was taken aback by the scene that awaited them. After hearing the reports of the approaching armada and concluding that the Barbarossas would attempt to retreat behind the castle walls; Mulay Muhammad had ordered the gates of the city to be shut. The sultan knew that the Barbarossas were damned by the Christians. They had set the Mediterranean on fire with that unquenchable spark of vengeance within them, the flames of which had eventually reached the sultan's door and turned his La Goulette into hell. From the very beginning, Huseyn was right in his assessments. Mulay Muhammad could not afford to let those pirates stay in La Goulette any longer.

He began riding in circles in front of the walls, yelling at guards, ordering them to open the gates; but the guards did not even move a finger. Andrea, on the other hand, had dispatched his men after them upon failing to find Khidr in La Goulette. Khidr could hear the beat of approaching hooves. It was not Andrea's men that he was concerned about. He was certain that his ferocious rage would knock them all down. But Aruj... Aruj could not stand the fight. Even if Khidr had the strength, his brother had not, thus Khidr needed to get him to a place where he could rest as soon as possible.

He yelled at the guards:
"I say open it! Open the gates!"

He, then, noticed Yusuf trying to get to them with his crippled leg and steered his horse toward him. Yusuf was panting for breath.
"Reis! Come, follow me. I know a way in."

The horses, terrified by the cannons bursting, were neighing and rearing in their stalls. Felipa needed to set them all free before the flames spread any further, or else they would all perish. After destroying the walls of La Goulette, the Genoese had made their way ashore and were either killing or capturing everyone they came across, dragging them to the galleons in chains. They had broken into almost all the homes in a short period of time and left behind rivers of blood flowing through the streets of La Goulette.

Felipa had released most of the horses. One of the remaining was her Viento. She had planned to jump on his back and get out of this hell after they were all set free. However, with the sudden entrance of Christian soldiers into the stables, all her plans went down the drain.

Felipa grabbed a shovel as they approached and broke the jaw of the first Genoese who made an attempt toward her; yet was unable to avoid being caught by the other two shortly after. The one who was treated with the shovel gathered himself, and as blood was streaming from his nose, he gave Felipa a hard slap on the face. Felipa stumbled; she was on the verge of passing out. It was clear that she would be taken captive. How preferable it certainly was for Felipa, on the other hand, if they simply put an end to her life at that very moment. If only she could stand up to them a little longer; if only she could bite and rip a piece of flesh from one of their arms, or break the nose of another maybe, and make them even more angry, there was no doubt that they would kill her there. Nonetheless, she had become so dizzy due to the blow on her face that she could only hazily see what was going on around her. The soldier with the broken jaw seemed higher in rank compared to the others. As he got closer, he started unbuckling his belt, determined to make Felipa pay for what she had just done.

Felipa was screaming and crying as she tried in vain to break free from their clutches. She was gasping. Her hair was all over her face, and her clothes were ripped apart. She spat the blood that had accumulated in her mouth onto the soldier's face who got closer but was unable to divert his attention. They dragged her over to the stack of hay bales on the corner. As the man tried to spread her legs apart Felipa was throwing strong kicks in the air. All of a sudden, they heard footsteps coming from the direction of the door, through which a thin beam of light was flowing in, and stopped. It was their commander, Andrea Doria, who had entered in the stables. He had heard the screams coming from inside and decided to check what had been going on. When the soldier gathered himself and stepped aside, Andrea saw Felipa was laid on the hay bales, pinned down by her wrists. He couldn't believe his eyes. He had finally found her. Whatever it was that their eyes had told each other in silence that Andrea quickly approached, drew his sword, and thrust it into the belly of the Genoese who was about to rape Felipa. The man collapsed on the ground. Felipa saw the blood leaking from his belly, spreading on the ground. The others, on the other hand, were nailed to the spot. Why on earth had their admiral been that much bothered by them having some fun with this woman, when he had remained silent while the people at the port were being slaughtered? When they loosened their grip on her wrists, Felipa quickly freed herself, yet did not try to escape. Andrea was standing there staring at Felipa.

"I knew it!"

She was brought to port on Viento's back; then made boarded Andrea's galleon. As the fleet left the port, it was the devil's dark breath rising into the air from La Goulette...

William rubbed his face. He then stood up, walked over to the window and gazed into the distance.

"Hell is empty... All the devils are here..."[143] Suddenly he turned to Cervantes. "Perhaps she had sensed..."

Cervantes hadn't understood what William meant.

"Felipa's tears..." William said; "Perhaps Felipa had sensed the previous night that it was her last night that she would be able to spend with Khidr."

The fires were put out. The lifeless bodies, the limbs and heads that had been severed were all gathered and buried. The blood that was flowing through the streets of La Goulette was washed away by the tears of Tunisians.

---

[143] William Shakespeare, The Tempest

Khidr, on the other hand, spent days searching for Felipa. As he looked at all those lifeless faces, he prayed to Allah that none of them belonged to Felipa, that he would not come across his Felipa among these dead bodies.

"There's no sign of her, Reis."

Khidr had sat on a rock at the ruined port, was watching the levends pull the sunken ships out of water.

"Should I be glad or sad about that, Yahya?"

"You should be glad, Reis. You should be glad that we didn't discover Felipa's lifeless body."

His gaze was drawn to Kurdoglu, who had just landed ashore, wiping his hands on a rag as he approached.

"It seems Kurdoglu was the last to see her. He said that he told Felipa that I was taking Aruj behind the city walls; that she should go and find me."

"Did you check the stables, Reis?"

"I did. It had been reduced to ash and dust. I saw Mustafa, lying on the ground covered in blood. As for the horses, none of them was there."

"It is likely that Felipa set all of them free. She must have been concerned that the fires would spread to the stables."

"She must have been captured while she was trying to save the horses."

His voice was devoid of color. Aruj was sick, Felipa was lost and there were no stone left on La Goulette that had not rolled down. Whereas how hard they had worked to strengthen those walls...

Kurdoglu drew closer and turned to Khidr:

"The ships are ready; we can sail to Djerba tomorrow morning. After that..."

"Allah knows what, after that..." Khidr muttered.

"One of the levends claims to have seen Felipa."

Khidr got excited.

"Who says so? He saw her where? When?"

"Slow down. He cannot say for certain, but it is possible that she was one of the enslaved women."

"Who knows how many women they took as slave. How would he know that the woman he saw was Felipa?"

"She was with the admiral, he says. It seems that she arrived at the port atop a jet-black horse, and the two of them boarded the flagship."

Yahya felt hopeful.

"It's possible that she's Felipa."

Khidr rubbed his face.

"She wouldn't leave her Viento..."

No one had a word to say. Felipa was taken captive and who knows where she was taken to. Khidr took out a small leather-bound notebook from his belt. Yahya immediately recognized the notebook.

"Doesn't that belong to Felipa?"

"It is Aruj's in fact. Felipa had told me that she found it in the captain's cabin on the day we met in Djerba. When I went to check on her late at night; I had found her sleeping on the couch with this notebook in her hands".

His hands flipped through the pages. It was almost as if he could smell Felipa's fragrance wafting from them. He simply opened a random page and began reading. His eyes welled up with tears..."

When Cervantes took his notebook as he told him the story, William had understood; that small leather-covered notebook Cervantes was holding in his hands was the very notebook that contained the lines that caused Khidr's eyes to well up with tears. Cervantes flipped through the pages and began reading.

"Do not grieve! If you can see, touch, breathe, walk, how happy for you! Do not tell me about what you do not have, tell me about what you do have, dear. Will the nights forever be lonely? Will those who left never return? Perhaps the one you lost will appear in front of you on a rainy night, or a spring morning. Know that there are also beauties in this life. Can you imagine a life without tides? Sorrow makes one mature, loss teaches patience..."[144]

He closed the notebook and turned to William:

"Whether it would be on a rainy night or a spring morning, he had no clue; but even if Khidr had to flip the Mediterranean upside down; he was going to find his Felipa."

---

[144] Rumi

Was she now Andrea's slave? Where was he taking her? Why was he taking her? Felipa was unaware that Andrea had been looking for her on every shore he had landed on, in all the bays of the Mediterranean since the day she managed to escape from the sheikh's men. She neither knew about the fire she had set within the admiral's heart the moment they had met.

As the waves of the Mediterranean rocked the galleon, Viento was getting restless. Inside the ship's hold was cold and dark. Felipa was sitting on the damp ground her head in between her hands, leaning against one of the posts that had been placed every two meters to support the upper deck. The rumble of the cannon fire that had destroyed La Goulette was still in her ears, and the vision of the dark thick blood that was oozing out from the Genoese soldier's belly, slowly spreading on the ground was in front of her eyes. If only she had more time... If only she had just a little more time, she would have hopped on her Viento and fled behind the city walls. If only Kurdoglu could have bought them a little more time, Felipa would be with Khidr now.

Khidr... How was Khidr, she wondered. What was he going to do when he found out that she had been taken captive? What could he possibly do? Even Felipa didn't know where she had been dragged.

She heard the door creak open. When a faint light streamed in and illuminated the hold; Felipa noticed that it was Andrea coming in. She did not move.

Andrea took off his jacket and placed it on Felipa's shoulders.

"You're trembling."

"Because it's cold."

"Come to the upper deck."

"I don't want to."

Andrea let out a sigh. They were back where they had started. Felipa had no intention to cooperate with him in any way. Every word that came out of her mouth had the sharpness of a knife.

"Then, what do you want?"

"To know why you kidnapped me!"

"Kidnap you? I saved you! I saved you from the clutches of those savage Muslims."

Lightning bolts flashed in Felipa's eyes.

"You rescued me? Who requested that you rescue me? I didn't need to be rescued from anyone, except from your men!"

Her voice was elevated. Her despair had mixed with her rage and was permeating every word she was saying at the time.

"I am not the one who kidnapped you! It was them! They were the ones who took you away from me; they were the ones who took you to Tunisia."

Felipa was perplexed. What was Andrea talking about?

"You must be out of your mind! As the king's gift, you took me to the sheikh. As a slave! With your own hands, you handed me over to the guards! If it hadn't been for Khidr, I was going to spend the rest of my life as a member of that stupid sheikh's harem. And you call those Muslims savages? You must have forgotten that I am a Muslim as well."

"I was going to buy you!"

Her words were cut short by Andrea's thunderous voice which was followed by an eerie silence descended upon the hold of the ship. Taking advantage of the silence, Andrea gathered his composure and repeated more calmly.

"I was going to buy you!"

Felipa was completely stunned.

"Buy me? So, I was going to be your slave rather than the sheikh's?"

"Not my slave... my wife... you were going to be my wife!"

It was the first time Felipa was witnessing Andrea's voice tremble. He was in love with her. Felipa had a better understanding now. She got on her feet and took a few steps toward him.

"Take me back to Khidr... please... I don't love you!"

They stood there in the dim light for a while, staring at each other. Andrea could see Felipa's intense desire for freedom in her eyes. He could see her despair as well as the courage and strength she displayed in the face of all the challenges she had faced. The last reflection he caught a glimpse of, on the other hand, was what was going to haunt him for the rest of his life. After splashing Felipa's face with the last words he had spoken in an icy tone, Andrea left the hold. It was Khidr whom he saw...

"You'll love in time."

She was startled by the slamming of the door. When the faint light that had been seeping through the partially open door vanished as well, Felipa was left in complete darkness. She sat down at her horse's feet and started crying. As she gently stroked Viento's velvet cheek with one of her hands, she wiped off the tears that wet her own cheek with the other. She recalled the hymn his father used to hum when she was little in an attempt to comfort her whenever she felt afraid or got lost in despair. "Do not let your heart, do not let your face become darkened just because the darkness has descended", Signor Faris would tell her; "Despair is the most beautiful sign that comes from Allah. It shows that it's time to pray. If tears were falling from your eyes, if your lovely face had been shadowed by sorrow, it means that your Lord had missed you, and wanted to hear your voice."[145]

She began humming.

The winds had ceased. The Genoese armada, proud of their victory, was slowly advancing towards the shores of Italy gliding through the tulle-like mist that had descended upon the vast sea. Felipa's voice rose in the silence and traveled down to the lower deck, where it reached the ears of the slaves and poured into the hearts of all those who had been chained to the oars. It had sounded familiar to them all. All of a sudden, it had given hope to them all. It did not take long for it to spread throughout the entire armada, and soon, thousands of Muslim slaves started to accompany Felipa.

"Allâhümme salli alâ… seyyidinâ… Muhammedinin Nebiyyil ümmiyyil… ve alâ… âlihî ve sahbihi ve sellim…"

---

[145] Rumi

Milan, Italy

These Templars... They live from a stone whose essence was most pure, If you have never heard of it I shall name it for you here. It is called Lapsit Exillis. By virtue of this Stone, The Phoenix is burned to ashes, in which he is reborn. Thus does the Phoenix moult his feathers. Which done, it shines dazzlingly bright and lovely as before.[146]

Leonardo was reading through his uncle's notebooks which were filled with ciphers and riddles; the notebooks, which, rather than providing answers to questions that have already exhausted his mind, plant the seeds for new questions...

All birds from others do derive their birth, but yet one fowl there is in all the earth, called by the Assyrians Phoenix, who the wain of age, repairs and sows herself again. Nor feeds on grain nor herbs, but on the gum of frankincense and of juicy amomum.[147]

How skillfully the sages had hidden their secrets. They had used hundreds of different words to describe the very same thing. Instead of putting in so much effort, Leonardo was thinking that it would have been better if they simply avoided writing altogether. How many lives had been ruined when those who were incapable of understanding the metaphors and who had taken everything that was written literally attempted to apply what was prescribed exactly as it was described... How many, who were ignorant of the

---

[146] Wolfram Von Eschenbach, Parzival, 13th century
[147] Ovid, Metamorphosis

laws of nature, had been dragged into poverty and misery, and died in this cause, as a result of digesting the poisonous sulfur and mercury...

Cervantes leaned back.

"Many had kept this knowledge hidden due to elitism. They had preferred to keep it for themselves because they believed that they were special, that they were far more deserving than others as God's chosen people. There was really no point in casting the pearls before the swine. There was really no need to invite more people at the table and end up hungry at the end of the night."

William's disappointment couldn't help but expressed itself.

"Whereas the Creator, in all humility, had shared the knowledge of creation with all of humanity."

Cervantes muttered from the Bible:

"God resists the proud but gives grace to the humble."[148]

William's heart was warmed by Jesus's wisdom.

"Just like love..." he muttered, "For, rather than becoming scarce, knowledge grows when it is shared, just like love..."

Wisdom begins with knowing that you do not know. For the mind has its limits; it cannot grasp what it cannot compare. Whereas love is eternal, immortal, and lights up all hearts. Love begins when one realizes that 'the other' is none other than himself. And peace can only be found within. The gift has already been gifted, you just need to wake up, Leonardo...

"Leonardo...Leonardo...Leonardooooooo!!!"

He was startled by Salai's voice. Leonardo had fallen into the arms of a brief nap on the couch while he was reflecting on his uncle's words with the notebooks on his lap. He straightened up.

"So, you showed up."

"I did."

---

[148] James 4:6

"Could you find the things that I've requested?"

Salai had gone inside to drop off the things that he had brought. He responded in a higher tone to ensure that he was heard.

"Not all of them. The rest, they said, you can find them in Florence, in Arte dei Medici e Speziali[149]. So, I'll go and check when we arrive, okay, Leonardo?"

"Master! You will call me Master!"

"So, I'll go and check when we arrive, okay MASTER?"

What Leonardo thought had in the end become his reality. Within a period of six months, the Swiss had driven the French out of Milan and handed over the city's administration to Massimiliano Sforza. The cannons had fallen silent, yet the city had nothing left to offer Leonardo from that point forward. After expressing his gratitude to the Melzis for their hospitality during his stay in Villa Melzi; Leonardo had taken Francesco with him and come to his vineyard in Milan to pack his belongings and bid farewell to his treasured vines.

Milan's gates were closed, but fortunately Florence's had been opened. The flames of republican freedom and religious reform fueled by Girolamo Savonarola's sermons, had been extinguished by the efforts of Giovanni di Lorenzo de Medici, who would later become Pope Leo X; and the Medicis had regained power in Florence.

Francesco's sudden entrance to the room startled Leonardo.

"How are you feeling, Leonardo? You seemed to be bit tired this morning."

"I'm fine Francesco, thank you. Though I'm a bit depressed. I have a lot to pack before we leave, but my aching bones are tying me to this couch."

Francesco smiled.

"Don't worry, we'll do whatever needs to be done with Salai."

He took a few steps forward and extended a letter to Leonardo.

"This is for you; perhaps you'd like to look at it."

As he reached for the letter, Leonardo muttered:

"I hope it's not from the cardinal."

---

[149] The physicians and pharmacists guild in Florence, founded in 1197

It was not. The letter was from Agrippa, whom Leonardo had been hoping to hear from for quite some time. He curiously opened it and started reading.

Dear Master Leonardo,

I apologize for not responding to your letter sooner. Life has compelled me to make the decisions that I was not willing to. As much as I wished to spend my days among the books, I found myself on the battlefields. My fingers with which I desired to hold a pen, gripped my blood-soaked sword. I followed the camp of the Emperor and the French King in many conflicts: gave no sluggish help: before my face went death, and I followed, the minstrel of death, my right hand soaked in blood, my left dividing spoil, my belly was filled with prey, and the way of my feet was over corpses of the slain. So I was made forgetful of my innermost honour, and wrapped round fifteenfold in Tartarean shade.[150] Now, as I'm in the service of the Marquise of Monferrat, I'm trying to save my soul from this agony and to recall the Truth that I had forgotten.

I understand from what you've written in your letter that you, too, are trying to awaken from the deep sleep in which you have no recollection of how or when you fell, and remember the Truth. Because a quest after the Ark of the Covenant is a quest after of the nature of reality; and it shows that you are in pursuit of the creation that has been evolving through the alchemy of time. However, fret not! Because the Truth is closer to you than your jugular vein and if you know what it is that you've been looking for, finding it will be much easier for you. As it is written; 'Ask and it will be given to you; seek and you will find; knock and the door will be opened to you. For everyone who asks receives; he who seeks finds; and to him who knocks, the door will be opened.' Knowing what you are looking for is knowing the location of the door that you would knock on. All religions, philosophers, teachers, and priests can only point to the path that leads to the door since the door is neither in any book nor in any teacher. And once you've found it, there is only one thing you need to do; and that is, to die and reborn. Because for the energy to be liberated, matter must be destroyed.

---

[150] Heinrich Cornelius Agrippa, Epistle 19, bk. 2

Leonardo let out a hearty laugh.

"Hah! And I'm already ready to die."

Agrippa had such an interesting way of explaining things. As soon as one thought that he was on the verge of understanding him, he was as well realizing that it was no more than a distant dream.

Having heard Leonardo partially, Salai reproached.

"I am not ready yet, Leonardo. There's a whole room of items to pack here! Do we have to hit the road today?"

"Master! You will call me Master!"

"Do we have to hit the road today, MASTER?"

Leonardo chuckled and turned his attention to the letter in his hands.

To die and reborn, yet of course while living. And as impossible as it may seem, I assure you it is not. Although it is not an easy task to save your soul from the torments of this corporeal world, to release the innermost 'You' that is aware of everything from the dungeons it was trapped in; it is in no way impossible. However, on this path of light as well as darkness, this path which includes both victories and defeats, one must first understand the importance of a focused mind that is passionate about its purpose as well as a strong faith free from doubt. And it should not be forgotten that what heals the patient is his love and faith towards the doctor and the medicine. Because when the mind is focused on something, regardless of what that something may be, it connects with the Mind of the Universe. And there is nothing that the Mind of the Universe cannot accomplish. As Hermes Trismegistus had said: two things God had bestowed on man beyond all mortal lives: mind and logos. Without the mind, the soul is an orphan. It cannot accomplish anything on its own, and man behaves in an irrational primitive manner. As for logos, it is the bright son of the mind. It is the expression of the expresser, the writing of the writer, the narration of the narrator, the creation of the creator! Because what makes the creator 'creator' is nothing but his 'creation'. And immortality would be the earned prize of one who uses these two gifts wisely. Therefore, even though the brain is in everyone, the mind has been placed between the souls like a gem so that they would strive to possess it and pursue wisdom. Just like the Philosopher's Stone the alchemists pursue.

He leaned back.

"The Secret of secrets. The Stone that is not a stone..."

He was wondering if he ever would figure it out. How exactly had he ended up being a part of this quest to solve the mystery of the Ark of the Covenant? It was the cardinal who had dragged Leonardo into this, in his pursuit of the Stones of Death that were allegedly inside the Ark.

"The Stones of Death..." he muttered. "The stones... the stone... THE STONE! THE PHILOSOPHER'S STONE! Hah! I found it! It is inside the Ark!"

When he got excited, Leonardo had leaped to his feet and shouted. Salai, who was at the time busy with gathering some of Leonardo's stuff in one of the rooms, responded by shouting back:

"If you're looking for your astrolabe. It's not inside your wooden ark. I just checked."

Leonardo had not even heard Salai. Now he couldn't wait to continue the letter from where he left off.

Some people believe that alchemy is the work of the devil, while others consider it to be sheer nonsense. But I can assure you, Master Leonardo, that those who simply deny its existence out of ignorance are no different than those in Plato's Cave who assume the shadows on the walls are real and deny the existence of the outside world. Pythagoras, Orpheus, Empedocles, Democritus, Plato, Platinus, Thales, and Anaximenes, along with many others, all attained the knowledge of this Great Secret; and after spending years of their lives studying it, they returned to their homes, founded schools, wrote books about it. The Greeks learned about the natural sciences in Egyptian Temples; they studied mathematics, astrology, geometry, philosophy, metallurgy, mineralogy. And it was only after they had gained an understanding of these sciences they realized that magic was not magic but rather the very Truth itself. But remember, one man's meat is another's poison and the line between philosophy and witchcraft is thin. If philosophy is the love of wisdom, witchcraft is the forbidden lust! And knowledge should never be used to challenge God, as was attempted to be used in the Tower of Babel. Because God is that infinite nothingness that is everything, which no human mind can fully comprehend. If a person who has climbed Jacob's Ladder falls into the trap of mistaking himself for God, he will shatter his most prized posses-sion, his stone. Because the power of thought is an actual force. A thought on the mental plane gives rise to an emotion on the astral plane, which then manifests as a substance on the physical plane. And it is cru-cial to treat this delicate substance with care.

He was, indeed, correct. There was no such thing as nothingness in the universe because everything was in some way some a 'thing' that differed from the other things in terms of quality and quantity. And if one were to make the effort to grasp nothingness, he would almost certainly lose his mind. He rubbed his aching wrists and sat back in his seat.

A Stone that is not a stone... A pillow for Jacob, the keystone of Solo-mon's Temple, the stone on which Muhammad had stepped and as-cended to the seventh heaven, and upon which Jesus had founded his church. The mysterious AZOTH of the alchemists, composed of the first and last letters of Latin, Greek and Hebrew alphabets. I AM that I AM, I am Alpha and Omega, I am the beginning and the end. The Foundation Stone that upon which the entire creation is built. 'Eben' in Hebrew, which has two words hidden in its core: "av" and "ben", the Father and the Son.

The path that leads to the City of Luz, where there is neither death nor pain, and where nothing but the Truth is spoken, passes through wisdom, Master. Wisdom is thought in its purest form, a state of pure awareness in which the mind is not involved. As you would also appreciate, one first has to be silent so as to be able to hear God's voice. Until the mind be-comes quiet, until the eyes are closed, the All-Seeing Eye would not open. As Jesus had said: 'The light of the body is the eye: if therefore thine eye be single, thy whole body shall be full of light.'[151] And you shouldn't forget that in the street of the blind, the one-eyed man is called the Guiding Light[152].

"The All-Seeing Eye...", muttered Leonardo. He thought of the organ the size of a pine nut that he had discovered right in the middle of the brain, just behind the eyes. Galen had called it Glandula Pinealis. And according to him,

---

[151] Matthew 6:22
[152] Genesis Rabbah 300-500 CE

this tiny gland, was serving the same function as the rest of the glands in the human body, which was to provide support for the blood vessels. Leonardo had felt a great deal of excitement when he discovered it, thinking that he had found the *All-Seeing Eye*. Yet, it seems that this phrase, too, was nothing but a metaphor. He turned his attention to Agrippa's letter.

> *Because the moment the All-Seeing Eye is opened, just as it happened to Jacob at Penuel, one finds himself face to face with God.*

"Penuel... the place where Jacob wrestled with God. The face of God..." Leonardo muttered. "Penuel... Peniel..." His mind is illuminated by a bolt of lightning. "Pinealis! Glandula Pinealis!"

Galen was wrong! Just as Leonardo had suspected; that little gland in the middle of the brain was the *All-Seeing Eye*! It was the eye of Horus! It was man's third eye! According to mythology, Horus had been born after Isis resurrected Osiris from the dead. This was the reason why the Pharaohs were choosing a Horus name for themselves before inheriting the throne. They would die in order to kill their old identities, connect with the Mind of the Universe, and then be reborn under a different name once they had attained the level of enlightenment required to rule. Leonardo let out a laugh. It seems that the real metaphor was in fact to die and then be reborn.

"All right, then, let's do it! I'm all set for this journey!"
He had not noticed Salai walk in.
"You can leave today if you want. We can set out and follow you as soon as we finish with the packing."
"Salai, mind your own business; I'm not talking to you."

He returned his gaze to the letter and continued reading.

> *A Stone that is not a stone... God's covenant with man, the throne of Shekhinah, the Ark of the Covenant! The place where the Essence of God dwells in man, the All-Seeing Eye! Or as we call it, the Philosopher's Stone!*

The alchemy he had avoided his entire life had eventually tangled around Leonardo's feet.

Alchemy is the art of transmutation. What nature achieves in its own time, the alchemist strives to achieve in his own. Nature is not in a hurry, but man certainly is. Because each passing day is another leaf that falls from his tree of life. And as you will appreciate, art can be swifter than nature. I hope you now understand why our stone is not a stone and that what we are discussing is an essence pregnant with the stone. An essence that envelops the soul and permeates everything in the universe. The source from which the four elements, all minerals, and everything that exists originate. The life energy the origin of which is a mystery to us though we cannot live without it. The Divine Breath! Ether! Or, as Aristotle put it, Quintessence[153]! Some people call it the chaos out of which thoughts are formed; some refer to it as the First Matter, while others describe it as the visible, the tangible form of God. The seed of life that descends from the heavens and falls upon us.

Leonardo muttered from the Torah: "*And when the dew fell upon the camp in the night, the manna fell upon it.*"[154]

William was puzzled.

"But, ether, Quintessence, is not something visible, not something tangible! It is neither hot, nor cold, nor is it dry, or wet. These are only the qualities of the four elements. The fifth element is just an idea, a theory!"

"Just like God, isn't it, Signor Shakespeare? And the *Manna* on the dew, the visible, tangible form of God..."

"The source of everything that exists in our corporeal world are the four elements. The fifth element is not a matter, how can it be tangible?"

"You are right, Signor, the fifth element is not a matter; it is not a thing. However, if you think that the universe is the sum total of things you see with your eyes, or touch with your hands; you are gravely mistaken."

"All right, then, explain to me how it is that something can be born from nothing? How can Non-Existence come to exist?"

Cervantes leaned back.

---

[153] Fifth Element
[154] Numbers 11:9

"There's no such thing as 'Absolute Non-Existence', Signor. Whatever you think of as "not existing", potentially exists in the universe. Just like a tree hidden in a seed. It has always been and always will be."

Leonardo rose to his feet. The letter slipped from his grasp, floated like a feather through the air, and eventually landed on the ground. He rubbed his face. All the observable laws of physics that he had clung to with his heart and soul up until that point had been toppled down like the Tower of Babel. He didn't even need to read the rest of the letter. For the first time in his entire life Leonardo believed that he had reached some level of understanding about the functioning of the universe.

"The Salt of the Earth..." he muttered, "the Prima Materia of the Great Art, the Vessel of Hermes... Salt, which condenses directly from vapor to solid, and sublimates from solid to gas, just like the Spirit. As pure and as white as it can possibly be..."

He felt that something was wrong with his blood pressure and gripped the edge of the couch to keep from falling. Had it not been for Francesco who came just in time and grabbed him by the arm, Leonardo would most likely have collapsed on the ground.

"Leonardo!"
He straightened himself with Francesco's help.
"I felt a bit dizzy."
Hearing Francesco's shout, Salai had also come running.
"Salt... I'll bring some salt!"

"Some people's faith would prevail over their minds causing them to spend their entire lives worshiping without ever questioning the reason why. While others' minds would triumph over their faith, and they would deny everything their mind failed to comprehend."
William muttered:
"And some first need to comprehend with their minds why this mystery can never be comprehended with the mind. Just like Leonardo..."

"Marsilio was right," said Cervantes, "One, first needed to understand Aristotle's 'form' in order to understand Plato's 'idea'. Leonardo had always believed that Aristotle had opposed his own teacher. However, it seemed that, what Aristotle had been trying to explain was that it was necessary to know about "the knowable" first, to get to know "the unknowable." Man, first needed to gain an understanding of how nature works. Hadn't 'the unknowable', hadn't 'the incomprehensible' created the universe to be known?"

With the help of his assistants, Leonardo sat back in his seat. And after downing the salty water that Salai had brought in a single gulp, he took a deep breath.

"Okay, I'm fine. Now you two can go about your own business."

Salai and Francesco looked at each other, concerned.

Leonardo raised his tone.

"Who am I talking to? Go! Go! Go!"

He picked up the letter and continued reading from where he had left off.

Nature is fertilized with this seed that falls from the heavens at any moment. Try it out for yourselves! Take a handful of soil, for instance, separate it, clean it, wash it and leave it out in the open for a while. You'll see that it will soon be teeming with life, with all those plants, worms, and other kinds of organisms that were brought forth. Because it is what rains from above that creates life, and the earth below what sustains and nourishes it. Just like a man and a woman, who require each other to create life, who need each other to become alive. You have stated that God was invisible, Master Leonardo. Now I ask you what is more visible in the entire universe than God? Our aim is nothing but to free this Essence, to release this energy that is constantly raining down, from the matter in which it is imprisoned. And once man has captured this Essence, once the alchemist succeeded in taking the Vessel of Hermes into his hands; he can then fill this Holy Grail with whatever he wants. Whether with gold or better with life...

It is Moses' Ark of the Covenant, Jesus' Holy Grail, Hermes' Vessel, Philosopher's Stone! And as a matter of fact, all the knowledge required to create the stone is already written in the scripture. Recall the burning bush that was not consumed. Think about the Ark, all the furnishings of the Temple, the Crown of Thorns and Jesus' Cross, and remember what they've all been made of... And reflect on, Master Leonardo, reflect on what the sacred geometry of the Tabernacle, the Temple, and the Ark might represent....

Great men may decline, mighty may fall, but an honest philosopher will maintain his station forever. A philosopher who has successfully created his stone can acquire riches, ward off illness and restore health, predict the future as well as see and know about things at great distances. Because it is the knowledge of creation he now possesses; with which he can condense God's light into matter and dissolve matter into light. The human body is innately endowed with the alchemist's most important apparatus, the furnace. It can easily separate the subtle from the gross. All that is required is to put the right food into this furnace because the soul needs nourishment just as much as the body does.

I hope you now have a better understanding of the gold the alchemists are after, the true meaning of Horus' eye, and the real worth of the treasure we inherited from Egypt.

"Do you not know, Asclepius, that Egypt is an image of heaven or, to be more precise, that everything governed and moved in heaven came down to Egypt and was transferred there? If truth were told, our land is the temple of the whole world. And yet, since it befits the wise to know all things in advance, of this you must not remain ignorant: a time will come when it will appear that the Egyptians paid respect to divinity with faithful mind and painstaking reverence - to no purpose. All their holy worship will be disappointed and perish without effect, for divinity will return from earth to heaven, and Egypt will be abandoned. The land that was the seat of reverence will be widowed by the powers and left destitute of their presence. When foreigners occupy the land and territory, not only will reverence fall *into neglect but, even harder, a prohibition under penalty prescribed by so-called law will be enacted against reverence, fidelity, and divine worship. Then this most holy land, seat of shrines and temples, will be filled completely with tombs and corpses. They will prefer shadows to light, and they will find death more expedient than life. No one will look up to heaven. The reverent will be thought mad, the irreverent wise; the lunatic will be thought brave, and the scoundrel will be taken for a decent person. Soul and all teachings about soul as I revealed them to you will be considered not simply laughable but even illusory."*[155]

William leaned back.

"All of his prophecies came true."

"The Coptic Christians who flocked to Alexandria from the monasteries dragged Hypatia naked through the streets, stoned her to death, ripped her body into pieces, and burned her in front of the Caesarium. The mystery of the occult, the legend of the giant worm *Shamir*[156], had filled the hearts of the Roman rulers of Alexandria with fear. They were saying that everything related to this knowledge had to be destroyed so that it wouldn't fall into the hands of their enemy and bring about the end of the empire. But, in reality, they had simply failed to understand what alchemy was all about, just as they had failed to understand Jesus, and become terrified. In the same way that people had throughout history been scared of God, they had been terrified of science."

After taking a moment to assemble himself, Cervantes went on.

"All manuscripts containing the alchemy of gold and silver were hurled into the fires; all the temples were razed to the ground. Following the destruction of the Library of Alexandria and that brilliant mathematician Hypatia's brutal murder, Europe plunged into its Dark Ages."

---

[155] Hermetica
[156] The legendary giant worm that could cut stones.

Now, I shall put an end to my words. I sincerely hope that I was able to provide you with some answers to your questions and that I brightened your mind a little. My only request is that you burn this letter and destroy it so that this knowledge does not fall into the hands of the wicked. If someone who is not pure in heart were to obtain this knowledge, he can take away the birthrights of all the princes of Christianity, overthrowing them all from their thrones. Because the beast we call man has such a large stomach that he swallows the entire world, yet never suffers from indigestion. Finally, I hope that the remedy that I gave to you in Pavia had helped to alleviate the pain in your hands, and with that, I conclude my letter.

Leonardo remembered the dark ruby crystals Agrippa had given him in Pavia, wrapped in a white handkerchief. He had mentioned that it would be helpful in alleviating his pains. When Leonardo returned home, however, he had put them in his drawer, and then, totally forgotten about them. Perhaps it would be better if he listened to the young scholar's words because his aches had recently become really intolerable.

He rose from his seat and poured himself a glass of wine. He took the crystals from his drawer and crushed them inside the handkerchief before dissolving the saffron-colored powder in his wine. He, then, turned to face Santa Maria delle Grazie and made a toast.

"And this is my last supper, Jesus... My last supper in Milan..."

He took a long sip of his wine and collapsed to his spot a few minutes later.

William was terrified.

"Oh God, I pray that nothing had happened to him!"

Cervantes reclined in his chair.

"Something did indeed happen to Leonardo, Signor Shakespeare; something very significant in Leonardo's life... But he did not mention anyone anything about it. When he came to himself, he told only one thing to Francesco and Salai who had spent the entire night trying to wake him up."

"Get up, we're going to Rome."

Salai was baffled.

"Rome? But, Leonardo, we were going to Florence!"

"Master! You'll call me Master!"

"Rome? But they were going to Florence!"

Cervantes let out a chuckle.

"Whatever had happened that night, Leonardo had suddenly changed his mind. At the time, his only concern was that the cardinal did not get his hands on the Ark before Leonardo solved its mystery and communicated with the pope."

William was surprised.

"Haven't you previously stated that the Ark was merely a metaphor?"

"I haven't, Signor. That's what Agrippa had said. Yet the young scholar was unaware of the fact that there was an Ark somewhere in the Mediterranean that was being passed from one hand to another. Fortunately, Leonardo had nothing to be concerned about at the time, because when Andrea found Felipa, he had forgotten why he had attacked La Goulette in the first place."

Ligurian Alps, Italy

The victory achieved by the Genoese in Tunisia was greeted with great enthusiasm throughout Italy. Andrea rose through the ranks and become the Admiral of the Genoese Navy. The nobles praised him and applauded him, stating that he had crushed the snake's head in its own nest. People living along Europe's coastline would finally breathe a sigh of relief.

The news had reached Spain's shores as well, but Spain had once more gotten in trouble with France. When the French seized control of Northern Italy and began marching toward Ravenna, just as Andrea was about to set sail, Pope Julius II had been compelled to seek assistance from Spain, and the armies had clashed around mid-April. Although the untimely death of their brilliant general Gaston de Foix had been a huge blow to the French, they had quickly recovered and successfully repelled the Spanish and papal armies. Pedro Navarro, on the other hand, who was the Head of the Spanish Infantry Troops, had suffered a great misfortune during this battle. Having been captured by the French, he was now waiting to be rescued in the dungeons of Loches.

"So, Pedro Navarro, too, ended up in Loches."
"In March 1512, the news of a strange infant's birth in Ravenna had provided Pope Julius II with the justification he needed to drag the King of Spain into a battle with France. The child was said to have been born with a horn on top of his head, and the wings of a bat in the place of his arms. On his

chest, the letters YXV were written; and as if having an eye on his right knee
was not horrifying enough, his left foot was looking like an eagle's claw. The
birth of the Monster of Ravenna prompted numerous prophecies throughout Italy. It was an omen sent by the Divine. The horn was meant to indicate
pride; the wings, mental frivolity, and inconstancy; the raptor's foot, rapa-
ciousness, usury, and every sort of avarice; and the eye on the knee, a mental orientation that was solely focused on earthly things. So, it meant, Italy
would be shattered into pieces by someone arrogant, mentally frivolous,
and inconsistent, rapacious, and solely oriented towards earthly power.
Who else could it be but the French King? Pope Julius II had not had a difficult time persuading Fernando. Despite the cardinal's repeated warnings
not to lose sight of North Africa, Fernando had turned his attention in the
final years of his life to the Italian territory occupied by the French at the
pope's request. And when the combined forces of Spain and Papacy were
defeated by the French armies led by Gaston de Foix, the Duke of Nemours,
the prophecy had been fulfilled. Ramón de Cardona, who had been appointed Commander of the Spanish Infantry Troops instead of Pedro Navarro simply because he was of noble blood, had fled the battlefield before
the first French attack. Pedro Navarro, on the other hand, had withstood the
French until the very end, attempting to seize control of the French artillery
despite knowing that he had no chance against the outmanned enemy
forces. He had failed. He had been captured and had waited in Loches for
three long years for Fernando to pay the ransom money demanded by the
French King. In a nutshell, it had been Pedro Navarro who had to walk the
plank and be fed to the sharks when Fernando refused to pay his ransom on
the grounds that he demonstrated military incompetence at Ravenna. In the
end, he would decide to play his cards right and inform the French King
about the Ark. And once he was released and entered the service of King
François I as Commander of the French troops, he would rush to Andrea."

"He must have learned about the victory Andrea had achieved in Tunisia."

"Andrea, however, didn't have any good news to deliver to Pedro Navarro
about the Ark. He had completely demolished La Goulette, leaving no stone
unturned at the port. His soldiers had broken into every house and every
shop, yet no one seemed to have any knowledge of an Ark rumored to contain stones of death. Andrea had even sent troops to the white city, but Mulay Muhammad had ordered the city gates to be shut as soon as he heard
about the assault. The forces Andrea had at his disposal were insufficient to

lay siege to Tunisia. Aside from that, if the Ark in question was, as claimed, an ark that bestowed victory on whoever possessed it, it was highly unlikely for it to be in the hands of the Barbarossas. After all, the Barbarossas had been defeated. Andrea had gotten what he wanted, and he had no further business in Tunisia. All he wanted to do at the time was lean against the fences and watch Felipa and Viento walk down the valley."

Autumn had arrived and the winds in the Ligurian Alps had begun to blow as if to tear the tired leaves that were clinging to life with their last bit of strength from the branches of the trees. It was possibly northern Italy's most beautiful season. Felipa's long dark hair was mingling with Viento's jet-black mane. She had tucked her hands into the sleeves of her cardigan and was taking weary steps alongside Viento. It appeared as if she was leaning against him, as though she was going to collapse on the ground if it were not for Viento. Andrea was concerned about seeing the woman he loved in such a state. Since the day he brought her to this farmhouse, Felipa had neither talked to him, nor had she eaten properly. Rosalie, Signor Roberto's wife, was possibly the first person to be able to communicate with Felipa. As for Signor Roberto, who had been working for Andrea for quite some time, he was not particularly a very social man, anyway. He would usually prefer to hide his gentle heart behind his frowning gaze.

With all those thoughts passing through his mind's sky, Andrea had been lost in the vision of the woman he loved as the day was about bid the valley farewell. He noticed Felipa came to a halt. She seemed to have stumbled a few steps. Was she all right? She was not looking all right. Felipa certainly was not looking all right! Holy Jesus, what was happening?

Andrea jumped over the fence and began running toward Felipa. "Felipa! Felipa!"

Felipa could hardly turn her head to look at Andrea. Shortly after that, her knees gave out and she collapsed on the spot.

"It's not surprising at all, Signor Cervantes, considering all that she had been through in her life. To tell you the truth, I've had a nagging fear from the very beginning that her sufferings would soon be manifested as a sickness in her frail body."

Cervantes leaned back.

"Felipa was a strong woman, Signor Shakespeare. Above all, her unwavering faith in God had been giving her the resilience to persevere through the challenges of her life. She had not given up hope when she lost her family, not even when she was taken to Mulay Muhammad's harem. There was something in her heart that was feeding her rebellious, her warrior spirit. Something that never left her side, like her Viento. On the other hand, it was true that her being taken captive by Andrea and brought to this farmhouse against her will had weakened her hopes significantly."

William inquired with a sense of wonder:

"What was wrong with her?"

Cervantes smiled.

"Wrong with her? There was nothing wrong with her, Signor Shakespeare? She just needed a reason to keep holding onto life, a reason to keep fighting for; and God had given her that. Felipa was pregnant. She was carrying Khidr's child."

Andrea crept a glance over at Felipa through the opening of the door as Doctor Ernesto prepared to leave the room. Her skin was pale, and she had sat on the edge of the bed and was listening to Rosalie.

He turned to the doctor and asked in curiosity.

"What's wrong with her? What illness rendered her bedridden?"

Doctor Ernesto chuckled.

"Illness? What illness?" He rested his hand on the admiral's shoulder. "Your wife is not ill, Signor Doria; she is pregnant."

Andrea was dumbfounded. Was Felipa pregnant? But... but... How could Felipa possibly be pregnant? Andrea hadn't even touched Felipa! The truth struck him like a bolt of lightning. It was not his, it was Khidr's child!

"What happened, Signor Doria? It seems the news came as quite a shock to you. Congratulations. You are going to be a father, soon."

After giving Andrea a few pats on the shoulder, Doctor Ernesto walked out of the room. Andrea, on the other hand, was nailed to the spot.

"Wow... That's literally God's retaliation!"

"Andrea was not only angry but also perplexed about how he should respond. After a few days of not seeing anyone and pondering about it, he called Rosalie and Roberto to him."

"I'll say it only once. I want you both to listen to me carefully."

They stood there silently waiting to hear what Andrea had to say.

"No one, including the child, will ever learn the fact that I am not the real father. The child will be given a Christian name. Rosalie, you will take care of Felipa until the time of delivery. Roberto, she is no longer allowed to ride. Viento will be your responsibility. And go tell Felipa that if she raises any objections to any of these conditions, she will neither see her baby nor Viento again."

"The orders were clear and concise. And judging from Andrea's resolute tone as he said all this, it was obvious that there would be no further negotiation on the matter."

"But, Signor Cervantes, the child has already a father! A real one!"

"His real father was on his way to Djerba, without even knowing that he was going to be a father. His mind was focused on a single goal, and that was regaining his strength and setting the Mediterranean on fire until Felipa was found."

"How could it be it possible for him to do it when he was in such a desperate state, with no proper fleet, money, artillery, or even enough men? Where did he get all that motivation and strength?"

"From his love, Signor Shakespeare, from his love for Felipa..."

Khidr toiled day and night all through the winter. Sending a portion of the loot he had seized in his expeditions to Djerba just prior to the Genoese attack had proven to be the wisest thing he had ever done. Khidr had loaded all that gold, silver, precious stones, and silk fabrics onto one of his galiots and then entrusted it to Piri, who had arrived in Djerba as soon as he received Khidr's letter. Piri was going to take Aydin and Seydi Ali along with him and set sail to Constantinople to present the treasure to Sultan Selim. Then, he was going to sail back to Djerba bringing with him the sultan's blessings as well as whatever support the Empire could provide. Khidr was of course hoping that this support would come in the form of ships, arms, and men.

Having completed all his preparations, Sultan Selim was almost ready to embark on his eastern campaign. Piri, knowing that he had no time to waste, had acted swiftly and arrived at Constantinople before the imperial army began its march.

Saray-ı Cedîd-i Âmire[157], built on eastern Roman Acropolis in Sarayburnu upon the order of Sultan Mehmed the Conqueror following the conquest of Constantinople, had a magnificent view overlooking not only the Bosporus but also the Golden Horn and the Sea of Marmara. Its architectural layout had been designed by the sultan himself, while its construction had been carried out by the laborers, stonecutters, carpenters, and masons the sultan appointed for the job who were the best of their era. Instead of being built as a single structure, Sultan Mehmed II had desired for the palace to be comprised of a number of buildings and pavilions that would serve for diverse

---

[157] New Royal Palace, the former name of Topkapi Palace

purposes opening into a series of courtyards that were surrounded by colonnades. It was not only the imperial residence, but more like a city built on an area of 700,000 square meters surrounded by walls known as the Sûr-ı Sultânî. The sultan's harem, viziers, tutors, eunuchs, and even his executioners would live here. Decisions would be made, records kept, heads severed right in this palace. The imperial mint, the treasury, and all the archives were all within its borders. Saray-ı Cedîd-i Âmire was the Ottoman Empire's heart and brain; it was the epicenter of imperial power.

Piri had been captivated by the magnificence before his eyes as soon as he entered through Bab-ı Hümâyun[158]. As he rode his horse forward on the Procession Road through the lined-up trees, he looked at all those buildings, gardens, and Hagia Irene Church, which at the time was being used as the imperial arsenal. Such a beloved was Constantinople that all the civilizations that had ever lived in the region had fallen in love with her with ecstatic passion. It must have had fourteen levels, seven of which belonged to heaven that one would see when he looked up the skies, and seven of which belonged to hell he would encounter when he turned his gaze to the ground.

"Just like Jerusalem..." thought Piri... "Who knows to how many civilizations you became a graveyard, beautiful Constantinople..."

The sound of church bells that tolled until recently had been replaced by the sound of prayer calls, yet the Christians who had been living in the city for a long time were still allowed to fulfill the requirements of their faith. Except for their bells, the churches were left untouched. Allah had taken the place of God, and that was all. Piri felt confused. Perhaps it would have been better for him if he didn't reflect much on this issue. How could he dare to question, anyway? When his attention was drawn to the people running around, all those thoughts flew off the branches of his mind.

The first courtyard, known as the Court of the Janissaries, was where all the regiments leaving the palace lined up. It was being used as a waiting area for the troops, servants, and horses before the ceremonies and during ambassador receptions. It was the only section of the palace open to public where any unarmed person was allowed to enter without the need of the sultan's permission. Inside were the offices of the Birûn officials, who did not

[158] Imperial Gate, a monumental two-story gate leading into the first courtyard.

have to stay in the palace at nights, as well as workshops and guilds of artists and artisans, warehouses for wood and supplies, and service buildings such as Enderûn[159] Hospital, and a bakery, which supplied the palace with bread and bagels.

Piri inhaled the aroma of freshly baked bread wafting from the ovens as he walked through the colorful flowers adorning the gardens. When he arrived at Bâbüsselâm[160], that was reminiscent of European castle gates with its octagonal towers rising on each side; he was startled by the Kapudji Bashi's[161] voice:

"Hooo... Hooo... That's where you'll stand, agha!"

Piri pulled back on the reins, bringing his horse to a sudden halt. He had not understood what the matter was.

"If to pass through Bâbüsselâm is your intention, you first need to dismount and pay me attention. On horseback, Kapudji Bashi will not let it, even the Grand Vizier is not allowed to pass it."

Piri had kind of liked the rhyme that had just spilled from the man's lips, who was standing guard at the gate in his brocade fur coat with a shining silver staff he was holding in his hand. After jumping off his horse and taking the reins, he replied in a cheerful tone:

"I'll certainly dismount if that's what you want. I meant no discourtesy, just wished to see His Majesty."

It was not intentional. The rhymes that came from his mouth were entirely spontaneous.

Kapudji Bashi flashed a grin.

"Well, what can I say? You're not bad with words either. Though, you need to work more on it."

Piri smiled and asked:

"Now that I've gotten off my horse, will I be allowed to pass, Kapudji Bashi?"

---

[159] From Persian andarûn, "inside", the term used to designate the "Interior Service" of the Imperial Court, concerned with the private service of the Ottoman Sultans, as opposed to the state-administrative "Exterior Service" (Birûn)
[160] The Middle Gate, an impressive entrance led to the second courtyard where the administrative authorities resided.
[161] Head of the gatekeepers

Kapudji Bashi leaned on his silver staff and squinted his eyes.

"You say you want to see the sultan, but is he expecting you?"

Piri took out from his caftan the letter Grand Vizier Hersekli Ahmed Pasha wrote to him and handed it over to Kapudji Bashi.

"Here, the Grand Vizier's invitation."

After a quick glance at the letter, Kapudji Bashi appeared to be convinced.

"Well, then you're allowed to pass, Piri Reis."

When Piri entered the second courtyard, which was more crowded than the first, Hersekli Ahmed Pasha greeted him. Piri had been acquainted with the Grand Vizier ever since he served as the governor of Gallipoli. They always had sympathy and respect for one another. He was a man of the sea as well. Prior to his appointment as Grand Vizier for the third time on the sultan's orders, he had been serving as Kapudan Pasha of the Ottoman Navy.

"Welcome, Piri Reis. The sultan is waiting for you in the Audience Hall."

After saluting the Grand Vizier, Piri followed began following his footsteps. He was as nervous as he was excited. After the unexpected visit of Muhyiddin, Piri had thought that it was time for him to appear before the sultan. He, therefore, had penned a letter to Hersekli Ahmed Pasha, in which he informed the Pasha briefly about the subject on which he wished to speak with the sultan. As far as he understood from his reply, the sultan was interested in hearing what he had to say, but... "but", Piri had thought to himself. After all, Piri had sailed in the Mediterranean for years under the patronage of Prince Korkud, who had only recently been strangled at the orders of Sultan Selim. How was he going to be greeted by the sultan? Piri was about to find out.

As the doors of the Audience Hall were opened, Piri walked in with his head bowed low. After making his way up to the sultan, he showed his reverence by kissing the hem of his caftan; then, he took a few backward steps without moving his gaze from the ground.

"My Sultan..."

And here he was, Piri was in the presence of the Ottoman Sultan, Selim the Stern, who had a height that was just slightly over average, a mustache that he continually twisted, teeth that were as white as snow, and a round face that was reddish white in color.

Selim was sitting on his throne with one hand on the knee, looking at him with a stern expression on his face. Piri felt himself shiver with fear.

"Welcome, Piri Reis. I knew and respected your uncle. He served the Empire a great deal. He was a loyal sword."

Piri was somewhat relieved. The sultan continued to speak:

"You mentioned in your letter that there was an important issue you needed to talk to me about an Ark that you and your uncle had taken hold of in the Mediterranean. Tell me more about it."

After clearing his throat, Piri started from the very beginning and told Sultan Selim the entire story and the sultan listened to him carefully without interrupting. When Piri had done speaking, the sultan posed him a single question:

"Well, Piri Reis, where is this ark now?"

"In Gallipoli, My Sultan, at my home. In the castle of Kilitbahir that your grandfather Sultan Mehmed Khan had ordered it be built."

"Kilitbahir?" William was perplexed. "But, Signor Cervantes, haven't you said that they took the Ark to Sultan Bayezid?"

"I haven't, Signor Shakespeare. That's what Kemal Reis had said. Kemal Reis had entrusted the Ark to Piri so that he would deliver it to Sultan Bayezid; he, then, had set sail to assemble the levends who were going to join the Barbarossas. They had planned to meet at Djerba on their way back."

"It appears that Piri had not obeyed his uncle."

"Upon the inexplicable death of two of his levends who were in charge of the Ark as they were on their way to Constantinople, Piri had not wanted to take this mysterious artifact into the heart of the Empire. Instead, he had steered his ship towards Gallipoli, stowed the Ark in one of the rooms in the castle, and had not spoken anything to anyone about it since."

"I was curious as to why Sultan Bayezid did not do anything about the Ark all this time. It turns out that the sultan hadn't even known about the existence of such an Ark."

"Bayezid had died oblivion of its existence, but his son, Selim, now knew about it. He ordered that the Ark be brought to Constantinople right away, and he asked Piri to learn everything about not only the Ark but also the maps he got from Colón, which clearly had connection with the Ark. As Sultan Selim embarked on his campaign against the Safavids, Piri would set out on his quest to solve the mystery of the Ark. Just like Leonardo, who had, at that time, recently settled in Rome in pursuit of the same mystery."

Rome, Italy

Leonardo had never liked Rome. With its streets being jammed with merchants, moneylenders, prostitutes, and inexperienced young artists yearning for jobs, this city was too congested for him. Rome had once again drawn all the attention onto itself, fueled by the passions of Leo X, who had just recently been elected Pope. Everyone was there. The arrogant Michelangelo who was painting on the ceiling of Cappella Magna[162] depicting the scenes of Genesis; Raphael, who was decorating the pope's private library with frescoes; his dear friend Bramante who was working on the great courtyard that would connect Saint Peter's Basilica to Villa Belvedere; and all the other artists who had heard that the Florentine Prince Giovanni de Medici, known for his devotion to being the Patron of Arts, had been elected Pope. Fortunately, the rooms that the pope's brother Giuliano had reserved for him in Palazzo Belvedere would offer Leonardo some peace and quiet, keeping him away from the chaos of the city. At this age, Leonardo had no intention to enter into any kind of competition with anyone.

With all these thoughts that had accompanied him on his journey, Leonardo had finally arrived at Villa Belvedere. Giuliano, pleased to have the master in Rome, was waiting at the door to greet him.

"Welcome to Rome, Master!"
Leonardo smiled.
"Good to see you, Giuliano."
"Come! My men will show you to your rooms."

---

[162] Sistine Chapel

Salai and Francesco began carrying the items they had unloaded from the carriage with the assistance of Giuliano's men. Leonardo and Giuliano followed them, taking slow steps.

"Even if I had thought about it for forty years, I would never have guessed that you would choose to live in Rome after this age. Did you want to be close to God, Leonardo, as you were about to leave?"

Leonardo chucked at Giuliano's remark, who was in his early thirties at the time.

"Giuliano, let alone thinking, you're not even living in this world for forty years. But you are absolutely correct about being close to God! I can't deny that it was the Medicis who created me out of clay."

Giuliano let out a hearty laugh.

"You are underestimating yourself, Leonardo. Many paint beautifully, but you fascinate!"

"I no longer want to paint for others, Giuliano; I'm unable to do, anyway. These pinpricks in my hands..." He paused. His hands... his hands did not seem to be aching as they had been a few days before. Leonardo's brief pause went unnoticed by Giuliano.

"Well, you're over sixty, it would be unfair to expect the performance of thirty-year-old Raphael from yourself."

"Does Raphael continue with his work in the library?"

"At full throttle; he is Giovanni's[163] favorite now."

"I guess you're still not used to calling Giovanni Leo."

"After thirty years of calling him Giovanni..." He came to a sudden halt and raised his hand to warn Leonardo.

"But you better address him as Leo; because he is a bit prickly er, I mean sensitive on this subject. As a matter of fact, if you address him as Your Holiness or Holy Father, you will be his best friend."

They chuckled.

Leonardo noticed that Bramante was approaching them in a brisk manner. They had not seen each other since the day Bramante paid him a visit in Milan. He had spread his arms wide and was getting ready to give his friend a warm embrace.

---

[163] Giovanni di Lorenzo de' Medici, Papa Leo X

They hugged each other.

"How are you Donnino?"

Bramante grabbed Leonardo by the arm and dragged him over to the window.

"Cortile del Belvedere! A single enclosed space filled with flowers of all hues that will connect the Villa to Saint Peter's in a series of six narrow terraces, that will regularize the slope, and be traversed by a monumental central stair leading to the wide middle terrace..."

Leonardo smiled. He was happy to see his old friend still full of life though he was almost seventy.

"What about the restoration of Saint Peter's?"

"Well, there are a few issues, but we'll certainly figure out a way!"

Saint Peter's Basilica, which had been designed inspired by the Temple of Solomon and built under the reign of Emperor Constantine I was the holiest home of Christianity. Its extremely high wall constructed over a continuous series of openings that had neither been strengthened by curves nor supported by buttresses had already been displaced more than six feet since the day it was built by the continual force of the wind. Italian architect Leon Battista Alberti had improved the apse and partially added a multi-story benediction loggia to the atrium facade; but the structure was in such disrepair due to weather, age, and neglect that no one was sure whether it would stand until the construction of the new basilica was complete.

"The House of God..." said Leonardo, "on the verge of collapse by the slightest breeze..."

Bramante added a mischievous seriousness to his smile.

"I said we'll figure it out!"

Leonardo confirmed his friend by putting his hand on his shoulder.

"Of course, you will, Donnino. If you can't figure it out, then who will?"

Bramante recalled the conversation about the Temple of Solomon they had in Milan. He couldn't help but ask:

"Did you talk to Agrippa?"

Leonardo's countenance turned serious. Giuliano's curiosity, on the other hand, was piqued.

"Yes, yes, I did. I'll tell you about it sometime."

"Definitely! But now, I shall leave. If there's no one there to supervise, everyone starts messing up the job."

Leonardo smiled and said goodbye to his friend with a slight head nod. After Bramante left, Giuliano turned to Leonardo and asked:

"You met with Agrippa?"

"Yes, there were a few questions that were bothering me."

"I asked Giovanni to have his excommunication revoked."

"I don't think Agrippa would care all that much about that, Giuliano."

"Did you find answers?"

"To what?"

"To the questions that were bothering you."

They had arrived at the door of the room reserved for Leonardo. Giuliano was standing there staring at Leonardo hoping to get a reply.

"I came to Rome to find answers to the new questions that Agrippa planted in my mind, Giuliano, and to spend some time in the library working if possible."

Giovanni de Medici was the second son of Lorenzo the Magnificent. He had been raised in Florence, possibly the first place in Europe where the Renaissance began to bloom, and been tutored by Marsilio Ficino and Pico della Mirandola. After being elected Pope and having the name Leo X, the first thing he did had been to transport all the Medici family's books and manuscripts that had been left to rot in San Marco Monastery to his private library in the Vatican. This library was the primary motivation for Leonardo's hasty trip to Rome after reading Agrippa's letter. He was going to try to solve the mystery of light as well as continue his studies in human anatomy at *Ospetale di Santo Spirito*[164]. And after compiling all the information he had gathered and assessing what was written in holy scripture in this context, he was going to appear before the pope and explain everything. And, of course, as the most educated Pope, the Vatican had ever seen, Leo X would do what was necessary.

---

[164] The oldest hospital in Europe, opened in 777

Cervantes reclined in his chair.

"But behold, man had been created as the recipient of God's blessings; egoism was his very nature. Even the most learned and seemingly virtuous ones would change in an instant as soon as they were endowed with power."

"What about his brother, Giuliano?"

"Giuliano was a well-educated and elegant Medici prince. His love of nature and his curiosity about its workings were at least as much as Leonardo's. He was identifying himself as a philosopher and not making an effort to hide from people his interest in geometry and alchemy."

"He must have been a good companion to Leonardo in Rome."

"Their friendship would soon become more cordial as a result of their common interests in philosophy and mathematics, and the patron-employee relationship would advance a step further. Giuliano would make every effort to provide Leonardo with everything he needed for his research, and Leonardo's workshop would be brimming with gadgets like magnifying glasses and distorting mirrors in no time. If all that existed outside was God's light, Leonardo needed to first solve the mystery of light."

"It appears that Leonardo had finally found the patron he'd been looking for his entire life."

"Giuliano was showing respect for his work and attending to his needs, but most importantly, he was not overburdening him. And at the time, it was all Leonardo needed; owing to the fact that he had a lot to learn before the Ark finally showed up." Cervantes folded his arms before finishing his sentence. "Luckily, there was no one who was looking for the Ark at the time..."

Ligurian Alps, Italy

Felipa's cries were reverberating off the cold stone walls. It had taken hours. She was in a great deal of pain. Every time Rosalie left the room to fetch some hot water from the kitchen, Andrea was searching for a flicker of hope in her eyes that would tell him everything was going to be okay; then, he was hearing Doctor Ernesto's voice.

"Come on, girl! Give it one more push! Push hard! Breathe Felipa, breath, do not pass out!"

Andrea was drenched in sweat as he stood at the door, hearing Felipa's cries and pleas. He didn't know how many times he had changed his shirt. Finally, he couldn't wait any longer and grabbed Rosalie by the arm as she was about to enter the room.

"Rosalie! What' going on? Why did it take so long?"
"It appears that the baby's cord has become entangled around the neck, Signor Doria."
Andrea had no idea what this meant.
"What does it mean?"
"It means, we might have to choose between the mother and the baby."

The door slammed in Andrea's face. Andrea was nailed on the spot. Roberto, sitting quietly by the window, slowly got to his feet, took Andrea by the arm, and led him to the stairs. Together they went down to the living room. After helping Andrea to sit down, Roberto took a small cross from his pocket and placed it in Andrea's hands.
"Pray, Admiral," he said; "There's nothing else you can do."

He then turned around and quietly left. While the last rays of sunlight poured through the drapes, casting long shadows on the Córdoba carpets on the floor, Andrea sat there in silence, looking at Jesus in his palms. Since he was not a man who was accustomed to leaving things up to chance or to prayer, he mumbled in a clumsy way.

"Would you accept my prayer? Would you not laugh at me if I asked you to spare these two lives after all the lives I'd taken?"
He leaned back. He was crying as he prayed.
"Please help me God. If this baby dies, I'll lose Felipa as well."

Soon, all the screams, wails, and pleas faded; and a sharp hush took their places. A few minutes later, Andrea heard footsteps coming down the stairs. He got up to his feet. It was Rosalie. In her arms, she was holding a baby wrapped in white linen.

"A boy..."
Andrea looked Rosalie in the eyes. He was curious as to how Felipa was.
"How about Felipa?"
"Exhausted... She is sleeping now."
He shut his eyes.
"Thank God!"
Rosalie handed the baby to Andrea.
"Would you like to have him in your arms, Signor Doria?"
Andrea eagerly reached out for him. but as soon as his eyes met the baby's, he took a step back.
"There's no need... You can give him to his mother when she wakes up."
He quickly turned around and exited the room. Rosalie turned her gaze to the baby and smiled.
"So that's how your father was looking."

There was both joy and sorrow in Cervantes's countenance.
"He looked so much like his father that whenever Felipa looked at her son, she was going to see Khidr."
William was curious.
"His name? What did they call the baby?"

"Peppino. But Felipa never called him Peppino. To Felipa, he was Hasan. Hasan meant good-looking, benefactor, doer of good... Hasan meant 'the one who was endowed with a kind of beauty beyond skin'... To Felipa, it meant love, serenity, and all the blessings of Allah that fell into her womb on that last night she spent with Khidr... As for Peppino, Felipa had no idea what Peppino meant."

Aruj had spent the entire winter with Khidr in Djerba and had finally recovered. Though he lacked his former joie de vivre, his temper tantrums that snatched him by the throat while in Tunisia, had become less frequent. He had initially been enraged at Khidr for losing La Goulette. Even though he knew Khidr would never leave his dear brother in such a situation, he had grumbled a lot about how he would not have been defeated if he had assisted Kurdoglu rather than trying to save him. Once his pains subsided and he finally made peace with his silver arm, Aruj had begun spending much of his days with his levends alongside his ships. They had been working day and night to prepare for the campaign that they planned to launch in the spring. Their target was clear. They were going to lay a second siege to Bejaia.

William was surprised.

"It is surprising to hear that they set sail in pursuit of bringing down the same walls, particularly after such a setback that not only cost Aruj an arm but also inflicted on his soul, significant harm. I'm curious as to what might have encouraged them. After all, they were unable to seize the castle the previous year with the troops and ammunition they had at their disposal. And over the period of time that passed until the Barbarossas regained their strength, the Spaniards must have strengthened the fortifications."

"After losing Bejaia, Abderrahmane had first negotiated a *modus vivendi* with the Spaniards which would soon be embodied in a treaty. The Spaniards, who were only interested in the African coastal line, had not left Bejaia to Abderrahmane; however, they had recognized the authority of these two princes in the hinterland, allowing them to establish their base in exchange for a yearly tribute that would be paid to Spain. Mulay Muhammad, on the

other hand, after witnessing the Barbarossas' swift recovery, was resolved
not to leave the matter to chance this time. Before they formed a new alliance with the traitor Abu Bakr, he was going to secure the Hafsid dominance
in eastern Algeria. He introduced an entirely new character into the scene.
In a letter that he wrote to Ahmad ben al-Qadi, he proclaimed him to be the
caliph of the entire region extending from Djidjelli to the Sahara."

"Who is Ahmad ben al-Qadi?"

"Ahmad Ben al-Qadi was a literate and educated state administrator from
one of the Bejaia's well-established families who had long served the Hafsids
as judges and civil servants. As a reward for his services thus far, the Sultan
of Tunisia, Mulay Muhammad, had granted him estates between Bona[165]
and El-Qal'a and recently appointed him as the governor of Bona. Having
worked for the dynasty for a long time, Ben al-Qadi had amassed a considerable fortune. He was a well-respected member of the community. His
opinions were being valued, his requests granted, and his calls were never
left unanswered. In short, if Bejaia were to be reclaimed, he was far more
competent than Abu Bakr, when it came to persuading the surrounding
tribes and leading a jihad against the Spaniards. The only issue about him,
according to Mulay Muhammad, was that he was not of Hafsid blood. Yet, it
was not an issue that constituted great significance for the sultan. Instead
of relying on Abu Bakr, who had given in to his ambitions and betrayed to
his own blood, Mulay Muhammad would much rather put his faith in a non-
Hafsid in matters pertaining to the security of his lands in eastern Algeria."

Even though Khidr had some reservations about laying another siege to
Bejaia, he was fully aware that seizing this castle was the only way to liberate
Aruj's soul. Furthermore, the number of tribes that had responded to Ben
al-Qadi's call in Kabylia were significantly higher than those that had rallied
around Abu Bakr in their previous attempt. It was possible. They could indeed be successful in seizing Bejaia this time. By the time the summer arrived and Piri, Aydin and Seydi Ali had returned to Djerba with the gifts Sultan Selim had sent to Barbarossas, they had completed all their preparations.

---

[165] A seaport city in the northeastern corner of Algeria, close to the border with
Tunisia, Modern day Annaba.

"Good to see you again, Piri!"

Having seen Piri's flag on the horizon, Aruj and Khidr had come to the shore to greet him.

"It's good to see you, too, Aruj Reis, doing well and looking strong, standing right beside your levends leading them."

"I've been through tough times, Piri."

"You can't avoid a fall, my uncle used to say; what matters is that you get back up."

"Man's effort is his wings.[166] And my brother is back with us, thanks to his efforts."

"First, let's set sail; that's when you'll see my wings."

Piri smiled.

"Well, if you say it's time, I have some good news for you. I brought you Sultan Selim's blessings, and alongside it, two fully equipped war galleys armed with bronze cannons." He turned his gaze to the harbor and pointed out the galleys shimmering like gold on the surface of the sea. "One for you, the other for Khidr. The sultan commissioned them to be built in Tersâne-i Âmire expressly for your use."

Aruj and Khidr were both fascinated by their beauty.

"May Allah, the Almighty, grant our Sultan long life and bless his reign."

"He also sent you each a crest and a sword with diamonds on the hilt. But more importantly..."

Piri paused. He had a flashy grin on his face. Both had their eyes fixed on Piri, waiting to hear what he had to say. Piri took out a letter from his belt.

"A letter from Sultan Selim to the Sultan of Tunisia."

"A letter?"

"Yes, a letter. Sultan Selim requests Mulay Muhammad to meet all your needs in your campaigns. He advises the sultan of Tunisia to support you in any given situation."

Aruj was surprised.

"Sultan Selim is literally warning Mulay Muhammad."

"Yes, Aruj; he is forcing him to pick his side, to make a choice between Spain and the Empire."

---

[166] Rumi

"Mulay Muhammad had found himself caught in between the devil and the deep blue sea."

"He must have been frustrated by the situation."

"Greatly, Signor Shakespeare."

Cervantes took his miniature ships and positioned them in front of the Castle of Bejaia.

"The day had finally come, and a thousand and one hundred levends and serdengectis[167] had furled the sails of twelve galiots. However, when they arrived in Bejaia, they saw that the Spaniards had also not sat idle all this time. Following the Barbarossas' previous assault, they had built inner walls in addition to those that already existed and had them fortified with cannons that had high firepower. The castle was formidable, yet still not enough to dissuade Aruj. The siege was going to be laid."

A group of levends and serdengectis disembarked, taking with them some of the cannons. Aruj set his camp on a hill overlooking the city. He knew that this time, he should not rely too much on the Moors who had come to his aid. They were no more than undisciplined tribal warriors with no understanding of tactics or strategy who switched their allegiances between *amirs* based on shifting power dynamics. Nevertheless, Aruj required every man who was willing to draw his sword and participate in the assault. Therefore, he divided them into groups and delegated command to his trusted levends. They were going to open cannon fire from the ships, and as soon as they were able to open a breach in the walls, they were going to swarm into the castle.

"The cannons spat fire for days. As soon as breaches were opened in walls, the Spaniards were mending them. The levends were on the verge of losing all drive, and the increasing unrest among the Moors had started getting on Aruj's nerves."

---

[167] The ones who give their heads; a military term used in the Ottoman army used for the soldiers who commit suicide attacks on the battlefield.

"It appears like history was repeating itself, Signor."

"The primary cause of the unrest was undoubtedly the provocations of the Spaniards. They were seeking to incite the tribes by reminding them that the rainy season was approaching and that if they did not return to their fields and attend to their crops, they were going to starve throughout the winter. Aruj needed an alternative plan."

When Khidr entered the tent, he found his brother pacing up and down. His fury was bubbling up from his turban like a volcano about to erupt. Khidr was aware of how essential it was for Aruj to seize control of this castle, but he also had recognized that he was correct in having reservations.

"In the end, this castle will take you away from me. Why is it so important to you, I don't understand."

Aruj yelled with rage.

"This castle cost me an arm; if necessary, I'd give my head as well."

Khidr was missing the Aruj he was familiar with, the one who attacked the enemy with arrows of laughter before drawing his sword from the sheath. Bejaia had snuffed out Aruj's zest for life and turned him into an aggressive, a ruthless man. He recalled the day his brother was giving instructions to Ahmad Reis when they had finally opened a small breach in the walls. Khidr had been so stunned to overhear the words that spilled from his brother's lips that he had given up all hope that Aruj he knew was still alive somewhere inside that broad chest. When Ahmad Reis had asked what to do with those who begged for mercy, Aruj had replied: "Pretend you don't know their language!"

Aruj came to a sudden halt. He had made up his mind.

"Tomorrow! Bring the ships to the river's mouth. We'll bring all the cannons ashore!"

Khidr turned his back to leave the tent. Just when he was about to get out, he heard Aruj's roar and paused.

"Did you hear what I said?"

He replied without turning to his brother:

"I did, brother..."

"Respond, then!"

"As per your command brother..."

This castle had long since taken Aruj from him. Khidr was just reluctant to admit it.

"When they finally opened a large enough breach on the outer walls, the Turks and the Moors swarmed inside. Then, the plunder began..."

"Plunder? Before the castle fell?"

"Aruj was watching all that was going on with dismay. The Moors were breaking into every house located between the outer and inner walls, defying all his commands. The Christians, on the other hand, although having lost around five hundred men, now had the opportunity to retreat to the inner keep."

William was listening intently.

"The assault continued for twenty days. They were about to run out of gunpowder, and Mulay Muhammad had once again left them in the lurch by failing to provide the support they expected. When the sultan learned that the Barbarossas were in trouble, he had said, "Let them get their just deserts!"

"Again? But,instead of Abu Bakr, they had joined forces with Ahmad Ben al-Qadi this time, in whom the sultan had trusted to the extent that he had given him authority for governing his lands in eastern Algeria? Why didn't the sultan come to their aid?"

"Because Mulay Muhammad had lost trust in Ben al-Qadi as a result of the things he did behind Mulay Muhammad's back."

William was at a loss for words.

"Is there anyone in North Africa, Signor Cervantes, on whom one can truly rely? I mean, siblings, cousins, uncles, friends, fathers, sons... Everyone is engaging in shady dealings behind each others' backs. Everyone is after digging a pit for the other, then using the stones that are removed from that pit to build a stronghold for themselves. Righteousness, honesty, merit, and loyalty seem that they had not sprouted in these lands..."

A bitter smile hit the shores of Cervantes' face.

"Is there anyone in this century of ours, Signor Shakespeare, on whom one can truly rely? Do you know of any place where those virtues you mentioned had indeed flourished. If so, I'd love to travel there with you, and I'd be more than glad to meet those people."

William was unable to respond. The Spaniard's questions appeared to have weighed heavy on him. On the other side, he was now inquisitive as to what had happened that had caused Mulay Muhammad to lose trust in Ben al-Qadi.

"I have mentioned to you previously that Ahmad Ben al-Qadi was not of Hafsid blood. He had status. He was affluent. And he had managed to rally around him the majority of the Kabylia tribes. However, he was able to accomplish all this because he had the support of the dynasty. On the other hand, he was aware that the Hafsids were declining in power, and he had predicted that the dynasty might soon lose all its grip over eastern Algeria. He was an official at the service of the state. What would have become of the official if the state would cease to exist? He had already made his calculations at the time when the Hafsids lost Bejaia to the Spaniards, and devised a plan to secure a future for himself as well as for his son Abdallah. Abdallah was going to travel to Bejaia, make a deal with the Spaniards, and seize power. He was going to declare his loyalty, pay them tribute and do as they said, while Ben al-Qadi would make Mulay Muhammad believe that he sent Abdallah there to act as a go-between and negotiate with the Spaniards on behalf of Abderrahmane and El-Abbas."

Cervantes observed the disappointment looking through William's eyes.

"But, the Truth, Signor Shakespeare, the truth may be stretched thin, but it never breaks, and it always surfaces above lies, as oil floats on water.[168]"

"How did the sultan learn about Ben al-Qadi's betrayal?"

"Thanks to the positive relations Huseyn had been cultivating with the Spanish for quite some time."

William had a better understanding now. Ahmad Ben al-Qadi had desired to be the victor in all conditions. Like everyone in this world who does not keep an account with their conscience...

---

[168] Miguel de Cervantes Saavedra, Don Quixote

"The Spaniards were suffering from extreme temperatures. They were not only short on food and water, but they were also coping with infections, a lack of sleep, and fatigue. The Moors, on the other hand, had begun to withdraw. But Aruj persisted. He kept fighting with all his might until the Spanish galleons under the command of Machín de Rentería appeared on the horizon. Khidr needed to do everything he could to persuade Aruj to lift the siege and retreat."

Two brothers talked for hours inside the tent that night. The levends had witnessed the tension rise at times and listened to the sound of an eerie calm at others. By the next morning, Aruj gathered his men around him. Everyone was waiting to hear what he had to say. Everyone was tired; nobody had any pep left in their step.

"We're retreating!"

They all remained silent. This time it seemed that Khidr had been successful in persuading his brother. September had arrived, and the stormy season was just about to begin. Spending more time in Bejaia would be no different than attempting a suicide.

"We're retreating to Djidjelli. We'll spend the winter there."

"When they returned to their ships, however, they encountered a scene that none of them had expected seeing. The waters of the river had receded, and their ships were stranded ashore."

"All will fall into the hands of the Spaniards!"

"They could not have allowed this to happen. Aruj needed to do something to prevent it. So, he set fire to all his ships that were stranded on the shore, gave Khidr command of the others, and dispatched them to Tunisia. He then mounted his horse and retreated to Djidjelli, nearly a hundred kilometers to the east, with his levends."

"A second setback in front of Bejaia... Two brothers, one sailing to Tunisia, the other, withdrawing to Djidjelli... Demoralized, weakened, and divided..."

"Had the Christians banded together they may have been able to put an end to this nightmare in the Mediterranean. Had the pope taken his attention away from the feasts and hunting parties, and Spain and France stopped beating one another up..."

Bologna, Italy

Following the death of King Louis XII of France, King François I of France had succeeded to the throne and was now preparing to seek vengeance for the Battle of Ravenna. Milan was the northern gate of the Italian Peninsula the control of which the youthful French King had no intention of relinquishing. Britain, Spain, and the Holy Roman Empire had forged an alliance against France, while François I had shaken hands with the German *landsknechts* and the Venetians who were known for their being early to every party and late to every fight. Concerning the pope, his heart was on the side of the victor, yet it was, of course, impossible to know for certain who would emerge victorious before the end of the war. Since he was unable to enjoy his papacy to its fullest due to the never-ending conflicts between these Christian princes, he was frustrated. He first had taken a step towards the Spanish; but when the French emerged victorious in the Battle of Marignano he had made the decision to throw himself into the arms of François I. At the time being, he was getting ready to welcome to this 'Most Christian King' in Bologna.

"The pope was ready to set out for the meeting, which was planned to take place in Bologna. As the crowded cortege, which also included Leonardo and Raphael as a part of the papal entourage, made its way to Florence, Florentines, who had begun a frenetic work months ago upon hearing that the pope would be passing through their city, had nearly completed their preparations."

"François was known as the 'Patron of Arts'. By including Leonardo and Raphael in his entourage, Leo seems that he had wanted to show the French King who the patron was."

"He was not mistaken in his assertion, because Leo was just as passionate about the arts as François I. He was the pope of the Renaissance. Since the day he had assumed the throne, received his scepter and tiara, Rome had been teeming with artists. And even though he would just be passing through the city, the Florentines had wanted to give him a warm welcome. He made a triumphal entry into Florence and greeted with festivities reminiscent of Ancient Roman processions arranged to celebrate the return of the armies, saluted the people expressing him affection as he passed beneath the decorated arches, and finally arrived at Bologna where he would be given a chilly welcome. François, on the other hand, was rumored to have been impatient to meet the pope. There was nothing he wanted more than to fling himself at his holy feet; of course, except for Parma and Piacenza to be left to French rule, the French abbots to be henceforth elected by himself, and the priceless artifact that had just recently been discovered in Rome to be transported to his own palace."

The pope welcomed the king in the public consistory in the great hall on the second floor of the Palazzo Publico, where a so large crowd had assembled that there had aroused a considerable concern that the floor on which they were standing might suddenly collapse. Leo X had already been drenched in sweat due to his sheer weight, yet he still put a smile on his fatty face, spread open his arms, and did not hesitate to give François I a big embrace.

"My son!"
François adapted to his role right away.
"Our Most Reverend Father!"
"There are no words that can adequately express how pleased I am to have finally been able to meet with you to discuss matters pertaining to the peace and prosperity of the Christian world. Come on, we have a lot to talk!"

As the pope and the French king disappeared from sight, Pedro Navarro, who had traveled to Bologna as a part of the king's retinue, took a few steps and approached Leonardo who was impatiently waiting for the ceremony to end so that he could find himself a place to rest.

"I'm delighted I finally had the opportunity to meet you, Master Leonardo."

Leonardo squinted his eyes to have a better look at the man who had just addressed him by name.

Pedro Navarro introduced himself.

"Pedro Navarro, the Commander of the French Troops."

"Please to meet you, Signor Navarro. How can I be of any assistance to you?"

"Perhaps, it would be best if we found ourselves a quiet place to talk."

William flashed a grin.

"It's not hard to guess about what the Commander wanted to talk with Leonardo."

"Leonardo, however, had at the time, nothing to say to anyone about the Ark. His thoughts were like a yarn of ball messed by a cat. He had been spending his days in the library, among the manuscripts, but he still had not yet arrived at a conclusion. He was on the verge, he could sense it, but first, he had to be certain that what he understood was correct. And then, he had to find the proper words to convey it."

After four days of religious ceremonies and a series of private discussions in which even the secretaries were not allowed to attend, Pope Leo X and François I had negotiated on the matters that had been troubling Europe and had finally come to an agreement regarding the action needed to be taken against the Turkish threat in the Mediterranean. François could now set out on his journey home.

During his stay, the king had built a cordial friendship with Leonardo, whom he had heard a great deal about but had never met in person. He invited Leonardo to travel to France with him, assuring him that if he accepted his invitation, he would never have to strive for the rest of his life to earn a living. But there were still loose ends that Leonardo needed to tie up in Rome.

"I have to say, Master Leonardo, that I am quite impressed by your mechanical lion. It really was marvelous. I was particularly awestruck when it opened its chest and presented me our *fleur-de-lis*; I could not believe my eyes."

"I'm glad that it gave you delight, Your Majesty."

François could not help reminding Leonardo of his invitation.

"Master, I ask you once more, please accept my invitation and come with me to France."

Leonardo bowed respectfully before the king.

"As soon as I finish my work in Rome, Your Majesty. However, I'd like to take this opportunity to express my gratitude for your offer once more."

"Let us hope that you get your tasks finished as quickly as possible, then," said the king. He then walked away and joined his retinue.

Leonardo was so focused as he looked behind the king that he had not noticed Pedro Navarro approaching him. He got startled by his voice.

"I would like to remind you once again, Master Leonardo, that we are looking forward to hearing more about the conclusions you will hopefully arrive at soon."

Leonardo turned to face Pedro Navarro and looked him directly in the eye to make sure that the commander understood him well.

"In case you find the Ark, Signor Navarro..."

The commander flashed a grin.

"Shall I bring it to you, Master Leonardo?"

"Hide it, Commander! If possible, hide it in a place where nobody ever finds it."

Leonardo said goodbye to Pedro Navarro with a small nod of the head and then joined the papal entourage that was getting ready to leave for the journey back.

Ligurian Alps, Italy

Neither the savory food that the cooks had prepared for the evening nor the flickering light that emanated from the candles illuminating the table had been able to warm the chilly air and make the room a little cozier place to be in. As Andrea had requested, Felipa had prepared herself for the evening and taken her place at the table. With her black dress that showed off her neck and shoulders and her hair tied in a bun; she was looking like a rare precious gem. And the tiny pearl earrings adorning her ears was adding an extra touch of elegance to the overall impression she gave with her appearance.

Pedro Navarro, having a difficult time tearing his gaze away from the young woman, was mesmerized by Felipa's beauty.

"I understand better now Signora, why Signor Doria had set the Mediterranean alight, searching for you. Such beauty does not come along very often."

Felipa slightly lowered in response to Pedro Navarro's compliments, but not a single word flowed from her lips.

Andrea turned to Pedro Navarro:

"I see that you are now working for the King of France, Signor Navarro. Whereas I had thought that Spain was the only country to which you totally devoted yourself. You had given me the impression that you were a true patriot."

"Oh, come on, Signor Doria, haven't you told me before that we're cut from the same cloth? We are mercenaries. François made me an offer that I could not refuse, so I accepted it."

"I don't remember you agreeing with me on this before, though. Did your perspective changed in those three years you spent in Loches waiting for Fernando to pay your ransom?"

Silence crept into the room. Pedro Navarro had come to a halt as he reached for his wine glass. Andrea was clearly attempting to corner him again. This man would never change, he thought. He took a deep breath and tried to conceal the fact that he was disturbed by his host's remarks. He took the crystal glass and brought it to his thirsty lips. After taking a sip of that exquisite wine, made from the finest grapes grown in the best vineyards of the Po Valley and stored in the admiral's vaults for years, he put the glass back on the table and turned his gaze to Andrea.

"Had it not been for the military competence I displayed in the Battle of Ravenna, Signor Doria, not a single member of the Spanish forces would have returned home alive. Therefore, if you're looking for a scapegoat for Spain's defeat, you should know that the goat you're looking for is not at this table right now."

"I truly wonder, whether it was François who made you an offer, or it was you who proposed a deal to him, Signor Navarro."

"It can be said that we had shared interests."

"Alternatively, it can as well be said that Fernando is no longer willing to entrust you with his troops."

Pedro Navarro could feel the anger building up inside of him. Even though he was trying to maintain his cool since he did not want to get into an argument with the host in a house where he was a guest, he could not prevent his voice from reflecting his annoyance, nonetheless.

"What do you want to learn, Signor Doria? If you ask me directly instead of trying to put out feelers, I might be able to quench your thirst."

"You are curious as to whether I found the Ark, right, Commander? This is the real purpose of your visit, isn't it? You made a promise to François that you would find the Ark and hand it over to him, and he appointed you as the Commander of the French troops."

"I suppose you've heard that France is getting ready to launch a large-scale campaign."

"Yes, Signor Navarro, I heard."

"The French will set sail from Toulon and Marseille, and a massive combine fleet comprised of French, Spanish and papal forces will be assembled along the line between Corsica and the Balearic Islands."

"They will then go after the Barbarossas and recover the Ark. And that's why you are here this evening. To learn whether I've already retrieved the Ark when I attacked La Goulette."

After taking a sip from his wine to clear his mouth from the remnants of his last bite, Pedro Navarro turned to Andrea:

"No one wants to pump a dry well, as you may understand. Besides, if you haven't already; perhaps the Republic of Genoa would like to join us as well."

Felipa was as if she was frozen. So, the French would soon set sail with a massive fleet... and having only a single target... Khidr... Her lashes tried hard to contain the anxiety that had welled up in her reddened eyes.

Andrea raised a toast.

"Then, Signor Navarro, let's raise our glasses in the hope that Europe will soon be rid of these barbarians troubling the Mediterranean, and that the Barbarossas will finally be drown in these waters."

Felipa could not stand any longer. Her tears were no longer able to hang on to her lashes. She stood up and ran upstairs. Andrea had attained what he wanted. The last candle of hope still burning in Felipa's heart that Khidr would one day come for her had been put out that evening. As he took his eyes away from the vacancy Felipa had left behind and turned his attention to Pedro Navarro, he saw the commander waiting for him with his glass raised high.

"I raise my glass to France! To the Ark and the Stones of Death that would soon be in François' hands!"

"The resentment he felt towards Spain must have been so great that he hadn't even paid heed to Leonardo's warnings," said William.

"Having been betrayed by one's own country is the greatest blow one could possibly suffer, Signor Shakespeare. If those for the sake of whom you're willing to lay down your life abandon you when you need them the most, you would one day forget what you've been fighting for."

Cervantes lost his mood. He had recalled those five years he spent in captivity waiting to be ransomed. He took a deep breath to fend off his past resentments that once again swarmed about him like flies and haunted his mind before continuing his words.

"Andrea, on the other hand, had become concerned. The commander did not know whether Andrea had retrieved the Ark, but Andrea knew. Given that Fernando had only recently died, if someone like François possessed such power, the death contained in the Ark would most certainly spread across Italian territory first, resulting in an all-out invasion of the lands that make up Italy. Andrea needed to tread carefully and speak with Cardinal Jiménez, who had taken over as the regent of Castile following Fernando's death."

La Goulette, Tunisia

Khidr had spent the winter in La Goulette. According to what he had learned from his brother, the inhabitants of Djidjelli had been suffering food shortage. The town had been in the hands of the Genoese since Andrea took possession of the port three years ago and had only just been reclaimed by the Barbarossas prior to their second siege of Bejaia. Aruj had demanded from Khidr that he take the ships he deemed appropriate, embark on a hunt in the spring, and bring the booty to Djidjelli. He knew that he first had to relieve people's hunger and free them from the influence of a handful of defiant tribal chiefs, before declaring himself the sultan.

Khidr had finished all his preparations and expanded his fleet with some additional ships just as his brother had advised. The hunting season was just about to start, and he was planning to set sail soon. Before he departed, he paid a visit to Mother Firuze, offered her gifts, and received her blessings in return. He, then, went to see Kalfa and they had a heart-to-heart conversation. Everything about Tunisia were reminding him of his Felipa. As Khidr made his way through the winding streets of this white city, he had the feeling that Felipa was going to show up around every corner he turned.

Khidr met Kalfa near the Séjoumi Lake, where they always used to do. When he arrived, he had found her lost in thoughts as she watched the waterfowls bathe in the lake. She had one hand on her neck, holding her shawl covering her hair, and with the other, she was holding a handkerchief which she used to wipe the tears wetting her cheeks.

"She was taking much delight watching these birds as she waited for you."

With his gaze on the fowls, Khidr stood there in silence, listening to Kalfa. There was nothing he could possibly say to make her feel better.

"She'd always arrive early for she wanted to relish every moment you saved for her. 'Hurry up, Kalfa!' she'd often say, rushing me off my feet, 'We're getting late!'"

She couldn't help but rested her head on Khidr and started sobbing. Khidr was at a loss for words. He, too, was feeling beyond grief. He held Kalfa from her shoulders and looked her in the eyes.

"I'll find her, Kalfa, I promise you."

After wiping her tears, Kalfa took a few steps back and re-draped her shawl that had landed on her shoulders over her hair.

"I got upset at her, from time to time, for being such a rebel, for acting recklessly without regard for the consequences; yet she was a free spirit, and it was all those qualities that made her so special."

"Pray, Kalfa. Pray that she never loses her zest for life; because the flame of vengeance with which I'll set ablaze those who stole her from me will never die out. Pray that she never loses hope, Kalfa. Just as I will never stop seeking for her, pray that she hangs on till the day I will find her."

"You two are constantly in my thoughts and prayers. May Allah, the Almighty, bestow you strength. May the wings of the angels shield you from all harm as the light of My Lord illuminate your path. May destiny brings you back together again, Khidr."

Khidr's mind took flight with the waterfowls and flew to Djerba. He remembered the day they first met... He recalled Felipa's affection for him, Aruj's hearty laughs... Time had taken so much from him...

"You would sweep the stars without realizing it, have the sun in your lap, but do not see. A child gazes into your eyes but you turn your back, the chorus would play in your heart, but you would not hear. What you've been living through is a profound love, but you fail to comprehend. And once it flies away, you cannot catch, even if you chase it..."

Cervantes took a breath of silence and reflected on William's words.

"Still, one should chase it, Signor Shakespeare. Even if it had long flown from the branches of his life, one should never give up on love. Because giving up on love is giving up on life; and contrary to what is thought to be, true love is a rare flower that does not blossom in every corner."

He stood up and walked over to the window. His gaze on the horizon, he started muttering to himself.

"Three, seven, eleven..."

William got curious.

"Fourteen, nineteen, twenty-one..."

William was perplexed as to what the old Spaniard was doing.

"Twenty-five, twenty-seven..."

He suddenly turned to face William.

"Twenty-eight!"

"Twenty-eight what?" asked William.

"Khidr was ready to set the Mediterranean on fire with twenty-eight ships at his disposal! He hadn't given up; he was never going to give up!"

"Twenty-eight ships? How could he have possibly found such many ships? It's a huge fleet!"

"Exactly, Signor. Khidr had sailed to La Goulette with three galiots and had purchased four more in the port; so, that sums up to seven. When the Turkish corsairs he met at the sailor's district expressed their wish to join him with seven galiots, his fleet grew to fourteen ships."

"What about the rest?"

"The rest had come as a great surprise for Khidr, as well. Kurdoglu had been summoned by Sultan Selim and assigned command of five galleys and nine galiots, six of which had twenty-four seats and three of which had eighteen."

"I had thought that Sultan Selim had turned his face towards east."

"After emerging triumphant from the Battle of Chaldiran that he fought against Shah Ismail, Sultan Selim had entered Tabriz with ceremonial processions. However, the fact that Mamluk Sultan Qansuh al-Ghawri's had supported the Safavids by providing his envoys a safe passage through Syria, and his refusal to congratulate the Ottoman Sultan after the battle, was something that Selim could not possibly turn a blind eye to. A feverish work had commenced in Tersâne-i Âmire. The sultan would advance by land and lead his janissaries, while competent sailors like Kurdoglu and Piri would provide the army with reinforcement from the seas. Judging by the reports of the envoy the knights had dispatched to the Vatican in the month of March, the armada that was at the time undergoing preparations was a huge armada."

"The news must have created a great deal of unrest across Europe."

"Its mission had been kept secret up until the very last moment, and the fact that Kurdoglu had set sail in the Mediterranean with a fleet of fourteen galiots at his command had struck fear into the hearts of Christians. But the first port Kurdoglu steered his fleet toward turned out to be La Goulette."

"It's been a long time since I've seen you in a good mood. I say, what if I were to steer the ships toward Saragossa without spending much time in the Strait of Messina, visit the castles of Agosta, Catania, and Messina one by one, while you salute the people of southern Sicily, and sail through the channel between the Island of Martyrs and the Cape of Trapani before arriving in Palermo? What if, we were to capture all the Genoese, Venetian, and Spanish ships we came across, turn into a storm, and wreak havoc on the infidel's shores and then return to Djidjelli with booty? What do you say, Khidr Reis?"

Khidr was delighted to see Kurdoglu. He first gave him a big embrace, then, a strong pat on the back.

"May our glory prevail!"

Cervantes reclined in his chair.

"When he had been given the command of such a powerful fleet, Kurdoglu had wanted to use this opportunity. If they set sail with Khidr in the Mediterranean until it was time for Kurdoglu to join the Ottoman navy and head to Alexandria, no one could possibly stand in front of them. They could seize every vessel they would come across, raid the coastlines, and pillage the towns. Who knows, perhaps in one of those towns Khidr would have found Felipa..."

Rome, Italy

Leonardo was working on *Saint John the Baptist* when there was a knock on his workshop's door.

"Come in!"

It was Salai.

"I thought you no longer want to paint."

One of his brushes tucked in the corner of his lips, Leonardo replied without taking his gaze away from John.

"I no longer want to paint for others."

Salai walked over to Leonardo's desk. His gaze fell on a few lively sketches drawn on a page of one of his notebooks lying open on the desk. Pillars of water rising up like serpents, ancient trees uprooted by the ferocious winds, fragments falling from the mountains that had been stripped naked by the torrents, fields submerged under the swollen waters, people that were swallowed by eddies... He picked up the notebook and started reading out loud:

"Ah! what dreadful screams were heard in the dark air rent by the fury of the thunder and the lightning it flashed forth which darted through the clouds bearing ruin and striking down all that withstood its course! Ah, you might see many stopping their ears with their hands in order to shut out the tremendous sounds made in the darkened air by the fury of the winds mingling with the rain, the thunders of heaven, and the fury of the thunderbolts! Others, not content to shut their eyes, laid their hands over them, one above the other to cover them more securely in order not to see the pitiless slaughter of the human race by the wrath of God. . . Ah, how many laments!"[169]

---

[169] From Leonardo da Vinci's notebooks

He turned to Leonardo:

"Is this about the Deluge?"

Leonardo confirmed with a nod.

"I see you can now read my mirror writing without a mirror."

"Do you know how long I've been your assistant?"

Leonardo raised his finger up.

"Master! You will call me Master!"

Salai turned his gaze to the drawings. His attention was drawn to a sketch of a seated old man, his chin resting on a staff he was leaning on.

"Is that you, MASTER?"

"He is Enoch!"

He returned the notebook to the desk and looked at all those mirrors and other gadgets that Leonardo used in his study of light.

"I'm beginning to think that you've become obsessed with this whole light thing. You act as if there's nothing else outside besides light."

"Because there isn't."

He took a few steps and approached Leonardo. He needed to say something to him but didn't know how to. He stood there for a while and tried to find the right words; then, he decided to be clear and concise and say it all at once.

"I do not want to travel with you to France."

Leonardo did not reply. He knew that this day would eventually come. Salai, now in his forties, was yearning to return to Milan and live there for the rest of his life. It was going to be the last time the two of them traveled together, and Salai would bid Leonardo farewell in Milan.

"Aren't you going to say something, Master?"

Leonardo did not look at Salai. He clearly didn't want him to notice the sadness that had settled on his eyes.

"I'll be fine with Francesco."

Silence crept in the room. They had spent a lifetime together, and now, separation was unable to find words to express itself. Like a pebble dropped into still water, a knock on the door disturbed the silence. It was Francesco.

"Leonardo, the pope wants to see you tomorrow morning. It seems those two empty-headed German mirror makers have accused you of sorcery."

When Leonardo let out a hearty laugh, the brush tucked in the corner of his lips fell to the ground. He bent down and picked it up; and after giving some final touches to John, he rose from his stool.

"I also want to see the pope."

After Francesco left, Salai turned to Leonardo.

"Why does he call you 'Leonardo'?"

At the time when the fingers of the golden sun began to touch Saint Peter's Square, located to the west of the River Tiber near the Hadrian's Mausoleum, there was no one else around other than the homeless who had spent the night sleeping on the damp stones under the starry blanket of the sky. Leonardo couldn't help but wonder how the garden of God could be so destitute when life in His house was so sumptuous. The table was so blessed that even the crumbs that would fall off it were enough to feed the birds. Of course, if there was someone willing to feed the birds...

His gaze was drawn to the ancient obelisk that stood on the central spina of the old Circus of Nero, which had once hosted many of the Emperor's violent games. To the silent witness of Peter's upside-down crucifixion... The four-sided, narrow-tapered monolithic obelisk made of reddish Aswan granite had been brought to Rome from Egypt by Caligula in 37 AD. With its 25.5-meter height, it resembled a giant needle, and the gilded ball atop was believed to contain the ashes of Julius Caesar.

When Leonardo arrived at the basilica, he climbed the stairs leading to the atrium, a large, enclosed courtyard in front of the main entrance encircled by colonnades. With one hand on his head, holding his hat, he was holding with the other his notebooks that he had tucked under his arm. When he came next to *Fontana della Pigna*, he paused for a moment and stared at the massive bronze pinecone, almost four meters high, with peacocks on its sides. He wondered whether the pope knew about what this former Roman fountain represented. He must certainly have known, he reasoned, in an attempt to refrain from thinking otherwise. After all, Leo had been tutored by Marsilio and Mirandola. He looked around as he made his way to the entrance. Even though he was in the Garden of Eden, his soul was somehow restless. The sun accompanied him as he entered the basilica by illuminating the five aisles with its golden rays. This eastward-facing edifice was as if it was enticing man so that he would turn his back to the apse at the west end and revere the sun god Ra rising from the east. With Bramante's untimely death, restoration had come to a halt. Leonardo wondered who would be the next architect that the pope would deem appropriate to complete the work. Whose task it was going to be to rebuild the House of God...

He walked through the marble columns retrieved from the previously de-molished pagan structures that were casting their shadows on the 250 feet long central nave. Leo, clad entirely in white with the exception of a scarlet cloak on his back, was reciting his morning prayer. Leonardo stood there in silence as he waited for the pope's demands from God to come to an end. It didn't take long, because Leo needed to attend the Cardinals Assembly, which he had ordered to be held right away. When he turned his back to Jesus to leave the basilica after concluding his prayers by drawing a cross on his chest, he noticed Leonardo waiting for him.

Leonardo took a few steps toward the pope.
"You wanted to see me, Your Holiness."
"Yes, but not at this hour. Come to Cappella Magna once the assembly is over."

The temperature of his already hefty body must have been even more elevated under this cloak, for he was continuously wiping the beads of sweat forming on his face.

"There was something I wanted to talk to you about as well."
"I told you later, Leonardo!"

When the pope walked away, Leonardo had no choice but to, once again, walk the same nave that he had just strode through. Had he come five minutes later, he would have run into the pope at the door.

When he stepped into the courtyard, he noticed someone else, standing by Fontana della Pigna, waiting for him.

"How are you, Master Leonardo?"

"The bells of the Vatican had started to toll. Leo had been able to escape from the clutches of Khidr at the very last moment, who had attacked Civitavecchia before turning his route to Channel of Piombino and landing on Giannutri and Elba to siege the fortress. And this misfortune had befallen the pope just when he was enjoying life at one of his favorite hunting parties. Khidr and Kurdoglu had set out with twenty-eight ships under their command, navigated their way to Liguria, and raided all the villages along the coastal line. And the eighteen Sicilian merchant galleons on their way to Genoa had paid dearly for their being in the wrong place at the wrong time. The corsairs had taken captive eight hundred locals from Apulia, and wreaked havoc in the Tyrrhenian Sea, completely disrupting the maritime trade in the vicinity of Civitavecchia."

"Khidr was looking for Felipa..." muttered William.

"Since the Fifth Council of the Lateran, which promulgated a decree prescribing war against the Turks, no steps had been taken to bring a definitive solution to the problem. Unable to unite behind a single holy cause, the Christian princes of Europe had failed to display their sharp fangs to those enemies of Christ, not accomplishing even one-tenth of what the Knights of Saint Jean had achieved as they carried out their operations from that tiny island of Rhodes. While Sultan Selim led his troops and march against the Mamluks, his pirates were sweeping across the Mediterranean, ravaging all its northern shores. Deprived of law, stability, and Christian brotherhood; Eastern Europe had literally been devastated. Churches had fallen into the hands of the adversary and Christians had been massacred and humiliated. What further catastrophes had to befall Christianity for its princes to set aside their enmities and band together against the Turks? Following Constantinople, did they want to lose Rome as well? Leo had written all this down, dispatched envoys all around Europe, and called for a Holy Alliance to be formed."

"After all, it was the duty of all the Christians to safeguard Rome."

"The pope had now turned to everyone for help in raising funds for the cause of Christianity. Because even though it had only been a few years since he took over the office; the Vatican had almost no money left, due to all of Leo's meaningless generosity, sumptuous feasts, and hunting parties."

"I have the impression that I've been followed, Signor Navarro."

Having been so excited about what he heard from Pedro Navarro, the King of France had been the first to respond to the pope's call. If this Ark which was claimed to contain the Stones of Death, was truly the legendary Ark of the Covenant that bestowed victories on God's Chosen People; then it would undoubtedly deliver victories on François as well. After all, hadn't God chosen François to be King of France? So, François too, was one of God's chosen people. However, since François had no idea to utilize its power, it was quite probable that the king would require the pope's help once he obtained the Ark.

"I've come at the king's behest to inform the pope that it would be an honor for us to serve him."

"It seems he kicked you out as well, just as he kicked me out."

Pedro Navarro laughed.

"Once the assembly is over, I'll see him at Cappella Magna. In the meantime, perhaps we could have a conversation with you."

Clearly, the commander was curious as to whether Leonardo was able to unravel the mystery of the Ark. Leonardo felt demoralized. He was unsure whether he should share with people the knowledge he obtained or keep all that he had learned to himself. Agrippa's words were reverberating in his mind, advising him once more by saying that this knowledge should not fall into the hands of the wicked. How could Leonardo possibly know whose soul was pure and whose was wicked? In fact, he was apprehensive of even the Church. The pope was employing his spiritual authority over the people to accomplish the worldly goals he had set for himself. He was no different than the secular European princes who did not think twice about letting their hands be soaked in blood. Even though he should have functioned as a spiritual leader, a teacher that would guide all Christians; with all those new posts he had made up and the indulgences he had sold to earn more cash; it appeared as though he had been trying to secure his Kingdom of Earth rather than the Kingdom of Heaven.

Leonardo took a deep breath and turned his gaze to Fontana della Pigna.

"Do you know what this pinecone represents, Signor Navarro?"

Pedro Navarro had not quite understood what Leonardo meant.

"Well... I must admit that my knowledge of the arts is not as extensive as my knowledge of military matters, Master Leonardo."

"Do you have faith, Signor Navarro?"

They were in the courtyard of Saint Peter's Basilica, the holiest of all Christian temples. The commander quickly made a cross on his chest.

"I believe in Jesus Christ with all my heart, all my being, Master Leonardo. My faith is as solid and unshakeable as a rock."

"Pedro..." muttered Leonardo, "Peter, Saint Peter...". He smiled.

"And I say also unto thee, That thou art Peter, and upon this rock I will build my church; and the gates of hell shall not prevail against it,"[170] said William.

Cervantes was smiling.

"Yes, Signor Shakespeare, it was a sign that had come from God, just when he had fallen into despair, uncertain as to whether or not he should speak up."

"So, Leonardo told Pedro Navarro everything he had learned about the Ark thus far."

"Leonardo poured knowledge as much as language allowed him to do so, and Pedro Navarro comprehended as much as the capacity of his grail."

The commander's gaze was on Fontana della Pigna, while his attention was on Leonardo.

"You, as Signor Navarro, are the reflection of God, Signor. You are his image in the mirror. And everything you see around you, including your own physical body, is the outward expression, a reflection of the deepest thoughts and beliefs you held; whether consciously or subconsciously. The Truth, on the other hand, is the mystery of the mirror. Is it possible to see the mirror, Signor Navarro? Or is it simply your image reflected from it that you will see when you look at it? Is there any reality to your image that is

---

[170] Matthew 16:18

independent of you? Does it have any existence in and of itself? Can you interfere and change it with your hands? You cannot, can you? There's only one thing you can do to change your reflection in the mirror, and that is to change yourself. Because if it is love that you harbor in your heart, then it will be love reflected back. However, if you are filled with hatred, then rage is what you'll get in the end."

"What about the Church? What about all those priests and bishops? Shouldn't they be aware of all this? Shouldn't they be telling us about the Truth and getting us ready for our rendezvous with God?"

"It has been unclear, in these lands, long since, where the Church ends, and the state begins. I can no longer say for certain that even the pope knows what his primary duty is. Particularly so, if we consider that Leo is currently looking to the Christian princes to assemble a combined military force that would serve him in securing his worldly dominion. Listen, Signor Navarro. Jesus was not a Christian. He was a rebellious Jew whose aspiration was in no way to create a brand-new religious tradition. He was upset, because the Truth, the core of this ancient teaching, was being covered up and transformed into something that was its polar opposite, into something incomprehensible. That's why he was angry with the Sanhedrin for slamming the Kingdom of Heaven's doors in people's faces; for he knew that it was everyone's birthright to attain Universal Consciousness, to realize that they were immortal beings, and to find the divine within."

"While God was waiting to be realized in man, they sought to hide God from its own reflection so as to serve their own interests."

"It was such an ancient teaching; it had been so firmly ingrained in history that it was literally a religion with no name. And the God of this religion, far from being a cruel despot who casts people into hellfire, was a loving, compassionate God. As a result, it reverberated within people's hearts like a sweet melody that had been playing for a very long time, playing since the times when there were no humans walking on the earth... It quickly spread and soon began captivating the hearts of an increasing number of people every day. When Emperor Theodosius realized that this would eventually cost him his authority, what other choice did he have other than to declare that he, too, was a Christian, issue the Edict of Thessalonica, and accept Christianity as the official religion of the Roman Empire? Which is fairer to say, Signor Navarro, did Rome become Christian or Christianity became Romanized in your opinion?"

As the love the commander had been harboring in his heart toward Jesus blossomed even further, the faith that he had in the church had been toppled down like the Tower of Babel.

"Jesus had given them so much that they had ample space to adapt the teaching into something that they themselves would benefit from."

"After all, it was inevitable for the people to bow down before those loving words that had spilled from a god-realized human being who was trying to help them comprehend that they were also immortal beings possessing the same divine potential within. Having seen the threat posed, Rome had to take the reins into its hands, laying a claim of ownership over the teaching as quickly as possible and elevating itself to a position of authority as the ultimate decision-maker with the power to dictate what the teaching meant. And the Emperor acted precisely as such! He ordered the temples to be destroyed, burned the majority of the corpus, labeled as pagan those who defended the aspects of the doctrine that he didn't find appropriate, eradicated all of its rituals from the annals of history, gathered all of the fruit, and pruned the tree in such a way that it would serve his own interests. During that last supper, when he referred to the bread as his flesh and the wine as his blood, Jesus was trying to explain to us what Moses had been trying to convey with the Ark of the Covenant." He squinted his eyes. "I suppose you must have already understood that neither the bread that they ate in the last supper was an ordinary bread nor that the wine they drank, was an ordinary wine. Now tell me, Commander; if a single grail is enough to lead man to his salvation, what other chance the Church had but breaking this holy grail to justify its own existence?"

Pedro Navarro rubbed his face.

"Do you think Leo knows what this pinecone represents?"

The tolling bells of Saint Peters informed them that the time had come for their meeting with the pope.

"Perhaps it's time to ask him in person, Signor Navarro."

When they entered *Cappella Magna*, Leonardo was welcomed by Michelangelo's scenes of Genesis. He felt his ears ringing. Those frescoes adorning the ceiling seemed to have come alive and were looking down at Leonardo from above. It was as if Leonardo was able to hear some strange whispers.

In the beginning, God created the heavens and the earth...

He rubbed his ears. The voices seemed to come from within rather than from without.

Now the earth was formless and empty...

Even though Leonardo had covered his ears, the sounds were still reverberating within his head.

Darkness was over the surface of the deep...

His vision had begun to darken. He reached out with difficulty and held onto Pedro Navarro's arm.

And the Spirit of God was hovering over the waters...

His heartbeat had quickened. Leonardo was having difficulty breathing.

And God said, "Let there be light"...

"And Leonardo's entire universe darkened."
William was petrified...

Djidjelli

Since it was a small harbor that was of little use to the Christians, Djidjelli had been nearly abandoned by the Genoese by the time the Barbarossas reclaimed its control. Even though it was true that the people who lived here had up until that day refused to comply living under the yoke of any sultan, Ben al-Qadi's reputation among the inhabitants was undeniable. Ben al-Qadi had taught Aruj everything he needed to know about the Moorish tribes, including their rituals and traditions which had made the majority of tribal leaders accept him as a member of their community. But "the majority" was not good enough for Aruj; "all" had to submit to him. As for Ibn al-Qadi, who had been hoping to put a harness on the Barbarossas to lead them as he pleased, he was now realizing that it was not a dream to be easily achieved. What he had failed to foresee, however, was the fact that Aruj had no intention of beginning a jihad against the Spaniards; rather, he was more dreaming about establishing a sultanate for himself.

Aruj's mental health had even more deteriorated after the second defeat they had suffered in front of Bejaia. His attitude towards Ben al-Qadi had become increasingly arrogant and aggressive; and his primary concern was, now, coercing the tribal leaders who refused to submit to his yoke voluntarily to bow down before him. And in the event that they resisted, Aruj would make certain that they no longer had a head above their shoulders to bow. Ben al-Qadi was now having a hard time to explain to these tribes that had banded together yelling war cries, why they had not yet embarked on an expedition against the Spaniards. An army mustered for jihad could not have been left standing idle for long. If a third assault on Bejaia was ruled out at the time; it was imperative that he needed to find a way to convince the

Barbarossas to launch a new campaign somewhere else. He dispatched spies to Algiers.

Khidr was not pleased with what he saw when he arrived in Djidjelli with a longing in his heart and galiots full of booty. The head of one of the tribal leaders who had refused to submit to Aruj was hanging from the castle walls. His brother, on the other hand, was now the Sultan of Djidjelli. After swiftly mounting the stairs and entering the hall, he found Aruj with two Moorish women in his arms.

"Brother?"

When Aruj raised his head after removing his lips from the breasts of the half-naked women and saw Khidr standing at the door, his initial response was one of surprise, followed by joy. Pushing the women aside with his hand, he rose to his feet; yet he was unable to stood tall and swayed. Was he drunk?

"Heyyy! Look who's here! My younger brother has come! If it had been someone else who had entered the room without knocking, I would have severed his head and hung it from the walls. But, of course, I have nothing to say to you."

Yes, Aruj was drunk, he was reeking of booze. Khidr turned his gaze to the women and ordered them to leave with a slight head move. As the women tidied up themselves and left, he stared at Aruj.

"I suppose severing heads off and dangling them from the castle walls is the latest trend, My Sultan. Is the owner of the head I saw hanging outside doomed to such a fate for he dared to do the same?"

Aruj had become enraged at Khidr's snide remarks. He made an attempt to approach him, but lost his balance, tripped, and fell into the arms of his younger brother. Khidr carried Aruj to the couch and took a deep sigh.

"If only you knew how much it grieves me to see you like this."

"See me like what? I am the Sultan of Djidjelli now, don't you see!"

"Sultan of Djidjelli? You look more like one of those tribal leaders, yet you are worse, for you don't even have a tribe of your own."

Aruj made an attempt to sit up straight.

"What do you mean, I don't have a tribe? All are under my command! All those tribes, all those men, warriors; they are all mine now! So, you'd better be careful with your words!"

"Take a thousand of these rotten hearts and they would not equal a single levend, a single Turk! They pretend to be on your side today; but tomorrow, they would not hesitate to stab you in the back if given the chance."

Khidr, gotten enraged, was unable to control his voice. Aruj did not reply.

"Anyway, brother. I'll go to the port and tell the men to unload the wheat we seized for your tribe. If you happen to be sober tomorrow, we'll sit down and talk."

He turned around and left.

"How closely linked the evolution of man is to the occurrences that take place in his life, to the conditions he finds himself in, the settings into which he's been dragged into mostly contrary to his will... To those whom he met on his path of life, those whom he loved... To his fears, predicaments, hopes, wishes, victories, setbacks, disappointments... In a life where change is the only constant, how futile it is to fight against it."

"Perhaps it's just the way that the nature works, and that in order for us to evolve into our own reality in the end, we have to go through all those stages of life."

Cervantes smiled.

"Like the Lipizzaner horses?"

"Precisely like the Lipizzaner horses, that are born with black coats, but die snow white..."

Cervantes' smile slowly faded, and the haze of sorrow settled in his eyes.

"Man, on the contrary..." he muttered. "...is born as white as a cloud but dies as black as a coal."

He closed his eyes.

"I think of all the sins I've committed thus far, Signor Shakespeare... I think of all the sins Aruj had committed... The sins of those kings, cardinals, commanders... of all the people... If I were God, I wouldn't forgive any of us."

William muttered from the Bible.

"Then said Jesus, Father, forgive them; for they know not what they do. And they parted his raiment, and cast lots."[171]

---

[171] Luke 23:34

While Khidr's presence in Djidjelli had assisted Aruj in regaining his poise, the grain he had brought with him had consolidated their authority in the region by obtaining them the recognition of both the town's inhabitants and the Kabylia tribes living nearby. But this modest port was not enough qualified to serve Aruj's future ambitions. And the fact that his brother had compared him to a tribal leader had hurt Aruj's pride. On the other hand, he knew that Khidr was right. What he needed was a real success story. Something lot more significant than hunting down a few Christian ships in the Mediterranean. A victory that would make his crimson beard leave its mark in history... A story just like the one that had recently been written by Selim the Stern at the Battle of Chaldiran when he crushed Shah Ismael's army and made a triumphal entry into Tabriz...

As he was contemplating his next steps, gazing at the Mediterranean, he was startled by Aydin's entry into the room.

"Baba Aruj, there are several men outside who claim to have been sent here by Sheikh Salim al-Tumi to meet you."

"Salim al-Tumi? The ruler Algiers? Invite them in, Aydin. Let's hear what they have to say."

Shortly after the three Algerians were welcomed in, Aruj called out to Aydin as he was about to leave.

"Aydin, stay with us. Khidr is out on the seas; you are a brother to me too. Let's together hear what these aghas have to say."

"As you requested, Baba Aruj!"

While Aydin took his seat next to Aruj, the others sat on the cushions laid on the floor. Aruj turned his attention to the men and asked:

"Tell us, aghas; why did Salim al-Tumi send you here? What does he want from me?"

After moving his turban slightly to the rear, the one with the rounder face and small eyes started speaking.

"He seeks your help, Aruj Reis. He invites you to Algiers."

"Why does he seek my help?"

"To drive those Spaniards away from our shores, of course."

After throwing a brief glance at Aydin, Aruj turned his attention back to Salim al-Tumi's envoys.

"Wasn't it Salim al-Tumi who bowed before the infidel, when the Spaniards captured the ports neighboring Algiers and drove Abderrahmane and El-Abbas to retire back into the highlands? What has changed since then, so that Salim is now turning away from his patrons, seeking my assistance?"

"Peñón de Argel."

The one with a thinner face than the former stepped in.

"We had enough of having to live with the sword of Christians over our necks. They do not allow boats to freely enter or leave the port. The slave markets are deserted. Algerians haven't been able to drag booty ashore for years. Since there are no goods to sell, almost all commercial activity came to a halt."

"Locals are not permitted to enter the port. They swore on all the scriptures of Allah that they would not engage in piracy, yet they're still not allowed to build boats, nor they are given the permission to mend those they already had. Their frigates are rotting before their very eyes."

"With their powerful artillery battery aimed at the city, they hunt down the muezzins reciting daily prayers merely for amusement and without even leaving the castle. People have no strength left to endure; a revolt is imminent."

"The notables of Algiers assembled and told Salim al-Tumi that he must either take Peñón or bear the consequences. How can Salim even think about taking Peñón, while all that he has at his disposal is his Arab cavalry with light lances in their hands?"

They were talking one after another. Aruj listened to all that they had to say; then, spoke:

"Be our guests tonight. Eat, drink, rest. I'll think about all that you've just said, talk to my levends and let you know my decision tomorrow."

They stood up, bowed their respects to Aruj and left the room. Once they left, Aruj turned to Aydin.

"Fernando is dead."

"I've heard. He lately had lost much of his popularity among the Castilians. They say only one nobleman had accompanied his corpse to Granada. It seems he had revised his will at the last moment and left the reign to Carlos, yet Carlos is only sixteen years old."

"The rules of Castile and Aragon stipulate that no prince can be entrusted with the kingdom before he reaches the age of twenty."

"There's a lot of political turmoil in Spain right now, Baba Aruj."

"Fernando's inheritance is a tricky one, Aydin. His marriage with Isabel may seem to have established a unified Spain, but in reality, Aragon is still Aragon and Castile is still Castile. Each still maintains its own institutions, laws, judiciaries and policies."

"Fierce debates are said to have been going on between those who backed Carlos' ascension to the throne and those who believed that he is too young for the crown to fit well on him. I've heard that the members of the nobility are claiming that his mother, Juana, is the legitimate successor to the kingdom, and that they would stage a rebellion if Carlos were to succeed to the throne."

"Juana la Loca?"

"Yes."

"Hah! It's going to be fun to watch."

He stood up, walked over to the window and set his gaze on the Mediterranean.

"What do you say, Aydin? Should we make the most of the rain clouds casting shadows on Spain?"

"Peñón is the most formidable of the Christian strongholds on the coast of the Maghreb, Baba Aruj. It is defended by two hundred soldiers equipped with powerful artillery on the largest of the four islets. With the number of men and munitions that we have at hand, it is not an easy task to lay siege to Peñón. Since its offshore we can't dig subterranean tunnels to blow up the walls with mines either. The only way into the castle is by opening a breach on the walls with heavy cannon fire. But I'm not sure how we're going to do that without getting within their firing range."

"I didn't ask why we can't do it, Aydin; I asked how we can do it."

"We need thirty thousand men as well as gunpowder that would last at least three months."

Aruj's expression turned sour. Aydin went on:

"I can equip sixteen galiots and dispatch them to Algiers with five hundred levends. It is likely that two thousand men join us from the Moors. There are a significant number of Andalusian immigrants in Algiers as well; and we may also find some more among the locals."

"Then, begin preparations, Aydin. We'll set out for Algiers."

"Baba Aruj, you know best, and we'll do as you say. But you know, Khidr is out at the sea..."

"Khidr may not be here, but I have you at my side, I have Seydi Ali, Salih..."

Aydin smiled.

"Well, then allow me to speak with the levends. Tomorrow morning, we'll give those three Algerians a positive response and send them back to Salim al-Tumi."

"You are free to go, Aydin."

Aydin stood up and made his way to the door. As he was just about to leave, he heard Aruj speaking.

"Aydin, inform those three Algerians that we'll first head to Oran."

Aydin was surprised yet remained silent. Aruj clearly had some sort of agenda.

"As you wish, Baba Aruj."

"There is a tide in the affairs of men, which taken at the flood, leads on to fortune. Omitted, all the voyage of their life is bound in shallows and in miseries."[172]

"Ben al-Qadi's spies had been successful in provoking the people of Algiers against the Spaniards in Peñón. Exasperated by the complaints, Salim al-Tumi had finally convened an assembly of scholars and elders. In some way or another they had to get rid of those Spaniards, or else a public revolt would very certainly dethrone Salim. However, Salim al-Tumi had neither men nor artillery. How could it be possible for him to even dream about seizing a stronghold like Peñón?"

---

[172] William Shakespeare, Julius Cesare

"Ben al-Qadi seems to have had found a channel to direct the troops he had mobilized for jihad."

"As a matter of fact, Ben al-Qadi was interested only in Bejaia, because he knew he would not have obtained the economic and political authority he desired over Kabylia otherwise. This was the primary reason for his moving his headquarters to Koukou and stoking the flames of jihad among the neighboring tribes. But when he was unable to convince Aruj to embark on a third expedition to Bejaia, he had decided to send his militia to Algiers before they lost their zeal, and drive the Spaniards out of Peñón. And also in this way, he could strike a serious blow to the Christians on the African shores and deprive Bejaia of support. Aruj, on the other hand, had other plans. Just as you said, Signor Shakespeare, he was thinking that the tide should be taken at the flood."

Cervantes rose from his seat, and after a brief look around, he picked a stone he found near the window and placed it off the coast of Algiers. He, then, took his miniature ships, positioned them around the stone, and turned his gaze to William.

"But Peñón was a formidable garrison, Signor Shakespeare; and Nicolás Quint was quite a capable commander."

"How are the preparations going on, Aydin?"

"Almost finished. We can haul up anchor and set sail within a couple of days if you give us the order."

Aruj was saddling up his horse and getting ready to depart.

"Mounted troops are ready as well. Eight hundred levends are waiting for you in the mountains to the west. As for the Moors, they are already on their way."

"The ships are entrusted to you, Aydin. I'll first stop by Cherchell."

Aydin was taken aback.

"Cherchell?"

"Yes, Aydin. I have things to settle with Kara Hasan."

Aydin had become concerned. He had not the slightest trust in Kara Hasan.

"Do you want me to ride along with you, Baba Aruj?"

"Didn't I just say that the ships were entrusted to you?"
"Yes, Baba Aruj, you said; okay, don't be concerned."

Aruj mounted on his horse, took the reins and circled around Aydin a few rounds.
"May the winds be with you, Aydin. We'll see each other in Algiers!"
"Good luck, Baba Aruj."

As Aruj disappeared in a cloud of dust rising from his horse's hooved, Aydin muttered to himself:
"May Allah keep you safe, Baba Aruj. I hope you know what you're doing."

"Who is Kara Hasan?" asked William.
"Kara Hasan was one of the Barbarossas' comrades with whom they had fought side by side up until not too long ago. However, particularly after the second unsuccessful siege on Bejaia, certain tribal leaders in Djidjelli, who were unwilling to submit to Aruj's authority, had begun to incite his men against him by taking advantage of his rapidly failing psychological condition, driving a rift between Aruj and his levends."
"Did they just draw their swords against their reis after battling side by side for so many years?"
"They did not draw their swords against him, but at the same time, they were no longer willing to draw their swords in his defense. When they were promised the amirship of minor towns, some of them were lured to accept the position. And Kara Hasan, who at the time had the loyalty of a few hundred men under his command, was one of those. He had been misled by the provocation, withdrawn to Cherchell with his followers and proclaimed himself to be the sultan of the region. And at that time, just like many fledgling rulers would do, he was getting along well with the Spaniards."
"So, they turned their backs to the man they called 'Baba', to whom they had been loyal for so long. And now, amid the deserts, blows a crimson-bearded wind of wrath..."
"Loyalty..." muttered Cervantes, "Though it may appear to be a quality that a man of dignity should already have, it is not a virtue that is commonly

seen among men. Consider the Muslims who abandoned their faith and converted to Christianity, or the Christians in North Africa who deserted their Savior... Consider those who joined the service of the French King, despite the fact that he had previously referred to himself as an ardent Spaniard..."

"Loyalty..." repeated William, in an attempt to create some room to ponder further on the concept. "Perhaps we should reconsider this very notion of loyalty in the light of the discussion that we just had about how profoundly man is changed as a result of the experiences he's been through in life. Pedro Navarro had waited for Fernando for a whole three years in the dungeons of Loches. Similarly, the levends... It is undeniable that Bejaia had costed Aruj much more than an arm, and that the defeat he suffered had awoken in him the sleeping dragon."

"A dragon that was about to turn North Africa into hell..."

"His changing demeanor toward his men, becoming haughtier and belligerent with each passing day; avarice and ruthlessness growing within his hardened heart... Don't you also think that the man to whom they had sworn their allegiance, who they had followed so far had long since passed away? Or Pedro Navarro's beloved Spain for which he was ready to lay down his life... Hadn't it been long since his country abandoned the commander?"

"The very heart of Aruj was a bloody battleground, Signor. At the moment, he was just striving to keep his head above water. As you would also know; the greatest war that man has to fight is the war that he would wage against himself."

"Every soul is fighting the very same war within the body it is trapped in. Aruj is not the only one cursed by an ego that casts shadows on him."

Cervantes muttered:

"The one who sows the wind will reap the storm..."

"Even though his essence is divine, man is at the same time is no less powerless than rest of the creatures. And in the same way as all the other living beings, his primary instinct is nothing but survival. We all have our valid reasons for the decisions we make. Consider yourself for a moment; for years, you shed blood to protect your country, to defend your faith. If even you yourself came to question in the end the primary motivation behind your decisions; if even you yourself are unsure whether all that you strived for was indeed for the sake of righteousness, and whether it is regret all that you are left with; who else can judge you but God?"

Cervantes muttered from the Bible:

"Judge not, and ye shall not be judged: condemn not, and ye shall not be condemned: forgive, and ye shall be forgiven..."[173]

Having seen Aruj approaching the castle with his eight hundred mounted troops, Kara Hasan called out to his men:

"He must have come to seek my assistance for Oran. Send out men to greet him properly!"

The men were perplexed.

"But, Reis, you promised the Spaniards..."

"Damn the Spaniards, now! Don't you see how many men he brought with him? We need to gain time and get him out of our territory as quickly as possible. I'll deal with him once the Spaniards arrive."

They were all frozen in place, trying to make sense of the situation. Kara Hasan became outraged.

"Come on, move! Didn't you hear what I said?"

"At your command, Reis!"

"Right away, Reis!"

They hastily left the room and sent men to welcome Aruj. Aruj, on the other hand, did not reveal his true colors; instead, he pretended as though he was really there to seek for help, took a couple of his trusted men along with him, and went to see Kara Hasan.

Kara Hasan greeted him with a phony smile glued to his face.

"The Sultan of Djidjelli! The fearless sword of the seas! Welcome to Cherchell!"

Aruj moved closer to Kara Hasan, and in less time than it takes a bird to flutter its wings, he drew his machete and placed it on Kara Hasan's throat.

"You're walking on eggshells, Kara Hasan. If you want your black head to remain attached to your body, tread lightly!"

---

[173] Luke 6:37

As the blood seeping from his throat soaked his shirt, beads of sweat had started to form on Kara Hasan's face. He wanted to say something, but his mouth was completely dried up. Aruj, on the other hand, having no intention of listening to him, knocked him down with a stroke of his silver arm. He then ordered his levends:

"Throw him into the dungeons; three hundred men will stay in the castle; the others will ride with me to Algiers!"

"Holy Jesus... Without the least hesitation, without a trembling of his hand, without even giving the man with whom he had fought back-to-back the opportunity to speak."

"That's something Aruj would do, not Barbarossa, Signor Shakespeare! Aruj was the sword of Damocles hanging over the necks of Christians, whereas Barbarossa, was hanging over the necks of anyone who would dare to challenge his authority."

Algiers

Upon his arrival in Algiers, Aruj was greeted by Salim al-Tumi, along with several other notables of the city. That night, at that big camp that had been set up at a distance of a crossbow shot away from the city walls, the candles were going to burn until dawn, and matters pertaining to Peñón would be discussed down to the smallest detail.

Salim al-Tumi was concerned.

"Do you believe the troops you brought for the siege will be sufficient, Aruj Reis?"

"You didn't expect me to commit all of my levends to this cause, did you, Sheikh Salim?"

"Well, not all of them, but I can't deny that I was also expecting to see Khidr and his men along with you."

"Khidr had to stay in Djidjelli; on such a slippery ground, I could not leave the ports I captured defenseless."

"I also heard that you left three hundred men in Cherchell"

Aruj got to his feet, clasped his hands behind and began walking in the tent.

"I have enough power to surround the fortress both from the sea and the land and pound it with heavy cannon fire for a long time. As soon as we open a breach in the walls, we are going to pour into the castle and take over the control together with your men."

Together with Salim's men? Was Aruj intending to drag his men into the battle as well? This could lead to a clash between Salim and the Spaniards. There would be no problem if Aruj succeeded in his endeavor; however, what if Aruj was unable to capture Peñón? In such a case, it would be Salim's turban which would be knocked down along with his head. Salim, on the other hand, had presumed that if the siege was unsuccessful, he could switch allegiances. He had planned to tell the Spaniards that he did not support Aruj and cruise through the situation easily. Salim had lost all his mood.

"What made you concerned, Sheikh Salim? Do you have any doubts about us seizing Peñón?"

"Of course, I don't, Aruj Reis. I have complete trust in you. I'm confident you'll triumph in a very short time."

"So, what's the reason behind the sour expression on your face?"

Salim drank a sip of the sorbet prepared from orange flower petals soaked in date syrup.

"It's because of the sorbet. It needs more sugar. It gave me a queasy feeling in my stomach."

"After Salim al-Tumi left the camp and returned to Algiers, Aruj composed a letter to Nicolás Quint offering a safe conduct to the garrison if he surrendered. He, then, handed it to two of his most trusted levends and told them to deliver it to the commander the next morning."

"If Nicolás Quint is a competent commander as you stated, his response must certainly have not been a positive one."

"Let alone giving a positive reply to Aruj, he had become tremendously enraged, Signor Shakespeare."

"He was spewing fire out of his mouth, Baba Aruj. I could hardly have escaped the flames. He was cursing and swearing, asking if you knew who he was and if you'd ever heard of his noble blood. He was yelling at us and saying that they were subjects of the mightiest monarch of Spain, and that they would not be intimidated by any of our threats, nor would they be enticed by any courtesies proffered."

"And what did you say in response to that?"

"I asked him, if the mightiest monarch of Spain whom he spoke of was the one whose corpse was said to have been accompanied by only one of the Castilian lords as it was being transported to Granada."

"Did he start spewing fire after that?"

Cemal paused for a little minute to reflect; then, he replied:

"No, Baba Aruj. He had already begun smoking sparky as soon as we got through the door. The fires swiftly grew out of control after that."

Aruj burst out laughing.

"You're a funny guy, Cemal!"

Cemal smiled as he looked at his reis.

"What are your orders, Baba Aruj?"

"Start the siege, Cemal. Let those cannons give his noble blood a good beating so that the commander, as well, gets an idea about who we are."

"As per your command, Baba Aruj!"

Cemal was just about to leave the tent to convey the orders to the levends, when he suddenly stopped and turned to Aruj.

"Baba Aruj..."

"What is it, Cemal?"

"It's so great to see you joyful again!"

Aruj replied with a playful smirk on his face.

"Go, Cemal, go! Get back to work!"

As Cemal walked away, Aruj's smile vanished. The crimson-colored flames of his beard quickly swept across his face, spiraled out of control, and engulfed his soul.

Cervantes' gaze was fixed on the stone he had positioned off the coast of Algiers.

"They pounded the castle walls for twenty days. All those firings of cannons, however, served no purpose other than to frighten the birds perched on the walls. Aruj's cannons were of small caliber, incapable of inflicting any damage on a stronghold as formidable as Peñón. He had even dispatched messengers to Djidjelli and asked Khidr to send reinforcements."

"It appeared that Salim al-Tumi's nightmares had become his reality."

"Salim was agitated to the limit. His anxiety levels were rising more and more with each passing day. He now had to find a way to get rid of this trouble that he had wrapped around his head like a turban."

It was one of those days when the levends had been desperately trying to open a breach in the walls, Salim al-Tumi had sent a note to Nicolás Quint telling him that he intended to pay him a secret visit on that Friday shortly before prayer time. They had already been exchanging letters for a while, and Salim had assigned the responsibility of delivering his letters to Peñón to an Algerian boy. To avoid attracting attention, it had seemed like a decent plan at first. But it hadn't taken long for Aruj's men to figure it out and buy the kid for a higher price than Selim had been paying. Salim's letters were leaving the city, but before they arrived at the castle, they were paying a brief visit to Aruj. In short, it had not been hard for Aruj to learn that Salim was going to take two of his men with him and go to see the commander on that Friday.

That Friday, Salim, sneaked out of the city while disguised under his cloak, accompanied by two of his guards. The guards were there to assure his safe entry into Peñón as well as his safe return to Casbah. After all, Selim's mistrust of Spaniards was on par with his mistrust of Turks.

"Always keep your hands on the hilts of your swords. Remember, these men are just as daunting as the Turks."

The guards gripped the hilts of their swords, remaining silent. When the gates were opened, they slipped into the castle.

Nicolás Quint was waiting for them in his room. As for his flames of fury fanned with the siege, they were now ready to spread across Salim's woodlands and destroy them all.

"You are the only one to blame for the assault, Sheikh Salim! If you hadn't resorted to Barbarossa for help, you wouldn't be standing in front of me right now, pleading for a way out of this mess!"

"I have nothing to do with any of this. It was not I who invited them to Algiers. Besides, you know, they are no less threatening to us than they are to you. Mulay Muhammad could hardly kick them out of La Goulette. If you want to know who's to blame for this, let me tell you; it is Ben al-Qadi. He sent out spies and inflamed the Algerians. When he saw that he couldn't subjugate that pirate, he decided to get rid of him by letting him loose on us. Let us join forces, and put an end to this pirate' presence in North Africa once and for all, Commander."

"Once you saw that they were going to fail, you decided to switch sides, didn't you, Salim? The number of lies you will resort to when you feel trapped is greater than the grains of sand on this beach. What were you hoping for, Salim? What else did you expect?"

Salim had nothing to say that could put out the commander's fires.

"Even the clay-tiled roofs of adobe houses would remain intact with that small caliber artillery that the barbarian is using against our walls. As for the men who appeared to follow Aruj's orders, you'll soon see that they all will abandon him. The wretches of the neighboring tribes carrying flimsy spears in their hands! What exactly were you expecting to get, Salim? Tell me!"

With his last words, Nicolás Quint had literally roared at the sheikh.

"They are backed up by Sultan Selim the Stern. I've heard that he gave Kurdoglu command of fourteen ships. Think about it, Commander; perhaps you keep your castle; but if they dethrone me and settle in Algiers, Spain will have to deal with the Ottomans rather than those wretches of the neighboring tribes in the near future."

Silence took over the reins. Commander Quint was pacing up and down his high-ceilinged room, trying to come up with a solution. Salim had brought up a crucial point. It was far easier to keep the tribes under control than to confront the Ottomans. He approached the window and gazed out at Aruj's anchored ships. He asked Salim without moving his gaze.

"What's your plan?"

Salim took a few steps and approached the commander. After focusing his sight on Aruj's fleet, he replied:

"We'll burn their fleet."

"Burn their fleet? How could Salim possibly burn Aruj's fleet at a time when the streets of Algiers were teeming with his levends? While he was even unable to fight against a handful of Spanish soldiers in Peñón, how was he going to prevent those people from razing down his city?"

"By laying an ambush, Signor. The Spaniards would set fire to Aruj's anchored galiots in the harbor. When the Turks ran to the port upon seeing their ships ablaze, Salim was going to shut the city gates against them, leaving Aruj and his men caught in the crossfire between the city and the castle."

"Sounds like a plan that might work."

"It might have. If Aruj hadn't known about this plot, Salim's plan might have worked out really well."

"How did he find out? As far as I know, there was no mention of a plot in Salim's letters to Commander Quint."

"Aruj had no idea what the sheikh was up to, but he was determined to find out. Therefore, he had murdered the two guards who were meant to accompany Salim to the castle that night and had assumed their roles."

William was confused.

"So, were those two men that Selim thought were his personal guards actually Aruj's men?"

"No, Signor Shakespeare. They were not his men; they were Aruj and Aydin themselves."

While Salim al-Tumi was making his way back to his palace, he was talking to himself.

"This plan should work! I might not have another chance."

His strides were short yet swift. The time for the Friday prayer had come and white flags had been raised atop the minarets to prevent any Spanish attack on the mosque. He was planning to do the ritual washing, go to the mosque, and pray to Allah so that He gives him the strength to cleanse his city of this Turkish plague. Friday was a holy day, so Allah would undoubtedly hear Salim's prayers and respond favorably. Salim had no doubts about it.

Aruj and Aydin, on the other hand, were right behind Salim. They proceeded by the flower gardens, passed through the cedar gates guarded by Salim's men, and followed the sheikh in silence until he arrived at the bath where he was going to perform his ablution. After Salim entered the bath, they looked at each other. Aydin could tell what Aruj was thinking by the expression on his face. They lingered at the entrance for a while and then followed Salim.

The hot steam of water inside the bath had made it difficult for Salim to foresee the impending calamity that was about to befall him. With a loin-cloth wrapped around his waist, he was rubbing his body with the scented oils contained in the crystal pitchers. Just as Aruj had planned, they were going to hunt the sheikh down when he least expected it.

When Aydin approached from behind and caught Salim by the arms, first he did not understood what was going on. Aruj, on the other hand, was twisting the turban that Salim had just taken off and set aside.

"What's happening? Aruj Reis? What are you doing?"
He first attempted to call out for help.
"Guaaaarddss! Guaaarrrdsss!"
After that, he began pleading.
"Please, don't hurt me, Aruj Reis, I made a mistake, please."
Aruj, holding Salim's twisted turban in his hands, faced the sheikh straight in the eye and asked:
"Aruj Reis? Who is Aruj Reis?"

His eyes were bloodshot, and the veins on his forehead and neck were swollen with wrath. Even Aydin could have sworn that this was the first time he had seen his Reis in such a state.

"I am Barbarossa, Salim Effendi. I am Barbarossa!"

He wrapped the turban around Salim's neck and strangled the ruler of Algiers on the spot.

William was at a loss for words. Even though the Spanish author had abstained from providing any details, it was as if he had heard the pounding sound that came from Salim's lifeless body as it fell on the marble floor.
Cervantes concluded the scene.
"And then they quietly walked out of the bath."

"Sheikh is deeeeaaad! Sheikh Salim al-Tumi is deeeeaddddd!"

The news echoed through the streets of Algiers, driving Algerians to rush out of their houses, stores, taverns, and baths. Salim al-Tumi's corpse had been discovered by his Sudanese servants, and the notables of the city had been the first to be notified about sheikh's death. But within a short period of time, there was not a single person in Algiers who was unaware of the sheikh's demise. Nicolás Quint's spies strolling the streets were alarmed. Sheikh Salim had died? Had he died, or had he been murdered?

People had started to gather in the town square. One among them got on a high platform and addressed the Algerians.

"Quiet! Calm down! Sheikh Salim is found dead in his bath. The physicians say that he may have passed away due to a heart attack he sustained while preparing for Friday prayer."

Grumblings had begun to rise from the crowd.

"So, it's true, Sheikh Salim is really dead."

"Such a pity, he was a sturdy man."

"Are the physicians certain that he died due to a heart attack?"

"They say he was lying on the marble floor."

"How do you know that he was not killed?"

"Yes, it's possible. Perhaps someone had killed him."

The people are speaking at the same time, each expressing their own opinion aloud.

"I agree! He's most likely been murdered!"

"But who would murder him?"

"The Spaniards must have killed him!"

"Yes, it must be the Spaniards!"

"Then he got what he deserved! He was the one who put us all into trouble by making a deal with the Spaniards!"

"Are we sure that it was the Spaniards who killed him?"

"Who else could it be?"

A voice broke through the commotion.

"Why not the Turks?"

All the voices buzzing in the air ceased for a moment, and that final claim rang in Aruj's ears, who was at that time standing in a corner and silently observing all that was taking place. He looked around in an attempt to find the man who made the claim. Then, he stepped onto the platform. Everyone was now waiting to hear what Aruj had to say.

Aydin, who had his attention firmly focused on Aruj, had thought that he would probably tell people about Salim's betrayal, but when Aruj started speaking, Aydin realized that he had not the slightest intention to take on the responsibility.

"O the people of Algiers! One among you just said something. I heard him! He claimed that we, the Turks, are responsible for the death of your sheikh. I tell you this so that you know! We came here all the way from Djidjelli because your sheikh appealed to us for help. We came here to expel the Spaniards out of Peñón so you might breathe a sigh of relief. Is it fair now that you are slandering us?"

The Algerians' murmurs gradually became a humming noise in the air.
"Yes! Reis is right! Turks are here to save us."
"Why would the Turks murder the sheikh anyway?"
"They're defending us against those Spaniards."
"But they still couldn't seize Peñón."
"The sheikh didn't even try, on the other hand."
"He's been living in prosperity while we've been struggling to make ends meet."
"Aruj Reis should be our new sheikh!"
"Yes, Aruj Reis should take Salim's place."
"I agree, it is in our best interests."
"But Sheikh Salim al-Tumi has a son!"

Once more, silence took over. A chill ran down Aruj's back. It was the same voice. It had the same depth and clarity. Salim al-Tumi had a son? Was there an heir to the throne of Algiers? His gaze met with Aydin's. Without showing much about how the news had caught him off guard, he continued his speech. Aydin's eyes, on the other hand, had started scanning the crowd. Whoever had uttered those words, he was going to find him in case he spoke again.

"Well, if your wish is to see me as your Sultan, then beginning today, I will do everything in my power to protect your interests. Your safety and well-being will be my primary concern. And the first thing I'll do to prove this to you will be capturing Peñón and driving those Spaniards away from our shores."

A storm of applauds broke out. Algerians, long fed up with Salim al-Tumi, were cheering and whistling for Sultan Aruj.

"After a *khutbah*[174] was read in his name in *Djamaa el Kebir*[175], Aruj moved to the Casbah. And the news of his taking over rulership in Algiers spread like wildfire not only in Africa, but in Europe as well."

"Who was that man?", asked William.

"Which man?"

"The one who claimed that Salim al-Tumi had a son, who said that Salim might have been murdered by the Turks."

"It was Yahya, Signor Shakespeare, Salim al-Tumi's son. And shortly after Aruj proclaimed himself the Sultan of Algiers, Yahya was first going to seek refuge in Oran; then, he was going to travel to Spain, to Cardinal Jiménez."

---

[174] Usually translated as "sermon" although it does not exactly correspond to a sermon in the Christian sense.
[175] The Great Mosque of Algiers

Spain

My Lord the Cardinal,

I regret to inform you that, following Salim al-Tumi's death, our collaboration with the notables of Algiers did not yield any fruitful results either. Twenty of our men, served as the ringleaders of the spirit of revolt, were identified by the Barbarossa's levends, exposed in front of a crowded congregation, bound with their own turbans, and beheaded for treason during the Friday prayer in Djamaa el Kebir. To ensure people's loyalty, the red-bearded pirate inspired fear in their hearts by mounting the heads on spikes and erecting them in several locations across the city. He also ordered the headless bodies to be tied behind donkeys and dragged along the streets. From this point on, I do not believe that any Algerian would look favorably upon making a collaboration with us regardless of the amount we offer. Nevertheless, due to the constant assaults of our Holy Church's arch adversary, the provisions provided from Spain to support our presence off the coast of Algiers do not arrive at their destination. We are suffering from thirst and famine at the extreme level. I plead you to find a solution to the serious challenges that our men have been facing for quite some time, and to somehow supply our garrison with the food, water and gunpowder it requires as well as the money that will be paid to our soldiers as swiftly as possible. It is of the utmost importance to cater to the requirements of our soldiers who serve as the eyes of the Kingdom of Spain along the Barbary Coast, in order to maintain the order and prevent any unrest that might break out in the castle. May God make your life long and prosperous.

Upon reading Nicolás Quint's letter, the cardinal had a rush of blood to his head. His limestone-colored face had turned to pomegranate red. Foamed with fury; he crumpled the letter in his hands.

"Damn you, Fernando! I had told you that we should never take our eyes away from North Africa."

He yelled out to his guards.

"Find me Admiral Don Diego de Vera now!"

Cervantes browsed through the jumbled papers and other items on the messy table, picking each one up one at a time and putting them back down with a disappointed expression on his face for not having been able to find what he was looking for.

"What is it that you're looking for, Signor?"

He rose from his chair, walked over to the sofa, kneeled, and looked under.

"They've got to be around here somewhere."

William was watching with interest.

"Ah, here they are..."

He reached beneath the sofa and struggled for a while to get that something he was looking for out.

William was just about to get up to lend Cervantes a hand when he heard his voice coming from under the sofa.

"I have them. No need for help."

He then returned to his desk, holding in his hands several more miniature models from his collection of linden wood.

He gave William a brief glance with a playful grin on his face before taking his seat.

"We wouldn't want your velvet coat, an indicator of your noble blood, to get stained; and we certainly wouldn't want your silk shirt, which in fact looks pretty good on you even though I hadn't previously praised it, to be torn here for a few wooden toys, would we Signor?"

William checked his outfits, particularly his coat and shirt.

"The apparel is not simply a covering for the body, Signor, it oft proclaims the man."

"Times are changing... The belts that women once used to wear over their petticoat skirts are replaced by corsets made of whalebone. Just because of these tight corsets that women wear for the sake of presenting a curvy waistline, babies who seek a chance for life in their mother's wombs are born dead if they are fortunate, and crippled if they are not. I can't help but marvel, from time to time, at the apparel with which the nobles prefer to proclaim themselves; especially when I compare them with a blacksmith who had chosen an apparel for himself that fits his occupation."

While William struggled to find a proper justification for the matter within the drawers of his mind, Cervantes' attention had already been drawn to Mancha, sleeping on the table, purring.

"It's all thanks to Mancha," said Cervantes as he arranged his miniatures on his desk one at a time, "With a single blow of his paw, he throws all these tiny boats, troops, and cannons off the desk; and after playing with them for a while, he leaves them where they've been dragged. Then, find them if you can." He gave his young buddy a friendly stroke on the head. "Cute little fellow, your mind is always at play."

Mancha purred in response, stretched himself, and then picked up his dreams from where he had left off.

William was curious.

"Since you felt the need to add more to those that are already on your desk, I presume it is a story of a great war which I'm about to hear from you."

"Not a single great war, Signor Shakespeare. What I'm about to tell you is a period during which a number of great wars were fought that shaped history. Because the events that took place in the years 1516 and 1517 were recorded in the annals of history not with ink, but rather with blood."

William's interest was piqued. Cervantes, his eyes on the map, took the remainder of his miniature troops and positioned them to the north of Aleppo.

"Following the loss of Djidjelli and Cherchell, the cardinal had lost control over Algiers as well. And the eastern winds had whispered in his ears that the feverish work going on at Tersâne-i Âmire had been completed. The Ottoman navy was now ready to set sail. And Selim the Stern had begun his march against the Mamluks with an army of sixty-five thousand men at his command."

"At long last, Kurdoglu can set sail."

Cervantes reached for his tiny ships and lined them up in front of Bizerte.

"It was time; but first Kurdoglu had to ward off the armada of Holy Alliance that had busted his home."

Bizerte, Tunisia

"Enemy shiiiiipppsss!"

When Kurdoglu spotted the thirty-three enemy ships approaching on the horizon he was having his breakfast under the awning covering the poop deck. He had been completely taken off guard. How was it possible that he had not been forewarned of the assault? The majority of the ships had already set sail a few days ago on the orders of Sultan Selim so that they joined the Ottoman armada. He had only four galleys moored in the harbor with which he had planned to set sail soon. How could Kurdoglu possibly stand up to a combined fleet of thirty-three ships with what he had at his disposal? It was impossible. His orders began to rain down.

"Carry everything onboard ashoreeee! Cannons, provisions, gunpowder, everythiiiiing!"

A commotion broke out at the port. While some of the levends dismantled the cannons, others began transporting ammo to the fortress. Kurdoglu kept on giving instructions.

"Inflict damage on the shiiiipssss! Render them useless if they are seized!"

The men carried out his orders as swiftly as they could; then, they retreated into the keep and started waiting. In a hurry, Kurdoglu penned four letters, gave them to his most trusted men and dispatched them to alert his regional allies about the attack, hoping for reinforcements. As his men raced out of Bizerte, he turned his attention to the approaching armada.

"The Franco-Spanish forces had been joined by the papal fleet under the command of Federigo Fregoso, which carried a force of a thousand soldiers. They later were joined by two galleys and three brigantines commanded by Paolo Vettori, four papal galleys of Giovanni and Antonio di Biassa, and escorted by the combined forces of Prégent de Bidoux, Bernardino d'Ornesan, and Servian, as well as, not surprisingly, the forces of Andrea Doria, who was commanding eight Genoese galleys at the time. After searching for the pirates in the vast area between Elba, Capraia, Corsica and Sardinia, the combined fleet had steered their ships to North Africa."

"This time it seems that Kurdoglu had not the slightest chance."

"What he needed, Signor Shakespeare, was support, not chance; and the reinforcements he was hoping to get would soon appear on the horizon off the coast of Bizerte."

"It is impossible for an armada of such a size, led by some of Europe's most capable admirals, to have failed to seize the fort."

"Seize the fort? While Kurdoglu was defending it?" Cervantes let out a laugh. "Let alone seizing the fort, the Christians had been caught in the crossfire between the fort and the forces of other Turkish levends on the Barbary Coast who had hurried to their comrade's aid as soon as they got Kurdoglu's message. They were at the time desperately trying to figure out a way to escape from this hell."

With arquebusiers stationed in the crow's nests and cannoneers waiting for their reis' command to open fire; the Turks were ready to launch the attack. When the rumbles of the war drums were accompanied by the high-pitched whistles coming from the brass cast horns, Christians had understood that they'd been trapped.

"Fireeeeee!"

Black powder caught fire, and the cannons began to discharge one after the other. When the screams of Allahu Akbar became a chorus filling the harbor, the chain of command in the Christian armada began to show the first signs of breakage.

They had been caught in between and were now trying to maneuver to evade the heavy cannon fire that was piercing their hauls, shattering their masts, and ripping their sails, but to no avail. After losing five of their galleons, the chain of command had been completely disrupted. As for the remainder of their ships, the Turks had inflicted on them serious damage. All those competent admirals were now infuriated knowing that there was no way that they could afford such a humiliating defeat. They simply had wanted to secure Bizerte before attacking Tunisia but failed. How could they possibly return to Europe while in such disgrace? They simply could not do that. As a result, they left Bizerte and headed for La Goulette.

"But attacking a man who was at the time trying to cope with the frustration of still not having found his Felipa, was going to turn out to be the worst decision that the Christians had ever made."

Marj Dābiq, Syria

When Selim the Stern arrived at the *Meadow of Dābiq*[176] with his twelve thousand janissaries and an additional forty thousand *timariots*[177] under his command, accompanied by ten thousand troops of the local *beys*[178] who had come to support him, it was the end of August. After staring for some time at Qansuh al-Ghawri's mounted troops that had already arrived at the plain waiting to confront him, the sultan, sitting tall on his horse in all his majesty, muttered to himself:

"Bedouin Arabs... You're now showing off on your beautiful mares, but when the battle horns blow, I really wonder how you are going to stand against my heavy artillery with those bows and lances in your hands..."

Cervantes' attention had been drawn to Mia and Mancha, who had begun teasing each other after waking up from their naps. William, who was also watching them play like Cervantes, was about to make a remark about how cute the scene was; when Mancha squawked and leaped on the Spanish author's lap, owing to a blow of paw he got on his face. The game was over; history could now resume its play. Cervantes returned his attention to William and began recounting the events leading up to the confrontation between Selim the Stern and Qansuh al-Ghawri from the very beginning.

---

[176] Marj Dābiq
[177] Sipahi cavalryman in the Ottoman army
[178] A Turkic title for a chieftain, and an honorific, traditionally applied to people with special lineages to the leaders or rulers of variously sized areas.

"By the spring of 1515, as the gardeners of Saray-ı Cedîd-i Âmire painted the seraglio with flowers of all hues; Sultan Selim had just returned from the eastern campaign he had undertaken against the Safavids, and generously rewarded his troops who had been fighting for him for over a year by giving them legions of honor, hosting banquets, and distributing money. He had to encourage his men; after all, they were not going to stay for long in Constantinople. As soon as the preparations were complete, they were going to march against the Mamluks. New swords were forged, strong cannons were cast; and the sultan, after meticulously weeding out the weakest links among his soldiers who had revealed themselves in the Battle of Chaldiran, replaced them with more reliable ones. Then, he took his quill pen and wrote a harsh letter to Qansuh al-Ghawri, in which he stated that he was perfectly aware of all the plots he'd been hatching behind his back, as well as the covert communication he'd been maintaining with the Safavids."

"It seems the sound of war drums rising from Constantinople had begun reverberating in Cairo."

"Qansuh al-Ghawri had realized that the question was no more 'whether' the Ottomans would march against them, but 'when' Selim the Stern would begin his march. It was imperative for Qansuh al-Ghawri to act fast and be the first to arrive on the battlefield in order for him to deploy his troops in a more advantageous position. He swiftly completed his preparations, took with him high officers of state, the sheikhs and courtiers as well as the Abbasid caliph Al-Mutawakkil III, left Cairo, and marched north in the sweltering heat of the summer. He led his army north from the Mediterranean side of the peninsula of sandstones and pebbles, which is the side that is relatively far from Sinai's floating sands and perilous canyons. He intended to disgrace Selim for raising his sword against a Muslim state and to rally Sunni Muslims to his side. That was the only reason why he had also dragged the Caliph into the conflict. Yet the question of how he could ever have hoped for gaining the favor of the Sunnis in a battle he was going to fight against a Sunni state, was an unanswerable one even for Caliph Al-Mutawakkil III. He made a stop in Jerusalem and prayed to Allah that he might prevail in his battle against the Ottomans. After that, he continued his march to Aleppo, sacking every village he passed through and coercively recruiting additional men, getting food, weapons, and supplies for his army from the people of the same Allah, receiving in return their damnation as a blessing."

"It looks like it was already evident from the beginning whose prayers God was going to accept."

"Aleppo, which is one of the oldest cities in the world, was at the time the second largest center for trade in the Middle East after Constantinople; it was the very heart of all the caravan routes to and from the Mediterranean. It had an elegant, covered souk that runs along for thirteen kilometers in which were bought and sold all kinds of goods. Having been located at the border it had long been serving as a buffer, a wall of defense, for the Mamluks that protected them against their adversaries lurking in the north. But when Qansuh al-Ghawri arrived at Aleppo with his troops, the inhabitants of the city could not understand whether it was their Sultan who had made an entrance or an invading army. Their homes were plundered, their property usurped, and their wives and daughters were raped. As the army was making its way out of the city, the people they left behind were bidding farewell by cursing and swearing at them, wishing Qansuh al-Ghawri that the upcoming battle would be his last."

After a brief pause, Cervantes turned his gaze to William and concluded his words.

"And it was going to turn out precisely as those people wished. The Mamluks, who refused to use firearms claiming that it was an invention of the infidel and faced the enemy with only a few sharp items in their hands, did not have the slightest chance of winning this war against the technologically superior Ottoman army."

Sultan Selim addressed his men:

"The day will come when every servant of Allah will die. No one can escape death by running away from it. If we are martyred today, eternal bliss will be awaiting us in the hereafter; yet, if we emerge triumphant, power and prosperity in this world will be our reward. The day is the day to put effort; come on, my valiant men, show no mercy to no one!"

Cannons were fired, and the swords clashed against each other. The Ottoman soldiers, upon seeing their Sultan his sword in his hand flinging himself into the battlefield, executed his command and showed no mercy. As cries of Allahu Akbar blended with the crimson screams and desperate moans of the wounded pleading to be quickly welcomed into the Garden of Eden, the *Meadow of Dābiq* became a graveyard for the Mamluks.

Mancha, long forgotten about the paw blow he suffered, was cleaning his face on Cervantes's lap. Cervantes' mind, however, was on the battlefield.

"It was not only the hottest hour of the day but the most intense moments of the battle, as well. Hayir Bey, the governor of Aleppo, who had been entrusted with the responsibility of commanding the Mamluks' left flank, entered Qansuh al-Ghawri's tent. His soldiers had been hemmed in by Selim's army on all sides. There was no longer even the tiniest glimmer of hope for Qansuh al-Ghawri to win this battle. If he wanted to live, he had no choice but to surrender. Hayir Bey had come to brief the sultan on the present situation and warn him. And as he was doing so, he had warned him a little louder so that if the sultan refused to surrender, all those meticulously planned conspiracies would not be for naught."

William was surprised.

"Conspiracies?"

"Hayir Bey had first visited Constantinople during the reign of Sultan Bayezid when he had been tasked with delivering the news of Sultan Qayitbay's death to throne city. This city of marvels, where he stayed for about a year, had enthralled him for all the richness, magnificence, and pleasures that it had to offer. The immense power the sultanate wielded, the breadth of the Empire's coffers, and the boundless generosity of the sultan were truly astounding. And Hayir Bey had seriously questioned the reliability of his eyes when he saw the sheer value of the booty that Kemal Reis had captured in a naval battle against the Knights of Saint John while returning from Egypt and presented to the sultan. Returning to Aleppo a year later, Hayir Bey had since served as the most reliable Ottoman spy in Mamluk territory, up until the Battle of Marj Dābiq. Of course, in exchange for the never-ending presents bestowed by the sultans."

"It seems Qansuh al-Ghawri had been nursing a viper in his bosom."

"Hayir Bey's words had scattered across the camp like sand blown by the desert winds. As they passed from one to another, their essence had undergone such a profound alteration that when the news had taken its ultimate form, the majority of the Mamluks believed that Qansuh al-Ghawri was murdered. by Sultan Selim in his tent. It did not take long before the right flank of the Mamluk army, which was commanded by Sibay, the governor of Damascus, fell apart. Soldiers set aside their lances and cued their mares to ride away, retreating. Qansuh al-Ghawri, on the other hand, had dashed out of his tent, was crying that he was not dead; yet no one was hearing him. After watching for a while, waiting to see how events would unfold, Hayir Bey eventually turned his steed and rode away from the battlefield together with the men under his command. As the day wore its twilight cloak, the Mamluk army had been utterly crushed; and there had remained no one on the battlefield save those who had already bid farewell to life, and those who were, at the time, groaning and praying to die as soon as possible. The survivors fled to Aleppo and Damascus, but after all the horrific things that they had done to the people, there was no one left in these cities who would welcome them. From that point on, only one sultan could enter through the gates, and that was Sultan Selim the Stern."

"It's no wonder that Qansuh al-Ghawri was not permitted into those cities, for he seems to have positioned himself as the protector of the land itself, rather than the protector of the people who lived in those lands."

"Qansuh al-Ghawri hadn't lived to see what had transpired, Signor Shakespeare. Having seen his armies destroyed had devastated the elderly sultan to such a degree that, gripped by paralysis, his jaw had dropped open. After taking a sip of water that was brought to him in a golden goblet, he had turned his horse to escape, but had fallen from his horse and surrendered his soul after two paces or so. With his well-disciplined and organized army that had a good chain of command and was armed with heavy artillery, Sultan Selim the Stern had won a decisive victory."

Castle of Aleppo, Syria

"The Temple of Hadad[179]... Son of Anu[180], the ruler of the skies, the King of the Gods..."

His charts under his arm, Piri was standing in front of the sky-rising stone stairs of the Citadel of Aleppo.

"The Storm God Adad... blesses his friends with his rains, and destroys his enemies by casting upon them darkness, poverty and death with his hurricanes..."

He paused for a moment.

"Tawba! What gods am I talking about? There's no god, but Allah! La Ilaha Illa Allah!"

As he climbed the stairs of the citadel, built on a natural limestone some thirty meters above the surrounding plain, Piri was grumbling to himself. How absurd it was for him to stand there babbling even though he was well aware that he did not have a second to waste. Following the victory at Marj Dābiq, Sultan Selim had marched to the Citadel of Aleppo, about forty kilometers south, and summoned Piri. Piri absolutely could not afford to be late. Though he knew that, he was still unable to keep himself from touching every stone, every wall that he passed by. Hittites, Assyrians, Akkadians, Greeks, Romans, Byzantines, Mongols... It was almost as if the scent of all

---

[179] The storm and rain god in the Canaanite and ancient Mesopotamian religions
[180] The divine personification of the sky, king of the gods, and ancestor of many of the deities in ancient Mesopotamian religion.

the civilizations that had formerly inhabited these lands had permeated into the walls. As Piri made his way through the maze of corridors, it was as if all those ancient souls were whispering into his ears...

He quickened his pace.

"Come on, Piri, run Piri... If you happen to be late and keep the sultan await, your soul will join those ancient souls as well. Then, they'll recite *Al-Fatihah* for us all."

When the guards let Piri in, Sultan Selim was on the balcony overlooking the city, talking to Hayir Bey. Piri, glad that he was not late, stood in a corner and waited for the sultan's meeting to come to an end. When Hayir Bey left the sultan's presence, Piri took a few humble steps and approached Selim.

"My Sultan..."

"Come, Piri Reis, come closer. I just made mention of your deceased uncle. Even though he finished his work and walked to Allah, the things he accomplished in his life, continue to serve us. Come tell me what you've been doing."

"Your Imperial Majesty, as you requested, I conducted research on the Ark of the Covenant to see whether the ark that we discovered with my deceased uncle in the Mediterranean may be the Holy Ark of Prophet Moses. It appears that I was correct in my assumptions."

"So, the Taboot, the herald of Mahdi's arrival, is finally found..."

Selim stood up and started walking with his hands clasped behind him.

"Their prophet further told them, "The sign of Saul's kingship is that the Ark will come to you—containing reassurance from your Lord and relics of the family of Moses and the family of Aaron, which will be carried by the angels. Surely in this is a sign for you, if you truly believe.""[181]

Piri remained silent; his gaze was on the floor. Sultan Selim's face lit up with a slight smile.

"So, it seems Allah the Almighty deemed me appropriate for this duty." He turned to Piri, "Perhaps, therefore no one has ever been able to locate the Ark thus far! Perhaps it has been waiting all this time for its rightful owner, Allah's chosen one, Ottoman Sultan Selim the Stern!"

---

[181] Qur'an, Surah Al-Baqarah, 248

"My Sultan, you may be correct in your assessment. But I've seen people who paid with their lives for having approached that Ark. I've seen dead bodies rot and fester."

"Because none of them who dared to approach the Ark was the Caliph, Piri! The Ark is now in my palace; and I'm in the Citadel of Aleppo facing Cairo, having Caliph Al-Mutawakkil III in my hands. What am I waiting for, Piri? What am I waiting for?"

Sultan Selim was excited. Piri, on the other hand, was almost certain that the secret of the Ark was hidden somewhere in Jerusalem, somewhere that he might discover if he followed the labyrinth that he came across on one of Colón's maps.

"My Sultan, please allow me to accompany you to Jerusalem, to set foot in the Holy land, and to seek an answer to this mystery in the place where the Ark was last seen, under the ruins of the Temple of Solomon. I'm certain that I'll come up with something. All I need is a little more time."

Selim took a deep breath. The pleading expression on Piri's face was indicating that there was something in his mind that was truly bothering him. In any case, before embarking on his expedition to Cairo, Selim had to circumambulate the Dome of the Rock and pray in *Masjid Aqsa* to express his gratitude to Allah for having been granted victory.

"All right, Piri, let it be as you say. But know that, in case you do not return to Constantinople having solved the mystery of the Ark, I'll make sure you wish you hadn't returned."

It was possible that the Ark that they found in the Mediterranean might cost Piri his life.

After bowing his respects, Piri left the sultan's presence.

He muttered to himself:

"So, it seems Allah the Almighty deemed me appropriate for this duty. Haci Ahmed Muhyiddin Piri , son of Haci Mehmed of Karaman, nephew of Ottoman Kapudan Pasha Kemal Reis..."

Algiers

After the Christians had been ushered back to the northern shores of the Mediterranean, Kurdoglu had embarked on his journey to Alexandria, while Khidr and his brother Isaac, who came from Lesbos not too long ago, had set sail to Algiers to see Aruj. The news that Isaac had brought from home was not good. Their blue-eyed, cotton-handed mother Katerina, whom they knew had been ill for some time, had eventually passed away.

"I was not there..."

Aruj was sad. Since the day he lost his arm, he had not visited his mother and always found an excuse to avoid traveling to Lesbos. Though he was not willing to admit it, his brothers knew; he hadn't wanted his mother to see him in such a shape. It did not matter for Aruj to remain in Katerina's memories as the same sturdy man with his white teeth, tanned skin, thick calves, and muscular body; but the shiny smile that he lost together with his arm, his mother should not have seen what had replaced it.

Isaac took a deep breath.
"You were there, Aruj..."
"How can you say that I was there, brother? It's been five years since the last time I caught a whiff of her beautiful fragrance."
"You were in her mind, in her heart, Aruj. As a matter of fact, we never set sail from her heart. During all those years we were away, she said there was never a single day she did not think of us."
Khidr muttered from Sappho:
"Death is an evil; the gods have so judged; had it been good, they would die."

Aruj shut his eyes.

"May Allah rest her soul in eternal peace and grant her the highest place in Jannah."

Isaac was wondering how Aruj had been doing since he last saw him in Tunisia.

"How you've been lately?"

"Me? I'm fine brother, thank you. Everyone is trying to kill me, so there's not much of a change."

Isaac threw a glance at Khidr.

"Why do you say so, Aruj? Haven't you subdued those rebellious tribes and made them pledge loyalty to you?"

"They switch sides faster than Mulay Muhammad. The real pests, though, are the Algerian spies. They do not go a single day without slitting someone's throat, and not a single day passes without them setting somewhere on fire." He leaped on his feet with rage. "Damn Spaniards! The nest of all the pestilence is this Peñón! They are inciting the people of my faith to turn against me." He had his eyes fixed on the Spanish garrison. "There is no peace for me until the day I toss you down from atop those walls!"

Khidr jumped in.

"I've heard Sultan Selim is marching on Cairo. According to what Piri wrote in his letter, the sultan is planning to take over the Caliphate."

"I heard..."

"You know, the people of North Africa have a lot of respect for the Caliph."

Khidr was obviously trying to say something, but Aruj was not thrilled to see him twisting the beans in his mouth.

"Don't turn it into a mastic in your mouth; and speak what you want to say all at once, Khidr."

Khidr took a deep breath.

"Look, brother! The people of Algiers have no faith in you. To them, you are no different than any other sheikh who comes to power only temporarily and exploits them. This is how they view you."

Aruj wanted to say something, but Khidr did not let him.

"Don't interrupt me, for once, and listen to what I have to say. They trust Spain more than they trust you."

Aruj was taken aback by what he heard. What on earth was his brother talking about?

"You must be out of your mind. They were the ones who invited me here to help fight off the Spaniards!"

Isaac had understood what Khidr was trying to say. They were now up against not just one, but two adversaries. In addition to fighting back against the Spaniards, they were also required to deal with the neighboring tribes. It was easy to brandish the sword against the infidel, but Khidr was reluctant to draw it against the people with whom they shared the same faith. They needed the support of the Algerians. They needed to establish some kind of governance system in Algiers that would safeguard the people's interests. If people would trust Aruj, nobody would be able to incite them against him.

Isaac turned to Khidr.
"You're talking about founding a state."
"That's exactly what I'm saying, brother!"
Aruj had not understood a thing.
"I declared myself Sultan, brought all those scattered Moors and Arabs under my rule; what else do you want me to do?"
"Instead of you, people should be proclaiming you the sultan, brother. They should not feel compelled to acknowledge you as their leader; but they themselves should be willing to do so. And for this to happen, they must have faith in you. They should trust that you have the required strength and the resilience to stand your ground against the Spaniards, and that Spain is not capable of crushing you like a fly whenever it gets irritated."
"Put your case forward, Khidr. Be clear and concise!"
"You need the backing of the Empire, brother. You should not assume the role of Sultan; rather, you should act as Sultan Selim's regent in Algiers."

Aruj had, at long last, understood what Khidr was getting at. However, the idea of sharing his authority with Sultan Selim had not appealed to him in the least.

Khidr continued speaking:
"You must establish a proper state administration. You should divide the land into provinces and appoint men for their governance if required. You need to set up *Odjaks*[182] and consolidate your power with the deployment

---

[182] Autonomous part of the Janissary Corps, the main element of land forces of the Regency of Algiers acting completely independently from the rest of the corps, also taking part in matters pertaining to internal administration, and politics.

of regular troops furnished by the empire, and train for yourself competent scholars and statesmen; people who would not look forward to stabbing you in the back when they get the slightest opportunity; people who would be comrades, brothers to you, to whom you would be able to entrust your lands when you are out at the seas. And to achieve all these, you need have the backing of the Empire; you need the backing of Sultan Selim."

"Djidjelli, Cherchell, Algiers... In any of the battles that I've fought up to this point, have I ever sought for the Empire's support, Khidr?"

"Don't talk like that, brother. If it hadn't been for the galleys the sultan had built and equipped for us in Tersâne-i Âmire, if it hadn't been for that fourteen ships he had given under Kurdoglu's command..." Khidr took a deep breath. "Take, for example, the knights. They are wielding the sword of Christianity in far-flung regions of the Mediterranean, where the arms of the kings are unable to reach. They have their own set of laws and regulations, but they have the Vatican's support behind them."

"Khidr is right, Aruj," said Isaac, confirming his younger brother. "He does not advise you to hand over your power to Sultan Selim. If the knights serve as the Christianity's cross in the Mediterranean, he says you to be the Crescent of Islam. In my opinion, you should think about it."

Aruj had cooled down a little.

"All right, I'll think about it."

"He was going to think about it, yet Aruj had such a strong ego that would not allow him to accept the yoke of any other sultan. The battles he would fight against the regional and local power holders in Maghrib were going to appear to him to be much easier to fight."

William flashed out a sarcastic smile.

"Aruj hadn't been able to come out victorious in any of the battles he fought against himself anyway."

"He had been engaging the adversary with his sword, Signor Shakespeare; the weapon that he knew how to use best. When he would confront his ego, however, he was aware that he had to fight with bare hands."

They were startled by a knock on the door. Aruj decided to invite the visitor in.

"Come in!"

It was Cemal.

"I'm sorry to interrupt, Baba Aruj, but there's a woman downstairs who says she needs to see you."
"A woman?" After a brief pause, Aruj asked: "Is she beautiful?"
Cemal had been caught off guard.
"Beautiful? Well... I don't know... I mean... She's quite pretty. As a matter of fact, she is more than that. With those eyes sparkling like two emeralds on her lovely face, and her hips that are so nicely rounded... She is stunning, Baba!"

Aruj had once again touched Cemal's soft spot, and Cemal, well known for his weakness for women, had stuttered not knowing what to say. They laughed out loud. Then, Khidr turned to Aruj:
"Hah! Brother, you've found the right man to ask about women. He was left with only a portion of his wits after Hanna of Tunisia, and he now lost that as well."
"Hanna of Tunisia? You need to update yourself, Khidr. After Hanna, he fell in love with Nerva in Djerba, then he found a girl called Zeyneb in Djidjelli, after Zeyneb came... What was her name, Cemal? The one you met in Cherchell?"
"But you're mocking me again, Baba Aruj."
"Swear to Allah I'm not." Aruj let out a laugh. "Come on, allow the woman in so we can see if her hips are as well-rounded as you claim."

"Ask Kurdoglu, if you want to know more about my hips. After all, he has navigated many times through my storms."

Aruj's cheeks were flushed with embarrassment. The woman who came to see him was Fatima, the Daughter of Granada. She hadn't bothered to wait for an invitation and barged into the room instead.

"My apologies, Fatima. If only I'd known it was you..."
Fatima laughed.
"What's the apology for, Aruj? I know of no woman who wouldn't take delight in seeing you men fantasizing about her well-rounded butts."

Aruj stood up, took a few steps towards Fatima. He, then, took her hand in his and brought it to his lips.

"Welcome, the Daughter of Granada..."

So, she was the Daughter of Granada. Khidr had heard a lot about her but had never met her in person. She was indeed as charming as they say, he thought. Then, he recalled his Felipa... and her jasmine-scented hair...

"My brothers and I have been talking about the next steps we should take in Algiers."

After saluting Isaac and Khidr with a quick emerald gaze, Fatima turned to Aruj:

"So it seems that my timing is excellent!"

"The intelligence you provide bring us victories in the Mediterranean. It's a pleasure to see you here, in Algiers, yet at the same time it is..."

"A cause of concern, isn't it Aruj? Seeing me to have traveled all the way from Tetouan, you're anxious as to whether you would like what I have to say."

"You've read my mind..."

"You're right, Aruj. I can't say that I have brought you good news. The Spanish are getting ready to set sail with a huge fleet."

"To hunt down who?"

"To hunt down you!"

Silence took over for a while. Then, Fatima continued:

"They seem to cooperate with the rulers of Tenes and Tlemcen. I was able to get a hold of a few letters exchanged between Admiral Diego de Vera and the ruler of Tenes, Hamid al-Abd. The admiral writes in his letter that he would set sail to North Africa with a sizable force under his command in order to specifically hunt down the Turks in the region. He also says that Cardinal Jiménez appreciated the support that Hamid would give to the Spaniards."

"What does Hamid say in response?"

"What do you expect from a man who claims his father entrusted him to the King of Spain before his death?"

"You are right..."

"There is also activity in Oran. The agreement you made with the tribe of Beni Rashid caused starvation among the Spaniards in Oran. Their stocks of barley, rice, and vinegar are said to be nearly depleted. I've heard that the soldiers are revolting by claiming that even the monks who took refuge in the mountains did not suffer from such scarcity."

"May they suffer more!"

"We all agree on that, but as you know, all these grievances will force the kingdom to expedite the preparations."

"How much time do you think we have?"

"Not much, no more than a few months. Will you be able to get ready by then?"

"Do I have another chance?"

Fatima took a deep breath.

"I wish I had better news for you. On the other hand, I'm confident that you'll easily repel the attack. I'll do everything in my power to assist you. Now, I shall leave. As a matter of fact, I've come to caution you more about Tenes and Tlemcen than about Spain. Don't trust the tribes, and don't march on Tenes or Tlemcen before you send those Spaniards into the depths of the sea."

"Okay Fatima, thank you."

She approached Aruj with a few steps. She looked him in the eye and smiled.

"You're most welcome Barbarossa."

She turned around and left the room as swiftly as she had entered. After staring from behind her for a while, Aruj turned to Isaac:

"See bro? I told you. Everyone is trying to kill me, so there's not much of a change.

"With each passing day, Aruj's annoyance at the existence of this formidable castle off the coast of Algiers was growing to a new extreme. First, he summoned Iskender, who was fluent in both Spanish and Italian, and dispatched him to Peñón, to speak with Nicolás Quint. Iskender had been tasked with informing the commander of Aruj's intention to give them one final opportunity to surrender the garrison and return to Spain."

"Aruj had already made this move on the day that he arrived in Algiers; however, I recall that he had not received a positive response to it," said William.

"You recall correctly, Signor Shakespeare, but circumstances had changed considerably since then. The Turks had been blocking the aid sent by the kingdom for quite some time, and Nicolás Quint had been going through hard times due to the lack of supplies. The commander was anxious that if Spain did not come to their help soon, he would be unable to prevent a mutiny in the garrison. Nonetheless, he refused Aruj's offer and returned Iskender by saying that he had been assigned this duty by His Majesty and would thus surrender the castle solely on His Majesty's orders."

"Aruj seems to have had no chance but to start preparations for the impending war."

"He began to study the area in detail. He carefully examined the city's plan and fortified the walls. He strengthened every key location that he deemed strategically important. He summoned more men from Djidjelli and ordered them to dig pits; then, to trap the Spaniards inside these pits, he gave the order for sharply pointed stakes to be placed inside, before covering them all with loose soil. He reinforced the city with heavy artillery, worked day and night, and kept his men awake. And while he was doing all this, he always kept an eye on Peñón."

"Like a leopard circling its prey..."

"As Fatima had foreseen, a few months later, a Spanish fleet of thirty-five galleons that had set sail from Valencia and Málaga alongside a hundred and forty troopships carrying fifteen thousand soldiers appeared on the horizon."

At the time that the Spanish Armada arrived at the shores of Algiers in tremendous disorder, Nicolás Quint was worried to such a degree that he was not even concerned about hiding his feelings. And his continual snapping of fingers, tapping of the foot, and biting his lips were revealing the truth as it was anyway. After anchoring under the shade of Peñón, Admiral Diego de Vera hastened to see the commander.

"First the galleons, then, the galleys. And, in the midst of all of this pandemonium, the admiral of the navy arrives at the harbor and drops anchor in broad daylight."

"I'm glad to see you as well, Signor Quint."

"You couldn't have warned the enemy to be on the lookout any louder, Admiral. Whereas I had thought that you intended to catch them off guard."

"Since the preparations took longer than anticipated, they had already been warned about the campaign, Commander. Common sense demanded hectoring around rather than trying to catch the enemy off guard."

Nicolás Quint did not reply. He walked over to his desk and sat down in his chair. He was concerned. Don Diego de Vera sought to calm him.

"I perfectly understand the situation you're in and all those troubles that you've been forced to deal with. But rest assured, Commander. We dropped anchor within range of your cannons. Tomorrow morning, about fifteen thousand soldiers will disembark. I can guarantee you that this will be the very last time that you ever see the Barbarossas."

"Your statements exacerbate my concerns, Admiral. I have no intention of questioning your authority or military prowess, but I'd like to draw your attention to the fact that the man you'll be facing on the battlefield tomorrow is Aruj Reis, the elder of the Barbarossas. He is no ordinary pirate; but rather a ferocious and daring warrior. After years of wreaking havoc throughout the Mediterranean, he eventually nested in Algiers, much like a scorpion. You may have observed that I did not say he 'took refuge' in Algiers; but rather, 'nested'. Because this red-bearded demon isn't interested in finding a safe harbor for his ships to spend the winter; his main objective is to establish a state that will ensure his name is written in gold letters in history."

"I understand your concerns, Commander, yet I find them unwarranted. This pirate appears to have really intimidated you. I'd like to remind you of the lesson we taught him in front of Bejaia."

"For quite some time, I've been living an inch away from this man, whom you claim I overestimate. If I were you, I would heed my words."

Don Diego de Vera smiled.

"I'll tell you what, Commander, you look pretty exhausted. Why don't you rest while I take Casbah and reinstate Spanish control over Algiers, and then we'll have dinner together?"

A forlorn smile formed on Nicolás Quint's face.

"As you wish, Admiral... as you wish..."

After paying respect to the Commander with a small nod of the head, Don Diego de Vera made his way to the door. Just as he was about to exit the room, he turned around.

"Oh, don't forget to make the table set for three people. I'm planning to bring that red-bearded devil's head with me so that he can join us for dinner."

Following his last words, he took a few confident steps and left the room.

Nicolás Quint muttered to himself:

"May God protect those fifteen thousand soldiers under your command, Admiral... As for you yourself, you'd somehow find a way to get out of this hell anyway."

The next day, when the Spanish forces disembarked close to *Oued El Harrach*, they were in complete disarray, and none of them appeared to have the smallest idea about what their admiral had planned. That day, Don Diego de Vera's contempt for the intelligence Nicolás Quint had supplied him regarding the city's weak points would cost the Christian troops dearly.

The sky was as if made of opal and the sea was sparkling like blue topaz. The only sound that could be heard in the stillness before the approaching storm was the call to prayer rising from the minarets. Don Diego de Vera had his camp set up on the river plain and had divided his troops into four main branches, ignoring all the objections his advisers had raised. According to Nicolás Quint, this was the worst possible maneuver that the admiral could have ever made, for he had deprived the Spaniards of the advantage of their having outnumbered the enemy. It appears the admiral was unaware of the gravity of the impending battle that was about to commence. Commander Quint had paid the admiral a visit at the camp to convey his final warnings, but Don Diego de Vera had shown no interest in what the commander had to say. As a man who is more blustering and vainglorious than brave, he had no intention of getting the advice of a castle commander regarding how to manage his fleet and command his armies.

Aruj, on the other hand, was standing atop the city walls, staring down at the admiral's flagship, rocking back and forth with the waves, which Don Diego de Vera had moored with its stern facing the city as if to express his scorn for Aruj. He muttered to himself:

"Well, at least he won't have to swerve the helm on the run..."

There was a deafening quiet. It was as if Algiers had been abandoned. When the spies he had dispatched in advance informed the admiral that the gates were open and there seemed to be no one around guarding the city, Don Diego de Vera flashed a sarcastic grin.

"Just as I had said, Commander Quint, you really had overestimated the Barbarossas."

When they entered in, there was no one around except for a handful of locals who were running away in what appeared to be a state of panic. The admiral speculated that Aruj had become frightened upon seeing the Spanish troops coming ashore and had fled the scene. He would soon realize the trap they were dragged into, but unfortunately, it was going to be too late for the admiral.

"When the drama titled *The Massacre of three thousand Spaniards* that Nicolás Quint watched from his fortress came to an end, a thousand men from the survivors had sought shelter in Peñón, while the rest had returned to their ships. However, a sudden shift in the weather combined with the rising tide threw them ashore and shattered the fleet on the rocks into pieces. As for Don Diego de Vera, he had somehow managed to get out of this hell just as the commander had anticipated. However, upon returning to Spain, covered with shame, he was going to be ridiculed even by the children for having been unable with his two arms to overcome the one-armed Barbarossa."

"A complete and utter destruction... It must have struck the cardinal hard."

"When the news reached Cardinal Jiménez, it was the end of October, and he was having a discussion with the theologians pertaining to religious matters. After having read the letters, he calmly turned to those around him and said, *'Our army has been defeated and partly destroyed. There is however one consolation in it: Spain is thereby ridden of a great manly idle and bad characters.'*. Then, knowing that his enemies would not lose a second to take advantage of this setback; he took his pen and wrote a letter to Carlos V, in which he informed the new sovereign of Spain that the North African campaign had failed and stated the number of Christians slain as one thousand.

Nonetheless, it must have been a hard blow to him, because he did not live to see the following expedition. Some claimed he was poisoned, while others claimed that his heart failed to take the heartbreaking news from Algiers."

Cervantes picked up the tiny wooden troops he had previously stationed in northern Aleppo and placed them over Jerusalem.

"By the time Don Diego de Vera fled the Barbary Coast, Sultan Selim the Stern had arrived in Jerusalem."
"The Holy land..."
"The clergy of Jerusalem welcomed the new sovereign of the Holy land with ceremonies. The splendor of *Al-Aqsa Mosque*, which had been decorated with twelve thousand lamps to honor the sultan's arrival had fascinated people to such an extent that it was going to be forever ingrained in their memories. Sultan Selim entered the Dome of Rock and prayed in front of *Hajar al-Muallaq*."
"The Floating Rock... The Stone of Foundation..." said William, "The holiest place on earth, where the Ark of the Covenant had once been kept..."

He had recalled Agrippa's letter. A stone that is not a stone... A pillow for Jacob, the keystone of Solomon's Temple, the stone on which Muhammad stood and ascended to the seventh heaven, the stone upon which Jesus founded his church... The throne of Shekhinah, the Foundation Stone upon which the entire creation is built, the Philosophers' Stone... All the puzzle pieces scattered throughout his mind were gradually settling into their proper places, leaving just one question William was still unable to find an answer to.

"I don't understand, Signor Cervantes. The more I think I get a better grasp on the teaching, the more I find myself unable to answer a single question. Even though all the traditions, the scripture, the prophets, and the philosophers, all strived to communicate the same wisdom, I have a hard time understanding why people who climb the same mountain via alternate paths are never weary of drawing swords against one another, why they hate one another to such a degree."

Dark clouds had descended on Cervantes' eyes.

"Who knows...", he muttered, "Maybe that's why the Qur'an begins with the command Iqra![183]"

Even though many would have spent a lifetime studying the scriptures, very few had been reading them with the eye of the heart, and even fewer had actually understood thus far, the core of the teaching the enlightened ones had tried to impart. Whereas there never had been a prophet whose words contradicted the previous ones. And as a matter of fact, it was more than enough for man to proceed to the next level of existence if he would simply refrain from doing a few things that had been prohibited in the scripture, rather than competing to do what had merely been advised. But just as Hermes had once said, the eyes blinded by the transient pleasures of this ephemeral world had been preferring shadows over light. And perhaps this was the reason why, at times when ignorance began to reign on the face of the earth and humanity entirely lost its way, there had always appeared someone who would become the light, who would pierce the sheer darkness and illuminate the minds. Because man was the sum total of all his likes and dislikes. Everyone whom he loved, everyone whom he hated was in fact no one other than man himself. Similar to an image reflected in a mirror, life would draw its sword against man, only in case man would draw his own sword against life. Yet time made man forget all that he innately knew. And those who one day come to realize that there really was something about life that did not feel quite right; those who struggle to make sense of the void that had nested in the depths of their hearts would, in the same way, that Cervantes did, try to remember the Truth.

Cervantes took a deep sigh.

"God's nature was altruistic. God had always been the one who bestowed. Man's nature, on the other hand, was egoistic, as he was created to be the one who would receive what was granted. Since one needed to be at the very beginning to start treading the path and reach the end, thus had man been created as the opposite pole, as God's reflection in the mirror. Man was the darkness which revealed the light; he was the black that absorbed the white. Had black emitted the white imprisoned within, had man allowed

---

[183] Read. God's first revelation proclaimed to Prophet Muhammad by Angel Gabriel

love and compassion to thaw his frozen heart, he would realize that his creator had always been closer to him than he had ever assumed." He gave a brief pause; then, added: "Like Piri, who, unaware that he was closer than he thought to discovering the secret of the Ark, was trying to find his way through Jerusalem's network of underground tunnels with Sinan."

Jerusalem

"So high, I can't get over it. So low, I can't get under it."

Piri had not understood. He brought the torch up to Sinan's face.
"What exactly do you mean? I'm not sure I understand."
"Neither do I, Reis. It baffles me how this city continues to stand without collapsing on top of us."

The dark underground tunnels of Jerusalem, through which they had been trying to find their way, were nothing short of a maze. Piri, who generally did not enjoy spending time indoors, became enraged at Sinan.

"Well done, Sinan! Continue to talk like that and you'll make me sweat even more."
Sinan let out a chuckle.
"What's the matter, Reis, are you scared or what?"
"I'm not scared, Sinan, I'm nervous. I am a man of the open seas who does not feel at ease in enclosed spaces."
"You are right indeed. It sometimes makes one feel as if he was buried alive."
Piri brought the torch up to Sinan's face once again.
"Sinan, for Allah's sake, shut your mouth up!"

Sinan was right. Beneath Jerusalem was like a molehill. And although Sinan was a genius of his time when it came to architecture, he was absolutely perplexed as to what this Holy City was standing on.

"The floating city..." said Piri, "The Temple of the Floating Rock..."

He handed the torch to Sinan.

"Hold this for me; I have a feeling that we're going around in circles. We'll get lost if we don't look at the maps."

Sinan reached out and took the torch. Piri checked the maps once more under the dim light.

"We must take the first left. If I've read the map correctly, a door should appear before us soon."

Sinan grumbled as they continued walking.

"I'm really curious as to how we'll be able to get out of this place. I hope you have an idea about where we are right now. Because I truly do not..."

When the door Piri had just mentioned suddenly appeared before them, both came to a halt. There was something inscribed on the door Piri felt familiar.

"And it repented the LORD that he had made man on the earth, and it grieved him at his heart."

"Torah!"

The news that the shores of Algiers had become a graveyard for Christians had become a source of concern among the North African rulers as well. If Spain was a scourge of God who could be reconciled, then the Turks were literally God's wrath personified. As the Arabs would say, God had assembled an army called the Turks, which he would unleash on those who infuriated him. And it seemed that this time, it was North Africa that was at the end of the rope. God had clearly become enraged at the so-called Muslim rulers of the Barbary Coast who did not hesitate to partner up with the Christians and oppress their own people for the sake of their own dynastic interests. On the other hand, why had God grown so furious at them; hadn't the Christians of Europe been doing the same? What was there to be so angry about the fact that man would grip the neck of the weak, as he sat at the wealthy's feet?

Africans were no different from the Europeans. After all, the man was the same no matter where he was. With the same lust for power, the former would fight in the name of Allah, while the latter would do the same in the name of God, and neither would think twice about strangling even their own brothers to attain their own ambitions. As if God had called the man at arms in the scripture, he would only put his sword down when his *nafs* was gratified... And such a cauldron *nafs* was, that was impossible to satisfy.

"O son, if you seek to know the form of the self, read the story of Hell with its seven gates,"[184] muttered Cervantes, and pointed at the Qur'an on his desk.

---

[184] Rumi

"Rumi equates the *nafs* to the hell mentioned in the Surah Qaf where it says, *'Beware of the Day We will ask Hell, "Are you full yet?" And it will respond, "Are there anymore?"'*[185]. As for Aruj, he had eventually fallen into the hands of that very hell's demons... Despite having been born from the same womb, despite having grown up together, Khidr and Aruj were not the same. Aruj would find an excuse at whatever cost and make those rulers of the Barbary Coast pay for their collaboration with the Spanish in an attempt to overthrow him.

Aruj had become enraged after receiving Khidr's letter, who was at the time in Telis. As he was pacing up and down the room, he was yelling.

"Look what he says, Yahya!" He held the letter up and showed it to Yahya. "I tell him that Hamid had conspired with the Spaniards and was now marching on me; I tell him to send me reinforcements so that I can set out and march on Hamid before he arrives at my doorstep and look how he replies!"

Yahya, who had been standing silently listening to Aruj up until that point, attempted to speak but was not allowed.

"Look! Look what he says!"

Aruj started reading aloud. His hands were trembling with anger.

"Do not forget, brother; when you took the throne, you also took on some responsibilities. You can't and shouldn't act only on your own initiative any longer. You must prioritize your subjects' interests over your own. If you continue giving your decisions by seeking the opinions of the Turks alone, they will get offended. We are currently laboring to restore law and order in the eastern provinces as you directed. Though we would surely send you the reinforcements you require, I feel it is imperative that you first consult with the Algerians and obtain their consent on the steps you intend to take in response to this threat. Until now, our adversary has been the infidel, but now we have co-religionists against us. You must convene the assembly of elders and take your decisions together with the notables of Algiers."

Yahya did not respond.

Aruj yelled at him.

"Say something, Yahya!"

---

[185] Qur'an, Surah Qaf, 30

As soon as Yahya opened his mouth, Aruj silenced him.

"Am I now going to ask these men to grant me permission, Yahya? Tell me, am I their Sultan or not?"

Yahya made another attempt to speak up but was hushed.

"I freed them from having to pay tribute to Spain. I restored order and peace to the city. When the Christians attacked, I was the one who stood against the enemy and defended the city! Am I going to ask these men to grant me permission, now? Am I wrong, Yahya? Tell me!"

Yahya finally had a chance to speak up:

"You are wrong, Baba Aruj!"

Aruj was baffled. What had Yahya just said? Had Aruj heard him right? Had he said to his reis that he was wrong? He couldn't help but yell out loud:

"Get the hell out of here, Yahya!"

"However, when Aruj saw that not only Yahya, but everyone around him, was thinking the same way, he was going to decide to lower his defenses and convene the council as Khidr had advised. Fortunately, this time, the notables of Algiers were going to be on the same page with Aruj."

He briefed the council members on Hamid's threat and then solicited their opinion on the course of action he intended to pursue.

"What do you say now, Aghas?" Is it halal[186] to march on and execute this traitor who has sown discord among the faithful?"

The notables gave their approval.

"It is halal, My Sultan!"

"Then, we'll begin making our preparations!"

---

[186] Permissible according to Islamic law

Cervantes reclined back.

"Aruj was a conqueror. He had to lead his warriors, bring the enemy to its knees, and make a ceremonial entry into the cities he captured. If he remained devoted for an extended period of time, he would become bored; not only from his cities but also from his women."

Cervantes picked up his little soldiers and placed them between Algiers and Tenes. He then turned to William.

"Aruj, accompanied by some thousand Turks armed with matchlocks, five hundred Moors, and a significant number of Arab sheiks he mustered, rode to greet Hamid al-Abd's six thousand mounted troops equipped with only bows and light spears. Despite the fact that Hamid's forces outnumbered the opponent, they did not have the slightest chance to stand against Aruj's firearms. It was a quick and decisive victory for Barbarossa resulting in Hamid's fleeing to the city without looking back. Hamid, then disguised himself as a merchant and set off for Sahara with several of his men."

"Like the Mamluks, who did not stand a chance against the heavily armed janissaries of Sultan Selim," said William.

"The age of knighthood has long since come to an end, Signor Shakespeare. Those legendary heroes of the past who donned their armor and drew their swords to fight for what they believed in, are now nothing but characters of a fairy tale."

"You've previously shared with me how this grieves you."

"Just the way he would like, the inhabitants of Tenes welcomed Aruj with celebrations held in his honor and presented him the keys to the city on velvet cushions. Aruj, on the other hand, after settling in Tenes and bringing ashore all the carbines, falconets, and catapults that Khidr had sent to provide him support, had his sights set on Tlemcen."

Tlemcen

Surrounded by walnuts and centuries-old olive groves, Tlemcen was situated on the far western edge of Maghrib kissing the Moroccan border. Due to its location at the crossroads connecting the west and east it had long been a place frequently visited by the merchants traveling along the Saharan caravan route. However, it had also faced a constant threat posed by the ruling dynasties of Tunisia and Morocco, who, enchanted by the city's wealth, had been fantasizing about seizing control of the land, continuously harassing the ruling Zayyanids. Despite having faced numerous hardships thus far, the people of Tlemcen had managed to survive, at least until Tlemcen's strength began to decline as a result of the struggles that members of the dynasty had over the throne. The true heir to the throne, Abu Zayyan, had been imprisoned by his uncle Abu Hammu. And the people of Tlemcen had been suffering under his Spain-biased politics since the day he took the throne and accepted vassalage to the Kingdom of Spain. In the end, the city's inhabitants had decided to send a delegation to Aruj and plead for help. How could such a brave and honorable man as Aruj possibly have turned them down, anyway?

"How could he have turned them down and lost out on another spectacular welcome?" said William with a sarcastic smile on his face. But his comment had elicited an emotion on the Spanish author's face that William was unable to comprehend. It was as if Cervantes had wanted to say something, but for reasons unclear to William, he had given up the idea at the last moment.

After swallowing up his thoughts that he had refrained from forming as words, Cervantes continued:

"Even though Abu Hammu had received reinforcements from the warriors that had escaped from Tenes, he still had no more than six hundred mounted troops in addition to three thousand infantries at his command. Therefore, it did not take Aruj very long to quickly disperse this worthless rabble that lacked strategy, tactics, and even weaponry that could compete with his."

"So, like Hamid, Abu Hammu, too, fled without looking back."

"Abu Hammu had not left much in Tlemcen that he would want to turn his head and look back, Signor Shakespeare. After abandoning his men on the battlefield and rushing to the city; he took with him thousands of dirhams of gold, the mugs inscribed with the names of the Moroccan sultans, inkpots of ebony, seals made of yellow amber, three-legged chinaware chests, golden treaded mats, and silk-embroidered Damascene fabrics, and fled to Morocco."

William let out a hearty laugh.

"For they say, if money go before, all ways do lie open."[187]

Cervantes continued his words.

"Leaving Isaac and Iskender at the Castle of Beni Rashid along with a few hundred men, Aruj made a ceremonial entrance into Tlemcen and was hailed by the notables of the city with laudatory words. As the verses of the Qur'an were recited out loud, he passed beneath the flags with silver fringes that were hanging from the poles and made his way through the gates of El Mechouar. When he finally arrived at the palace, the first thing he did was to free Abu Zayyan from the pit in which he was imprisoned."

"I have a sneaking suspicion that Aruj would not be willing to leave such a priceless city in the hands of Abu Zayyan."

"As he traveled all the way down to Tlemcen, he had reflected on Khidr's words which reminded Aruj that it was improper for a Muslim to brandish his sword against another Muslim. There was nothing wrong with his march against Tenes because Hamid had sown strife among the people of their own faith. However, Tlemcen... Was it really appropriate for Aruj to intervene in dynastic fights? It was true that Abu Hammu had consented to

---

[187] William Shakespeare, The Merry Wives of Windsor

Spain's vassalage, but hadn't his father done the same? Aruj was well aware of the fact that he had given in to his greed. It was possible that he could amass an immense amount of wealth due to Tlemcen's proximity to Morocco and its geographically strategic location for being at the crossroads; but, on the other hand, this place was right under the nose of Spain. How would Aruj be able to establish his authority in Tlemcen, given that he had not yet consolidated his rule in Algiers? The most prudent course of action would be to reach an arrangement with Abu Zayyan and then return to Algiers. He had come here for help; he should not have deposed a Muslim ruler without a legitimate basis. On the other hand, he was unwilling to abandon a city for which so many wars had been waged. Fortunately, Abu Zayyan would soon give him a valid reason, and Aruj was not going to feel any guilt as he overthrew him."

"You cannot allow this pirate to stay in Tlemcen any longer!"

"Forging an alliance with him will bring the Spaniards' wrath upon us."

"My Sultan, Tlemcen is neither Tunisia nor Algiers. The Kingdom of Spain is our neighbor. We must get along with the Spaniards."

"We are already being confronted by a persistent Moroccan threat."

"Do you want the same thing to happen to you as it did to Salim al-Tumi?"

"You know that the Turks are a worse scourge than the Spaniards."

"Enough!"

"My Sultan..."

"I said enough!"

"Abu Zayyan was not much of a strong-willed ruler, but rather he was someone easily influenced. Perhaps it was because, this was his personality, or because he had been kept in that dungeon pit for quite some time. Aruj had come to his aid. He couldn't say that he liked this red-bearded, self-centered man whose arrogance often manifested itself as insolence, but Abu Zayyan was thinking..."

"If his thoughts were to be reflected in his deeds, Aruj would notice it and take the appropriate attitude in..."

"In no time flat, exactly, Signor Shakespeare. Aruj was already aware that the notables of Tlemcen were getting increasingly restless about his prolonged presence in the city. Regarding Abu Zayyan's demeanor toward him, it was less friendly and more aloof with each passing day. Despite all of this, Aruj made an effort to rein in his ego which he had been battling against for quite some time. He had even begun to seriously consider returning to Algiers and dealing with the city's administrative affairs. However, the unpleasant news came from the Castle of Beni Rashid awoke the sleeping Barbarossa inside Aruj."

Oran

You witnessed all that had happened because of the Turks. You have been deprived of all those supplies that have been provided to you not only by the Castle of Beni Rashid but the neighboring sites as well. If you had collaborated with me to fight against Aruj, you would not be suffering from such scarcity today. Think about and evaluate the outcomes brought about by your decision to let Aruj bully around. Use whatever methods necessary to prevent this flood by treating it at its source. Or else, you risk falling prey to your own recklessness and losing everything including your fortress.

Abu Hammu was right. The governor of Oran, Marquis de Comares, could no longer postpone taking action. He gave the command for his ten thousand cavalries to ride from Almeria to Oran to meet up with Abu Hammu's mounted troops. And when Commander Martin D'Aragote's army of three thousand soldiers joined this force, he dispatched them all to the Castle of Beni Rashid which had been under the command of Isaac and Iskender for the last six months.

Cervantes placed his finger over the Castle of Beni Rashid, located about fifty kilometers south of Tenes.

"They had neither enough men nor weapons. As a result of the fireballs launched by the catapults, the castle was totally engulfed in flames in a very short time. The casualties they incurred were innumerable. Corpses had begun to pile up on top of each other. They had no option but to surrender."

"So, it was the rumbling of cannon fire that roused the sleeping Barbarossa."

"It was Isaac's final breath, Signor, he exhaled due to a misunderstanding as they surrendered the castle, that roused the sleeping Barbarossa."

William was taken aback by what he had just heard.

"Did Isaac die?"

"Isaac, Iskender, and the rest of the civilians who had been granted safe passage... They all perished."

"Did the Spaniards kill unarmed civilians and the fighters of a commander who had already surrendered?"

"Because of the speed with which the events unfolded, nobody was able to comprehend what had taken place. Isaac and Commander Martin D'Aragote had reached an arrangement over the surrender of the castle, and Isaac and his comrades had in fact been promised safe passage. But when they were leaving the castle, a young man from Tlemcen couldn't prevent his rage from erupting like a volcano when he saw Iskender carrying the shield that belonged to his father who had been killed a few days ago; and the fight evolved into a bloodbath. Not a single levend survived the massacre. And the ring, which Isaac had entrusted to a Sudanese in his last breath so that he may deliver it to Aruj, was soon in Aruj's palms."

Tlemcen

When Aruj stormed into Abu Zayyan's bedroom, wearing Isaac's jasper ring and the flames of vengeance were burning in his eyes, it was late at night. Aruj approached him, opened the mosquito net that covered his bed, and clutched his throat. Abu Zayyan had been caught off guard.

"Aruj Reis, what's happening?"

Aruj was aware that Abu Zayyan had secretly been communicating with the Spaniards for a while. Since their relationship began to fall apart, he had been keeping a close eye on the sultan, watching every step he had been taking. Aruj had been trying to maintain his cool and be patient with Abu Zayyan. But it seemed that he had been way too tolerant. His goodwill had been abused, and their rotten friendship had given way to a burgeoning animosity. Abu Zayyan had stabbed Aruj in the back. This wretched, this miserable man clearly had lacked the guts to look him straight in the eye and challenge him. Aruj had lost his brother; he had lost his friend, his comrade. He leaped on his throat with his silver claw.

"Aruj Reis? Who is Aruj Reis? I am Barbarossa!"

The ground was shaking with each footstep the soldiers took in unison as the marching troops carrying Aragon, Castile, and Toledo flags approached Tlemcen. The clanking of the armors, hooks, and swords, the rumblings from the axles, and the creaking of the catapults were draining the little bit of zeal left in his levends. Ben al-Qadi, on the other hand, was retiring with his troops, abandoning Aruj, arguing that it was not their war. Aruj was now witnessing the fulfillment of what Khidr had once said when he warned him about the fact that a thousand nomads would not equal a single Turk, and that he could not trust any of them. As for those who Aruj had taken to his side by force in the aftermath of Abu Zayyan's death, they were now waiting for the time when they would exact their revenge. One of them had once yelled at him, "You will end up in both hells, both the hell of Christians' as well as of the Muslims'!" just before Aruj drowned him with his own hands in the fountain of *Jami' al-Kabir*. Aruj was aware that only his levends would fight alongside him till the last drop of blood was spilled. Other than his levends, he knew that he had no one else.

He did his utmost to stand against the enemy; he would rather die than surrender the city. What he dreaded the most, on the other hand, was having to see the demise of his companions. The protracted siege had resulted in uprisings in Tlemcen, which Aruj tried hard to suppress; and Martin D'Aragote had put a bounty on the pirate's head by taking advantage of the civil unrest.

One day, when he and his men were ambushed as they were praying in the El Mechouar Mosque, Aruj ran out of patience. They were going to retreat. Even though Tlemcen had slipped through his fingers, all was not lost. Aruj could return to Algiers, bandage his wounds, assemble his troops, and retake the city the following year. He gathered his men around him.

"Are we going to die or retreat?"
Nobody said a word. Aruj asked them once more, this time in a louder tone.
"I said, are we going to die or retreat?"
"Whatever you command Baba Aruj."
None of the levends raised an objection. Aruj rubbed his face.
"Then we'll retreat."

They had spent a considerable amount of time in Tlemcen. Aruj knew practically every street in the city. He had discovered about all the secret passages, tunnels, and underground galleries that might come in handy if they needed to leave this place unnoticed. He led his men down a musty-smelling, damp underground tunnel leading to a nearby village.

Cervantes got to his feet and walked up to the fireplace.

"They moved in such a stealthy and cautious manner that just as Aruj had intended nobody realized they were fleeing... Except Martin D'Aragote... And for Barbarossa, it was now the beginning of the final act."

William had straightened himself in his chair and was now attentively listening to Cervantes.

"In an attempt to stall the Spaniards who were chasing them, they began scattering gold coins, silver plates, jeweled crests, and many other precious items that they had taken with them along the route that was trodden by the hooves of their horses." Cervantes gave a sarcastic smile. "And you know what, Signor Shakespeare, all Spanish cavalries, with the exception of forty-five, went after the spoils."

"Money makes the world go around... Not faith, nor ideals..."

"Just as they were about the cross a creek, the Spaniards caught up."

Together with several of his men, Aruj had made his was across. However, as soon as he heard the battle cries coming from the rest of his levends, he recrossed the stream and flung himself into the fray. Enough was enough. Aruj was shouting at the top of his lungs:

"Who gave you permission to die? Who gave you permission to die without me!"

He leaped from his horse, snatched an axe from the ground, and attacked the Spaniards while swinging it above his head like a mace.

Cervantes' gaze was on the dying embers.

"He must have fought with such zeal until he collapsed to the ground that some claimed that he ripped a Spaniard's throat with his teeth, some said he knocked down twelve men with a single stroke."

He was gasping for breath. His clothes were in shreds, and his sharp-featured face was covered in sweat, dust, and blood. Dazed by a blow on the head, he had fallen onto his knees. As he was just about to gather himself and stand up, Garcia de Tineo's spear pierced him in the chest, causing him to collapse. The clashing of the swords and the shrieks of the levends had come to a halt. The blazing fire in Aruj's eyes had begun to cloud over. Garcia de Tineo stood over and stared at his waning flames; then, with one final thrust of a sword, he severed the red devil's head from his body.

The flames dancing in the fireplace had gone out. Cervantes' eyes were now on the still-smoldering ashes.

"His head, with nerves hanging from underneath, his silver arm, and his gold-embroidered caftan were carried to Spain, while his headless body journeyed across the Maghreb. The Spanish armada, which had returned from the Barbary Coast victorious this time, was greeted with jubilation by the Christians of Europe. Weeks of festivities were held, and Carlos V bestowed the title of nobility to Garcia de Tineo, as well as the privilege of embroidering the red devil's head, crown, flag, and scimitar on his coat of arms."

"The news must have reached Felipa as well."

"As soon as it reached Andrea, Signor Shakespeare."

"Felipa, are you aware of how risky what you're about to do is?"

Felipa was packing up as she was wiping the tears falling from her eyes.

"I should have done it long ago, Rosalie. I'm already too late."

"How could you put Hasan in such danger, I don't understand. How could his frail body withstand such a journey? Why don't you wait a bit longer and leave when he's a little older?"

"Wait till when, Rosalie? Should I wait till I also hear out about Khidr's death? Hasan is a strong boy; much like his father. He'd get through it."

They were startled by a knock on the door. It was Roberto.

"The horses are ready."

"All right, Roberto, we're coming."

Felipa roused Hasan from his sleep and took him into her arms.

"Come on, sweetie. Hold onto mummy."

Hasan rubbed his eyes.

"What's going on, Mom? Where are we going?"

Felipa gave him a warm smile.

"To your father, son; we're going to your father."

"Khidr..." muttered Cervantes... "Khidr, on the other hand, contrary to expectations, had responded to his brother's death with great fortitude and banned mourning throughout Algiers. He avoided speaking with anyone for a while. It was as if he was waiting for something. He was strolling along the city walls, looking out the windows as if he were expecting a late visitor. When his visitor finally arrived, he stood in front of the mirror and applied the henna his servants prepared for him to his reddish-brown beard, which made it appear even redder. After a while of staring at the mirror, he muttered..."

"Welcome, brother..."

REFERENCES

Abraham Lees, The Cyclopedia, or, Universal Dictionary of Arts, Sciences and Literature Vol. I., London, 1819

Alan G. Jamieson, Lords of the Sea: A History of the Barbary Corsairs, London, 2012

Alan Mikhail, God's Shadow: Sultan Selim, His Ottoman Empire, and the Making of the Modern World, New York, 2020

Alexander Donaldson, The History of The Knights Hospitallers of St. John of Jerusalem; styled afterwards, The Knights of Rhodes and at present, The Knights of Malta Vol. V. (Translated from the French Mons. L'Abbe de Vertot), Edinburg, 1770

Ali Bektan, Kanuni Devri Gizli Tarihi, İstanbul, 2012

Allison Lee Palmer, Leonardo da Vinci: A Reference Guide to His Life and Works, USA, 2019

Amiral Jurien de La Gravière, Doria et Barberousse, Paris, 1886

André Clot, Soliman le magnifique, translated by Matthew J. Reisz, London, 2012

Andrew C. Hess - The Forgotten Frontier_ A History of the Sixteenth-Century Ibero-African Frontier (Publications of the Center for Middle Eastern Studies)-University of Chicago Press, 2010

Andrew M. Reid, Paul J. Lane, African Historical Archaeologies, New York, 2004

Angus Konstam, The Barbary Pirates 15th-17th Centuries, United Kingdom, 2016

Anna T. Saddlier, Names That Live in Catholic Hearts: Memoirs of Cardinal Ximenes, Michael Angelo, Samuel de Champlain, Archbishop Plunket, Charles Carroli, Henri de Laroche Jacquelein, Simon de Montfort, Canada, 1882

Anonymous, The Book of Aquarius: Alchemy and The Philosophers Stone, edited by Wanda Priday, 2012

Aurea Catena Homeri, The Golden Chain of Homer, translated from German Edition of 1781 by Gregory S. Hamilton and Philip N. Wheeler, Indiana, 1984

Aryeh Kaplan, Sefer Yetzirah: The Book of Creation, Massachusetts, 2004

Barbara Keevil Parker, Duane F. Parker, The Great Hispanic Heritage, Miguel de Cervantes, Philadelphia, 2003

Barnaby Rogerson, The Last Crusaders, East, West and the Battle for the Centre of the World, London, 2009

Barrington Barber, William Wray, Through the Eyes of Leonardo Da Vinci, London 2004

Bekir Büyükarkın, Suların Gölgesinde, İstanbul, 2010

C.S Forester, The Barbary Pirates, New York, 2007

Céline Dauverd, Imperial Ambition in the Early Modern Mediterranean: Genoese Merchants and the Spanish Crown, Genoese Merchants and the Spanish Crown, New York, 2015

Charles Nicholl, Leonardo da Vinci: The Flights of The Mind, New York, 2004

Christopher Partridge, The Occult World, New York, 2015

Commander E. Hamilton Currey, Seawolves of the Mediterranean: The Grand Period of the Moslem Corsairs, Ria Press Edition, 2005

D.M Murdock, Did Moses Exist, The Myth of the Israelite Law Giver, USA, 2014

David Flynn, Temple at the Center of Time: Newton's Codex Finally Deciphered and the Year 2012, USA, 2008

Doç. Dr. Murat Yıldız, Celalzâde'nin Rodos Fetihnamesi, İstanbul, 2011

Dr. Jay Winter, The Complete Book of Enoch, California, 2017

Emrah Safa Gürkan, Sultanın Casusları:16. Yüzyılda istihbarat, Santaj ve Rüşvet Ağları, İstanbul 2017

Emrah Sefa Gürkan, Sultanın Korsanları: Osmanlı Akdenizi'nde Gaza Yağma ve Esaret, İstanbul, 2018

Dursun Saral, Oruç Barbaros Sultan, İstanbul 2014

Ernle Dusgate Selby Bradford, The Knights of the Order, London, 1998

Ernle Dusgate Selby Bradford, The Shield and the Sword, London, 2002

Ernle Dusgate Selby Bradford, The Sultan's Admiral, London, 1968

Ertuğrul Düzdağ, Barbaros Hayreddin Paşa'nın Hatıraları, İstanbul, 2012

Fernand Braudel, The Mediterranean and the Mediterranean World in the Age of Philip II Vol:1,2,3 , California, 1996

Florian Ebeling, Hermes Trismegistus'un Gizemi, Çeviren Mehmet Ali Erbak, İstanbul, 2017

Fray Diégo de Haëdo, Histoire des Rois D'Alger, Valladolid, 1612

H.D de Grammont, Histoire D'Alger: Sous La Domination Turque, Paris, 1887

H. Erdem Çıpa, The Making of Selim: Succession, Legitimacy and Memory in the Early Modern Ottoman Word, Indiana, 2017

Heinrich Cornelius Agrippa of Nettensheim, Three Books of Occult Philosophy, Completely Annotated with Modern Commentary, The Foundation Book of Western Occultism, translated by James Freake, edited and annotated by Donald Tyson, USA, 1995

Helena Lehman, The Language of God in Humanity: An in-Depth Study of the Bible, As Seen in the Rituals, Covenants, Symbols, & People That Serve As Living Parables In God's Eternal Kingdom, 2006

Henry Corbin, Histoire de la philosophie islamique (İslam Felsefesi Tarihi), Çeviren Prof. Dr. Hüseyin Hatemi, İstanbul, 1986

Herbert M. Vaughan, The Medici Popes, USA, 1908

Hermes Trismegistus, Hermetica, The Greek Corpus Hermeticum and the Latin Asclepius with Notes and Introduction by Brian P. Copenhaver, Cambridge, 1992

Hugh Bicheno, Crescent and Cross: The Battle of Lepanto 1571, London, 2004

Hugh Roberts, Berber Government: The Kabyle Polity in Pre-colonial Algeria (Library of Middle East History), 2017

İbrahim Sarıçam, İslam Tarihi El Kitabı: Afrika'da Kurulan Bağımsız İslam Devletleri, Ankara, 2017

James Reston Jr., Defenders of The Faith: Charles v, Suleiman the Magnificent and the Battle for Europe 1520-1536, New York 2009

James McDougall, A History of Algeria, USA, 2017

Jamil M.Abun-Nasr, A History of The Maghrib in the Islamic Period, New York, 1987

Jay Williams, Leonardo da Vinci, 1965

Jean Louis Belachemi – Nous, les frères Barberousse, corsaires et rois d'Alger (Barbaros Kardeşler: Fırtına'nın Oğlulları), çev. Nihan Önol, İstanbul, 2006

John Finnemore, Barbary Rovers, California, 2019

Jonathan Hughes, The Rise of Alchemy in Fourteenth-Century England Plantagenet Kings and the Search for the Philosopher's Stone, India, 2012

Jonathan Riley-Smith, The Knights Hospitaller in the Levant, c.1070–1309, New York, 2012

Judith E. Tucker, The Making of the Modern Mediterranean: Views from the South, California, 2019

Kadir Mısırlıoğlu, Barbaros Hayreddin Paşa, İstanbul, 2009

Kemalettin Çalık, Suya Düşen Gölge: Bir Piri Reis Romanı, İstanbul, 2007

Kenneth M. Setton, The Papacy and The Levant (1204-1571) Vol.1, Philedelphia, 1976

King James, The King James Version of the Bible, E-Kitap Projesi, 2014

Laurence Bergreen, Columbus: The Four Voyages, USA, 2011

Leo Africanus, The History and the Description of Africa and of the Notable Things Thereein Contained Vol. 1,2 , translated by John Pory in year 1600, edited by Dr. Robert Brown, London, 2010

Leonardo da Vinci, 1452–1519 Notebooks / Leonardo da Vinci; selected by Irma A. Richter, New York, 2008

Leonardo da Vinci, The Notebooks of Leonardo da Vinci, Translated by Jean Paul Richter, London 1888

Lionel Casson, Illustrate History of Ships and Boats, New York, 1964

Lütfi Filiz, Noktanın Sonsuzluğu, İstanbul, 2015

María Antonia Garcés, Cervantes in Algiers: A Captive's Tale, Nashville, 2002

Massimo Di Muzio, Leonardo da Vinci, the Alchemy, and the Universal Vibration, 2016

Metin Bobaroğlu, Batıni Gelenek, İstanbul, 2002

Metin Soylu, Piri Reis'in Hazineleri, İstanbul, 2006

Mevlana Celaleddin Rumi, Mesnevi Tam Metin, Çeviren Mehmed Bahaeddin Çelebi (İzbudak), E-Kitap Projesi, 2018

Michael White, Leonardo: İlk Bilgin, Çeviren Ahmet Aybars Çağlayan, İstanbul, 2000

Miguel de Cervantes Saavedra, Don Quixote, Çeviren Edith Grossman, New York, 2005

Miguel de Cervantes Saavedra, Novelas ejemplares (The Exemplary Novels of Cervantes), translated from Spanish by Walter K. Kelly, London, 1881

Miguel de Cervantes Saavedra, The Bagnios of Algiers and The Great Sultana, edited and translated by Barbara Fuchs and Aaron J. Ilika, Philadelphia, 2010

Mircea Eliade, Histoire des croyances et des idées religieuses (A History of religious ideas), translated by Willard R. Trask, Vol: 1,2,3, London, Chicago, 1981

Mons. L'Abbe de Vertot, The History of the Knights Hospitaller of the St John of Jerusalem, Styled Afterwards The Knights of Rhodes and at present The Knights of Malta, New York, 1923

Muhyiddīn Ibn 'Arabī, Al-Ittihad Al-Kawni (Universal Tree & the Four Birds: Treatise on Unification), translated by Angela Jaffray, Oxford ,2006

Muhyiddīn Ibn 'Arabī, Ḥilyat al-abdāl (The Four Pillars of Spiritual Transformation), translated by Stephen Hirtstein, Oxford, 2008

Niccolò Capponi, Victory of the West: The Great Christian-Muslim Clash at the Battle of Lepanto, USA, 2007

Nicolas Flamel, Alchemical Hieroglyphics, Paris, 1980

Norman Roth, Conversos, Inquisition and the Expulsion of the Jews from Spain, Wisconsin 2002

Geoffrey Parker, Emperor: A New Life of Charles V Yale University Press, 2021

George F. Nafziger, Mark W. Walton, Islam at War, London 2003

Giancarlo Casale, The Ottoman Age of Exploration, New York, 2010

Özlem Kumrular, Dünyada Türk İmgesi, İstanbul, 2005

Özlem Kumrular, Türkler ve Deniz, İstanbul, 2007

Özlem Kumrular, Türk Korkusu, İstanbul, 2008

Palmira Brummet, Osmanlı Denizgücü: Keşifler Çağında Osmanlı Denizgücü ve Doğu Akdeniz'de Diplomasi, Çeviren Nazlı Pişkin, İstanbul, 2009

Piri Reis, Kitâb-ı Bahriyye, 1973

Prof. Dr. Afet İnan, Life and Works of the Turkish Admiral Piri Reis, Çeviren Dr. Leman Yolag, Ankara, 1954

Prof. Dr. Feridun M. Emecen – Zamanın İskenderi, Şarkın Fatihi: Yavuz Sultan Selim, İstanbul, 2010

Prof. Gershom G. Scholem, Zohar ihtişamın Kitabı: Kabala'dan Temel Öğretiler, Çeviren Ebru Yetiş, İstanbul 2008

Prophet Jasher, The Book of Jasher, translated by R.H. Charles, USA, 2013

Raif Karadağ, Deryaları Dize Getirenler, İstanbul, 2014

Raphael Patai, The Jewish Alchemists: A History and Sourcebook, New Jersey, 1995

Rav Michael Laitman PhD, Basic Concepts of Kabbalah, Canada, 2006

Rav Michael Laitman PhD, The Path of Kabbalah, Canada, 2006

Rav Michael Laitman PhD, The Secrets of the Eternal Book: The Meaning of the Stories of The Pentateuch, Canada 2014

Rav Michael Laitman PhD, The Zohar: annotations to the Ashlag Commentary (Secrets of the Bible Package), Canada, 2019

Rav Michael Laitman PhD, Unlocking the Zohar, New York, 2011

Rav Yehuda Ashlag, Introduction to the Book of Zohar vol. 1,2 , Commentary by Rav Michael Laitman, 2005

Renaissance and Reformation 1500–1620: a biographical dictionary, edited by Joe Eldridge Carney, USA, 2001

Richard Laurance, Richard Charles, Rutherford H. Platt, İdris Peygamber'in İki Kitabı Çeviren Oğuz Eser, İstanbul 2012

Richard Shaw Pooler, Leonardo da Vinci's Treatise of Painting: The Story of the World's Greatest Treatise on Painting Its Origins, History, Content and Influence, Delaware, 2014

Robert C. Davis, Christian Slaves, Muslim Masters: White Slavery in the Mediterranean, The Barbary Coast, and Italy, 1500-1800 (Early Modern History: Society and Culture), New York, 2003

Robert Temple, The Sirius Mystery, 1976

Rodney S. Quinn, The Sword of Islam, Canada, 2006

Sharan Newman, The Real History Behind the Templars, New York, 2007

Sidney Lee, The Complete Works of William Shakespeare: All 214 Plays, Sonnets, Poems & Apocryphal Plays, e-artnow, 2016

Sigmund Freud, Eine Kindheitserinnerung des Leonardo da Vinci (Leonardo Da Vinci, A Memory of His Childhood), Edited by Peter Gray, New York 1964

Stanley Lane-Poole, The Story of The Barbary Corsairs, London, 1890

S.J. Hodge, Secrets of the Knights Templar: The Hidden History of the World's Most Powerful Order, United Kingdom, 2013

Stuart Nettleton, The Alchemy Key: Unraveling the Single Tangible Secret in all Mysteries, Australia, 2004

Susan Sorek, The Jews Against Rome: War in Palestine AD 66-73, New York, 2008

Süheyl Seçkinoğlu, Mesnevi'den Hikayeler, İstanbul 2010

Talha Uğurluel, Dünyaya Hükmeden Sultan-2: Kanuni'nin Akıl Oyunları, İstanbul 2013

The Cambridge of Islam, History of Islam Volume 2A The Indian Sub-Continent, Southeast Asia, Africa and the Muslim West, edited by P.M. Holt, Ann K.S. Lambton and Bernard Lewis, United Kingdom, 1970

The Metropolitan Museum of Art, Leonardo da Vinci, Master Draftsman, New York, 2003

The Newry Magazine or Literary and Political Register Vol. IV., Ireland, 1819

The Qur'an and Sayings of Prophet Muhammad, Annotations by Sohaib N. Sultan Translated by Yusuf Ali, USA, 2007

Thomas Shaw, Travels or Observations Relating to Several Parts of Barbary and The Levant, Edingburg, 1808

Tobias Daniel Wabbel, The Templar Treasure: An Investigation, Chicago, 2014

Toshihiko Izutsu, A Comparative Study of The Key Philosophical Concepts in Sufisim and Taoism/Ibn 'Arabi and Lao Tzü, Çuang Tzü, 2008

Uwe Neumar, Miguel de Cervantes: Deli Dolu Bir Hayat, Çeviren Erol Özbek, İstanbul, 2018

Üç İnisiye, Kybalion: Yedi Kozmik Yasa, Antik Mısır ve Yunan Hermetik Felsefesi, Çeviren Murat Sağlam, İstanbul, 2015

Walter Isaacson, Leonardo da Vinci, New York, 2017

Washington Irwing, The Life and Voyages of Christopher Columbus, London, 1828

William C. Chittick, Ibn 'Arabi Heir to the Prophets, London , 2005

William C. Chittick, The Sufi Path of Knowledge: Ibn Al-Arabi's Metaphysics of Imagination, New York, 1989

Yılmaz Öztuna, Kanuni Sultan Süleyman, İstanbul, 2014

Yılmaz Öztuna, Yavuz Sultan Selim, İstanbul, 2006

ARTICLES

Ahmet Durak, Akdeniz'de Osmanlı Korsanlığı ve Osmanlının Korsanlıkla Mücadelesi (1530-1571), ETÜ, Sosyal Bilimler Enstitüsü Dergisi, I/2, Temmuz 2016, Sayfa: 131-148

Christopher W. Tyler, PhD, DSc, Leonardo da Vinci's World Map, Cosmos and History: The Journal of Natural and Social Philosophy, vol. 13, no. 2, 2017

David M. Gitlitz, Conversos and The Spanish Inquisiton, edited from an interview by David Rabinovitch

Diego Cuoghi, The Mysteries of the Piri Reis Map, English translation by Roberto Patriarca, with valuable help of James Gill

Dr. Henri Arroyo, The Ottoman Coinage of Tilimsan, Oriental Numismatic January 1979 Occasional Paper No. 12, 1980

Emrah Safa Gürkan, Batı Akdeniz'de Osmanlı korsanlığı ve gaza meselesi, Kebikeç: İnsan Bilimleri İçin Kaynak Araştırmaları Dergisi, 33 (2012), pp. 173-204.

Emrah Safa Gürkan, Ottoman Corsairs in the Western Mediterranean and Their Place in the Ottoman-Habsburg Rivalry, 2006

Fernando Fernández Lanza, Hassan Aga and his Government in Algiers. The Consolidation of a Mediterranean Myth

Heath W. Lowry, Halil İnalcık, Nejat Göyünç, İsmail Erünsal, The Journal of Ottoman Studies X: From Trabzon to İstanbul: The Relationship between Suleiman the Lawgive and His Foster Brother Yahya Efendi

Geert J. Verhoeven, Stefaan J. Missinne, Unfolding Leonardo da Vinci's Globe (AD 1504) To Reveal its Historical World Map

Mehmet Tütüncü, Cezayir'de Barbaros'un Bilinmeyen Kitabesi, Yedikıta Dergisi Temmuz 2017

M.L Tarizzo, Early Arab Coins of Tunisia The Hafsid - AH 627-982 (1230-1574 AD), Oriental Numismatic January 1980

Information Sheet No. 22, 1980

Roberto Barazzutti, Andrea Doria, Genous Admiral and Mercenary, Wars and Stories No:57

Sefa Duran, 16. Yüzyıl Osmanlı Donanmasında Süreklilik ve Değişim: Osmanlı İmparatorluğu'nun Açık Deniz Politikası, Edirne, 2017

Serhat Kuzucu, XVIII. Yüzyılda Uluslararası Bir Sorun Olarak Garp Ocak-ları'nın Akdeniz'deki Korsanlık Faaliyetleri Akademik Bakış Cilt 9 Sayı 17 Kış 2015

Steve Kalec, The Blood Of Osiris, DMT, and The Acacia Tree

Svat Soucek, Piri Reis and Ottoman Discovery of the Great Discoveries, Studia Islamica, no. 79, 1994, pp. 121–142.